DOWN AND OUT IN PURGATORY

The Collected Stories of
TIM POWERS

Books by Tim Powers

⁜ ⁜ ⁜

The Skies Discrowned
An Epitaph in Rust
The Drawing of the Dark
The Anubis Gates
Dinner at Deviant's Palace
On Stranger Tides
The Stress of Her Regard

Fault Lines series
Last Call
Expiration Date
Earthquake Weather

Declare
Three Days to Never
Hide Me Among the Graves
Medusa's Web
Alternate Routes (Upcoming from Baen Books)

Short story collections
Night Moves and Other Stories
Strange Itineraries
The Bible Repairman and Other Stories

DOWN AND OUT IN PURGATORY

BY

TIM POWERS

DOWN AND OUT IN PURGATORY: THE COLLECTED STORIES OF TIM POWERS

"Salvage and Demolition" © 2013 by Tim Powers. First published as *Salvage and Demolition* (Burton, MI: Subterranean Press).

"The Bible Repairman" © 2006 by Tim Powers. First published as *The Bible Repairman* (Burton, MI: Subterranean Press).

"Appointment at Sunset" © 2014 by Tim Powers. First published as *Appointment at Sunset* (Catskill, NY: Charnel House).

"The Better Boy" © 1995 by James P. Blaylock and Tim Powers.
First appeared in *Isaac Asimov's Science Fiction Magazine* (February 1991).

"Pat Moore" © 2004 by Tim Powers. First appeared in *Flights: Extreme Visions of Fantasy* (New York: Roc).

"The Way Down the Hill" © 1982 by Tim Powers. First appeared in *The Magazine of Fantasy & Science Fiction* (December 1982).

"Itinerary" © 1999 by Tim Powers. First appeared in *999* (New York: Avon Books).

"A Journey of Only Two Paces" © 2011 by Tim Powers. First appeared in *The Bible Repairman and Other Stories* (San Francisco, Cali.: Tachyon). (A shorter version of this story first appeared in 2009 in "LX Eastercon: The Souvenir Book" edited by Steve Cooper (Bradford, United Kingdom).

"The Hour of Babel" © 2008 by Tim Powers. First appeared in *Subterranean: Tales of Dark Fantasy*, edited by William Schaefer (Burton, MI: Subterranean Press).

"Where They Are Hid" © 1995 by Tim Powers. First published as *Where They are Hid* (New York: Charnel House).

"We Traverse Afar" © 1995 by James P. Blaylock and Tim Powers. First appeared in *Christmas Forever* (New York: Tor Books).

"Through and Through" © 2003 by James P. Blaylock and Tim Powers. First appeared in *The Devils in the Details* (Burton, Mich.: Subterranean Press).

"Night Moves" © 1986 by Tim Powers. First published as *Night Moves* (Seattle, Wash.: Axolotl Press).

"A Soul in a Bottle" © 2006 by Tim Powers. First published as *A Soul in a Bottle* (Burton, MI: Subterranean Press).

"Parallel Lines" © 2010 by Tim Powers. First appeared in *Stories*, edited by Neil Gaiman and Al Sarrantonio (New York: HarperCollins).

"Fifty Cents" © 2003 by James P. Blaylock and Tim Powers. First appeared in *The Devils in the Details* (Burton, MI: Subterranean Press).

"Nobody's Home: An Anubis Gates Story" © 2014 by Tim Powers. First published as *Nobody's Home* (Burton, Mich.: Subterranean Press).

"A Time To Cast Away Stones" © 2008 by Tim Powers. First published as *A Time to Cast Away Stones* (Catskill, NY: Charnel House).

"Down and Out in Purgatory" © 2016 by Tim Powers. First published as *Down and Out in Purgatory* (Burton, Mich.: Subterranean Press).

"Sufficient Unto the Day" © 2017 by Tim Powers. First appeared at *Baen.com* (October 2017).

Foreword © 2017 by David Drake
Introduction © 2017 by Tony Daniel
All other material © 2017 by Tim Powers

A Baen Books Original

Baen Publishing Enterprises
P.O. Box 1403
Riverdale, NY 10471
www.baen.com

ISBN: 978-1-4814-8279-0

Cover art by Adam Burn

First Baen printing November 2017

Distributed by Simon & Schuster
1230 Avenue of the Americas
New York, NY 10020

Printed in the United States of America

10 9 8 7 6 5 4 3 2 1

To John Berlyne

⇥ TABLE OF CONTENTS ⇤

FOREWORD
⊰ PATHS THROUGH DARK WOODS ⊱
by David Drake

THIS IS A COLLECTION of horror stories. The contents won't make you think of a mad slasher movie, nor are they kin to HP Lovecraft's work. (Amusingly that's true even of the story in which Lovecraft himself is a character.) What these most put me in mind of is Walter de la Mare's horror stories, in that they're (generally) quiet, closely observed, and very damned frightening by the end.

Time is always an important factor, but it's time in human increments—not the vistas of eternity for which Lovecraft strove. Here people revisit their pasts—sometimes literally. Books and more generally literature are often factors, and both are described by a writer who knows and loves them.

The stories have a California ambiance, though a few are set at considerable distances in space and time. This California is neither glittery Hollywood nor the industrial giant in which my uncle worked for Bethlehem Steel. It's a fringe California in which the viewpoint characters are as clearly defined as the settings, but they're outside mainstream society.

They aren't criminals, nor are they opposed to society for political reasons; they're just folks who aren't quite making it and are being paid off-book. Intelligent people, often creative people, but people who don't fit into organized structures. That's at least part of the reason the stories work so well: they start with a skewed perspective, so the reader is never quite sure where the fantasy begins or whether there is supernatural fantasy at all.

This is particularly true of *A Time to Cast Away Stones*. The viewpoint character is Edward John Trelawny, a 19th century literary figure who was as real as Dante Gabriel Rossetti (whom he knew well).

As it chances I've read both of Trelawny's published books, and I've recently stood on the slopes of Mount Parnassus, where much of the story's action takes place. Events in the story are in keeping with geography and the historical record. Things going on in Trelawny's head are fantastic—

But as I said, I've read Trelawny. The life he created and claimed for true in his autobiographical books is no less fantastic than the causes the author posits here. Trelawny is exactly the sort of fringe character who people many of the other stories in this collection, and who are just as real and vivid to the reader.

I began by saying that these are different horror stories. There is another fashion in which they differ from most horror—and certainly from the horror stories that I once wrote: these are stories in which there is hope.

Characters start with very little and may lose much even of that in the course of the story. Nonetheless, they have a chance of salvation even though they themselves are never looking for it. They have given up on god, but God—in the broadest sense—has not given up on them.

Tim Powers' paths really do come out on the other side of the darkness.

—Dave Drake

INTRODUCTION
⊰✠ THE POWERS EFFECT ✠⊱
by Tony Daniel

THE FIRST HALF HOUR after you come away from reading work by Tim Powers can be a disorienting experience. You've entered a world where the rules don't quite match our own, but are close enough so that you can almost juxtapose the two realities over one another. Or rather, it sometimes seems that you have been living in the real word while reading Powers (or perhaps that phrase should take capitalization: "Real World"), and now you're back to the shadow existence that Plato and Socrates were always going on about, and trying to escape. You've been banging up against the giant tuning forks of existence, the archetypes, when you are in a Powers story, and afterwards you're only bumping into common walls, desks, and chairs.

But one of the fun things about reading a Powers story— perhaps the best thing of all—is that you come away from the story seeing *people* not as sacks of meat bludgeoned around by a dumb universe, but as strange conglomerations of collective archetypes, souls, memories, and possible states. Unlike an LSD experience, which woefully does not produce the years of intense flashbacks promised in the advertisements, you can find yourself having Tim Powers flashbacks at odd moments for the rest of your life. It truly feels as if a new sense has been added onto your normal five. What's great, and a little scary, is that once you have it, the "Powers Effect" doesn't go away.

The writer Dean R. Koontz, who is an old friend of Tim Powers from college days, is keenly aware of the Powers Effect on himself.

✢ ✢ ✢

> Goodbye little chocolate doughnuts sold in neat cellophane packages; hello, chocolate gyroidal pastries produced by a secret priesthood dating back to first-century Rome and sold by street vendors who provide them three at a time in a red cardboard pix, with a knowing wink.

That's the way it is after you read a novel by Tim Powers. This might be his breakthrough time travel and science fiction genre-bender, *The Anubis Gates,* or the book on which they based half the story and most of the magical system of the fourth of the Pirates of the Caribbean films, *On Stranger Tides.* It might be World Fantasy award winner *Last Call*, or it might be *Alternate Routes*, an August 2018 Baen original Powers novel set along a ghost-ridden stretch of the Los Angeles freeway system that *must* exist in some universe that is slightly more real than ours.

It is also an effect that each Powers story delivers. So here you have in your hands an extremely effective set of needles for altering the warp and woof of everyday existence and sewing a few threads of forever into the fabric.

The archetypes you will be banging up against come from a deeply imbued sense of a purposeful world. The philosophers have a word for this, which is "teleological." Tim Powers stories are deeply teleological. In almost every story a character discovers that the random universe he thought he inhabited is instead charged with meaning and is driving toward a purpose that could be good, but that could also be evil.

"Noumena" is another ten-dollar philosophical term that is sometimes useful to pull out of the old trunk we saved from the good ship *Immanuel Kant* and bandy about like our great-great-great grandfather's sword allegedly from the Spanish-American War. A "noumenon" (the singular form) simply means something (we can't quite say *what*, and it isn't really a "thing" at all) that is beyond our sensations. Okay, maybe it isn't *that* simple a concept. Anyway, you could look at the human mind as a sorting device that only lets in the kinds of stuff that will not blast our brains to pieces. We call this stuff "things that happen," or phenomena. The phenomena get let in. The noumena are kept out.

Except in a Tim Powers story, the noumena *aren't* kept out.

That is, I think, what the Powers Effect is. It is a lingering ability to sense the noumena in our everyday surroundings. Of course, if you are anchored in the soon-to-be-outmoded concepts of early twenty-first century philosophy and insist on "seeing through" such premodern Kantian nonsense right down to the whistle of darkness that is your nutty little heart, you will have to fool yourself into thinking of a Powers story as "mere words" that evoke a "self-perpetuating response." In either case, Powers will get to you. That's because he does it with magic, not philosophy, so there's no thinking your way out of it.

A Powers story is a kind of spell—which is the fun of reading it.

Take one of the greats in this volume, "The Bible Repairman." What alternate purgatory have we landed in? It seems that Bibles come defective from the source. They just *won't* let us do what we wish to do. So Terry Torrez fixes them. It seems like the perfect metaphor for modern folk. Think a certain truth should not be *your* truth? Hire a dude to sprinkle some special sauce on it and wipe it out. Adultery? Envy? Gluttony? No longer *your* problem, bub. We have the sacred technology to solve those little glitches. And were they really glitches at all, but just something some old patriarch *said* was wrong in order to wield a little sadistic power? Give your guilt the heave-ho.

The problem is, truth *is* true. Wrong is not right. You don't wipe it away so much as push it below until it bobs back to the surface elsewhere. Terry is all too aware of this inconvenient fact. That is why only a lost soul should become a bible repairman. Because somebody *always* pays the price. Better if you deserve it.

But this is only the first layer in a deeply affecting tale. Because Terry *isn't* so doomed as he imagines himself to be. Ghosts haunt him because he doesn't want to let go of those he loves. In a way, the more he loses of himself by performing his brujo's magic for the good of others, the closer he comes to redeeming his own mortal sin. It's a heartbreaking story that will, in the end, leave you oddly hopeful.

Which is another thing about Powers. His stories are *real* stories with beginnings, middles, and ends. He may be a literary craftsman with the metaphors and spare and evocative word choices and such, but he always, *always* has a hell of story to tell. You can see this is in the beautifully crafted plot of "Salvage and Demolition," with its delightfully overlapping time travel narrative lines. But it's just as true with a completely out-there tale such as the story from which the collection takes its title, "Down and Out in Purgatory," or the hilarious amalgamation of personal names, life-greedy ghosts, and chain letters, "Pat Moore."

Once you buy into the magic, into the *teleology* and the glimpses of *noumena*, the story makes perfect sense—always in a certain twisted and delightful manner.

Another Powers staple you see in "Down and Out in Purgatory" is a wry . . . well, it may as well be said . . . traditional Catholic and broadly Christian take on things. There is a great deal of C.S. Lewis's *The Great Divorce* in the idea of the afterlife in "Down and Out in Purgatory," with its characters doing their best to constantly misunderstand the situation they are in, and the eternal consequences they are careening toward. But there's also a lot of straight-up baroque excess you might find in the world of Fritz Leiber's Fafhrd and the Gray Mouser tales, Jack Vance's Dying Earth stories, and Gene Wolfe's Book of the New Sun series.

Tim Powers may be a Catholic intellectual, but he's also a dyed-in-the-wool science fiction and fantasy geek who wears a "Miskatonic University" class ring around for kicks.

There are not subtle and nearly insubstantial differences between good and evil in these stories. That's because there are not subtle and insubstantial differences between good and evil in the world we live in, where the distinctions between the two are fairly stark and self-defining. In a Powers story it is *people* who are subtle and interesting; it's people who are confused, and limited, and tempted to do the wrong thing for gain, but who usually find a way through to some sort of revelation and resolution that allows good to triumph in its way. In other words, Powers stories usually have happy endings. Or at least bittersweet endings that are deserved based on the story, and that don't come out of the blue. These are traditional stories in the very best sense, even though their subject matter is weirder than hell.

There are a few other matters that deserve to be pointed out to increase your enjoyment of this collection. One is that a number of the stories here are written with James P. Blaylock. Powers and Blaylock have been friends since their college days, not at Miskatonic University—perhaps unfortunately—but at Cal State Fullerton, where they were part of the literary set that included science fiction writer K.W. Jeter and, later, Koontz. Powers and Blaylock have fed off each other like aesthetic vampires ever since (well, perhaps the relationship is more symbiotic), and their influence on each other's work is profound.

Powers and Blaylock are the coinventors of the Romantic poet William Ashbless. You will find mention of him in several spots in the collection. They have put so much work into Ashbless that he almost seems to be real. He is, in fact, one of the main characters in the great Powers novel *The Anubis Gates*. But there is no real William Ashbless. At least on our plane of existence.

One influence that is not so much literary, but personal, is the late Philip K. Dick. If you know even a bit of Dick's biography, you'll see several characters that are reflections of Philip K. Dick in these stories. As a young man, Tim Powers was friends with Phil Dick, and a protégé of sorts.

Whatever you may think of Philip K. Dick's work— I am a big fan of his short stories from the sixties—there is no gainsaying the fact that Dick was an extraordinarily generous and kind fellow who went out of his way to encourage and help fledgling writers and others who may have chosen equally grim roads in life. Powers was the beneficiary of that magnanimity and has himself paid it forward in many ways by teaching and mentoring others through the years. As an editor, I often run into authors who have had happy and encouraging encounters with Tim Powers.

Powers stories are often about love: its missed opportunities, disappointments, but mostly its subtle antidote to life's evil, and its casual, even brutal, victory against all manner of twisted geniuses determined to turn affection against itself for their own dastardly ends. In fact, a Powers "ghost" is often the psychic resonance of possibilities set in motion by love, for both good and ill. It cannot be a coincidence that at science fiction conventions, writing conferences, and elsewhere, Tim and his wife Serena can usually be regarded as an inseparable unit.

There is another inspiration in Powers' work that is even stronger than love or friendship.

The Los Angeles greater metropolitan area.

L.A. is the setting for a majority of the stories in this collection, and Tim Powers has turned that basin of teeming humanity into a landscape as seething with delirium, mystery, depravity, wonder, and magic as William Faulkner's Yoknapatawpha County or J.R.R. Tolkien's Middle-Earth. There are ancient apartment buildings hidden away up tiny canyons whose roads are overhung with eucalyptus trees and jacaranda rank with blue blossoms where secret sects attempt to cheat death itself by weaving together their souls into cobweb-like group minds. There are burnt out San Bernardino lots where family houses used to stand filled with ghosts from all of yesterday's tragedies, some of whom don't even realize that they are dead. There is the freeway system, which for Tim Powers is as symbolic, rich, dangerous, and unfathomable as the Mississippi River was for Mark Twain. And stitching it altogether are the hopes and dreams of millions of people lapping and overlapping against one another, creating psychic eddies and holes in space time where strange things thrive.

The collection ends with "Sufficient Unto the Day," a new story that was first published at the Baen website and that appears here for the first time in good old traditional print. This one is about Thanksgiving and, for those who have ever had kids who can't take their eyes off video games, YouTube personalities, and/or binge-inducing television shows, this one will resonate. For with great technology comes the possibility of great evil, and the better your reception the better chance that the technology can receive *you*. Tech is not always a medium. When it becomes and end in itself, it can and will reach out and grab you, pull you in, and take you away forever.

Sometimes we need a reminder that all the magical technology of the witch doctors and shamans from our past, and the game designers and YouTubers of our present, can be dangerous distractions. Even the great temptation that comes up again and again in stories by Tim Powers, the lure of everlasting Earthly life, turns out to be a mere diversion from the true path.

And what is that path? Love. Family. Hewing to what is right even when we can't see it so well, when we're confused, tipsy from drink or life, and susceptible to illusion. Throughout all the weirdness in a Tim Powers story, these are the only constants we can depend on, the only method of escape from a hangman's sentence of spiritual oblivion and material dissipation in an insensible universe. It's the hallmark of a Tim Powers hero, as well. To survive, you have to figure out how the magic works, sure, but even then, you must hold on to what you know is right, see yourself as the imperfect person you are, have faith—and leap into the weirdness. The leap of faith may not save your world, but it will absolutely get you off the mad carousel of materialistic determinism and magic-induced repetition where so many die after never having really lived. It may even set you free forever.

That's the real Powers Effect.

⊰ SALVAGE AND DEMOLITION ⊱

⊰ I ⊱

THE LAST OF the three boxes just seemed to contain litter—a dozen cigarette butts and a dusting of ash scattered across the middle pages of an old issue of the San Francisco *Chronicle* and a 1957 copy of *TV Guide* with a very youthful-looking Pat Boone on the cover.

Blanzac sat back, tapping the ash off his own cigarette onto the old carpet under his chair, and took off his reading glasses to peer past the narrow glow of the desk lamp at the sunlit bougainvillea vines outside the window. The first two boxes had yielded up a first edition of Ginsberg's *Howl*, inscribed by the author to Sophia Greenwald, and several TLS—typed letters signed—to the same person from Jack Kerouac . . . and a few lesser but still remarkable items. That was treasure enough, but still he wished he'd opened this unexciting box first.

He sighed and slid his glasses on again, and lifted out the *TV Guide* and the newspaper, and then his hopes brightened again. Under an old science fiction paperback below them lay a disordered stack of handwritten manuscript.

There was no name or title on the top sheet, but the handwriting looked feminine to him. Perhaps it was something of Sophia Greenwald's—he seemed to remember that she had been a minor poet in San Francisco in the '50s, though her niece, who had given him the boxes on consignment, had seemed unaware of that and he hadn't mentioned the vague recollection to her. Were there any Sophia Greenwald collectors?

He turned to his computer and called up the Google screen and typed in her name. According to Wikipedia she'd been born in 1926, lived in San Francisco, had two books of poetry published, in 1953 and 1955, left San Francisco in 1957 and died of cholera in Mexico in 1969 at the age of forty-three.

He picked up the top sheets of the manuscript. It did appear to be poetry—many of the lines ended well short of the right-hand edge of the paper.

He puzzled out a few lines from the middle of the page—

. . . And, slick with juice, it slipped, but quick his hand
Caught firm a hold, and brought it to his face—
To hesitate a heartbeat—God's command
Still seemed to echo in this sylvan place;
And Adam saw before him stretch two lives:
One to move in God's shadow, acquiesce
In all responses, reflexes and drives;
The other . . . ah, the other! To express
His own *will, print* himself *upon this world!*
He chose—and bit—and dimmed each future dawn—
As helplessly as shadows fall unfurled
To west instead of east as dusk come on,
As fated as the phases of the moon . . .

He read through several pages of it, pausing sometimes to puzzle out a word, and the narrative gradually shifted from a distorted retelling of Genesis to an oddly compelling view of the old Ptolemaic earth-centered universe, with the sun and planets fixed on crystal spheres that spun like clockwork inside a vast ultimate sphere . . . then the focus returned to Adam and Eve and Cain and Abel, and their vividly detailed sacrifices and crimes were made to seem as mechanical as the motions of the spheres.

He forgot about the other items in the boxes, absorbed in the fluid narrative of the poem, but after a few minutes he jumped at a cold tap on the back of his neck, and then drops of water were pattering on his desk.

He lunged out of his chair and spread his corduroy jacket to cover the Kerouac letters and the Ginsberg book, and as he cursed and fumbled them into the last box and hugged it against his shirt he squinted over his shoulder, certain that the window was open and a sprinkler had come on—

But even before he snatched off his glasses to see clearly across the room, he was aware of the dry-white-wine smell of rain on pavement, and a whiff of chocolate; and he caught a familiar melody, and a hissing like tires on a wet street, growing more audible and then fading.

A moment later the falling water had stopped, the music was gone, and the room once again smelled only of cigarette smoke and coffee and old book paper.

His desk was dry. Still clutching the box to himself, with his free hand he slapped around among the catalogues and invoices littering the surface, but there were no drops of water anywhere. And the window, he saw, was closed.

He glanced up—the ceiling was dry and uncracked.

He sat down and carefully slid the box back onto the desk, but for several seconds he simply stared at it and took reassurance from breathing in and out. The flaps of the box had sprung open, and he could see that the books and papers in it were perfectly dry.

The brief moment of impossible rain had apparently never happened.

At last he sighed deeply and sat back in his chair.

You had a hallucination, he told himself cautiously, but it's over. Probably you shouldn't open the Wild Turkey bottle before noon anymore; this was a warning, I'll cut back, no problem. I'm glad the books and letters didn't actually get wet!

It was late afternoon now, though, so he let himself reach out, a bit shakily, and pick up his glass. He wasn't aware of the rigidity of his neck until the resonant warmth of the swallowed bourbon loosened his muscles.

The hallucinated melody, he realized belatedly, had been "How Little We Know." Long time since I heard that one, he thought.

Then his face went cold again, for his gaze had fallen on the science fiction paperback, and, though he hadn't given it more than a glance a few moments earlier, he was sure that it was now a different book; its cover had been dark purple, some kind of outer space scene with planets or rockets or something of that sort, but now it was green and yellow—giant lizards chasing men in a jungle with *What Vast Image* in lurid lettering across the top.

He put down his glass and picked up the book, hoping that it would somehow look purple again viewed close up. It was still green and yellow, but when he flipped it over and looked at the back cover he barked out a couple of syllables of relieved laughter.

It was two books bound together *tête-bêche*, back to back, one upside-down to the other, and the reverse cover was the remembered purple one, titled, he saw, *Seconds of Arc*. The author of both was Daniel Gropeshaw, a name Blanzac didn't recognize. Now he noticed the blue band at the top of each cover: ACE DOUBLE NOVEL BOOKS TWO COMPLETE NOVELS, and he recalled that William Burroughs' first book had been published by Ace Books as one half of a similar pair.

He looked at both title pages, but neither was signed, and he tossed it onto the desk. A moment later the telephone rang.

He cleared his throat and hummed a few notes of "How Little We Know" to be sure his voice wouldn't come out shrill, then picked up the receiver and said, "Hello?"

"Richard Blanzac? I'm Amy Mathis with Goldengrove Retirement Community, in Oakland, and one of our residents asked us to call you. Her name is Betty Barlow, Elizabeth Barlow, and she wishes to talk to you about . . . some books, she said."

"Books?" Blanzac was still blinking doubtfully at the desk and the closed window and the dry, unblemished ceiling. "Books, you say. To sell?"

"Some books you have, I gathered."

"She wants to what, buy some?"

A sigh came down the line. "That might be. She asked that you visit her here. I gather from your area code that you're in the Bay Area?"

"Yes, in Daly City, but . . ." He forced himself to pay attention. "Retirement community, was it? How old is she?"

A bit snippily, the woman replied, "She's entirely alert and competent to handle her affairs, sir."

"Can I talk to her, ask what this is about?"

"She'd be happier talking directly."

He sighed, and was about to recommend that the old lady contact him through the mail, but the narrow office he'd made in the spare bedroom of his house suddenly seemed oppressive, even threatening.

He glanced again at the window and the ceiling, and impulsively said, "What's your address?"

Goldengrove was a tranquil collage of green lawns and patios and winding brick walkways around a tan Romanesque tower and a long structure that looked like a new apartment complex. Regularly spaced cypress trees stood up behind the building, swaying against the blue late-afternoon sky.

The lobby was in the central tower, and the cathedral-high ceiling and the elegant Chippendale-style furniture made him wish he had put on a tie and a newer jacket. But the young lady at the receptionist desk cheerfully copied his name from his driver's license and directed him down one of the carpeted halls. The place smelled of violet air-freshener and rubbing alcohol.

Betty Barlow's door was open; the doorway was easily four feet wide, and Blanzac wasn't surprised to see a motorized wheelchair and an aluminum walker parked against the wall below the window, beside some rounded metal apparatus that might have been a humidifier. The blinds were open, and several frail old men in shorts and T-shirts were slumped in white plastic chairs on a patio out there.

The woman in the bed blinked at him through thick bifocals from under a thin haze of curly white hair. Her narrow body lay so straight under the smooth blanket that Blanzac thought the bed couldn't really be said to be unmade.

"Betty—Elizabeth Barlow?" he said, standing in the doorway. "I was told you want to see me."

"You're Richard Blanzac?" she said, her voice high and scratchy. When he assented, she said, "Sit down here. Those are my books you've got, you can't have them."

He moved a recent issue of *Time* magazine and a bottle of Tabasco from a nearby chair, and set them beside a telephone on a wheeled formica table by the bed. He noticed a big magnifying glass lying next to the telephone.

Barlow nodded at the Tabasco. "I go through a bottle of that a week," she said. "The food here is so bland you can't tell the puree beef from the flan. I'm the literary executor for the Sophia Greenwald estate. Have been since she died in '69." From under the blankets she produced a manila envelope. "This was in the safe, but

I made them bring it to me after I got the call from Greenwald's idiot niece. Edith."

Edith Tillard was the name of the woman who had given Blanzac the three boxes of books on consignment.

The old woman reached up above her head and switched on a bright reading lamp, then picked up the magnifying glass as she slid a sheaf of folded documents out of the envelope. She riffled through them, peering at them through the glass, then handed several sheets to Blanzac.

They were a death certificate for Sophia Greenwald from a town in Mexico called Otatoclan, and letters of administration from a court in Texas, all dated in 1969. Elizabeth Barlow was indeed named executor of the Greenwald estate.

"You have a young voice," Barlow said. "How old are you?"

"I'm forty, ma'am."

"I've been executor of her estate longer than you've been alive."

Blanzac shifted uncomfortably and handed the papers back to her. "I got the books on consignment from her niece, her heir."

"You smell like cigarettes. Let me have one."

Blanzac pulled the pack of Camels from his shirt pocket and shook the pack toward her so that one cigarette stuck out; she took it with steady fingers and put it in her mouth as he fetched a lighter out of his pants pocket.

From behind him a woman's voice said, "And how are we—ah! Miss Barlow, you know there's no smoking in the building."

Blanzac turned and saw a woman in a nurse-like uniform staring past him.

"And if I get myself together to go outside," said Barlow bitterly, "those old breadsticks cough and wave their hands, even if I'm a dozen yards downwind." But she handed the cigarette back to Blanzac, who tucked it back into the pack.

Barlow glared at the woman until she retreated into the hallway, then turned to Blanzac. "Sometimes I suffer from what these people like to call dementia. You could more accurately call it something like religious ecstasy, though it does make me self-destructive sometimes. Self-destructive," she repeated, nodding. "Boxes, was it?"

"Boxes?"

"The books, Murgatroyd, the books! Ginsberg, Kerouac, Rexroth? I made some calls after idiot Edith called me—I shouldn't have."

"You called me," he said.

"I didn't call you, I had the receptionist call you." She waved at the telephone on the wheeled table. "I shouldn't have called anyone from this phone. It's in my name. The books Edith gave you are mine, you're not to touch them." She blinked at him. "Have you?"

"I've looked through Miss Tillard's boxes," he said. "Books, mainly, the 1950s San Francisco poets, as you say."

"Mainly?"

Blanzac took a deep breath. "There's what appears to be a substantial stack of autograph manuscript, as well, which might be Greenwald's work—I can give you a photocopy of it. As literary executor, you should have the text."

For several seconds she said nothing. Then, "A *manuscript*!" Her voice was hoarse. "What sort of manuscript?"

"Poetry, iambic pentameter—it looks like a hundred pages or so."

Barlow had closed her eyes, and was breathing in short gasps.

Alarmed, Blanzac started up from his chair, but she opened her eyes and stared at him. "Burn the manuscript," she whispered; then went on more loudly, "I'm her executor, you saw that. I have the authority to order you to destroy it. I—was with Sophia Greenwald when she died, and her last words were . . . burn that manuscript!"

"You don't know what it is!" protested Blanzac. "I don't either. It might be anything—!"

"What else was in *that* box, with the manuscript?"

Blanzac exhaled and spread his hands. "An old newspaper. A science fiction paperback. A lot of cigarette butts."

"Ach, burn the paperback too. I can compel this, legally. You don't want a lawsuit. And you must give me the books, the Ginsbergs and Rexroths, all of them."

Those belong to the niece, Blanzac thought; but let's not get into a fight about that right now. "This manuscript—you seem to know what it is. Is it something by Sophia Greenwald?"

"What if it is? She was a worthless poet. Michael McClure and Gary Snyder both said she was no good. Her books have been out of print ever since she wasn't around to boost them anymore."

He shook his head, baffled. "You're her literary executor? Wouldn't it be—"

"She made a mistake when she chose me as executor. I despise her work. For a few years I had to turn down requests to print her stuff, but—hah!—it's been decades now since anybody's even asked."

She closed her eyes, and tears were running down her wrinkled cheeks now. "Damn her vanity! Why didn't she—I can't know if you've destroyed it—even if you bring it here and burn it out on the patio where I can see, I can't know you haven't made a Xerox of it!"

And I would, thought Blanzac.

"I'll buy it," she said finally. "The manuscript and the paperback book. Calculate a fair price. And I'll have to trust your professional ethics not to make a copy of the manuscript before you sell it to me— part of what I'll be paying for is exclusivity. Is that acceptable, can you assure me of that condition?"

Blanzac paused before agreeing, to make it seem that he was seriously considering the terms.

Barlow went on, "Do you *care* about Sophia Greenwald's poetry? Are you a big fan?"

He smiled. "I've never read any of her work."

"It's rubbish, completely forgotten."

Forgotten because you've kept it out of print, Blanzac thought. He leaned back and crossed his arms. "Very well," he said. "Exclusivity."

"How much will it cost me?"

"I haven't even looked at it yet! How can I—"

"Give me your price, Murgatroyd," she said scornfully.

"Oh hell." The Ginsberg *Howl* would probably bring in five thousand dollars, and each of the Kerouac letters would probably do the same or better, and there were a dozen other worthwhile books in the lot. "A hundred dollars, and I sell the rest of the stuff for the niece."

The old woman scowled fiercely at him, her mouth pinched. At last she said, "And I get the science fiction paperback too."

"I'll throw that in free." And I *will* photocopy the Greenwald manuscript, he thought. After you're dead, I'll see what I can do with that.

"Go now. And talk to me here, don't call me on the telephone."

Blanzac got to his feet. "I'm sorry if I—"

She waved him away. "Get out of my sight, small-fry."

✠ ✠ ✠

As Blanzac was walking through the Goldengrove lobby toward the front doors, squinting as he passed through horizontal bars of sunlight from the high western windows, a portly man in a wide-lapelled business suit rose from one of the Chippendale chairs and stepped in front of him. He was older than Blanzac, though he didn't look old enough to be a resident here.

"Is it Mr. Blanzac?" The man was smiling and rocking on his heels. "I hoped I'd catch you. I'm Jesse Welch, from the University of California Special Collections, and I gather you've come into possession of some literary items that concern Sophia Greenwald?"

Blanzac looked past the man toward the parking lot, then back toward the receptionist's desk.

"How did you know I'd be here?" he asked.

"She's not herself these days. What's the nature of these items?"

"Some books on consignment," said Blanzac after a moment's pause, "that belonged to Sophia Greenwald. I gather Miss Barlow is the literary executor of the Greenwald estate."

"Just books? No letters, papers?" His smile disappeared, and he was now frowning and nodding. "Miss Barlow has some unreasoning old grudge against Greenwald, and opposes any suggestion that Greenwald's work receive scholarly attention. Did the consignment include any manuscripts that might be Greenwald's?" He stared at Blanzac. "I'd see that you were well paid for turning any such over to me."

The man's insistence was a curious new factor, and Blanzac was suddenly cautious. "I've only glanced at the boxes," he said, shrugging and hoping he sounded casual. "It seems to be all books. No . . . papers."

"I could help you inventory the material."

"I won't be able to get to it right away. Do you have a business card? I could call you when I'm ready."

"Certainly. And could I have one of yours?"

Blanzac pulled out his wallet, pinched up one of his *Blanzac Rare Books* cards, and exchanged it with the card Welch handed him, which did appear to be genuine.

"I'll call you if I don't hear from you," said Welch.

Blanzac nodded, opened his mouth as if to say something more, then just nodded again and walked past the man, toward the doors to the parking lot. But Welch's face had seemed remotely familiar.

⇥ II ⇤

BACK IN HIS spare-bedroom office, Blanzac peered suspiciously at the window and the ceiling, then, reassured, allowed himself another splash of Wild Turkey as he sat down at his desk.

He took a sip of the lukewarm bourbon and then opened the third box and carefully lifted out the book and letters he had tossed into it during his hallucination an hour ago, and set them aside. It was the contested manuscript that interested him now.

He carefully gathered it up, nudged the box aside and set the stack of papers down on a clear spot on the desk, and riffled through the age-tanned pages.

The top twenty or so pages were handwritten verse, and he had read most of those earlier; below that were carbon copies of typescript. The carbons were easier to read than the inked pages had been, but after scanning a couple of lines—

> *Two Streams: one flowing South, the other North,*
> *As if from mirror'd Springs they issu'd forth*

—he returned his attention to the top pages, which at least were in relatively modern English. What the hell sort of poet had Greenwald been, anyway? What he had read was hardly in any "1950s Beat poets" style. That Welch guy, impostor or not, had seemed to be familiar with her work.

Blanzac shifted in his chair to pull out his wallet, and he laid it on the desk and shuffled through the cards till he found the one Welch had given him. Welch hadn't explained how he had come to be at Goldengrove, and he'd been awfully pushy, even for a scholar. It should be easy enough to call some central office of the University of California and verify that he was what he claimed to be.

Blanzac pulled a cigarette out of the pack in his shirt pocket and tucked it between his lips, then groped around for a lighter.

There wasn't one on the desk, and he hiked his chair around to face the nearest bookshelves.

But the bookshelves weren't there—

He had an astonished moment of looking instead down a grubby white-painted hallway with an upright piano at the far end of it, and then he had sat down hard on a linoleum floor as pieces of wood clattered around him.

He gasped, and caught the smells of Beef Stroganoff and cigarette smoke on the warm air, and from behind him shivered the babble of a lot of people talking.

He scrambled to his feet, panting and looking around wildly. In front of him was a door with a wooden Men sign on it, and now an unsteady young man in horn-rimmed glasses and a white shirt and striped tie came shuffling down the hall from the direction of the crowd noise. The young man kicked a piece of wood aside before lurching into the men's room, and Blanzac looked down.

He recognized the seat and disattached arms of his office chair, and there were some rectangular scraps of paper and cloth, too. He looked more closely and saw that one of them was the shaved-off spine of a first edition of *For Whom the Bell Tolls*, alongside the spine of the dust jacket. The young man in the men's room had stepped on the cigarette Blanzac had had in his mouth.

Blanzac crouched and picked up one arm of his chair; he turned it in his shaking hands, noting the smooth, faintly-concave cut, and on an impulse he lifted it and bit it. He tasted varnish and wood.

He tossed it aside, then rubbed his palm down the painted wall, noting the coolness and the slightly gritty texture.

This could not be a hallucination.

Alcoholic blackout, he thought, almost eagerly. That's not too bad, lots of people have those. Wherever this is, you must have walked into this place, probably with someone, and now you've forgotten the past few hours. You can walk back out into the—restaurant, apparently— and fit yourself into whatever's going on, and probably figure out who you're with and bluff your way through a conversation until it all comes back to you—

Then his chest went cold and he looked down again. The wood pieces and strips of book-spine still lay on the linoleum floor.

Obviously he had not broken up his chair and torn the spine from a book and then chosen to bring the pieces along on a dinner date.

And he noticed his trousers, and then held his arms up to look at his jacket and shirt-cuffs. He was wearing the same clothes in which he had visited the Goldengrove place.

His fingertips were tingling and, though he had been panting a moment before, he was suddenly unable to take a deep breath.

There's a crowd, he thought. I can mix in a crowd and seem normal and inconspicuous while I . . . figure this out.

His pulse was pounding in his wrists and temples, but he walked steadily enough down the hall toward the rattle of cutlery and conversation. He tried to catch words or phrases, afraid that they might not be in English.

But as soon as he stepped out into the long, high-ceilinged room at the end of the corridor, a woman grabbed his elbow.

"Wow," she said, speaking loudly to be heard over the conversations at the crowded tables, "you're good!" She was looking in evident wonderment from the hall behind him to the other end of the room and back. "Even if there's a back door there by the restrooms, I don't see how you could have run around to there so quick!" Her breath smelled of gin.

Blanzac glanced down at her. She looked to be in her early thirties, a narrow pale face squinting up at him from under dark bangs and dark eyebrows, and she was wearing a black dress that seemed too big for her. Blanzac looked out across the noisy crowd, and every man he could see was wearing a sport coat and tie.

"I've got to say it's good to see you again," the woman said wryly. "But of course you're the *other* one now, the *previous* one, and you don't know who I am. Right? Hah!" She pulled him out across the floor, her black pumps knocking awkwardly on the wood. "I hope nobody took our table," she said over her shoulder.

The room was lit by white globe lamps hung from the ceiling, and Blanzac glimpsed a painted menu on the wall to his right through the layers of cigarette smoke.

She sat down at a table with two drinks and an ashtray on it and waved him to the other chair. Blanzac joined her and tried to hide the eagerness with which he picked up the drink in front of him. It proved to be bourbon, and he took a deep gulp.

"I can see for myself later," she said, "but you do have a scar in your groin from a hernia operation, right? Looks like this," she added, drawing a squiggle in the air.

"Well," he said, and the heat in his face might simply have been from the alcohol, "well, yes." Quickly he went on, "Uh, what's the name of this place again?"

"It's the Tin Angel, but you supposedly have no idea where you are. But I do *not* believe you're from the year 2012."

Blanzac swallowed the rest of his drink and exhaled. "What year," he asked carefully, "do you think it is?"

"This is 1957," she said patiently. "You said 2012 was pretty much the same, except everybody has little computers that nobody does math on, but I *know* they'll have flying cars and colonies on the moon by then."

"1957." He looked around at the room again. This could hardly be a California restaurant, with everyone smoking. Well no, it might be some sort of private club. "And we're . . . where?"

"The Embarcadero. San Francisco." She frowned speculatively at him. "You said you were pretty scared, right now. Are you pretty scared?"

He began laughing, and he made himself stop. "I think that's what it is," he agreed dizzily. He still didn't seem to be able to take a deep breath. "You said I'm the other one. The previous one. What . . . how does one get another drink? What did you mean by that?"

"The fellow who just left, who looks just like you but his clothes were damp, this afternoon he told me you'd be showing up in that hallway tonight. He remembered showing up there himself, on this night." She shook her head, not smiling now. "I'll get more drinks. I'm scared too. Same again? It's on me, I know you don't have any money."

He touched his back pocket and realized that she was right—his wallet was still on his desk in his office. "Yes, please."

She got up and sidled her way toward the bar, and Blanzac slumped in his chair and took sidelong glances at the people at the tables around him. The men all had fairly short haircuts, nothing unusual; many of the women wore more make-up than Blanzac would have expected, but that didn't prove anything. It was certainly odd, though, that just about everybody he could see was smoking a cigarette!

He got up and crossed to a table that was not next to his own. "Excuse me," he said to the couple sitting there, "maybe you could settle a bet. Who is currently President of the United States?"

The man gave Blanzac an unfriendly look, possibly because of his open shirt and jeans. "Eisenhower," he said, emphasizing each syllable.

Blanzac nodded and went back to his own table.

Why, he asked himself, would I have come to this place? Well, I didn't come here, I fell here out of my office chair, taking pieces of it with me. But *whatever that was,* this is obviously one of those retro theme clubs, and my . . . date? I don't even know her name! . . . is playing along with the pretence; so is that Eisenhower guy. No wonder they all smoke—it's a '50s cliché, part of the costume.

The woman came shuffling back with two filled glasses, and when she had set them down beside the ashtray she looked around at the nearby tables.

"So did you ask somebody?" she said, pulling her chair out and sitting down. "I guess I shouldn't prompt you, if you haven't yet."

"You know what I asked him?"

"Who's President. He said Eisenhower. You told me half an hour ago that you did that. How fast can you drink that?"

Blanzac considered it. "Pretty fast."

"Good, get busy. Nobody will be looking for me in *this* place, but we've got things to do. I'm supposed to explain everything to you in a taxi. So drink up."

Blanzac downed half of his drink and then hastily set it down to catch his breath.

"Who," he said hoarsely, "are you?"

She rolled her eyes. "You knew all about me when we met this afternoon—and now after all that you *really* don't know me at all?" Her expression was rueful. "I'm Sophie Greenwald. I write poetry, or I have done that, at least, and I—do translation now, for rent money. I want to quit that." She shivered and for a moment looked like a scared twelve-year-old.

Blanzac didn't move, but looked at her carefully—her wide mouth, brown eyes—and wished he had seen a picture of the real Sophia Greenwald.

Her drink was clear, with a lime slice sitting on the ice cubes, possibly a gin and tonic, and she picked it up in both hands and took a long sip of it. "And you," she said, "are Richard Vader, you're in salvage and demolition work, whatever that is, you're forty years old, unmarried though two years ago you nearly married that horrible

Gillian woman who went to work for Tiny Softs, which makes those little computers."

"Microsoft," said Blanzac faintly. It was true about Gillian—but salvage and demolition? And *Vader*? As in Darth?

"And, oh, you majored in English at City College of San Francisco, and, and—and you like the British mystery writer Ian Fleming and you don't like back rubs." She laughed and added, "And you worked for a while at a tobacco shop where the boss's name was Ted! I didn't forget!"

This was all true. Blanzac stood up, wishing he hadn't gulped the bourbon. "Let's get outside."

She tilted up her glass, then set it down empty, whistled, and got to her feet.

As they made their zig-zag way through the tables toward the front door, Blanzac's hands were trembling and he paid particular attention to moving his legs, for he was afraid his knees might buckle. He saw many matchbooks and cigarette lighters on the tables and in people's hands, but the lighters were all metal, he saw no plastic Bics at all.

A gust of chilly sea air ruffled his hair when the woman who claimed to be Sophia Greenwald pushed open the door, and the yellow glow of streetlights gleamed on the wet, dark lanes of a highway beyond. Ragged clouds half-hid the moon in the black sky.

"I'm glad the rain finally stopped," said Greenwald. She raised one hand and stepped to the curb, looking toward the oncoming headlights. Blanzac walked up beside her—slowly, for he was watching the cars that swept past. The cars were the boxy, bulbous Chevys and Fords and Studebakers of the 1950s.

Out past the lanes of the highway and a low warehouse he could see a couple of piers and the masts of moored boats, and the patchily moonlit ocean.

"What's this street?" he asked.

"This is the Embarcadero." She turned and pointed at the street on the far side of the building and added, "That's Greenwich, and Filbert's behind us."

Blanzac frowned in puzzlement, then sprinted to the corner. The street sign over his head said Greenwich, and when he walked out to the center of the street and looked inland, he saw a steeply ascending slope of lights in the windows of bay-fronted buildings, and at the top of the hill the silhouette of Coit Tower.

He trudged back to where Greenwald was waving at an approaching taxi.

"Greenwich doesn't connect to the Embarcadero," he said. He took a deep breath. "Anymore. All this," he added as he waved around at the street and the neon Tin Angel sign over the doors behind them, "got torn out when they built the Embarcadero Freeway."

"I'd rather they'd build a spaceport," she said. The taxi, a green Chrysler that Blanzac thought looked like a big toaster, had swerved in to the curb, and Greenwald pulled open the back door and gave the driver an address on Divisadero Street, then folded herself onto the rear seat and moved over to make room for Blanzac. And when he had got in too and pulled the door shut, she slid the plexiglass partition closed.

She raised her hands, then let them drop in her lap as the cab accelerated away from the curb. "Earlier today you told me what I'm going to say to you now. You said it was disjointed. I work for a group of scholars, or something—"

"God!" The cab had turned right on Pacific Avenue, and though Blanzac vaguely recognized the buildings they were passing, the Transamerica pyramid no longer reared its tapering forty-eight stories above the rooftops to his left. "I'm sorry, go on—uh, scholars. In goddamn *1957*!"

"What, you think we're all dumb, way back here in the past?"

"No, I'm just beginning to believe it really *is* 1957." He gripped his elbows and rocked back and forth on the seat.

She gave him a puzzled look in the dimness. "*I'm* actually beginning to believe you really *are* from 2012," she said, almost to herself. She reached across the seat and thoughtfully rubbed a pinch of his jacket between her thumb and forefinger. "But yes," she went on briskly, dropping her hand, "scholars. They've hired me to translate parts of a very old Sumerian text, and I'm probably the only person alive qualified to do it, but—but I want to quit, and they don't want to let me." She shook her head. "Damn it, when I met you on North Point today you already *knew* all this!"

Blanzac shrugged, only half listening to her. Am I here, now, forever? he wondered. I *think* she's saying that I'm soon to jump from this night back to an earlier point in this day. After that, do I stay here?

My God, Hemingway and Faulkner are still alive! I bet signed first editions of things like *Three Stories and Ten Poems* and *The Marble Faun* are under a hundred bucks!

She was staring at him, and he mentally replayed her last statements. "You're what, the premier scholar in ancient Sumerian?"

Of course a hundred dollars is probably two or three months' rent here, he thought, and those signed firsts won't be worth fortunes for a while yet, here.

"No," she said, "that'd be Samuel Kramer at the University of Pennsylvania. I'm not the best translator, per se, but I'm the best translator for the purposes of my employers. For them it has to be someone who has done effective—*affective*—work in rhyme and meter, they want the translation to have the authority rhyme and meter have. And—"

"Rhyme and meter," echoed Blanzac. He was peering mistrustfully out at the skyline, but he forced himself to pay attention. "Uh—isn't that kind of old fashioned?" He preferred free verse poets like Sylvia Plath. "Even . . . now?"

"Oh hell, Vader, *beer* is old fashioned, *salt* is old fashioned. Why do you think magic spells in stories always rhyme? And kids' jump-rope rituals? And political slogans? The subconscious, the prerational part of your brain, thinks a statement must be important if it rhymes. And meter, that drum-beat—imagine how *un*inspiring the St. Crispin's Day speech in Henry V would have been if it wasn't in iambic pentameter!"

The cab had swept through the dimly-lit Columbus Street intersection and the engine was louder now as the driver downshifted for the climb up Russian Hill.

"And," she went on, "the parts I've been assigned apparently have to be translated by a woman. Most Sumerian script is in a dialect called *eme-gir*, but certain mystery-cult poems are written in another, called *eme-sal*, a special dialect that was ascribed to women. The poem has several sections in *eme-sal*, and my employers had me translate all of them, though that's a good deal more than is considered healthy for one translator. Chatterton didn't translate near as many lines, and look at him."

Blanzac nodded, leaning back now and just frowning out the window at the slanted-looking buildings they passed. "Tell me about this duplicate of me."

"Keep your fluffy little pants on, I'm getting there. Of course men can translate the *eme-sal* sections, but the Sumerian script has a lot of homonyms, words that are spelled the same but have different meanings. At those points the translator has to just intuit the intended meaning, and my employers believe the job requires a woman, a woman poet, to divine the intended flow."

"Chatterton, you said? Not the 18th century suicide?"

"Yes." She slid the partition aside as the cab turned south on Divisadero and said to the driver, "That's it on the left."

The night had got chillier, and when they had got out Blanzac shivered on the sidewalk in his light corduroy jacket as Greenwald paid the driver.

Stepping up to the gate of the turreted old apartment building, she said, "I'm on the top floor, in what used to be Larry Ferlinghetti's flat; he and his wife are living over on Chestnut now."

"Ferlinghetti? The poet Ferlinghetti?"

"That's the one."

The thought of Lawrence Ferlinghetti still in his forties, without a white beard, made Blanzac think of his own parents—in 1957 they were newly married, and living in a rented house in Richmond across the bay.

"What's the date?" he asked Greenwald as she swung open the wrought-iron gate.

"April seventeenth."

And my mother, he thought, age twenty, is over there in Richmond right now, pregnant with her first, my older brother! I'm not even going to be conceived for another fourteen years!

"Let's get inside," he said, suddenly afraid that his twenty-one-year-old father might somehow drive down Divisadero and see him—a figure who shouldn't exist here, now—and be, to some initially small but incrementally escalating extent, nudged out of his predestined course.

⊰ III ⊱

AT THE TOP of two flights of narrow stairs, Greenwald's apartment was three rooms: a hexagonal living room with three tall

windows overlooking the street, a bedroom, and a tiny kitchen. There might have been a bathroom, but Blanzac didn't immediately see a door for one. In the living room, two standing lamps with parchment shades threw a mellow glow over mismatched rugs, an old table and couch and overstuffed chair, and high shelves haphazardly filled with books. Between the windows hung unframed abstract paintings. The room smelled of oranges and dusty central heating.

Greenwald waved Blanzac toward the chair and hurried into the kitchen, emerging a moment later with a half-full bottle of Gordon's gin and a glass.

"Damn it, I'm still too sober," she said as she sat down on the couch and twisted the cap off the bottle. She tipped it up for a couple of swallows right from the neck of it, then splashed several inches of gin into the glass. "They can sense my thoughts when I'm clear-headed— even what direction I'm in, from them. I've read *way* too much of that damn poem, and so have they. It's an inconvenient link." She clanked the bottle onto the table and gulped a mouthful from the glass and then scowled at Blanzac. "I don't know why *you're* drunk, they don't have hooks into *you*."

Blanzac wondered uneasily how unstable she might be. "Who?" he ventured. "And what sort of hooks do they have in you?"

"The poem, the translation! My employers, they work for—they're disciples of—this fake Swami Rajgah, the self-unrealization guru, who is due back in town tomorrow. He's dying of cancer, you see, so they're all in a hurry."

Blanzac shrugged. "Okay."

She giggled and drank some more gin. "Have you ever heard of Philipp Mainlander? German philosopher, killed himself in 1876? No? He had the idea of a god that did the same thing, killed itself, before time started, though I guess 'before' doesn't mean anything in that context. My employers think it's true, and lately I think so too. Allen Ginsberg can translate Latin, and they offered him the job of translating parts of a late Latin version of the poem, but he turned 'em down, said he wouldn't participate. He said the god was this primeval Mayan deity called Akan, who was apparently always portrayed cutting off his own head; but every culture, in their oldest mythologies, has been aware of it. In Egypt it was remembered as Aker, the god who had to be asked for permission to go to the underworld, and in the oldest European cults it was the Horned God."

She paused, so Blanzac nodded. "Old suicide god," he said. "I'm with you."

"One theory," she went on, "is that this god was sort of an anti-particle to the Judeo-Christian God. Opposite in every way, including in the wish to exist. Which it decided not to. Supposedly it left a— what you could call a hole in reality, shaped like itself, as it were, and—and if you cram a whole lot of people into an empty round room with a domed ceiling, pile 'em on top of each other till there's no more empty space left, you've got a mass of protoplasm in the shape of a cupcake."

Blanzac wondered where he could go, if Greenwald became downright crazy. Not to his eventual parents' house in Richmond, for sure. Maybe he could find some mission for the homeless, south of Market Street . . .

". . . I suppose so," he said.

"But it's still a gap in the architecture." She gave him a haggard smile. "I'm not making sense, am I?"

Blanzac spread his hands. "Not so's anybody'd notice."

"Was you ever stung by a dead bee?"

At that Blanzac laughed, cautiously relieved, for it was a quote from the Bogart movie *To Have And Have Not.*

"They can still sting you," he said, trying to quote the Walter Brennan character accurately, "especially if they was mad when they died."

Greenwald sighed and sat back. "I guess this old dead god was mad. I'm afraid he's stung me." She stared across the table at him. "And then *you* showed up a few hours ago. From the future, allergedly. Allegedly. Why are *you* here?"

"I have no idea." He didn't want to get into speculations that would surely involve the fact that she was to die in 1969. "I was sitting at my desk in 2012, and then I was sitting on nothing in that restroom hallway. But you say you talked to me this afternoon, right? I guess I didn't have any explanation then either?" She shook her head, and he went on, "I think you'd better tell me about the *me* you met today."

"Okay." Greenwald reached across and touched his hand with one unsteady finger, as if to make sure he was physically present. "This afternoon my boss and a couple of the Swami's fellows tried to grab me and throw me into a car, on North Point Street by the Ghirardelli chocolate factory, but there were people around—a drunk on the other side of the street had just yelled something at me, and there was a woman walking a dog who started yelling, I mean the woman, not the dog, well, the dog was barking too, and then you were there right next to me, and you pulled me away from my, my would-be kidnappers. You threw a cup of coffee in one of them's face, and the lady and the dog were still yelling and barking, and Devriess, the guy you threw coffee at, cussed and got back in the car and took off." Her finger was still touching his hand. "And then you and I had some Irish coffee, and then we came back here, and—and—well, it *is* 1957, and you *had* just saved me from maybe torture, and you were . . . a lot more charming than you are tonight."

He opened his mouth, uncertain of what he should say here, but she stood up and crossed to the nearest window and pulled the long curtain across the view of the night sky.

"And you said," she went on briskly, returning to the couch and sitting farther away from him, "that it was the second time you had met me; you told me you first met me at the Tin Angel *tonight*— though, when you said it, tonight was still a couple of hours in the future. And you knew everything I'm telling you now, and you warned me that when I met you tonight you wouldn't know any of it. You came with me to the bar tonight, but when it was time for *you* to appear, in the rest room hallway, you left by the front door. I didn't believe your story until you damn well *did* appear from the hallway, and you really *didn't* know any of this stuff." She leaned forward, and Blanzac guessed she had looked at the clock on the stove when she added, "You said you disappeared from here tonight at around ten. We've got an hour or so yet."

He stared at her, dizzy to realize that, at least at this moment, he believed her. If it was possible for him to fall into the past at all, it wasn't implausible that he would touch down in a couple of places like a skipped stone, and not in the local chronological order. At last he said, "And I told you my name is Richard Vader."

"Yes. Isn't it?"

If I did prevent a kidnapping this afternoon, he thought—if that event really does lie in my personal retrograde future, though in this world's immediate past—it may have called attention to me, among some dangerous-sounding people.

And they might still succeed in grabbing her, and she might tell them my name. I certainly don't want anyone, even just her, interfering with any Bay Area people named Blanzac.

"Yes," he said.

"Hmm. Well, Vader will do, I suppose. You didn't tell me much about what's going to happen. You're supposedly from . . . fifty-five years in the future! I gather the United States still exists."

"Uh, yes. And the Soviet Union has collapsed." What else? The Kennedy assassinations? 9/11? A list of presidents?

"Do you know a Betty Barlow?" he asked finally.

Greenwald blinked. "She's a friend of mine, works at the Discovery bookstore on Columbus. We're always planning to go to Mexico together someday. Why?"

"I just figured you'd know her. Along with Ferlinghetti and Ginsberg and all." He glanced at the two uncurtained windows. "Won't these swami boys come looking for you here?"

"No. They, my employers, have an old address of mine, and I get mail at a post office box, and this place is rented under somebody else's name."

A big long-haired calico cat walked out of the bedroom, stretched one hind leg straight out behind it for a moment and then yowled reproachfully. Greenwald sighed and stood up.

"Keep your fluffy little pants on," she told the cat as she walked back into the kitchen. "She doesn't live here, but I've got to feed her," she called over her shoulder. "I'll be back in a moment."

As the cat trotted after her toward the kitchen, it occurred to Blanzac that it did seem to have fluffy pants on. He heard the pop and *grind, grind, grind* of a manual can opener being worked, and he leaned back in his chair and looked at the bookcase.

He could see a copy of Ginsberg's *Howl*, and he was sure that it was a first edition, signed, and that he knew what the inscription was.

And he recognized a stack of five paperbacks as having the red-and-blue striped spines of Ace Double novels; he stood up and crossed the old carpet to the bookshelves and picked up one of the copies—noting that all five were identical—and he wasn't surprised to see that it was *Seconds of Arc* on one side and *What Vast Image* on the other.

"I already gave you a copy of that, this afternoon," Greenwald remarked, wiping her hands on a towel as she walked back to the couch, accompanied by a whiff of tuna. She looked at the table and then at the floor. "It's around here someplace. I wrote both the novels, and Allen Ginsberg got Ace Books to publish the pair after he made a deal with them for a William Burroughs book. I swore Allen to secrecy, and I thought the pseudonym would hide me, but I guess my damned *employers* found my name in the copyright office. They bought up just about the entire run, and burned them."

Blanzac was peering at the byline on one of the lurid covers. "Unless I'm mistaken—" he said slowly, "and no, I'm not mistaken!— they probably didn't have to go to the copyright office. 'Daniel Gropeshaw' is an anagram of Sophia Greenwald."

She looked crestfallen. "My God, is it that obvious? Auctorial vanity—it *is* my work, and I suppose I just couldn't resist putting at least a disguised version of my name on it."

Blanzac shook his head impatiently. "So who *are* these, these *employers* of yours?—who want to *kidnap* you? And why did they burn all the copies of this? And—some kind of *swami*?"

She picked up a pack of Camels from the table and held it toward him; he took one, though they were unfiltered, and he leaned forward to the match she held out after she had lit one of her own.

"It's the damned *poem*," she said, exhaling smoke. "They've been trying to get it effectively translated for . . . God, at least three hundred years. They had Christopher Smart and Thomas Chatterton trying to unravel the Latin version in the 18th century, but nobody knew then that it's like exposure to radiation, you can't have one translator do too much of the thing, or he gets sick, his perceptions get screwy, he pretty much goes nuts." She gave Blanzac a bright-eyed smile. "*I've* done more lines than I should, and that's from the original Sumerian, all the sections of it that are in the *eme-sal* dialect! Chatterton got a lot of the Latin version translated, but he apparently had a moment of sanity, and destroyed his manuscript and then killed himself."

Blanzac managed to catch his cigarette when it fell out of his mouth. "What the hell *is* it?"

"It was ogrig—'scuse me—*orig*inally a cuneiform text on ten big limestone tablets in a place called Al Hillah in Iraq, used to be Babylon. Crusaders from Levantine Edessa destroyed the tablets in 1098, but a

French clerk had copied out the inscriptions, and there was already a fairly messy Greek translation, and Irenaeus had quoted a few lines in one of his treatises against heresies in the second century. And a differently-messy Latin translation showed up in the 15th century, apparently rendered from the Greek but with some fixes that imply acquaintance with the original. And—"

She paused to take a long drag on the cigarette and a hasty gulp of the gin. "And," she went on hoarsely through the smoke, "What the poem is, is the definition, the *apologia pro deletu meo,* of this god that killed itself before the beginning of time. The images—no, the reader's *responses* to the images, to the kamikaze *theses* and *antitheses* of the poem's dialectic—lead the reader to the negating *synthesis* which this god consisted of. It's a *reductio ad nihilum.* And if enough people read the thing all at about the same time, like in a newspaper, then—"

"Ah," said Blanzac, "they fill in the empty room?"

Greenwald frowned at him. "What room? Are you too drunk to follow what I'm—"

"We're both on the same drunk wavelength," he assured her. "I mean what you said before, cram a whole lot of people into an empty round room—"

"Oh, right. Sorry. Yes, all together they take on the shape of the empty space. The god, call it Akan, is still dead, still absent, but their clustered living minds take on what you could call its shape, its features, like water filling a particular circuitous dry riverbed. A sort of Moebius riverbed."

"It's like the SETI project," said Blanzac, half to himself. "They need a supercomputer that's too big for anybody to ever actually make, so they get a million volunteers to remotely connect their little individual computers together." He squinted at her as if against a headwind. "What happens to the people?—who read the poem in the paper?"

"Well, it's never happened before. Maybe they'd just have a blackout as the god's lifeless shape passed across them, and be fine again next day. Maybe they'd all go crazier than Smart and Chatterton. Maybe they'd all spontaneously die, from being pieces of the mosaic that filled in the dead god's spiritual outline."

Blanzac shook his head dubiously. "Why would your swami want this to happen?"

"He's not a covert Communist, if that's what you're thinking. He, and his aides, his disciples, want to read the poem themselves, shortly after a whole lot of other people have read it—they hope to ride the wave of helplessly conforming minds right into . . . the state Akan is in, though you can't really use the verb 'is' about Akan. Nonexistence." She opened her mouth as if searching for another word, then just repeated, "Nonexistence."

"Well, what—why don't they just kill themselves? Like their god did? Why the—"

"That wouldn't get them nonexistence! It did for this god—it's the essence of Akan not to exist, it's the definition of it—but for humans to achieve that, they have to fall sideways through that god-shaped hole, right out of reality! If they just *die,* suicide or not—and over the centuries most of them *have died* without the escape hatch of the poem—they go on to whatever the afterlife is. And Swami Rajgah is supposed to be in the last stages of cancer, so he needs the poem to be armed and fired right away."

"They're scared of—what, Hell?"

Blanzac jumped then, and lost his cigarette again, for the front door lock snapped and the door swung open and a dark-haired young man in a gray suit and tie stepped into the room. He was holding a revolver pointed at the carpet.

"Miss Greenwald," he said, and his voice seemed to have a trace of some European accent, "you are insufficiently drunk." Then he noticed Blanzac and hastily raised the revolver. "Remain sitting, my friend—you've no coffee to throw tonight, eh?"

Greenwald eyed the intruder warily. "You're too late, Devriess," she said. "Did you think I wouldn't burn it, after your tricks this afternoon? Get another poet and start over." Devriess leaned toward her and sniffed, then smiled. "Your anxiety is too . . . immediate. You fear that I will find it, not that I will administer some penalty."

Another man, heavier and older and wearing a tan overcoat, had stepped in beside Devriess. "It's her best work," he said. "She won't have burned it." He crossed to the bookshelves, keeping a wary eye on Blanzac, and picked up one of the Ace Double paperbacks.

"Look," he said, "she even squirreled away a pile of these." He glanced down at the book—"The inoculation," he sneered, "hah!"—and tossed it back onto the others. He put his arm out straight and began slowly to turn around. "Tell me when I'm getting warm," he said.

Devriess sniffed the air over Greenwald's head again, and after a few moments said, "Stop."

His partner's hand was pointing at a hi-fi console below one of the windows, and the man crossed to it and knelt to pull open one of the doors of the cabinet below the turntable. He fumbled inside and then slid out a wooden box like a cigar humidor, and when he swung back the lid Blanzac glimpsed a stack of papers inside, and lines of handwriting on the top sheet.

"That's it," said Devriess. "She is very not happy."

His partner rolled the manuscript into a thick cylinder and straightened up, holding it in one hand.

"Damn you," whispered Greenwald. "You might go to Heaven, Valhalla, Paradise, the Elysian Fields . . . !"

"And see, there," agreed Devriess with a brightly false smile, "and act, and comprehend, and think! 'When but to think is to be full of sorrow and leaden-eyed despairs'—*Non, merci*." To his companion he said, "carry the inoculation book away too."

The older man nodded and with his free hand shoved the five paperbacks into various pockets of his overcoat.

Devriess stepped back toward the open door. "You can even now come along," he said to Greenwald. "We do not hold this against you. We do not hold anything."

"*Non, merci,*" she said through clenched teeth.

"Certain? How is your vision, depth perception, your memory? No irrational rages, fears, dreams of falling? The candle is not burning so unevenly as to merit blowing out? 'To cease upon the midnight with no pain'? No?" He shrugged, beckoned to his companion who was carrying the manuscript, and both of them stepped out into the hall, pulling the door closed.

Greenwald snatched up the gin bottle and took several gulps as the two men's footsteps receded down the stairs, and Blanzac winced at the juniper reek of it. He opened his mouth, but she made a sharp chopping motion to silence him.

At last they heard the building's front gate slam and footsteps knocking on the sidewalk, and she exhaled and glared at Blanzac.

"*You son of a bitch,*" she whispered, "*why didn't you tell me about that?* You told me I'd meet you tonight, and that we'd come back here, and that you'd disappear—why didn't you tell me that they'd come and *take the manuscript?* I could have—" She shook her head and spat.

"*I* don't know!" protested Blanzac. "I don't know that I *do* come back here earlier today! But if I do, I'll tell you this time, I promise—"

She blinked. "You'll . . . tell me? This afternoon? But no, if you tell me—" And then abruptly she was laughing, and she got up from the couch and leaned over him to give him a messy gin-flavored kiss on the mouth. "I'm sorry!" she said, smiling down at him. "They'd have known, if—you see? They'd have *known,* if I'd hidden it somewhere else! I *believed* they were taking the Akan translation, and Devriess could *sense* that I believed that. Did it look like my handwriting, in that box they took?"

Blanzac had not got a close look at the top page in the box. "I don't know," he said, "I'm not—"

"Never mind, you wouldn't know, would you—but it looked like it to Devriess, so it probably was. What would I—" She snapped her fingers. "I bet I know what it was! It was probably my old translation of Hesiod's *Theogony.* Wait a moment."

She straightened up and swayed into the bedroom, and a few moments later came out again waving a lidless cardboard box in one hand.

"It's empty all right," she said, frowning and nodding. "My Hesiod translation was in this. I took a shower this afternoon, and you were alone for ten minutes—you will be, that is, from your point of view—and you must have put the Hesiod manuscript into that box." She waved at the now empty wooden box beside the hi-fi cabinet.

She stared at him fiercely. "You've got to do that, you understand? This is probably why you were sent here from the future! Come in here."

He followed her into the bedroom and she pointed to an empty space between two books with German titles on a crowded bookshelf over her narrow bed. "That's where this box was," she said with careful articulation. She held the cardboard box up to the gap to make it clear. "Right? When I'm in the shower a couple of hours ago, you've got to come in here, take the papers out of this box, and put them into that wooden box they emptied. Right? Okay?"

Blanzac was dizzy and his mouth tasted of second-hand gin, and wanted to go sit down again. "Okay," he said. "And what do you want me to do with the, the Akan translation?—after I take it out of the wooden box in the stereo?"

"Stereo! Hide it. Uh, hide it under my pillow, all right? This pillow right here." She pointed at the bed.

Blanzac shrugged. "Okay."

Greenwald lifted the pillow. There were no papers under it.

"What the hell!" she said. "I just told you to put it there!"

Blanzac spread his hands. "Maybe you change your mind about where to hide it. That's not a very good place, really."

"It's good enough, we know they didn't search the apartment. Dammit—okay, hide it under the sink in the bathroom, will you do *that*?"

"Sure."

They shuffled through a doorway into a closet-sized bathroom, and when Greenwald hiked up her black dress and sat down on the green-and-white tiled floor and opened the low cabinet, Blanzac had to step into the still-damp shower. His shoulder clinked a couple of shampoo bottles together on a tile shelf, and he realized they were glass.

"It's not in here, either," said Greenwald, her voice muffled, "though you'd have had plenty of room!" She sat back and scowled up at him. "What the *hell* did you *do* with it?"

"Maybe in a minute you're going to tell me to burn it, and so this afternoon I threw it down the incinerator shaft! Have you got those in this building?"

"Yes, but my God, don't do that!" She got to her feet and smoothed out the black dress. "It's the only copy, and—and all my notes on the Sumerian grammar are in there too, and carbons of Christopher Smart's version—"

Blanzac stepped out of the shower. "You want it *preserved*?"

"No, I just don't want it destroyed! Jesus! I'm not sure the originals of the Smart lines still exist anywhere. *Don't* do that, even if I tell you to in the next—" She glanced at the kitchen clock, "in the next hour!" She stamped her foot. "If you'd only put it under the pillow like I *said* to!"

"I still could," he said; then he grimaced and added, "no, sorry, right, it'd be there now."

She didn't seem to have heard him. "Maybe," she said slowly, "it's good *not* to have it in the apartment. Hesiod's not a bad decoy, but one of those guys might be familiar with the Latin version of my text, and see that what they took isn't part of that. Swami Rajgah will know, for sure, when they show it to him." She was snapping her fingers rapidly. "We've got to get out of here right now, out of town, I can't come back here. I'll take the Fleming book. Can you drive a car?"

"Sure." He took a deep breath and let it out. He was suddenly feeling dizzy. "Maybe after some black coffee."

"I've got my sister's Volkswagen in the garage downstairs, but I can't drive anymore, 'specially at night. No depth perception, misinterpretation of images. Wages of sin. Wages of Sumerian. We'll think of a place outside the building for you to hide it." She watched as he stepped carefully to the couch and sat down. "Come on, Murgatroyd, they might be back here any second!"

"Right, right." He sighed and pressed down on the arm of the couch, but it seemed to yield under his palm like brittle foam, and for a moment he caught the familiar whiff of coffee and book paper from his office in 2012.

He held still, then cautiously inhaled—and there were only the faint citrus and burnt dust smells of Greenwald's apartment. The upholstered arm of the couch was solid again, but he didn't put any weight on it.

"I think I'm . . . going," he said. His voice was a careful monotone. "Disappearing."

"What, right now? It's earlier than you said! But *where's the manuscript*?"

He heard a telephone ringing—the resonance sounded oddly constricted in the big volume of Greenwald's living room, and its tone was recognizably that of the one on his own desk.

"You don't hear a phone ringing," he said quietly, not daring to move.

"No." She knelt beside him and reached out as if to take his hand, then hesitated, apparently fearful that touching him might hasten his disappearance. Tears glittered on her eyelashes. "Look—just make sure they don't get it, okay?"

He nodded, shaking her living room out of focus for a moment. "I'll see you earlier today."

"But *I* won't see *you* again—maybe ever!" She grabbed for his hand,

and her hand went through his as if through a shadow, and just thumped the upholstery; and as the couch gave way beneath him he caught four last fading syllables which might have been, "Read what I wrote!"

He raised his arms and straightened his legs to keep from falling, and then the light shifted and he was hopping to keep his balance on the carpet in his office. His hands slapped against his desk and he turned around and leaned against it.

⊰ IV ⊱

HE WAS BREATHING hard and squinting around at the familiar shelves and file cabinets, which were still lit by early evening sunlight slanting in through the window. A round section was missing from the carpet, and some pieces of the vanished chair lay in a dished concavity in the exposed floorboards. The nearest bookshelf showed a round patch of pale shaved wood across the shelf edges, and the sewn quires of a book deprived of its spine. That Hemingway is worthless now, he thought automatically, and that was a first-state dust jacket.

There were no fragments of Greenwald's couch on the floor. Apparently the bounce-back had returned only himself to the present, not any surrounding bits that belonged to the past. He was at least still wearing his clothes.

The telephone was still ringing, and he picked up the receiver. He tried to say Hello, but could only pant into the mouthpiece.

From up the hall came the bong of the doorbell, and from the phone Blanzac heard a man's voice: "Mr. Blanzac, this is Jesse Welch, we met half an hour ago at the Goldengrove Retirement Community. I noticed on your business card that you're on my way, and I thought I'd stop by to take a quick look at the Greenwald items."

"Just a minute," Blanzac said, "there's somebody at my front door."

Welch chuckled. "That's me. My route home takes me right past your exit, so I thought, Why not visit? Could I have just a few minutes of your time?"

With an unreasoning chill, Blanzac remembered Welch's question half an hour ago: *Did the consignment include any manuscripts that might be Greenwald's?*

"A minute of my time," echoed Blanzac as he hastily made a decision. "Certainly! I—I just got out of the shower, I'll be with you as soon as I . . . throw on some clothes."

He hung up the phone, picked up the manuscript and the Ace Double paperback and shoved them over the top of a row of Einstein biographies on a high shelf so that they fell down behind the books, out of sight. Then he hurried down the hall to the kitchen and opened the door to the carport on the east side of the house; the kitchen door creaked, so he left it open as he stepped around the front of his white Chevy Blazer and carefully levered open the driver's side door. He got in and released the parking brake, and then, without closing the door all the way, he started the SUV and immediately shifted it into reverse and accelerated backward down the driveway.

Out in the street, while the vehicle was still rocking, he pulled the shift lever into Drive and stomped on the gas pedal; laughing with mingled alarm and embarrassment, he looked in the rear-view mirror and glimpsed someone moving from his front door toward the curb.

He swung left onto Washington Street; the lanes were clear and the sun was behind him now. There was an onramp for the northbound 280 ahead, and if he could get onto that freeway without Welch seeing the move, he should be safely lost in the infinite every-which-way traffic of the San Franisco peninsula . . . if in fact his anxiety was justified and Welch was indeed trying to follow him.

A police car passed him going the other way, and Blanzac lifted his foot from the accelerator. He told himself to drive carefully—he had left his wallet, again, on his desk at home, and in any case, he was still somewhat drunk, from bourbon he had drunk fifty-five years in the past.

The receptionist at Goldengrove called Betty Barlow's room phone to ask if she was free to see her earlier visitor again, and, though the reply filled several seconds, she finally hung up the phone and told Blanzac, "She'll see you. Don't tire her or excite her."

"No," Blanzac assured her, though as he strode down the familiar hall he reflected that he was unlikely to follow that instruction. While crossing the Bay Bridge during the half hour drive from Daly City, an odd idea about old Betty Barlow had become a strong suspicion.

She was still lying in the bed when he stepped through the wide doorway into her room, and she was glaring in his direction from under her thin white hair. An overhead fluorescent light had been switched on since his last visit, dimming the light from outside and making the hour seem later.

"You again," she snapped. She peered around through her thick glasses. "You've burned the manuscript and the science fiction book? I want to see ashes."

"Keep your fluffy little pants on, Murgatroyd," he said. "I haven't been paid yet." He sat down in the chair beside the bed. "Remember that cigarette of mine that you put in your mouth this afternoon, and then gave back to me?"

"What? I *did* give it back to you. Did you come here again to get back one cigarette? You're drunk, I can smell it. Edith is a fool to have—"

"Yes yes, you gave it back to me. And I'm pretty sure I put that same cigarette in *my* mouth, when I got home," he said. "And it wasn't Betty Barlow I found waiting for me when the merry-go-round stopped. I'm—"

"Fluffy little pants," she interrupted, frowning past him. "That—that was about a cat."

"In your apartment on Divisadero," he agreed, "that Ferlinghetti used to live in." He took a deep breath and resolutely went on, "I imagine the authorities in a little Mexican town like Otatoclan don't really question the alleged identity of an American tourist who dies there, when they issue a death certificate. Especially back in 1969, when you didn't even need passports to be there."

The old woman's wrinkled face held no expression. After several seconds, she said, "That was a long time ago."

"Yes."

"I doubt anything could be established at this late date. Neither of us was ever fingerprinted."

"I imagine you're right."

"So why are you here?" Before Blanzac could frame an answer, she went on, "Isn't this the real manuscript, after all? Hah! Have you still just got, who was it, Hesiod? There's nothing I can do about it now. I swear to you I don't remember any of the Sumerian grammar or vocabulary anymore."

Blanzac shivered and stared at the withered old face on the pillow. Until this moment he had not truly believed that this really was Sophia Greenwald herself, the dark-haired young woman who had kissed him less than an hour ago, fifty-five years ago.

Blanzac said, gently, "I'm not one of the Swami's crowd, Sophie."

This time the silence lasted nearly a full minute, and if he hadn't seen her eyes blinking behind the thick lenses he might have thought she had gone to sleep.

"You have a young voice," she said finally. "But I might have heard it before today. *Blanzac* means nothing to me—who are you?"

Blanzac sighed and gripped his knees. "Back then I told you that my name was Richard Vader."

"Richard— ?" She gasped and, in an oddly childlike gesture, she pulled the sheet up over her face.

"I wasn't going to see you," came her frail, scratchy voice through it, "if you somehow found me! And you *especially*, you were supposed to believe it was me that died in Otatoclan—Betty had no family, so it was easy to become her, after the cholera did her in, and then just stay in Mexico. *Rare books—*" She dropped the sheet and glared at him. "You said salvage and demolition!"

"I haven't said it yet," he told her. "I just fell out of your Divisadero living room half an hour ago. Devriess was just there, and took— probably took—your Hesiod translation." He spread his hands. "That was the evening. I'm apparently still due to go back, for the afternoon."

"Devriess!" she said with a visible shudder. "That's right, you arrived out of sequence, didn't you. What, that cigarette? This happened in the hour since you were last here? And—and right now you've still got that afternoon ahead of you?" She rolled her eyes toward the ceiling. "Oh my." She shook her head sharply and looked at him. "Did you really just . . . find the manuscript in a box of papers? Lately?"

"This afternoon," he said. "This long afternoon."

"All this time, and *they* might have found it as easily as you! Where did you put it, on that day?"

"I don't know, I haven't done it yet."

"Where is it now?"

"Hidden in my office, at home. There's a guy who seems to want it—Welch? He even came to my house, half an hour ago. I ditched him and drove here. He said he was from the University of California."

"That you may be sure he was not. They still want it—Swami Rajgah died in '57, right on schedule, without finding his door into nothing, but his people still hope to find it, to save themselves . . . from existence." She tried to sit up in the bed, then fell back, panting. "You need to destroy it, Richard. Go straight home and burn it, please! I translated too much of it back then, and I think now it's . . . I'm very afraid that it's extending itself! In my dreams! Like crystals forming in salt water as it evaporates, as my mind is evaporating in this damn place. I'm afraid—I'm truly afraid that if they do it now, I'll be swept out through the hole with them! 'I have been half in love with easeful death,' but I want to, I *do* want to, take my memories with me, even if that means taking them to Hell."

"An hour ago you insisted that I *not* destroy it."

"Nonsense, the first thing I said to you here was—"

"Sorry, I mean in 1957. It was almost the last thing you said to me before I fell back to now."

"Well, I was closer to it then. It was my work—hard work, good work. But it was evil work too. I had a gift, but I used it in the service of the void. 'Then on my tongue the taste is sour of all I ever wrote.'"

Blanzac stirred in his chair. "Your earlier work wasn't corrupted. Why keep it out of print?"

"Penance. Expiation."

"Don't you think the penance has gone on long enough? You said that your poetry was worthless. Your poetry, not the translation. Did you mean it?"

"Yes. I don't know. Who cares, now?"

"I think . . . you do. Do you believe it was worthless?"

"Why *ask*?"

"I think the answer is important. To you." For several seconds she was silent; then she sighed heavily and pulled a Kleenex from a box on the table and took off her glasses to blot her eyes.

"No," she whispered. "It was as good as I could make it, and I was no slouch."

Blanzac opened his mouth to speak, but she went on quickly, "And the two science fiction novels—those were expiation too. They, published upside down to each other, they're made of images I believed would stay in a reader's head and deflect the disassembly-logic of the Sumerian poem, disarm its images by . . . *pre-emptively* hanging distracting contrary associations on them. The two novels are really the same plot, one set in the Amazon jungle and the other set in outer space, so I could use contrasting archetypes to fragment the Akan logic from all sides." She fitted her glasses back on. "And you still have the afternoon ahead of you, God help us! I wonder if this time you can do things differently than you did, and destroy it then."

Blanzac frowned and shook his head. "We wouldn't be talking about it now, if I had done it then. It's all happened already—I just haven't walked through my second-act part yet. First-act, I mean."

She waved a hand. "Of course," she said bleakly. "Free will versus determinism. That was the core contradiction behind the sequence of images in the poem. They're both true, so there's no place to stand. The synthesis, the net result, is zero, consciousness winks out."

"Really." Blanzac flexed his fingers. "You, uh, just explained it to me, and I'm still conscious."

"Well so am I, Murgatroyd," she said. It was the first time Blanzac had seen the old woman smile, and he winced as he recognized—for a moment, among the sagging wrinkles—the woman he had spent an hour with in 1957. "You need to read at least a good extent of the poem, visualize and vicariously experience each sequential juxtaposition of images, internalize them—the poem starts mild, and then escalates. Whoever put that thing together could have made Jung swallow his own head."

"Who *did* put it together?"

She sniffed. "You do smell like bourbon. You didn't *bring* any liquor, did you? Huh! Negligent. 'O for a draught of vintage!' Who put it together? It must have been a group, each man writing one section in the sequence. Astrologers maybe? And it must have been a relay team that cut the cuneiform into the Al Hillah limestone—or else somebody who couldn't read, and just copied the symbols."

Blanzac looked at her wrinkled, spotted hand on the bedsheet, and he remembered her touching his hand half a century ago.

"I should go," he said, standing up. "I'll burn the Akan text as soon as I get home."

She reached out a withered arm and turned the phone around to face him. "There's my number. Call me, please, as soon as it's surely gone."

He leaned forward and read the number taped onto the phone, and repeated it to himself.

"I've got it," he said, "and yes, I'll call you the minute it's done. But I'm going to get hold of your two poetry collections, and I hope you'll begin trying to find a publisher for them."

"They're," she began, scowling; then her expression softened, and she went on more quietly, "they're not really too bad, if the Akan translation is gone."

"We'll find a publisher," he told her, "or publish them ourselves. Get 'em on Amazon." He nodded and then left the room.

The sky was dark and the streetlights were on when he got home, and he paused in the kitchen to put a cup of water in the microwave oven. He noticed that he had left the kitchen door ajar, and he pulled it closed and locked it. Then the microwave binged, and he fetched down a jar of instant coffee and stirred a spoonful into the steaming water.

When, he wondered, do I go back to enact the 1957 afternoon? It was that cigarette that triggered the last jump, presumably because it had some of her saliva on it, constituted contact with her. Would I have jumped back if I had touched her during this last visit to Goldengrove?

It could be that I'll *stay* back there, this time, and simply disappear from 2012! I could go to Mexico with her—though tonight she talked as if I hadn't done that. Still, I should bring some things, have some useful items in my pockets—a gun, gold, a list of Kentucky Derby winners!

He picked up the coffee cup, blowing across the top of it, and hurried down the hall to his office.

He had taken two steps across the now-holed carpet and turned toward his desk, when he froze. In the dimness he could see two men standing by the bookshelves below the window.

"Mr. Blanzac," said one of them, "do please turn on the light."

Blanzac reached out to the side with his left hand and found the wall switch, and when the overhead light came on he recognized Welch. The other man was very old—bald and stooped in a baggy lime-green leisure suit, blinking through bifocals and leaning heavily on an aluminum walker.

Welch, Blanzac noticed belatedly, was holding a revolver pointed at the floor.

The very old man began wheezing and trembling in frail excitement. "This is the fellow!" he croaked.

"What," said Welch, not taking his eyes off Blanzac, "you've seen him before?"

"He was with her, in San Francisco! He stopped us from capturing her—" The effort of speaking was making him drool. "He was with her when we—took what we *thought* was her translation!"

"That was in the '50s," said Welch irritably. "This isn't the same guy."

The old man's mouth was opening and shutting. "It was! It is! He's still young—"

"For God's sake, Devriess! Shut up." Welch raised the gun and pointed it at Blanzac's face. "We want the manuscript that was in that box. I'm sure it's here, and if I have to kill you I'll eventually find it, but you can save me some time. Oh, and your life."

But Blanzac was staring at the old man clinging to the walker. Devriess! He tried to recognize in this shaking, wet-eyed ruin the handsome young man who had politely taken Greenwald's Hesiod translation from the apartment on Divisadero fifty-five years ago.

"I really will kill you," remarked Welch. "And I really will find the manuscript, afterward. I imagine it's right in this room."

"Yes," said Blanzac, exhaling. If I had any hope, he told himself, of saving Sophie's soul by resisting here, I might resist; but he *would* find the manuscript, in any case.

He slowly put the cup down on the desk, and raised his hands. "I've got to pull some books down from a high shelf."

Welch nodded. "Pull down a gun and you'll be dead before you can aim it."

Blanzac nodded too, then turned around and reached up for the Einstein biographies. He gripped half a dozen of them and pulled them out, then crouched to set them on the carpet; he straightened up and reached in behind where they had been, and when he turned around again he was holding the sheaf of manuscript.

He laid it on the desk and picked up his coffee and stepped back to take a cautious sip of it. "So now what?" he asked. "You get a lot of people to read it, so you can step out of reality?"

Welch had relaxed at the sight of the stack of papers, and he smiled. "I wasn't actually sure you had it! Yes, lots of people." He waved toward

Devriess. "Their plan back in the '50s was to buy a few pages of a magazine and publish the thing that way, but we're ready to hack it into a thousand high-traffic online blogs. Millions of people will read it on the same morning!" Assuming a Peter Lorre accent, he said, "And then, *adio* Casablanca."

Blanzac laughed, for he had all at once dizzily decided to try to take the gun away from the man. "Your letters of transit," he said.

Welch smiled, nodding. "You played it for her," he said, in a Bogart imitation now, "you can play it for me." He shifted the gun to his left hand in order to reach for the stack of papers—and Blanzac lunged forward and with his free hand chopped down at Welch's wrist before the man could get his finger into the trigger-guard.

⊰ V ⊱

THE EDGE OF Blanzac's hand collided hard with the bones of Welch's wrist, knocking the man's arm sharply away—

And then the light was gone and the floor was tilted and Blanzac stumbled forward into a man who was somehow right in front of him. Blanzac had raised both hands to stop his fall, and he inadvertently splashed hot coffee into the stranger's face.

A cold wind that smelled of chocolate was blowing rain into Blanzac's eyes, and as the stranger recoiled away, cursing in French, Blanzac caught hold of a woman's arm and nearly pulled her over backward, skipping on wet pavement to regain his balance.

Across the street—he was outdoors, he realized, on a street!—a woman was shouting and a dog was barking, and the woman Blanzac had grabbed was hastily stepping backward away from an old Buick idling at the curb, and she was pulling Blanzac back with her. His arm was tangled in the strap of her purse.

"Out of here!" came a muffled shout from inside the car—the passenger door was open—and the man Blanzac had splashed with coffee threw himself in across the seat.

The Buick roared and accelerated away, the tires leaving brief tracks on the wet asphalt. People on the other side of the street were staring and pointing and waving umbrellas, and one man had dropped a newspaper. Blanzac freed his elbow from the woman's purse-strap and peered at her in the dim street lamp glow.

She was Sophia Greenwald, again looking no more than thirty years old.

She blinked at him, then glanced across the street at the pedestrians on the opposite sidewalk. "Never mind," she said breathlessly, "let's get out of here."

"Where," he asked in a strangled voice as he matched her hurrying footsteps, "is here?" He waved his emptied coffee cup and then left it to fill with rainwater on a chest-level wall they were passing. "I mean, I bet it's San Francisco, but where?"

"North Point Street, by Ghirardelli. You know, the chocolate factory. Are you lost?" She looked over her shoulder, blinking against the rain. "Thanks for helping me, mister, but I should get out of sight."

What do I say? he thought. "Sophie, I can help you."

She paused, and after glancing narrowly up and down the street she looked closely at his face; she reached up and brushed the wet hair off his forehead with cold fingers, and shook her head. "Who are you? I don't recognize you. Come on," she added, pulling him along and steering him around the lefthand corner onto the Hyde Street sidewalk. He could see the red neon Buena Vista sign shining against the gray overcast sky ahead of them. Beyond it through the veils of rain he could just see a cable car slowly rotating on the Hyde Street turnaround, with a man in a yellow raincoat pushing it.

Icy water was running down inside Blanzac's collar. "I believe we have some Irish coffee now," he said through clenched teeth.

She was still scanning the street, but she gave him a nervous smile. "I believe you're right."

They hurried down the slanted sidewalk to the Beach Street corner and Blanzac held open the door of the Buena Vista Café as she hurried inside.

He glanced at his hand on the door, and his jaw clenched in shock to see what appeared to be rain-diluted blood all over his right hand; with his other hand he slapped at his wrist and forearm, but felt no pain. He let the door close and hurried back across the sidewalk to a gushing rain-gutter and rinsed his hand, wiggling his fingers in the icy water. He flapped his arm, but no more red fluid appeared, and as far back as he could push the cuff of his jacket and shirt he could see no wound. Apparently it had not been blood, or not his, at any rate—perhaps young Devriess had been bleeding when Blanzac stumbled into him a few moments ago . . . though the man would seem uninjured when he would appear later this evening.

Blanzac heaved a deep sigh of relief and ran back to the Buena Vista door and pulled it open again.

The lights in the long yellow hall made the dark day outside the tall windows seem like night. Only a few people were sitting at the tables, but Greenwald had made straight for the tall wooden bar along the left-hand wall and was perched on a stool with her purse at her elbow, staring back at him. Getting his first clear look at her since inadvertently pulling her away from the Buick, Blanzac noticed that she was wearing a loose blue sweater, now beaded with moisture, and tight black Capris that ended at mid-calf. When, he wondered, does she put on the black dress?

He glanced at his watch—noting with a fresh surge of relief that there was still no blood to be seen—but then remembered that there would be no correspondence between his personal time and this local time.

"Do you," he began as he sat down on the stool next to her, then said to the bartender who leaned in, "Two Irish coffees, please. Wait, sorry, I don't have any money!" To Greenwald he said, awkwardly, "Order something if you like, I'll just . . . sit here and get warm."

"Don't be silly, you just saved me from God knows what, a kidnapping or something. Two Irish coffees, please," she repeated to the bartender. "And you started to say, 'Do you—'?"

"Oh, do you know what time it is?" He wished he had noted what time it was that he arrived—was to arrive—in the restroom hallway at the Tin Angel tonight.

She looked at her own wristwatch. "Five-thirty." As the bartender dropped sugar cubes into two glasses and poured coffee and Bushmill's whiskey into them, she squinted at Blanzac. "I still don't recognize you. How do you know me?"

"Ah, this will be hard to believe." Go ahead and be direct, he thought, you know it works out. "I'm from the future, from the year 2012. This right now," he said, tapping the bar, "is my second tumble back in time to this day, but they're out of order; on my *first* one I met you *tonight*—about three hours from now—at a bar called the Tin Angel."

She grinned delightedly and picked up her drink and took a sip of the fortified coffee through the cream layer on top, and there was a line of cream on her upper lip when she put it down and said, "Is it more like Pohl and Kornbluth in 2012, or Heinlein?"

Blanzac recognized the names of science fiction writers. "It's very like this, actually. Cars, gas stations, traffic signals, TV, movie theaters. The only difference you'd notice is that everybody in 2012 has a computer no bigger than a TV set."

She rested her elbow on the bar and cupped her chin in her hand. "Why do you all need computers? Are you forever calculating trajectories to other planets?"

He smiled and shook his head. "To write notes to each other, mainly. They're all hooked together via the phone lines."

She glanced at the dark windows and turned to face the bar. "So how do you really know me," she said in a level tone, "and who are you?"

"My name is—" He sighed. "—is Richard Vader. I was born in 1972, and I was an English major at San Francisco City College and got a BA in '94. I met you for the first time later this evening, and you told me about your translation work, the Sumerian poem."

She stood up, her face stony. "You leave right now, mister. When you're gone I'll call a cab."

Waving placatingly at the tensed bartender, Blanzac said with quiet urgency, "Sophie, I don't want it, I don't want to dive through the Akan hole! I very much want to help you keep it away from Devriess and Swami Gaga or whatever his name is."

"It's *Rajgah*." She eyed him skeptically but slowly resumed her seat. "Are you from the Vatican or something?" She shivered and hugged herself inside the wet sweater. "Well, I could *use* some help now, actually. But I gotta say it's a very outlandish sort of cover story you've chosen."

"I think you'd agree it's a pretty outlandish situation." He took a solid sip of the hot Irish coffee and sighed as the whiskey in it seemed to relax his chilled scalp. "Thanks for the drink. I'm afraid you buy me two more before the evening's out."

"A poorly equipped time traveler," she said. She opened her purse and took out a pack of Camels and slid an ashtray closer. "Didn't think to bring contemporary money, eh?"

"No wallet at all. I hadn't planned on coming." She held the pack of cigarettes toward him, and he took one. "Thanks," he said. "You can't smoke in public places anymore, in 2012." She struck a match and he leaned over her hand to get a light. "I was in my office at home both times, when with no warning I found myself," he said with an all-around wave of his cigarette, "here. 1957."

"Office? What do you do?"

"Uh—" He thought about the Sumerian manuscript. "Salvage and demolition, lately."

She had lit a cigarette of her own, and now her syllables were accompanied by little puffs of smoke. "So how is it that you know about the translation, and the Swami and Devriess?"

"You explain it all to me on my first visit—later tonight, starting when we're taking a cab from the Tin Angel back to your apartment." He smiled crookedly, remembering the conversation. "It's a fairly disjointed account, but eventually I get the story."

"You did stop Devriess just now from grabbing me and I don't know what, torturing me, maybe, to get the translation. But you didn't come here to help me, specifically."

"No, I fell into it somehow. But I landed squarely on your side." He paused for a moment. "I don't want," he went on, thinking of a frightened old woman in an assisted living home in 2012, "I *don't* want them to win."

"You said you landed on my side. I hope you're not kidding. There's nobody else on my side, and a big serious crowd against . . . us?"

"Us," he agreed.

She held out her right hand, and he shook it.

"Drink up, Captain Future," she said. "We should grab a taxi back to my place. You know where that is?"

"Divisadero, half a block south of Pacific."

She shivered again in her damp sweater. "I surely hope you're on my side—nobody's supposed to know that." She looked across at the bartender. "Could you call us a cab?"

⁜ ⁜ ⁜

"I think I'm going to have to leave town," she said as she closed the apartment door and clicked the wall switch that lit the two living room lamps, "at least for a while. I've completed my part of the translation—"

"The women's dialect," said Blanzac.

He had sat down on the couch, and she stepped into the kitchen. "Okay," she called, "now how do you know about that? Nobody knows about that except the Swami's crowd."

"And you. You tell me about it, in a few hours."

She came back into the living room carrying the bottle of Gordon's gin Blanzac had seen on his last visit here, visibly fuller now. "Live your cover," she said. "You don't want to say who you work for. I really hope you're a right guy, 'cause you're all I've got."

She picked up one of the stack of identical Ace Double science fiction novels—he noticed that there were six of them now—and waved it at him. "I wrote this," she said. "You should have a copy, it'll do you good." She shoved some books back to make room to set the bottle down, and then picked up a ball-point pen from the table and scribbled something in the middle pages of the book and tossed pen and book onto the table. Rain thrashed against the dark windows.

Bottle in hand again, she joined him on the couch and took another gulp of the gin. "You want some of this? I could get a glass. I have to stay fairly drunk at all times."

He nodded. "So they can't track you, because you've all read too much of the poem. No, I'm fine for now, thanks."

She put it down on the table beside an ashtray and pushed her wet hair back from her forehead with both hands. Blanzac felt the hairs on his arms stand up as he saw a TV *Guide* and a copy of the San Francsico *Chronicle* lying beside the ashtray. The cover of the TV *Guide* was a picture of Pat Boone.

"How long do you stay here today," Greenwald asked, "altogether?"

"I leave around ten, I think."

"Is there a Mrs. Vader, up there in the future?"

He smiled. "No."

"Never?" she asked, picking up the gin bottle again. "That's a long stretch of future." Bubbles gurgled up through the clear liquor as she drank.

"Never. I came close once, but she wanted me to be more ambitious. Big house with a pool, new cars . . . she eventually got a job with Microsoft and found a guy like that." Seeing her raised eyebrows, he added, "Microsoft makes . . . things to do with computers."

"A square like that would be all wrong for you, Captain Future." Greenwald clanked the bottle down again. "What was her name?"

"Gillian."

"I hate her. I've got beer, if you'd rather."

"No, I—soon we'll be—" He paused, for her cold fingers were on his neck.

"You're all tense," she said, and began to knead the muscles of his shoulder under his wet collar. "And getting tenser! 'Tenser, said the tensor'! You don't like back rubs?"

He shifted around to face her, which pulled his shoulder free. Her hand fell onto the knee of his damp jeans. "Never got used to them," he admitted.

"God, we're both soaked." She stood up and looked away from him. "We should . . . get out of these damp clothes."

"Sophie," said Blazac unsteadily, "you've had a lot to drink—"

"I always do, these days."

"I'm apparently going to be disappearing—"

"Right, but then your three-hour-younger self will step in. So? Damn it, I'm not some—I'm thirty-one years old, and—and if we're—I need to know you. Right now you're a stranger."

"I'm afraid I'll never be much more than that," he said, but he got to his feet.

⊰ VI ⊱

WHEN SHE SLEEPILY got out of bed and said she'd take a shower before they left for the Tin Angel, Blanzac followed her into the bathroom and waited until she had turned on the water and stepped into the narrow shower stall—where he would be standing in a couple of hours while she looked for the manuscript under the sink—and then he hurried back to the bedroom. As he pulled on his clothes and shoved his feet into his shoes, he stole glances at the furnishings of her room, and in that hurried moment the rocking chair and the framed pictures of silent-era movie stars and the couple of bowler hats on the wall all struck him as oddly endearing, and he wondered if he could be falling in love with Sophia Greenwald.

He found the box between the two German books on the shelf over the bed, quickly lifted out the sheets of the Hesiod translation, and slid the empty box back into its place on the shelf.

He was panting. Later tonight she would tell him that she stayed in the shower for ten minutes, and he hoped that was accurate.

There had to be another box, *the* box, ready to hand—he stepped into the living room and glanced around but didn't see one, then hurried into the kitchen. The window over the sink was open, and he nearly dropped the Hesiod papers when the calico cat startled him by leaping in and bounding to the floor, but after a few moments he found a box on the counter with three big 20-ounce jars of pickled garlic in it. He juggled them out one-handed and set them on the counter, then carried the box and the Hesiod translation into the living room and knelt to lay them on the carpet beside the hi-fi

The wooden box was in the cabinet below the turntable, right where Devriess' companion would find it in an hour or so, and Blanzac pulled it out and opened it.

There was the remembered handwritten text—

As helplessly as shadows fall unfurled, he read, *To west instead of east as dusk comes on,/ As fated as the phases of the moon . . .*

—and he lifted the stack of papers out and dropped them into the cardboard box the jars of garlic had been in, then laid the Hesiod translation into the wooden box, closed it, and pushed it back in place and shut the cabinet doors.

Sweating, he stood up with the cardboard box in his hands.

And even though he knew he would be getting this box again in fifty-five years, the manuscript looked dangerously conspicuous all by itself in there.

He hurried to the table and tossed the Ace Double paperback in alongside the handwritten pages, and unfolded the outer sheet of the newspaper and threw that and the *TV Guide* in on top. For good measure he dumped the ashtray over it all, then folded the box's flaps closed and straightened up, holding it.

And he bared his teeth in agonized indecision. Where *was* he to put it? He couldn't hide it in the apartment, even though Devriess and his companion wouldn't search the apartment during their visit tonight; they might come back and do a thorough search when they discovered that what they had taken was the wrong manuscript, and it might not take them long to discover that.

Just throw it in a trash can on the street? But then he would not have got it in 2012, and would not visit the old woman who would claim to be Betty Barlow, and would therefore not be here now. If he removed himself from this chain of events, Greenwald would be alone when Devriess and that other man would come here tonight, and the Akan manuscript would be in the hi-fi cabinet.

Then he remembered her saying, *I've got my sister's Volkswagen in the garage downstairs, but I can't drive anymore,* and, *We've got to get out of here, out of town, I can't come back here.*

The Volkswagen will surely be returned to her sister somehow when Sophie disappears to Mexico, he thought. And the sister will apparently get the books, including the signed *Howl* and the Kerouac letters.

Greenwald had dropped her purse on the floor beside the couch, and he knelt by it and felt past her wallet and hairbrush and cigarettes to a set of keys at the bottom. One of the keys was a short brass Master, the only one that could fit a probable padlock on the garage door.

He pocketed the keys, opened the front door and carried the box down the stairs.

When Greenwald emerged from the steamy bathroom in a terrycloth robe, rubbing her hair with a towel, he had been standing by the bookshelves for thirty seconds, and he had stopped panting.

"Is that what you're going to wear to the Tin Angel?" she asked. "You don't seem to be drying out."

"I didn't bring a change of clothes," he said. "I'll be fine." He was holding a book in a gray dust-jacket with red hearts on it. "This is the British first edition of *Casino Royale*," he remarked. It hadn't been among the books he was to get in 2012.

She peered at it from under the towel. "Oh, Ian Fleming. Is it worth something?"

"It will be."

"Is he good? Maybe I'll take it with me."

"He'll—I think he'll write better books, but yes. Keep the dust-jacket in good condition." He put it back carefully.

She laughed. "Look at you, future boy, your fly's down and your shoes are untied. Fix up and I'll call for a taxi."

She disappeared into the bedroom as he hastily zipped his fly and sat down in the upsholstered chair to tie his shoes, and shortly she had emerged again wearing the remembered black dress and black leather pumps, brushing her hair.

"What do we do at the Tin Angel?" she asked.

"Well, I apparently disappear." He thought about the situation he had left in his office in 2012. "I don't know what happens to me after that. But then I'll appear out of the restroom hallway, but it'll be my first visit, the earlier me, who won't have met you yet and won't know any of the things we've talked about. I'll be pretty scared—I won't even believe it's really 1957—I'll ask a guy at another table who's president, and even when he tells me Eisenhower I still won't believe it."

"You know, sweetie, you seem so sane most of the time." She shook her head as she stooped to pick up her purse. "We can wait downstairs in the entryway till we see the cab."

⇥ VII ⇤

WHEN THEY GOT out of the cab in front of the Tin Angel, Blanzac blinked around in the rain. In spite of everything, he was disoriented anew to see the Greenwich Street sign at the corner.

She was holding the door for him, and he hurried forward. The air was warm inside and rich with the remembered smells of tobacco smoke and Beef Stroganoff, which he now saw listed on the wall blackboard as the Wednesday special.

He led her down the long high-ceilinged room through the maze of tables to the one he remembered, and no one was sitting at it and the table was bare except for an empty ashtray.

"I'll get drinks," she said as he sat down.

"No," he said, catching her hand. "Sophie, there are drinks on the table when I come here for the first time—when I won't know you, and *this* me disappears. That can't happen until there's drinks."

She gave him a wry smile with her eyes half closed, but sat down. He still held her hand. "You won't remember this afternoon," she said.

"I won't have lived through this afternoon yet. *I'll* remember this afternoon as long as I live."

She squeezed his hand and then released it. "And you'll help, with this situation? The Swami, Devriess, the Akan translation?"

"I'll at least help, I can promise you that. You escape them, I promise."

"I hope so." She frowned, though still smiling. "Why—and if you won't say, I want to know why you won't say—*why* the story about coming from the future? How does that help?"

He shook his head, looking down at his hands. "It's the crazy truth. But I do want to tell you that I—"

She reached across the table and touched his lips. "Save it. I'll get drinks. What'll you have? I'm buying."

He opened his mouth, wanting to say that he loved her and that he wished it weren't impossible for them to stay together . . .

He sighed. "Bourbon on the rocks, as I recall."

She laughed softly and stood up.

He watched her step lithely away toward the bar, and he restrained a sudden impulse to run after her, hold onto her. She's going to be standing by the restroom hallway soon, he told himself; she's got to be, for all this to work out.

Greenwald came back with two glasses and slid one in front of him as she took her seat.

"I suppose this earlier self of yours won't have any money either," she said.

"Thanks. No, both times I've left my wallet sitting on my desk, back home. Oh," he added, "and I once worked at a tobacco shop, and the boss's name was Ted."

She was squinting at him. "What?"

"It's true, and I apparently mention that to you. Covering all the bases here." He looked into her brown eyes. "You can't . . . imagine," he said with quiet intensity, "how much I wish I could stay here with you."

She nodded and looked away toward the back of the room. "1957 girls are easy. Were these drinks full, when you arrived here . . . now?"

"No. About half."

She picked up her glass and took several gulps. "Drink up," she said. "I think it's time I met the other you. Hah! A line of iambic pentameter there for you to take away with you."

She pushed her chair back and got to her feet.

He stood up too. "I'll go out the front," he said. "You go stand by the hallway back there." She nodded and turned away.

The floor began to wobble as he walked to the street side door, and several of the people at the tables gave him irritated glances as he lurched past them, and when he put out his hand to take hold of the door handle, it seemed to dissolve at his touch like a stack of soap suds. He took a deep breath and stepped forward, right through the closed door.

And then he was stumbling across the carpet of his office, and Welch was spinning away from him and rebounding off the desk, and the revolver bounced off of the bottom edge of a file cabinet.

Blanzac let his stumble become a crouch, and he snatched up the gun and turned to face the room.

Welch had slid off the desk and was now sitting on the floor, wheezing and clutching his left forearm; his left hand gleamed bright red with blood and his face was pale. Blanzac could see blood drops scattered across the desk top and falling rapidly now onto the carpet. He noticed that the hole in the carpet was more of an oval now, and bigger.

Old Devriess was just leaning on his walker by the window and gaping in confusion.

Blanzac shifted the gun in his hand. The bottom of the grip was oddly cut away on the left side, and it was awkward to hold.

Welch's mouth was opening and shutting, and finally he whispered, "I think you cut off my little finger!" His eyes darted around the diminished carpet. "Where is it? They can sew it back on." He squinted up at Blanzac. "What did you cut me with?"

Blanzac remembered the blood he had belatedly noticed on his hand outside the Buena Vista Café. "You're lucky," he panted, swallowing hard against nausea, "that I was knocking your hand *away*, when I touched you. Otherwise—you'd probably have lost the whole hand."

But why, he wondered, should touching *him* have propelled me back? What intimacy have I ever shared with *him*—especially in 1957?

Blanzac glanced at Devriess. "Who is he?" he asked, waving the gun at the bleeding figure sitting on the floor. "Where did you recruit him?"

A sigh. "Far from here, long ago."

Blanzac crossed cautiously to the desk and with his free hand shook out one sheet of the old San Francisco *Chronicle* and laid it out flat. "Tell him where his missing finger is." Devriess rocked his bald head back and stared at the ceiling. "It is probably in the gutter on North Point Street. Or it was, fifty-five years ago." He lowered his head and gave Blanzac a frail smile. "The coffee cup you were holding a moment ago—it is there too, yes?"

"Overflowing with rainwater by now," Blanzac agreed. He lifted the stack of papers that were the Akan translation and laid them in the middle of the big square of newsprint.

"Find my goddamn *finger*," Welch sobbed, scuffing his heels on the carpet.

The revolver was shaking in Blanzac's fist. "It's in San Francisco!" he said, more shrilly than he'd meant to. "Weren't you listening? Fifty-five years ago!"

Looking at Welch's contorted face and sweaty gray hair, Blanzac thought: Fifty-five years ago. And touching him propelled me back there.

He glanced across at Devriess and then back at Welch.

"Welch," said Blanzac slowly, forcing his voice to be level, "listen to me. I'll let you two leave, so you can get to a hospital. But first, throw me your wallet."

"Screw you. Find my finger!" The man's face was as pale as old bedsheets, and gleaming with sweat.

"Throw me your wallet or bleed to death right there." After a few seconds he added, "I've got all night."

Whining, the older man loosened his grip on his wrist to reach around behind himself, and then he threw a wallet onto the carpet and clutched his wrist again. "Take it," he said hoarsely. "I'll cancel all the credit cards."

Blanzac crouched, picked up the wallet, and flipped it open as he straightened up. He glanced again at Devriess, who rolled his eyes and nodded.

Jesse Lewis Welch had been born on January 20, 1958. May, June, July—yes, almost exactly nine months later.

"We adopted, yes, *recruited* him," said Devriess quietly, "as a possible lever." He shrugged. "But we could not find her, and when we learned where she was, nine years later, it was because she had died."

Blanzac's chest felt hollow as he turned to stare at the gray-haired, bloody, dishevelled figure of Welch sitting on the blood-spattered carpet. Blanzac ached to say something important, but after standing with his mouth open for ten seconds, "You deserved better," was all he could think of. He added, "From me, from everybody."

Then he folded the newspaper around the manuscript and tucked the bundle under his arm; the posture meant he couldn't swing the gun from one man to the other as easily, but neither looked aggressive right now.

Finally Blanzac stretched out his free arm, reached into the box and lifted out one of the old Camel cigarette butts.

"What do you think?" he asked Devriess. "One more time?" He bent his knees, took a deep breath, and then put the dry cigarette butt between his lips.

And abruptly the light went dim and gray, and cold rain stung his face, and in his involuntary gasp the smells of diesel exhaust and chocolate were blended on the gusty breeze.

He shuffled to get his footing on the wet cement of the tilted sidewalk, spitting out the instantly-soaked cigarette butt, and though he hugged the newspaper-wrapped bundle to his chest, the oddly narrowed grip of the revolver slipped out of his hand; the gun splashed into the overflowing gutter.

He would instinctively have crouched to retrieve it, but he had to step out of the way of a woman in a white raincoat walking a dog on a leash. A car hissed past beyond the curb, and through its partly-rolled-down window he heard a familiar melody, and of course it was "How Little We Know."

Blanzac squinted through the rain at the other side of the street, and after a few seconds of blinking water out of his eyes he saw a slim figure hurrying east along the sidewalk over there, and then his heart was pounding, for he had recognized her even before he made out the dark hair and blue sweater and black Capri pants.

"Sophie!" he yelled over the wind and the thrashing of the rain. "I love you!"

He knew she hadn't been able to make out his words, but she peered across the lanes in his direction. He waved and slipped on the wet pavement and scrambled to catch his balance, nearly losing the newspaper-wrapped bundle.

Then a darkly-gleaming Buick had pulled to the curb on her side of the street, and a man got out quickly and grabbed her arms; the two figures rocked as she struggled. The woman in the raincoat was shouting something, and the dog was barking; Blanzac unthinkingly took a step out onto the street, letting go of the bundled papers—but a moment later there were *two* men beside the Buick across the street, apparently fighting, and then the first man got hastily back into the car, which sped away to the west.

The newcomer was now walking quickly away to the east with Sophia Greenwald, toward Hyde Street.

A close, loud car-horn made Blanzac jump back onto the curb, and this time he did lose his footing, and he sat down on the wet sidewalk as a taxi hissed past a yard beyond his shoes.

He got back to his feet, rubbing his chilled and abraded palms on his jacket, and he saw that the taxi had run over the bundle—the newspaper was torn and already soaked, and the handwritten pages were fanned out across the asphalt, rapidly darkening with moisture.

Stepping back from the curb, he watched as the tires of two more cars slashed over the papers, scattering them in wet pieces.

He looked up, but Greenwald and her companion had already turned down Hyde Street.

I believe you have some Irish coffee now, he thought, and, even in the moment he thought it, he was blinking in the relatively bright radiance of the overhead light in his office, and both Welch and Devriess were staring at him.

"The translation!" said Devriess. "Where is it?"

"He's dropped the gun," said Welch. "Grab him now!"

"Don't be absurd," said Devriess. He looked more closely at Blanzac, whose hair was now wetly plastered down. "That same day?"

Blanzac nodded. "I threw it in the street. Cars ran over it."

Welch had got to his feet, bracing himself on the desk. "What?" he asked plaintively. "Did I pass out?"

"Get to a hospital," Blanzac told him.

"But—" He looked at the desk and the floor. "Where's the Greenwald translation?"

"Destroyed," said Devriess, hiking his walker forward. "Long ago."

"What the hell are you—it was right here a second ago—wasn't it?"

"I will explain," said Devriess, "in the car."

Welch gave Blanzac a wide-eyed look. "I'll kill you for this." It wasn't clear whether he meant his maimed hand or the lost translation. Probably both, Blanzac thought.

"You don't want that sin too," said Devriess, reaching out to turn the injured man toward the door. To Blanzac he said, "We don't hold this against you. We don't hold anything."

⇥ VIII ⇤

WHEN THE TAILLIGHTS of their car had disappeared around the nearest corner, Blanzac locked the front and kitchen doors and trudged back up the hall to his office, and then just stood in the doorway and looked around.

At his feet the carpet pattern was obscured by the wide dark patch of Welch's blood; a yard farther it was missing a broad oval section over concave floorboards with scraps of his chair in one end of it. The Einstein biographies still sat on the floor in the corner. He leaned on the desk, lifted the telephone receiver, and dialed the number he had memorized at some earlier point in this fragmented evening.

After two rings a man answered with an impatient, "Yes?"

"Uh, could I talk to . . . Betty Barlow, please?"

"Not now. Who is this?"

"My name's Richard Blanzac, I visited her about—"

"Blanzac! One moment."

A woman's voice now said, "Mr. Blanzac? yes, you visited Miss Barlow an hour ago. We were going to call you shortly, since you were the last one to speak with her. Was there anything . . . did she seem well?"

"Yes," he said; and to test his sudden fearful suspicion, he said, "I'm a book dealer, and she asked me to hold some books for her, awaiting payment."

"I'm afraid she . . . I'm afraid you can consider the order cancelled."

"She died?"

"She—*was* eighty-six."

Blanzac thanked her and hung up.

She was eighty-six, but in some direction, like a figure seen through the wrong end of a telescope, she was still thirty-one, running down the rainy slope of Hyde Street with him toward the Buena Vista Café.

He picked up another cigarette butt out of the box that had once long ago held jars of pickled garlic, and put it in his mouth, and closed his eyes.

But the air remained still and warm, and when he opened his eyes he was still leaning against his desk in the office.

The discontinuity circuit was apparently closed now; or rather, it had always been closed and would always be there, but he had now irrevocably moved past it in time. And he wondered if, by some law of conservation of reality, the Akan text always necessarily destroyed itself, because it was a doorway to the god who had destroyed itself.

He put the cigarette butt back in the box, and stood up and stretched, then crossed to the bookcase and reached up into the gap where the Einstein biographies had been, and pulled out the Ace Double.

He crossed back to the desk, pushed the box out of the way and sat down.

Read what I wrote, she had said to him as he'd disappeared from her apartment for the first time—the last time she was ever to see him, until his visit to Goldengrove today. And earlier in that long-ago day she had written something in the book, in the middle pages.

He riffled through it until the pages of *Seconds of Arc* became the upside-down pages of *What Vast Image,* and he had glimpsed ink writing. He flipped back through the pages and found the end of *Seconds of Arc,* right next to a page listing Ace Science Fiction Novels; Greenwald's novel ended halfway down the left-hand page, and below it she had scrawled, *I hope you love me—Sophie.*

The fifty-five-year-old ball-point ink lines had blurred slightly in the yellowed pulp paper.

"And I hope you loved me," he said to the empty room.

He turned to the first page and began to read.

✢ AUTHOR'S NOTE ✢

Any time travel story written since 1941 owes, or should owe, a huge debt to Heinlein's groundbreaking story "By His Bootstraps," in which it was first noted that a time-traveler might participate in a particular scene as multiple characters, at different stages in his personal chronology; and it occurred to me that several visits to a day in the past need not be experienced in sequential order.

And, of course, any story about a text that is perilous to read owes something to Robert W. Chambers' The King in Yellow and H. P. Lovecraft's stories involving the Necronomicon . . . and, nowadays, maybe to the Monty Python idea of a joke so funny that anyone hearing it dies laughing, so that it has to be pronounced phonetically in a language the teller doesn't understand.

Incidentally, the town where Sophia Greenwald faked her death, Otatoclan, is the fictional town where Terry Lennnox faked his own suicide in Raymond Chandler's The Long Goodbye; and the name of my assisted living home, Goldengrove, is from Gerard Manley Hopkins' poem "Spring and Fall."

And, like that poem, this story is propelled by a constant rueful bafflement that the world of the past is inaccessible to us. "I see the country far ago where I will never stand," as A. E. Housman almost said.

⚛ THE BIBLE REPAIRMAN ⚛

"It'll do to kiss the book on still, won't it?" growled Dick, who was evidently uneasy at the curse he had brought on himself.

"A Bible with a bit cut out!" returned Silver derisively. "Not it. It don't bind no more'n a ballad-book."

"Don't it, though?" cried Dick, with a sort of joy. "Well I reckon that's worth having, too."

—*Treasure Island,*
Robert Louis Stevenson

ACROSS THE HIGHWAY was old Humberto, a dark spot against the tan field between the railroad tracks and the freeway fence, pushing a stripped-down shopping cart along the cracked sidewalk. His shadow still stretched halfway to the center-divider line in the early morning sunlight, but he was apparently already very drunk, and he was using the shopping cart as a walker, bracing his weight on it as he shuffled along. Probably he never slept at all, not that he was ever really awake either.

Humberto had done a lot of work in his time, and the people he talked and gestured to were, at best, long gone and probably existed now only in his cannibalized memory—but this morning as Torrez watched him the old man clearly looked across the street straight at Torrez, and waved. He was just a silhouette against the bright eastern daylight—his camouflage pants, white beard and Daniel Boone coonskin cap were all one raggedly backlit outline—but he might have been smiling too.

After a moment's hesitation, Torrez waved and nodded. Torrez was not drunk in the morning, nor unable to walk without leaning on something, nor surrounded by imaginary acquaintances, and he meant to sustain those differences between them—but he supposed that he and Humberto were brothers in the trades, and he should show some respect to a player who simply had not known when to retire.

Torrez pocketed his Camels and his change and turned his back on the old man, and trudged across the parking lot toward the path that led across a weedy field to home.

He was retired, at least from the big-stakes dives. Nowadays he just waded a little ways out—he worked on cars and Bibles and secondhand eyeglasses and clothes people bought at thrift stores, and half of that work was just convincing the customers that work had been done. He always had to use holy water—*real* holy water, from gallon jugs he filled from the silver urn at St. Anne's—but though it impressed the customers, all he could see that it actually did was get stuff wet. Still, it was better to err on the side of thoroughness.

His garage door was open, and several goats stood up with their hoofs on the fence rail of the lot next door. Torrez paused to pull up some of the tall, furry, sage-like weeds that sprang up in every stretch of unattended dirt in the county, and he held them out and let the goats chew them up. Sometimes when customers arrived at times like this, Torrez would whisper to the goats and then pause and nod.

Torrez's Toyota stood at the curb because a white Dodge Dart was parked in the driveway. Torrez had already installed a "pain button" on the Dodge's dashboard, so that when the car wouldn't start, the owner could give the car a couple of jabs—*Oh yeah? How do you like this, eh?* On the other side of the firewall the button was connected to a wire that was screwed to the carburetor housing; nonsense, but the stuff had to look convincing.

Torrez had also used a can of Staples compressed air and a couple of magnets to try to draw a babbling ghost out of the car's stereo system, and this had not been nonsense—if he had properly opposed the magnets to the magnets in the speakers, and got the Bernoulli effect with the compressed air sprayed over the speaker diaphragm, then at speeds over forty there would no longer be a droning imbecile monologue faintly going on behind whatever music was playing. Torrez would take the Dodge out onto the freeway today, assuming the old car would get up to freeway speeds, and try it out driving north, east, south and west. Two hundred dollars if the voice was gone, and a hundred in any case for the pain button.

And he had a couple of Bibles in need of customized repair, and those were an easy fifty dollars apiece—just brace the page against a piece of plywood in a frame and scorch out the verses the customers found intolerable, with a wood-burning stylus; a plain old razor wouldn't have the authority that hot iron did. And then of course drench the defaced book in holy water to validate the edited text. Matthew 19:5-6 and Mark 10:7-12 were bits he was often asked to burn out, since they condemned remarriage after divorce, but he also got a lot of requests to lose Matthew 25:41 through 46, with Jesus's promise of Hell to stingy people. And he offered a special deal to eradicate all thirty or so mentions of adultery. Some of these customized Bibles ended up after a few years with hardly any weight besides the binding.

He pushed open the front door of the house—he never locked it— and made his way to the kitchen to get a beer out of the cold spot in the sink. The light was blinking on the telephone answering machine, and when he had popped the can of Budweiser he pushed the play button.

"Give Mr. Torrez this message," said a recorded voice. "Write down the number I give you! It is important, make sure he gets it!" The voice recited a number then, and Torrez wrote it down. His answering machine had come with a prerecorded message on it in a woman's voice—*No one is available to take your call right now*—and many callers assumed the voice was that of a woman he was living with. Apparently she sounded unreliable, for they often insisted several times that she convey their messages to him.

He punched in the number, and a few moments later a man at the other end of the line was saying to him, "Mr. Torrez? We need your help, like you helped out the Fotas four years ago. Our daughter was stolen, and now we've got a ransom note—she was in a coffee pot with roses tied around it—"

"I don't do that work anymore," Torrez interrupted, "I'm sorry. Mr. Seaweed in Corona still does—he's younger—I could give you his number."

"I called him already a week ago, but then I heard you were back in business. You're better than Seaweed—"

Poor old Humberto had kept on doing deep dives. Torrez had done them longer than he should have, and nowadays couldn't understand a lot of the books he had loved when he'd been younger.

"I'm not back in that business," he said. "I'm very sorry." He hung up the phone.

He had not even done the ransom negotiations when it had been his own daughter that had been stolen, three years ago—and his wife had left him over it, not understanding that she would probably have had to be changing her mentally retarded husband's diapers forever afterward if he had done it.

Torrez's daughter Amelia had died at the age of eight, of a fever. Her grave was in the dirt lot behind the Catholic cemetery, and on most Sundays Torrez and his wife had visited the grave and made sure there were lots of little stuffed animals and silver foil pinwheels arranged on the dirt, and for a marker they had set into the ground a black plastic box with a clear top, with her death-certificate displayed in it to show that she had died in a hospital. And her soul had surely gone to Heaven, but they had caught her ghost to keep it from wandering in the noisy, cold half-world, and Torrez had bound it into one of Amelia's cloth dolls. Every Sunday night they had put candy and cigarettes and a shot-glass of rum in front of the doll—hardly appropriate fare for a little girl, but ghosts were somehow all the same age. Torrez had always lit the cigarettes and stubbed them out before laying them in front of the doll, and bitten the candies: ghosts needed somebody to have *started* such things for them.

And then one day the house had been broken into, and the little shrine and the doll were gone, replaced with a ransom note: *If you want your daughter's ghost back, Mr. Torrez, give me some of your blood.* And there had been a phone number.

Usually these ransom notes asked the recipient to get a specific tattoo that corresponded to a tattoo on the kidnapper's body—and afterward whichever family member complied would have lost a lot of memories, and be unable to feel affection, and never again dream at night. The kidnapper would have taken those things. But a kidnapper would always settle instead for the blood of a person whose soul was broken in the way that Torrez's was, and so the robbed families would often come to

Torrez and offer him a lot of money to step in and give up some of his blood, and save them the fearful obligation of the vampiric tattoo.

Sometimes the kidnapper was the divorced father or mother of the ghost—courts never considered custody of a dead child—or a suitor who had been rejected long before, and in these cases there would be no ransom demand; but then it had sometimes been possible for Torrez to trace the thief and steal the ghost back, in whatever pot or box or liquor bottle it had been confined in.

But in most cases he had had to go through with the deal, meet the kidnapper somewhere and give up a cupful or so of blood to retrieve the stolen ghost; and each time, along with the blood, he had lost a piece of his soul.

The phone began ringing again as Torrez tipped up the can for the last sip of beer; he ignored it.

Ten years ago it had been an abstract consideration—when he had thought about it at all, he had supposed that he could lose a lot of his soul without missing it, and he'd told himself that his soul was bound for Hell anyway, since he had deliberately broken it when he was eighteen, and so dispersing it had just seemed like hiding money from the IRS. But by the time he was thirty-five his hair had gone white and he had lost most of the sight in his left eye because of ruptured blood-vessels behind the retina, and he could no longer understand the plots of long novels he tried to read. Apparently some sort of physical and mental integrity was lost too, along with the blood and the bits of his hypothetical soul.

But what the kidnappers wanted from Torrez's blood was not vicarious integrity—it was nearly the opposite. Torrez thought of it as spiritual botox.

The men and women who stole ghosts for ransom were generally mediums, fortune-tellers, psychics—always clairvoyant. And even more than the escape that could be got from extorted dreams and memories and the ability to feel affection, they needed to be able to selectively blunt the psychic noise of humans living and dead.

Torrez imagined it as a hundred radios going at once all the time, and half the announcers moronically drunk—crying, giggling, trying to start fights.

He would never know. He had broken all the antennae in his own soul when he was eighteen, by killing a man who attacked him with a knife in a parking lot one midnight. Torrez had wrestled the knife away from the drunken assailant and had knocked the man unconscious by slamming his head into the bumper of a car—but then Torrez had picked up the man's knife and, just because he could, had driven it into the unconscious man's chest. The district attorney had eventually called it self-defense, a justifiable homicide, and no charges were brought against Torrez, but his soul was broken.

The answering machine clicked on, but only the dial tone followed the recorded message. Torrez dropped the Budweiser can into the trash basket and walked into the living room, which over the years had become his workshop.

Murder seemed to be the crime that broke souls most effectively, and Torrez had done his first ghost-ransom job for free that same year, in 1983, just to see if his soul was now a source of the temporary disconnection-from-humanity that the psychics valued so highly. And he had tested out fine.

He had been doing Bible repair for twenty years now, but his reputation in that cottage industry had been made only a couple of years ago, by accident. Three Jehovah's Witnesses had come to his door one summer day, wearing suits and ties, and he had stepped outside to debate scripture with them. "Let me see your Bible," he had said, "and I'll show you right in there why you're wrong," and when they handed him the book he had flipped to the first chapter of John's gospel and started reading. This was after his vision had begun to go bad, though, and he'd had to read it with a magnifying glass, and it had been a sunny day—and he had inadvertently set their Bible on fire. They had left hurriedly, and apparently told everyone in the neighborhood that Torrez could burn a Bible just by touching it.

He was bracing a tattered old Bible in the frame on the marble-topped table, ready to scorch out St. Paul's adverse remarks about homosexuality for a customer, when he heard three knocks at his front door, the first one loud and the next two just glancing scuffs, and he realized he had not closed the door and the knocks had pushed it open. He made sure his woodburning stylus was lying in the ashtray, then hurried to the entry hall.

Framed in the bright doorway was a short stocky man with a moustache, holding a shoebox and shifting from one foot to the other.

"Mr. Torrez," the man said. He smiled, and a moment later looked as if he'd never smile again. He waved the shoebox toward Torrez and said, "A man has stolen my daughter."

Perhaps the shoebox was the shrine he had kept his daughter's ghost in, in some jelly jar or perfume bottle. Probably there were ribbons and candy hearts around the empty space where the daughter's ghost-container had lain. Still, a shoebox was a pretty nondescript shrine; but maybe it was just for travelling, like a cat-carrier box.

"I just called," the man said, "and got your woman. I hoped she was wrong, and you were here."

"I don't do that work anymore," said Torrez patiently, "ransoming ghosts. You want to call Seaweed in Corona."

"I don't want you to ransom a ghost," the man said, holding the box toward Torrez. "I already had old Humberto do that, yesterday. This is for you."

"If Humberto ransomed your daughter," Torrez said carefully, nodding toward the box but not taking it, "then why are you here?"

"*My* daughter is *not* a ghost. My daughter is twelve years old, and this man took her when she was walking home from school. I can pay you fifteen hundred dollars to get her back—this is extra, a gift for you, from me, with the help of Humberto."

Torrez had stepped back. "Your daughter was kidnapped? Alive? Good God, man, call the police right now! The FBI! You don't come to *me* with—"

"The police would not take the ransom note seriously," the man said, shaking his head. "They would think he wants money really, they would not think of his terms being sincerely meant, as he wrote them!" He took a deep breath and let it out. "Here," he said, extending the box again.

Torrez took the box—it was light—and cautiously lifted the lid.

Inside, in a nest of rosemary sprigs and Catholic holy cards, lay a little cloth doll that Torrez recognized.

"Amelia," he said softly.

He lifted it out of the box, and he could feel the quiver of his own daughter's long-lost ghost in it.

"Humberto bought this back for you?" Torrez asked. Three years after her kidnapping, he thought. No wonder Humberto waved to me this morning! I hope he didn't have to spend much of his soul on her; he's got no more than a mouse's worth left.

"For you," the man said. "She is a gift. Save my daughter."

Torrez didn't want to invite the man into the house. "What did the ransom note for your daughter say?"

"It said, Juan-Manuel Ortega—that's me—I have Elizabeth, and I will kill her and take all her blood unless you *induce* Terry Torrez to come to me and him give me the ransom blood instead."

"Call the police," Torrez said. "That's a bluff, about taking her blood. Why would he want a little girl's blood? When did this happen? Every minute—"

Juan-Manuel Ortega opened his mouth very wide, as if to pronounce some big syllable, then closed it. "My Elizabeth," he said, "she—killed her sister last year. My rifle was in the closet—she didn't know, she's a child, she didn't know it was loaded—"

Torrez could feel that his eyebrows were raised. Yes she did, he thought; she killed her sister deliberately, and broke her own soul doing it, and the kidnapper knows it even if you truly don't.

Your daughter's a murderer. She's like me.

Still, her blood—her broken, blunting soul—wouldn't be accessible to the kidnapper, the way Torrez's would be, unless . . .

"Has your daughter—" He had spoken too harshly, and tried again. "Has she ever used magic?" Or is her soul still virginal, he thought.

Ortega bared his teeth and shrugged. "Maybe! She said she caught her sister's ghost in my electric shaver. I—I think she did. I don't use it anymore, but think I hear it in the nights."

Then her blood will do for the kidnapper what mine would, Torrez thought. Not quite as well, since my soul is surely more opaque—older and more stained by the use of magic—but hers will do if he can't get mine.

"Here is my phone number," said Ortega, now shoving a business card at Torrez and talking too rapidly to interrupt, "and the kidnapper has your number. He wants only you. I am leaving it in your hands. Save my daughter, please."

Then he turned around and ran down the walkway to a van parked behind Torrez's Toyota. Torrez started after him, but the sun-glare in his bad left eye made him uncertain of his footing, and he stopped when he heard the van shift into gear and start away. The man's wife must have been waiting behind the wheel.

I should call the police myself, Torrez thought as he lost sight of the van in the brightness. But he's right, the police would take the kidnapping seriously, but not the ransom. The kidnapper doesn't want money—he wants my blood, me.

A living girl! he thought. I don't save living people, I save ghosts. And I don't even do that anymore.

She's like me.

He shuffled back into the house, and set the cloth doll on the kitchen counter, sitting up against the toaster. Almost without thinking about it, he took the pack of Camels out of his shirt pocket and lit one with his Bic lighter, then stubbed it out on the stovetop and laid it on the tile beside the doll.

The tip of the cigarette glowed again, and the telephone rang. He just kept staring at the doll and the smoldering cigarette and let the phone ring.

The answering machine clicked in, and he heard the woman's recorded voice say, "No one is available to take your call, he had me on his TV, Daddy, so I could change channels for him. 'Two, four, eleven,' and I'd change them."

Torrez became aware that he had sat down on the linoleum floor. Her ghost had never found a way to speak when he and his ex-wife had had possession of it. "I'm sorry, Amelia," he said hoarsely. "It would have killed me to buy you back. They don't want money, they—"

"What?" said the voice of the caller. "Is Mr. Torrez there?"

"Rum he gave me, at least," said Amelia's voice. "It wouldn't have killed you, not really."

Torrez got to his feet, feeling much older than his actual forty years. He opened the high cupboard and saw her bottle of 151-proof rum still standing up there beside the stacked china dishes he never used. He hoisted the bottle down and wiped dust off it.

"I'm going to tell him how rude you are," said the voice on the phone, "this isn't very funny." The line clicked.

"No," Torrez said as he poured a couple of ounces of rum into a coffee cup. "It wouldn't have killed me. But it would have made a mindless . . . it would have made an idiot of me. I wouldn't have been able to . . . work, talk, think." Even now I can hardly make sense of the comics in the newspaper, he thought.

"He had me on his TV, Daddy," said Amelia's voice from the answering machine. "I was his channel-changer."

Torrez set the coffee cup near the doll, and felt it vibrate faintly just as he let go of the handle. The sharp alcohol smell became stronger, as if some of the rum had been vaporized.

"And he gave me candy."

"I'm sorry," said Torrez absently, "I don't have any candy."

"Sugar Babies are better than Reese's Pieces." Torrez had always given her Reese's Pieces, but before now she had not been able to tell him what she preferred.

"How can you talk?"

"The people that nobody paid for, he would put all of us, all our jars and boxes and dolls on the TV and make us change what the TV people said. We made them say bad prayers."

The phone rang again, and Amelia's voice out of the answering machine speaker said, "Sheesh" and broke right in. "What, what?"

"I've got a message for Terry Torrez," said a woman's voice, "make sure he gets it, write this number down!" The woman recited a number, which Torrez automatically memorized. "My husband is in an alarm clock, but he's fading; I don't hardly dream about him even with the clock under the pillow anymore, and the mint patties, it's like a year he takes to even get halfway through one! He needs a booster shot, tell Terry Torrez that, and I'll pay a thousand dollars for it."

I'll want more than a thousand, Torrez thought, and she'll pay more, too. Booster shot! The only way to boost a fading ghost—and they all faded sooner or later—was to add to the container a second ghost, the ghost of a newly deceased infant, which would have vitality but no personality to interfere with the original ghost.

Torrez had done that a few times, and—though these were only ghosts, not souls, not actual people!—it had always felt like putting feeder mice into an aquarium with an old, blind snake.

"That'll buy a lot of Sugar Babies," remarked Amelia's ghost.

"What? Just make sure he gets the message!"

The phone clicked off, and Amelia said, "I remember the number."

"So do I."

Midwives sold newborn ghosts. The thought of looking one of them up nauseated him.

"Mom's dead," said Amelia.

Torrez opened his mouth, then just exhaled. He took a sip of Amelia's rum and said, "She is?"

"Sure. We all know, when someone is. I guess they figured you wouldn't bleed for her, if you wouldn't bleed for me. Sugar Babies are better than Reese's Pieces."

"Right, you said."

"Can I have her rings? They'd fit on my head like crowns."

"I don't know what became of her," he said. It's true, he realized, I don't. I don't even know what there was of her.

He looked at the doll and wondered why anyone kept such things.

His own Bible, on the mantel in the living room workshop, was relatively intact, though of course it was warped from having been soaked in holy water. He had burned out half a dozen verses from the Old Testament that had to do with witchcraft and wizards; and he had thought about excising "thou shalt not kill" from Exodus, but decided that if the commandment was gone, his career might be too.

After he had refused to ransom Amelia's ghost, he had cut out Ezekiel 44:25—"And they shall come at no dead person to defile themselves: but for father, or for mother, or for son, or for daughter, for brother, or for sister that hath had no husband, they may defile themselves." He had refused to defile himself—defile himself any further, at least—for his own dead daughter. And so she had wound up helping to voice "bad prayers" out of a TV set somewhere.

The phone rang again, and this time he snatched up the receiver before the answering machine could come on. "Yes?"

"Mr. Torrez," said a man's voice. "I have a beaker of silence here, she's twelve years old and she's not in any jar or bottle."

"Her father has been here," Torrez said.

"I'd rather have the beaker that's you. For all her virtues, her soul's a bit thin still, and noises would get through."

Torrez remembered stories he'd heard about clairvoyants driven to insanity by the constant din of other people's thoughts.

"My daddy doesn't play that anymore," said Amelia. "He has me back now." Torrez remembered Humberto's wave this morning. Torrez had waved back.

Torrez looked into the living room, at the current Bible in the burning rack, and at the books he still kept on a shelf over the cold fireplace—paperbacks, hardcovers with gold-stamped titles, books in battered dust-jackets. He had found—what?—a connection with other people's lives, in them, which since the age of eighteen he had not been able to have in any other way. But these days their pages might as well all be blank. When he occasionally pulled one down and opened it, squinting through his magnifying glass to be able to see the print clearly, he could understand individual words but the sentences didn't cohere anymore.

She's like me.

I wonder if I could have found my way back, if I'd tried. I could tell her father to ask her to try.

"Bring the girl to where we meet," Torrez said. He leaned against the kitchen counter. In spite of his resolve, he was dizzy. "I'll have her parents with me to drive her away."

I'm dead already, he thought. *Her father came to me, but the book says he may do that for a daughter. And for me, the dead person, this is the only way left to have a vital connection with other people's lives, even if they are strangers.*

"And you'll come away with me," said the man's voice.

"No," said Amelia, "he won't. He brings me rum and candy."

The living girl who had been Amelia would have been at least somewhat concerned about the kidnapped girl. *We each owe God our mind,* Torrez thought, *and he that gives it up today is paid off for tomorrow.*

"Yes," said Torrez. He lifted the coffee cup; his hand was shaky, but he carefully poured the rum over the cloth head of the doll; the rum soaked into its fabric and puddled on the counter.

"How much is the ransom?" he asked.

"Only a reasonable amount," the voice assured him blandly.

Torrez was relieved; he was sure a reasonable amount was all that was left, and the kidnapper was likely to take it all anyway. He flicked his lighter over the doll, and then the doll was in a teardrop-shaped blue glare on the counter. Torrez stepped back, ready to wipe a wet towel over the cabinets if they should start to smolder. The doll turned black and began to come apart.

Amelia's voice didn't speak from the answering machine, though he thought he might have heard a long sigh—of release, he hoped.

"I want something," Torrez said. "A condition."

"What?"

"Do you have a Bible? Not a repaired one, a whole one?"

"I can get one."

"Yes, get one. And bring it for me."

"Okay. So we have a deal?"

The rum had burned out and the doll was a black pile, still glowing red here and there. He filled the cup with water from the tap and poured it over the ashes, and then there was no more red glow.

Torrez sighed, seeming to empty his lungs. "Yes. Where do we meet?"

✛ AUTHOR'S NOTE ✛

I wrote this story after watching the movie Man on Fire, *caught up with the idea of a kidnap negotiator who finds that he has somehow got to the point where he must sacrifice himself in order to free the victim. And I used my current San Bernardino neighborhood as a setting, which led inevitably to the peculiarly pragmatic Hispanic style of magic.*

Like Torrez in the story, I was once visited by proselytizers for some variety of Christian faith, and when I told them that we were Catholic, they replied that Catholicism was a false religion. I offered to show them, in their own Bible, why they were mistaken, and they handed it over—but, again like Torrez, I need a magnifying glass to read, and it was a sunny day, and I did inadvertently set their Bible on fire. I'm told that they still go door to door, but they now avoid our whole street.

⚔ APPOINTMENT ON SUNSET ⚔

THE CONCENTRIC CIRCLES filled the white wall, very fine black lines so tightly crowded that the wall would appear plain gray if viewed from more than five feet away; illusory colors seemed to flicker and spread in the dense curves, and after a few moments they abruptly sprang into full daylight, with a wide wedge of blue sky above clusters of foreshortened black and white rectangles that were expanding and moving to left and right away from the center.

Aware now of having a body, he shifted on the plastic chair, squinting. He could feel the alertness of being alive returning to him—he hoped he would see the cement truck here, and his right foot tapped the linoleum floor, impatient to feel the slant of a gas pedal instead. Do this right, he told himself tensely, and you'll add fourteen years to your life.

"I'm nearly in," he said quietly, his voice flat and unechoing in the big studio. "Still a bit blurry."

He concentrated, and then was able to see the field in depth. He was viewing low, crowded-together buildings through the windshield of a moving car. There seemed to be a lot of billboards above the buildings, and a line of telephone poles was swinging past to his right, and he could see the revolving yellow-and-red sign of a Shell station; that was good, there was supposed to be a Shell station, but was this the right one? He'd done a lot of driving in alcoholic blackouts. And then he saw, closer at hand, the vertical blue sign of Angel's Corner Liquor.

He exhaled, and he could hear it in the tense silence of the unseen studio.

"I'm on Sunset all right," he said, with relief. The red, yellow and blue colors of the nearby signs were invigorating.

The lumpy pale shapes on the arc of the steering wheel resolved into his hands. They appeared to be steady.

"I'm stepping in."

Breuer relaxed into it; his posture changed, and the air was abruptly warmer and smelled of Popov vodka and old Camel cigarettes, and his hands could feel the curved plastic hardness of the steering wheel as the surface he was sitting on became upholstered padding. That British rock and roll song, "I Want to Hold Your Hand,"was playing on the radio.

For nearly a minute he didn't speak, just concentrated on breathing evenly as he watched his hands move the wheel to stay in his lane. The big white cement truck was there in the lane ahead of him, and of course he was tailgating, as he always had, but no overriding exertion was called for yet. The stacked capitals of the LARGO sign loomed to the right now—he could remember when the burlesque club had been the Westside Market. And just past it was the Villa Nova, where he had once seen Marilyn Monroe dining with Joe DiMaggio.

Breuer had lived in Los Angeles for years, and even without having partially re-experienced this few minutes several times here in the last couple of days, he knew this stretch of Sunset well. He passed Doheny Drive, and noted the familiar curved red LIQUOR sign over Turner's liquor store, and he grinned nervously to realize that, as always, he had noticed it sooner than the much larger Coca Cola sign.

Sunset Boulevard had a hallucinatory vividness to him now, like a dream in a fever, and he wondered how he would fit into his life in the days that would follow this one.

He was breathing more rapidly, and bracing himself. Only another couple of blocks to where it happened, he thought—and this time it'll happen differently. He flexed his hands on the wheel.

The cement truck was pulling ahead, speeding up to make the light where Sunset curved south at Cory Avenue, and Breuer's heart was thudding in his chest. Beyond the truck he could see the black and white sign of the Cock 'n Bull restaurant ahead on the left, and closer on the right was the Frascati Grill. The man in the sweatshirt and baseball cap was standing on the sidewalk out in front of it, as he had been in each of these flashbacks, watching him drive past. This time Breuer effortfully lifted a hand from the wheel to wave, and the man waved back.

"Concentrate," said Harris, who was standing behind his chair in the studio.

"Shut up!—and let me drive here."

But, whether because he had waved at the man or because Harris had spoken, the view of Sunset Boulevard flickered; Breuer tried to focus on the cement-caked discharge hopper of the receding truck, but it all folded away, and he was staring at the tight circular lines on the wall four feet away and sitting on the hard surface of the plastic chair again, and the smells of vodka and cigarettes were gone, faintly replaced, once again, by his personal default smell of gasoline.

He still felt his old body clearly enough to brace his hands on his knees as he stood up.

"Hey!" said Harris.

"I fell out again, this time just before the Cock 'n Bull."

"Cement truck still in the lane ahead of you?"

Breuer nodded tiredly. "Right place, right minute. Next time don't talk to me while I'm in it."

His alertness was fading, and the accidental rhyme of *minute* with *in it* stuttered in his consciousness, shaking his frail thoughts to fragments.

Harris pressed his lips together under his gray moustache, but nodded. "We're trying to save your life here."

"Here? What?"

"Damn it, I said We're *trying to save your life.*"

"Oh. Yes. Save my life." Breuer was forcing himself to pay attention. "As a side-effect, anyway."

"An effect, nevertheless."

"I still die, though—before you were even born."

"Well what do you want? You'd be what, a hundred something today?"

"It's 2014 now?" Breuer's ectoplasmic form shivered. "I'd be . . . a hundred and seven."

"And if you can just get past the crash in this blackout, you'll live to 1978. You'll have lived to seventy-one. That's plenty for anybody, especially . . ." He waved it away and turned to lean over the microphone. "Derailed again," he said. "We'll try it again in five."

Breuer mentally supplied the end of Harris' unfinished sentence: Especially an alcoholic who didn't have sense enough to wear a seatbelt and never should have got a driver's license in the first place.

"Side effect," he muttered, recalling that it had seemed to be a relevant remark recently.

Harris sighed. "Go get your refreshments."

Breuer nodded vaguely and moved toward the open door of the break room in the south wall, consciously swinging his insubstantial legs back and forth beneath him.

Unless he concentrated on having a pair of eyes, his view was in all directions, and as he looked ahead at the treats laid out on the desk in the break room he was also aware of the plexiglas cube in the far corner, in which the scorched and broken steering wheel of his 1962 Dodge Dart hung on some special kind of wires in a nitrogen atmosphere under a strobing black light. It was his anchor, Harris said, the object that had killed him.

Good thing I wasn't propelled through the windshield, Breuer thought; they'd have had to get at least the back end of that cement truck in here.

But outside of the flashbacks his dispersed vision was almost totally black-and-white. Only in the moire patterns of the tight circles on the north wall was he still capable of seeing colors, and those were an optical illusion.

He paused in the doorway, staring at the broken Hershey bars and the cigarettes on the desk, all at once completely unaware of where he was. The old drunk's reflexes came back to him—act like you know what's going on, give vague and cheerful answers to any questions, and watch for clues to why you're here and what day it is. His clothes would be a clue—suit and tie, jeans and a sweatshirt?—but when he looked down at himself he saw the carelessly imagined and hardly separate trousers and shirt that didn't hide his insubstantial body, and recent memories fitfully resurfaced, like images on a film negative in a pan of metol and hydroquinone.

That's right, I *died*, he thought; I'm a, a *ghost*, and these people— Harris and . . . others, have conjured me up from my wrecked Dodge. They want me to go back and drive it again. Actions I took in alcoholic blackouts are dice still tumbling, according to Harris— fields of uncollapsed probability!—and so he wants me to go back to that blank interval in 1964 and do something besides die when I died.

He focused his sight on the far wall of the studio, the million concentric circles blurred to a uselessly gray disk from this distance, and for a moment he started to drift toward it, impelled to sink through the moire flickers into a flashback and experience colors and textures and continuity of thought once more; but he could also see the chocolate and the cigarettes. And they were closer.

The studio was a big room, three of its walls panelled with bumpy tinfoil and with only a few chairs and trestle tables on the wide cement floor, and bright lights were hung from the high ceiling; the break room was smaller, and clearly meant to be more hospitable—a couch, a cork bulletin board on one wall, an old oak desk, several padded chairs. Probably it was warmer too, but Breuer wasn't able to tell.

His attention was focused on the desk. The chocolate pieces had all been bitten by somebody already, and the cigarettes had all been lit and then stubbed out—in his present state Breuer needed somebody to visibly have started such things for him.

The cigarettes and the chocolate fragments were light enough for his virtual fingers to lift, if he kept his mind wholly on the task. It involved forgetting his situation again, but he experienced a minimal sort of contentment masticating the toothmarked chocolate and imagining that he could puff visible smoke from one of the cigarettes.

After a minute, though, they fell through his hands, and he was emptily looking at the break room in all directions. On one wall various bits of paper had been tacked to the bulletin board, and several of them snagged his memory and drew his cloudy attention.

There was a red and gold matchbook from Chasen's, and he remembered chili con carne and Ballantine's scotch whisky, and the red leather booth in which he had asked Margaret to marry him, in . . . 1958. To some extent he could remember Margaret too—dark hair, red lipstick . . . nobody else in the memory, they had never had any children. That guy, Harris, had called this collection of stuff a clarification aid. And here was a picture of himself—from a driver's license, passport, employee of the month poster?—light-colored hair, a lean face, faint self-deprecating grin. Amiable but not forceful.

Below it were a couple of photographs of buildings, and he had the idea that he had been the photographer.

And there were copies, and even some originals, of grade-school report cards; he seemed to have been a Bs and Cs sort of student. And there was a library card from 1918; he looked at his eleven-year-old self's signature, and wondered if his mature signature had differed much.

Behind him he saw Harris striding toward the break room, and so Breuer had turned to face him by the time the man stepped through the door.

Harris looked at the chocolate bits and the cigarette on the floor. "Are you . . . restored? Ready to try it again?"

Breuer had no idea who the man was or what he was talking about. "Oh, sure!" he said. "Bright eyed and horny toad."

"What?"

"What?" echoed Breuer.

Harris made an impatient sound with his teeth and absently picked up one of the cigarettes from the desk. "If you can't do it, you know, we drop you. We'll take your steering wheel out of that case and throw it in the trash, and you'll just wink out of existence here. We can't maintain this facility indefinitely, and if she never became a senator we can still work with the situation we've got." He stared at Breuer. "And you can go ahead and die at fifty-seven instead of seventy-one." Harris looked around, but there were no matches or lighters in the room, and he threw the cigarette back onto the desk.

That's right, thought Breuer, I died, but I could have more years to live—whatever the difference is between fifty-seven and seventy-one; a lot, probably.

And they want me to . . . *not* rear-end the cement truck this time, to drive up onto the sidewalk and run over a mailbox instead. Not die. Yes, Harris already told me this—some woman who was going to run for the Senate met a guy while they were watching me burn up in my car in the middle of Sunset Boulevard, and they went and had drinks afterward to stop the shakes, and they wound up engaged and she withdrew from the race. Somebody had fixed the election, but I screwed it up by giving her and this guy a spectacle to go away and talk about together. But if I drive up onto the sidewalk, Harris says, I'll block them from even seeing each other. They'll walk away separately.

"We really are willing to just snuff you right now," Harris went on.

"We did it to another guy, in this project—another damn drunk that was walking along Sunset in a blackout on that morning. He was too dumb to do what we asked, so we threw away his anchor, and his— briefly reawakened—ghost disappeared from 2014."

"Did *he* die on that day too? In 1964?"

Harris blinked at him, evidently surprised that he was paying attention. "No. This was before we were able to locate your car, the remains of it, in a closed-down wrecking yard in Long Beach. Before we found you, our best hope was this guy Nelson. We gave him a couple of horserace winners for the following month and told him to write them down after he made sure the man and woman didn't meet—you remember me telling you about them?"

"Sure," said Breuer airily. "She was supposed to win a rigged election for the Senate, but she went and had drinks with a guy instead."

Harris managed to smile. "There's hope for you yet. But Nelson didn't manage to stop them from meeting and going away together. He was hospitalized later that day, is how we knew about his blackout. I don't know if he placed the bets or not. He did die of cirrhosis only a few years later, though, dead broke. We told him to write that down, too, but if he did, it didn't change anything." Harris ran his hands through his close-cropped gray hair. "You dead guys are frustrating."

"I'm sure you'll be the same way," said Breuer.

Harris frowned and started to say something, then just shook his head. "I'm not going to leave any anchors," he said.

Breuer waved toward the bulletin board. "Maybe nobody will want to call you back anyway."

"Is it such a treat?" Harris seemed unreasonably angry. "You get to gum the candy bars, suck on the cigarettes?"

"I'm here." Breuer shrugged.

Harris shook his head. "Fine. And as long as you're here, do you want to try it one more time?"

Whoever this guy is and whatever he's talking about, thought Breuer, agree. "Sure," he said.

"Sunset Boulevard," said Harris as Breuer sat down again in the chair in front of the wall with all the tight circles on it. "You're in your old Dodge Dart—not that old, in fact, it's a 1962 model. You start at

Horn Avenue, and you're moving west, toward the Cock 'n' Bull restaurant. You remember the way, right?"

"I remember." Breuer was staring at the center point of the universe of circles, and vivid blue and purple moire patterns flickered in his peripheral vision. "I die right out in front of the place."

"No," came Harris' anxious voice from behind him, "you swerve and go up the northside curb, hit the mailbox instead of the truck."

"Right, right. Swerve. Mailbox. Senator. Now shut up."

A patch of dazzling blue sprang out of the tight rings, above the center; and then he saw, opening out on either side of the pavement moving past under his car, the sunlit sidewalks and shops, the parking meters and palm trees and striped awnings, of Sunset Boulevard. He watched it all hungrily, with the perspective of a man brought back from the dead. His hands gripped the steering wheel as he inhaled the vivid smells of vodka and cigarettes, and his right shoe pressed the gas pedal and he hummed along with the rock and roll song.

As on his previous re-experiences of this time-segment, he noticed a heavy inertia to his motions—if he relaxed, he wasn't aware of it and his body moved smoothly and with no sensation of impediment, but if he tried, for instance, to take his hand from the wheel and reach into his pocket, there was resistance, as if he were moving under water. He had concluded that the actions requiring particular effort were ones he had not done in that original blackout, and so he made a point now of twisting his head around as he drove, and flexing his hands on the wheel, so that he'd be ready to overcome the inertia and pull the wheel sharply to the right when the moment came.

He was sweating. It was particularly difficult to keep his right foot from pressing hard on the gas pedal; no wonder I rear-ended the cement truck on my original pass through this time, he thought. Damn fool.

On his first re-enactment he had decided to simply avoid the site of the alleged accident altogether, and turn right on Doheny, two blocks short of it; but as he had clicked the turn indicator and begun to make the right-angle turn, the sensation of moving under water had quickly become more like straining against hard rubber, and the Dodge had swerved only a few degrees before righting itself in the lane. Apparently there was some sort of law of conservation of reality at work. He was going to have to throw all his weight into missing the cement truck.

I suppose I'll be arrested for drunk driving again, he thought as he watched the high windows of the Scandia restaurant pass on the left—and for wrecking a mail box—and maybe I'll spend some time in jail for it and Margaret will be furious with me and maybe not pay my bail this time. But I'll live fourteen more years.

And now he was crossing Doheny Drive, with Turner's well-remembered liquor store on the corner. The next big street would be the leftward slant at Cory Avenue, but he wasn't going to make it that far.

Ahead of him he could see the black and white sign for the Cock 'n Bull, and he felt his heart begin to pound in his chest as his foot pushed on the accelerator to foolishly try to catch up with the truck; he glanced to his right, and there was the man in the sweatshirt and baseball cap out in front of the Frascati Grill, and Breuer started to raise his hand against the inertial resistance to wave to him again—but this time he met the man's gaze.

And as the man's eyes seemed to bore into him, Breuer saw the familiar flicker as his view of the street began to fold away and the song on the radio faded to silence, and he waited for the studio wall to replace it. The smells were gone, replaced by the usual faint aroma of gasoline.

"I fell out again," he said unhappily; but he didn't see the studio wall—and then his chest went cold and his pulse was thudding in his temples.

What he saw was twisted shapes in a red illumination; and a moment later he realized that it was a warped view of Sunset Boulevard. The nine-story City Bank building on the far side of Cory Avenue was bent out over the boulevard, and the telephone poles on this side curved across as if to meet it in the dark sky. The cars he could see were motionless, and looked like boats with upswept bows and sterns.

For several seconds he just stared, and in his mind was nothing but a wail of horror—I waited to long! I hit the truck, I'm dead!

But the silence was broken by a tapping from his right; and when he swung his head that way—against no resistance now—he saw the man in the sweatshirt standing beside the passenger door. When he caught Breuer's eye, he smiled and opened the door.

"You're obviously Breuer, re-doing your blackout," he said, his voice sounding closely constricted in the stilled air. "Mind if I join you?" He was already sliding into the passenger seat.

Breuer opened his mouth, but couldn't say anything. His heart was still racing.

"You're the guy," the stranger went on, "who's supposed to crash your car; I mean, *avoid* crashing your car, this time. Jump the damn sidewalk! I was supposed to distract the guy from meeting the woman too, though less dramatically. I even had a plan—I was going to just punch him in the nose by surprise. They told me they'd try to get you up and running if I didn't do it."

He looked more closely at Breuer. "Hey, don't look so scared! Did you think this," he said, waving at the distorted buildings and cars in the red glow, "was death or something? It's just the view half folded—it's stuck 'cause I intruded on you just now. I'm in the way, like I got my arm keeping an elevator door from closing all the way. When I step out of your picture, you'll either be right back where you were—my guess is that you were headed straight for the back end of that cement mixer—or else you'll be back in their damn studio. That's what happens when you fall out of a session, you're right back in that chair, ghost-stupid again, looking at all those circles on the wall."

"I know," Breuer managed to croak. "This isn't my first attempt. I keep falling out." He took a deep breath. "You're . . . Nelson," he added in a more normal tone.

"They told you about me, hey? Yeah, I decided not to do it, and I'm not even gonna bet on their alleged horseraces. The whole thing stinks. Why should I keep the girl from being born, just to make those yucks rich? Harder choice for you, though, I can see that."

Breuer shook his head, looking out at the warped buildings and cars. "Girl from being born?"

"Maybe you're supposed to run over the guy, or the woman," said Nelson. "Is the rest of your life worth murder?"

"No, I'm just supposed to run over a mailbox! I'm not going to kill anybody! I'm just going to stop them meeting, so she doesn't run for Congress."

"Run for Congress? Nobody runs for Congress, at least not in the story they gave me. What I heard was that these two," he said, waving at the curled sidewalk ahead, "meet and have a daughter, and the daughter patents some kind of router when she grows up, and Harris' gang came up with the same gadget but a bit too late, didn't get the patent. It's worth a fortune, see. So—eliminate the daughter from the picture and there's no contest, Harris gets the patent."

"A . . . router."

"Lots of stopped-up drains in L.A. in the future, I guess. No, that's rooter—I guess they want to cut a lot of grooves in wood?" He shook his head. "They told you somebody was going to run for Congress, hey?"

Breuer nodded toward the twisted wall of Frascati's. "The woman. That's what Harris said." The half-melted red-lit buildings looked ready to fall down. Harris changed the story for me, he thought. The couple will have a daughter, who will grow up, meet people, go places, do things. Or not. Or not.

"I guess," Breuer said slowly, "after you didn't do it, he decided it was too much to ask somebody—even a ghost!—to prevent a person from being born. From being conceived at all."

He found that he was trying to picture the girl, but could imagine nothing but an empty patch of cork on Harris' bulletin board.

"It's pretty bad," Nelson agreed. "Worse than murder, if you think about it. At least somebody you murder had a life."

"But—but I'll get fourteen more years of *my* life," said Breuer, sounding petulant even to himself, "if I miss the truck and go up the curb."

"Well I can't really shed any tears for somebody that never existed," said Nelson; "but I wouldn't want to be the one to *make* 'em not exist, either." He looked out the windshield at the molten view. "Awful sight, ain't it? Can't blame you for thinking it was death." He swung one leg out of the car. "Nice meeting a fellow blackout drunk—but I'm apparently due to pass out on the sidewalk and get taken to a hospital. Can't keep 'em waiting. If you *do* happen to go through with the original event, I'll find 'em one day and tell 'em they owe you."

Nelson got out of the car and slammed the door, then strode back over the bent pavement to the sidewalk, turned, and waved.

And as he waved, sunlight flared in the blue sky and in glare on gleaming symmetical car bodies and vertical white walls of buildings, and Breuer was slammed back against the seat by sudden acceleration. The traffic light at Cory Avenue switched to yellow, but the cement truck was apparently aiming to catch the tail end of the yellow light, and the inertial heaviness in Breuer's right foot indicated the intention to follow it.

He could still yank the wheel to the side—he could now even see the blue-and-red mailbox on the sidewalk to the right.

The bright clarity of the shop windows and the green leaves on the curbside trees, the tactile reality of the very steering wheel and the dusty dashboard in front of him, were alien to his new perspective, and made him suddenly ashamed. I don't belong here any longer, he thought—I'm a ghost, whether I die today or in 1978—and how can I take those fourteen useless years now, at the expense of a baby being conceived and born, of somebody's real life . . .

He let his foot stay heavy on the gas pedal, even when the truck driver apparently changed his mind and hit the brakes, the truck screeching to a halt just short of the Cory Avenue intersection.

Breuer remembered Nelson saying, *If you do happen to go through with the original event, I'll tell 'em they owe you.*

Tell *her,* was Breuer's last thought, and then there was just the stunning crash and the always-waiting smell of gasoline.

❖ AUTHOR'S NOTE ❖

This is another story deriving from my wish that the past was accessible to us! Faulkner said, "The past isn't dead. It isn't even past." You sure can't get there from here, though. I wish I could walk down Sunset Boulevard in 1964, or '44 or '34. I can see them in movies, they obviously exist!

And alcoholic blackouts are a mysterious state. Who's minding the store, where are you? And are you really firmly locked into sequential time? (This is fictional speculation only, don't try it for real!)

⚜ THE BETTER BOY ⚜
written with James P. Blaylock

KNOCK KNOCK.

Bernard Wilkins twisted the scratched restaurant butter-knife in his pudgy hand to catch the eastern sun.

There was a subtle magic in the morning. He felt it most at breakfast—the smells of bacon and coffee, the sound of birds outside, the arrangement of clouds in the deep summer sky, and the day laid out before him like a roadmap unfolded on a dashboard.

This morning he could surely allow himself to forget about the worms and the ether bunnies.

It was Saturday, and he was going to take it easy today, go home and do the crossword puzzle, maybe get the ball game on the radio late in the afternoon while he put in a couple of hours in the garage. The Angels were a half game out and were playing Oakland at two o'clock. In last night's game Downing had slammed a home run into the outfield scoreboard, knocking out the scoreboard's electrical system, and the crowd had gone flat-out crazy, cheering for six solid minutes, stomping and clapping and hooting until the stands were vibrating so badly that they had to stop the game to let everybody calm down.

In his living room Wilkins had been stomping right along with the rest of them, till he was nearly worn out with it.

He grinned now to think about it. Baseball—there was magic in baseball, too . . . even in your living room you could imagine it, beer and hot dogs, those frozen malts, the smell of cut grass, the summer evenings.

He could remember the smell of baseball leather from his childhood, grass-stained hardballs and new gloves. Chiefly it was the dill pickles and black licorice and Cokes in paper cups that he remembered from back then, when he had played Little League ball. They had sold the stuff out of a plywood shack behind the major league diamond.

It was just after eight o'clock in the morning, and Norm's coffee shop was getting crowded with people knocking back coffee and orange juice.

There was nothing like a good meal. Time stopped while you were eating. Troubles abdicated. It was like a holiday. Wilkins sopped up the last of the egg yolk with a scrap of toast, salted it, and put it into his mouth, chewing contentedly. Annie, the waitress, laid his check on the counter, winked at him, and then went off to deal with a wild-eyed woman who wore a half dozen tattered sweaters all at once and was carefully emptying the ketchup bottle onto soda crackers she'd pick out of a basket, afterward dropping them one by one into her ice water, mixing up a sort of poverty-style gazpacho.

Wilkins sighed, wiped his mouth, left a twenty percent tip, heaved himself off the stool and headed for the cash register near the door.

"A good meal," he said to himself comfortably, as if it were an occult phrase. He paid up, then rolled a toothpick out of the dispenser and poked it between his teeth. He pushed open the glass door with a lordly sweep, and strode outside onto the sidewalk.

The morning was fine and warm. He walked to the parking lot edge of the pavement, letting the sun wash over him as he hitched up his pants and tucked his thumbs through his belt loops. What he needed was a pair of suspenders. Belts weren't worth much to a fat man. He rolled the toothpick back and forth in his mouth, working it expertly with his tongue.

He was wearing his inventor's pants. That's what he had come to call them. He'd had them how many years? Fifteen, anyway. Last winter he had tried to order another pair through a catalogue company back in Wisconsin, but hadn't had any luck. They were khaki work pants with eight separate pockets and oversized, reinforced belt loops. He wore a heavy key chain on one of the loops, with a retractable ring holding a dozen assorted keys—all the more reason for the suspenders.

The cotton fabric of the trousers was web-thin in places. His wife had patched the knees six different times and had resewn the inseam twice. She wasn't happy about the idea of him wearing the pants out in public. Some day, Molly was certain of it, he would sit down on the counter stool at Norm's and the entire rear end would rip right out of them.

Well, that was something Wilkins would face when the time came. He was certain, in his heart, that there would always be a way to patch the pants one more time, which meant infinitely. A stitch in time. Everything was patchable.

"Son of a bitch!" came a shout behind him. He jumped and turned around.

It was the raggedy woman who had been mixing ketchup and crackers into her ice water. She had apparently abandoned her makeshift breakfast.

"What if I *am* a whore?" she demanded of some long-gone debating partner. "Did he ever give *me* a dollar?"

Moved somehow by the sunny morning, Wilkins impulsively tugged a dollar bill out of his trousers. "Here," he said, holding it out to her.

She flounced past him unseeing, and shouted, at no one visibly present, a word that it grieved him to hear. He waved the dollar after her halfheartedly, but she was walking purposefully toward a cluster of disadvantaged-looking people crouched around the dumpster behind the restaurant's service door.

He wondered for a moment about everything being, in fact, patchable.

But perhaps she had some friends among them. Magic after all was like the bottles on the shelves of a dubious-neighborhood liquor store—it was available in different proofs and labels, and at different prices, for anyone who cared to walk in.

And sometimes it helped them. Perhaps obscurely.

He wasn't keen on revealing any of this business about magic to anyone who wouldn't understand; but, in his own case, when he was out in the garage working, he never felt quite right wearing anything except his inventor's pants.

Somewhere he had read that Fred Astaire had worn a favorite pair of dancing shoes for years after they had worn out, going so far as to pad the interior with newspaper in between resolings.

Well, Bernard Wilkins had his inventor's trousers, didn't he? And by damn he didn't care what the world thought about them. He scratched at a spot of egg yolk on a pocket and sucked at his teeth, clamping the toothpick against his lip.

Wilkins is the name, he thought with self-indulgent pomposity— invention's the game.

What he was inventing now was a way to eliminate garden pests. There was a subsonic device already on the market to discourage gophers, sure, and another patented machine to chase off mosquitoes.

Neither of them worked worth a damn, really.

The thing that *really* worked on gophers was a wooden propeller nailed to a stick that was driven into the ground. The propeller whirled in the wind, sending vibrations down the stick into the dirt. He had built three of them, big ones, and as a result he had no gopher trouble.

The tomato worms were working him over hard, though, scouring the tomato vines clean of leaves and tomatoes in the night. He sometimes found the creatures in the morning, heavy and long, glowing bright green with pirated chlorophyll and wearing a face that was far too mammalian, almost human.

The sight of one of them bursting under a tramping shoe was too horrible for any sane person to want to do it twice.

Usually what he did was gingerly pick them off the stems and throw them over the fence into his neighbor's yard, but they crawled back through again in the night, further decimating the leaves of his plants. He had replanted three times this season.

What he was working on was a scientific means to get rid of the things. He thought about the nets in his garage, and the boxes of crystal-growing kits he had bought.

Behind him, a car motor revved. A dusty old Ford Torino shot toward him from the back of the parking lot, burning rubber from the rear tires in a cloud of white smoke, the windshield an opaque glare of reflected sunlight. In sudden panic Wilkins scuffed his shoes on the asphalt, trying to reverse his direction, to hop back out of the way before he was run down. The front tire nearly ran over his foot as he yelled and pounded on the hood, and right then the hooked post from the broken-off passenger-side mirror caught him by the keychain and yanked his legs out from under him.

He fell heavily to the pavement and slid.

For one instant it was a contest between his inventor's pants and the car—then the waistband gave way and the inseam ripped out, and he was watching his popped-off shoes bounce away across the parking lot and his pants disappear as the car made a fast right onto Main.

License number! He scrabbled to his feet, lunging substantially naked toward the parking lot exit. There the car went, zigging away through traffic, cutting off a pickup truck at the corner. He caught just the first letter of the license, a G, or maybe a Q. From the mirror support, flapping and dancing and billowing out at the end of the snagged keychain, his inventor's pants flailed themselves to ribbons against the street, looking for all the world as if the pant legs were running furiously, trying to keep up with the car. In a moment the car was gone, and his pants with it.

The sight of the departing pants sent him jogging for his own car. Appallingly the summer breeze was ruffling the hair on his bare legs, and he looked back at the restaurant in horror, wondering if he had been seen.

Sure enough, a line of faces stared at him from inside Norm's, a crowd of people leaning over the tables along the parking lot window. Nearly every recognizable human emotion seemed to play across the faces: surprise, worry, hilarity, joy, disgust, fear—everything but envy. He could hear the whoop of someone's laughter, muffled by the window glass.

One of his pennyloafers lay in the weeds of a flowerbed, and he paused long enough to grab it, then hurried on again in his stocking feet and baggy undershorts, realizing that the seat of his shorts had mostly been abraded away against the asphalt when he had gone down.

Son of a bitch, he thought, unconsciously echoing the raggedy woman's evaluation.

His car was locked, and instinctively he reached for his key chain, which of course was to hell and gone down Seventeenth Street by now. "Shit!" he said, hearing someone stepping up behind him. He angled around toward the front of the car, so as to be at least half-hidden from the crowd in Norm's.

Most of the faces were laughing now. People were pointing. He was all right. He hadn't been hurt after all. They could laugh like zoo apes and their consciences would be clear. Look at him run! A fat man in joke shorts! Look at that butt!

It was an old man who had come up behind him. He stood there now in the parking lot, shaking his head seriously.

"It was hit and run," the old man said. "I saw the whole thing. I was right there in the window, and I'm prepared to go to court. Bastard didn't even look."

He stood on the other side of the car, between Wilkins and the window full of staring people. Someone hooted from a car driving past on Sixteenth, and Wilkins flinched, dropping down to his hands and knees and groping for the hide-a-key under the front bumper. He pawed the dirty underside of the bumper frantically, but couldn't find the little magnetic box. Maybe it was on the rear bumper. He damned well wasn't going to go crawling around after it, providing an easy laugh . . .

A wolf-whistle rang out from somewhere above, from an open window across Sixteenth. He stood up hurriedly.

"Did you get the license?" the old man said.

"What? No, I didn't." Wilkins took a deep breath to calm himself.

The goddamn magnetic hide-a-key. It had probably dropped off down the highway somewhere. Wouldn't you know it! Betrayed by the very thing . . .

His heart still raced, but it didn't pound so hard. He concentrated on simmering down, clutching his chest with his hand. "Easy, boy," he muttered to himself, his eyes nearly shut. That was better. He could take stock now.

It was a miracle he wasn't hurt. If he were a skinny man the physical forces of the encounter would probably have torn him in half. As it was, his knee was scraped pretty good, but nothing worse than ten million such scrapes he had suffered as a kid. His palms were raw, and the skin on his rear-end stung pretty well. He felt stiff, too.

He flexed his leg muscles and rotated his arms. The wolf-whistle sounded again, but he ignored it.

Miraculously, he had come through nearly unharmed. No broken bones. Nothing a tube of Ben-Gay wouldn't fix, maybe some Bactine on the scrapes.

He realized then that he still had the toothpick in his mouth. Unsteadily, he poked at his teeth with it, hoping that it would help restore the world to normalcy. It was soft and splintered, though, and no good for anything, so he threw it away into the juniper plants.

"You should have got his license. That's the first thing. But I should talk. I didn't get it either." The old man looked back toward the window, insulted on Wilkins's behalf, scowling at the crowd, which had dwindled now. "Damned bunch of assholes . . ." A few people still stood and gaped, waiting to get another look at Wilkins, hoping for a few more details to flesh out the story they would be telling everyone they met for the next six weeks. Six months, more likely. It was probably the only story they had, the morons. They'd make it last forever. "Got your car keys, didn't they?"

Wilkins nodded. Suddenly he was shaking. His hands danced against the hood of his car and he sat back heavily on the high concrete curb of a planter.

"Here now," the old man said, visibly worried. "Wait. I got a blanket in the car. What the hell am I thinking?" He hurried away to an old, beaten Chevrolet wagon, opening the cargo door and hauling out a stadium blanket in a clear plastic case. He pulled the blanket out and draped it over Wilkins's shoulders.

Wilkins sat on the curb with his head sagging forward now. For a moment there he had felt faint. His heart had started to even out, though. He wanted to lie down, but he couldn't, not there on the parking lot.

"Shock," the old man said to him. "Accompanies every injury, no matter what. You live around here?"

Wilkins nodded. "Down on French Street. Few blocks."

"I'll give you a ride. Your car won't go nowhere. Might as well leave it here. You can get another key and come back down after it. They get your wallet, too?"

His wallet gone! Of course they had got his wallet. He hadn't thought of that. He wasn't thinking clearly at all. Well, that was just fine. What was in there? At least thirty-odd dollars and his bank card and gas card and Visa—the whole magilla was gone.

The old man shook his head. "These punks," he said. "This is Babylon we're living in, stuff like this happens to a man."

Wilkins nodded and let the old man lead him to the Chevy wagon.

Wilkins climbed into the passenger seat, and the man got in and fired up the engine. He backed out terrifically slowly, straight past the window where a couple of people still gaped out at them. One of the people pointed and grinned stupidly, and the old man, winding down the window, leaned out and flipped the person off vigorously with both hands.

"Scum-sucking pig!" he shouted, then headed out down the alley toward Sixteenth, shaking his head darkly, one wheel bouncing down off the curb as he swerved out onto the street, angling up Sixteenth toward French.

"Name's Bob Dodge," the man said, reaching across to shake hands.

Wilkins felt very nearly like crying. This man redeems us all, he said to himself as he blinked at the Good Samaritan behind the wheel. "Bernard Wilkins," he said, shaking the man's hand. "I guess I'm lucky. No harm done. Could have been worse." He was feeling better. Just to be out of there helped. He had stopped shaking.

"Damn right you're lucky. If I was you I'd take it easy, though. Sometimes you throw something out of kilter, you don't even know it till later. Whiplash works that way."

Something out of kilter! Wilkins rejected the thought. "I feel . . . intact enough. Little bit sandpapered, that's all. If he'd hit me . . ." He sighed deeply; he didn't seem to be able to get enough air. "Take a right here. That's it—the blue house there with the shingles." The car pulled into the driveway, and Wilkins turned to the old man and put out his hand again. "Thanks," he said. "You want to step in for a moment, and I'll give you the blanket back. I could probably rustle up a cup of java."

"Naw. I guess I'll be on my way. I left a pal of mine back in the booth. Don't want to stiff him on the check. I'll see you down to Norm's one of these days. Just leave the blanket in the back of your car."

"I will."

Wilkins opened the car door, got out, and stood on the driveway, realizing for the first time that the blanket he was wearing had the California Angels logo on it, the big A with a halo. He watched Bob Dodge drive off. An Angels fan! He might have known it. Had he been there when Downing wrecked the big scoreboard? Wilkins hoped so.

Some destructions didn't matter, like the scoreboard, and those clear plastic backboards that the basketball players were routinely exploding a few years ago, with their energetic slam dunks. There were repairmen for those things, and the repairmen probably made more money in a week than Wilkins pulled down from Social Security in a year. He thought of his pants, beating against the street at forty miles an hour. Where were they now? Reduced to atoms? Lying in a ditch?

Hell.

He went in through the front door, and there was Molly, drinking coffee and reading the newspaper. Her pleasant look turned at once to uncomprehending alarm.

"What ?" she started to say.

"Lost the pants up at Norm's," he said as breezily as he could. He grinned at her. This was what she had prophesied. It had come to pass. "A guy drove me home. No big deal!" He hurried past her, grinning and nodding, holding tight to the blanket so that she wouldn't see where his knee was scraped. He didn't want any fuss. "I'll tell you in a bit!" he called back, overriding her anxious questions. "Later! I've got to . . . damn it—" He was sweating, and his heart was thudding furiously again in his chest. "Leave me alone! Just leave me alone for awhile, will you?"

There had to be something that could be salvaged. In his second-best pair of fancy-dinners pants, he plodded past the washer and drier and down the back steps.

His backyard was deep, nearly a hundred feet from the back patio to the fence, the old boards of which were almost hidden under the branches and tendrils and green leaves of the tomato plants. Sometimes he worried about having planted them that far out. Closer to the house would have been safer. But the topsoil way out there was deep and good. Avocado leaves fell year round, rotting down into a dark, twiggy mulch. When he had spaded the ground up for the first time, he had found six inches of leafy humus on the surface, and the tomatoes that grew from that rich soil could be very nearly as big as grapefruit.

Still, it was awfully far out, way past the three big windmilling gopher repellers. He couldn't keep an eye on things out there. As vigilant as he was, the worms seemed to take out the tomatoes, one by one. He had put out a pony-pack of Early Girls first, back in February. It had still been too cold, and the plants hadn't taken off. A worm got five of the six one night during the first week in March, and he had gone back to the nursery in order to get more Early Girls. He had ended up buying six small Beefsteak plants too, from a flat, and another six Better Boys in four-inch pots, thinking that out of eighteen plants, plus the one the worms had missed, he ought to come up with something.

What he had now, in mid-June, were nine good plants. Most of the Early Girls had come to nothing, the worms having savaged them pretty badly. And the Beefsteaks were putting out fruit that was deformed, bulbous, and off-tasting.

The Better Boys were coming along, though. He knelt in the dirt, patiently untangling and staking up vines, pinching off new leaves near the flower clusters, cultivating the soil around the base of the plants and mounding it up into little dikes to hold water around the roots. Soon he would need another bundle of six-foot stakes.

There was a dark, round shadow way back in there among the Better Boys, nearly against the fence pickets; he could make out the yellow-orange flush against the white paint. For a moment he stared at it, adjusting his eyes to the tangled shadows. It must be a cluster of tomatoes.

He reached his arm through the vines, feeling around, shoving his face in among them and breathing in the bitter scent of the leaves. He found the fence picket and groped around blindly until he felt them—

No. It.

There was only one tomato, one of the Better Boys, deep in the vines.

It was enormous, and it was only half-ripe. Slowly he spread his hand out, tracing with his thumb and pinky finger along the equator of the tomato.

"Leaping Jesus," he said out loud.

The damned thing must have an eight-inch diameter, ten-inch, maybe. He shoved his head farther in, squinting into the tangled depths. He could see it better now. It hung there heavily, from a stem as big around as his thumb.

Knock, Knock, he thought.

Who's there?

Ether.

Ether who?

Ether bunnies.

No ball game today, he thought. No crossword puzzle.

He backed out of the vines and strode purposefully toward the garage. He hadn't planned on using the ether nets this year, but this was a thing that needed saving. He could imagine the worms eyeing the vast Better Boy from their—what, nests? Lairs?—and making plans for the evening. Tying metaphorical napkins around their necks and hauling out the silverware.

He pulled open the warped garage door and looked at the big freezer in the corner and at the draped, fine-mesh nets on the wall. The crystals might or might not be mature, but he would have to use them tonight.

He had read the works of Professor Dayton C. Miller, who had been a colleague of Edward Williams Morley, and, like Miller, Wilkins had become convinced that Einstein had been wrong—light was not in any sense particles, but consisted of waves traveling through a medium that the nineteenth-century physicists had called ether, the luminiferous ether.

"Luminiferous ether." He rolled the phrase across his tongue, listening to the magic in it.

Ordinary matter like planets and people and baseballs traveled through the ether without being affected by it. The ether passed through them like water through a swimming-pool net. But anything that *bent* light, anything like a magnifying glass, or a prism, or even a Coke bottle, *participated* with the ether a little, and so experienced a certain drag.

Molly had a collection of glass and crystal animals—people had offered her serious money for them, over the years—and Wilkins had noticed that in certain seasons some of them moved off of their dust-free spots on the shelf. The ones that seemed to have moved farthest were a set of comical rabbits that they had picked up in Atlantic City in—it must have been—1954. He had come to the conclusion that the effect occurred because of the angle and lengths of the rabbits' ears.

A correctly shaped crystal, he reasoned, would simply be stopped by the eternally motionless ether, and would be yanked off of the moving Earth like . . . like his pants had been ripped off of his body when the car-mirror post had hooked them.

And so he had bought a lot of crystal-growing kits at a local hobby store, and had "seeded" the Tupperware growing environments with spatially customized, rabbit-shaped forms that he'd fashioned from copper wire. It had taken him months to get the ears right.

The resulting crystalline silicon-dioxide shapes would not exhibit their ether-anchored properties while they were still in the refractive water—frozen water, at the moment—and he had not planned to put them to the test until next year.

But tonight he would need an anchor. There was the Better Boy to be saved. The year, with all of its defeats and humiliations, would not have been for nothing. He grinned to think about the Better Boy, hanging out there in the shadows, impossibly big and round. A slice of that on a hamburger . . .

Knock knock.

Who's there?

Samoa.

Samoa who?

Samoa ether bunnies.

He whistled a little tune, admiring the sunlight slanting in through the dusty window. The Early Girls and the misshapen Beefsteaks would have to be sacrificed. He would drape the nets under them. Let the worms feast on them in outer space if they had the spittle for it, as Thomas More had said.

Molly's Spanish aunt had once sent them a lacy, hand-embroidered bedspread. Apparently a whole convent-full of nuns had spent the bulk of their lifetimes putting the thing together. *Frank Sinatra* couldn't have afforded to buy the thing at the sort of retail price it deserved. Wilkins had taken great pains in laying the gorgeous cloth over their modest bed, and had luxuriated in lying under it while reading something appropriate—Shakespeare's sonnets, as he recalled.

That same night their cat had jumped onto the bed and almost instantly had vomited out a live tapeworm that must have been a yard long. The worm had convulsed on the bedspread, several times standing right up on its head, and in horror Wilkins had balled the bedspread up around the creature, thrown it onto the floor and stomped on it repeatedly, and then flung the bundle out into the yard. Eventually Wilkins and his wife had gone to sleep. That night it had rained for eight hours straight, and by morning the bedspread was something he'd been ashamed even to have visible in his trash.

When the obscuring ice melted, the rabbit-shaped crystals would be the floats, the equivalent of the glass balls that Polynesian fishermen apparently used to hold up the perimeters of their nets. The crystals would grab the fabric of the celestial ether like good tires grabbing pavement, and the lacy nets—full of tomato worms, their teeth in the flesh of the luckless Early Girls and Beefsteaks—would go flying off into space.

Let them come crawling back *then,* Wilkins thought gravely. He searched his mind for doubt but found none. There was nothing at all wrong with his science. It only wanted application. Tonight, he would give it that.

Still wearing his go-out-to-dinner pants, Wilkins expertly tied monkey-fist knots around the blocks of ice, then put each back into the freezer. Several times Molly had come out to the garage to plead with him to quit and come inside. He had to think about his health, she'd said. Remonstrating, he called it. "Don't *remonstrate* with me!" he shouted at her finally, and she went away in a huff. Caught up in his work, he simmered down almost at once, and soon he was able to take the long view. Hell, she couldn't be expected to see the sense in these nets and blocks of ice. They must seem like so much lunacy to her. He wondered whether he ought to wake her up around midnight and call her outside when the nets lifted off . . .

Luckily he had made dozens of the rabbit-forms. There would be plenty for the nets. And he would have to buy more crystal kits tomorrow.

Knock knock.
Who's there?
Consumption.
Consumption who?
Consumption be done about all these ether bunnies?
He laughed out loud.

By dinnertime he had fastened yellow and red twist ties around the edges of the nets. It would be an easy thing to attach the ether bunnies to the twist ties when the time was just right. He had spread the nets under all the tomato plants around the one that bore the prodigious Better Boy, pulling back and breaking off encumbering vines from adjacent plants. He hated to destroy the surrounding plants, but his eggs were all going into one basket here. If you were going to do a job, you did a job. Wasn't that what Casey Stengel always said? Halfway measures wouldn't stop a tomato worm. Wilkins had found that out the hard way.

Molly cooked him his favorite dinner—pork chops baked in cream of mushroom soup, with mashed potatoes and a vegetable medley on the side. There was a sprig of parsley on the plate, as a garnish, just like in a good restaurant. He picked it up and laid it on the tablecloth. Then, slathering margarine onto a slice of white bread and sopping up gravy with it, he chewed contentedly, surveying their kitchen, their domain. Outside, the world was alive with impersonal horrors. The evening news was full of them. Old Bob Dodge was right. This was Babylon. But with the summer breeze blowing in through the open window and the smell of dinner in the air, Wilkins didn't give a damn for Babylon.

He studied the plate-rack on the wall, remembering where he and Molly had picked up each of the souvenir plates. There was the Spokane plate, from the World's Fair in '74. And there was the Grand Canyon plate and the Mesa Verde one next to that, chipped just a little on the edge. What the hell did a chip matter? A little bit of Super Glue if it was a bad one . . .

There was a magic in all of it—the plates on the wall, the little stack of bread slices on the saucer, the carrots and peas mixing it up with the mashed potatoes. There was something in the space around such things, like the force-field dome over a lunar city in a story. Whatever it was, this magic, it held Babylon at bay.

He remembered the cat and the Spanish bedspread suddenly, and put his fork down. But hell—the ether bunnies, the saving of the enormous tomato—tonight things would go a different way.

He picked up his fork again and stabbed a piece of carrot, careful to catch a couple of peas at the same time, dredging it all in the mushroom gravy.

He would have to remember to put the stadium blanket into the trunk. Bob Dodge. . . . Even the man's name had a ring to it. If God were to lean out of the sky, as the Bible said He had done in times past, and say "Find me one good man, or else I'll pull this whole damned shooting match to pieces," Wilkins would point to Bob Dodge, and then they could all relax and go back to eating pork chops.

"More mashed potatoes?" Molly asked him, breaking in on his reverie.

"Please. And gravy."

She went over to the stove and picked up the pan, spooning him out a big mound of potatoes, dropping it onto his plate, and then pushing a deep depression in the middle of the mound. She got it just right. Wilkins smiled at her, watching her pour gravy into the hole.

"Salt?"

"Doesn't need it," he said. "It's perfect."

Molly canted her head and looked at him: "A penny?"

He grinned self-consciously. "For my thoughts? They're not worth a penny—or they're worth too much to stick a number on. I was just thinking about all this. About us." He gestured around him, at the souvenir plates on the wall and the plates full of food on the table.

"Oh, I see," she said, feigning skepticism.

"We could have done worse."

She nodded as if she meant it. He nearly told her about the ether bunnies, about why he had bought the old freezer and the nets, about Einstein and Miller—but instead he found himself finally telling her about Norm's, about having nearly got run down in the parking lot. Earlier that day, when he had borrowed her keys and gone down to retrieve the car, she hadn't asked any questions. He had thought she was miffed, but now he knew that wasn't it. She'd just been giving him room to breathe.

"Sorry I shouted at you when I got home," he said when he had finished describing the ordeal. "I was pretty shook up."

"I guess you would be. I wish you would have told me, though. Someone should have called the police."

"Wouldn't have done any good. I didn't even get the guy's license number. Happened too fast."

"One of those people in Norm's must have got it."

Wilkins shrugged. Right then he didn't give a flying damn about the guy in the Torino. In a sense there had not been any guy in the Torino, just a . . . a force of nature, like gravity or cold or the way things go to hell if you don't look out. He hacked little gaps in his mashed potatoes, letting the gravy leak down the edges like molten lava out of a volcano, careful not to let it all run out. He shoveled a forkful into his mouth and then picked up a pork chop, holding it by the bone, and nibbled off the meat that was left. "No harm done," he said. "A few bucks . . ."

"What you ought to have done after you'd got home and put on another pair of pants was drive up Seventeenth Street. Your pants are probably lying by the roadside somewhere, in a heap."

"First thing in the morning," he said, putting it off even though there was still a couple hours worth of daylight left.

But then abruptly he knew she was right. Of course that's what he should have done. He had been too addled. A man didn't like to think of that sort of embarrassment, not so soon. Now, safe in the kitchen, eating a good meal, the world was distant enough to permit his taking a philosophical attitude. He could talk about it now, admit everything to Molly. There was no shame in it. Hell, it was funny. If he had been watching out the window at Norm's, he would have laughed at himself, too. There was no harm done. Except that his inventor's pants were gone.

Suddenly full, he pushed his plate away and stood up.

"Sit and talk?" Molly asked.

"Not tonight. I've got a few things to do yet, before dark."

"I'll make you a cup of coffee, then, and bring it out to the garage."

He smiled at her and winked, then bent over and kissed her on the cheek. "Use the Melitta filter. And make it in that big, one-quart German stein, will you? I want it to last. Nothing tastes better than coffee with milk and sugar in it an hour after the whole thing has got cold. The milk forms a sort of halo on the surface after a while. A concession from the Brownian motion."

She nodded doubtfully at him, and he winked again before heading out the back door. "I'm just going down to Builders Emporium," he said at the last moment. "Before they close. Leave the coffee on the bench, if you don't mind."

Immediately he set out around toward the front, climbing into his car and heading toward Seventeenth Street, five blocks up.

He drove east slowly, ignoring the half a dozen cars angrily changing lanes to pass him. Someone shouted something, and Wilkins hollered "That's right!" out the window, although he had no idea what it was the man had said.

The roadside was littered with rubbish—cans and bottles and disposable diapers. He had never noticed it all before, never really looked. It was a depressing sight. The search suddenly struck him as hopeless. His pants were probably caught on a tree limb somewhere up in the Santa Ana mountains. The police could put their best men on the search and nothing would come of it.

He bumped slowly over the railroad tracks, deliberately missing the green light just this side of the freeway underpass, so that he had to stop and wait out the long red light. Bells began to ring, and an Amtrak passenger train thundered past right behind him, shaking his car and filling the rear window with the sight of hurtling steel. Abruptly be felt cut off, dislocated, as if he had lost his moorings, and he decided to make a U-turn at the next corner and go home. This was no good, this futile searching.

But it was just then that he saw the pants, bunched up like a dead dog in the dim, concrete shadows beneath the overpass. He drove quickly forward when the light changed, the sound of the train receding into the distance, and he pulled into the next driveway and stopped in the parking lot of a tune-up shop closed for the night.

Getting out, he hitched up his dinner pants and strode back down the sidewalk as the traffic rushed past on the street, the drivers oblivious to him and his mission.

The pants were a living wreck, hopelessly flayed after having polished three blocks of asphalt. The wallet and keys were long gone.

He shook the pants out. One of the legs was hanging, pretty literally, by threads. The seat was virtually gone. What remained was streaked with dried gutter water. For a moment he was tempted to fling them away, mainly out of anger.

He didn't, though.

Would a sailor toss out a sail torn to pieces by a storm? No he wouldn't. He would wearily take out the needle and thread, is what he would do, and begin patching it up. Who cared what it looked like when it was done? If it caught the wind, and held it. . . . A new broom sweeps clean, he told himself stoically, but an old broom knows every corner.

He took the pants with him back to the car. And when he got home, five minutes later, there was the cup of coffee still steaming on the bench. He put the pants on the corner of the bench top, blew across the top of the coffee, and swallowed a big slug of it, sighing out loud.

The moon was high and full. That would mean he could see, and wouldn't have to mess with unrolling the hundred-foot extension cord and hanging the trouble-light in the avocado tree. And he was fairly sure that moonlight brought out the tomato worms, too. The hypothesis wasn't scientifically sound, maybe, but that didn't mean it wasn't right. He had studied the creatures pretty thoroughly, and had come to know their habits.

He set down the styrofoam ice chest containing the ice-encased ether bunnies, studied the nets for a moment, and then opened a little cloth-covered notebook, taking out the pencil clipped inside the spine. He had to gauge it very damned carefully. If he tied on the ice-encased bunnies too soon or too late, it would all come to nothing, an empty net ascending into the stratosphere. There was a variation in air temperature across the backyard—very slight, but significant. And down among the vines there was a photosynthetic cooling that was very nearly tempered by residual heat leaking out of the sun-warmed soil. He had worked through the calculations three times on paper and then once again with a pocket calculator.

And of course there was no way of knowing the precise moment that the worms would attempt to cross the nets. That was a variable that he could only approximate. Still, that didn't make the fine-tuning any less necessary. All the steps in the process were vital.

He wondered, as he carefully wired the ether bunnies onto the nets, if maybe there wasn't energy in moonlight, too—a sort of heat echo, something even his instruments couldn't pick up. The worms could sense it, whatever it was—a subtle but irresistible force, possibly involving tidal effects. Well, fat lot of good it would do him to start worrying about that now. It clearly wasn't the sort of thing you could work out on a pocket calculator.

He struggled heavily to his feet, straightening up at last, the ice chest empty. He groaned at the familiar stiffness and shooting pains in his lower back. Molly could cook, he had to give her that. One of these days he would take off a few pounds. He wondered suddenly if maybe there weren't a couple of cold pork chops left over in the fridge, but then he decided that Molly would want to cook them up for his breakfast in the morning. That would be good—eggs and chops and sourdough toast.

She had come out to the garage only once that evening, to remonstrate with him again, but he had made it clear that he was up to his neck in what he was doing, and that he wasn't going to give himself any rest. She had looked curiously around the garage and then had gone back inside, and after several hours she had shut the light off upstairs in order to go to sleep.

So the house was dark now, except for a couple of sconces burning in the living room. He could see the front porch light, too, shining through the window beyond them.

The sky was full of stars, the Milky Way stretching like a river through trackless space. He felt a sudden sorrow for the tomato worms, who knew nothing of the ether. They went plodding along, inexorably, sniffing out tomato plants, night after night, compelled by Nature, by the fleeing moon. They were his brothers, after a fashion. It was a hard world for a tomato worm, and Wilkins was sorry that he had to kill them.

He fetched a lawn chair and sat down in it, very glad to take a load off his feet. He studied the plants. There was no wind, not even an occasional breeze. The heavy-bodied tomato worms would make the branches dip and sway as they came along, cutting through the still night. Wilkins would have to remain vigilant. There would be no sleep for him. He was certain that he could trust the ether bunnies to do their work, to trap the worms and propel them away into the depths of space, but it was a thing that he had to see, as an astronomer had to wait out a solar eclipse.

He was suddenly hungry again. That's what had come of thinking about the pork chops. He was reminded of the tomato, nearly invisible down in the depths of the vines. How many people could that Better Boy feed, Wilkins wondered, and all at once it struck him that he himself was hardly worthy to eat such a tomato as this. He would find Bob Dodge, maybe, and give it to him. "Here," he would say, surprising the old man in his booth at Norm's. "Eat it well." And he would hand Dodge the tomato, and Dodge would understand, and would take it from him.

He got up out of his chair and peered into the vines. The ice was still solid. The night air hadn't started it melting yet. But the worms hadn't come yet either. It was too soon. He found a little cluster of Early Girls, tiny things that didn't amount to anything and weren't quite ripe yet. Carefully, he pulled a few of them loose and then went back to his chair, sucking the insides out of one of the tomatoes as if it were a Concord grape. He threw the peel away, tasting the still-bitter fruit.

"Green," he said out loud, surprised at the sound of his own voice and wishing he had some salt. And then, to himself, he said, "It's nourishing, though. Vitamin C." He felt a little like a hunter, eating his kill in the depths of a forest, or a fisherman at sea, lunching off his catch.

He could hear them coming. Faintly on the still air he could hear the rustle of leaves bending against vines, even, he'd swear, the munch-munch of tiny jaws grinding vegetation into nasty green pulp in the speckled moonlight. It was a steady susurration—there must have been hundreds of them out there. Clearly the full moon and the incredible prize had drawn the creatures out in an unprecedented way. Perhaps every tomato worm in Orange County was here tonight to sate itself.

And the ice wasn't melting fast enough. He had miscalculated.

He forced himself up out of the lawn chair and plodded across the grass to the plants. He couldn't see the worms—their markings were perfect camouflage, letting them blend into the shifting-patches of moonlight and shadow—but he could hear them moving in among the Early Girls.

Crouched against the vines, he blew softly on the ice blocks at the outside corners of the net. If only he could hurry them along. When they warmed up just a couple of degrees, the night air would really go to work on them. They'd melt quickly once they started. Abruptly he thought of heading into the garage for a propane torch, but he couldn't leave the tomato alone with the worms now, not even for a moment. He kept blowing. Little rivulets of water were running down the edges of the ice. Cheered at the sight of this, he blew harder.

Dimly, he realized that he had fallen to his knees.

Maybe he had hyperventilated, or else had been bent over so long that blood had rushed to his head. He felt heavy, though, and he pulled at the collar of his shirt to loosen it across his chest. He heard them again, close to him now.

"The worms!" he said out loud, and he reached out and took hold of the nearest piece of string-bound ice in both hands to melt it. He didn't let go of it even when he overbalanced and thudded heavily to the ground on his shoulder, but the ice still wasn't melting fast enough, and his hands were getting numb and beginning to ache.

The sound of the feasting worms was a hissing in his ears that mingled with the sound of rushing blood, like two rivers of noise flowing together, into one deep stream. The air seemed to have turned cold, chilling the sweat running down his forehead. His heart was pounding in his chest, like a pickaxe chopping hard into dirt.

He struggled up onto his hands and knees and lunged his way toward the Better Boy. He could see them.

One of the worms was halfway up the narrow trunk, and two more were noodling in along the vines from the side. A cramp in his chest helped him to lean in closer, although he gasped at the pain and clutched at his shirt pocket. Now he could not see anything human or even mammalian in the faces of the worms, any more than he had been able to see the driver of the hit-and-run Torino behind the sun glare on the windshield.

He made his hand stretch out and take hold of one of the worms. It held on to the vine until he really tugged, and then after tearing loose it curled in a muscular way in his palm before he could fling it away. In his fright and revulsion he grabbed the next one too hard, and it burst in his fist— somehow horribly still squirming against his fingers even after its insides had jetted out and greased Wilkins's thumb.

He spared a glance toward the nearest chunk of ice, but he couldn't see it; perhaps they were melting at last.

Just a little longer, he told himself, his breath coming quick and shallow. His hands were numb, but he seized everything that might have been a worm and threw it behind him. He was panting loud enough to drown out the racket of the feasting worms, and the sweat stung in his eyes, but he didn't let himself stop.

His left arm spasmed in pain when he took hold of another one of the creatures, and he half believed the thing had somehow struck back at him, and then at that moment his chest was crushed between the earth and the sky.

He tried to stand, but toppled over backward.

Against the enormous weight he managed to lift his head—and he was smiling when he let it fall back onto the grass, for he was sure he had seen the edges of the nets fluttering upward as the ether bunnies, freed at last from the ice, struggled to take hold of the fabric of space— struggled inadequately, he had to concede, against the weight of the nets and the plants and the worms and the sky, but bravely nevertheless, keeping on tugging until it was obvious that their best efforts weren't enough, and then keeping on tugging even after that.

He didn't lose consciousness. He was simply unable to move. But the chill had gone away and the warm air had taken its place, and he was content to lie on the grass and stare up at the stars and listen to his heart.

He knew that it had probably been a heart attack that had happened to him—but he had heard of people mistaking for a heart attack what had merely been a seizure from too much caffeine. It might have been the big mug of coffee. He'd have to cut down on that stuff. Thinking of the coffee made him think of Molly asleep upstairs. He was glad that she didn't know he was down here, lying all alone on the dewy grass.

In and out with the summer night air. Breathing was the thing. He focused on it. Nothing else mattered to him. If you could still breathe you were all right, and he felt like he could do it forever.

When the top leaves of his neighbor's olive tree lit gold with the dawn sun he found that he could move. He sat up slowly, carefully, but nothing bad happened. The morning breeze was pleasantly cool, and crows were calling to each other across the rooftops.

He parted the vines and looked into the shadowy depths of the tomato plants.

The Better Boy was gone. All that was left of it was a long shred of orange skin dangling like a deflated balloon from its now foolish-looking stout stem. The ether bunnies, perhaps warped out of the effective shape by the night of strain, lay inert along the edges of the nets, which were soiled with garden dirt now and with a couple of crushed worms and a scattering of avocado leaves.

He was all alone in the yard—Molly wouldn't wake up for an hour yet—so he let himself cry as he sat there on the grass. The sobs shook him like hiccups, and tears ran down his face as the sweat had done hours earlier, and the tears made dark spots on the lap of his dinner pants.

Then he got up onto his feet and, still moving carefully because he felt so frail and weak, walked around to the front of the house.

The newspaper lay on the driveway. He nearly picked it up,

thinking to take a look at the sports page. He had been so busy yesterday evening that he had missed the tail end of the ballgame. Perhaps the Angels had slugged their way into first place. They had been on a streak, and Wilkins wanted to think that their luck had held.

He turned and went into the silent house. He didn't want to make coffee, so he just walked slowly from room to room, noticing things, paying attention to trifles, from the bright morning sun shining straight in horizontally through the windows to the familiar titles of books on shelves.

He felt a remote surprise at seeing his inventor's pants on the top of the dirty clothes in the hamper in the bathroom, and he picked them up.

No wonder it had been late when Molly had finally turned out the bedroom light. She had sewn up or patched every one of the outrageous tears and lesions in the old pants, and now clearly intended to wash them. Impulsively he wanted to put them on right then and there . . . but he wouldn't. He would let Molly have her way with them, let her return the pants in her own good time. He would wear them again tomorrow, or the day after.

There was still a subtle magic in the morning.

Knock knock.

Who's there?

Samoa.

He let the pants fall back onto the pile, and then he walked slowly, carefully, into the kitchen and opened the refrigerator door. He would make breakfast for her.

❖ AUTHOR'S NOTE ❖

I find that my short stories—probably because I don't want to do a year's research to write one—tend to use, as plot springboards, a lot of places and incidents taken from my day-to-day life. In this case, my wife and I were growing tomatoes in the backyard of our apartment on 16th Street in Santa Ana, California, and we did discover one enormous tomato, still too green to pick, hidden among the leaves; and when one morning I found hideous tomato hornworms chewing at the bottom of it, I tried all sorts of tricks to keep the worms from getting the rest of it. But in spite of my modestly heroic efforts, each dawn revealed a diminished remnant of the once-huge tomato, and the day came when all that was left of it was a shred of still-green skin hanging from the stem. The hornworms had prevailed.

Jim Blaylock and I decided that this called for a scaled-down horticultural version of Hemingway's The Old Man and the Sea, *with a tomato instead of a marlin.*

And my wife's parents did get a bedspread exaclty like the one described, from a relative in Spain, and its fate was exactly as described in the story.

⇥ PAT MOORE ⇤

"IS IT OKAY if you're one of the ten people I send the letter to," said the voice on the telephone, "or is that redundant? I don't want to screw this up. 'Ear repair' sounds horrible."

Moore exhaled smoke and put out his Marlboro in the half inch of cold coffee in his cup. "No, Rick, don't send it to me. In fact, you're screwed—it says you have to have ten friends."

He picked up the copy he had got in the mail yesterday, spread the single sheet out flat on the kitchen table and weighted two corners with the dusty salt and pepper shakers. It had clearly been photocopied from a photocopy, and originally composed on a typewriter.

> *This has been sent to you for good luck. The original is in*
> *San Fransisco. You must send it on to ten friend's, who, you*
> *think need good luck, within 24 hrs of recieving it.*

"I could use some luck," Rick went on. "Can you loan me a couple of thousand? My wife's in the hospital and we've got no insurance."

Moore paused for a moment before going on with the old joke; then, "Sure," he said, "so we won't see you at the lowball game tomorrow?"

"Oh, I've got money for *that*." Rick might have caught Moore's hesitation, for he went on quickly without waiting for a dutiful laugh: "Mark 'n' Howard mentioned the chain letter this morning on the radio. You're famous."

> *The luck is now sent to you—you will recieve Good Luck*

115

*within three days of recieving this, provided you send it on.
Do not send money, since luck has no price.*

On a Wednesday dawn five months ago now, Moore had poured a tumbler of Popov Vodka at this table, after sitting most of the night in the emergency room at—what had been the name of the hospital in San Mateo? Not St. Lazarus, for sure—and then he had carefully lit a Virginia Slims from the orphaned pack on the counter and laid the smoldering cigarette in an ashtray beside the glass. When the untouched cigarette had burned down to the filter and gone out, he had carried the full glass and the ashtray to the back door and set them in the trash can, and then washed his hands in the kitchen sink, wondering if the little ritual had been a sufficient goodbye. Later he had thrown out the bottle of vodka and the pack of Virginia Slims too.

A young man in Florida got the letter, it was very faded, and he resovled to type it again, but he forgot. He had many troubles, including expensive ear repair. But then he typed ten copy's and mailed them, and he got a better job.

"Where you playing today?" Rick asked.

"The Garden City in San Jose, probably," Moore said, "the six-and-twelve-dollar Hold 'Em. I was just about to leave when you called."

"For sure? I could meet you there. I was going to play at the Bay on Bering, but if we were going to meet there you'd have to shave—"

"And find a clean shirt, I know. But I'll see you at Larry's game tomorrow, and we shouldn't play at the same table anyway. Go to the Bay."

"Naw, I wanted to ask you about something. So you'll be at the Garden City. You take 280, right?"

Pat Moore put off mailing the letter and died, but later found it again and passed it on, and recieved threescore and ten.

"Right."

"If that crapped-out Dodge of yours can get up to freeway speed."

"It'll still be cranking along when your Saturn is a planter somewhere."

"Great, so I'll see you there," Rick said. "Hey," he added with forced joviality, "you're famous!"

Do not ignore this letter
ST LAZARUS

"Type up ten copies with your name in it, you can be famous too," Moore said, standing up and crumpling the letter. "Send one to Mark 'n' Howard. See you."

He hung up the phone and fetched his car keys from the cluttered table by the front door. The chilly sea breeze outside was a reproach after the musty staleness of the apartment, and he was glad he'd brought his denim jacket.

He combed his hair in the rearview mirror while the Dodge's old slant-six engine idled in the carport, and he wondered if he would see the day when his brown hair might turn gray. He was still thirty years short of threescore and ten, and he wasn't envying the Pat Moore in the chain letter.

The first half hour of the drive down 280 was quiet, with a Gershwin CD playing the *Concerto in F* and the pines and green meadows of the Fish and Game Refuge wheeling past on his left under the gray sky, while the pastel houses of Hillsborough and Redwood City marched across the eastern hills. The car smelled familiarly of Marlboros and Doublemint gum and engine exhaust.

Just over those hills, on 101 overlooking the bay, Trish had driven her Ford Granada over an unrailed embankment at midnight, after a St. Patrick's Day party at Bay Meadows. Moore was objectively sure he would drive on 101 some day, but not yet.

Traffic was light on 280 this morning, and in his rearview mirror he saw the little white car surging from side to side in the lanes as it passed other vehicles. Like most modern cars, it looked to Moore like an oversized computer mouse. He clicked up his turn signal lever and drifted over the lane-divider bumps into the right lane.

The white car—he could see the blue Chevy cross on its hood now—swooped up in the lane Moore had just left, but instead of rocketing on past him, it slowed, pacing Moore's old Dodge at sixty miles an hour.

Moore glanced to his left, wondering if he knew the driver of the

Chevy—but it was a lean-faced stranger in sunglasses, looking straight at him. In the moment before Moore recognized the thing as a shotgun viewed muzzle-on, he thought the man was holding up a microphone; but instantly another person in the white car had blocked the driver— Moore glimpsed only a purple shirt and long dark hair—and then with squealing tires the car veered sharply away to the left.

Moore gripped the hard green plastic of his steering wheel and looked straight ahead; he was braced for the sound of the Chevy hitting the center-divider fence, and so he didn't jump when he heard the crash—even though the seat rocked under him and someone was now sitting in the car with him, on the passenger side against the door. For one unthinking moment he assumed someone had been thrown from the Chevrolet and had landed in his car.

He focused on the lane ahead and on holding the Dodge Dart steady between the white lines. Nobody could have come through the roof, or the windows; or the doors. Must have been hiding in the back seat all this time, he thought, and only now jumped over into the front. What timing. He was panting shallowly, and his ribs tingled, and he made himself take a deep breath and let it out.

He looked to his right. A dark-haired woman in a purple dress was grinning at him. Her hair hung in a neat pageboy cut, and she wasn't panting.

"I'm your guardian angel," she said. "And guess what my name is."

Moore carefully lifted his foot from the accelerator—he didn't trust himself with the brake yet—and steered the Dodge onto the dirt shoulder. When the car had slowed to the point where he could hear gravel popping under the tires, he pressed the brake; the abrupt stop rocked him forward, though the woman beside him didn't shift on the old green upholstery.

"And guess what my name is," she said again.

The sweat rolling down his chest under his shirt was a sharp tang in his nostrils. "Hmm," he said, to test his voice; then he said, "You can get out of the car now."

In the front pocket of his jeans was a roll of hundred-dollar bills, but his left hand was only inches away from the .38 revolver tucked into the open seam at the side of the seat. But both the woman's hands were visible on her lap, and empty.

She didn't move.

The engine was still running, shaking the car, and he could smell the hot exhaust fumes seeping up through the floor. He sighed, then reluctantly reached forward and switched off the ignition.

"I shouldn't be talking to you," the woman said in the sudden silence. "*She* told me not to. But I just now saved your life. So don't tell me to get out of the car."

It had been a purple shirt or something, and dark hair. But this was obviously not the person he'd glimpsed in the Chevy. A team, twins?

"What's your name?" he asked absently. A van whipped past on the left, and the car rocked on its shock absorbers.

"Pat Moore, same as yours," she said with evident satisfaction. He noticed that every time he glanced at her she looked away from something else to meet his eyes, as if whenever he wasn't watching her she was studying the interior of the car, or his shirt, or the freeway lanes.

"Did you—get threescore and ten?" he asked. Something more like a nervous tic than a smile was twitching his lips. "When you sent out the letter?"

"That wasn't me, that was *her*. And she hasn't got it yet. And she won't, either, if her students kill all the available Pat Moores. You're in trouble every which way, but I like you."

"Listen, when did you get into my car?"

"About ten seconds ago. What if he had backup, another car following him? You should get moving again."

Moore called up the instant's glimpse he had got of the thing in front of the driver's hand—the ring had definitely been the muzzle of a shotgun, twelve-gauge, probably a pistol-grip. And he seized on her remark about a backup car because the thought was manageable and complete. He clanked the gearshift into park, and the Dodge started at the first twist of the key, and he levered it into drive and gunned along the shoulder in a cloud of dust until he had got up enough speed to swing into the right lane between two yellow Stater Brothers trucks.

He concentrated on working his way over to the fast lane, and then when he had got there, his engine roaring, he just watched the rearview mirror and the oncoming exit signs until he found a chance to make a sharp right across all the lanes and straight into the exit lane that swept toward southbound 85. A couple of cars behind him honked.

He was going too fast for the curving interchange lane, his tires chirruping on the pavement, and he wrestled with the wheel and stroked the brake.

"Who's getting off behind us?" he asked sharply.

"I can't see," she said.

He darted a glance at the rearview mirror, and was pleased to see only a slow-moving old station wagon, far back.

"A station wagon," she said, though she still hadn't turned around. Maybe she had looked in the passenger-side door mirror.

He had got the car back under control by the time he merged with the southbound lanes, and then he braked, for 85 was ending ahead at a traffic signal by the grounds of some college.

"Is your neck hurt?" he asked. "Can't twist your head around?"

"It's not that. I can't see anything you don't see."

He tried to frame an answer to that, or a question about it, and finally just said, "I bet we could find a bar fairly readily. Around here."

"I can't drink, I don't have any ID."

"You can have a Virgin Mary," he said absently, catching a green light and turning right just short of the college. "Celery stick to stir it with." Raindrops began spotting the dust on the windshield.

"I'm not so good at touching things," she said. "I'm not actually a living person."

"Okay, see, that means what? You're a *dead* person, a ghost?"

"Yes."

Already disoriented, Moore flexed his mind to see if anything in his experience or philosophies might let him believe this, and there was nothing that did. This woman, probably a neighbor, simply knew who he was, and she had hidden in the back of his car back at the apartment parking lot. She was probably insane. It would be a mistake to get further involved with her.

"Here's a place," he said, swinging the car into a strip-mall parking lot to the right. "Pirate's Cove. We can see how well you handle peanuts or something, before you try a drink."

He parked behind the row of stores, and the back door of the Pirate's Cove led them down a hallway stacked with boxes before they stepped through an arch into the dim bar. There were no other customers in the place at this early hour, and the room smelled more like bleach than beer; the teenaged-looking bartender barely gave them a glance and a nod as Moore led the woman across the worn carpet and the parqueted square to a table under a football poster. There were four low stools instead of chairs.

The woman couldn't remember any movies she'd ever seen, and claimed not to have heard about the war in Iraq, so when Moore walked to the bar and came back with a glass of Budweiser and a bowl of popcorn, he sat down and just stared at her. She was easier to see in the dim light from the jukebox and the neon bar-signs than she had been out in the gray daylight. He would guess that she was about thirty—though her face had no wrinkles at all, as if she had never laughed or frowned.

"You want to try the popcorn?" he asked as he unsnapped the front of his denim jacket.

"Look at it so I know where it is."

He glanced down at the bowl, and then back at her. As always, her eyes fixed on his as soon as he was looking at her. Either her pupils were fully dilated, or else her irises were black.

But he glanced down again when something thumped the table and a puff of hot salty air flicked his hair, and some popcorn kernels spun away through the air.

The popcorn remaining in the bowl had been flattened into little white jigsaw-puzzle pieces. The orange plastic bowl was cracked.

Her hands were still in her lap, and she was still looking at him. "I guess not, thanks."

Slowly he lifted his glass of beer and took a sip. That was a powerful raise, he thought, forcing himself not to show any astonishment—though you should have suspected a strong hand. Play carefully here.

He glanced toward the bar; but the bartender, if he had looked toward their table at all, had returned his attention to his newspaper.

"Tom Cruise," the woman said.

Moore looked back at her and after a moment raised his eyebrows. She said, "That was a movie, wasn't it?"

"In a way." *Play carefully here.* "What did you—is something wrong with your vision?"

"I don't have any vision. No retinas. I have to use yours. I'm a ghost."

"Ah. I've never met a ghost before." He remembered a line from a Robert Frost poem: *The dead are holding something back.*

"Well, not that you could see. You can only see me because . . . I'm like the stamp you get on the back of your hand at Disneyland; you can't see me unless there's a black light shining on me. *She's* the black light."

"You're in her field of influence, like."

"Sure. There's probably dozens of Pat Moore ghosts in the outfield, and *she's* the whole infield. I'm the shortstop."

"Why doesn't . . . *she* want you to talk to me?" He never drank on days he intended to play, but he lifted his glass again.

"She doesn't want me to tell you what's going to happen." She smiled, and the smile stayed on her smooth face like the expression on a porcelain doll. "If it was up to me, I'd tell you."

He swallowed a mouthful of beer. "But."

She nodded, and at last let her smile relax. "It's not up to me. She'd kill me if I told you."

He opened his mouth to point out a logic problem with that, then sighed and said instead, "Would she know?" She just blinked at him, so he went on, "Would she know it, if you told me?"

"*Oh* yeah."

"How would she know?"

"You'd be doing things. You wouldn't be sitting here drinking a beer, for sure."

"What would I be doing?"

"I think you'd be driving to San Francisco. If I told you—if you asked—" For an instant she was gone, and then he could see her again; but she seemed two-dimensional now, like a projection on a screen—he had the feeling that if he moved to the side he would just see this image of her get narrower, not see the other side of her.

"What's in San Francisco?" he asked quickly.

"Well if you asked me about Maxwell's Demon-n-n-n—"

She was perfectly motionless, and the drone of the last consonant slowly deepened in pitch to silence. Then the popcorn in the cracked bowl rattled in the same instant that she silently disappeared like the picture on a switched-off television set, leaving Moore alone at the table, his face suddenly chilly in the bar's air conditioning. For a moment "air conditioning" seemed to remind him of something, but he forgot it when he looked down at the popcorn—the bowl was full of brown BBs—unpopped dried corn. As he watched, each kernel slowly opened in white curls and blobs until all the popcorn was as fresh-looking and uncrushed as it had been when he had carried it to the table. There hadn't been a sound, though he caught a strong whiff of gasoline. The bowl wasn't cracked anymore.

He stood up and kicked his stool aside as he backed away from the table. She was definitely gone.

The bartender was looking at him now, but Moore hurried past him and back through the hallway to the stormy gray daylight.

What if she had backup? he thought as he fumbled the keys out of his pocket; and, *She doesn't want me to tell you what's going to happen*

He only realized that he'd been sprinting when he scuffed to a halt on the wet asphalt beside the old white Dodge, and he was panting as he unlocked the door and yanked it open. Rain on the pavement was a steady textured hiss. He climbed in and pulled the door closed, and rammed the key into the ignition—

—when the drumming of rain on the car roof abruptly went silent, and a voice spoke in his head: *Relax. I'm you. You're me.*

And then his mouth opened and the words were coming out of his mouth: "We're Pat Moore, there's nothing to be afraid of." His voice belonged to someone else in this muffled silence.

His eyes were watering with the useless effort to breathe more quickly.

He knew this wasn't the same Pat Moore he had been in the bar with. This was the *her* she had spoken of. A moment later the thoughts had been wiped away, leaving nothing but an insistent pressure of *all-is-well.*

Though nothing grabbed him, he found that his head was turning to the right, and with dimming vision he saw that his right hand was moving toward his face.

But *all-is-well* had for some time been a feeling that was alien to him, and he managed to resist it long enough to make his infiltrated mind form a thought—*she's crowding me out.*

And he managed to think, too, *Alive or dead, stay whole.* He reached down to the open seam in the seat before he could lose his left arm too, and he snatched up the revolver and stabbed the barrel into his open mouth. A moment later he felt the click through the steel against his teeth when he cocked the hammer back. His belly coiled icily, as if he were standing on the coping of a very high wall and looking up.

The intrusion in his mind paused, and he sensed confusion, so he threw at it the thought, *One more step and I blow my head off.* He added, *Go ahead and call this bet, please. I've been meaning to drive 101 for a while now.*

His throat was working to form words that he could only guess at, and then he was in control of his own breathing again, panting and huffing spit into the gun barrel. Beyond the hammer of the gun he could see the rapid distortions of rain hitting the windshield, but he still couldn't hear anything from outside the car.

The voice in his head was muted now: *I mean to help you.*

He let himself pull the gun away from his mouth, though he kept it pointed at his face, and he spoke into the wet barrel as if it were a microphone. "I don't want help," he said hoarsely.

I'm Pat Moore, and I want help.

"You want to . . . take over, possess me."

I want to protect you. A man tried to kill you.

"That's your pals," he said, remembering what the ghost woman had told him in the car. "Your students, trying to kill all the Pat Moores—to keep you from taking one over, I bet. Don't joggle me now." Staring down the rifled barrel, he cautiously hooked his thumb over the hammer and then pulled the trigger and eased the hammer down. "I can still do it with one pull of the trigger," he told her as he lifted his thumb away. "So you—what, you put off mailing the letter, and died?"

The letter is just my chain mail. The only important thing about it is my name in it, and the likelihood that people will reproduce it and pass it on. Bombers evade radar by throwing clouds of tinfoil. The chain mail is my name, scattered everywhere so that any blow directed at me is dissipated.

"So you're a ghost too."

A prepared ghost. I know how to get outside of time.

"Fine, get outside of time. What do you need me for?"

You're alive, and your name is mine, which is to say your identity is mine. I've used too much of my energy saving you, holding you. And you're the most compatible of them all—you're a Pat Moore identity squared, by marriage.

"Squared by—" He closed his eyes, and nearly lowered the gun. "Everybody called her Trish," he whispered. "Only her mother called her Pat." He couldn't feel the seat under him, and he was afraid that if he let go of the gun it would fall to the car's roof.

Her mother called her Pat.

"You can't have me." He was holding his voice steady with an effort. "I'm driving away now."

You're Pat Moore's only hope.

"You need an exorcist, not a poker player." He could move his right arm again, and he started the engine and then switched on the windshield wipers.

Abruptly the drumming of the rain came back on, sounding loud after the long silence. She was gone.

His hands were shaking as he tucked the gun back into its pocket, but he was confident that he could get back onto 280, even with his worn-out windshield wipers blurring everything, and he had no intention of getting on 101 anytime soon; he had been almost entirely bluffing when he told her, *I've been meaning to drive 101 for a while now.* But like an alcoholic who tries one drink after long abstinence, he was remembering the taste of the gun barrel in his mouth: That was easier than I thought it would be, he thought.

He fumbled a pack of Marlboros out of his jacket pocket and shook one out.

As soon as he had got onto northbound 85 he became aware that the purple dress and the dark hair were blocking the passenger-side window again, and he didn't jump at all. He had wondered which way to turn on 280, and now he steered the car into the lane that would take him back north, toward San Francisco. The grooved interchange lane gleamed with fresh rain, and he kept his speed down to forty.

"One big U-turn," he said finally, speaking around his lit cigarette. He glanced at her; she looked three-dimensional again, and she was smiling at him as cheerfully as ever.

"I'm your guardian angel," she said.

"Right, I remember. And your name's Pat Moore, same as mine. Same as everybody's, lately." He realized that he was optimistic, which surprised him; it was something like the happy confidence he had felt in dreams in which he had discovered that he could fly, and leave behind all earthbound reproaches. "I met *her,* you know. She's dead too, and she needs a living body, and so she tried to possess me."

"Yes," said Pat Moore. "That's what's going to happen. I couldn't tell you before."

He frowned. "I scared her off, by threatening to shoot myself." Reluctantly he asked, "Will she try again, do you think?"

"Sure. When you're asleep, probably, since this didn't work. She can wait a few hours; a few days, even, in a pinch. It was just because I talked to you that she switched me off and tried to do it right away, while you were still awake. *Jumped the gun,*" she added, with the first laugh he had heard from her—it sounded as if she were trying to chant in a language she didn't understand.

"Ah," he said softly. "That raises the ante." He took a deep breath and let it out. "When did you . . . die?"

"I don't know. Some time besides now. Could you put out the cigarette? The smoke messes up my reception, I'm still partly seeing that bar, and partly a hilltop in a park somewhere."

He rolled the window down an inch and flicked the cigarette out. "Is this how you looked, when you were alive?"

She touched her hair as he glanced at her. "I don't know."

"When you were alive—did you know about movies, and current news? I mean, you don't seem to know about them now."

"I suppose I did. Don't most people?"

He was gripping the wheel hard now. "Did your mother call you Pat?"

"I suppose she did. It's my name."

"Did your . . . friends, call you Trish?"

"I suppose they did."

I suppose, I suppose! He forced himself not to shout at her. She's dead, he reminded himself.

She's probably doing the best she can.

But again he thought of the Frost line: *The dead are holding something back.*

They had passed under two gray concrete bridges, and now he switched on his left turn signal to merge with northbound 280. The pavement ahead of him glittered with reflected red brake lights.

"See, my wife's name was Patricia Moore," he said, trying to sound reasonable. "She died in a car crash five months ago. Well, a single-car accident. Drove off a freeway embankment. She was drunk." He remembered that the popcorn in the Pirate's Cove had momentarily smelled like spilled gasoline.

"I've been drunk."

"So has everybody. But—you might be her."

"Who?"

"My wife. Trish."

"I might be your wife."

"Tell me about Maxwell's Demon."

"I would have been married to you, you mean. We'd *really* have been Pat Moore then. Like mirrors reflecting each other."

"That's why *she* wants me, right. So what's Maxwell's Demon?"

"It's . . . she's dead, so she's like a smoke ring somebody puffed out in the air, if they were smoking. Maxwell's Demon keeps her from disappearing like a smoke ring would, it keeps her . . ."

"Distinct," Moore said when she didn't go on. "Even though she's got no right to be distinct anymore."

"And me. Through her."

"Can I kill him? Or make him stop sustaining her?" And you, he thought; it would stop him sustaining you. Did I stop sustaining you before? Well, obviously.

Earthbound reproaches.

"It's not a him. It looks like a sprinkler you'd screw onto a hose to water your yard, if it would spin. It's in her house, hooked up to the air conditioning."

"A sprinkler." He was nodding repeatedly, and he made himself stop. "Okay. Can you show me where her house is? I'm going to have to sleep sometime."

"She'd kill me."

"Pat—Trish—" Instantly he despised himself for calling her by that name. "—you're already dead."

"She can get outside of time. Ghosts aren't really in time anyway, I'm wrecking the popcorn in that bar in the future as much as in the past, it's all just cards in a circle on a table, none in front. None of it's really now or not-now. She could make me not ever—she could take my thread out of the carpet—you'd never have met me, even like this."

"Make you never have existed."

"Right. Never was any *me* at all."

"She wouldn't dare—Pat." Just from self-respect he couldn't bring himself to call her Trish again. "Think about it. If you never existed, then I wouldn't have married you, and so I wouldn't be the Pat Moore squared that she needs."

"If you *did* marry me. Me, I mean. I can't remember. Do you think you did?"

She'll take me there, if I say yes, he thought. She'll believe me if I say it. And what's to become of me, if she doesn't? That woman very nearly crowded me right out of the world five minutes ago, and I was wide awake.

The memory nauseated him.

What becomes of a soul that's pushed out of its body, he thought, as *she* means to do to me? Would there be *anything* left of *me*, even a half-wit ghost like poor Pat here?

Against his will came the thought, You always did lie to her.

"I don't know," he said finally. "The odds are against it."

There's always 101, he told himself, and somehow the thought wasn't entirely bleak. Six chambers of it, hollow-point .38s. Fly away.

"It's possible, though, isn't it?"

He exhaled, and nodded. "It's possible, yes."

"I think I owe it to you. Some Pat Moore does. We left you alone."

"It was my fault." In a rush he added, "I was even glad you didn't leave a note." It's true, he thought. I was grateful.

"I'm glad she didn't leave a note," this Pat Moore said.

He needed to change the subject. "*You're* a ghost," he said. "Can't you make *her* never have existed?"

"No. I can't get far from real places or I'd blur away, out of focus, but she can go way up high, where you can look down on the whole carpet, and—twist out strands of it; bend somebody at right angles to *everything*, which means you're gone without a trace. And anyway, she and her students are all blocked against that kind of attack, they've got ConfigSafe."

He laughed at the analogy. "You know about computers?"

"No," she said emptily. "Did I?"

He sighed. "No, not a lot." He thought of the revolver in the seat, and then thought of something better. "You mentioned a park. You used to like Buena Vista Park. Let's stop there on the way."

✤ ✤ ✤

Moore drove clockwise around the tall, darkly wooded hill that was the park, while the peaked roofs and cylindrical towers of the old Victorian houses were teeth on a saw passing across the gray sky on his left. He found a parking space on the eastern curve of Buena Vista Avenue, and he got out of the car quickly to keep the Pat Moore ghost from having to open the door on her side; he remembered what she had done to the bowl of popcorn.

But she was already standing on the splashing pavement in the rain, without having opened the door. In the ashy daylight her purple dress seemed to have lost all its color, and her face was indistinct and pale; he peered at her, and he was sure the heavy raindrops were falling right through her.

He could imagine her simply dissolving on the hike up to the meadow. "Would you rather wait in the car?" he said. "I won't be long."

"Do you have a pair of binoculars?" she asked. Her voice too was frail out here in the cold.

"Yes, in the glove compartment." Cold rain was soaking his hair and leaking down inside his jacket collar, and he wanted to get moving. "Can you . . . hold them?"

"I can't hold anything. But if you take out the lens in the middle you can catch me in it, and carry me."

He stepped past her to open the passenger-side door, and bent over to pop open the glove compartment, and then he knelt on the seat and dragged out his old leather-sleeved binoculars and turned them this way and that in the wobbly gray light that filtered through the windshield.

"How do I get the lens out?" he called over his shoulder.

"A screwdriver, I guess," came her voice, barely audible above the thrashing of the rain. "See the tiny screw by the eyepiece?"

"Oh. Right." He used the small blade from his pocketknife on the screw in the back of the left barrel, and then had to do the same with a similar screw on the forward end of it. The eyepiece stayed where it was, but the big forward lens fell out, exposing a metal cross on the inside; it was held down with a screw that he managed to rotate with the blade-tip—and then a triangular block of polished glass fell out into his palm.

"That's it, that's the lens," she called from outside the car.

Moore's cell phone buzzed as he was stepping backward to the pavement, and he fumbled it out of his jacket pocket and flipped it open. "Moore here," he said. He pushed the car door closed and leaned over the phone to keep the rain off it.

"Hey Pat," came Rick's voice, "I'm sitting here in your Garden City club in San Jose, and I could be at the Bay. Where are you, man?"

The Pat Moore ghost was moving her head, and Moore looked up at her. With evident effort she was making her head swivel back and forth in a clear *no* gesture.

The warning chilled Moore. Into the phone he said, "I'm—not far, I'm at a bar off the 85. Place called the Pirate's Cove."

"Well, don't chug your beer on my account. But come over here when you can."

"You bet. I'll be out of here in five minutes." He closed the phone and dropped it back into his pocket.

"They made him call again," said the ghost. "They lost track of your car after I killed the guy with the shotgun." She smiled, and her teeth seemed to be gone. "That was good, saying you were at that bar. They can tell truth from lies, and that's only twenty minutes from being true."

Guardian angel, he thought. "You killed him?"

"I think so." Her image faded, then solidified again. "Yes."

"Ah. Well—good." With his free hand he pushed the wet hair hack from his forehead. "So what do I do with this?" he asked, holding up the lens.

"Hold it by the frosted sides, with the long edge of the triangle pointed at me; then look at me through the two other edges."

The glass thing was a blocky right-triangle, frosted on the sides but polished smooth and clear on the thick edges; obediently he held it up to his eye and peered through the two slanted faces of clear glass.

He could see her clearly through the lens—possibly more clearly than when he looked at her directly—but this was a mirror image: the dark slope of the park appeared to be to the left of her.

"Now roll it over a quarter turn, like from noon to three," she said.

He rotated the lens ninety degrees—but her image in it rotated a full 180 degrees, so that instead of seeing her horizontal he saw her upside down.

He jumped then, for her voice was right in his ear. "Close your eyes and put the lens in your pocket."

He did as she said, and when he opened his eyes again she was gone—the wet pavement stretched empty to the curbstones and green lawns of the old houses.

"You've got me in your pocket," her voice said in his ear. "When you want me, look through the lens again and turn it back the other way."

It occurred to him that he believed her. "Okay," he said, and sprinted across the street to the narrow stone stairs that led up into the park.

His leather shoes tapped the ascending steps, and then splashed in the mud as he took the uphill path to the left. The city was gone now, hidden behind the dense overhanging boughs of pine and eucalyptus, and the rain echoed under the canopy of green leaves. The cold air was musky with the smells of mulch and pine and wet loam.

Up at the level playground lawn the swingsets were of course empty, and in fact he seemed to be the only living soul in the park today. Through gaps between the trees he could see San Francisco spread out below him on all sides, as still as a photograph, under the heavy clouds.

He splashed through the gutters that were made of fragments of old marble headstones—keeping his head down, he glimpsed an incised cross filled with mud in the face of one stone, and the lone phrase "*in loving memory*" on another—and then he had come to the meadow with the big old oak trees he remembered.

He looked around, but there was still nobody to be seen in the cathedral space, and he hurried to the side and crouched to step in under the shaggy foliage and catch his breath.

"It's beautiful," said the voice in his ear.

"Yes," he said, and he took the lens out of his pocket. He held it up and squinted through the right-angle panels, and there was the image of her, upside down. He rotated it counterclockwise ninety degrees and the image was upright, and when he moved the lens away from his eye she was standing out in the clearing.

"Look at the city some more," she said, and her voice now seemed to come from several yards away. "So I can see it again."

One last time, he thought. Maybe for both of us; it's nice that we can do it together.

"Sure." He stepped out from under the oak tree and walked back out into the rain to the middle of the clearing and looked around.

A line of trees to the north was the panhandle of Golden Gate Park, and past that he could see the stepped levels of Alta Vista Park; more distantly to the left he could just make out the green band that was the hills of the Presidio, though the two big piers of the Golden Gate Bridge were lost behind miles of rain; he turned to look southwest, where the Twin Peaks and the TV tower on Mount Sutro were vivid above the misty streets; and then far away to the east the white spike of the Transamerica Pyramid stood up from the skyline at the very edge of visibility.

"It's beautiful," she said again. "Did you come here to look at it?"

"No," he said, and he lowered his gaze to the dark mulch under the trees. Cypress, eucalyptus, pine, oak—even from out here he could see that mushrooms were clustered in patches and rings on the carpet of wet black leaves, and he walked back to the trees and then shuffled in a crouch into the aromatic dimness under the boughs.

After a couple of minutes, "Here's one," he said, stooping to pick a mushroom. Its tan cap was about two inches across, covered with a patch of white veil. He unsnapped his denim jacket and tucked the mushroom carefully into his shirt pocket.

"What is it?" asked Pat Moore.

"I don't know," he said. "My wife was never able to tell, so she never picked them. It's either *Amanita lanei,* which is edible, or it's *Amanita phalloides,* which is fatally poisonous. You'd need a real expert to know which this is."

"What are you going to do with it?"

"I think I'm going to sandbag her. You want to hop back into the lens for the hike down the hill?"

He had parked the old Dodge at an alarming slant on Jones Street on the south slope of Russian Hill, and then the two of them had walked steeply uphill past close-set gates and balconies under tall sidewalk trees that grew straight up from the slanted pavements. Headlights of cars descending Jones Street reflected in white glitter on the wet trunks and curbstones, and in the wakes of the cars the tire tracks blurred away slowly in the continuing rain.

"How are we going to get into her house?" he asked quietly.

"It'll be unlocked," said the ghost. "She's expecting you now."

He shivered. "Is she. Well I hope I'm playing a better hand than she guesses."

"Down here," said Pat, pointing at a brick-paved alley that led away to the right between the Victorian-gingerbread porches of two narrow houses.

They were in a little alley now, overhung with rose bushes and rosemary, with white-painted fences on either side. Columns of fog billowed in the breeze, and then he noticed that they were human forms—female torsos twisting transparently in the air, blank-faced children running in slow motion, hunched figures swaying heads that changed shape like water balloons.

"The outfielders," said the Pat Moore ghost.

Now Moore could hear their voices: *Goddamn car—I got yer unconditional right here—excuse me, you got a problem?—He was never there for me So I told him, you want it you come over here and take it—Bless me Father, I have died—*

The acid smell of wet stone was lost in the scents of tobacco and jasmine perfume and liquor and old, old sweat.

Moore bit his lip and tried to focus on the solid pavement and the fences. "Where the hell's her place?" he asked tightly.

"This gate," she said. "Maybe you'd better—"

He nodded and stepped past her; the gate latch had no padlock, and he flipped up the catch. The hinges squeaked as he swung the gate inward over flagstones and low-cut grass.

He looked up at the house the path led to. It was a one-story 1920s bungalow, painted white or gray, with green wicker chairs on the narrow porch. Lights were on behind stained-glass panels in the two windows and the porch door.

"It's unlocked," said the ghost.

He turned back toward her. "Stand over by the roses there," he told her, "away from the . . . the outfielders. I want to take you in in my pocket, okay?"

"Okay."

She drifted to the roses, and he fished the lens out of his pocket and found her image through the right-angle faces, then twisted the lens and put it back into his pocket.

He walked slowly up the path, treading on the grass rather than on the flagstones, and stepped up to the porch.

"It's not locked, Patrick," came a woman's loud voice from inside.

He turned the glass knob and walked several paces into a

high-ceilinged kitchen with a black-and-white-tiled floor; a blonde woman in jeans and a sweatshirt sat at a formica table by the big old refrigerator. From the next room, beyond an arch in the white-painted plaster, a steady whistling hiss provided an irritating background noise, as if a teakettle were boiling.

The woman at the table was much more clearly visible than his guardian angel had been, almost aggressively three-dimensional—her breasts under the sweatshirt were prominent and pointed, her nose and chin stood out perceptibly too far from her high cheekbones, and her lips were so full that they looked distinctly swollen.

A bottle of Wild Turkey bourbon stood beside three Flintstones glasses on the table, and she took it in one hand and twisted out the cork with the other. "Have a drink," she said, speaking loudly, perhaps in order to be heard over the hiss in the next room.

"I don't think I will, thanks," he said. "You're good with your hands." His jacket was dripping rainwater on the tiles, but he didn't take it off.

"I'm the solidest ghost you'll ever see."

Abruptly she stood up, knocking her chair against the refrigerator, and then she rushed past him, her Reeboks beating on the floor; and her body seemed to rotate as she went by him, as if she were swerving away from him; though her course to the door was straight. She reached out one lumpy hand and slammed the door.

She faced him again and held out her right hand. "I'm Pat Moore," she said, "and I want help."

He flexed his fingers, then cautiously held out his own hand. "I'm Pat Moore too," he said.

Her palm touched his, and though it was moving very slowly his own hand was slapped away when they touched.

"I want us to become partners," she said. Her thick lips moved in ostentatious synchronization with her words.

"Okay," he said.

Her outlines blurred for just an instant; then she said, in the same booming tone, "I want us to become one person. You'll be immortal, and—"

"Let's do it," he said.

She blinked her black eyes. "You're—agreeing to it," she said. "You're accepting it, now?"

"Yes." He cleared his throat. "That's correct."

He looked away from her and noticed a figure sitting at the table—a transparent old man in an overcoat, hardly more visible than a puff of smoke.

"Is he Maxwell's Demon?" Moore asked.

The woman smiled, baring huge teeth. "No, that's . . . a soliton. A poor little soliton who's lost its way. I'll show you Maxwell's Demon."

She lunged and clattered into the next room, and Moore followed her, trying simultaneously not to slip on the floor and to keep an eye on her and on the misty old man.

Moore stepped into a parlor, and the hissing noise was louder in here. Carved dark wood tables and chairs and a modern exercise bicycle had been pushed against a curtained bay window in the far wall, and a vast carpet had been rolled back from the dusty hardwood floor and humped against the chair legs. In the high corners of the room and along the fluted top of the window frame, things like translucent cheerleaders' pompoms grimaced and waved tentacles or locks of hair in the agitated air. Moore warily took a step away from them.

"Look over here," said the alarming woman.

In the near wall an air-conditioning panel had been taken apart, and a red rubber hose hung from its machinery and was connected into the side of a length of steel pipe that lay on a TV table. Nozzles on either end of the pipe were making the loud whistling sound.

Moore looked more closely at it. It was apparently two sections of pipe, one about eight inches long and the other about four, connected together by a blocky fitting where the hose was attached, and a stove stopcock stood half-open near the end of the longer pipe.

"Feel the air," the woman said.

Moore cupped a hand near the end of the longer pipe, and then yanked it back—the air blasting out of it felt hot enough to light a cigar. More cautiously he waved his fingers over the nozzle at the end of the short pipe; and then he rolled his hand in the air-jet, for it was icy cold.

"*It's* not supernatural," she boomed, "even though the air conditioner's pumping room-temperature air. A spiral washer in the connector housing sends air spinning up the long pipe; the hot molecules spin out to the sides of the little whirlwind in there, and it's them that the stopcock lets out. The cold molecules fall into a smaller whirlwind inside the big one, and they move the opposite way and come out at the end of the short pipe. Room-temperature air is a mix of hot and cold molecules, and this device separates them out."

"Okay," said Moore. He spoke levelly, but he was wishing he had brought his gun along from the car. It occurred to him that it was a rifled pipe that things usually come spinning out of, but which he had been ready to dive into. He wondered if the gills under the cap of the mushroom in his pocket were curved in a spiral.

"But this is counter-entropy," she said, smiling again. "A Scottish physicist named Maxwell p-postulay-postul—guessed that a Demon would be needed to sort the hot molecules from the cold ones. If the Demon is present, the effect occurs, and vice versa—if you can make the effect occur you've summoned the Demon. Get the effect, and the cause has no choice but to be present." She thumped her chest, though her peculiar breasts didn't move at all. "And once the Demon is present, he—he—"

She paused, so Moore said, "Maintains distinctions that wouldn't ordinarily stay distinct." His heart was pounding, but he was pleased with how steady his voice was.

Something like an invisible hand struck him solidly in the chest, and he stepped back.

"You don't touch it," she said. Again there was an invisible thump against his chest. "Back to the kitchen."

The soliton old man, hardly visible in the bright overhead light, was still nodding in one of the chairs at the table.

The blonde woman was slapping the wall, and then a white-painted cabinet, but when Moore looked toward her she grabbed the knob on one of the cabinet drawers and yanked it open.

"You need to come over here," she said, "and look in the drawer."

After the things he'd seen in the high corners of the parlor, Moore was cautious; he leaned over and peered into the drawer—but it contained only a stack of typing paper, a felt tip laundry-marking pen, and half a dozen yo-yos.

As he watched, she reached past him and snatched out a sheet of paper and the laundry marker; and it occurred to him that she hadn't been able to see the contents of the drawer until he was looking at them.

I don't have any vision, his guardian angel had said. *No retinas. I have to use yours.*

The woman had stepped away from the cabinet now. "I was

prepared, see," she said, loudly enough to be heard out on Jones Street, "for my stupid students killing me. I knew they might. We were all working to learn how to transcend time, but I got there first, and they were afraid of what I would do. So *boom-boom-boom* for Mistress Moore. But I had already set up the Demon, and I had xeroxed my chain mail and put it in addressed envelopes. Bales of them, the stamps cost me a fortune. I came back strong. And I'm going to merge with you now and get a real body again. You accepted the proposal—you just called, you said 'Yes, that's correct'—you didn't raise this time to chase me away."

The cap flew off the laundry marker, and then she slapped the paper down on the table next to the Wild Turkey bottle. "Watch me!" she said, and when he looked at the piece of paper, she began vigorously writing on it. Soon she had written *PAT* in big sprawling letters and was embarked on *MOORE*.

She straightened up when it was finished. "Now," she said, her black eyes glittering with hunger, "you cut your hand and write with your blood, tracing over the letters. Our name is us, and we'll merge. Smooth as silk through a goose."

Moore slowly dug the pocketknife out of his pants pocket. "This is new," he said. "You didn't do this name-in-blood business when you tried to take me in the car."

She waved one big hand dismissively. "I thought I could sneak up on you. You resisted me, though— you'd probably have tried to resist me even in your sleep. But since you're accepting the inevitable now, we can do a proper contract, in ink and blood. Cut, cut!"

"Okay," he said, and unfolded the short blade and cut a nick in his right forefinger. "*You've* made a new bet now, though, and it's to me." Blood was dripping from the cut, and he dragged his finger over the *P* in her crude signature.

He had to pause halfway through and probe again with the blade-tip to get more freely flowing blood; and as he was painfully tracing the *R* in *MOORE*, he began to feel another will helping to push his finger along, and he heard a faint drone like a radio carrier-wave starting up in his head. Somewhere he was crouched on his toes on a narrow, outward-tilting ledge with no handholds anywhere, with vast volumes of emptiness below him—and his toes were sliding—So he added quickly, "And I raise back at you."

By touch alone, looking up at the high ceiling, he pulled the mushroom out of his shirt pocket and popped it into his mouth and bit down on it. Call-and-raise, he thought. Sandbagged. Then he lowered his eyes, and in an instant her gaze was locked onto his.

"What happened?" she demanded, and Moore could hear the three syllables of it chug in his own throat. "What did you do?"

"*Amanita*," said the smoky old man at the table. His voice sounded like nothing organic—more like sandpaper on metal. "It was time to eat the mushroom."

Moore had resolutely chewed the thing up, his teeth grating on bits of dirt. It had the cold-water taste of ordinary mushrooms, and as he forced himself to swallow it he forlornly hoped, in spite of all his bravura thoughts about the 101 freeway, that it might be the *lanei* rather than the deadly *phalloides*.

"He ate a mushroom?" the woman demanded of the old man. "You never told me about any mushroom! Is it a poisonous mushroom?"

"I don't know," came the rasping voice again. "It's either poisonous or not, though, I remember that much."

Moore was dizzy with the first twinges of comprehension of what he had done. "Fifty-fifty chance," he said tightly. "The Death Cap Amanita looks just like another one that's harmless, both grow locally. I picked this one today, and I don't know which it was. If it's the poison one, we won't know for about twenty-four hours, maybe longer."

The drone in Moore's head grew suddenly louder, then faded until it was imperceptible. "You're telling the truth," she said. She flung out an arm toward the back porch, and for a moment her bony forefinger was a foot long. "Go vomit it up, now!"

He twitched, like someone mistaking the green left-turn arrow for the green light. No, he told himself, clenching his fists to conceal any trembling. Fifty-fifty is better than zero. You've clocked the odds and placed your bet. Trust yourself.

"No good," he said. "The smallest particle will do the job, if it's the poisonous one. Enough's probably been absorbed already. That's why I chose it." This was a bluff, or a guess, anyway, but this time she didn't scan his mind.

He was tense, but a grin was twitching at his lips. He nodded toward the old man and asked her, "Who *is* the lost sultan, anyway?"

"Soliton," she snapped. "He's you, you—dumb-brain." She stamped one foot, shaking the house. "How can I take you now? And I can't wait twenty-four hours just to see if I *can* take you!"

"Me? How is he me?"

"My name's Pat Moore," said the gray silhouette at the table.

"Ghosts are solitons," she said impatiently, "waves that keep moving all-in-a-piece after the living push has stopped. Forward or backward doesn't matter to them."

"I'm from the *future*," said the soliton, perhaps grinning.

Moore stared at the indistinct thing, and he had to repress an urge to run over there and tear it apart, try to set fire to it, stuff it in a drawer. And he realized that the sudden chill on his forehead wasn't from fright, as he had at first assumed, but from profound embarrassment at the thing's presence here.

"I've blown it all on you," the blonde woman said, perhaps to herself even though her voice boomed in the tall kitchen. "I don't have the . . . sounds like 'courses' . . . I don't have the energy reserves to go after another living Pat Moore *now*. You were perfect, Pat Moore squared— why did you have to be a diehard suicide fan?"

Moore actually laughed at that—and she glared at him in the same instant that he was punched backward off his feet by the hardest invisible blow yet.

He sat down hard and slid, and his back collided with the stove; and then, though he could still see the walls and the old man's smoky legs under the table across the room and the glittering rippled glass of the windows, he was somewhere else. He could feel the square tiles under his palms, but in this other place he had no body.

In the now-remote kitchen, the blonde woman said, "Drape him," and the soliton got up and drifted across the floor toward Moore, shrinking as it came so that its face was on a level with Moore's.

Its face was indistinct—pouches under the empty eyes, drink-wrinkles spilling diagonally across the cheekbones, petulant lines around the mouth—and Moore did not try to recognize himself in it.

The force that had knocked Moore down was holding him pressed against the floor and the stove, unable to crawl away, and all he could do was hold his breath as the soliton ghost swept over him like a spiderweb.

You've got a girl in your pocket, came the thing's raspy old voice in his ear.

Get away from me, Moore thought, nearly gagging.

Who get away from who?

"I can get another living Pat Moore," the blonde woman was saying, "if I never wasted any effort on you in the first place, if there was never a you for me to notice." He heard her take a deep breath. "I can do this." She crossed the floor to stand over him.

Her knee touched his cheek, slamming his head against the oven door. She was leaning over the top of the stove, banging blindly at the burners and the knobs, and then Moore heard the triple click of one of the knobs turning, and the faint thump of the flame coming on. He peered up and saw that she was holding the sheet of paper with the ink and blood on it, and then he could smell the paper burning.

Moore became aware that there was still the faintest drone in his head only a moment before it ceased.

"Up," she said, and the ghost was a net surrounding Moore, lifting him up off the floor and through the intangible roof and far away from the rainy shadowed hills of San Francisco.

He was aware that his body was still in the house, still slumped against the stove in the kitchen, but his soul, indistinguishable now from his ghost, was in some vast region where *in front* and *behind* had no meaning, where the once-apparent dichotomy between *here* and *there* was a discarded optical illusion, where comprehension was total but didn't depend on light or sight or perspective, and where even *ago* and *to come* were just compass points; everything was in stasis, for motion had been left far behind with sequential time.

He knew that the long braids or vapor trails that he encompassed and which surrounded him were lifelines, stretching from births in that direction to deaths in the other—some linked to others for varying intervals, some curving alone through the non-sky—but they were more like long electrical arcs than anything substantial; they were stretched across time and space, but at the same time they were coils too infinitesimally small to be perceived, if his perception had been by means of sight; and they were electrons in standing waves surrounding an unimaginable nucleus, which also surrounded them— the universe, apprehended here in its full volume of past and future, was one enormous and eternal atom.

But he could feel the tiles of the kitchen floor beneath his fingertips.

He dragged one hand up his hip to the side-pocket of his jacket, and his fingers slipped inside and touched the triangular lens.

No, said the soliton ghost, a separate thing again.

Moore was still huddled on the floor, still touching the lens—but now he and his ghost were sitting on the other side of the room at the kitchen table too, and the ghost was holding a deck of cards in one hand and spinning cards out with the other. The ghost stopped when two cards lay in front of each of them. The Wild Turkey bottle was gone, and the glow from the ceiling lamp was a dimmer yellow than it had been.

"Hold 'Em," the ghost rasped. "Your whole lifeline is the buy-in, and I'm going to take it away from you. You've got a tall stack there, birth to now, but I won't go all-in on you right away. I bet our first seven years—Fudgsicles, our dad flying kites in the spring sunsets, the star decals in constellations on our bedroom ceiling, our mom reading the Narnia books out loud to us. Push 'em out." The air in the kitchen was summery with the pink candy smell of Bazooka gum.

Hold 'Em, thought Moore. I'll raise.

Trish killed herself, he projected at his ghost, *rather than live with us anymore. Drove her Granada over the embankment off 101. The police said she was doing ninety, with no touch of the brake.* Again he smelled spilled gasoline—

—and so, apparently did his opponent; the pouchy-faced old ghost flickered, but came back into focus. "I make it more," said the ghost, "the next seven. Bicycles, the Albert Payson Terhune books, hiking with Joe and Ken in the oil fields, the Valentine from Teresa Thompson. Push 'em out, or fold."

Neither of them had looked at their cards, and Moore hoped the game wouldn't proceed to the eventual arbitrary showdown—he hoped that the frail ghost wouldn't be able to keep sustaining raises.

I can't hold anything, his guardian angel had said.

It hurt Moore, but he projected another raise at the ghost: *When we admitted we had deleted her poetry files deliberately, she said, "You're not a nice man." She was drunk, and we laughed at her when she said it, but one day after she was gone we remembered it, and then we had to pull over to the side of the road because we couldn't see through the tears to drive.*

The ghost was just a smoky sketch of a midget or a monkey now, and Moore doubted it had enough substance even to deal cards. In a faint birdlike voice it said, "The next seven. College, and our old motorcycle, and—"

And Trish at twenty, Moore finished, grinding his teeth and thinking about the mushroom dissolving in his stomach. *We talked her into taking her first drink. Pink gin, Tanqueray with Angostura bitters. And we were pleased when she said, "Where has this been all my life?"*

"All my life," whispered the ghost, and then it flicked away like a reflection in a dropped mirror.

The blonde woman was sitting there instead. "What did you have?" she boomed, nodding toward his cards.

"The winning hand," said Moore. He touched his two face-down cards. "The pot's mine—the raises got too high for him." The cards blurred away like fragments left over from a dream.

Then he hunched forward and gripped the edge of the table, for the timeless vertiginous gulf, the infinite atom of the lifelines, was a sudden pressure from outside the world, and this artificial scene had momentarily lost its depth of field.

"I can twist your thread out, even without his help," she told him. She frowned, and a vein stood out on her curved forehead, and the kitchen table resumed its cubic dimensions and the light brightened. "Even dead, I'm more potent than you are."

She whirled her massive right arm up from below the table and clanked down her elbow, with her forearm upright; her hand was open.

Put me behind her, Pat, said the Pat Moore ghost's remembered voice in his ear.

He made himself feel the floor tiles under his hand and the stove at his back, and then he pulled the triangular lens out of his pocket; when he held it up to his eye he was able to see himself and the blonde woman at the table across the room, and the Pat Moore ghost was visible upside down behind the woman. He rotated the glass a quarter turn, and she was now upright.

He moved the lens away and blinked, and then he was gripping the edge of the table and looking across it at the blonde woman, and at her hand only a foot away from his face. The fingerprints were like comb-tracks in clay. Peripherally he could see the slim Pat Moore ghost, still in the purple dress, standing behind her.

"Arm-wrestling?" he said, raising his eyebrows. He didn't want to let go of the table, or even move—this localized perspective seemed very frail.

The woman only glared at him out of her irisless eyes. At last he leaned back in the chair and unclamped the fingers of his right hand from the table-edge; and then he shrugged and raised his right arm and set his elbow beside hers. With her free hand she picked up his pocketknife and hefted it. "When this thing hits the floor, we start." She clasped his hand, and his fingers were numbed as if from a hard impact.

Her free hand jerked, and the knife was glittering in a fantastic parabola through the air, and though he was braced all the way through his torso from his firmly planted feet, when the knife clanged against the tiles the massive power of her arm hit his palm like a falling tree.

Sweat sprang out on his forehead, and his arm was steadily bending backward—and the whole world was rotating too, narrowing, tilting away from him to spill him, all the bets he and his ghost had made, into zero.

In the car the Pat Moore ghost had told him, *She can bend somebody at right angles to* everything, *which means you're gone without a trace.*

We're not sitting at the kitchen table, he told himself; we're still dispersed in that vaster comprehension of the universe.

And if she rotates me ninety degrees, he was suddenly certain, I'm gone.

And then the frail Pat Moore ghost leaned in from behind the woman, and clasped her diaphanous hand around Moore's; and together they were Pat Moore squared, their lifelines linked still by their marriage, and he could feel her strong pulse in supporting counterpoint to his own.

His forearm moved like a counterclockwise second hand in front of his squinting eyes as the opposing pressure steadily weakened. The woman's face seemed in his straining sight to be a rubber mask with a frantic animal trapped inside it, and when only inches separated the back of her hand from the formica tabletop, the resistance faded to nothing, and his hand was left poised empty in the air.

The world rocked back to solidity with such abruptness that he would have fallen down if he hadn't been sitting on the floor against the stove.

Over the sudden pressure release ringing in his ears, he heard a scurrying across the tiles on the other side of the room, and a thumping on the hardwood planks in the parlor.

The Pat Moore ghost still stood across the room, beside the table; and the Wild Turkey bottle was on the table, and he was sure it had been there all along.

He reached out slowly and picked up his pocketknife. It was so cold that it stung his hand.

"Cut it," said the ghost of his wife.

"I can't cut it," he said. Barring hallucinations, his body had hardly moved for the past five or ten minutes, but he was panting. "You'll die."

"I'm dead already, Pat. This—" She waved a hand from her shoulder to her knee "—isn't any good. I should be gone." She smiled. "I think that was the *lanei* mushroom."

He knew she was guessing. "I'll know tomorrow."

He got to his feet, still holding the knife. The blade, he saw, was still folded out.

"Forgive me," he said awkwardly. "For everything."

She smiled, and it was almost a familiar smile. "I forgave you in mid-air. And you forgive me too."

"If you ever did anything wrong, yes."

"Oh, I did. I don't think you noticed. Cut it."

He walked back across the room to the arch that led into the parlor, and he paused when he was beside her.

"I won't come in with you," she said, "if you don't mind."

"No," he said. "I love you, Pat."

"Loved. I loved you too. That counts. Go."

He nodded and turned away from her.

Maxwell's Demon was still hissing on the TV table by the disassembled air conditioner, and he walked to it one step at a time, not looking at the forms that twisted and whispered urgently in the high corners of the room. One seemed to be perceptibly more solid than the rest, but all of them flinched away from him.

He had to blink tears out of his eyes to see the air-hose clearly, and when he did, he noticed a plain on-off toggle switch hanging from wires that were still connected to the air-conditioning unit. He cut the hose and switched off the air conditioner, and the silence that fell then seemed to spill out of the house and across San Francisco and into the sky.

He was alone in the house.

He tried to remember the expanded, timeless perspective he had participated in, but his memory had already simplified it to a three-dimensional picture, with himself floating like a bubble in one particular place.

Which of the . . . jet trails or arcs or coils was mine? he wondered now. How long is it?

I'll be better able to guess tomorrow, he thought. At least I know it's there, forever—and even though I didn't see which one it was, I know it's linked to another.

❖ AUTHOR'S NOTE ❖

This story started with my discovery, while idly taking apart an old busted pair of binoculars, of a "poro lens." I was astonished to see that when I peered through the two shorter faces of the glass triangle, and then rotated it a quarter turn, the image I saw through the glass rotated a hundred and eighty degrees, and was now upside-down. I rotated it another quarter turn, and the image was now right-side-up again. It was obvious to me that this crazy lens was somehow twisting the fabric of space, so I hastily rotated it a hundred and eighty degrees back the other way, restoring local space to normal, and put the thing away.

Given the reality-violating properties of the thing, it seemed a natural means for capturing a ghost. And then I got one of those silly chain letter in the mail ("Send this on to ten people for Good Luck!"), and it immediately occurred to me that a widely mailed chain letter could be chain mail, as in armor. I wondered, could a ghost find that sort of chain mail valuable? Well, since you ask, of course . . .

⚜ THE WAY DOWN THE HILL ⚜

Then I was frightened at myself, for the cold mood
That envies all men running hotly, out of breath,
Nowhere, and who prefer, still drunk with their own blood,
Hell to extinction, horror and disease to death.
> —George Dillon,
> from the French of Charles Baudelaire

I HADN'T BEEN to the place since 1961, but I still instinctively downshifted as I leaned around the curve, so that the bike was moving slowly enough to take the sharp turn off the paved road when it appeared. The old man's driveway was just a long path of rutted gravel curling up the hillside, and several times I had to correct with my feet when the bald back tire lost traction, but it was a clear and breezy afternoon, with the trees and the tan California hillside making each other look good, and I was whistling cheerfully as I crested the hill and parked my old Honda beside a couple of lethal-looking Harley-Davidsons.

I was late. The yard spread out in front of the old man's Victorian-style house was a mosaic of vans, Volkswagens, big ostentatious sedans, sports cars and plain anonymous autos. There were even, I noticed as I stuffed my gloves into my helmet and strode up to the front steps, a couple of skateboards leaning on the porch rails. I grinned and wondered who the kids would be.

The heavy door was pulled open before I could touch the knob, and Archie was handing me a foaming Carlsberg he'd doubtless fetched for someone else. Somehow I can always recognize Archie.

"Come in, sibling!" he cried jovially. "We certainly can't expect Rafe yet, so you must be Saul or Amelia." He studied my face as I stepped inside. "Too old to be Amelia. Saul?"

"Right," I said, unknotting my scarf. "How's the old man, Arch?"

"Never better. He was asking just a few minutes ago if you'd showed up yet. Where the hell have you been, anyway, for . . . how many years?"

"Twenty—missed the last three meetings. Oh, I've been wandering around. Checked out Europe one more time and took a couple of courses back east before the old boredom effect drifted me back here. Living in Santa Ana now." I grinned at him a little warily. "I imagine I've got a lot of catching up to do."

"Yeah. Did you know Alice is gone?"

I tossed my helmet onto a coat-buried chair, but kept my leather jacket because all my supplies were in it. "No," I said quietly. I'd always liked Alice.

"She is. Incognito underground, maybe—but more likely . . ." He shrugged.

I nodded and took a long sip of the beer, grateful for his reticence. Why say it, after all? People do let go sometimes. Some say it's hard to do, as difficult as holding your breath till you faint—others say it's as easy as not catching a silver dollar tossed to you. Guesses.

Archie ducked away to get another beer, and I walked across the entry hall into the crowded living room. The rich, leathery smell of Latakia tobacco told me that old Bill was there, and I soon identified him by the long, blackened meerschaum pipe he somehow found again every time. The little girl puffing at it gave me a raised eyebrow.

"Howdy, Bill," I said. "It's Saul."

"Saul, laddie!" piped the little girl's voice. "Excuse the nonrecognition. You were a gawky youth when I saw you last. Been doing anything worthwhile?"

I didn't even bother to give the standard negative reply. "I'll talk to you later," I said. "Got to find something for this beer to chase."

Bill chuckled merrily. "They laid in a dozen bottles of Laphroaig Scotch in case you came." He waved his pipe toward the dining room that traditionally served as the bar. "You know your way down the hill."

It was a longstanding gag between us, deriving from one night when a girlfriend and I had been visiting a prominent author whose house sat on top of one of the Hollywood hills; the girlfriend had begun stretching and yawning on the couch and remarking how tired she was, and the prominent author obligingly told her she could spend the night right there. Turning briefly toward me, he inquired, "You know your way down the hill, don't you?" Bill and I now used the phrase to indicate any significant descent. I smiled as I turned toward the bar.

I stiffened, though, and my smile unkinked itself, when I saw a certain auburn-haired girl sipping a grasshopper at a corner table.

I could feel my face heat up even before I was sure I recognized her. It hadn't been long ago, a warm August evening at the Orange Street Fair, with the blue and rose sky fading behind the strings of light bulbs that swayed overhead. I'd been slouched in a chair in the middle of Glassell Street, momentarily left in a littered clearing by an ebb in the crowd. The breeze was from the south, carrying frying smells from the Chinese section on Chapman, and I was meditatively sipping Coors from a plastic cup when she dragged up another chair and straddled it.

I don't remember how the conversation started, but I know that through a dozen more cups of beer we discussed Scriabin and Stevenson and David Bowie and A. E. Housman and Mexican beers. And later she perched sidesaddle, because one of the passenger foot pegs fell off long ago, on the back of my motorcycle as I cranked us through the quiet streets to my apartment.

She went out for a newspaper and ice cream the next afternoon, and never came back. I'd been wryly treasuring the memory, in a two-ships-that-pass-in-the-night way, until now.

Restraining my anger, I crossed to her table and sat down. The girl's face looked up and smiled, obviously recognizing me.

"Hello, Saul."

"Goddamn it," I gritted. "All right, who are you?"

"Marcus. Are you upset? Why? Oh, I know! I still owe you for that newspaper." Marcus started digging in his purse.

"Less of the simpering. You knew it was me?"

"Well, sure," he said. "What's wrong? I broke an *unwritten law* or something? Listen, you haven't been around for a while. Customs change, ever notice? What's wrong with members of the clan having relations with each other?"

"Christ. Lots of things," I said hoarsely. Could the old man have sanctioned this? "It makes me sick." I could remember going bar-hopping with Marcus in the 1860s when he was a bearded giant, both of us drunkenly prowling the streets of Paris, hooting at women and trading implausible and profane reminiscences.

"Don't run off." Marc caught me by the arm as I was getting up. "There are a few things I've got to tell you before the ceremony at six. Sit down. Laphroaig still your drink? I'll get a bottle—"

"Don't bother. I want to go talk to the old man. Save whatever you've got to say until the meeting."

"It's old Hain I want to talk about. You've got to hear this sooner or later, so—"

"So I'll hear it later," I said, and strode out of the bar to find Sam Hain, our patriarch. I'd been there only about five minutes, but I was already wishing I hadn't come. If this was the current trend, I thought, I can't blame Alice for disappearing.

Back in the high-ceilinged living room I caught the eye of a little boy who was pouring himself a glassful of Boodle's. "Where's our host?" I asked.

"Library. Amelia?"

"Saul. Robin?" Robin was always fond of good gin.

"Right. Talk to you later, yes?" He wandered off toward the group around the piano.

From the corner of my eye I saw Marcus—who'd put on a bit of weight since that night, I noted with vindictive satisfaction—hurry out of the bar. I braced myself, but he just crossed to the entry and thumped away up the stairs. Doubtless in a snit, I thought.

I pictured old Marc sniffling and dabbing at his mascara'd eyes with a perfumed hankie, and shook my head. It always upset me to consider how thoroughly even the keenest-edged minds are at the mercy of hormones and such biological baggage. We are all indeed windowless gonads, as Leibnz nearly said.

Old Sam Hain was asleep in his usual leather chair when I pushed open the library door, so I sipped my beer and let my eyes rove over the shelves for a minute or two. As always, I envied him his library. The quarto *Plays of Wharfinger, Ashbless' Odes,* Blaylock's *The Wild Man of Tanga-Raza,* all were treasures I'd admired for decades—though, at least in a cursory glance, I didn't notice any new items.

I absently reached for the cigar humidor, but my fingers struck polished tabletop where it should have been. Suddenly I noticed an absence that had been subconsciously nagging at me ever since I'd arrived—the house, and the library particularly, was not steeped in the aroma of Caribbean cigars anymore.

Behind me the old man grunted and raised his head. "Saul?"

"Yes sir." It never failed to please me, the way he could always recognize me after a long separation. I sat down across the table from him. "What's become of the cigars?"

"Ahh," he waved his hand, "they began to disagree with me." He squinted speculatively at me. "You've been away twenty years, son. Have you, too, begun to disagree with me?"

Embarrassed and a little puzzled, I shifted in my chair. "Of course not, sir. You know I just wander off for a while sometimes—I missed four or five in a row at the end of the last century, remember? Means nothing. It's just to indulge my solitary streak once in a while."

Hain nodded and pressed his fingertips together. "Such impulses should be resisted —I think you know that. We are a clan, and our potentially great power is . . . vitiated if we persist in operating as individuals."

I glanced at him sharply. This seemed to be an about-face from his usual opinions —more the kind of thing I'd have expected from Marcus or Rafe.

"Ho. It sounds as if you're saying we should go back to the way we were in the days of the Medici—or as Balzac portrayed us in *The Thirteen*." I spoke banteringly, certain he'd explain whatever he'd actually meant.

"I've been doing some deep thinking for a number of years, Saul," he said slowly, "and it seems to me that we've been living in a fantasy daydream since I took over in 1861 and made such drastic changes in traditional clan policy. They were well-intentioned changes, certainly—and in a decent world they'd be practical. But we're not living in a decent world, ever notice? No, I no longer think our isolation and meek, live-and-let-live ways are realistic. Ah, don't frown, Saul. I know you've enjoyed this last hundred and twenty years more than any other period . . . but surely you can see you've—we've all— been ignoring certain facts? What do you think would happen if the ephemerals ever learned of our existence?"

"It wouldn't matter," I cried, unhappily aware that I was taking the side he'd always taken in this perennial question. "They'd kill some of us, I suppose, but we've all had violent deaths before. I prefer quick deaths to slow ones anyway. Why can't we just leave them alone? *We're* the parasites, after all."

"You're talking rot," he snapped. "Do you really think killing us is the worst they could do? What about perpetual maintenance on an artificial life-support system, with no means of suicide? What about administering mind-destroying drugs, so you spend the rest of your incarnations drooling and cutting out paper dolls in one half-wit asylum after another? And even if you could get to your suicide kit or jump in the way of a car before they seized you . . . do you think it's still absolutely impossible for them to track a soul to its next host?"

"I don't know," I muttered after a pause. In spite of my convictions his words had shaken me, touching as they did our very deepest fears. Maybe he's right, I thought miserably. We *are* parasites—all the liquor and food and music and poetry we enjoy is produced by the toiling ephemerals—but surely even parasites have to defend themselves?

"Saul," he said kindly, "I'm sorry to rub your nose in it this way, but you see we have to face it. Go have a drink and mix with the siblings; this will all be discussed after dinner. By the way, have you talked to Marcus?"

"Briefly."

"Talk to him at more length, then. He's got something important to tell you before the meeting."

"Can you tell me?"

"Let him. Relax, it's good news. Now if you'll excuse me, I'll finish my nap. It seems to be ripening to a real Alexandrian feast out there, and if it's going to last on into tomorrow I'd best catch some shut-eye."

"Right, sir."

I closed the door as I left, and went back to the bar, slumping into the same chair I'd had before. Archie was tending bar now, and I called my order to him, and when it arrived I tossed back a stiff gulp of the nearly warm Scotch and chased it with a long draft of icy Coors.

Being a member of the clan, I was used to seeing cherished things come and go—"This too will pass" was one of our basic tenets—but the old man had, in only a hundred and twenty years, become a rock against the waves of change, an immortal father, a symbol of values that outlast individual lifetimes. But now *he* had changed.

One corner of my mind was just keening. Even *this*, it wailed, even *this* will pass?

I remembered the meeting at which he'd first appeared, on a chilly night in 1806 at Rafe's Boston mansion. Sam was then a boy of about ten, and though he knew everyone and greeted the mature ones by name, he never did say who he'd been before. This upset a lot of us, but he was cordially firm on that point; and we couldn't deduce it by a process of elimination, either—a number of siblings had suicided in the early 1790s, after the tantalizingly hopeful French Revolution had degenerated into the Terror, and several apparently let go, never to come back. There was, of course, a lot of speculation about which one he was . . . though a few whispered that he wasn't any one of our lost siblings, but a new being who'd somehow infiltrated us.

The crowd in the bar slacked off. Most of the clan had carried their drinks out into the backyard, where the barbecue pit was already flinging clouds of aromatic smoke across the lawn, and the dedicated drinkers who remained were now working more slowly, so Archie came out from behind the bar and sat down at my table.

"Have a drink, Archimago," I said.

"Got one." He waved a tequila sour I hadn't noticed.

I took a long sip of the Laphroaig. "Are we all present and accounted for?"

"Nearly. The count's at forty these days now that Alice is gone—and there are thirty-eight of us here. Not a bad turnout."

"Who's missing?"

"Amelia and Rafe. Amelia's currently a man, about forty years old. Maybe she killed herself. And of course Rafe just died two months ago, so we can't expect to see him for another decade."

"How'd he go this time?" I didn't care, really. Marcus and Rafe were fast friends, but though in some incarnations I liked Marcus, I could never stand Rafe.

"Shot himself through the roof of the mouth in his apartment on Lombard Street in San Francisco. Nobody was surprised, he was nearly fifty." Archimago chuckled. "They say he managed to pull the trigger twice."

I shrugged. "If a thing's worth doing, it's worth doing thoroughly," I allowed.

Archie looked across the room and got to his feet. "Ah, I see Vogel is out of akvavit. Excuse me."

Most of us choose to die at about fifty, to ride the best years out of a body and then divorce ourselves from it by means of pills or a bullet or whatever strikes our fancy, so that our unencumbered soul can— though we rarely talk about it—dart through the void to the as yet unfirmly rooted soul of some unborn child, which we hungrily thrust out into the darkness, taking its embryonic body for ourselves. It sounds horrible baldly stated, and there's a mournful ballad called "The Legion of Lost Children," which none of us ever even hums, though we all know it, but it's hard to the point of impossibility to stare into the final, lightless abyss, and feel yourself falling, picking up speed . . . and not grab the nearest handhold.

Sam Hain, though, seemed to be an exception to this. He was born in mid-1796 and never died once after that, somehow maintaining his now one-hundred-and-eighty-five-year-old body on red wine, sashimi, tobacco and sheer will power. His physical age made him stand out among us even more than the obscurity of his origin did, and being patient, kindly and wise as well, he was elected Master at our 1861 meeting.

Up until then the Master post had meant little, and carried no duties except to provide a house and bountiful food and liquor for the five-yearly meetings. I was Master myself for several decades in the early part of the sixteenth century, and some of the clan never did find out—or even ask—who the host of the meetings was. Sam Hain, though, made changes: for one thing, he arbitrarily changed the date of the meetings from the thirty-first of October to November first; he began to cut back on the several vast, clan-owned corporations that provide us all with allowances; and he encouraged us to get more out of a body, to carry it, as he certainly had, into old age before unseating some unborn child and taking its fresh one. I believe it was Sam, in fact, who first referred to us all as "hermit crabs with the power of eviction."

I looked up from my drink and saw Marcus enter the bar and signal Archie. The alcohol had given me some detachment toward the whole business, and I admitted to myself that Marc had certainly drawn a good body this time—tall and slender, with cascades of lustrous coppery hair. I could no longer be attracted to it, but I could certainly see why I'd been so entranced at the street fair.

"Hello, Marc," I said levelly. "Sam says you've got some good news for me."

"That's right, Saul." He sat down just as Archie brought him his creamy, pale green drink, and he took a sip before going on. "You're going to be a father."

For several moments I stared at him blankly. I finally choked, "That night . . . ?"

He nodded, grinning, and fished from his purse a slip of folded paper. "Tested out positive."

"Goddamn you," I said softly. "Was it for this that you picked me up in the first place?"

He shrugged. "Does it matter? I should think your main concern at this point is the welfare of the child."

Though sick and cold inside, I nodded, for I saw the teeth of the trap at last—if one of us dies while in physical contract with a pregnant woman, it is her fetus that that one will take. And though we of the clan can generally have children, the hermit-crab reincarnation ability doesn't breed true—our children are all ephemerals.

"A hostage to fortune," I said. "You're holding my unborn child for ransom, right? Why? What do I have that you want?"

"You catch on fast," Marc said approvingly. "Okay, listen—if you cooperate with me and a couple of others, I'll allow your child to be born, and you can take it away or put it up for adoption or whatever. We'll even triple your allowance, and you don't use more than half of it now." He had another sip of his disgusting drink. "Of course, if you don't cooperate, one of the clan is likely to die while holding my hand, and . . . well, the Legion would have one more squalling member."

I didn't flinch at the reference to the strictly tabooed song, for I knew he'd hoped to shock me with it. "Cooperate? In what?"

He spread his hands. "Something I don't think you'd object to anyway. The, uh," he patted his abdomen, "hostage is just insurance. Would you like a fresh drink? I thought so. Arch! Another boilermaker here. Well, Saul, you've heard the good news—take it easy!—and now I'm afraid I've got some bad." He just sat and watched me until I'd had a sip of the new drink.

"Sam Hain is dead," he said, very quietly. "He blew his head off, in this very house, late in 1963. Please don't interrupt! Rafe and I found his body only a few hours afterward, and came to a decision you might disapprove of—the next meeting wasn't for three years, so we had one of the secret, advanced branches of our DIRE Corporation construct a simulacrum."

I opened my mouth to call him a liar, but closed it again. I realized I was certain it was true. "What does smoke do, clog the thing's circuits or something?"

He nodded. "It's rough on the delicate machinery, so we had him give up the cigars, as you noticed. It was me speaking to you through the simulacrum, from the controls upstairs."

"I saw you run out of the bar." Marc started to speak, but I interrupted him. "Wait a minute! You said '63? That can't be—he'd be . . . eighteen now, and he'd be here today. If this is—"

Marc took my hand. "He *would* be eighteen, Saul. If he came back . . . but he didn't. He let go. We were pretty sure he would, or we wouldn't have gone to the trouble of having the sim built."

I jerked my hand away. I didn't doubt him—Sam Hain was just the sort who'd choose to drop away into the last oblivion rather than cheat an unborn child of life—but I wanted no intimacy with Marc.

"All right, so you've got this robot to take his place. Why involve me in—"

I broke off my sentence when a dark-haired man with a deeply lined face lurched into the bar; his tie was loose, his jacket looked slept in, and he'd clearly been doing some preliminary drinking elsewhere. "Who's doling out the spirits here?" he called.

Archimago waved to him. "Right here, Amelia. We didn't think you were going to show. What'll you have?"

"Ethanol." Amelia wove with drunkard dignity across the room and ceremoniously collapsed into the third chair at our table. "Okay if I join you? Who are you anyway?"

I overrode Marc's brushing-off excuses, wanting some time to consider what he'd been saying. "Sure, keep your seat, Amelia. I'm Saul, and this is Marcus."

"Yeah," Amelia said, "I know. I visited Marc last year at his apartment in Frisco. Still living there, Marc? Nice little place, on that twisty street and all. 'Member that night we drove to—"

"You're late," Marcus said coldly, "and drunk. Why is that?"

Amelia's eyes dulled, and though her expression grew, if anything, more blank, I thought she was going to cry. "I had a stop to make this morning, a visit, before coming here."

Marc rolled his eyes toward the ceiling. "This *morning?* Where, in New York?"

Archie brought a glass of some kind of whiskey, and Amelia seized it eagerly. "In Costa Mesa," she breathed, after taking a liberal sip. "Fairview State Mental Hospital."

"I hope they didn't say they were too full to take you," Marc said sweetly.

"Shut up, Marc," I said. "Who were you visiting?"

"My . . . fiancé, from my last life," Amelia said, "when I was a woman."

The incongruity of a woman talking out of a man's body rarely bothered me, but it did now.

"He's seventy-two years old," she went on. "White hair, no teeth . . . a face like a desert tortoise."

"What's he doing in the hatch?" Marc inquired.

His sarcasm was lost on the inward-peering Amelia. "We were engaged," he said, "but we got into a fight one evening. This was in 1939. I'd gone out to dinner with a guy I'd met at a party, and Len said I shouldn't have. I was drunk, of course, and I laughed and told him . . . the truth, that I'd slept around long before I met him, and would be doing it long after he was dead."

"Can this romance be saved?" said Marc, looking tremendously bored.

"Anyway, he belted me. First time . . . only time . . . he ever did. God I was mad. I can't now, as a man, *imagine* being that mad. So you know what I did? I went into the kitchen and got a big knife out of the drawer and, while he stood there muttering apologies, I shoved the blade up to the handle into my stomach. And I pulled it out and laughed at him some more and called him every filthy name I knew, for three whole goddamned hours, as I lay there on the floor and bled to death. He never moved. Well, he sat down."

Even Marc was looking a little horrified. "I don't wonder the poor bastard's in Fairview now," he said. "And you *visited* him?"

"Yeah. I forget why. I think I wanted to apologize, though I was a thirty-year-old woman when he last saw me . . . I told them I was a relative, and quoted enough family history to get in." She took another big sip of the whiskey. "He was in a little bed, and his dried-up body didn't raise the blankets any more than a couple of brooms would. I was looking respectable, freshly shaved, dressed like you see, smiling . . . and yet he *knew* me, he recognized me!" Amelia gulped her whole drink. "He started yelling and crying and, in his birdy old voice, begging me to *forgive* him." She grinned, her man's face wrinkling. "Can you beat that? Forgive him."

"Absolutely fascinating," pronounced Marcus, slapping the table. "Now why don't you go find somebody else to tell it to, hmm? Saul and I have to talk."

"I want to talk to the old man," said Amelia weakly as she got to her feet and tottered away.

"Oh, God," Marc moaned, exasperated.

"Hadn't you better dash upstairs again?" I suggested. "With no one at the sim's controls she'll think it's a corpse."

"No," he said, staring after Amelia, "it's equipped to run independently, too. Speaks vague platitudes and agrees with nearly everything that's said to it. Oh, well, she's too lushed to notice anything. Okay, now, listen, Saul, you started to ask why we dragged you in on this—I'll tell you, and then you can call me a son of a bitch, and then do what I ask, and then, if you want, take the hostage when it shows up and disappear and never come back. As I say, you and the kid will be financially provided for.

"Through the simulacrum, Rafe and I have been gradually changing clan policy, restoring things to the way they were before Hain took over in 1861. DIRE is going to resume the genetic and conditioning researches Hain made them stop in the 1950s, and, oh, we've bought and cultivated acres of farmland near Ankara for . . . certain lucrative enterprises he would never have permitted, and—anyway, you see? As a matter of fact, we hope soon to be able to maintain a farm of healthy perpetually pregnant ephemerals, so that we can have our deaths performed under controlled conditions and be sure the fetus we move on to is a healthy, well-cared-for one. Honestly, wouldn't it be nice not to find yourself born in slums anymore? Not to have to pretend to be a child for a dreary decade until you can leave whatever poor family you elbowed your way into? And we can begin taking hormone injections quite young, to bring us more quickly to a mature—"

Suddenly I was sorry I'd had so much to drink. "That's filthy," I said. "All of it. More abominable than . . . than I can say."

He pursed his painted lips. "I'm sorry you can't approve, Saul. We'd hoped your long absence was a sign of dissatisfaction with the way things were. But with our . . . hostage to fortune, as you put it, we don't need your approval. Just your cooperation. Some siblings have commented on the changes in the old man, and we can't afford to have them even suspect that what they see is a phony. If they knew he was gone it would be impossible to get them to work together, or even allow . . . Anyway, if they all see you, Sam's traditional favorite, drinking with the old man and reminiscing and laughing and agreeing with everything that comes out of his mouth, why, it'll be established in their minds, safely below the conscious level, that this is certainly the genuine Sam Hain they've unquestioningly obeyed for more than a century."

"You want me to kiss him?"

Marc frowned, puzzled. "That won't be necessary. Just friendly, like you've always been. And of course, if you don't, then I'll go hold Amelia's hand in one of mine and," he patted his purse, "blow her head off with the other. And then it'll be her I give birth to in six months. Maybe she'd even be able to visit that poor son of a bitch at Fairview again, as a baby this time."

"I know, I know," I told him impatiently. "I comprehended the threat the first time. Shut up and let me think."

I've had a number of children, over the centuries, and they're all as dead-and-gone as Marc was threatening to make this one. It never bothered me much, even when, in a few cases, I'd actually seen them die—they'd had their little lives, and their irreversible deaths. And of course the . . . eviction of unborn babies from their bodies, though not a concept I was really at ease with, was anything but a new one to me. Still . . . I didn't want a child of mine to get just alive enough to die and then be pushed away to sink into the dark. "They give birth astride a grave," Beckett said, "the light gleams an instant, then it's night once more." That's how it is for the ephemerals, certainly. But let them have that instant's gleam of light!

"All right," I said dully. "If Sam's gone, I don't care what becomes of you all anyway. I'll take the kid and go incognito underground."

"The wisest choice," approved Marcus with a grin that brought out smile lines in his cheeks. What, I wondered, would this girl have been like today, if Marc hadn't taken over her embryonic body years ago? Perhaps we'd still have met at the street fair, and talked about Stevenson.

It took me a few seconds to stand up, and I heard my chair clatter over behind me, but I felt coldly sober. "Trot upstairs and get in the driver's seat," I said. "I'd like to get home by midnight."

"Archimago will run the sim," Marc said, giving a thumbs-up to Archie, who nodded and strode out of the bar without looking at me.

"I'm going to take a walk out back," I said. "Clear the fumes out of my head . . . and give your wind-up man time to join the others ahead of me. You don't want this to look rehearsed."

"I suppose not. Okay, but don't wander off or anything."

"You're holding the stake," I reminded him.

Scattered between the house and the backdrop of trees silhouetted against the darkening sky, my siblings were beginning to deal with dinner. The fire-pit blazed fiercely, seeming to lack only a bound martyr for some real nostalgia, and the crowd, as if to supply it, was dragging up a whole side of beef wired to a revolving black iron frame. They'd got into the cellar, and I picked my way through a litter of half-empty Latour and Mouton bottles on my way to the unlighted, vine-roofed patio on the west side of the house.

After dark we of the clan generally prefer noisy, bright-lit groups to solitude, and I wasn't surprised to find the deep-shadowed patio empty. I fished a cigarette from my left jacket pocket and struck a match on the side of the bench I was sitting on, and drew a lungful and then let the smoke hiss out and flit away on the cool, eucalyptus-scented breeze.

I stared at the dark bulk of the old house and wondered where its master was buried. Though it was like Sam to have let go, I blamed him for having killed himself. Surely he must have known we'd slide back into our old, ruthless ways once he was gone, like domesticated dogs thrown back out into the wilderness.

A dim green glow defined a window in the third story, near where several heavy cables were moored to the shingles. Doubtless the room, I thought, where Archie is hunched over whatever sort of controls a simulacrum requires. I picked a loose chip from one of the flagstones and cocked my arm to pitch it at the window—then sadly decided the move would be a mistake, and let it fall back to the pavement instead.

I was aware that it would be quite a while before I'd know whether Marc had kept his end of the bargain. I shook my head and flicked away the cigarette. Marc and his crew were maneuvering me around—from the seduction three months ago to the curt orders of tonight—like a scarecrow, no more independent than their mechanical Sam Hain. Predictable is what you are, I told myself bitterly, and as helplessly useful as one of those keys for opening sardine cans.

Before I knew what I was doing I found myself standing on the seat of the concrete bench and gripping one of the horizontal beams that the vine trellises were nailed to. By God, I thought, I'll at least give Archie a scare, make him tangle the puppet strings a little. I chinned myself up and, driving my legs through the brittlely snapping trellis, jackknifed forward and wound up sitting on the beam, brushing dust, splinters and bits of ivy from my hair.

I stood up on the beam cautiously. It dipped here and there, but took my weight without coming unmoored, and in a moment I had flapped and tottered my way to the house wall, and steadied myself by grabbing a drainpipe that, overhead, snaked right past the window I wanted to get to. Not wanting to lose my drunken impetus, I immediately swarmed up it in my best rock-climbing style, leaving most of the skin of my palms on the rough seams of the pipe.

I reached the level of the dim green window and braced a foot on one of the pipe's brackets; then I leaned sideways, gripped the windowsill and made a fearsome wide-eyed, open-mouthed face while scrabbling at the glass with the nails of my free hand.

There was no response—just an uninterrupted, muted hum of machinery. I banged the pane with my forehead and made barking sounds. Still nothing.

I was beginning to get irritable. I dug in my right jacket pocket and pulled out the compact but heavy pistol I always kept there, and knocked in the glass. There were a few glass splinters in the frame when I was done, but I knew my leather jacket would protect me from them.

I brought my other hand quickly to the sill, heaved, and dove into the room, landing on my fingertips and somersaulting across a linoleum floor.

"I'll take over the controls, Arch," I gasped, springing to my feet. "How do you make the thing do a jig? Or—"

I stopped babbling. The room was empty except for a long plastic case on the floor, about three feet deep and connected by tubes to a bank of dimly illuminated dials on one wall.

I sagged. My only concern at this point was to get out of there without having to answer any questions as to why I had thought it worth my while to break into what was doubtless the room housing the building's air-conditioning unit. I hurried toward the metal door in the far wall, but jerked to a halt when I peripherally glimpsed a face under the curved plastic surface of that suddenly-recognizable-as-coffin-sized case.

Sweat sprang out on my temples—I was afraid I'd recognized the face, and I didn't want to look again and confirm it. You didn't see anything, my mind assured me. Go rejoin the party.

I think I'd have taken its advice if its tone hadn't been so like Marc's. I knelt in front of the case and stared into it. As I had thought, the sleeping face inside was Sam Hain's, clearly recognizable in spite of the fact that the head had been shaved of its curly white hair and a couple of green plastic tubes had been poked into the nostrils and taped down beside the jaw.

There didn't seem to be any way to open the case, but I didn't need to—I was certain this was the real Sam Hain, maintained, imprisoned, in dim, lobotomized half-life in this narrow room. So much for Marc's story of a suicide and refusal to be reborn! Marc and his friends had gone to a lot of trouble to make sure Sam was out of the picture without being freed from his old body.

I was still holding the little gun with which I'd broken the window, and I set it down on the plastic case long enough to whip off my jacket; then I picked it up and wrapped it and my hand tightly in the folds of leather. It was a little two-shot pistol I'd had made in 1900 for use on myself if I should ever want to leave a body quickly—its two bullets were .50 caliber hollow-points, pretty sure to do a thorough job at close range—and I didn't grudge Sam one of them.

I braced my wrist with my free hand and pressed the leather-padded muzzle against the section of plastic over Sam's head. "The cage door's open, Sam," I whispered. "Take off." I squeezed the trigger.

There was a jarring thump, but the layers of leather absorbed most of the noise. I untangled the gun and put on the jacket, slapping it to dispel clinging smoke. One glance at the exploded ruin under the holed case was enough to tell me I'd freed Sam, so I tucked the gun back into my jacket pocket and turned to the window.

Getting out wasn't as easy as getting in had been, and I had a gashed finger, a wrenched ankle and a long tear in the left leg of my pants by the time I stood wheezing on the flagstones of the still-empty patio. I combed my hair, straightened my now-perforated jacket, and walked around the corner, through the fire-lit mob in the backyard, to the living room.

It was a superficially warm and hearty scene that greeted me as I let the screen door bang shut at my back; yellow lamplight made the smoke-misty air glow around the knot of well-groomed people clustered around the piano, and the smiling, white-haired figure with his hand on the pianist's shoulder fairly radiated benign fatherly wisdom. A stranger would have needed second sight to know that several of the company, particularly Amelia, were dangerously drunk, and that perhaps a third of them were currently a physical gender that was at odds with their instinctive one, and that their beaming patriarch was, under his plastic skin, a mass of laboring machinery.

Marcus, perched on the arm of the couch, raised his thin eyebrows at my rumpled, dusty appearance, then gave me a little nod and glanced toward the simulacrum. I obediently crossed the room and stood beside the thing.

"Well, Saul!" the machinery said. "It's good to see you, lad. Say, have you thought about what we were discussing earlier in the library?"

"Yes, Sam," I said with as warm a smile as I could muster, "and I can see it all makes perfect sense. We really do need to establish a position of power, so we can defend ourselves against the ephemerals . . . if that should ever become necessary."

I wanted to gag or laugh. I hope, I mentally told the embryo in Marcus, you may some day appreciate what I'm doing right now to buy you a life.

"I'm glad," nodded the simulacrum. "Some truths are hard to face . . . but you never were one to flinch, Saul." It smiled at the company. "Well, siblings, another song or two and then we'll get down to the meeting, hmm? Saul and Marcus and I have a few proposals to air."

Mirabile resumed banging away at the piano, and we went through a couple of refrains each of "Nichevo" and "Ich Bin Von

Kopf Bis Fus" as a bottle of Hennessy made the circuit and helped the music to lend the evening an air of pleasantly wistful melancholy. I took a glass of cognac, and winced to see Marc working on still another grasshopper.

"Here, Mirabile," muttered Amelia, edging the pianist off the bench. "I learned to play, last life." After finding a comfortable position, she poised her unsteady hands over the keys, and then set to.

And despite all her hard drinking she played beautifully, wringing real heartbreak out of "St. James Infirmary," which we all sang so enthusiastically that we set the glasses to rattling in the cupboard.

We were all singing the last lines when it became clear that Amelia was playing and singing a different song, and our voices faltered away as the new chords moaned out of the piano and Amelia's lyrics countered ours.

She was handling her man's voice as well as she handled the piano, and some of us didn't immediately realize what song it was that she was rendering.

"*. . . Throw on another log,*" she sang, "*—but draw the curtains shut!*
For across the icy fields our yellow light
Spills, and has raised a sobbing in the night.

"*Sing louder, friends! Drown out that windy, wavering song*
Of childish voices, and step up the beat,
For a rainy pattering, like tiny feet,
Draws nearer every moment. For so very long
They've wandered, wailing in a mournful chorus,
Searching through all of hell and heaven for us."

I don't know whether it was the vapors of the cognac that caused it, or the mood of gentle despair that hung about us like the tobacco smoke, but a couple of voices actually joined her in the nearly whispered refrain:

"*And at the close of some unhappy Autumn day,*
From their cold, unlighted region,
Treading soft, will come the Legion
Of Lost Children and they'll suck our souls away."

Then a number of things happened simultaneously. Marc's little fist, as he lunged from the couch arm, cracked into Amelia's jaw and sent her and the heavy bench crashing over on the hardwood floor; Mirabile slammed the cover down over the keys, producing one final rumbling chord; the simulacrum just stood and gaped stupidly, and the rest of the company, pale and unmoving, registered varying mixtures of anger, embarrassment and fear.

Marc straightened, shot a look toward the sim, and then glanced furtively at me—and snatched his eyes away immediately when mine met them.

"Get her out of here," he rasped to Mirabile. "Don't be gentle."

"To hell with the songs," said the Sam Hain replica expressionlessly. "It's time for the meeting."

I reached into my right jacket pocket. "Just a minute," I said. They all looked up, and I could see a dew of sweat on Marc's forehead—he was wary, even a little scared, and I believed I knew why. "I'll be back in a moment," I finished lamely, and walked into the kitchen.

Just outside the window over the sink was a thermometer, and I cut the screen with a butter knife to reach it. It unsnapped easily from the clamp that held it to the wall, and I pulled the glass tube off and slipped it into my pants pocket. To explain my exit I took a can of beer from the refrigerator and tore the tab off as I strolled back into the living room.

"Sorry to hold everybody up," I said. "We rummies need our crutch."

"Sit down, Saul," said Bill quietly. His pipe lay across his bony knees, and his little-girl fingers were busy stuffing it with black tobacco. "Marc went out back to drag everybody in."

I didn't sit down—for one thing, I found myself vaguely disturbed to see discolored teeth and red, wrinkle-bordered eyes in what should have been the face of an eight-year-old girl—but crossed to Marc's place instead. His creamy green drink was still cold, so I fished the thermometer tube from my pocket and, leaning over to hide the action, snapped it in half and shook the glittering drops of mercury into the drink.

Oddly, I felt only a tired depression as I moved away, and not the sorrow I'd have expected—but perhaps the empathy circuits in all of us were fused and blown out centuries ago, and we don't notice it because we so seldom care to call upon those circuits. The knowledge that my child had been killed two months ago, at any rate, grieved me only a little more than would news of the cancellation of some concert I'd been looking forward to.

For I'd figured it out, of course; the pieces were all there, and it had been Marc's involuntary, worried glance, after that song, that put them all together for me. Rafe, Marc's closest friend in the clan, had shot himself two months ago in an apartment on Lombard Street; and Marc, Amelia had said, was also living in an apartment on that street—the same one, I was certain. Obviously they'd been living together, in accord with Marc's new clan ethics. I wondered with a shudder whether Rafe had been jealous when Marc came down for the street fair.

Probably Marc *had* intended to keep my unborn child as a hostage . . . but then Rafe must have got sick or injured or something, and decided to ditch his middle-aged body . . . and was Marc going to let his old buddy take his chances with whatever fetus randomness might provide, when there was a healthy one so ready to hand?

And so Marc had taken Rafe's hand—and the gun too, I think, judging from the report that Rafe shot himself twice—and held on until the ruined body was quite still and he could be sure his friend's soul was safely lodged in the month-old fetus that had been my child's.

Standing there by the piano that night, I was certain of all this. At my leisure, since, I have occasionally had sick moments of doubt, and have had to fetch the Laphroaig bottle to dull my ears to any "sobbing in the night."

Marc led in those who'd been out back, many of them still gnawing bones and complaining about being taken from their dinner.

"Shut up now, damn it," Marc told them. "The meeting's going to be a short one this time, you'll be back to your food in ten minutes. Saul and Sam have just got a few ideas to propose."

He nodded to the simulacrum, which stood up, smiled and cleared its throat convincingly. "Siblings," it said, "we all—"

I palmed my little gun and stood up. "Excuse me, Sam," I said, "I'd like to begin, if you don't mind."

"Sit down, Saul," Marc said through clenched teeth.

"No," I said, pointing the gun at him, "you sit down. Don't let your damned drink get warm. I want to open the meeting."

The rest of the clan began showing some interest, hoping for some diverting violence. Marc pursed his lips, then shrugged and sat down, not relishing the idea of losing his current body while it was still so young and usefully good-looking. I smiled inwardly to see him snatch up his glass and down the remainder of his drink at one gulp, and apparently not even notice, under the thick crème de menthe and cream, whatever taste mercury has.

For all I knew, the mercury might just pass through him, as inertly harmless in that form as a wad of bubble gum, but I hoped not—I wanted to throw acid on the wiring of his mind, sand in the clockwork of his psyche, so that, though he might be reborn again and again until the sun goes out, every incarnation would be lived in a different home for the retarded. I hoped—still hope—the mercury could do the job, and with any luck get Rafe too.

"Siblings," I said, "I haven't been around for the last three meetings, but I gather there have been new trends afoot, fostered mainly by him," I jabbed the gun toward Marc, "and *him*," toward the simulacrum. "Quiet, don't interrupt me. For more than a century Sam Hain tried to civilize us, and now these two are eroding his efforts, throwing us back to the cruel, greedy old days of pretending to be gods to the ephemerals . . . when actually we're a sort of immortal tapeworm in humanity's guts. What's that, Bill? No, I'm not drunk. Sit down, Marc, or I swear I'll blow that beautiful face out through the back of your head—no, I'm not drunk, Bill, why? Oh, you're saying if these two are wrecking Sam Hain's teaching, then who do I think the guy with the white beard is? I'll show you."

I raised my arm and pulled the trigger, and the barrel clouted my cheek as the gun slammed back in recoil. My ears were ringing from the unmuffled report and the gunpowder smoke had my eyes watering, and I couldn't see the simulacrum at all.

Then I saw it. It was on its hands and knees in the middle of the rug, and all of its head from the nose upward had been taken out as if by a giant ice-cream scoop. Bits of wire and tubing and color-coded plastic were scattered across the floor, and two little jets of red liquid—artificial blood meant to lend verisimilitude in case of a cut in the cheek—fountained out onto the rug from opposite sides of the head.

The eyes, three-quarters exposed now, clicked rapidly up and down and back and forth in frantic unsynchronized scanning, and the mouth opened: "I'm hurt," the thing quacked, as the automatic damage circuits overrode anything Archie might be trying to do. "I'm hurt. I'm hurt. I'm hurt. I'm—"

I gave it a hard kick in the throat that shattered its voice mechanism and knocked it to the floor. "The real Sam Hain is upstairs," I said quietly, prodding my bruised cheek. "He was being maintained unconscious on a life-support system—and probably would have been forever if I hadn't shot him fifteen minutes ago." Marc stood up. "Give my regards to Rafe when he's born, in six months," I said. After a moment Marc sat down again. I faced the crowd. "Leave the clan," I told them, tossing my gun away. "Take all your money out of DIRE stocks. Stop coming to these horrible meetings and supporting the maniac ravings of people like Marcus and Rafe. Go incognito underground—any of you can afford to live well anywhere, even without your allowances."

No one said anything, so I strode around them to the entry hall and found my helmet. "And when you die this time," I called back as I opened the door, "take the death you've had coming for so long! Let go! The Legion has members enough."

I left the door slightly ajar and trudged down the dark path toward my bike. It started up at the first kick, and the cool night air was so restoring that I snapped my helmet to the sissy bar and let the wind's fingers brush my hair back as the bike and I coursed down the curling road toward the winking lights of Whittier. The headwind found the bullet holes in my jacket and cooled my damp shirt, and by the time I stopped at the traffic signal on Whittier Boulevard my anger had dissipated like smoke from an open-windowed room.

And so I've decided to let go, this time. It occurs to me that we've all been like children repeating eighth grade over and over again, and finally coming to believe that there's nothing beyond it. And when a century goes by and I haven't shown up, they'll say, What could have made him do it? Not realizing the real question is, What stopped preventing him?

❖ AUTHOR'S NOTE ❖

This is my first published short story, and it appeared in The Magazine of Fantasy and Science Fiction *in 1982. I'd had three novels published previous to that, and I wasn't intending to write a short story, but George Scithers, editor of* Isaac Asimov's Science Fiction Magazine *at the time, asked if I'd like to do one, so I did. Scithers was also editor of the fanzine* Amra, *and I'd sporadically had drawings and limericks published in it since I was seventeen.*

As it happened, Scithers didn't like "The Way Down the Hill"—he said the world didn't need another we'd-all-be-better-off-dead story—but I thought, Oh, I bet there's room for one more, *and I sold it instead to F&SF, and Scithers and I continued to have an amiable relationship.*

For Sam Hain's house I was thinking of the Muckenthaler Mansion in Fullerton, California, though for the story I moved it to the Whittier Hills. I had been in an amateur production of Lysistrata *at the Muckenthaler in 1974—I played a senator, a role that required me merely to stand in the background and nod or frown—and it struck me as an appropriate place for the old patriarch to live.*

⊰ ITINERARY ⊱

THE DAY BEFORE the Santa Ana place blew up, the telephone rang at about noon. I had just walked the three blocks back from Togo's with a tuna-fish sandwich, and when I was still out in the yard I heard the phone ringing through the open window; I ran up the porch steps, trying to fumble my keys out of my pocket without dropping the Togo's bag, and I was panting when I snatched up the receiver in the living room. "Hello?"

I thought I could hear a hissing at the other end, but no voice. It was October, with the hot Santa Ana winds shaking the dry pods off of the carob trees, and the receiver was already slick with my sweat. I used to sweat a lot in those days, what with the beer and the stress and all. "Hello?" I said again, impatiently. "Am I talking to a short circuit?" Sometimes my number used to get automatic phone calls from an old abandoned oil tank in San Pedro, and I thought I had rushed in just to get another of those.

It was a whisper that finally answered me, very hoarse; but I could tell it was a man: "Gunther! Jesus, boy—this is—Doug Olney, from Neff High School! You remember me, don't you?"

"Doug? Olney?" I wondered if he had had throat cancer. It had been nearly twenty years since I'd spoken to him. "Sure I remember! Where are you? Are you in town—"

"No time to talk. I don't want to—change any of your plans." He seemed to be upset. "Listen, a woman's gonna call your number in a minute; she's gonna ask for me. You don't know her. Say I just left a minute ago, okay?"

"Who is she—" I began, but he had already hung up.

As soon as I lowered the receiver into the cradle, the phone rang again. I took a deep breath and then picked it up again. "Hello?"

It was a woman, sure enough, and she said, "Is Doug Olney there?" I remember thinking that she sounded like my sister, who's married, in a common-law and probably unconsummated sense, to an Iranian who lives at de Gaulle Airport in France; though I hadn't heard from my sister since Carter was president.

I took a deep breath. "He just left," I said helplessly.

"I bet." A shivering sigh came over the line. "But I can't do any more." Again I was holding a dead phone.

We grew up in a big old Victorian house on Lafayette Avenue in Buffalo. The third floor had no interior partitions or walls, since it was originally designed to be a ballroom; by the time we were living there the days of balls were long gone, and that whole floor was jammed to capacity with antique furniture, wall to wall, floor to twelve-foot ceiling, back to front. My sister and I were little kids then, and we could crawl all through that vast lightless volume, up one canted couch and across the underside of an inverted table, squeezing past rolled carpets and worming between Regency chair legs. Of course there was no light at all unless we crowded into a space near one of the dust-filmed windows; and climbing back down to the floor, and then tracing the molding and the direction of the floor planks to the door, was a challenge. When we were finally able to stand up straight again out in the hall, we'd be covered with sour dust and not eager to explore in there again soon.

The nightmare I always had as a child was of having crept and wriggled to the very center of that room all by myself in the middle of the night, pausing roughly halfway between the floor and ceiling in pitch darkness on some sloped cabinet or sleigh bed—and then hearing a cautious scuffle from some remote cubic yard out there, in that three-dimensional maze of Cabriole legs and cartouches that you had to touch to learn the shapes of. And in the dream I knew it was some lonely boy who had hidden away up there with all the furniture years and years ago, and that he wanted to play, to show me whatever old shoe buckles or pocket watches or fountain pens he had found in drawers and coat pockets. I always pictured him skeletal and pale, though of course he'd be careful never to get near enough to the windows to be seen, and I knew he'd speak in a whisper.

I always woke up from that dream while it was still dark outside my window, and so tense that I'd simply lie without moving a muscle until I could see the morning light through my eyelids.

I was in the yard of the Santa Ana house early the next morning, sipping at a can of Coors beer and blinking tears out of my eyes as I tried to focus on the tomato vines through the sun glare on the white garden wall, when I heard a pattering like rain among the leaves. I sat down abruptly in the damp grass to push the low leaves aside.

It was bits of glass falling out of the sky. I touched one shard, and it was as hot as a serving plate. A cracking and thumping started up behind me then, and I fell over backward trying to stand up in a hurry. Red clay roof tiles were shattering violently on the grass and tearing the jasmine branches. The air was sharp with the acid smell of burned, broken stone, and then a hard punch of scorchingly hot air lifted me off my feet and rolled me over the top of the picnic table. I was lying facedown and breathless in the grass when the bass-note boom deafened me and stretched my hair out straight, so that it stood up from my scalp for days; I still have trouble combing it down flat, not that I try frequently.

The yard looked like a battlefield. All the rose bushes were broken off flush with the ground, and the ceramic duck that we'd had forever was broken into a hundred pieces. I was dimly glad that the duck had been able to tour California once in his otherwise uneventful life.

The eastern end of the house, where the kitchen had been, was broken wide open, with tar-paper strips standing up along the roof edge like my hair, and beams and plaster chunks lay scattered out across the grass. Everything inside the kitchen was gone, the table and the refrigerator and the pictures on the wall. Propane is heavier than air, and it had filled the kitchen from the floor upward, until it had reached the pilot light on the stove.

The explosion had cracked my ribs and burned my eyebrows off and scorched my throat, and I think I got sick from radon or asbestos that had been in the walls. I took a daylong ride on a bus out here to San Bernardino to recuperate at my uncle's place, the same rambling old ranch-style house where we lived happily for a year right after we moved from New York, before my mother found the Santa Ana house and began making payments on it.

The ceramic duck might have been the first thing my mother bought for the house. He generally just sat in the yard, but shortly after my sister and I turned seven he was stolen. We didn't get very excited about that, but we were awestruck when the duck mysteriously showed up on the lawn again, six months later—because propped up against him in the dewy grass was a photo album full of pictures of the ceramic duck in various locations around the state: the duck in front of the flower bank at the entrance to Disneyland, the duck on a cable-car seat in San Francisco, the duck sitting between the palm prints of Clark Gable; along with a couple of more mundane shots, like one of the duck just leaning against an avocado tree in somebody's yard out behind a weather-beaten old house. I think all the stories you hear about world-travelling lawn gnomes these days started with the humbler travels of our duck, back in '59. Or vice versa, I suppose.

My uncle's place hasn't changed at all since my sister and I explored every hollow and gully of the weedy acre and climbed the sycamores along the back fence so many years ago—our carved initials are still visible on the trunk of one of them, I discover, still only a yard above the dirt, though my sister isn't interested in seeing them now. There's a surprising lot of our toys, too, old wooden Lincoln Logs and Nike missile launchers; I've gathered them from among the weeds and put them near the back of the garage where my uncle supposedly keeps his beer, but she doesn't want to see them either.

Always in San Bernardino you see women on the noonday sidewalks wearing shorts and halter tops, and from behind they look young and shapely with their long brown legs and blonde hair; but when the car you're in has driven past them, and you hike around in the passenger seat to look back, their faces are weary, and shockingly old. And at night along Base Line, under the occasional clusters of sodium-vapor lights, you can see that the bar parking lots are jammed with cars, but you can generally also see four or five horses tied up to a post outside the bar door. My uncle says this is a semi-desert climate, right below the Cajon Pass and Barstow in the high desert, and so we get a lot of patches of mirage.

I'll let my sister drive me as far as the Stater Brothers market on Highland, though that doesn't cheer her up, probably because I mostly shoplift the fruits and cheese and crackers that are all I can keep down anymore. She flew back from France after I hurt myself, and when she can borrow an old car from a friend she drives out to visit me. She keeps trying to trick me into coming back to live in Santa Ana again, or anywhere besides my uncle's house—she wants to drive me to a hospital, actually—but I don't dare. I've told her not to tell anyone where I am, and I've taken a false name, not that anyone asks me.

Her family, I have to admit, has given her a lot of grief. Her husband was born in a part of Iran that was under British jurisdiction, and when he tried to go back there after going to school in England the Iranians said he was an enemy of the Shah; they took his passport and gave him some papers that permitted him to leave but never come back, and he got as far as Charles de Gaulle Airport, but France wouldn't let him in without a passport and Customs wouldn't let him get on another plane. He's lived on the Boutique Level of Terminal One now for decades, sleeping on a plastic couch and watching TV, and Lufthansa flight attendants give him travel kits so that he can shave and brush his teeth. My sister met him there during a layover on a European tour my mother bought for her right after high school, and now she's got a job and an apartment in Roissy so she can be near him. I keep telling her she's going to lose her job, staying away like this, but she says she has no choice, because nobody else can get through to me the way she still can. I'm *backward,* she says.

My uncle makes himself scarce when she drives up the dirt track out front in one beat old borrowed car or another; so does everybody. When I hobbled off the bus at his warped chain-link front gate, all scorched and blinking and hoarse and dizzy from the radon, he was waiting for me out in the front yard with his usual straw hat pulled down over his gray hair; all you really see is the bushy mustache. The house is empty now, just echoing rooms with one old black Bakelite telephone on the kitchen floor and a lot of wires sticking out of the walls where there used to be lights, but he told me I could sleep in my old room, and I've carried in some newspapers to make a nest in the corner there. I'm thinking about moving the nest into the closet.

"Don't bother anybody you might see here," my uncle told me on that first day. "Just leave 'em alone. They probably live here." And I have seen a very old man in the kitchen, always crying quietly over the sink, and wearing one of those senior-citizen jumpsuits that zip up from the ankle to the neck; I've just nodded to him and discreetly shuffled past across the dusty linoleum. What could we have to say to each other that the other wouldn't already know? And a couple of times I've seen two kids out at the far end of the backyard. Let them play, I figure. My uncle is generally walking around in circles behind the garage trying to find his beer. There's a patch of mirage out there—if you step into the weeds by the edge of the driveway, walking away from the house, you find with no shift at all that you've just stepped *onto* the driveway, *facing* the house.

"It's been that way forever," he told me one day when he was taking a break from it, sitting on the hood of his wrecked old truck. "But one night a few winters ago I stepped out there and *wasn't* facing the house; and I was standing on one of your mom's long-ago rosebushes. The flowers were open, like they thought it was day, and the leaves were warm. Time doesn't pass in mirages, everybody knows that—so I hopped right in the truck and bought two cases of Budweiser out of the cooler at Top Cat, and stashed 'em there right by the rosebush. The next morning it was the two-for-one-step mirage again, but whenever it slacks off, I know where there's a lot of cold beer."

I nodded a number of times, and so did he, and it was right after this conversation with him that I started keeping all our old toys back there.

Yesterday my sister came rocking up the dirt driveway in a shiny green Edsel, and when she braked it in a cloud of dust and clanked the door open I could see that she'd been crying at some point on the drive up. It's a long drive, and it takes a lot out of her.

My voice is gone because of the explosion having scorched my throat, so I stepped closer to her to be heard. "Come in the house and have . . . some water," I rasped—awkwardly, because she's doing all this for my sake. We don't have any glasses, but she could drink it out of the faucet. "Or crackers," I added.

"I can't stand to see the inside of the house," she said, crossly. "We had good times in this house, *when we were all living* in it." She squinted out past the dogwood tree at the infinity of brown hillocks that is the backyard. "Let's talk out there."

"You're testy," I noted as I followed her up the dirt driveway, past the house. She was wearing a blue sundress that clung to her sweaty back.

"Why do you suppose that is, Gunther?"

I glanced around quickly, but there wasn't even a bird in the empty blue sky. "Doug," I reminded her huskily, trying to project my frail voice. The name had been suggested by the phone call I'd got on the day before the explosion, and certainly Doug Olney himself would never hear about the deception, wherever he might be. "Always, you promised."

We were walking out past the end of the driveway among the burr-weeds now, and I saw her shoulders shrug wearily. "Why do you suppose that is—Mr. Olney?" she called back to me.

I lengthened my stride to step up beside her. The soles of my feet must be tough, because the burrs never stick in my skin. "I bet it's expensive to rent a classic Edsel," I hazarded.

"Yes, it is." Her voice was flat and harsh. "Especially in the summer, with all the Mexican weddings. It's a '57, but it must have a new engine or something in it—I could hardly see the signs on the old Route 66 today. Just 'Foothill Boulevard' all the way. I may not be able to come out here again, get through to you, not even your own *twin*, who *lived* here, *with* you! Not even in a car from those days. And Hakim needs me too." She turned to face me and stamped her foot. "He could figure some way to get out of that airport if he really wanted to! And look at you! Damn it—Doug—how long do you think a comatose body can *live*, even in a hospital like Western Medical, with its soul off hiding *incognito* somewhere?"

"Well, *soul* . . ."

"This is certainly unsanctified ground. Is it a crossroads? Have you got *rue* growing out here with the weeds?" She was crying again. "*Propane leak*. Why were you found out in the yard, out by the duck? You changed your mind, didn't you? You were trying to walk away from it. Good! Keep *on* walking away from it, don't stop here in the, in the . . . terminal, the nowhere in-between. Walk right now to that silly old car back there, and let me drive you to Western Medical while I still can, while you can still make the trip. You can *wake up*."

I smiled at her and shook my head. I know now that I was never scared of the boy in the dark ballroom. I was tense with fear of each fresh unknown dawn, which the boy had found a way to hide from, but which always did come to me mercilessly shining right through my closed eyelids. I opened my mouth to croak some reassurance to her, but she was looking past me with an empty expression.

"Jesus," she said then, reverently, in a voice almost as hoarse as mine, "this is where that other picture was taken. The photo of the duck by the avocado tree. In the photo album, remember?" She pointed back toward the house. "There's no tree here now, but the angle of the house, the windows—look, it's the very same view, we just didn't recognize it then because we remembered this house freshly painted, not all faded and peeled like it is now, and like it was in the picture, and because in the picture there was a big distracting avocado tree in the foreground!"

I stood beside her and squinted through watering eyes against the sun glare. She might have been right—if you imagined a tree to the right, with the poor duck leaning against the trunk, this view was at least very like the one in that old photo album.

"The person with the camera was standing right here," she said softly.

Or *will* be standing, I thought.

"Could you drive me to Stater Brothers?" I said.

Several times I've gone out and looked, since she drove away, and I'm still not sure she was right. The trouble is, I don't remember the photograph all that clearly. It might have been this house. All I can do is wait.

I don't imagine that I'll be going to Stater Brothers again soon, if ever. The trip was upsetting, with so many curdles and fractures of mirage in the harsh daylight that you'd think San Bernardino was populated by nothing but walking skeletons and one-hoss shays. I did get an avocado, along with my crackers and processed cheese-food slices, and my sister left off a box of our dad's old clothes because I've been wearing the scorched pants and shirt still, and she said it broke her heart to see me walking around all killed. I haven't looked in the box, but it stands to reason that there's one of those jumpsuits in it.

I know now that she's going back, at last, to poor stalled Hakim at the airport in Roissy. I called her from the phone in the kitchen here.

"I'm on my way to the hospital," I told her. "You can go back to France."

"You're—Gunth—I mean, *Doug*, where are you calling from?"

"I'm back in Santa Ana. I just want to change my clothes, try to comb my hair, before I get on a bus to the hospital."

"Santa Ana? What's the number there, I'll call you right back." That panicked me. Helplessly I gave her the only phone number I could think of, my old Santa Ana number. "But I didn't mean to take up any more of your time," I babbled, "I just wanted to—"

"That's our old number," she said. "How can you be at our old number?"

"It—stayed with the house." If I could still sweat, I'd have been sweating. "These people who live here now don't mind me hanging around." The lie was getting ahead of me. "They like me; they made me a sandwich."

"I bet. Stay by the phone."

She hung up, and I knew it was a race then to see which of us would be able to dial the old number most rapidly. She must have been hampered by a rotary-dial phone too, because I got ringing out of the earpiece; and after it had rung four times I concluded that the number must be back in service again, because I would have got the recording by then if it had not been. My lips were silently mouthing, *Please, please,* and I was aching with anxious hope that whoever answered the line would agree to go along with what I'd tell them to say.

Then the phone at the other end was lifted, and the voice said, breathlessly, "Hello?"

Of course I recognized him, and the breath clogged in my numb throat.

"Hello?" came the voice again. "Am I talking to a short circuit?"

Yes, I thought.

That oil tank in San Pedro hadn't been in use for years, but it had once been equipped with an automatic-dial switch to call the company's main office when its fuel was depleted; a stray power surge had apparently turned it on again, and the emergency number it called was by that time ours. Probably the oil tank hadn't had any fuel in it at all anymore, and only occasionally noticed. Certainly there had been nothing we could do about it.

"Gunther!" It hurt my teeth to say the name. "Jesus, boy—this is— Doug Olney, from Neff High School! You remember me, don't you?"

"Doug?" said the half-drunk, middle-aged man at the other end of the line, befuddledly wondering if I had throat cancer. "Olney? Sure I remember! Where are you? Are you in town—"

"No time to talk," I said, trying not to choke. What if Doug Olney, the real one, *had* been in town, in Santa Ana? Would this unhappy loser have suggested that the two of them get together for lunch? "I don't want to—" Stop you, I thought; save you, for damn sure. "—change any of your plans." My eyes were watering, even in the dim kitchen. "Listen, a woman's gonna call your number in a minute; she's gonna ask for me. You don't know her," I assured him; I didn't want him to be at all thinking he might. "Say I just left a minute ago, okay?"

"Who is she—"

I just hung up. You'll find out, I thought.

My uncle's beer appeared in the yard today, two cases of it, still cold from the cooler at Top Cat. The roses are still fresh, and I looked at the clip-cuts on some stems and tried to comprehend that my mother had cut the flowers only a few hours earlier, by the rosebush's time; the smears in the white dust on the rose hips were probably from her fingers. Sitting in the dirt driveway in the noonday sun, my uncle and I got all weepy and sentimental, and drank can after can of the Budweiser in toasts to missing loved ones, though probably nobody was in the house, and the two children were by then long gone from the backyard.

I've planted the golf-ball-sized seed from the avocado, right where the tree was in the picture—if it was in fact a picture of this house. Eventually it will be a tree, and maybe one day the duck will be there, leaning on the trunk, on his way back from Disneyland and Grauman's Chinese Theatre to the house where my sister and I are still seven years old. I plan to tag along, if he'll have me.

✣ AUTHOR'S NOTE ✣

An incidental benefit of using occurrences and places from my own life in my short stories is that I can take my small, personal accidents and bafflements and put them into a fictional context in which they count for something. I did once get the two unexplained phone calls that Gunther gets at the beginning of this story, and there was never any follow-up explanation from "Doug Olney." So in this story I tried to come up with a context in which those calls might logically occur—well, "logically" if you allow the idea of a ghost into the picture.

And the house I gave Gunther is the apartment I was living in at that time, though it never actually blew up.

⊰ A JOURNEY OF ONLY TWO PACES ⊱

SHE HAD ORDERED STEAK TARTARE and Hennessy XO brandy, which would, he reflected, look extravagant when he submitted his expenses to the court. And God knew what parking would cost here.

He took another frugal sip of his beer and said, trying not to sound sour, "I could have mailed you a check."

They were at one of the glass-topped tables on the outdoor veranda at the Beverly Wilshire Hotel, just a couple of feet above the sidewalk beyond the railing, looking out from under the table's umbrella down the sunlit lanes of Rodeo Drive. The diesel-scented air was hot even in the shade.

"But you were his old friend," she said. "He always told me that you're entertaining." She smiled at him expectantly.

She had been a widow for about ten years, Kohler recalled—and she must have married young. In her sunglasses and broad Panama hat she only seemed to be about twenty now.

Kohler, though, felt far older than his thirty-five years.

"He was easily entertained, Mrs. Halloway," he said slowly. "I'm pretty. . . lackluster, really." A young man on the other side of the railing overheard him and glanced his way in amusement as he strode past on the sidewalk.

"Call me Campion. But a dealer in rare books must have some fascinating stories."

Her full name was Elizabeth St. Campion Halloway. She signed her paintings "Campion." Kohler had looked her up online before driving out here to deliver the thousand dollars, and had decided that all her artwork was morbid and clumsy.

"He found you attractive," she went on, tapping the ash off her cigarette into the scraped remains of her steak tartare. He noticed that the filter was smeared with her red lipstick. "Did he ever tell you?"

"Really. No." For all Kohler knew, Jack Ranald might have been gay. The two of them had only got together about once a year since college, and then only when Kohler had already begged off on two or three email invitations. Kohler's wife had always thought Jack was inwardly mocking her—*He forgets me when he's not looking right at me,* she'd said—and she wouldn't have been pleased with these involvements in the dead man's estate.

Kohler's wife had looked nothing like Campion.

Campion was staring at him now over the coal of her cigarette—he couldn't see her eyes behind the dark lenses, but her pale, narrow face swung carefully down and left and right. "I can already see him in you. You have the Letters Testamentary?"

"Uh." The shift in conversational gear left him momentarily blank. "Oh, yes—would you like to see them? and I'll want a receipt—"

"Not the one from the court clerk. The one Jack arranged."

Kohler bent down to get his black vinyl briefcase, and he pushed his chair back from the table to unzip it on his lap. Inside were all the records of terminating the water and electric utilities at the house Jack had owned in Echo Park and paying off Jack's credit cards, and, in a manila envelope along with the death certificate—which discreetly didn't mention suicide—the letters he had been given by the probate court.

One of them was the apparently standard sort, signed by the clerk and the deputy clerk, but the other had been prepared by Jack himself.

Kohler tugged that one out and leaned forward to hand it across the table to Campion, and while she bent her head over it he mentally recalled its phrases: *. . . having been appointed and qualified as enactor of the will of John Carpenter Ranald, departed, who expired on or about 28 February 2009, Arthur Lewis Kohler is hereby authorized to function as enactor and to consummate possession . . .* In effect it was a suicide note. It had been signed in advance by Jack, and Kohler had recently been required to sign it too.

"Kabbalah," she said, without looking up, and for a moment Kohler thought he had somehow put one of his own business invoices into the briefcase by mistake and handed it to her. She looked up and smiled at him. "Are you afraid to get drunk with me? I'm sure one beer won't release any pent-up emotions, you can safely finish it. What *is* the most valuable book you have in stock?"

Kohler was frowning, but he went along with her change of subject. Jack must have told her what sort of books he specialized in.

"I guess that would be a manuscript codex of a thing called the *Gallei Razayya*, written in about 1550. It, uh, differs from the copy at Oxford." He shrugged. "I've got it priced high—it'll probably just go to my," he hesitated, then sighed and completed the habitual sentence, "my heirs."

"Rhymes with prayers, and you don't have any, do you? Heirs? Anymore? I was so sorry to hear about that."

Kohler stared at her, wondering if he wanted to make the effort of taking offense at her flippancy.

"No," he said instead, carefully

But it's about transmigration of souls, isn't it? Your codex book? Maybe you could . . . bequeath it to yourself."

She pushed her own chair back and stood up, brushing out her white linen skirt. "Have you tried to find the apartment building he owned in Silver Lake?"

Kohler began hastily to zip up his briefcase, and he was about to ask her how she knew about the manuscript when he remembered that she was still holding the peculiar Letter Testamentary.

"Uh . . . ?" he said, reaching for it.

"I'll keep it for a while," she said gaily, tucking it into her purse. "I bet you couldn't find the place."

"That's true." He lowered his hand and finished zipping the case; the letter signed by the clerks was the legally important one. "I need to get the building assessed for the inventory of the estate. The address on the tax records seems to be wrong." Finally he asked, "You . . . know a lot about Kabbalah?"

"I can take you there. The address is wrong, as you say. Do you like cats? Jack told me about your book, your *codex*."

Kohler got to his feet and drank off half of the remaining beer in his glass. It wasn't very cold by this time. Jack had always wanted to hear about Kohler's business—Kohler must have acquired the manuscript shortly before they had last met for dinner, and told Jack about it.

"Sure," he said distractedly. She raised one penciled eyebrow, and he added, "I like cats fine."

"I'll drive," she said. "I have no head for directions, I couldn't guide you." She started toward the steps down to the Wilshire Boulevard sidewalk, then turned back and frowned at his briefcase. "You've followed all the directions he left in his will?"

Kohler guessed what she was thinking of. "The urn is in the trunk of my car," he said.

"You can drive. Your car is smaller, better for the tight turns."

Kohler followed her down out of the hotel's shadow onto the glaring Wilshire sidewalk, wondering how she knew what sort of car he drove, and when he had agreed to go right now to look at the apartment building.

She directed him east to the Hollywood freeway and then up into the hills above the Silver Lake Reservoir. The roads were narrow and twisting and overhung with carob and jacaranda trees.

Eventually, after Kohler had lost all sense of direction, Campion said, "Turn left at that street there."

"That? That's a driveway," Kohler objected, braking to a halt.

"It's the street," she said. "Well, lane. Alley. Anyway, it's where the apartment building is. Where are you living these days?"

In an apartment building, Kohler thought, probably not as nice as the one we're trying to find here. The old house was just too unbearably familiar. "Culver City."

"Did you like him? Jack?"

Kohler turned the wheel sharply and then steered by inches up onto the narrow strip of pavement, which curled away out of sight to the right behind a hedge of white-blooming oleander only a few yards ahead. Dry palm-fronds scattered across the cracked asphalt crunched under the tires. The needle of the temperature gauge was still comfortably on the left side of the dial, but he kept an eye on it.

"I liked him well enough," he said, squinting through the alternating sun-glare and palm-trunk shadows on the windshield. He exhaled. "Actually I didn't, no. I liked him in college, but after his father died, he—he just wasn't the same guy anymore."

"It was a shock," she said, nodding. "A trauma. He had heartworms."

Kohler just shook his head. "And Jack was sick, he said. What was wrong with him?"

She shrugged. "What does it matter? Something he didn't want to wait for. But—" And then she sang, "We're young and healthy, so let's be *bold*." She giggled. "Do you remember that song?"

"No."

"No, it would have been before your time."

The steep little road did seem to be something more than a driveway—Kohler kept the Saturn to about five miles an hour, and they slowly rumbled past several old Spanish-style houses with white stucco walls and red roof-tiles and tiny garages with green painted doors, the whole landscape as apparently empty of people as a street in a de Chirico painting. Campion had lit another cigarette, and Kohler cranked down the driver's-side window, and even though it was hot he was grateful for the sage and honeysuckle breeze.

"It's on the right," she said, tapping the windshield with a fingernail. "The arch there leads into the parking court."

Kohler steered in through the chipped white arch between tall trees, and he was surprised to see five or six cars parked in the unpaved yard and a big Honda Gold Wing motorcycle leaning on its stand up by the porch, in the shade of a vast lantana bush that crawled up the side of the two-story old building.

"Tenants?" he said, rocking the Saturn into a gap beside a battered old Volkswagen. "I hope . . . what's-his-name, the guy who inherited the place, wants to keep it running." A haze of dust raised by their passage across the yard swirled over the car.

"Mister Bump. He will, he lives here." She pointed at the motorcycle. "Jack's bike—running boards, a windshield, stereo, passenger seat—it's as if his RV had pups."

Kohler hadn't turned off the engine. "I could do this through the mail, if I could get a valid address."

"They get mail here, sort of informally. Somebody will tell you how to address it." She had opened her door and was stepping out onto the dry dirt, so he sighed and twisted the ignition key back and pulled it out. Now he could hear a violin playing behind one of the upstairs balconies—some intricate phrase from *Scheherazade*, rendered with such gliding expertise that he thought it must be a recording.

With the wall around it, and the still air under the old pepper trees, this compound seemed disconnected from the surrounding streets and freeways of Los Angeles.

"These were Jack's friends," Campion said. "Bring the urn."

Kohler was already sweating in the harsh sunlight, but he walked to the trunk and bent down to open it. He lifted out the heavy cardboard box and slammed the trunk shut.

"Jack is who we all have in common," said Campion, smiling and taking his free arm.

She led Kohler across the yard and up the worn stone steps to the porch, and the French doors stood open onto a dim, high-ceilinged lobby.

The air was cooler inside, and Kohler could hear an air-conditioner rattling away somewhere behind the painted screens and tapestries and potted plants that hid the walls. Narrow beams of sunlight slanted in and gleamed on the polished wooden floor.

Then Kohler noticed the cats. First two on an old Victorian sofa, then several more between vases on high shelves, and after a moment he decided that there must be at least a dozen cats in the room, lazily staring at the newcomers from heavy-lidded topaz eyes.

The cats were all identical—long-haired orange and white creatures with long fluffy tails.

"Campion!"

A tanned young man in a Polo shirt and khaki shorts had walked into the lobby through the French doors on the far side, and Kohler glimpsed an atrium behind him—huge shiny green leaves and orchid blossoms motionless in the still air.

"You *bitch*," the man said cheerfully, "did you lose your phone? Couldn't at least *honk* while you were driving up? ''Tis just like a summer birdcage in a garden.'"

"Mr. Bump," said Campion, "I've brought James Kohler for the, the *wake*."

"No," said Kohler hastily, "I can't stay—"

"Can I call you Jimmy?" interrupted Mr. Bump. He held out his hand. "Mentally I'm spelling it J-I-M-I, like Hendrix."

Kohler shook the man's brown hand, then after several seconds flexed his own hand to separate them.

"No time to go a-waking, eh?" said Mr. Bump with a smile.

"I'm afraid not. I'll just—"

"Is that Jack?"

Kohler blinked, then realized that the man must be referring to the box he carried in his left hand.

"Oh. Yes."

"Let's walk him out to the atrium, shall we? We can disperse his ashes in the garden there."

Over Mr. Bump's shoulder, one of the orange cats on a high shelf flattened its ears.

"I'm supposed to—" Kohler paused to take a breath before explaining Jack Ranald's eccentric instructions. "I'm supposed to give him—his ashes—to somebody who quotes a certain poem to me. And I think it would be illegal to . . . pour out the ashes in a, a residence."

Behind him Campion laughed. "It's not a *poem*."

"Jimi isn't literary, is all," said Mr. Bump to her reprovingly. He crouched to pick up a kitten that seemed to be an exact miniature copy of all the other cats.

I'm a rare-books dealer! thought Kohler, but he just turned to her and said, "What is it?"

"I quoted a bit of it just now," said Mr. Bump, holding the kitten now and stroking it. "'Tis just like a summer birdcage in a garden; the birds that are without despair to get in, and the birds that are within despair and are in a consumption for fear they shall never get out.'"

Kohler nodded—that was it. The will had specified the phrase, *Consumption for fear they shall never get out*, and he had assumed it was a line of anapestic quatrameter.

"What's it from?" he asked, setting the box on a table and lifting out of it the black ceramic urn.

"A play," said Campion, taking his free arm again, apparently in anticipation of walking out to the atrium. "Webster's *The White Devil*."

"It's a filthy play," put in Mr. Bump.

The cats were bounding down from their perches and scurrying out the far doors into the atrium, their tails waving like a field of orange ferns in a wind.

The three people followed the cats out into the small, tiled courtyard that lay below second-floor balconies on all four sides. The atrium was crowded with tropical-looking plants, and leafy branches and vines hid some corners of the balconies—but Kohler noted uneasily that more than a dozen young men and women were leaning on the iron railings and silently looking down on them. The air smelled of jasmine and cat-boxes.

"The character who says the birdcage business," remarked Campion, "rises from the dead, at the end."

"And then gets killed again," noted Mr. Bump.

Campion shrugged. "Still." She looked up at the audience on the balconies. "Jack's back!" she called. "This nice man has been kind enough to carry him."

The men and women on the balconies all began snapping their fingers, apparently by way of applause. Kohler was nervously tempted to bow.

They didn't stop, and the shrill clacking began to take on a choppy rhythm.

The cats had all sat down in a ring in the center of the atrium floor—no, Kohler saw, it wasn't a ring, it was a triangle, and then he saw that they were all sitting on three lines of red tile set into the pavement. The space inside the triangle was empty.

Campion had stepped away to close the French doors to the lobby, and Mr. Bump leaned close to Kohler and spoke loudly to be heard over the shaking rattle from above. "This is the last part of your duty as executor," he said. The kitten he was holding seemed to have gone to sleep, in spite of the noise.

"It's not the last, by any means," said Kohler, who was sweating again. "There's the taxes, and selling the house, and—and I don't think this *is* part of my duties." He squinted up at the finger-snapping people—they were all dressed in slacks and shirts that were black or white, and the faces he could make out were expressionless. *Something's happening here,* he thought, *and you don't know what it is.* The sweat was suddenly cold on his forehead, and he pushed the urn into Mr. Bump's hands.

"I have to leave," Kohler said, turning back toward the lobby. "Now."

Campion stood in front of the closed doors, and she was pointing a small black automatic pistol at him—it looked like .22 or .25 caliber. "It was so kind of you to come!" she cried merrily. "And you are very nice!"

Kohler was peripherally aware that what she had said was a quote from something, but all his attention was focused on the gun muzzle.

Campion's finger was inside the trigger guard. He stopped moving, then slowly extended his empty hands out to the side, his fingers twitching in time to his heartbeat.

Mr. Bump shook his head and smiled ruefully at Kohler. "Campion is so *theatrical!* We just, we'd be very grateful if you'd participate in a—memorial service."

The people on the balconies must have been able to see the situation, but the counterpoint racket never faltered—clearly there would be no help from them, whoever they were. "Then," said Kohler hoarsely, "I can go?"

"You might very well prefer to stay," said Campion. "It's a leisurely life."

Stay? Kohler thought.

"What," he asked, "do I do?"

"You were his closest friend," said Mr. Bump, "so you should—"

"I hardly knew him! Since college, at least. Maybe once or twice a year—"

"You're who he nominated. You should step over the cats, into the open space there, and after everybody has recited Jack's Letter Testamentary, you simply break the urn. At your feet."

Mr. Bump pressed the urn into Kohler's right hand, and Kohler closed his fingers around the glassy neck of it.

"And then I—can leave."

Campion nodded brightly. "Yours will be a journey only of two paces into view of the stars again," she said.

Kohler recognized what she had said as lines from a Walter de la Mare poem, and he recalled how the sentence in the poem ended—*but you will not make it.*

And belatedly he recognized what she had said a few moments ago: *It was so kind of you to come! And you are very nice!—* that was from Lewis Carroll's "The Walrus and the Carpenter," spoken by the Walrus just before he and the Carpenter began devouring the gullible Oysters.

Kohler was grasping the urn in both hands, and now he had to force his arms not to shake in time to the percussive rhythm of all the rattling hands. He glanced at Campion, but she was still holding the gun pointed directly at the middle of him.

"You really should have had more to drink," she called.

God only knew who these people were, or what weird ritual this was, and Kohler was considering causing some kind of diversion and just diving over some plants and rolling through one of the ground-floor French doors, and then just running. Out of this building, over the wall, and away.

It seemed unrealistic.

He obediently stepped over the cats into the clear triangle of pavement.

"Now wait till they've recited it all," said Mr. Bump loudly.

With her free hand Campion dug the peculiar Letter Testamentary out of her purse and flapped it in the still air to unfold it.

And then a young woman on one of the balconies whispered, "*Having* . . ." and a man on a balcony on the other side of the atrium whispered, ". . . *been* . . ." and another followed with ". . . *appointed* . . ."

The hoarse whispers undercut the shrill finger-snapping and echoed clearly around the walled space. They were reciting the text of Jack's letter, and each was enunciating only one word of it, letting a pause fall between each word.

The glassy bulge of the urn was slippery in Kohler's sweating hands, and he assembled some of the disjointed phrases in his mind: *enactor of the will of John Carpenter Ranald . . . Arthur Lewis Kohler . . . to consummate possession . . .*

And he recognized this technique—in first century Kabbalistic mysticism, certain truths could be spoken only in whispers, and the writing of certain magical texts required that a different scribe write each separate word.

As clearly as if she were speaking now, Campion's words at lunch came back to him: *But it's about transmigration of souls, isn't it?* and *I can already see him in you.*

And he recalled saying, *after his father died, he just wasn't the same guy anymore.*

Jack Ranald had been executor of his father's will.

"*To*," whispered one of the black-or-white-clad people on the balconies. "*Consummate*," whispered another. "*Possession*," breathed one more, and then they stopped, and the finger-snapping stopped too. The silence that followed seemed to spring up from the paving stones, and the cats sitting in a triangle around Kohler shifted in place.

Mr. Bump nodded to Kohler and raised the kitten in both hands.

"Where do you want to go, from here?" whispered Campion. "Is there anything *you* want to wait for?"

Kohler sighed, a long exhalation that relaxed all his muscles and seemed to empty him. Go? he thought. Back to my studio apartment in Culver City . . . Wait for? No. I *could* do this—I *could* stay here, hidden from everything, even from myself, it seems.

He could hear the cats around the triangle purring. It's a leisurely life, Campion had said.

"What have you got to lose?" whispered Campion.

Lose? he thought. Nothing—nothing but memories I don't seem to have room for anymore.

And he remembered again what his wife had said about Jack—*He forgets me when he's not looking right at me.* Kohler couldn't look at her anymore—

—but to do this, whatever it was, would pretty clearly be to join Jack.

Kohler took a deep breath, and he felt as if he were stepping back out of a warm doorway, back into the useless tensions of a cold night.

And he flung the urn as hard as he could straight up. Everyone's eyes followed it, and Kohler stepped out of the triangle and, in a sudden moment of inspiration, picked up one of the cats and leaned forward to set it down in the clear triangular patch before hurrying toward a door away from Campion.

The urn shattered on the pavement behind him with a noise like a gunshot as Kohler was grabbing the doorknob, but two sounds stopped him—the cat yowled two syllables and, in perfect synchronization, a voice in his head said, in anguish, *Jimmy.*

It was Jack's voice. Even the cat's cry had seemed to be Jack's voice.

Helplessly Kohler let go of the doorknob and turned around.

The rest of the cats had scattered. Campion had hurried into the triangular space, the gun falling from her fingers and skittering across the paving stones, and she was cradling the cat Kohler had put there. Mr. Bump had let the kitten jump down from his arms now and was just staring open-mouthed, and the people on the balconies were leaning forward and whispering in agitation—but their whispers now weren't audible.

"Jack!" Campion said hitchingly through tears, "Jack, darling, what has he done, what has he done?"

The cat was staring over Campion's shoulder directly at Kohler, and Kohler shivered at its intense amber glare.

But he nodded and said softly, "So long, Jack." Then he recalled that it was probably Jack's father, and looked away.

He took two steps forward across the tiles and picked up the little automatic pistol that Campion had dropped. There seemed to be no reason now not to leave by the way he'd come in.

Mr. Bump was shaking his head in evident amazement. "It was supposed to be you," he said, standing well back as he held the lobby door open, "into the kitten, to make room for Jack. That cat's already got somebody—I don't know how that'll work out." He stepped quickly to keep up with Kohler's stride across the dim lobby toward the front doors. "No use, anyway, they can't even write. Just not enough brain in their heads!" He laughed nervously, watching the gun in Kohler's hand. "You're—actually going to *leave* then?"

At the front doors, with his hand on one of the old iron handles, Kohler stopped. "I don't think anybody would want me to stay."

Mr. Bump shrugged. "I think Campion likes you. Likes *you*, I mean, too." He smiled. "'Despair to get in,' and I think you've paid the entry fee. Stay for dinner, at least? I'm making a huge cioppino, plenty for everybody, even the cats."

Kohler found that he was not sure enough about what had happened, not *quite* sure enough, to make the impossible denunciations that he wanted to make. It might help to read some of the books in his stock, but at this moment he was resolved never to open one again except to catalogue it.

So "Give Jack mine," was all he said, as he pulled the door open; and then he hurried down the steps into the sunlight, reaching into his pocket for his car keys and bleakly eyeing the lane that would lead him back down to the old, old, terribly familiar freeway.

❖ AUTHOR'S NOTE ❖

Los Angeles is my favorite city. Anybody can fall in love with San Francisco or New Orleans in ten minutes, but Los Angeles is more circumspect. There are lots of odd, secluded spots down in the canyons or up on the hilltops between the freeways—domed temples from the

1920s that still host some furtive sorts of worship, eccentric private gardens that stretch implausible distances, nearly inaccessible old apartment buildings whose tenants seem to be covertly united in some secret cause. The odd place in this story was based on one such apartment building where my wife and I one day found the street-side lobby door unlocked.

⚜ THE HOUR OF BABEL ⚜

A GUST OF RAINY WIND wobbled the old 350 Honda as it made a right turn from Anaheim Boulevard into the empty parking lot, but the rider swerved a little wider to correct for it, and the green neutral-light shone under the water-beaded plastic window of the speedometer gauge as he coasted to a stop in one of the parking spaces in front of the anonymous office building.

He flipped down the kickstand and let the bike lean onto it without touching his shoe to the gleaming black pavement, and he unsnapped his helmet and pulled it off, shaking out his gray hair as he stared at the three-story building. In sunlight its white stucco walls were probably bright, but on this overcast noon it just looked ashen.

He shifted around on the plastic shopping bag he had draped over the section of black steel frame where the padded seat had once been, and squinted across the street. Past the wet cars hissing by in both directions he could see the bar, though it had a different name now. Probably the last person he knew from those days had quit going in there twenty years ago.

He looked back at the office building in front of him and tried to remember the Firehouse Pizza building that had stood there in 1975. It had sat further back, it seemed to him, with a wider parking lot in front. The spot where he used to park his bike was somewhere inside this new building now.

He reached a gloved hand below the front of the gas tank and switched off the engine.

✢ ✢ ✢

"Is he coming in?"

The bald man at the computer monitor stared at the red dot on the map-grid. "I don't—"

"Look out the window," said Hartford Evian with exaggerated clarity.

"Oh, right." Scarbee got up from the computer and crossed to the tinted window that overlooked Anaheim Boulevard, and peered down. "He's just sitting on his motorcycle, with his helmet off." He rubbed his nose. "It's raining."

"Was this visit on the schedule?"

"I suppose so. Why should they show *me* the schedule? It must have been."

Evian had flipped open a cell phone and begun awkwardly punching numbers into it, when Scarbee added, "Now Kokolo just drove in."

Evian swore and quickly finished pushing the tiny buttons.

"Perry," he said a moment later, "don't look at the guy on the motorcycle to your right, it's Hollis. *Hollis.* Yes, that one. It's not on any schedule *I* ever saw. Just walk in, ignore him." After listening for a moment, he went on, "Wait, wait! Felise is with you? Tell Felise not to get out of the car!"

Scarbee was still looking out the window. "Felise is already out of the car," he said.

"Get in here, both of you, quick, don't look around," said Evian, and then he snapped the phone closed. "Did Hollis look at her?"

"Well," said Scarbee, "he looked over at both of them."

Evian opened his mouth as if to speak, hesitated, then said, "Call Hoag Hospital. We've got to get Lyle back here right now, not later today."

Scarbee turned around to face the desk. "That's earlier than we said. His doctors won't—"

"Keep watching Hollis!" When Scarbee turned back to the window, Evian said, "They'll go along if Lyle insists. I'm sure that's what happens. Tell him we'll give his family more money. Double."

"I hope they've got an ambulance free, to drive all the way here from Newport. Now he's putting his helmet back on. Hollis, down there."

Evian hit a button on the intercom. "You guys see the biker out front?" he asked.

"We see him," came a woman's voice from the speaker.

Scarbee said, "I think he's trying to start his motorcycle. It looks like he's jumping on it."

"Get him inside," said Evian, "polite if possible." He released the button.

A moment later Scarbee said, "Couple of security guys, running out. And—huh! I think they just stun-gunned him. Now they're walking him back in, but I think he's unconscious. His motorcycle fell over."

"Not very polite." Evian stood up and ran his fingers through his graying hair. "Now I guess we all talk to Hollis. I swear this wasn't in the goddamn schedule! Get him into the conference room—and remind them to be sure the area of measurement is locked. And get somebody to prop his silly motorcycle up again."

Kurt Hollis was still shaky and nauseated, but he sat back and sighed when the bald man slid a bowl of M&Ms across the table toward him. Hollis looked past the four people on the other side of the table at the windows high in the white cinder-block wall, then glanced at the two men standing by the door behind him.

At last he focused on the four people sitting across from him. Two of them he had seen a few minutes ago in the parking lot—the dark-haired young woman in a lumberjack shirt with the sleeves rolled back, and the blond man in a silver-fabric windbreaker. All the other men were in jackets and ties.

The bald man waved at the M&Ms. "The electric shock made your muscles go into rapid spasms," he said. "All your blood sugar was converted to lactic acid."

Hollis stared at him, and the bald man looked at the ceiling, apparently reconsidering what he had said. "You should eat these . . . candies," he said finally.

"Cigarettes," said Hollis. It was the first time he had spoken in several days, and his voice was hoarse. He spread his hand, then slowly reached into his damp brown leather jacket and pulled out a crumpled pack of Camels and hooked a Bic lighter out of one side of it.

"Smoking!" said the bald man. "No, you can't use those in here."

Hollis let go of the cigarette pack and the lighter. "You've mistaken me for somebody," he said. "Check it out. Let me go and this whole thing is just my word against yours."

The blond man in the silver windbreaker leaned forward. "You are Kurt Hollis," he said, "fifty-one years old, apartment on 16th Street in Santa Ana."

The gray-haired man beside him shifted in his chair and said, "We think you recognized Felise here." He waved at the young lady.

Hollis stared at her. Fluorescent lights in the ceiling were bright enough for him to see her clearly against the muted gray daylight from the windows.

"No," he said. "And I don't know anybody named Felise. I'm Kurt Hollis, but you've got crossed wires somewhere." He rubbed his eyes, then dropped his hands to the tabletop and tucked the lighter back into the cigarette pack. "I'm going to walk out of here," he said, shifting his chair back on the carpet. "Where'd you put my helmet?"

Felise reached out and took a handful of the M&Ms. "You can't possibly eat all of them," she said, and her voice was light and amused.

And Hollis recognized her.

"Liquor," he said, and reached into his jacket again, to pull out a flat half-pint bottle of Wild Turkey bourbon. His hand was shaking now as he unscrewed the cap and tilted the bottle up for a mouthful.

In 1975 he had been twenty years old, working at Firehouse Pizza until late June, and one weekday night in April he had been clearing away the litter a departed family had left on one of the picnic tables out in the dining area, when a dark-haired young woman sitting by herself at a nearby table had said, "Hey."

Hollis had turned to look at her. "Hey." She had seemed to be about his age, possibly a year or two younger.

He could remember the smells of the place, even now—the sharp reek of tomato sauce and garlic, the stale smell of the beer-soaked wood-slat floor behind the bar, the harsh odor of the ashtrays on all the tables.

She had nodded toward the aluminum pizza pans he had picked up. "What happens to the pizzas people don't finish?"

Hollis looked down at the pans. Several triangular slices of pizza had been left uneaten, pepperoni in one pan and sausage and bell pepper in the other.

"We just throw 'em out," he said. "Hard luck on the starving children in China, but . . . that's what we do."

"Oh," she said. "I wondered."

Hollis hesitated, then glanced to the bar and back to her. "Sometimes I leave them at the end of the bar," he said. "Till I have time to take them to the back room, where the sinks are."

After another pause, he nodded and carried the pans to the bar, and set them in front of one of the empty stools on the side of the cash register away from the kitchen. There were no customers at the bar, so he walked on into the kitchen, where two other young men in aprons and red-and-white-striped shirts were listlessly painting tomato sauce onto disks of dough. Hollis took the long-handled spatula from the top of the oven and pulled open the narrow top door—probably he had burned his forearm on the door-edge, as he often did—and turned the pizzas that sat on the flour-dusted iron floor inside.

When he looked through the doorway to the bar a few minutes later, he saw the girl sitting at the end of the bar, chewing. When he looked again, she was gone, and later when he went to pick up the pans he saw that they were empty.

Hollis and the girl never spoke again, though she had come in about once a week, always on a slow weekday night, and sat at the stool beyond the cash register, and Hollis had every time found an opportunity to leave a half-finished pizza or two near her.

And she had been there, he recalled now, on that last night, June 21, 1975; the night Firehouse Pizza closed down, and he had thus lost the last real job he'd ever had; the night that had been intruding so stressfully into his dreams lately that he had actually ridden his bike over here today. The night of which he had no recollection past about 8 PM, though he had awakened the next day at noon in his apartment, his face stiff with dried tears and stinging with impossible sunburn.

You can't possibly eat all of them.

He stared at her now as she sat chewing M&Ms across the table from him, stared at the corners of her eyes, the skin on her throat and the backs of her hands. It was all still smooth—she still looked to be about twenty years old.

"That," he said carefully, "was thirty-one years ago. A bit more."

"That's recommended retail time," she said. "We get it wholesale."

"You do recognize her," said the blond man.

"Who are these guys?" Hollis asked Felise. "Why is he wearing that Buck Rogers jacket?"

"It's a uniform," said Felise, "or will be. Could I—?" she added, with a wave toward the bottle of Wild Turkey. When Hollis nodded she reached over and slid it to her side and took a sip from it. "But I've got to admit," she said, exhaling around the whiskey, "that it makes him look like a baked potato that was taken too young from its mother."

"My name is Perry Kokolo," the blond man said, apparently unruffled. "The citizens beside me are Hartford Evian and Zip Scarbee. We employ Felise as a consultant. Do you remember a man named Don Lyle?"

"Yes!" Don had been working that night too, Hollis recalled now. The boss had left for the night, and he and Don had been drinking beers as they worked, pausing occasionally to sing old Dean Martin songs over the loudspeaker that was meant for calling out pick-up numbers.

"He'll be joining us soon," Kokolo went on. "He's done some consulting for us too, on a more freelance basis. We'd like your help as well."

"They pay very nice," said Felise. "I can afford my own pizzas now."

"Did they recruit you with a stun-gun?"

Felise said, "Probably," as gray-haired Evian said, "Apologies, apologies! It was urgent, our people got carried away. And we do pay well."

"Help . . . with what?" asked Hollis.

"We simply want to find out what happened here on June 21,1975."

"The night God vomited on Firehouse Pizza," said Felise, nodding solemnly.

Hollis took a deep breath and let it out. "I don't remember anything about that night after about eight." He looked at the four people across from him. "Why is it important? Now?"

"You're finally starting to remember, I think," said Evian. "You drove your motorcycle here today, and you recognized Felise, eventually. As to why it's important—"

"They can't," interrupted Felise, "we can't, that is, time-travel to that night. They can't get closer than a half hour on either side of it, and if they get there early and then try to walk in, they find they're walking out. Without changing direction. Even me, and I'm already *in* there."

The bald man, Scarbee, spoke up: "Cameras we leave in there disappear on that evening."

"It's like an island in the time stream," agreed Evian. "We're confined to the metaphorical water, and so we find we've gone by the incident, or we're short of it, but we can't get *to* it. And something important happened thex. Then by there, I mean."

Felise said, "He means 'then and there.'"

"Time-travel," said Hollis flatly. He took the bourbon bottle and drank a mouthful, then glanced around at the featureless room.

"Congress approved a new super-collider in Dallas in 2012," said the bald-headed man, "and the National Security Agency got Fermilab in Chicago. Charged tachyons in a mile-wide magnetic ring. It can project power fifth-dimensionally for a range of about fifty years back and twenty forward—there's some kind of Lorentzian ether headwind. We get shut down in 2019."

Hollis frowned and opened his mouth, but before he could speak, Felise said, "It's true. Look at me."

For several seconds none of them spoke.

"So," said Hollis finally, with no expression, "you can change the past?"

"Apparently not," said Evian. "But we can usually find out what it is. What happened that night?"

"Ask Felise," said Hollis, "or Don. They were both there too, then. Thex."

"I hid behind the bar," said Felise, "after the devil's hula-hoops and basketballs started spinning."

Hollis's forehead was suddenly cold with sweat. *That's right,* he thought—*hoops and balls.*

The deteriorating scar wall he had built up around the memory had been severely shaken by seeing Felise again, still as young as she had been on that night, and now, with this prompt from her, it gave way at last.

He had been on the phone by the front cash register when his vision had begun to flicker—he had been looking out past the counter at the tables, but suddenly without shifting his head he had seen curled segments of the pinball machines at the back end of the dining room, and even of the dumpster out back.

And then the spheres and rings had appeared in the air, rapidly expanding and sending tables flying in a clatter, or shrinking down to nothing. They were zebra-patterned in black and silver, and the stripes shifted as rapidly as the size of the impossible things.

Probably the intrusion had lasted no more than ten seconds. Five.

There had never been any police investigation later, but people had died there. Hollis could remember seeing a man explosively crushed against one of the walls as an expanding ring punched most of his body right through into the alley.

How could I have forgotten this? he thought now; how could I *not* have forgotten it?

And then he seemed to recall that he had met it—

Only after he choked on warm bourbon did he realize that he had snatched up the bottle. He coughed, and then drank what remained in three heroic gulps.

"It was a hallucination," he said hoarsely, wondering if he was going to be sick. "There would have been cops, ambulances—"

"Yes," said Evian, "if we hadn't stepped in and asserted national security. Pre-emptive jurisdiction. Nerve gas, terrorists, plausible enough. We were in place around the building and had it cordoned off even before the first survivor came out."

"That was me, I think," said Felise with a visible shiver. "And I think you guys *did* stun-gun me, now that I think of it." She gave Hollis a haunted look. "It's only six months ago, for me."

"What," said Evian, leaning forward, "was it?"

"It was silver-and-black balls," snapped Hollis, "and donut-shaped things, that busted the place up and killed people."

"Silver and black," whispered Felise, nodding.

"What did it say?"

Hollis's chest was suddenly cold, and his hands were tingling, and he couldn't take a deep breath.

"Say? It didn't *say* anything! Good God!"

Had it *said* anything?

"It didn't say anything," said Felise, still whispering, "I swear."

"What do you think you . . . *learned* from it?"

"Nothing," said Hollis. "Stay out of pizza parlors."

Evian smiled. "When's the last time you've seen a doctor, got a, a check-up?"

"What, radiation? After thirty-one years?" When Evian just continued to smile at him, Hollis thought about it. "When I was in college, I guess."

"That's a long time."

Hollis shrugged. "All I want to hear from a doctor is, 'If you had come in six months ago we could have done something about this.'"

"You were going to college, but you never went again after that night."

"Sure. What's the use of knowing anything?"

"And you've never married."

"I don't know any women well enough to hate 'em that much."

Felise laughed with apparent delight. "Lyle says the same thing! It was redundant for that thing to crush people *physically*."

Evian went on, "I gather you share Felise's opinion that it was one thing, that appeared as a lot of inconstant shapes?"

Hollis sighed deeply. "You guys actually know something about . . . all that?"

"We've been looking into it for thirty years," said Evian.

"Across thirty years, anyway," said Felise.

Hollis rubbed his face. "Yes," he said, then lowered his hands and looked down at them. "It was one thing. It . . . passed through our, our what, our space, like somebody diving into a pond through a carpet of water lilies. If the diver's arms and legs were spread out, the water lilies might think it was lots of things diving through them." He looked at Felise. "And how have you been, these last six months?"

"I sleep fourteen hours a day," she said brightly. "Lyle's dying of cancer, probably because he wants to. We all have low self of steam."

"What made you come here today?" asked Evian quietly. "We've been monitoring you closely ever since that night. You never came back here before. In fact according to our schedule you weren't supposed to come here today."

Kokolo looked sharply at Evian. "You're saying this is an anomaly? I don't believe it."

"I'll query Chicago in the window, but I'm pretty sure." Evian looked back at Hollis. "So why?"

Hollis realized that he was drunk. Good enough for now, but he'd have to get them to fetch another bottle soon.

"Lately," he began. He frowned at Evian, then went on, "Lately I've been dreaming that what happened here, after the part of that night that I could remember, was that I met myself, finally. And that in fact there isn't anybody else besides me. Like you're all just things I'm imagining because I'm separated from myself now and trying to fill the absence. I guess I came here today to see if I could meet myself again, somehow, so I can be me and stop being this, this flat roadkill."

"Solipsism," said Felise. "I thought that too, for a while, but it was so obvious that my cat didn't think so, didn't think I was the only thing in the universe, that I decided it wasn't true."

"That's hardly an argument against solipsism!" said Hollis, smiling in spite of himself. "Especially to convince somebody else."

"I could show you the cat," she said.

Kokolo touched his ear and cocked his head. "Lyle's here," he said. "I know that was on the schedule, at least. We should go to the area of measurement."

"We think it was an alien," said Evian as he pushed his chair back and stood up. "Not just a, some creature from another planet, you know, but something that ordinarily exists in more dimensions than the four we live in. Or the five we move in when we travel through time."

Felise had paused to listen to him, and she nodded. "We need more liquor," she said. "Lyle can't drink anymore, but it'd mean a lot to him to see other people still fighting the good fight."

One of the two silent men who had stood by the door now opened it and led the way down a carpeted hall to the right; Kokolo and Evian and Scarbee were right behind him, and Hollis and Felise followed more slowly, with the second door-guard coming along last.

The men ahead stopped beside a steel door, and Kokolo pressed his thumb against a tiny glass square above the lever handle.

"This might be disorienting," he said over his shoulder to Hollis, and then he pushed the lever down and opened the door. A puff of chilly air-conditioning ruffled his blond hair.

"It still freaks me," Felise said.

Hollis glimpsed the pool-cue racks mounted on the red-painted walls while the men ahead of him were shuffling into the big room, so he knew what this place was; and when he had stepped through and was standing on the green linoleum floor again for the first time in thirty one years, he was able to look around at the counters and the bar and the restroom doors in the far wall without any expression of surprise. The lights were all on, and the pinball machines glowed.

"We had the place eminent-domained before you even got outside," said Evian.

The picnic tables and pool tables were still scattered and broken across the floor, and black smears on the linoleum were certainly decades-old blood. The holes in the plaster walls were still raw white against the red paint, though there seemed to be a lighted hallway on the other side now, instead of the alley he remembered. The jagged glass of the front window now had white drywall behind it.

Still dizzy from the stun-gun shock—or freshly drunk—Hollis walked carefully across the littered floor, past the spot at the bar where Felise had always sat when he didn't know her name, and stepped behind the bar to the cash register. He punched in "No Sale," and tore off the receipt. The date on it was June 21,1975.

On the shelf below the register was the paperback copy of J. P. Donleavy's *The Ginger Man* that Hollis had been reading at the time. He had never bothered to pick up another copy of the book.

Felise had followed Hollis, and now set up one of the fallen barstools and sat down at what used to be her customary place.

Hollis sniffed. The bar, the whole big room, had no smells at all any more, just a faint chilly whiff of metal.

There was a stack of black bakelite ashtrays on the bar, and he lifted the top one off and pulled the cigarette pack out of his pocket and shook a cigarette onto his lip.

"It's 1975 in here," he called to Scarbee, "check the register tape. Smoking's allowed."

"Five people died here that night," said Evian, who still stood with the others near the door. "Nine survived, though five of them were unresponsively catatonic afterward. And we did try to get responses!

"The four that survived sane—relatively so—were you, Felise, Lyle, and a four-year-old male child. He died three years ago at the age of thirty-two, in a misadventure during a sadomasochistic orgy."

Felise snickered. "Strangled himself. Can I bum a smoke?"

Hollis slid the pack across to her, then clicked his lighter, but apparently rain had got into it. He picked a Firehouse matchbook out of a box on the shelf and struck one of the matches for her, then held it to his own cigarette.

"Where's Lyle?" he asked as he puffed it alight.

"They're bringing him in," said Evian. "Nurses, IV poles."

"You can't cure him in the future?"

Evian shrugged and widened his eyes. "The past is unalterable! Or we thought so, before you showed up just now where you shouldn't be. Lyle is supposed to die a week from hex. But we've debriefed him very thoroughly, many times, over the years, everything he can give us."

Evian, Kokolo, and Scarbee had begun cautiously stepping out into the room.

"We debriefed *you*," Evian went on, "with narcohypnosis, right after getting you and your motorcycle back to your apartment, and several times thereafter—you were encouraged to think these interview periods were alcoholic blackouts—and you appeared to remember nothing. But now that you *have* begun to remember what happened, we may as well see if any input from you can manage to prompt something more from Lyle."

"Set up a query transmission to the Chicago window," said Kokolo. "We need to find out for sure that Hollis's visit today isn't an anomaly— the schedule signals aren't always complete, but Chicago can check it against the big chronology. I'm sure he is scheduled to be here—that's probably why we summon Lyle."

"We don't have much bandwidth left in their allotment for hex, it'll have to be a very tight frequency," said Scarbee, edging hesitantly across the linoleum and looking around wide-eyed. Perhaps he had never been in here before. To Hollis he said, "Time may be infinite, but the time-window of our control of the Fermilab accelerator isn't. It uses up a long piece of that duration to negotiate a transmission. They allot us segments of it. And it's not cheap."

"You guys talk pretty freely to strangers," Hollis said.

Kokolo laughed, for the first time. "Like you might tell somebody, call the L.A. *Times*? We know you don't." To Evian he went on, "Check his resonance, then, you can do that with just the carrier-wave link itself, no need for a message. If his resonance is the same as what we've got recorded, we can be pretty sure he hasn't deviated from his plotted time-line."

Evian nodded to Scarbee. "Get a link-station," he said, and Scarbee hurried, with evident relief, out of the preserved pizza parlor.

Hollis stepped through the doorway onto the cement floor of the kitchen. There wasn't much dust on the counter surfaces—higher air pressure maintained in this whole place, he thought—and the two disks of dough on the work table were clean, though clearly dry as chalk.

Kokolo stepped up on the other side of the counter, and Hollis stopped himself from reflexively reaching for the order pad, which was still right below the telephone.

"We're going to look at your life-line resonance," said Kokolo. "It's a jab in your finger, just enough to hurt."

"You're supposed to die in March of 2008," called Felise cheerfully. "Suicide, while you're on Prozac. At first I thought they said it would be while you had *Kojak* on." She had stepped around behind the bar and was walking toward the kitchen. "I die at forty-eight, but nobody's looked up what year it'll happen in."

"What takes *you* so long?" asked Hollis, turning toward her.

"We both survive it by about thirty years. Subjective years." She smiled at him. "I call that pretty good."

Scarbee had shuffled back into the room, wheeling a cart with something on it that looked like a fax machine. He steered it around the pieces of broken wood.

"We think you survived," said Evian, "weathered the encounter, because you had referents that let you partly roll with the blow; fragment it, deflect it. In your debriefing you talked about Escher prints and Ivan Albright paintings, and William Burroughs, and Ligeti's music. Ionesco, Lovecraft. You were babbling, throwing these things out like cancelled credit cards or phony IDs."

"And I'm still here," said Felise as she lifted one of the hardened dough-disks and let it drop with a clack, "according to these guys, because I was a street girl and a doper. It wasn't a *big* step to get stomped right out of the world." She hiccuped. "Into the cold void between the stars. I wish you still served beer here."

Hollis thought now that he remembered that cold void too. "And Lyle?" said Hollis.

"Lyle was a Christian," Evian said. "Though he stopped being, after that night."

"They figure the four-year-old was abused," said Felise. She rapped the center of one disk with a knuckle, and it broke in a star pattern.

Scarbee had wheeled the device up beside Evian on the other side of the counter. "Give me your hand," he said to Hollis.

Hollis looked at Felise, who nodded. "We've all done it," she said. "It's just a jab, to plug into your nervous system for a second."

"The machine," said Evian, "has a gate in it that's always connected to Fermilab in Chicago in 2015. The time-line of your nervous system is like a long hallway with a mirror at each end—this will tachyonically ring the whole length of it, birth to death, and the resulting, uh, 'note' will show up as a series of lines on a print-out. Interference fringes."

"It's got special cranberry glass rods in it," said Felise helpfully.

"They're colloidal photonic crystals," agreed Scarbee as Hollis reluctantly laid his hand across the order-pickup counter. "Expensive to make. They act as a half-silvered mirror hex, and the machine measures the Cherenkov radiation the tachyons produce as they hit the glass."

He jabbed a needle into Hollis's fingertip. Hollis recoiled and stepped back, blood dripping rapidly from his finger. Felise slid the unbroken dough-disk onto the counter below his hand to catch the drops.

The machine buzzed as a sheet of paper slid out from the front of it, and Scarbee held it up and compared it to a sheet he had brought in. "They don't match," he said flatly. "His time-line has changed."

"Do I die sooner or later than you thought, now?" asked Hollis, idly drawing a question mark in blood on the dough-disk. But he was aware that his heartbeat had speeded up. The faint metal smell of the room had taken on an oily tang, like ozone.

"Let me see those," snapped Kokolo, stepping over and snatching the papers from Scarbee.

"Can't tell from this," said Scarbee quietly to Hollis, though his eyes were on Kokolo. "Just that it's changed."

"Okay," said Kokolo, dropping the papers, "okay, this seems to be an anomaly. Get Chicago on the line, even if you have to use up all the bandwidth we've got left."

Hollis looked past them at several figures who had entered the room. One was in a wheelchair, and another was pushing a wheeled IV stand beside it.

Hollis squinted at the wasted, bald, skeletal figure in the wheelchair. Presumably it was Don Lyle, but there was apparently nothing left of the cheerful young man Hollis had known.

Scarbee finished pushing a series of buttons on the machine, and paused and then pushed them again. "No connection with Chicago," he said. His voice was hoarse.

Kokolo glanced around quickly with no expression, then reached into his silver jacket and yanked out what looked like a black rubber handlebar-grip.

"You can't leave us hex!" shouted Evian even as Kokolo seemed to squeeze the thing.

Nothing happened. Kokolo stared at his own gripping hand—blood had begun to drip from it—and Evian and Scarbee and Felise stared at him with their mouths open, and Lyle's wheelchair continued to roll forward across the floor.

"Your ejection seat didn't fire," said Felise merrily. "The gate's down—no connection with Chicago at all."

Hollis leaned against the counter, nauseated by the sight of his blood and the taste of the bourbon, and he thought he heard faint voices singing "*Everybody Loves Somebody Sometime*" over the speakers mounted above the take-out counter.

He looked at Felise beside him, but saw curls of color rippling across the room, passing over her face: quick views of the broken pool tables, and the corridors outside the room, and even a night-time parking lot lit by sodium lights—the parking lot that was no longer out front.

His face and hands felt hot.

"Get Lyle out of here!" screamed Kokolo. "It's too similar!"

Then the heavy identity was present again like a subsonic roar, and they were all subsumed in its perspective like confetti in a fire.

And rings and spheres appeared in the lamplit air and expanded rapidly, seeming to rush toward Hollis as they grew and rush away from him as they shrank back down to nothing, and more burst into swelling existence everywhere, so that he seemed to be standing in the lanes of some metaphysical freeway.

He had not remembered the noise of it. Tables snapped into pieces and clattered against the walls, masonry broke with booms like cannon shots, and the chilly air whistled around the instantly changing shapes.

The counter he was leaning on crashed backward into the kitchen in a spray of splinters, tumbling him against the base of the oven.

But his frail consciousness was engulfed by the personality that overwhelmed and became his own through its sheer power and age— a person that existed in darkness and infinite emptiness because it had renounced light and everything and everyone that was not itself.

As Hollis's mind imploded it threw up remembered fragments of surrealist paintings, and images from symbolist poems and fairy tales.

This time, though, Hollis's identity wasn't completely assimilated into the thing—he was aware of himself remembering that this had happened before, and so he was able to see it as something separate from himself, though he was sure that his self must at any moment be crushed to oblivion under the infinite psychic weight of the other.

(The cement floor shook under him, and he was remotely aware of screams and crashing.)

This time he was able to perceive that the other was static, unaware of him—rushing through space-time but frozen in one subjective moment of hard-won ruin. And he was aware that it was rushing away from, being powerfully repelled by, something that was its opposite.

Then it was gone and space sprang back into the gap and Hollis was retching and sobbing against the steel foot of the oven, peripherally convinced that the room must be dotted with smoldering fires like a blackened field after a wildfire has passed across it.

A hand was shaking his shoulder, and when he rolled over and looked up at the cracked ceiling he managed to tighten his focus enough to see that someone was bending over him—it was the girl, Felise. Blood was dripping from her nose.

"Out of here," she said. "Lyle too."

Still partly in the perspective of the other, Hollis despised her for her physical presence and the vulgarity of communicating, especially communicating by causing organic membranes to vibrate in air-clotted space—but he struggled to his feet, bracing himself against the oven because he was viscerally aware that he himself was a body standing on a planet that was spinning as it fell through an empty void.

The two of them stumbled out of the kitchen. The bar had been flattened, and they dizzily stepped over the ripped boards and brass strips onto the floor of the dining area. It was difficult for Hollis, and for Felise too, to judge by her hunched posture and short steps, to resist the impulse to crawl on hands and knees.

Evian lay across one of the wrecked picnic tables, his body from the chest down crushed into a new crater in the floor. Scarbee was nowhere to be seen, and Kokolo was standing against the far wall, his lips compressed and his eyes clenched shut.

Lyle's wheelchair was gone, but he lay on his back by the door, and Hollis saw him raise one bloody hand to brush his forehead, chest and shoulders in the sign of the cross, before the last of his blood jetted from the stump where his left leg had been.

Hollis's ears were shrilling as if someone had fired a gun in front of his face.

Supporting each other, Hollis and Felise limped out of the pizza parlor into the unlit corridor, and Hollis noticed that she was carrying the link-station machine Scarbee had brought in.

The lights were all out. Part of the wall had been blown in plaster chunks across the corridor, and in the dimness Hollis saw three motionless bodies on the carpet, two of which might have been alive.

"Front door," said Felise hoarsely, stumbling over the pieces of plaster as she led Hollis toward relative brightness ahead.

"My bike," said Hollis. "Away from here."

Felise shook her head. "They'll be out front." She coughed and spat. "Again. Cordoned off again. Stun-guns."

But they both continued toward the gray daylight of the front door, and when Hollis had pushed it open they were both panting as they stepped out onto the breezy pavement, as if they had been holding their breaths.

The parking lot under the overcast sky was empty except for Kokolo's car and Hollis's motorcycle. Cars rushed past on Anaheim Boulevard, but none turned into the lot.

"A bigger area," said Felise, "this time. They'll be closing in any moment."

But Hollis crossed to his motorcycle and swung one leg over it. The key was still in the ignition. He switched it on and tromped on the kick-starter, and the engine sputtered into life. He pushed the kickstand up with his foot and wheeled the bike around to face the street.

"Come on," he called, and Felise, still carrying the steel box, shrugged and walked carefully over to the bike.

"There's no passenger footpegs," she said.

"They fell off," he panted, "a long time ago. Hook your feet over my legs."

She climbed on and folded her legs around him with her feet on the gas tank, clutching him with her hands linked over his chest and the box between his back and her stomach.

He clicked the bike into gear and let the clutch out, and it surged forward into a right turn onto the street.

"How far?" he called over his shoulder as the cold wind ruffled his wet hair.

"Another block or two," she said, and when the bike had roared and bounced through two green-light intersections, she called, "Pull over somewhere."

Hollis downshifted and leaned the bike into a wide supermarket parking lot, and when he had braked it to a halt Felise pushed herself off over the back, hopping on the blacktop to keep her balance while holding the metal box.

"They don't have a cordon," she said. "They're not hex—not here, now." When Hollis got off the bike too and stretched, she laid the box on the frame plate where the seat should have been and pushed buttons on it. "Nothing," she said. "No link to Chicago hex either."

"Maybe the battery's dead," said Hollis.

"The battery is Fermilab in 2015. *That* battery's dead. I better call the New York office." She pulled an ordinary cell phone out of her shirt pocket and tapped in a number. After a moment she said, "Felise, from the field team in Anaheim. I can't raise Chicago. The gate in the link-station seems to be dead." For several seconds she listened, then said, "Right," and closed the phone.

She was frowning. "They say they've lost the link too. But *they* weren't in this locus, for sure." She blinked at Hollis. "No contact here or in New York, not even the carrier-wave signal, no team from the future to move in on the disaster at the Anaheim office—the whole thing's broken down."

For several seconds neither of them spoke, and people parked cars and got out of them to walk toward the supermarket.

Hollis touched his face, and it stung. "Sunburn again," he said.

"Yeah," she said absently, staring at the inert link-station box, "me too."

"The thing," Hollis said, "that passed through—I could perceive more about it this time."

She nodded. "They never were able to change the past, though it's changed now—they had no notes on their charts of anything like this. God knows when you and I die, now. I bet they can't jump at all anymore—I bet we're all left high and dry where we are, now. Some of us in interrupted segments, out of sequence."

She looked around the parking lot as if still hoping a team from the future might come rushing up to debrief them. None did.

"It wasn't . . . objective," Hollis went on awkwardly. "This time I could tell that I *wasn't* it, and what it let us see was its own chosen situation, not—maybe not—reality. God help us."

"They pushed it too hard," she said sadly, "drilling five-dimensional paths through the solid continuum to jump from point to point of our four-dimensions. Something too heavy rolled over it and it all fell down, like the Tower of Babel. The hour of Babel."

"The thing," he said, "was an opposite of something else, something that's apparently stronger than it, that expelled it."

Felise finally looked at him in exasperation. "Yes, it was a fallen angel, falling at some speed-of-light through space-time, in dimensions that make all this—" She waved at the store and the street and the sky, "—look like figures on a comic-book page. It tore right through our pages, punching one hole that showed up twice in our continuity. Looks like more than one, but it's one."

"Could it have been . . . *wrong?*" He gave her a twitchy, uncertain smile. "It can't have been *wrong,* can it? After all this time?"

"I don't know. I've spent six months—you've spent thirty-one years!—carrying its perspective." She blinked at him. "What do you suppose the world is really like?"

"I—have no idea."

She shivered. "We thought it was true, didn't we?"

"Or attractive." He climbed back on the idling bike and raised his eyebrows, though it made his forehead sting. "It's still attractive." With his right hand he twisted the throttle, gunning the engine. "Should we get moving?"

"Sure. I think the rain's passed." She carelessly pushed the link-station box off onto the asphalt and climbed on behind him again. "Where to?"

He rubbed his left hand carefully over his face and sighed. Then he laughed weakly. "I think I'd like to see your cat."

❖ AUTHOR'S NOTE ❖

When I was working at a place called Firehouse Pizza in the mid-'70s, there was a homeless-looking girl who would come in on slow nights and sit at the far end of the bar, where I would, as if by accident, set trays of half-finished pizzas on their way to the trash cans and sinks in the back room, and eventually she would be gone and the trays would be empty. I don't think she and I ever spoke, beyond her first question about what became of the pizzas left unfinished by customers, and I've wanted to use her in a story ever since.

Firehouse Pizza was exactly how and where I describe it here, and, as in the story, the place where it once stood is now some sort of office building. So for the story I resurrected the old motorcycle I was riding in those days and went back to see what had become of the place, and of that girl. I wound up wrecking the place, but at least I got to talk to her, finally.

⊰ WHERE THEY ARE HID ⊱

WHEN HE STEPPED out of the doorway and sniffed the warm air, he had a feeling that he'd finally finished the reluctant, years-long, trial-and-error journey—and he was sure of it when, after squinting around for a couple of moments, he saw the woman pushing the baby carriage along the sidewalk. And though now that it was all over he felt like staring in horror, or crying, or just running away, he forced himself to do nothing more than pat the pockets of his coat and smile casually as he strolled up to her. He said good afternoon and peered into the carriage.

He remarked on what a nice-looking son she had, and the mother gave him a smile, but then let it relax back into her habitual bored pout when it became clear that the man really had stopped only to admire the baby. The man pulled a pair of glasses out of his coat pocket, and when a wad of bills tumbled to the sidewalk the young mother darted around to the front of the carriage, recovered the money, and handed nearly all of it back to him.

He had been leaning over the carriage, doing something with the baby's bottle, and when the mother handed him the bills he thanked her with as good a show of surprise and sincerity as he could muster.

The woman nodded and began pushing the carriage on down the sidewalk. Neither she, nor, probably, the baby, had noticed that the stranger had switched bottles. Certainly neither of them was aware of the paper he'd tucked under the blanket.

When the man turned away, his face stiff with grief and fear, he let his left hand fall out from under his coat, and he was gripping the snatched baby bottle so tightly that his knuckles were white.

Just from habit—for there was certainly no need to look sharp for the visitor he was expecting—the secret ruler of the world glanced at himself in the full-length closet door mirror, and then he leaned forward and pressed a lever on his desktop intercom.

The lever broke right off. "Damn it," he muttered, glancing at his watch and pushing his chair back to stand up. The casters emitted a loud squeal, and his secretary was already looking up when he yanked the connecting door open.

"No calls or visitors for the next fifteen minutes," he said distinctly.

The girl's eyebrows went up. "But Mr. Stanwell, I thought you were having lunch with the Trotsky Youth rep."

"That's at eleven," said Stanwell irritably. "It's only a quarter after ten now."

"So you want . . . what was it? A sno-cone and ribs, did you say? And—"

"I said *no calls or visitors. For the next fifteen minutes.* For God's sake. Now repeat that back to me."

She managed to, despite the stutter that seemed to be fashionable or epidemic or something these days, and he went back into his office and crossed to the window.

"Good news about something," he whispered, looking out across the Santa Ana business district and trying to notice the trucks zooming efficiently past on Main Street rather than the work crew that was somehow still finding something to fool with under the ripped-up pavement of Civic Center Drive. "The labor unions deciding to rejoin us at last, employment up," he was whispering with his eyes shut now, "the colors getting brighter again, the hallucinations stop—bring me good news about *something.*"

When the familiar *thump* jarred him and rattled the window he opened his eyes and turned around.

There was a man standing on the other side of the desk now, and though the newcomer was dressed in blue jeans and a flannel shirt with a heavy coat over his arm, and kept alternately looking at and sucking on a cut thumb, he was otherwise an identical twin to Stanwell.

"Glad to see you," said Stanwell. "We okay? What happened to the thumb?"

The other man waved impatiently. "Little cut," he said. "I'd explain what I did, but you'd probably be tempted to fix it so it wouldn't happen."

Stanwell frowned. "You know I'm always careful to—"

"Sure. Look, I'm not really in the mood to stay back here very long, you know? I'm damn busy, and of course I've been through this conversation once before."

Stanwell looked hurt, but asked, "Anything you'd like me to change? Anything I should buy, anybody to—"

"Nope," said his double. "Just hang in there. We're doing fine."

Stanwell was frowning as he turned to the liquor cabinet and reached down a bottle of Stolichnaya. "I gather," he said a little stiffly, "that something goes right, and you're afraid that if I know about it in advance I'll fumble the ball." He tonged ice cubes into two glasses and poured vodka over them. "Well, if genuine spontaneity is absolutely necessary, I understand. But I'd like at least *some* answers." He turned and held one glass out toward the visitor. "For example, in what direction do Poland and Mexico—"

"No, thank you, we've given up drink. And I've got to go. Just wanted to show you we're okay."

"What, already?" asked Stanwell, disconcerted. "But usually we stay—"

"Not this time, old buddy," said the double, who was obviously not enjoying the conversation. He shut his eyes—then opened them and hesitantly held out his right hand. "I wish," he said quietly as the mystified Stanwell took it, "that we could have got to know each other."

Abruptly the visitor disappeared, and Stanwell stumbled forward, his ears ringing and his wrist almost sprained from the sudden, close implosion of air. He flexed his fingers ruefully.

"You okay, Mr. Stanwell?" came his secretary's call from beyond the closed door.

"Yes," he shouted. "Don't interrupt." Some soundproof door, he thought bitterly.

It was his turn now to reassure the next man back, but he sat down first and took a long sip of the vodka. What can I tell him? he wondered helplessly. Well of course I'll *tell* him whatever it was that I *heard* a year ago; but the next-up man then sure looked more confident than I feel now.

He glanced at the neat stack of typed pages on the bookshelf, and he wished he could still read his unfinished autobiography and derive inspiration and that sense of high purpose from it; but during the last year it had seemed to him that the margins were wider than he remembered, and that the text had become a little murky and ambiguous, and that all the moving or funny or tragic anecdotes had had the pith leached out of them.

Though he modestly intended that the book should be published after his death, he had put together a selection of accompanying photographs, and had even commissioned a painting for the cover. He swivelled his chair around now so that he faced the big canvas that occupied most of one wall.

It he still liked. It was an impressionist view of a tree, with an infant—looking almost embarrassingly Christ-child-like—perched in the high branches. Years ago Stanwell had tried to locate the very tree in which he'd been mysteriously found in 1950, but he learned that they'd built the Pasadena Freeway right over the field in which the tree had stood. He'd considered going back and making them build the damn freeway along a different route, in case subsequent generations might want to make a shrine or something around the tree, but he'd decided that such a move would be a needlessly egotistical strain on the fabric—and besides, the real tree probably hadn't looked half so imposing as this painted one.

He drained the drink and stood up. Hell, he thought, take the long view. What if we haven't made a lot of progress *this* year? The man ahead had seemed busy, if rude, and things have been getting steadily better ever since I engineered Roosevelt's death to occur in '44 instead of '45, so that it was Henry Wallace, not Harry Truman, who inherited the presidency. Stanwell smiled out the window at the multitudes below. Hardly any of you know who I am, he thought, and not one of you knows my real function, but I prevented the bomb and Korea and Vietnam and Nixon for you. I don't look for thanks—how could you thank me for deflecting calamities you never heard of?—I do it only so that we may all have a better world to live in. Mine is a . . . where did I once read this phrase? . . . a high and lonely destiny.

Feeling confident enough now to go and give encouragement to the next man back, he stepped into the middle of the room, frowned for a moment in concentration, and then disappeared.

The implosion of air cracked the window and snatched the top few pages of his autobiography off the stack; they whirled to the floor, and one of them hid the impression his shoes had left in the carpet.

The telephone was still ringing when Keith Bondier blinked back into awareness of his surroundings.

Should have known better than to try and answer it, he thought groggily as he rolled over on the kitchen floor. You knew today was the day you can *count* on the fainting fits—every July first, at exactly fifteen minutes after ten, and then another one a while later. Usually, though, the second fit happens at least half an hour after the first one. I really thought I could get to the phone and then back to bed before it hit.

His kneecaps were resonating with pain and his shoulder throbbed, but his head only stung a little above one ear, so it couldn't have been a bad fall.

The phone was still ringing, though, so he struggled wincingly to his feet and fumbled the receiver off the hook. "*Ah.* Yeah?"

"Keith? You okay?"

"Yeah yeah, fine. Hi Margie. What's up?"

"Shopping. Errands. You want to come along?"

He smiled, his aches forgotten. "Sure, and I just got my disability check, so I can buy us lunch."

"Oh, I'll pay my half."

"No, Marge, you always have to drive."

"Keith, as soon as they get you on the right medication you'll be able to get a license—then I'll make you drive all the time. Today we'll go Dutch."

"Nah, I'll get it," he said hastily. "Let me, while I've got a fresh check." He figured that paying for her lunch would make it a real *date*, rather than just two friends out wandering around. "When can you get here?"

"Hm? Oh, five minutes. I'm ready to go."

"Great. See you soon."

After he hung up the phone he sat down and rubbed his knees as he looked around his apartment. The place looks neat enough, he thought. Only a few clothes on the floor. If I straighten it up, she'd be able to tell, and it'd put her on guard. Right. Got to strive to make it look spontaneous. I'd better brush my teeth, though, for the old breath's sake.

Halfway to the bathroom he stopped, a pained expression on his face, for once again he had caught a tart-sweet whiff of garbage. He was sure it was just another olfactory hallucination, that visitors couldn't smell it, but it was hardly the sort of thing to get him in the mood to try and seduce Margie; and while the smell was—just barely!—tolerable, he couldn't say the same for the sort of auditory and visual hallucinations that occasionally followed. He fervently hoped this wasn't going to be one of his bad days.

But just as he was squeezing a dab of toothpaste onto his toothbrush he heard a hoarse voice cry, "You better put all that trash back in them barrels, lady!"—and though it sounded as though the man who'd yelled was standing right beside him, the cry had an unconfined sound, as if it had occurred outdoors.

The sudden voice had startled Bondier, and the curl of toothpaste had wound up on the mirror. He swore under his breath and steeled himself against any further intrusions, and he managed to get a blob of toothpaste onto the brush in spite of an old woman's voice snarling, "Screw yaself, I'm on public propitty," as he lifted his hand.

He resolutely brushed his teeth, then spat and rinsed his mouth. It occurred to him that he ought to shave, and during the task he was subjected to no further phantom noises except a few bangs and clatters, which he ignored.

The doorbell rang just as he'd sat down and got a cigarette lit, which pleased him, for he thought he looked less like an invalid when he was smoking. "Come on in, Marge, it's not locked."

The door opened and Margie bustled inside. She was a bit older than Bondier, but her pale skin, wool skirt, eye-magnifying glasses and brown hair—pulled functionally back in a bun—made her seem younger, or at least made the question of her age somehow irrelevant. Her head and hands and feet were just perceptibly bigger than scale, and sometimes when he was in a bad mood he thought she looked like one of those human-body drawings that exaggerated the bits that had greater nerve sensitivity.

"Ready to go?" she asked, brightly cheerful as always.

Bondier could hardly hear her over the new hallucinatory noise, a measured series of sharp metallic crunchings, as if someone was methodically stomping a line of flimsy toy cars. "Sure," he said, trying not to raise his voice. "But you just got here—sit down. Can I get you a cup of coffee?"

"Lady, you can't flatten 'em here, my tenants gotta park here," rasped the man's voice again, and Bondier had missed Margie's answer.

"What?"

"I said no thanks, let's go before the rain starts." Margie cocked her head and blinked at him. "You sure you're all right?"

"Well," said Bondier, unable to think of any other way to make her alight, "I did have one of my blackouts a few minutes ago. A couple of 'em, actually."

He heard a car start up, sounding like it was right in the room with them, and he was wearily glad that Margie didn't share his hallucinations, for the following gust of engine fumes would have driven her out of the apartment if she'd been able to smell them. He stubbed out his cigarette in a coffee cup.

"Oh, you poor thing," Margie said with sudden concern, shutting the door and crossing to join him on the couch. "Did you fall?"

"Stupid old bitch," the man's voice growled.

"Just a . . . sort of tumble," said Bondier. He draped an arm around her shoulder. "I'm still a little dizzy, though." Start, rain, he thought. Start hard.

Trying not to seem either hesitant or hurried, he leaned over to kiss her.

A sharp but silent flash in the room made him jerk around involuntarily—and then it took all his control not to yell in surprise, for his kitchen was gone, and his living room now opened onto a brightly sunlit parking lot, and, standing only a few yards away from him, facing away toward the cars, was a fat old man in overalls who was meditatively scratching his rear end.

Oh, God, it's bigger and vivider than my *apartment*, than *I* am, thought Bondier shrilly; but it'll go away. I'm getting worse, but it *will go away*—if I ignore it, don't acknowledge it, really act as if it's not—intolerably!—there.

He turned back to Margie, squinting against the impossible glare and hoping his voice wouldn't quaver when he apologized for having jumped, but she was leaning back against the couch-arm, with her eyes closed, and really didn't seem to have noticed. Her lips were open and working, and at first he thought she was somewhat grotesquely inviting a kiss, but then he saw that her arms were extended to form a ring, as though she was in the *process* of kissing someone, someone invisible.

And a moment later he actually shrieked, for he had looked down and seen that there was a hole that extended across her belly and part of the couch, and through the hole he could clearly see a trash can full of old milk cartons and sour cream tubs and crumpled bags from some takeout restaurant he'd never heard of called McDonald's.

He was on his feet, gagging and near panic.

The front end of his apartment, he noted numbly, not only still showed a gray day behind the blinds, but also wasn't even a bit lighted by the—yes, it was all still there—bright sunlight on the other side of the room.

"I'm sorry, Marge," he said in a constricted voice as he stared hard at the room's normal half. "I think I took more of a knock than I realized. Let's get some fresh air, okay?"

There was no answer, so he forced himself to turn around.

On the couch—between Bondier and the fat man in overalls, who was still scratching his rear end—Margie was now reclining on her back, making soft sounds of protest but still working her mouth and caressing empty air. As Bondier watched, her blouse rippled and the top button slowly undid itself.

"*Marge*," he said loudly, fear putting a whining tone in his voice.

She didn't hear him.

"*Marge!*" he shouted, suddenly so dizzy that he grabbed the arm of a chair in case he had another blackout.

The old man stopped scratching and turned around to stare unseeingly in Bondier's direction. "Who's that?" he called.

"*Goddamn it, Marge, can't you hear me?*" screamed Bondier.

"Hey, keep it down, there," said the old man. "Where are you, anyway?"

The old man started forward, and Bondier's nerve broke; he whirled around, snatched open his front door and bolted down the walkway toward the street. A cat scampered out of his path and ran straight up a wooden fence.

He desperately wished there was someone he could talk to, someone who was close enough to him to listen without making judgments about his sanity. He had a few friends, but none of them would welcome this kind of confidence.

Family, he thought, that's what I wish I had right now, people who would have known me since I was a baby. A brother to share this with, a mother on whose lap to tearfully dump it all. Of course I *do* have a mother—somewhere, if she hasn't died by now.

He smiled bitterly at the thought. He'd never known his mother, hadn't even seen her since the court took him away from her when he was still a baby, but she didn't seem to have been the sort of woman who could be bothered with comforting an upset son. She almost certainly *had* thrown his twin brother off that overpass onto the Pasadena Freeway in 1954, as several witnesses had attested; and if the little corpse hadn't evidently been carried right away by one of the passing vehicles, she'd have had to put up with the inconvenience of a murder trial . . . and she hadn't made even a token protest when the authorities subsequently relieved her of the remaining member of the pair.

Sure, he told himself, trying desperately to be adult and jocularly independent about it. Look *her* up. *That'd* make you feel better. Jesus.

He'd slowed to a walk, and now stopped and turned to look at his apartment, two blocks back. It looked the same as it always did, a pair of windows in the long rust-streaked building, and Margie's battered old Volkswagen sat as placidly as ever by the curb. A young man had ducked behind a tree across the street, probably—knowing this neighborhood—to take a piss.

It occurred to him that the cars in the hallucinated parking lot had all been models he'd never seen. They'd been littler, and rounder.

He took several deep breaths. It must have been an aftereffect of the two blackouts, he thought. This was the worst yet, but it seems to be over. I ought to head back.

But he decided to clear his head with some brisk walking and fresh air first, and let the chilly breeze brush even the memory of the garbage-reek out of his hair. He walked randomly for ten minutes, up this alley and down that street, and his heartbeat was nearly back to normal, his mouth beginning to lose the dry taste of unreasoning fear, when he turned onto Main Street, aiming to get a beer at Trader Joe's, and to hell with the doctor's warnings about drinking while on medication. Some medication it had turned out to be.

He heard brakes and a sudden metallic crunch a couple of blocks behind him, and when he turned he saw that a delivery van had backed into a parked car—several cardboard boxes toppled out and split open, and cigarette cartons spilled into the gutter. He started back, hoping to be first among the mob that would quickly be gathering to snatch them up, but then he saw the thing striding massively down the sidewalk toward him.

Keeping his face very stiff so as not to let his aides know that something was wrong, Stanwell walked steadily from the cab to the door of the Corday Hotel.

The hardest part was to keep from alternately narrowing and unnarrowing his eyes as the hallucination of a bright, sunny day flashed on and off every few seconds. It was easier when he'd got inside Andre's, the ground-floor restaurant, and been shown to a table, for though the room kept changing from an elegant restaurant to a shabby laundromat and back again, as abruptly as if the restaurant scene was a photograph someone kept shoving in his face and then yanking away, he could lean back and shut his eyes. At least the feel of his chair, and the tablecloth under his hands, were steady.

"You're certain you're all right, sir?"

Stanwell nodded without opening his eyes. "Gribbin be here soon?"

"That's what his man said on the phone, sir. Of course, you know how the subways are. But if you feel at all bad, it'd be easy to—"

"I'm fine, damn it," Stanwell snapped, his eyes still shut. "Tired, is all."

He thought, if only that son-of-a-bitch, year-older version of me could have said whether or not these damned hallucinations have let up by his time! Or if only I could circumvent him, break the now-barrier: travel farther into the future than the somehow-constant now-line, which moves forward only at the agonizingly slow rate of a day per day.

He sighed, opened his eyes long enough for the restaurant to appear, and grabbed his water glass.

I suppose, he thought as he took a sip and replaced the glass by touch, that if an ordinary person, condemned, as each of them is, to be a steadily moving point on the time chart, unable to edge even one second further ahead or back than the instant of now—if one of them could know of my capabilities, he'd probably think I had incalculable freedom . . . the fool.

I guess I can see why there is the now-barrier—it's the freshly woven edge of the fabric, beyond which is only emptiness and God's moving shuttle—or uncollapsed probability waves—but what's the problem with the *other* direction? Why in hell can't I jump forward again from any point further back than 1953?

Thank God, he thought with a shiver, I didn't have to jump any further back than 1943 to learn that. *That* was a horrible decade for me, unable to jump and concluding that the talent had been lost; having to get jobs and apartments, and simply *live* my way ploddingly up the years, until mid-1953 finally rolled around again, and I found the talent had been restored, and I could jump up to *now*, which had been . . . what, 1975 then.

And why in hell should it be the case that I can only do it if I'm in—of all places—downtown Santa Ana, California? It's as if there's some kind of psychic power-station locally.

"Ah, I see Gribbin coming up the steps now, sir," said one of his aides, and Stanwell ventured to open his eyes.

The hallucinatory tug-of-war seemed to have been settled in favor of the restaurant, he noted with relief, and he beckoned to the drink steward. Being from New York, Stanwell reasoned, Gribbin might like to take the opportunity to try some tequila—just as whenever I'm back east I always make it a point to get hold of some real Scotch.

A few moments after Stanwell had placed the drinks order, Gribbin's driver walked up to the table and pulled out a chair, and then after a pause pushed it in again.

"Where's Mr. Gribbin?" Stanwell asked him.

The man didn't answer.

"Excuse me, I asked you where Mr. Gribbin is."

The man on Stanwell's right leaned forward and shook hands with the empty air over the ashtray. "And I'm Bob Atkins, Mr. Gribbin," he said respectfully

The drink steward returned and set down two glasses of tequila, one in front of Stanwell and one at the empty place across the table. "I trust you'll enjoy that, sir," said the steward to the empty chair.

✣ ✣ ✣

The thing was no taller than Bondier, but it was so broad—from its shopping-cart shoulders to its fringed, elephantine feet—that it seemed to loom over him as it advanced up the street, filling the sidewalk and spinning heedless pedestrians out of its way. Its mouth was a wide square hole, studded with bits of jagged metal, and its eyes were two big tin pie-plates, with riddlings of tiny holes at their centers like the holes boys punch into jar lids to let captive insects breathe; but the eyes were spinning back and forth on the front of the rubbish head, and a harsh roaring was echoing out of the mouth.

It was rushing at him fast, and the pure, idiot ferocity that glared like tropical sunlight off of the blunt face made Bondier cry out in shock and cringe back against the wall.

It slid to a halt, dust and smoke bursting from its substance and whirling away in spirals, and then it turned its terrible head toward him, and for the first time he realized that it was composed of trash. Bags and cans and old bits of cloth heaved as it flexed itself, and then a long, shapeless limb had lashed out and a paw made of coat hangers and branches had grabbed Bondier under the chin and was crushing him against the wall.

Bondier managed to force out a choked scream, but the people on the sidewalk were oblivious of both the monster and him; even as he sobbed and tore uselessly at the garbage cable that had him pinned, several pedestrians at once collided with the trash-creature's back, then expressionlessly righted themselves and resumed their walking.

The thing's steady roaring became recognizable as many voices only when all of them began to speak in unison; suddenly it was a senilely shrill babble that came rasping out of the big hole in the face, and Bondier was able to catch words: "*. . . see who pays the piper now, Stanwell, you can dish it out, all right, but now we'll see . . . throat out, rip his balls off, right here in front of God'n'everybody . . . but wait a minute, any of you remember, we saw him, just a minute ago, at that restaurant, that André's fency-shmency . . . back the street . . . yeah . . . this ain't him, this is got no gray hair—young, too young, this boy.*"

For a moment the wires and branches pressed a little less tightly against Bondier's larynx, and he got his legs braced for a breakaway and mad sprint, but before he could choose his moment the inhuman grip tightened again, so tight this time that his breath whistled in his throat and his vision started to darken.

"*It's the* twin, *then, we* knew *there was a twin . . . maybe if we kill the twin, Stanwell will die—and then we can have our real lives!*"

And then, without releasing his throat, it had crowded up to the wall and was embracing him, hugging him to its greasy, crumbling chest, and when he opened his mouth to scream again an oil-soaked rag wormed in between his jaws; cigarette butts and old straws had found his nostrils and were burrowing up into his head, and cords and lengths of cloth looped around his arms and legs and began pulling them upward and inward. Pressed rib-crackingly hard against the wall, he was simultaneously being folded up into a fetal position and smothered.

More bits of trash were forcing their way into his nose and mouth—he coughed gaggingly, but only wound up letting them get further in; they were well down his throat by now, with more packing themselves in every second. Then there was a sharp pain in his side, and instantly afterward a feeling of heat and running wetness, and he realized that some jagged component of the thing had stabbed him, and that the garbagey member was about to begin probing the interior of his abdomen.

It galvanized him. He gave one last, mighty convulsion—but it wasn't a physical one, and he felt the whole world jump with him.

In an instant the thing was gone, every bit of it, and he had fallen forward hard onto his hands and knees, and he was retching and coughing up all kinds of litter onto the sidewalk. After a few moments he was able to breathe, and when he stopped whooping he sat up and pulled up his shirt—the cut in his side wasn't bleeding too badly, and didn't look nearly as deep as it had felt. He folded his handkerchief into a pad and unlooped his belt to rebuckle it across his stomach, pressing the handkerchief against the cut, and then he tucked in his shirt. Finally he stood up, shakily, grinning in embarrassment at the people near him, but they weren't looking at him, just as they hadn't seemed to be able to see the trash-thing.

He hurried away, and all he permitted himself to think about on the way back to his apartment was how he was going to crawl into bed and pull the covers over his head . . . and then see the doctor tomorrow morning and request, demand, some vastly more potent medication. He assured himself that the trash monster had just been one more hallucination . . . and that probably the bruise on his throat and the cut in his side were imaginary too.

He was even beginning to relax as he rounded the last corner and saw his apartment—and Margie's car, still! Bless her—ahead. But then he saw his front door yanked open, and a young man came running out, scaring a cat out of his path, and Bondier realized he wasn't clear of it yet, for the obviously terrified young man sprinting up the sidewalk on the other side of the street was himself.

Okay, he told himself tensely, you're still in it, it's the same hallucination. It's even got a certain consistency—that's probably the twin that that monster referred to. See? It's just *one* of your fits, not even several. You're probably still on the couch, actually. Don't start crying.

But the air felt too cold, and the street was too normally wide, and the building was at once too detailed and too insignificant-looking for him to believe that this was a hallucination. He cowered behind a tree and watched while the young man paused and looked back.

Then he remembered the cat that had run out of his path . . . and with the irrational certainty of real nightmares he was sure he knew what the frightened young man was thinking at this moment: *Too bad I don't have a family, ought to go back, no, bit of a walk first, clear my head, and then maybe swing by Trader Joe's for a beer and who's that guy taking a piss behind the tree across the street there?*

When the other Bondier had rounded the corner, Bondier stepped out from behind the tree. A crazy thought had come to him, so crazy that it was in itself pretty good evidence that he was in some kind of dream state.

That last convulsion of mine, he thought, when the trash-creature was about to choke me or rip out my entrails—which way did I jump? The thing wasn't even around afterward. Could I have . . . *jumped back?*

In which corner of the compass is ago?

He glanced at his watch. Five minutes to eleven. He wondered if that other Bondier's watch read about twenty of. He walked slowly back to the apartment and pushed open the door. Marge was still on the couch, and he was relieved to see that the kitchen was restored, but the very first thing he glanced at was the clock over the oven.

It read 10:41.

If it was right, he had gained fifteen minutes on the world.

"All *along*," Margie said, evidently emphasizing some point she'd made in the minute or two when neither of him had been there. She was wrapped up in the tapestry he covered the threadbare couch with, and though her glasses were off she was staring at the chair he usually sat in. He crossed to it, stepping over her discarded skirt and blouse and underwear, and sat down.

Now she was staring right at him, and it was suddenly much harder to suppose that this scene was automatic, and would continue whether he stayed or not.

"Hi, Marge," he said helplessly as he unbuttoned his blood-spotted shirt. "The universe or me—one of us is real sick."

"Oh *don't* tell me that," she groaned, tossing her head. He noticed that without glasses her eyes were smaller and seemed to have too much white skin around them. "You don't mean it," she went on, "you're just . . . throwing that to me, the way you'd throw a dog a bone to make it stop bothering you."

He tossed the bloody shirt onto the floor, stood up and ducked into the narrow bathroom, and reappeared with a glass bottle of Bactine. He splashed some onto his reddening handkerchief-bandage and put the bottle down. "Listen, Marge," he said, leaning forward and forcing his voice to come out in a reasonable tone, "can you hear me?"

She didn't answer.

"Well," he went on, picking up a comparatively clean shirt from the floor, "I saw a thing today, walking around like a human, but it was entirely . . . made out of *trash*, I swear, it—was just *made out of trash*." He laughed hollowly as he buttoned the fresh shirt. "And this trash-thing could talk. It said I was—some kind of twin—of some guy they're afraid of. I should have said it talks in lots of voices, shouldn't I? I can't tell this right. But these voices said that this twin is right now having lunch at Andre's. That's the posh place in the Corday." He sat down again so that when she talked it would be toward him.

"You knew I wasn't ready for this kind of thing," said Margie unhappily. "Just friends, we agreed."

"Jesus, Marge, I'll tell you the truth, it's hard for me to feel . . . *to blame* about whatever's been going on here, you know? But listen, Marge, I *did* have a twin. I never told you about this, but I did. My mother pitched him off a pedestrian overpass onto the Pasadena Freeway in '54, when he and I were both a year old. She only wanted to keep *me*, though they took me away from her too. But—this just occurred to me, and you're gonna think I'm really nuts—what if my one-year-old brother's reaction to total terror was the same as what I right now suspect mine is? To jump backward in time? Then maybe he *isn't* dead. Maybe in mid-fall he jumped back, maybe all the way to a time before the freeway was built, and wound up in a field somewhere, and was found alive. He'd never know he had a twin brother."

Margie had been muttering for the last several seconds, and when he paused he heard her saying, ". . . as a free lunch, and there has to be *commitment,* and I frankly—(sniff)—don't think you're capable of that."

"You're probably right, Marge, though I'll bet I wind up committed." The joke, muffled by the stained carpet and drapes, sounded dead even to him. "You know what I get lately when I'm walking down the street? Claustrophobia. I feel like I'm in a diorama, you know, like the statues of Neanderthals in the museum, I'm afraid I'll notice that the sun's a light bulb, and my buddies are just painted statues, and the sky's got corners."

In spite of his efforts his voice had got whimpery, and he took a few deep breaths.

Suddenly Margie looked up, and he gathered that he'd been supposed to get to his feet. He stayed where he was.

"No, don't touch me," Margie cried, shoving herself backward across the couch and getting one bare foot caught in a hole in the fabric.

"I'm just sitting here, Margie," he said, bleakly sure that no one in the universe could hear him.

"You do?" she quavered now, looking up toward the ceiling light. "Really, Keith? It isn't just a . . . sop to my pride? You *do* love me?"

"*I* don't know, Marge," said Bondier unhappily, still in his chair. "I don't know if I'm even—"

"Oh, Keith, I love you too," she whispered, and let the tapestry fall from her white shoulders.

He felt as though cold water had been splashed in his face. The breath caught in his throat, and all at once he was ashamed of himself; of course it had all been hallucinations—this was *Margerie,* not some figure from a nightmare, and he *did* love her.

He unbent himself out of the chair and fitted himself beside her on the couch, kissing her as he had always meant to, running his trembling, bloodstained hands over her bare breasts . . . but she was stiff, and though her lips were obviously responding, they weren't responding to *him*, and he broke free of the off-center embrace and stood up, panting with renewed fear.

She rocked over onto her back, and Bondier found himself almost able to gauge the actions of her invisible partner by her motions. What if he should begin to see a cloudy figure there—and what if it were to look up at him?

Again he ran out of the apartment, and again the pavements and buildings were too clear for him to believe that they weren't real. He began walking, and the only destination he could think of was the restaurant where, maybe, his twin was. He didn't want to think, so he walked faster instead, and when he sped up he discovered that he'd been correct when he'd thought the passersby couldn't see him. Okay, that makes sense, he told himself desperately—keep the fear at arm's length, boy. Of course they can't see you, you're out of your slot, you're fifteen minutes away from where you're supposed to be at this moment.

But even before I time-jumped, he thought, Margie couldn't see or hear me. She was kissing the nonexistent me even *before*.

There were young women in the crowds on Main Street, office workers out for lunch, and he found himself looking at them speculatively—until he remembered that the many-voiced garbage-giant might still be able to see him, and he couldn't know which window or rooftop or trash can it might be peering at him from, preparing to rush at him again.

The thought started him moving again, and when he tried to imagine what Margie might be up to by this time, all alone back in his shabby apartment, he began to hurry toward the Hotel Corday.

Moving through the blind, mechanical crowd required a specialized pace that seemed similar to both broken-field running and bullfighting cape-work; and just as Bondier was beginning to get accustomed to the lateral hops and quick backtracking and the occasional necessity of a close whirl around a straight-oncoming pedestrian, a flash of light blinded him.

The light stayed on, and he winced and braced himself for the first collision, determined at least not to fall under the inexorable feet—but nothing touched him, and the air was warmer suddenly, and smelled fresher, and after a few seconds he squintingly looked up.

It was a bright summer day with a few clouds sailing past

unbelievably high overhead, and though the sidewalk wasn't as crowded now, a number of people—all of whom seemed more three-dimensional than the people he'd been dodging moments ago—were staring at him in surprise.

"Where'd you drop from, son?" one man wonderingly inquired, and Bondier had just opened his mouth to stammer a reply when the sunlight went out again and a fat lady rammed him broadside and propelled him against the wall of the Corday Hotel.

He glanced around wildly, wondering for the first time if this whole *world* might be the hallucination, and the sunlit world the real one. In comparison, this one seemed so . . . dark and gray and depthless.

A bright blue dot flared in the sky, then slowly became a line like a luminous jet trail. The first crack, he thought.

He edged his way to the entrance of Andre's and shoved against the glass door, and then pulled, but it didn't open, didn't even rattle against a bolt—it was as if he'd grabbed a section of brickwork.

What is this, he thought, they can't be *closed,* it isn't even noon yet, and I can see people inside.

He saw a portly, toothpick-chewing man striding up the hall toward the entrance, and he took a step back in case the glass should break when the man hit the immovable door, but to Bondier's surprise the door swung open easily at the man's push. Bondier sprang forward and caught the edge of the door as the man joined the street throng—but the door swung shut, no faster or slower than normal, despite Bondier's straining, heel-dragging effort to hold it open, and finally he had to let go in order to save his fingers.

I'm not a member of this world at all anymore, he thought. Maybe I was never more than half-connected, but now all these things are as impervious to me as objects in a newspaper photograph would be to a fly crawling over the paper. A tossed bottle-cap might knock me down—or punch right through me. Christ, is this world's oxygen still willing to combine with the hemoglobin in my blood, or whatever it is it's supposed to do?

He glanced desperately at the sky. The bright blue line was longer now, and branched at one end. Hurry, he thought.

Another patron, a woman, left the restaurant, and this time Bondier scuttled in around her and rolled inside before the irresistible door closed.

Every table in the elegant dining room was occupied, but the talking and the clatter of cutlery was muffled. There were no smells— and as Bondier walked in and looked around for someone who looked like himself, he noted that the carpeting under his feet seemed to be frozen, or shellacked; and then he realized that it simply wasn't yielding under him. I'd probably break a tooth if I tried to eat a forkful of mashed potatoes, he thought.

He heard a crash out on Main Street, and he knew it was the delivery truck bumping the car and spilling the cigarette cartons, right on schedule. He glanced toward the noise.

When he turned back to the dining room he saw him, the man he knew must be his twin, sitting with a couple of other men at a table by the window. The man was older, his hair gray at the temples, but the eyes, nose and chin were the same ones Bondier saw every morning in the mirror. The twin was talking angrily—and, it seemed to Bondier, a little fearfully—to a man who'd just walked up to the table; but the new arrival, and the others at the table too, were ignoring him and talking cheerfully among themselves.

I do believe, thought Bondier, that my brother is also beginning to notice a bit of dislocation. Bondier had just opened his mouth to call out a greeting when his twin abruptly went limp and collapsed face down on the tablecloth.

Alarmed, Bondier hurried forward. The other men at the table were now quiet, and were looking attentively at a point over the inert twin's head, and then at an empty chair on the other side of the table, and then over the twin's head again, and Bondier guessed that, according to the universe's script, a dialogue was going on.

Bondier hoisted up his unconscious brother and let him slump back in the chair. He was breathing, at least.

"Uh, that was last Tuesday, sir," put in the man by the window.

"Who asked you, clown," said Bondier absently. He took one of the slack wrists. The pulse was steady and strong.

It's just like one of my blackout fits, he reflected. In fact it's probably the same malady, something that runs in the family. I wonder if *his* doctors have been able to diagnose it. He looks like he could afford private practice ones. Well, if that's what it is, he ought to be coming out of it in a minute or two.

Bondier glanced at his watch. Exactly eleven. Right about now, he thought, a block or two south of here, that trash-thing is jumping on the fifteen-minutes-younger me, and I'm disappearing.

"That's correct, sir," said the window-seat man.

"Shut up," Bondier told him. As a matter of fact, he thought, my time-jump and his blackout were, as far as I can tell, simultaneous. I wonder if my time-jump—only a few seconds ago by every watch but mine—could be the *cause* of this blackout.

And has that all along been the cause of mine? That *he's* been jumping? If so, why the hell does he every year make two jumps on the morning of July first?

Like someone trying to deduce the reason behind a puzzling chess move, Bondier mentally put himself in his twin's place—and he was beginning to get a glimmer of an answer to his question, when Stanwell inhaled sharply, stiffened, opened his eyes and glanced around.

"I seem to have passed out," he said uncertainly to the man by the window, who happened to be looking at him.

"They can't hear you," said Bondier quietly, crouched beside Stanwell's chair.

Stanwell jumped, then turned on Bondier a glare with more than a little fear in it. "And just who the hell are—" he began, then his eyes widened and he reached down and gripped Bondier's shoulder. "My God," he said softly, "is this a . . . a trick? Is your hair dyed? But it's thicker, too . . . and no facelift could have restored my youth so perfectly . . . My God, boy, you've broken the barrier, you jumped forward past your local now! Tell me how you did it—and then we can *all* get together, and dispense with this business of the once-a year backward relay of reassurance messages."

"It was getting tiresome," hazarded Bondier, pretty sure of his guess now, "every July first."

Stanwell's face had lost its look of reined-in panic, and he laughed jovially. "You don't know how tiresome, my boy," he said. "I wish you'd been in my office earlier today and seen the me—the us, I should say—from next year. Un*pardonably* rude, abrupt, wouldn't tell me anything . . . hah! But now we can cross the barrier and go have some fun with him, pretend we won't tell him how—but wait a minute! Have you tried—you might not have—have you tried to jump *forward* again from earlier than 1953? *I* can't do it, though I don't know why. Maybe . . ."

Stanwell's voice drifted off and he glanced around the restaurant uneasily. "This is lasting a little long," he said. "Maybe you've already noticed instances of it back when you're from, times when people can't see or hear you . . . sometimes if you *shout* they can, but then if you can get them to answer, it's just stuttering, as if you're forcing a machine . . . But this has been several minutes now, it's bound to click in again soon. Why don't you stand back by the hall there, so no one will see you just appear out of nowhere, and then I'll introduce you as my younger brother."

"I don't think we'll show up for a while yet," said Bondier gently. He stood up and stepped around to the empty chair that was Gribbin's, and sat down in it. "This guy's just plain gone," he observed, patting the arms of the chair. "Has that ever happened before? One of the actors just doesn't show up, but everyone else carries on as if he were present and following the script?"

"Well, no," Stanwell admitted. "I think we ought to jump ahead and make sure everything's—"

"I need some filling in," said Bondier. "You've been fooling with history?"

"Well, certainly," said Stanwell. "How young are you, anyway? That's my—our—purpose. That's why God put us in that tree."

Bondier blinked at him. "Tree? Wait, wait a minute, I've got it—in a place now occupied by the Pasadena Freeway, right?"

"Of course. You knew that. We knew that when we were seven."

Another guess confirmed. "Just wanted to be sure."

There was a conclusion implicit in all this, and he knew it was going to be terrifying, and he knew too that he'd suffer it whether he learned its nature or not—but he found that he couldn't back away from it and, even for the little time he might have left, never know. "Have you killed many people?"

Stanwell stared at him. "When *are* you from? You look like about 1970, and we were jumping pretty frequently by the late sixties; it only took a couple of jumps to learn how to do it without having to be scared to death in order to provoke it. We'd done plenty by your time, hadn't we? Or hadn't we started *facing* it yet? I hadn't thought we were so cowardly. Yes, we've shortened some world-lines, and probably eliminated some altogether, but always for the world's good. Christ, you must remember the original version more clearly than I do— Vietnam, Nixon—"

"Do these people *stay* erased? Don't you worry that maybe you've stretched the fabric so tight with your alterations that . . . I don't know . . . it starts to crack and split a little, here and there, faster than you can scramble with your needle and thread?"

"That's nonsense, of course they stay erased, what are you—"

"Have you . . . have you ever seen a thing made of animated trash that walks around and talks with a lot of voices?"

"I think he's got a point, sir," piped up the man beside Stanwell. Both twins looked at him, but the man was still oblivious of them.

Stanwell had turned pale. "How can you know about that thing? You look like you're from absolutely no later than '72 or so, and I only first saw it last year—and I've *never* heard it," he shuddered, "*speak.*"

"Maybe you *can't* erase people," said Bondier, smiling nervously as he shifted back and forth on the unyielding seat cushion. "Maybe you can eliminate the bodies they would have got, cut their lifelines out of the four-dimensional hypercube, but their minds hang around anyway . . . faded and imbecilic let's say, and malevolent as nasty children, but present . . . and if they get together, enough of them, maybe they can animate lightweight stuff and come looking for the guy who evicted them from the story." He shook his head and reached for Gribbin's glass of tequila, but it stuck to the table as if bolted there. "I don't think you've rerouted history. I think the real world, the original version, is still going on, independent of this. You've just engineered a . . . an interesting short circuit.

"I guess it's pretty clear what I've got to do," he said, and as Stanwell opened his mouth to say something further, Bondier closed his eyes and, finally, let himself realize that his identity—the whole neurally-coded accumulation of memories, prejudices, fears and ambitions that was himself—was about to wink out of existence along with the fake world that had collaborated in their creation.

His twin brother was speaking, but Bondier had opened his eyes and looked down at his lap, and instead of his hands he saw a wire basket full of dirty T-shirts and jeans—he was even now falling out of the world, and he convulsed in icy vertigo at the realization.

And the whole world imploded.

Bondier looked back over his shoulder and though he was still squinting in the sunlight he could see the young mother and the baby carriage moving steadily away. I wonder, he thought, what she's planning to buy with the five dollar bill she palmed from the roll I let fall? A drink to steady her nerves afterward? A new dress? How far does a fiver go in '54, anyway?

But you'll never get to spend it, Mom. This time they'll find the little corpse.

Reaching into his flannel shirt, he touched his side and felt the scar he would now never acquire. It hadn't healed quickly; for the entire first year of this clumsy, backward-jumping journey it had been inflamed and infected . . . and even now, after years of searching and time-jumping and searching some more, it still sometimes woke him up with a sudden twinge.

He walked away, looking around at the buildings and the bulbous, incongruously shiny cars. What have I got, he wondered, ten minutes? It'll take her about that long to wheel that thing to the freeway overpass, and by then my poor brother will have consumed enough of that codeine-laced milk to have rendered himself unconscious, and unable to feel any fear when the moment comes.

He remembered something his brother had said—*Have you tried to jump forward again from earlier than 1953? I can't do it . . .*

Of course he couldn't do it, Bondier thought now. Before 1953 we weren't *born* yet—he couldn't jump back up from before then, because I was his overdrive time-jumping engine, and before 1953 I didn't exist.

I could still stop her.

Sure, he thought with a fragile grin, I could let him live and then have my *own* try at rewriting history, use *his* mind as *my* overdrive engine for the time-jumps, let *him* be the invalid with the blackouts this time, as I was in his version. But my version would certainly run down and stop too.

He hoped the police would find the epitaph he had written on a piece of paper and tucked into his infant brother's blanket. It was from A.E. Housman:

> *But I will go where they are hid*
> *That never were begot,*
> *To my inheritance amid*
> *The nation that is not.*

I wonder, he thought, what Keith Bondier's life is like in the real world. I hope I don't get involved with Margie. I hope I still like Beethoven and Hemingway and Monet and Housman. I hope the real world isn't as bad off as my poor doomed brother thought it was. At least it'll be the real one.

He looked back toward the freeway again, but he couldn't see them anymore. So long, Mom and brother, he thought. Though I'll see you one more time, brother. It'll only take me a couple of jumps to get up to that July first where you're waiting for that progress report. The last one—when, according to you, I'll be "unpardonably rude and abrupt" and not tell you anything. I suppose I'll seem that way. What could I say, though?

In his tight-clutching hand the baby bottle broke, spattering the dusty pavement with milk. Bondier absently dropped the pieces, and after a few moments he noticed that his thumb was bleeding. He sucked on it.

And then, having no reason to delay here any longer, he disappeared, and this time there was no sound to mark his passage, nor any slightest ripple in the dust.

✢ AUTHOR'S NOTE ✢

I think I got the idea for this when I saw a startled kitten jump straight up into the air; at one moment it was fast asleep, and in the next moment it was three feet above the floor. Of course, it wasn't actually teleportation, but with just a few tenths of a second shaved off, it would have been.

It's an interesting response to a suddenly pereived threat, but the kitten did land right back where he had been. (Luckily the "threat" was just something like me dropping a book.) A better reflex would be to jump through time, rather than space, and land, alert, a little while before the threat appeared.

But physical jumps require muscle. What would a chrono-jump require? Arguably a nearby mind to provide a psychic boost—so that as the fleeing mind jumps out of the local picture, the traction-providing mind gets pushed down.

The notion of the world as a clockwork mechanism that keeps operating according to its unalterably determinist script, even if individual players have got out of their proper place or disappeared altogether, I got from the Fritz Leiber novella, "You're All Alone." Not the first idea I've found in his work!

⊰ WE TRAVERSE AFAR ⊱
written with James P. Blaylock

HARRISON sat in the dim living room and listened to the train. All the sounds were clear—the shrill steam whistle over the bass chug of the engine, and even, faintly, the clatter of the wheels on the track.

It never rained anymore on Christmas Eve. The plastic rain gauge was probably still out on the shed roof; he used to lean over the balcony railing outside the master bedroom to check the level of the water in the thing. There had been something reassuring about the idea of rainwater rising in the gauge—nature measurably doing its work, the seasons going around, the drought held at bay . . .

But he couldn't recall any rain since last winter. He hadn't checked, because the master bedroom was closed up now. And anyway the widow next door, Mrs. Kemp, had hung some strings of Christmas lights over her back porch, and even if he *did* get through to the balcony, he wouldn't be able to help seeing the blinking colors, and probably even something like a Christmas wreath on her back door.

Too many cooks spoil the broth, he thought, a good wine needs no bush, a friend in need is one friend too many, leave me alone.

She'd even knocked on his door today, the widow had; with a paper plate of Christmas cookies! The plate was covered in red and green foil and the whole bundle was wrapped in a Santa Claus napkin. He had taken the plate, out of politeness; but the whole kit and caboodle, cookies and all, had gone straight into the dumpster.

To hell with rain anyway. He was sitting in the old leather chair by the cold fireplace, watching snow. In the glass globe in his hand a little painted man and woman sat in a sleigh that was being pulled by a little frozen horse.

He took a sip of vodka and turned the globe upside down and back again, and a contained flurry of snow swirled around the figures. He and his wife had bought the thing a long time ago. The couple in the sleigh had been on their cold ride for decades now. Better to travel than to arrive, he thought, peering through the glass at their tiny blue-eyed faces; they didn't look a day older than when they'd started out. And still together, too, after all these years.

The sound of the train engine changed, was more echoing and booming now—maybe it had gone into a tunnel.

He put the globe down on the magazine stand and had another sip of vodka. With his nose stuffed full of Vicks VapoRub, as it was tonight, his taste buds wouldn't have known the difference if he'd been drinking VSOP brandy or paint thinner, but he could feel the warm glow in his stomach.

It was an old LP record on the turntable, one from the days when the real hi-fi enthusiasts cared more about sound quality than any kind of actual music. This one was two whole sides of locomotive racket, booming out through his monaural Klipschorn speaker. He also had old disks of surf sounds, downtown traffic, ocean waves, birds shouting in tropical forests . . .

Better a train. Booming across those nighttime miles.

He was just getting well relaxed when he began to hear faint music behind the barreling train. It was a Christmas song, and before he could stop himself he recognized it—Bing Crosby singing "We Three Kings," one of her favorites.

He'd been ready for it. He pulled two balls of cotton out of the plastic bag beside the vodka bottle and twisted them into his ears. That made it better—all he could hear now was a distant hiss that might have been rain against the windows.

Ghost rain, he thought. I should have put out a ghost gauge.

As if in response to his thought, the next sip of vodka had a taste—the full-orchestra, peaches-and-bourbon chord of Southern Comfort. He tilted his head forward and let the liquor run out of his mouth back into the glass, and then he stood up and crossed to the phonograph, lifted the arm off the record and laid it in its rest, off to the side.

When he pulled the cotton out of his ears, the house was silent.

There was no creaking of floorboards, no sound of breathing or rustling. He was staring at the empty fireplace, pretty sure that if he looked around he would see that flickering rainbow glow from the dining room; the glow of lights, and the star on the top of the tree, and those weird little glass columns with bubbles wobbling up through the liquid inside. Somehow the stuff never boiled away. Some kind of perpetual motion, like those glass birds with the top hats, that bobbed back and forth, dipping their beaks into a glass of water, forever. At least with the Vicks he wouldn't smell pine sap.

The pages of the wall calendar had been rearranged sometime last night. He'd noticed it right away this morning when he'd come out of what used to be the guest bedroom, where he slept now on the single bed. The pink cloud of tuberous begonias above the thirty-one empty days of March was gone, replaced by the blooming poinsettia of the December page. Had he done it himself, shifted the calendar while walking in his sleep? He wasn't normally a sleepwalker. And sometime during the night, around midnight probably, he'd thought he'd heard a stirring in the closed-up bedroom across the hall, the door whispering open, what sounded like bedroom slippers shuffling on the living room carpet.

Before even making coffee he had folded the calendar back to March. She'd died on St. Patrick's Day evening, and in fact the green dress she'd laid out on the queen-size bed still lay there, gathering whatever kind of dust inhabited a closed-up room. Around the dress, on the bedspread, were still scattered the green-felt shamrocks she had intended to sew onto it. She'd never even had a chance to iron the dress, and, after the paramedics had taken her away on that long-ago evening, he'd had to unplug the iron himself, at the same time that he unplugged the bedside clock.

The following day, after moving out most of his clothes, he had shut the bedroom door for the last time. This business with the calendar made him wonder if maybe the clock was plugged in again, too, but he was not going to venture in there to find out.

Through the back door, from across the yard, he heard the familiar scrape of the widow's screen door opening, and then the sound of it slapping shut. Quickly he reached up and flipped off the lamp, then sat still in the darkened living room. Maybe she wasn't paying him another visit, but he wasn't taking any chances.

In a couple of minutes there came the clumping of her shoes on the front steps, and he hunkered down in the chair, glad that he'd turned off the train noise.

He watched her shadow in the porch light. He shouldn't leave it on all the time. It probably looked like an invitation, especially at this time of year. She knocked at the door, waited a moment and then knocked again. She couldn't take a hint if it stepped out of the bushes and bit her on the leg.

Abruptly he felt sheepish, hiding out like this, like a kid. But he was a *married man*, for God's sake. He'd taken a *vow*. And a vow wasn't worth taking if it wasn't *binding. She will do him good and not evil all the days of her life,* said Proverbs 31 about a good wife; *her lamp does not go out at night.*

Does not go out.

His thoughts trailed off into nothing when he realized that the woman outside was leaving, shuffling back down the steps. He caught himself wondering if she'd brought him something else to eat, maybe left a casserole outside the door. Once she'd brought around half a corned beef and a mess of potatoes and cabbage, and like the Christmas cookies, all of it had gone straight into the garbage. But the canned chili he'd microwaved earlier this evening wasn't sitting too well with him, and the thought of corned beef . . .

He could definitely hear something now from the closed-up bedroom—a low whirring noise like bees in a hive—the sewing machine? He couldn't recall if he had unplugged it too, that night. Still, it had no excuse. . . .

He grabbed the cotton balls, twisting them up tight and jamming them into his ears again. Had the bedroom door moved? He groped wildly for the lamp, switched it on, and with one last backward glance he went out the front door, nearly slamming it behind him in his haste.

Shakily, he sat down in one of the white plastic chairs on the porch and buttoned up his cardigan sweater. If the widow returned, she'd find him, and there was damn-all he could do about it. He looked around in case she might have left him something, but apparently she hadn't. The chilly night air calmed him down a little bit, and he listened for a moment to the sound of crickets, wondering what he would do now. Sooner or later he'd have to go back inside. He hadn't even brought out the vodka bottle.

Tomorrow, Christmas day, would be worse.

What would he say to her if the bedroom door should *open,* and she were to step out? If he were actually to *confront* her. . . . A good marriage was made in heaven, as the scriptures said, and you didn't let a thing like that go. No matter what. Hang on with chains.

After a while he became aware that someone up the street was yelling about something, and he stood up in relief, grateful for an excuse to get off the porch, away from the house. He shuffled down the two concrete steps, breathing the cold air that was scented with jasmine even in December.

Some distance up the block, half a dozen people in robes were walking down the sidewalk toward his house, carrying one of those real estate signs that looked like a miniature hangman's gallows. No, only one of them was carrying it, and at the bottom end of it was a metal wheel that was skirling along the dry pavement.

Then he saw that it wasn't a real estate sign, but a cross. The guy carrying it was apparently supposed to be Jesus, and two of the men behind him wore slatted skirts like Roman soldiers, and they had rope whips that they were snapping in the chilly air.

"Get along, King of the Jews!" one of the soldiers called, obviously not for the first time, and not very angrily. Behind the soldiers three women in togas trotted along, shaking their heads and waving their hands. Harrison supposed they must be Mary or somebody. The wheel at the bottom of the cross definitely needed a squirt of oil.

Harrison took a deep breath, and then forced jocularity into his voice as he called, "You guys missed the Golgotha off-ramp. Only thing south of here is the YMCA."

A black couple was pushing a shopping cart up the sidewalk from the opposite direction, their shadows stark under the streetlight. They were slowing down to watch Jesus. All kinds of unoiled wheels were turning tonight.

The biblical procession stopped in front of his house, and Harrison walked down the path to the sidewalk. Jesus grinned at him, clearly glad for the chance to pause amid his travail and catch his breath.

One of the women handed Harrison a folded flier. "I'm Mary Magdalene," she told him. "This is about a meeting we're having at our church next week. We're on Seventeenth, just past the 5 Freeway."

The shopping cart had stopped too, and Harrison carried the flier over to the black man and woman. "Here," he said, holding out the piece of paper. "Mary Magdalene wants you to check out her church. Take a right at the light, it's just past the freeway."

The black man had a bushy beard but didn't seem to be older than thirty, and the woman was fairly fat, wearing a sweatsuit. The shopping cart was full of empty bottles and cans sitting on top of a trash bag half-full of clothes.

The black man grinned. "We're homeless, and we'd sure like to get the dollar-ninety-nine breakfast at Norm's. Could you help us out? We only need a little more."

"Ask Jesus," said Harrison nervously, waving at the robed people. "Hey Jesus, here's a chance to do some actual *thing* tonight, not just march around the streets. This here is a genuine homeless couple, give 'em a couple of bucks."

Jesus patted his robes with the hand that wasn't holding the cross. "I don't have anything on me," he said apologetically.

Harrison turned to the Roman soldiers. "You guys got any money?"

"Just change would do," put in the black man.

"Nah," said one of the soldiers, "I left my money in my pants."

"Girls?" said Harrison.

Mary Magdalene glanced at her companions, then turned back to Harrison and shook her head.

"Really?" said Harrison. "Out in this kind of neighborhood at night, and you don't even have quarters for phone calls?"

"We weren't going to go far," explained Jesus.

"Weren't going to go far." Harrison nodded, then looked back to Mary Magdalene. "Can your church help these people out? Food, shelter, that kind of thing?"

The black woman had walked over to Jesus and was admiring his cross. She liked the wheel.

"They'd have to be married," Mary Magdalene told Harrison. "In the church. If they're just . . . living together, we can't do anything for them."

That's great, thought Harrison, coming from Mary Magdalene. "So that's it, I guess, huh?"

Apparently it was. "Drop by the church!" said Jesus cheerfully, resuming his burden and starting forward again.

"Get along, King of the Jews!" called one of the soldiers, snapping his length of rope in the air. The procession moved on down the sidewalk, the wheel at the bottom of the cross squeaking.

The black man looked at Harrison. "Sir, could we borrow a couple of bucks? You live here? We'll pay you back."

Harrison was staring after the robed procession. "Oh," he said absently, "sure. Here." He dug a wad of bills out of his pants pocket and peeled two ones away from the five and held them out.

The man took the bills. "God bless you. Could we have the five too? It's Christmas Eve."

Harrison found that he was insulted by the *God bless you.* The implication was that these two were devout Christians, and would assuredly spend the money on wholesome food, or medicine, and not go buy dope or wine.

"No," he said sharply. "And I don't care what you buy with the two bucks." Once I've given it away, he thought, it shouldn't be my business. Gone is gone.

The black man scowled at him and muttered something obviously offensive under his breath as the two of them turned away, not toward Norm's and the dollar-ninety-nine breakfast, but down a side street toward the mini-mart.

Obscurely defeated, Harrison trudged back up to his porch and collapsed back into the chair.

He wished the train record was still playing inside—but even if it had been, it would still be a train that, realistically, had probably stopped rolling a long time ago. Listening to it over and over again wouldn't make it move again.

He opened the door and walked back into the dim living room. Just as he closed the door he heard thunder boom across the night sky, and then he heard the hiss of sudden rain on the pavement outside. In a moment it was tapping at the windows.

He wondered if the rain gauge was still on the roof, maybe measuring what was happening to Jesus and the black couple out there. And he was glad that he had had the roof redone a year ago. He was okay in here—no wet carpets in store for him.

The vodka bottle was still on the table, but he could see tiny reflected flickers of light in the glassy depths of it—red and green and yellow and blue; and, though he knew that the arm of the phonograph was lifted and in its holder, he heard again, clearly now, Bing Crosby singing "We Three Kings."

To hell with the vodka. He sat down in the leather chair and picked up the snow globe with trembling fingers. "What," he said softly, "too far? Too long? I thought it was supposed to be forever."

But rainy gusts boomed at the windows, and he realized that he had stood up. He pried at the base of the snow globe, and managed to free the plug.

Water and white plastic flecks bubbled and trickled out of it, onto the floor. In only a minute the globe had emptied out, and the two figures in the sleigh were exposed to the air of tonight, stopped. Without the refraction of the surrounding water the man and the woman looked smaller, and lifeless.

"Field and fountain, moor and mountain," he whispered. "Journey's done—finally. Sorry."

He was alone in the dark living room. No lights gleamed in the vodka bottle, and there was no sound but his own breath and heartbeat.

Tomorrow he would open the door to anyone who might knock.

❖ AUTHOR'S NOTE ❖

This encounter between a homeless couple and a band of generic Christians happened one Christmas Eve night right outside of our apartment on 16th Street in Santa Ana, and my wife and I went out and ended up giving two dollars to the homeless couple when the people in the crucifixion procession turned out to have no money in their robes. And when David Hartwell asked Blaylock and I for a short story to include in an anthology of Christmas stories, this encounter seemed like a good thing to hang a story on. The scene seemed to carry some implicit moral of its own, and we decided to let it play out the way it actually did, with no help . . . except to add a Christmas haunting.

⚞ THROUGH AND THROUGH ⚟

ALREADY when he walked in through the side door, there were a few people sitting here and there, separately in the Saturday afternoon dimness. The air was cool, and smelled of floor wax.

He almost peered at the shadowed faces, irrationally hoping one might be hers, come back these seven days later to try for a different result; but most of the faces were lowered, and of course she wouldn't be here. Two days ago, maybe—today, and ever after, no.

The funeral would be next week sometime, probably Monday. No complications about burial in consecrated soil anymore, thank God . . . or thank human mercy.

His shoes knocked echoingly on the glossy linoleum as he walked across the nave, pausing to bow toward the altar. In the old days he would have genuflected, and it would have been spontaneous; in recenter years the bow had become perfunctory, dutiful—today it was a twitch of self-distaste.

There were fewer people than he had first thought, he noted as he walked past the side altar and started down the wall aisle toward the confessional door, passing under the high, wooden Stations of the Cross and the awkwardly lettered banners of the Renew Committee. Maybe only three, all women; and a couple of little girls.

They never wanted to line up against the wall—a discreet couple of yards away from the door—until he actually entered the church; and then if there were six or so of them they'd be frowning at each other as they got up out of the pews and belatedly formed the line, silently but obviously disagreeing about the order in which they'd originally entered the church.

Last week there had been five, counting her. And afterward he had walked back up to the front of the church and stepped up onto the altar level and gone into the sacristy to put on the vestments for 5:30 Mass. Had he been worrying about what she had said? *What sins you shall retain, they are retained.* Probably he had been worrying about it.

As he opened the confessional door now, he nodded to the old woman who was first in line. The others appeared to be trying to hide behind her—he could see only a drape of skirt and a couple of shoes behind her. He didn't recognize the old woman.

He stepped into the little room and pulled the door closed behind him. They wouldn't begin to come in until he turned on the red light over the door, and he needed a drink.

The little room was brighter than the interior of the church, lit by a pebbled glass window high in the wall at his back. He opened the closet and shook out his surplice, a white robe that he pulled over his head. Then he undraped from a hanger the stole, a strip of cloth like a long, double-wide necktie, purple silk on one side and white on the other; and he draped it over his head and down the front of his surplice, with the purple side showing. The audience demands the costume, he thought as he bent down to snag a pint bottle of Wild Turkey from behind an old pair of shoes.

A couple of little girls out there, he thought. Chinese-restaurant style confessions, those will be, one from column A and two from column B: *I quarreled with my brothers, I disobeyed my parents.* They look to be a little young yet for *impure thoughts.*

He unscrewed the plastic cap and took a mouthful of the warm bourbon, letting the vapors fill his head before he swallowed. And for their penances I'll tell them, *Say five Our Fathers and five Hail Marys.*

No use in being imaginative. Once he had told a young boy, *For your penance, I want you to tell your mother and father that you love them.* Later he'd learned that the boy had found this flatly impossible—apparently in the boy's family the declaration would have been taken as a symptom of insanity—and the boy had lived in silent fear of Hell for two weeks before his family had finally gone to Confession again, at which point the boy had taken the same old sins to another priest, one who would reliably give the conventional sort of penance.

Confession is good for the soul. I still believe that's true, he thought. It can make life easier to bear, after all, letting in the fresh air, sharing your secrets with another. But not when it's so tied in with the dread of Hell. That woman last week—

He took another sip of the bourbon to take the edge off the memory. And it hadn't been his fault—how could he have known how strangled she was with scruples and legalisms? She didn't need—hadn't needed—a sympathetic human being to talk to; what would have served her best would have been an 800 number—*If your sin has to do with the 6th Commandment, press 6 now.*

In his early years as a priest, he had seemed to feel heavier after hearing confessions, especially the marathon sessions before Easter, as if some residue of the absolved sins clung to him; and he had whimsically speculated that clouds of evicted sins polluted the air afterward, interfering with TV reception and making cars hard to start. Now he just felt tired afterward, as if he had spent the afternoon helping a lot of people to get their checking accounts unscrambled.

The woman last week hadn't wanted any *help*, not from him. She had sat her thin frame down in the chair across from his, awkwardly, tucking in her skirt and glancing around, clearly uneasy about the face-to-face style of Confession. She'd have been happier with the old booth arrangement, he thought, whispering through a screen so that priest and penitent saw each other only as dim silhouettes; though she had hardly looked more than thirty years old.

He took one more mouthful of the liquor now, and then screwed the cap back on and put the bottle away.

She had made the sign of the cross and then started right in, exhaling as she spoke: "Bless me, Father, I have sinned." Her voice was shaky. "My last Confession was . . . at least five years ago, before '96. I've meant to come—it's scary, though, a big speed bump to get over—last week I went to a wedding—" He noted that her left ring finger didn't have a ring on it; "—and there were family people there, people I hadn't seen since college. I took Communion. At the Mass."

He had nodded, and when she didn't go on he raised his eyebrows.

"I took Communion while in a state of mortal sin," she said.

"The Eucharist provides forgiveness of sins," he told her. He had preferred *Eucharist* to *Communion* ever since Whitley Strieber's book about space aliens had taken the latter term as its title.

"Father," she had said uncertainly, "not mortal sins. Which I'll get to a lot of, here, I hope. If you're not in a state of grace, Communion is like sugar to a diabetic—uh, damaging?" She spread her hands as if to catch a ball.

He had smiled at her, and he hoped now that his smile had not been patronizing. "God understands—" he began.

"But it's God, literally coming into us, right?" she interrupted. "If there's oily rags and newspapers around, you'll catch fire from the heat of Him, your soul gets scorched, right?" She laughed nervously. "And I've got a lot of oily rags in my soul. I don't like the idea that I've . . ." She shook her head and closed her mouth.

"Sin," he had said expansively. "What do we mean by it? Isn't the only *real* sin cruelty, to others—or to yourself?"

For a moment neither of them spoke, and he hoped this wouldn't take too long. How many more people were waiting out there?

"I came a long way to get here," she had said finally. "I didn't really think I'd get this far. I don't need to talk about 'What's sin?' with some *guy*. I've done some terrible things, and right now I think I can say them out loud; I think. I want absolution."

"Well," he said, "I'm not going to *absolve* you for something that isn't a *sin*."

Her mouth was open in evident disbelief. "As a favor to me," she said.

"No, it's ridiculous." He noticed her bony hands clutched together, and it occurred to him that she might be an addict—amphetamines, probably. "Don't trouble yourself over these—"

"'What sins you shall forgive, they are forgiven,'" she said, her voice getting brittle, "I remember that part. And 'What sins you shall retain, they are retained.' You're telling me you're retaining this one." Her smile made her cheekbones prominent. "I bet you'd retain them all, if you heard them. I bet none of them are sins anymore . . . according to you."

"I'm not *retaining* anything! So far I haven't heard anything you've done wrong. Tell me—"

"No." She had stood up. "This was a mistake."

And she had walked out.

And on Thursday morning she had been found dead in a back pew of the church. Dead of an overdose of drugs—a speedball, he'd been told, cocaine and heroin. Her parents were long-time parishioners, and her funeral would be in this church. Luckily she had not left a note.

How long will it take, he wondered as he reached for the switch that would turn on the red light over the door outside, before people are ready to abandon the crude supernatural templates that obscure God's love? When will they see that God is in all of us, and that what we most need is to forgive ourselves?

The knob turned, and the door swung inward and a little girl in blue jeans and a green sweater stepped in, Reeboks scuffing the carpet. She appeared to be about eight years old, with short-cropped dark hair.

He wondered if she had shoved in ahead of the old woman he'd seen at the front of the line. The girl's face was narrow, with horizontal wrinkles in the lower eyelids already.

"Do sit down," he told her.

He had forgotten to put a stick of Doublemint gum in his mouth, but she didn't appear to notice any smell of liquor, and he'd remember to do it before the old woman came in.

She climbed into the chair, and her shoes didn't touch the carpet.

"Bless me, Father," she said, "I have sinned. My last Confession was too long ago to remember. These are my sins—I killed myself on Thursday." She looked at him mournfully. "I know that's very bad."

He was aware of cold air on his face—his forehead was suddenly dewed with sweat.

"That's not funny," he said, "a woman did—was found dead—"

"I want absolution," the little girl said. "I want the sacrament. I came a long way to get here. I didn't really think I'd get this far."

Abruptly he remembered that the door to the confessional opened outward.

He turned to look at it—it was closed now, and its frame didn't appear to have been tampered with any time lately—and when he turned back, it was a white-haired old woman who sat opposite him.

He jumped violently in his chair, inhaling in a whispered screech. High blood pressure made a ringing wail in his head, and his peripheral vision had narrowed to nearly nothing.

He blinked several times, and exhaled. "Who are you?" he asked in a rusty voice. His fingers were tingling, gripping the arms of his chair.

"And before that," quavered the old woman, "I took Communion while in a state of mortal sin." She had been looking down at her bony old hands, and now she looked up at him; and her eyes were empty holes in the wrinkled parchment of her face.

Through the holes he could see the fabric of the chair, bright in the afternoon light from the window at his back. She wasn't even casting a shadow.

It's a ghost, he told himself as he made himself breathe deeply.

It's the ghost of that woman who was here a week ago. Priests have seen ghosts before.

He flexed his legs under the surplice. He didn't want to find that his legs had gone to sleep when he made a bolt for the door. He would say there'd been an electrical short, he smelled gas, felt faint, and if they found the Wild Turkey, blame it on the Vietnamese priest.

But the old woman had reached out one papery hand as slow as drifting smoke, and now touched his knee; he shouldn't even have been able to feel the touch, through the fabric of the surplice and his slacks, but the impact punched another shrill wheeze out of him, and numbed his whole leg. His heart beat several times very fast, then seemed to stop; and he began panting in relief when his pulse began beating regularly again, though it was still fast.

"And before that," she said, in the same frail voice, "you took Communion in a state of mortal sin."

He remembered a Tennyson line: *The dead shall look me through and through.* It was probably true—he had not been to another priest for Confession in . . . months . . . and he took Communion many times a week, at every Mass he said.

She might kill him if she touched him again. Would it be deliberate, did she mean to hurt him?

He was dizzy, and he became aware that he could feel the late afternoon light on his face—but he was sure he hadn't turned his chair around in the spasm of her touching him. He blinked, but he couldn't see anything except a gray fog. Quickly he darted a hand to his right eye, and his dry fingers found only a hole in a numb, crackling surface.

"Bless me, Father," came his own voice from a few feet away, "I have sinned. My last Confession was a thousand years ago. I want absolution."

He jumped with all his will, but not physically—and then his hands were gripping the arms of his own chair, and the window was at his back and he could see again, and it was the little girl in the chair across from him now.

"Don't—do that again," he whispered. His heart was hammering again.

"I firmly resolve to sin no more," the little girl said, "and to avoid the near occasions of sin. Amen."

She can't do anything deliberately, he thought. She can't sin anymore, she's dead. She might kill me, but with no more moral responsibility than a sick dog would have.

She was waiting.

His sister baptized dogs and cats—just a lick of spit on a fingertip to make a cross on the furry forehead, a whispered *I baptize thee . . .* Why couldn't he just say the words here, give this lost revenant what it wanted? *Ego te absolvo a peccatis tuis* but those were the old Latin phrases; these days it was *I absolve you from your sins in the name of the Father, and of the Son, and of the Holy Spirit.*

But this thing can't have contrition, he thought, it can't repent. Its living soul is with God—this is just a suffering cast-off shell.

But it is suffering, as dogs and cats do, and they don't have souls either.

Why was she appearing as a girl and an old woman? Why was she so widely avoiding the appearance she'd had when she'd come to Confession last week, the appearance she'd had when she'd died? Was it too traumatic?

And suddenly, with something like the intimacy of sore muscles, he knew that he was responsible for the form she took; when she walked in, she had been an uncollapsed wave of possible appearances, all the appearances she'd ever had; it was his guilt that had collapsed all the percentages of possibilities down to this small "one." A few moments ago he had even forced on her the appearance of an old woman, which was just a sheet of old skin because she would never actually live to that age.

Would a better priest, a better man, have seen the woman as she had appeared last week, when she'd been alive?

The world, before the first sentient man left the Garden of Eden and *looked* at it, had not yet been defined by attention—it had been a spectrum of worlds-in-potential that had not included humanity, an

infinity of possible prehuman histories; but by the time Adam stepped
out and turned his attention on it, he had sinned mortally, and so the
history that came to the fore as the actual one was a history of
undeserved suffering and death. When Adam's foot touched the soil,
when his eyes took in the landscape, it stopped being many potentials
and became one actual: a landscape that had been a savage killing-
ground for millennia.

Light turns out to be particles if you measure for particles, he
thought, waves if you measure for waves. Adam had helplessly
measured for misery. What sort of world would a sinless first man have
found pre-existent out there? Animals that had never starved, cats that
had never killed?

I've measured for . . . evasion, he thought. Even last week, here.

"*Ego te—*" he began; then halted.

She might kill him if she touched him again. And where would he
be then? A moment ago he had told himself that her soul was now
with God—but what if it weren't? What if it were still sentient, but
somewhere else?

What if Purgatory and Hell are real? It had been a long time since
he had entertained any such notions; in fact it had been a long time
since he'd believed in the existence of any sort of actual Heaven.

But this dead penitent sitting in front of him made all sorts of
horrible ideas possible. Did he want to die right after using his priestly
powers—*thou art a priest forever, according to the order of
Melchizedek*—to perform the mockery of a sacrament? He had started
to do it—*Ego te . . .*

And I'm not in a state of grace anyway, he thought, if all these
damned *legalisms* actually *apply,* if all the awful old supernatural
stories are *true!*

He wasn't aware of being scared, but he was shivering in the warm
room, and his hands were tingling.

I'd probably go to—everlasting punishment!—and a snakeskin
half-wit piece of me would join her in her lost ghosthood, to be
another specter forever haunting confessionals, looking for
impossible absolution. Visible, perhaps, only to other doomed
priests.

"Can you *have* a firm purpose of amendment?" he asked her
unhappily. "*Can* you . . . mend your ways, go and sin no more?"

The little girl held out her hand; not threateningly, but he flinched back from the offered touch.

"I came for the sacrament," she said.

He was suddenly sure that there was no one waiting outside the door—the others he had seen had only been *her,* fragmented as if in a kaleidoscope, and this conversation was taking place in some corner outside of normal time. If he were to open the door, *pull* it open, he'd see beyond the door frame only the gray fog he had seen when he had been in the shell of the old woman.

"There's nobody else," she said. "Nobody else talks to me but you. Hollowed be thy name."

The dead shall look me through and through.

"Give me the sacrament," she said. "Deliver us from evil."

Or to it, he thought.

Her hand came up again, but hovered between them as if undecided between touching him and making the sign of the cross.

"Okay," he said.

The hand wavered sketchily in the air, and then subsided into her lap.

God help me, he thought. If I'm not dead already myself, and beyond all help.

He stood up slowly, his head bobbing; and the little girl just watched him solemnly. He stepped to the closet and slid from a high shelf one of his sick-call kits, a six-inch black leather box with hinges and a latch.

He returned to his chair and sat down, and he opened the box on his lap. Inside, tucked into fitted depressions in red velvet, were a silver crucifix, a silver holy-water sprinkler, a round silver box that held no consecrated hosts at the moment, a spare folded stole . . . and a little silver jar of oil.

It was olive oil, and it would probably be rancid by this time, but he recalled that the oil in this kit was real *Oleum Infirmorum,* blessed by the bishop.

In recent years he had come to the conclusion that the oil had no efficacy on its own—whether it was olive oil or motor oil, blessed or not—and was simply a comfort to sick people with heads full of biblical imagery; but now he was cautiously glad this was precisely the prescribed kind.

"I've got a lot of oily rags in my soul already," the little girl said. She was frowning and shifting on the chair.

She looks me through and through, he thought. "I'm going to give you the sacrament," he said, forcing his voice to be steady.

He unscrewed the lid of the little silver jar, and leaned over it. "God of mercy," he said, "ease the suffering and comfort the weakness of your servant—uh—" He looked up at her with his eyebrows raised. He could feel drops of sweat on his forehead.

"Jane," the girl said. "This—isn't Confession."

"Jane . . ."

The breath caught in his throat as he abruptly remembered what would shortly be required of him here.

After several seconds he exhaled and went on, bleakly, "Jane, whom the Church anoints with this holy oil. We ask this through Christ our Lord."

"Amen," said Jane. "This is last rites."

"Yes," he said.

He would have to touch her. The sacrament of Extreme Unction— or Anointing of the Sick, as they called it now—would require that he touch her forehead.

Her light touch, through two layers of cloth, had nearly killed him a few moments ago. This would be virtually skin-to-skin, with only the insulation of the oil.

And was this just another mockery of a sacrament? The rules permitted this sacrament to be administered to a person who appeared to have been dead for as much as two hours, who might in fact very well *be* dead, since no one could be sure precisely when the soul left a body that had died.

But two days?—and anointing *this,* while the body was at a mortuary somewhere? Briefly he imagined explaining it to his bishop: *But she was still speaking!*

He dipped his right forefinger into the oil and lifted it out—but just sat staring at it while two drops formed and fell silently back into the jar.

He thought of his sister, baptizing cats and dogs; and he thought of Adam, who had imposed suffering and death on all soulless things.

And he dipped his finger again, and leaned forward. "*Per istam sanctam unctionem—*" he said, and he touched his finger to Jane's forehead.

Her skin was as cold as window-glass, and though he felt no impact and his heartbeat didn't accelerate wildly this time, his finger, and then his knuckles, were numb.

He drew the sign of the cross on her forehead with the oil and went on speaking, remembering now to do it in English, "—may the Lord in His love and mercy help you with the grace of the Holy Spirit."

Jane was motionless, looking up at him.

"Amen," she whispered.

Oil trickled down and collected under her eye sockets like tears. The numbness was gone from his hand, and he dipped his finger again.

With his left hand he took hold of her right hand—it was as cold as her forehead—and then made the sign of the cross on the back of her hand.

"May the Lord who frees you from sin save you and raise you up," he said.

"Amen," she said again. Her voice was remote now, as if she were speaking from the far end of a corridor.

He reached for her other hand, but it was gone; her face, alone, hung over the chair like a reflection of sunlight on a wall, and for an instant it was the face of the woman who had come in here a week ago.

He couldn't see her mouth move, but he heard the receding voice say, "And what's my penance?"

Five Our Fathers? Tell your parents you love them? You don't get a penance with Extreme Unction, he thought—but she seemed to need it. He was at a loss, and cast in his mind for some prayer out of the Bible.

Only after he had said it, and the face had seemed to smile and then disappeared, did he realize that what he said had not been from the Bible:

"Go gentle into that good night," he had told her. "Rest easy with the dying of the light."

Bastardized Dylan Thomas! But it seemed to have been adequate— he was alone in the room.

When his pulse and breathing had slowed to normal, he made the sign of the cross, spotting his surplice with oil, and he thought, was that all right?

There was only silence in his mind for an answer, but for once it was not an empty silence.

And so he sat motionless until the door opened—outward, giving him a glimpse, as he looked up, of the dim church beyond.

A young man stepped in hesitantly, sniffed the air, then shuffled to the chair that had so recently been Jane's.

"Bless me, Father," the young man said huskily as he sat down, "I have sinned."

And the priest listened, nodding, as the young man began talking, and he absently replaced the lid on the oil jar and put the sick-call kit aside.

✤ AUTHOR'S NOTE ✤

I'm Catholic, and I get impatient—to say the least—with the generation of now-roughly-70-year-old priests who would probably call themselves progressive. I've had priests tell me in the confessional, "Oh, we don't really consider that a sin anymore," and I've replied, testily, "Well, I meant it to be a sin when I did it."

A priest who, perhaps out of a desire to be liked or to seem young at heart, softens or denies the inconvenient doctrines of the Church is like a doctor who'd tell you smoking isn't really bad for you. I can come up with my own rationalizations, thanks—what I want from the experts is the often unwelcome truth.

This story came about because I was wondering what a priest would do if a ghost came into the confessional. And it was more fun to spring the ghost on one of these old progressive priests than on a younger and more orthodox one who would be able to handle it better.

⩵ NIGHT MOVES ⩵

WHEN A WARM MIDNIGHT WIND sails in over the mountains from the desert and puffs window shades inward, and then hesitates for a second so that the shades flap back and knock against the window frames, southern Californians wake up and know that the Santa Ana wind has come, and that tomorrow their potted plants will be strewn up and down the alleys and sidewalks; but it promises blue skies and clean air, and they prop themselves up in bed for a few moments and listen to the palm fronds rattling and creaking out in the darkness.

Litter flies west, papers and leaves and long veils of dust from lots where the tractors wait for morning, and tonight a dry scrap cartwheeled and skated through Santa Margarita's nighttime streets; it clung briefly to high branches, skipped over the roofs of parked cars, and at one point did a slow jiggle-dance down the whole length of the north window sill at Guillermo's Todo Noche Cantina. The only person who noticed it was the old man everybody called Cyclops, who had been drinking coffee at the counter for hours in exchange for a warm, lighted place to pass the night, and until the thing tumbled away at the west end of the windowsill he stared at it, turning his head to give his good eye a clear look at it.

It looked, he thought, like one of those little desiccated devilfish they sell at swap-meets; they cut three slits in the fish's body before they dry it, so after it dries it looks as if it has a primate body and stunted limbs and a disproportionately large head with huge, empty eye sockets. When you walk out of the swap-meet area in the late afternoon, out of the shadow of the big drive-in movie screen, you sometimes step on the stiff little bodies among the litter of cotton candy and cigarette butts and bits of tortilla.

Cyclops had noticed that it danced west, and when he listened he could hear the warm wind whispering through the parallel streets outside like a slow breath through the channels of a harmonica, seeming to be just a puff short of evoking an audible chord. Realizing that this was no longer a night he needed shelter from, Cyclops laid two quarters on the counter, got to his feet and lumbered to the door.

Outside, he tilted back his devastated hat and sniffed the night. It was the old desert wind, all right, hinting of mesquite and sage, and he could feel the city shifting in its sleep—but tonight there was a taint on the wind, one that the old man smelled in his mind rather than in his nose, and he knew that something else had come into the city tonight too, something that stirred a different sort of thing than leaves and dust.

The night felt flexed, stressed, like a sheet of glass being bent. Alertly Cyclops shambled halfway across Main Street and then stopped and stared south.

After eleven o'clock the traffic lights stopped cycling and switched to a steady metronomic flashing, all the north-south lights flashing yellow for caution while the east-west ones, facing the smaller cross-streets, flashed red for stop. Standing halfway across the crosswalk Cyclops could see more than a mile's worth of randomly flashing yellow lights receding away south down Main, and about once every minute the flashes synchronized into one relayed pulse that rushed up the long street and past him over his head, toward the traffic circle at Bailey, half a mile north of where he stood.

He'd stood there often late at night, coming to conclusions about things by watching the patterns of disorder and synchronization in the long street-tunnel of flashing yellow lights, and he quickly realized that tonight they were flashing in step more frequently than normal, and only in pulses that swept north, as if delineating a landing pattern for something.

Cyclops nodded grimly. The night was warped, all right—as much curvature as he'd ever seen. The Great Gray-Legged Scissors Men would be out tonight in force.

He squared his shoulders, then strode away purposefully up Main, the once-per-minute relay-pulse of yellow light sweeping past him overhead like luminous birds.

Benny Kemp carried his drink out to the dark porch and sat down on the bench that his father had built there more than fifty years earlier. Someone had once tried to saw it away from the wall, but the solid oak had proved too hard, and the attempt had apparently been abandoned before any serious damage had been done. Running his hand over the wood now in the absolute darkness, Kemp couldn't even find the ragged groove.

He took a sip of his wine, breathing shallowly and pretending that the air carried the scent of night-blooming jasmine and dewy lawns instead of the smell of age-soured wood and rodent nests, and that it moved. In his imagination he watched moths bumble against the long-gone porch light.

He never turned on the real light; he knew that his cherished fantasy wouldn't survive the sight of the solid wall that crowded right up against the porch rail. There was a doorway where the porch steps had once been, but it led into the entry hall of the apartment building his father's house had been converted into, and all that was out there was a pay phone, cheap panelling peeling off the new walls, and, generally, a shopping cart or two. The entry hall and office had been added right onto the front of the old house—completely enclosing the porch and making an eccentric room of it—but he seldom entered or left the building through the new section, preferring the relatively unchanged back stairs.

He leaned back now and let the wine help him pretend. He'd never told any of the long string of renters and landlords that this was the house he had grown up in—he was afraid that sharing that information would diminish his relationship with the old building, and make it impossible for him to sit here quietly like this and, late at night, slide imperceptibly into the past.

The moths thumped and fluttered softly against the light, and, inhaling through the wine fumes, Kemp caught a whiff of jasmine, and then a warm breeze touched his cheek and a moment later he heard a faint pattering as jacaranda flowers, shaken from the tree out front, fell like a sower's cast of dead butterflies to the sidewalk and the street.

He opened his eyes and saw the tree's branches shift slowly against the dark sky, and coins of bright moonlight appeared, moved and disappeared in the tree's restless shadow. Kemp stood up, as carefully as a man with a tray of fragile, antique glass in his hands. He moved to the porch steps, went gingerly down them and then stole down the walkway to the sidewalk.

To his right he could see the railroad yard and, beyond it, the agitated glow that was the freeway. Too . . . hard, Kemp thought, too solidified, too much certainty and not enough possibility. He looked left, toward the traffic circle. It was quieter in that direction and aside from the moon the only source of illumination was the flashing yellow of the traffic lights. The wind seemed warmer in that direction, too. Trembling, he hurried toward the circle; and though he thought he glimpsed a couple of the tall, lean people in gray leotards—or maybe it was just one, darting rapidly from this shadowed area to that— tonight, for once, he was not going to let them frighten him.

The wind was tunnelled stronger under the Hatton Park bridge, and a plastic bag in a shopping cart bellied full like the sail of a ship, and pulled the cart forward until it stopped against the sneakered foot of an old woman who slept next to it. Mary Francis woke up and looked around. The trash-can fires had all burned out—it had to be closer to morning than to dusk.

She sniffed the intrusive desert wind, and her pulse quickened, for there were smells on it that she hadn't known in forty years, not since the days when this area was more orange groves than streets.

She fumbled in her topmost coat for one of her mirrors, and after she'd pulled out the irregular bit of silvered glass and stared into it for a few moments she exhaled a harsh sigh of wonder.

She had known this would happen if she worked hard enough at her collecting—and it seemed she finally had. Still staring into the mirror, she stood up and pushed her shopping cart out from under the bridge. In the moonlight all the scraps of cloth in her cart should have looked gray, but instead they glowed with their true color, the special sea-green that was the only hue of rag she would deign to pick up in her daily circuit of the trash cans and dumpsters—the never-forgotten color of the dress she'd worn at her debut in 1923. In recent years it had occurred to her that if she could find even a scrap of that dress, and then hang onto it, it might regenerate itself . . . slowly, yes, you couldn't be in a hurry, but if you were willing to wait . . . and she suspected that if the cloth were with her, it might regenerate her, too . . . banish the collapsed old wrinkled-bedsheet face and restore her real face, and figure, not only re-create the dress but also the Mary Francis that had worn it . . .

And look, now on this magic night it had happened. The face in the mirror was blurry, but it was clearly the face of the girl she'd never really stopped being. Oval face, big dark eyes, pale, smooth skin . . . that unaffected, trusting innocence.

She turned east, and the focus became clearer—but it was the what's-this-I-found-in-the-back-of-yer-old-garage face. Quickly she turned west, and was awed by the beauty of her own smile of relief when the girl-face returned, more clearly now.

She was facing the traffic circle. Keeping her eyes fixed on the ever-more-in-focus image in the mirror, she began pushing her shopping cart westward, and she didn't even notice the agile, faceless gray figures that dropped from trees and jackknifed up out of the sewer vents and went loping silently along toward the circle.

The traffic circle at Main and Bailey was the oldest part of town. Restaurants wanting to show a bit of local color always had to hang a couple of old black-and-white photographs of the circle with Pierce-Arrows and Model-T Fords driving around it and men in bowler hats and high collars sitting on the benches or leaning on the coping of the fountain. People in the restaurants would always look at the old photographs and try to figure out which way was north.

The flattened leathery thing that Cyclops had thought was a dried devilfish sailed on over the roof of the YMCA, frisbeed over the motorcycle cops who were waiting for someone to betray drunkenness by having trouble driving around the circle, and then like a dried leaf it smacked into the pool of the old fountain. It drifted to the tiled pillar in the center and wound up canted slightly out of the water against the tiles, its big empty eyes seeming to watch the rooftops.

"Are you okay?"

"Yes," he croaked, concealing his irritation at her tone, which had seemed to imply that he must be either crazy or having a fit to jump out of bed that way; but if he had objected she'd reply, in hurt surprise, "All I said was, 'are you okay?,'" which would put him two points down and give her the right to sigh in a put-upon way and make a show of having trouble getting back to sleep. "Just a dream," he said shortly.

"*Fine*," she said, and then added, just a little too soon, "I only *asked*."

He suppressed a grin. She'd been too eager, and done a riposte when there had only been a feint. He gave her a wondering look and said, "Gee, relax, hon. Maybe you were in the middle of a dream too, huh?" He chuckled with a fair imitation of fondness. "We *both* seem to be acting like *lunatics*." One-all, his advantage.

"What was the dream about?" she asked.

Oh no you don't, he thought. "I don't remember." He walked to the window and looked down at Main Street. The palm trees were bending and he could hear the low roaring of the wind.

Debbie rolled over and began breathing regularly, and Roger knew that until she really did go to sleep any noise he made would provoke the rendition of a startled awakening, so he resolved to stand by the window until he was certain she wasn't shamming. Of course she'd know what he was thinking and try to draw him into an error with convincing breathing-hitches and even—a tactical concession—undignified snortings.

He would wait her out. He stared down at the street and thought about his dream.

It was a dream he used to have fairly frequently when he was a child, though he hadn't had it since coming to California. Jesus, he thought, and I came to California in '57, when I was six years old. What does it mean, that I'm having it again after almost thirty years? And—I remember now—that dream always heralded the arrival of Evelyn, my as-they-like-to-call-it imaginary playmate.

The dream tonight had been so exactly the same as before that when he woke up he'd thought at first that he was in one of the many bedrooms he'd had back east, in the year—1956, it must have been—when his parents had been moving around so much. The dream always started with a train, seen from a distance, moving down a moonlit track across a field, with buildings a remote unevenness on the dark horizon. Then, and it was never *quite* scary in the dream, the whistle wailed and the smokestack emitted a blob of white smoke; the smoke didn't dissipate—it billowed but kept its volume like a splash of milk in a jug of clear oil, and when the train had disappeared in the distance the blob of smoke slowly formed into a white, blank-eyed face. And then, slow as a cloud, the face would drift into town and move up and down the dark streets, and at every bedroom window it would pause and silently peer in . . . until it came to Roger's window. When it came to his, it smiled and at last dissolved away, and then there was the sense of company in his mind.

He remembered, now, the last time he'd had the dream; it had been the night before his parents abandoned him. He had awakened early the next morning, and when his mother had walked into the kitchen to put on the coffee pot he'd already fixed himself a bowl of Cheerios.

"Up already, Rog?" his mother asked him. "What have we told you about getting into the fridge without asking?"

"Sorry," he'd said, and for at least a year afterward he had been certain that they'd abandoned him because he'd broken the rule about the refrigerator. "Evelyn's back," he remarked then, to change the subject.

His mother had frozen, holding the can of ground coffee, and her face had seemed to get leaner. "What—" she began harshly; then, in a desperately reasonable tone, "What do you mean, honey? She can't be. I know she found us again after we moved from Keyport to Redbank, and all those other times since, but we're in *New York* now, almost all the way to Buffalo, she can't have followed us all that way. You're just . . . *pretending*, this time, right?"

"Nah," he'd replied carelessly. "But she says it was a long trip. How long since we moved away from Atlantic City?"

His mother had sat down across the table from him, still holding the coffee can. "Five months," she whispered.

"Yeah, she flew over a river, the . . . she says Del Ware? And then she had to go around Phil-a-delph-ia, 'cause there was too many people there, and they—them all thinking, and wishing for things—started to bend the air, like too many people on a trampoline, and it would have bent all the way around and made a bubble, and she wouldn't a been able to get out of it, back to real places. And then, she says, she went around Scranton and Elmira, and now here she is."

The six-year-old Roger had looked up from his cereal then, and he realized for the first time that his mother was afraid of Evelyn. And now, standing at his bedroom window in Santa Margarita while

Debbie pretended to be asleep in the bed behind him, it suddenly and belatedly occurred to him that it might have been Evelyn's remarkable tracking abilities that had made his parents move so frequently during that year.

But why, he wondered, would they both so fear a child's imaginary playmate? It wasn't as if Evelyn could be seen, or move things, or say where lost watches and rings had got to . . . much less hurt anyone, like the "imaginary playmate" in the story by John Collier. The only one she got even remotely forceful with was me, censoring my dreams whenever I dreamed about things she didn't like. And hell, when I first started talking about her, my Mom was just amused . . . used to ask me how Evelyn was, and even cut a piece of cake for her on my fifth birthday. It wasn't until I started telling Mom things that Evelyn had told me—like that Evelyn was three years older than me, to the month—that Mom stopped finding the idea of an imaginary playmate charming.

Roger thought about the current unpaid bill from the private investigator. If he can find you before I become too broke to pay for his services, he thought, I'll get a chance to *ask* you what bothered you about Evelyn, *Mom*—after I get through asking you and Dad about the ethics of sending a six-year-old boy into a drug store with a quarter to buy candy with, and then driving away, forever, while he's inside. And it might be soon—if the investigator's deductions from studying money-order records and Social Security payments are correct, and you and Dad really do live within blocks of here.

Someone was shouting furiously, down the street . . . and walking this way, by the sound of it. A male voice, Roger noted—probably old Cyclops. What the hell is it that makes so many street bums shout? Old women at bus stops who make heads turn two blocks away with the volume and pure rage of their almost totally incoherent outbursts, men that walk out into traffic so that screeching brakes punctuate their wrathfully delivered catalogue of the various things they are not going to stand for anymore . . . and people who, like Cyclops here tonight, simply walk up and down the empty nighttime streets shouting warnings and challenges to imaginary enemies: it must be some kind of urban malady, new to civilization as far as I know. Maybe it's contagious, and sometime it'll be me and Debbie down there shaking our fists at empty stretches of sidewalk and screaming, *Oh yeah, you sons of bitches?*

He glanced back at Debbie. Her sooner than me, he thought. If her parents didn't live in Balboa and own a boat and a cabin up at Big Bear, and lots all over hell, would I be intending to marry her? No way. And if I do succeed in finding my parents, and if they prove to be as affluent as my memories of their cars and houses indicate they were, I'll send her back to her parents. My gain and their loss.

He shivered. The room wasn't cold, but he'd felt a draft of . . . of success passing by; a breath of impending squalor stirring the dust under the bedroom door, and he thought the bills on the desk were softly rustled by a stale shift of air that somehow carried the smell of gray hair and temporary jobs, and trash bags full of empty cans of creamed corn and Spam and corned beef hash.

I can't let go of her, he thought, until I'm *certain* about my parents—until I've not only found them, but found out how much they're worth, and then shamed or even blackmailed them into giving me a lot of money, and making me their heir. Only then will I be able to ditch poor loony Debbie . . . as any less avaricious man would have done right after that first time she ran back to her parents.

It had been about four months earlier. As soon as he'd realized she had left him, he had known where she must have gone. He had taken the bus down to her parents' house the next day. He'd been prepared to claim that he loved their daughter, and to explain that the two of them had been living together only because they couldn't get married yet; he'd braced himself for a lot of parental disapproval, even for violence . . . but he had not been prepared for what awaited him.

Debbie's mother had opened the door when he knocked, but when, nervously defiant, he introduced himself, she only smiled. "Oh, you're Roger! I'm so pleased to meet you, Debbie's told us so *much* about you! Do come in and say hello, I know a visit from you will cheer her up . . ." He wanted to explain that he'd come to take her back with him, but her mother was still speaking as she led him inside, out of the sunlight and into the living room, where curtains had been drawn across all the windows and no lights were on. There was a chair standing in the middle of the floor. "Yes, our Debbie likes to go out and make new friends," the mother was saying cheerfully, "but," she added with a wave toward the chair, "as you can see, she always comes home again."

Peering in the dimness, Roger had finally noticed that Debbie was sitting motionless in the chair, staring blankly . . . and then that she was *tied* into the chair, with belts around her waist, wrists and ankles. Without conscious thought he had left the house, and he walked quite a way up Main before remembering that he would have to get a bus if he wanted to get home before dark.

Later he had gone back again to that house, and caught Debbie in a more accessible segment of whatever her doomed mood-cycle was, and he talked her into returning to the apartment they'd been sharing: in his more fatuous moments he told himself that he'd gone back for her in order to save her from that environment and her evidently demented mother, but late on frightened nights like this one he could admit, to himself at least, that his concern for her was the concern a man feels for his last uncancelled credit card.

Debbie now emitted a prolonged sound that was halfway between a snore and a sentence, and he knew she must really be asleep. I'll wait till old Cyclops has gone by, Roger thought, and then crawl carefully back into bed. I wonder if Evelyn will still censor my dreams. What was it she used to object to? The dreams she didn't like were all prompted by something I experienced, so she was probably just my subconscious mind suppressing memories which, in some unacknowledged way, I found traumatic. I still remember the time my parents took me to the Crystal Lake amusement park in New Jersey— they were jovial during the first half of the drive, but when we got off the turnpike they seemed to unexpectedly recognize the area, and they got very tense—and, after that, Evelyn wouldn't let me dream about that neighborhood. And once I saw a cowboy movie in which, at one point, a cavalry soldier was shot and fell off his horse but had one foot caught in the stirrup and got dragged along, bouncing like a rag doll over the prairie—Evelyn always squelched any dream that began to include that bit. And after I got my tonsils taken out, she wouldn't let me dream about the smell of the ether; I was free to dream about the hospital and the sore throat and the ice cream, but not that smell.

"*Climb back down into your holes, you bastards!*" shouted Cyclops on the sidewalk below. Debbie shifted and muttered, and Roger mentally damned the noisy old bum. "*Dare to come near me,*" Cyclops added, "*and I'll smash your gray faces for you! Break your scissor legs!*"

Interested in spite of himself, Roger glanced down at the street— and then peered more closely. Cyclops, as usual, was lurching along the sidewalk and shaking his fists at dire adversaries, but tonight, for once, he seemed to be yelling at people who were actually there. A half-dozen dark figures were bounding about on the shadowed lawns and turning fantastic cartwheels in the dimness between streetlights. Roger's first guess was that they must be young theater majors from some local college, out larking and wino-hassling after some rehearsal or cast-party, for the figures all seemed to be dressed in gray leotards and wearing gray nylon stockings pulled down over their faces. Then he saw one of them spring from a grasshopper-crouch . . . and rise all the way up to the third floor of an office building, and cling to the sill of a dark window there for a moment, before spider-jumping back down to the pavement.

The yellow-flashing traffic lights were strangely coordinated, flinging relayed pulses past at the height of his window, and he felt Evelyn's presence very strongly. *Come out, Roger,* she called to him from out in the warm-as-breath night. *Decide what you want, so I can give it to you.*

"Can you find my Mom and Dad?" he whispered.

Debbie instantly sat up in bed behind him. "What?" she said. "Are you crazy?"

Yes, came Evelyn's answer from outside. *Look. Here they are. I'll bring them out for you.*

Roger stepped away from the window and began pulling on his pants.

"Roger!" said Debbie sharply, real concern beginning to show through her reflexive malice. "You're walking in your sleep. Get back in bed."

"I'm awake," he said, stepping into his shoes without bothering about socks. "I'm going out. You go back to sleep."

Aware that she was being left out of something, Debbie bounded out of bed. "I'm coming with you."

"No, damn it," he said almost pleadingly as he buttoned alternate buttons on his shirt. "What do you want to come for?"

"Because you don't want me to," she said, her voice muffled under the dress she was pulling on over her head. She stepped into shoes on her way to the door and had it open before he'd even finished tucking in his shirt. "At least I'm waiting for you."

They left the apartment by the front door and hurried down the stairs to the pavement. Leaves and flattened paper cups whirled through the air like nocturnal birds, and Cyclops was already a block ahead of Roger and Debbie. Looking past the old man, Roger could see that the stop lights north of the traffic circle were sending synchronized yellow pulses south; the pulses from south and north Main met at the circle like tracer bullets from two directions being fired at a common target.

His feet were suddenly warmer, and, glancing down, he noticed that he had socks on; also, every button of his shirt was fastened, and his shoes looked polished.

He began running toward the bending palms that ringed the circle. Debbie, running right behind him, called out in a voice made timid by fright or wonder, "Where are we going?"

"I could be wrong," he shouted without looking back, "but I think that, tonight at least, it's the place where dreams come true."

Jack Singer straightened the knot of his tie and then stood back from the mirror and admired his reflection. A well-tailored suit certainly did things for a man—not only did he look lean and fit, with somehow no trace of projecting belly, but even his face seemed tanned and alert, his hair fuller and darker. He patted his breast pocket and felt the slim billfold there, and without having to look he knew it contained a Diner's Club card, and a Visa—one with that asterisk that means you're good for more than the average guy—and a gold American Express card, and a few crisp hundred dollar bills for tips.

He stepped away from the mirror and took a sip of brandy from the glass on the bureau. Good stuff, that five-star Courvoisier. "You about ready, dear?" he called toward his wife's dressing room.

"In a minute," she said. "The diamond fell out of one of my fingernails, and I've got it Super Gluing."

He nodded, and though his smile didn't falter, his fine-drawn eyebrows contracted into a frown. Diamonds in her *what? Her fingernails?* He'd never heard of such a thing . . . but he knew better than to ask her about it, for it was clearly just one more part of this weirdly wonderful evening.

For just a moment, after they had awakened an hour ago, he had thought it was the middle of the night, and their apartment seemed to be . . . a shabby one they had lived in once. But then the hot Santa Ana wind had puffed in at the window and he had remembered that it was early evening, and that his wife and he were due to attend the dinner being given in their honor at the . . . what was the name of the hotel? . . . just the finest hotel in the state . . . the *Splendide,* that was it.

He glanced out the window. "The limo is here, darling," he called.

"Coming." His wife appeared from her dressing room. Fine clothes had done wonders for her, too—she looked twenty pounds slimmer, and would be described as voluptuous now instead of just plain damn fat.

The chauffeur knocked quietly at the door, and Singer held out his arm for his wife to take.

They dutifully had a drink apiece in the limousine as it carried them smoothly west on Bailey, and though they couldn't recall gulping them the glasses were empty by the time the chauffeur made the sweeping turn around three-quarters of the traffic circle and then with never a jiggle turned south onto Main and drew in to the curb in front of the *Hotel Splendide.* A man in an almost insanely ornate red coat and gold-crusted hat opened the door for them.

Singer got out and then helped his wife out, and he noticed that the sidewalk, which had the *Splendide* insignia inset into the cement every yard or so, was so brightly lit by spotlights on the lawn and the dozen huge chandeliers in the lobby that he and his wife cast no shadows.

"They are awaiting you in the Napoleon Lounge, M'sieur," said the doorman, bowing obsequiously, "drinks and hors d'oeuvres there, and then you are to dine in the Grand Ballroom." Out of sight somewhere, an orchestra was richly performing a medley of favorites from the 1940s.

Singer produced a hundred-dollar bill and let it disappear into the man's gloved hand. "Thank you, Armand."

They strolled across the carpeted floor, surreptitiously admiring their reflections in the tall mirrors that alternated with marble panels on all the walls, and when they walked through the gilded arch into the Napoleon Lounge the other guests all greeted their appearance with delighted cries.

And they were all elegant—the lovely young woman in the striking sea-green dress, the piratically handsome old fellow with the eyepatch, the young couple who had been filling two plates over at one of the hors d'oeuvre tables . . . and especially the woman who was walking toward them with her hands out in welcome, a smile on her porcelain-pale face . . .

"Good evening," the woman said, "we're all so glad to see you. I'm your hostess this evening—my name is Evelyn."

Roger, looking up from the plate he'd been filling with caviar and thin slices of some black bread that was thick with caraway seeds, saw the newcomers flinch, just perceptibly, when Evelyn introduced herself, and instantly he knew that this couple must be his parents. They quickly recovered their poise and allowed Evelyn to lead them in, and Roger studied them out of the corner of his eye as, trying not to betray the trembling of his hands and the hard thudding of his heart, he forked a devilled egg and a tiny ear of pickled baby corn onto his plate. They do look prosperous, he thought with cautious satisfaction.

Evelyn was leading the couple straight toward the table beside which Roger and Debbie stood. "Jack and Irma," she said to Roger's parents, "this is Debbie and Roger." Again his parents flinched, and Irma stared hard and expressionlessly at Roger for a couple of seconds before extending her hand. She opened her mouth as if to say something, but Evelyn spoke first.

"Ah, here come the stewards," she said. "The cocktails are all first-rate here, of course, and on the table there is a list of the particular specialties of the house. And now you must excuse me—I think our Mr. Kemp has a question." She smiled and spun away toward a middle-aged man who was eyeing the stewards with something like alarm. As much to postpone confronting his parents as from thirst, Roger squinted at the sheet of apparently genuine vellum on which, in fancy calligraphy, the specialty drinks were described, but they were all frothy things like Pink Squirrels and White Russians and Eggnog, and he decided to follow his usual custom in dressy bars and ask for Chivas Regal Royal Salute 25-Year-Old. . . in a snifter. That always impressed people.

The steward who approached their table, a tall, thin fellow in dark gray, bowed and said, "Can I bring you anything from the bar?"

"I'll have one of your Pink Squirrels, but made with *whiskey* instead of *bourbon*," said Debbie in her best misconception-squared style.

Roger looked up to give the steward a *humor-her* wink, but he stepped back quickly with a smothered exclamation, for the man's face, just for a fraction of a second, had seemed to be a featureless gray angularity, like a plastic trash bag stretched taut across the front of a skull.

A moment later it was just an indistinct face, but Roger said, "Uh, right, and a Scotch for me, excuse me," and took a couple of steps toward the center of the room.

The dignified man with the eyepatch was staring at him, and Roger realized that it was Cyclops, not looking nearly as ridiculous in antique Navy dress blues as one might have expected. Cyclops, who wasn't holding a drink, crossed to him and said quietly, "You saw that one, didn't you? For a second you saw it wasn't a waiter, but one of the Great Gray-Legged Scissors Men."

Oh Jesus, thought Roger unhappily. Where in hell is my Scotch? "One of the *what?*"

"Oh, sorry, right—I just call 'em that 'cause they look like that guy in the old kids' rhyme, remember? The Great Red-Legged Scissors Man, who dashes up with a huge pair of scissors and cuts the thumbs off kids that suck their thumbs? How's it end?—'I knew he'd come . . . to naughty little suck-a-thumb.'"

"They're . . ." began Roger, so wildly disoriented that it was hard to take a deep breath or refrain from giggling, "They're going to cut off our thumbs, are they?"

Cyclops looked disgusted. "No. Are you drunk? I *said* I just call 'em that 'cause they look like the guy in the picture that went with that poem. Except these here guys are all gray. No, *these* guys appear out o' nowhere when somebody who can boost dreams comes along, the way raindrops appear out o' nowhere when a low-pressure area comes along. Maybe the gray guys are the deep roots of our own minds, curled back up so they poke out o' the ground near us and seem separate, like the worm that got himself pregnant; or maybe they're ghosts that you can only see in the spirit light that shines from one of these imagination-amplifier people." He nodded toward Evelyn, "She's the one doing it here tonight. The trouble is, such people warp the night, and the more minds she's overdriving the sharper the angle of the curve, like blowing in one of those kid's-toy loops that holds a flat surface of soap-film, you know? You blow harder and harder, and the film bellies out rounder and rounder, and then—pop!—it's a bubble, broke loose and drifting away."

"Right," Roger said, nodding repeatedly and looking around for, if nothing else, a drink someone had abandoned. "Right—a bubble floating away, gotcha. Scissors men. You don't see a *drink* anywhere, do—"

"It's gonna happen tonight," said Cyclops harshly. "Damn soon. Did you notice the traffic signals? You know why they're all flashing at the same second so often now? 'Cause we're only still intersecting with a few of 'em, what seems like many is just lots o' reflections of only a couple. When they're perfectly in step that'll mean there's only one left, and the connection between this bubble and the real world is just a thin, thin tunnel."

"Okay, but . . ."

"I'm leaving now," Cyclops interrupted. "If you got any sense, you'll come too. In five minutes it may be too late."

"Uhh . . ." Roger looked thoughtfully down at the elegant Yves St. Laurent suit he'd found himself wearing when he had approached the hotel, and he looked back at the low-cut, sequined gown that Debbie was—just as inexplicably—wearing. Now he held his hand out, palm up, fingers slightly curled, and he concentrated—and then suddenly he was holding a snifter that had an inch of amber fluid swirling in the bottom of it. He smiled up at the stern old man. "Imagination-amplifier, hey?" he said slowly. "I'll stay for just a little while, thanks. Hell, five minutes—that's plenty of time."

Cyclops smiled with pity and contempt, then turned and strode out of the room. Roger stared over at Evelyn. Who *was* she, *what* was she? Clearly something more than a child's imaginary playmate, or—what had he guessed her to be, earlier?—just a function of his subconscious mind. Of course, maybe he was better off not knowing, not asking inconvenient questions.

He carried his drink back to where Debbie and his parents were standing. "Well!" he said heartily. "Mom, Dad—it's good to see you again after all these years."

He was shocked by the physical change these words produced in the couple—his father shrank, and was suddenly balding and gray, and the gaps between the buttons of his ill-fitting suit were pulled wide by an abrupt protrusion of belly, and his mother became ludicrously fat, her expression of well-bred amusement turning to one of petulant unhappiness—and belatedly it occurred to Roger that their apparent affluence might be as ephemeral as his own suit and snifter of Scotch.

"You . . . *are* Roger, aren't you?" the old woman whispered. "And," she added, turning in horror toward their hostess, "that is Evelyn."

"Yes," Roger said, a little surprised to realize that his adventurous delight in this evening had, all at once, evaporated, leaving him feeling old and bitter. "She only found her way back to me tonight. The trip took her more than twenty-five years . . . but, you remember, she always avoided very populated areas."

"Until tonight," his father pointed out quietly.

"Until tonight," Roger agreed.

His father's smile was sickly. "Look," the old man said, "we've got lots to discuss, I'll admit—lots to, uh, beg forgiveness for, even—but can we get *out* of here right now? Without attracting the attention of . . . our hostess?"

Roger looked around. Evelyn was chatting gaily with the group on the other side of the room, and every time she glanced up the chandeliers brightened and the trays of hors d'oeuvres came into clearer focus, but the stewards were getting leaner and taller, and their features were fading like images cast by a projector with a dimming bulb, and peripherally Roger saw one of them out in the lobby leap right up to the ceiling and cling there like a big fly.

"Yeah," said Roger, suddenly frightened and taking Cyclops' warning seriously. He let his drink evaporate, glass and all. "If anybody asks, say we're just going out for some fresh air—and go on about what a great time you're having." He took Debbie's arm. "Come on," he said.

"No, I'm staying. You know what they put in this drink, after I *told* them not to?"

"We're only going for a stroll, just to take a look at the front of the building—but sure, stay if you want."

"No, I'm coming." She put her drink down, and Roger noticed that the glass broke up silently into an unfocussed blur when she let go of it.

The four of them made their way to the lobby unhindered—Evelyn even saw them go, but looked more exasperated than angry—and Roger led them around the faceless, ceiling-crouching thing and across the carpeted floor, through the front doors, and down the marble steps to the sidewalk.

"South on Main, come on," he said, trying not to panic in spite of how synchronized the traffic signals were, "away from the circle." As they trudged along, Roger felt a sudden slickness against his feet, and he realized that his socks had disappeared. He didn't have to glance to the side to know that Debbie was back in the old sack dress she'd pulled on over her head right after leaping out of bed. Behind him the ticktack of his mother's heels and the knock of his father's shoes became a flapping—bedroom slippers, it sounded like. Good, Roger thought— I guess we weren't too late.

He looked up, and the whole sky was turning slowly, like a vast, glitter-strewn wheel, and he couldn't decide whether to take that as a good sign or a bad one. Funny how the night moves, he thought nervously. I don't think this is what Bob Seger meant.

And then his feet were comfortable again, and even though they'd been walking in a straight line he saw the traffic circle ahead, and, from around the corner to the right, the glow of the *Splendide's* main entrance.

The others noticed it too, and slowed. "We were walking south on Main," Debbie said, ". . . away from the traffic circle."

"And now, without having changed course," said Roger wearily, "we're headed east on Bailey, toward it. We waited too long."

Jack Singer was smiling broadly. "Screw this," he said, and his voice was cheerful, if a bit shrill. "I'll see you all later." He turned and fled back the way they'd come, his newly restored suit and shoes disappearing within a few yards, leaving him an overweight man in pajamas and slippers, puffing and flapping like a clown as he ran.

Roger's mother took a hesitant step after him, but Roger took her arm. "Don't bother, Mom—I'm pretty sure the quickest way to catch up with him is to just keep going straight ahead."

Debbie was patting the fabric of her sequined gown. "I hope I get to keep this," she said.

The traffic lights were in perfect step now. Roger considered leading the two women around the circle and straight out Bailey, eastward, but he was fatalistically sure that Bailey Boulevard, as they proceeded along it, would within half a block or so become Main Street, and they'd be facing the circle again. Neither his mother nor Debbie objected when he turned right at Main, toward the *Splendide*.

The entrance was more brightly illuminated than ever, but it was a harsh glare like that cast by arc lights, and the cars pulling up and driving away moved in sudden hops, like spiders, or like cars in a film from which a lot of the frames have been cut. The music was a weary, prolonged moaning of brass and strings. Jack Singer, once again in his suit, slouched up from the far side of the hotel and joined them on the steps.

Roger thought of making some cutting remark—something like, "Not so easy to ditch me this time, huh, Pop?"—but both his parents looked so unhappy, and he himself was so frightened, that he didn't have the heart for it.

"Oh, God," wailed his mother, "will we ever get back home?"

Roger was facing the hotel, but he turned around when he heard splashing behind him. It was the fountain—the traffic circle was now right in front of the hotel, and the pavement below the steps wasn't the Main Street sidewalk any longer, was now just a concrete walkway between the grass of the circle and the steps of the hotel.

Dark buildings, as nondescript as painted stage props, crowded up around the other sides of the circle, and Roger could see only one traffic light. It was flashing slower, and its yellow color had a faint orange tint.

"Do come in," called Evelyn from the open lobby doors. "It's just time to sit down for dinner." Her face was paler, and she seemed to be trembling.

Roger glanced at his mother. "Maybe," he said. Then he turned toward the circle and concentrated; it was harder than making a snifter of Scotch appear, but in a moment he had projected, blotting out the dim traffic circle, a downtown street he remembered seeing on the way to the Crystal Lake amusement park in New Jersey. It was one of the things Evelyn had never permitted him to dream about.

He was surprised at how clearly he was able to project it—until he saw that the sky behind the shabby New Jersey office buildings was overcast and gray instead of the brilliant blue he remembered, and he realized that someone else, perhaps unintentionally, perhaps even against their will, was helping to fill out the picture, using their own recollections of it.

Behind him Evelyn gasped—and the one visible traffic signal began to flash a little faster, and to lose some of the orange tint.

Okay, Roger thought tensely, the cord isn't quite cut yet. What else was there? Oh yeah . . .

He made the New Jersey street disappear and instantly replaced it
with a prairie, across which a horse and rider galloped. At first the
rider was a cavalry soldier, as in the movie scene Roger remembered,
but again someone else's projection changed the scene—the rider was
smaller now, and not dressed in blue . . . it was hard to see clearly, and
again Roger got the impression that this altering of what he was
projecting was unintentional . . . and when the rider fell off the horse
it was hard to tell which foot had caught in the stirrup . . .

The pavement below him had widened, and now he could see
another traffic light. The two were still in step, but were at least flashing
in their normal pace and color.

He replaced the vision of the galloping horse and the suffering
figure behind it with a rendition of the hospital room in which he'd
awakened after the removal of his tonsils . . . and this time the picture
was altered instantly and totally, though the lingering-in-the-back-of-
his-throat smell of ether grew stronger. He saw a windowless room
with newspapers spread neatly all over the floor, and there was a sort
of table, with . . .

The night shuddered, and suddenly he could see down Main
Street—and, way down south, he saw one yellow light blinking out of
synch. "This way out," he said, stepping to the sidewalk and walking
south. "Walk through the visions—I'm building us a bridge."

Again the downtown New Jersey street appeared, and without his
volition a young couple—hardly more than teenagers—entered the
picture. They both looked determined and scared as they walked along
the sidewalk looking at the address numbers on the buildings.

Roger kept leading his group southward, and when the New Jersey
picture faded he saw that the out-of-step signal was closer. Debbie was
walking carefully right beside him. Thank God, he thought, that she
hasn't chosen this occasion to be difficult—but where are my parents?

He couldn't turn to look behind him, for the next projection was
appearing, cleaving a path out of Evelyn's imploding fake world.
Obviously Evelyn's aversion to these memories was strong, for her own
projection simply recoiled from these the way a live oyster contracts
away from lemon juice squeezed onto it.

The cowboy movie memory was now altered out of recognition,
though it was the most effective yet at rerandomizing the traffic lights;
now it was a girl instead of a cavalry soldier, and somehow she still

had *both* feet in the stirrups, and though there was blood she didn't seem to be being dragged over any prairie . . . in fact she was lying on a table in a windowless room with newspapers all over the floor, and the ether reek was everywhere like the smell of rotten pears, and her young boyfriend was pacing the sidewalk out in front of the shabby office and at last the overcast sky had begun dropping rain so that he needn't struggle to hold back his tears any longer . . .

"Woulda been a girl, I think," came the multiply remembered voice of a man . . .

Shock and sudden comprehension slowed Roger's steps, and involuntarily he turned and looked back at Evelyn as bitterness and loss closed his throat and brought tears to his eyes. The man knew his business, he thought. "Goodbye, Evelyn," he whispered.

Goodbye, Roger, spoke a voice—a receding voice—in his head.

The projected scene ahead was even clearer now, but beyond it lay the real pre-dawn Santa Margarita streets. "Come on," said Roger, stepping forward again. "We're almost out of it."

Debbie was right beside him, but he didn't hear his parents, so he paused and turned.

They were stopped several yards back, staring at the pavement.

"Come on," Roger said harshly. "It's the way out."

"We can't go through it," his father said.

"Again," added his mother faintly.

"We weren't *married* yet, then, in—'48 . . ." his father began; but Roger had taken Debbie's hand and resumed their forward progress.

They moved slowly through the windowless room, every full stride covering a few inches of newspaper-strewn floor, and then there was the fluttering thump of something landing in a paper-lined wastebasket and they were out in the streets and the air was cold and Roger didn't have socks on and the traffic signals, ready for all the early-morning commuters, were switching through their long-green, short-yellow, long-red cycles, and the one-eyed old hobo standing in the street nodded curtly at them and then motioned them to step aside, for an ancient woman was puffing along the sidewalk behind them, pushing a shopping cart full of green scraps of cloth, and behind her trotted a lean little old fellow whom Roger remembered having seen many times walking the streets of Santa Margarita, lingering by empty lots when the workmen had gone home and the concrete outlines of long-gone houses could still be seen among the mud and litter and tractor tracks. There was no one else on the street. The sky was already pale blue, though the sun wasn't up yet.

Debbie glanced down at herself and pursed her lips angrily to see that her fine gown had disappeared again. "Are you through with your games?" she snapped. "Can we go home now?"

"You go ahead," Roger told her. "I want to walk some."

"No, come back with me."

He shook his head and walked away, slapping his pants pockets for change and trying to remember where he'd seen the all-night Mexican diner with the sign about the menudo breakfast.

"When you do come back," Debbie called furiously, "I won't be there! And don't bother going to my parents' house, 'cause I won't be there either!"

Good for you, he thought.

And as the first rays of the sun touched the tall palms around the traffic circle a scrap of something, unnoticed by anyone, sank to the bottom of the fountain pool, at peace at last.

❖ AUTHOR'S NOTE ❖

When we watched the movie The Amityville Horror, *I was struck by the development that the demon or demons followed the terrorized family when they fled to another residence—but that it took the demons a couple of weeks to get to the new place. Did they walk? Get lost for a while on the way? The new residence was apparently not far from the original haunted house—how long would it have taken the demons to catch up if the family had moved all the way to the West Coast?*

To use demons seemed a little too remeniscent of The Amityville Horror, *so I decided that a suppsedly imaginary playmate would be more useful—and then I had to figure out what a not-so-imaginary-after-all playmate would in fact be.*

⊰ DISPENSATION ⊱

"I am content to survey my ample height and pallid complexion (bleach'd by the deep Saxon forests and Scandinavian snows) . . ."

—H. P. Lovecraft, in a letter to
Frank Belknap Long, 11 December 1923

"On my expedition of the 20th [of October], a particularly congenial bodyguard or retinue attended me through the sunlit arcades of the grove—in the person of *two tiny kittens,* one gray and one tortoise-shell, who appeared out of nowhere in the midst of the sylvan solitudes."

—H. P. Lovecraft, in a letter to
James Ferdinand Morton, March, 1937. His last letter.

IT WAS CLEAR that the man was going to die soon—certainly before the next summer, and already the leaves of the oaks and maples in the Squantum Woods had fallen to make a rustling carpet, gold in the sunset light that filtered between the trunks.

Though his back ached and his feet were swollen in his old lace-up boots as he picked his way through the woods, and an hour ago he had unbuttoned his celluloid collar and stuffed it into his coat pocket, he had walked five miles here from the house he leased on College Street in Providence. For decades he had explored the Providence environs, but he had never been to this part of the east shore of Narraganset Bay, and he might very well have sensed that the time left to him was short.

He paused and closed his eyes clenching his fists against a spasm of pain in his abdomen —

And fifteen miles south of where he stood, the ancient Newport Tower shivered imperceptibly on its 11th century foundations, and to the east, in the shallows of the Taunton River, the petroglyphs on the long stone known as the Dighton Rock were momentarily more clearly incised; and half a dozen yards behind the man, four tiny paws stepped onto the dry leaves.

It was not too long a step, for they had been here before, long ago, and in Freyja's realm of Folkvangr it was always the sunset hour.

The screen of an i-Phone briefly lit the faces of two young men crouched beside a gravestone in the Swan Point Cemetery, and then they were once again silhouettes faintly backlit by moonlight. Down the slope behind them the broad Seekonk River swept silently past, and the breeze fluttered the leaves of the surrounding beech trees.

"Ten to midnight," said one of the men softly.

The other man nodded` and shrugged a knapsack off his shoulders. Laying it on the damp grass, he unbuckled it and pulled out four hardcover books, a short cylindrical cardboard carton, and an old crank-style telephone.

He clicked on a pencil flashlight and shined it on the spine of one of the books. *"Elements of English Composition,"* he read, *"Grammatical, Rhetorical, Logical, and Practical."*

"Grammar books were on the west wall of his study," said his companion, and the man with the flashlight set the book upright on the grass on one side of the gravestone.

The other three books were a battered copy of Milton's *Poems*, Dunsany's *Chronicles of Rodriguez*, and a 1904 edition of the *Farmer's Almanac*. As he set each one down in the compass point the other man indicated, he flipped to the front flyleaf of each to make sure the same one-time owner's name was inked there.

"They're the right ones, Trevor," said the other man. "You think I have a lot of copies of Dunsany books lying around?"

"Too bad we couldn't have got some of his furniture too."

"The books are what he'll recognize. And we could hardly have dragged tables and chairs out here anyway, even if they still exist."

Trevor shrugged, then worked the lid off of the cardboard cylinder, which was still very cold. The scent of vanilla blotted out the faint tidal smell of the river.

He carefully set the carton on top of the gravestone, then pushed the antique telephone across the grass and sat back. "It's close enough to midnight. Call him up."

The other man lifted the two wires that were attached to the back of the bakelite box and thrust each of them through the grass into the soil, a foot apart; then he lifted the earpiece from its cradle on the side of the telephone and pressed it to his ear.

With his free hand he began turning the crank, and as the armature spun inside the fixed magnets in the magneto, he said, speaking distinctly, "Howard Phillips Lovecraft, call for Howard Phillips Lovecraft."

Trevor sprang to his feet. "Jeez, Max, the wet grass—I'm getting a shock!"

"Sit down," hissed his companion. "So's he. And it won't dissolve *you*." He went on, "Call for Howard Phillips Lovecraft . . ."

In the twilit afterlife realm called Folkvangr, where time is distance and distance is unmeasurable, the goddess Freyja's chariot was paused, motionless, the harnesses empty and lying loose on the perpetual grass.

The October evening breeze was chilly on Lovecraft's sweaty forehead when the pain had passed, and he leaned against the trunk of an oak tree to catch his breath. Looking up through the boughs which shook against the cold, above the distant glow of the lights of Providence he could see the bright spots in the darkening sky that were Venus and Saturn—for some reason he found himself thinking of them as Alfheimr and Muspelheim, two of the worlds on the cosmic Yggdrasil tree in Norse mythology—and he turned when he heard a stirring among the leaves behind him.

Two kittens had appeared from somewhere and were stepping toward him. Glad of the distraction, Lovecraft carefully braced one hand against the trunk and lowered himself to sit in the leaves. "Blithe spirits of the ancient wood," he whispered, smiling as he pulled his watch free of his waistcoat pocket and waved the chain where the kittens could see it. "What brings you here?"

One of the little cats began purring and batting at the chain, but when Lovecraft extended his hand to the other, a paw darted out and claws raked the back of his hand.

"Oh, you're a fierce one, aren't you?" Lovecraft said, gently drawing his hand back to look at the scratches.

In the twilight glow through the trees he saw one thin straight line of blood, with two parallel lines angling up from it on the right side.

Having marked him, that kitten joined its fellow in swatting the watch chain.

Trevor was aware of a deepening in the shadows beside him, and when he glanced to the side he inhaled sharply—for a patch of shadow now imposed against the dim landscape was in the shape of a standing man.

Trevor's heart was pounding, and the breath was caught in his throat.

Max had obviously seen it too, for the buzz of the cranking paused, and then resumed, faster. "Ask him!" he said shrilly, flexing the fingers of his free hand on the telephone's earpiece.

Without looking away from the shadow, Trevor whispered, "What if it's not —"

"Dammit, who else could it be?" Max nodded toward the books on the grass and the carton of ice cream on the headstone. "This current will dissolve him to nothing in a minute or so—he's been dead nearly eighty years! *Ask him.*"

Trevor took a deep breath and peered nervously at the spot where the shadow's eyes would be.

"In 1926," he said quickly, "Harry Houdini was performing in Providence, and he approached you, hired you to write a book—it was to be called *The Cancer of Superstition*—do you remember?"

The shadow was raising its smoky arms. Trevor glanced toward Max, who shook his head and muttered, "Nothing yet."

Trevor went on, speaking to the shadow, "Okay, Houdini suggested a line of research, but a couple of weeks later he was killed—somebody hit him so hard that it ruptured his appendix—and the manuscript you were working on for him was stolen. Right?"

Max made a chopping motion and sat up straight, and even in the dimness Trevor could see a gleam of sweat on the man's forehead. "Apparent evidence," Max said in a harsh whisper, clearly repeating what he was hearing on the phone; "survive death, spirit undiminished . . . forever." After a few moments he continued, still repeating, "Obviously nonsense, but . . . material was stolen . . . before I could pinpoint inevitable flaws . . ."

"We need to know what it was," pressed Trevor, facing the shadow again. "What was the line of research that Houdini asked you to pursue?"

The shapes that seemed to be the ghost's hands had merged now with the dark oval that was its head; and then a shape glowed there in red. It looked like a capital F with the pair of arms bent upward.

Abruptly Max yanked the earpiece away from his head. "Trouble," he gasped. "I got the infinity tone, we're shut down. He's claimed after all."

"Claimed?" protested Trevor. "No—by who or what? Dammit, the man was a total atheist!"

"*I* don't know! But that sign," said Max, nodding toward the shadow without looking at it, "is a Norse rune." He yanked the wires out of the ground and shoved the bakelite telephone across the grass toward his companion. "We gotta get out of here—we just tried to boil out somebody's citizen."

"A rune?" Trevor was hastily tucking the telephone into the knapsack. "That's Vikings? There were never Vikings around here."

"Sure there were, that tower in Newport—and a rock with runes on it that's in a museum now, that used to be in a river east of here. Leave the stuff, the sooner we're —"

The shadow was gone, freed to shimmer away at last into the direction of sunset, but two large, low shapes were approaching from the direction of the river.

In timeless Folkvangr, the goddess Frejya forever rides in a chariot drawn by two cats, and receives the souls of Viking who die in battle. Once, at the behest of the cats, she granted a dispensation which allowed for the entry of a skald, a descendant of Vikings and composer of stories, who had befriended their mortal kin, and who had memorably written a piece called "The Cats of Ulthar." That skald dwells in the sunset meadows of Folkvangr for eternity.

✤　✤　✤

The bodies of two Brown University students, viciously slashed, were found the following morning in Swan Point Cemetery; and until the theory proved to be unsustainable, the coroner speculated that the killings were the work of some escaped lion or tiger. All that was found beside the bodies were a knapsack and an antique telephone. Anything else that might have been there had been taken away.

✤ AUTHOR'S NOTE ✤

When our friend Bill Wu asked me for a story about animals for inclusion in an anthology being put together to fund animal adoption programs, I thought of H. P. Lovecraft's last letter, written in 1937, less than a month before his death. In that letter he mentions having gone for one last walk in the woods around his home, and two kittens who "appeared out of nowhere" and escorted him through "the sylvan solitudes."

They had stuck in my memory because one day when my wife and I were walking through Providence, Lovecraft's home town, I told her about how the kittens had kept Lovecraft company on his last ramble . . . and as I was speaking, two kittens emerged from an arichaic street-side courtyard, as if summoned by the story. We naturally assumed that these were the same kittens—supernatural entities of some sort.

Lovecraft has been one of my favorite writers since I first read "The Rats in the Walls" at about age thirteen, and I was happy to have this chance to send him to the sort of pagan afterlife he'd have enjoyed.

⊰⊱ A SOUL IN A BOTTLE ⊰⊱

THE FORECOURT of the Chinese Theater smelled of rain-wet stone and car exhaust, but a faint aroma like pears and cumin seemed to cling to his shirt-collar as he stepped around the clustered tourists, who all appeared to be blinking up at the copper towers above the forecourt wall or smiling into cameras as they knelt to press their hands into the puddled handprints in the cement paving blocks.

George Sydney gripped his shopping bag under his arm and dug three pennies from his pants pocket.

For the third or fourth time this morning he found himself glancing sharply over his left shoulder, but again there was no one within yards of him. The morning sun was bright on the Roosevelt Hotel across the boulevard, and the clouds were breaking up in the blue sky.

He crouched beside Jean Harlow's square and carefully laid one penny in each of the three round indentations below her incised signature, then wiped his wet fingers on his jacket. The coins wouldn't stay there long, but Sydney always put three fresh ones down whenever he walked past this block of Hollywood Boulevard.

He straightened up and again caught a whiff of pears and cumin, and when he glanced over his left shoulder there was a girl standing right behind him.

At first glance he thought she was a teenager—she was a head shorter than him, and her tangled red hair framed a narrow, freckled face with squinting eyes and a wide, amused mouth.

"*Three* pennies?" she asked, and her voice was deeper than he would have expected.

She was standing so close to him that his elbow had brushed her breasts when he'd turned around.

"That's right," said Sydney, stepping back from her, awkwardly so as not to scuff the coins loose.

"Why?"

"Uh . . ." He waved at the cement square and then barely caught his shopping bag. "People pried up the original three," he said. "For souvenirs. That she put there. Jean Harlow, when she put her handprints and shoe prints in the wet cement, in 1933."

The girl raised her faint eyebrows and blinked down at the stone. "I never knew that. How did you know that?"

"I looked her up one time. Uh, on Google."

The girl laughed quietly, and in that moment she seemed to be the only figure in the forecourt, including himself, that had color. He realized dizzily that the scent he'd been catching all morning was hers.

"Google?" she said. "Sounds like a Chinaman trying to say something. Are you always so nice to dead people?"

Her black linen jacket and skirt were visibly damp, as if she had slept outside, and seemed to be incongruously formal. He wondered if somebody had donated the suit to the Salvation Army place down the boulevard by Pep Boys, and if this girl was one of the young people he sometimes saw in sleeping bags under the marquee of a closed theater down there.

"Respectful, at least," he said, "I suppose."

She nodded. "'Lo,'" she said, " 'some we loved, the loveliest and the best . . .'"

Surprised by the quote, he mentally recited the next two lines of the Rubaiyat quatrain—*That Time and Fate of all their Vintage prest, / Have drunk their cup a round or two before*—and found himself saying the last line out loud: "'And one by one crept silently to Rest.'"

She was looking at him intently, so he cleared his throat and said, "Are you local? You've been here before, I gather." Probably that odd scent was popular right now, he thought, the way patchouli oil had apparently been in the '60s. Probably he had brushed past someone who had been wearing it too, earlier in the day.

"I'm staying at the Heroic," she said, then went on quickly, "Do you live near here?"

He could see her bra through her damp white blouse, and he looked away—though he had noticed that it seemed to be embroidered with vines.

"I have an apartment up on Franklin," he said, belatedly.

She had noticed his glance, and arched her back for a moment before pulling her jacket closed and buttoning it. "'And in a Windingsheet of Vineleaf wrapped,'" she said merrily, "'So bury me by some sweet Gardenside.'"

Embarrassed, he muttered the first line of that quatrain: "'Ah, with the grape my fading life provide . . .'"

"Good idea!" she said—then she frowned, and her face was older. "No, dammit, I've got to go—but I'll see you again, right? I like you." She leaned forward and tipped her face up—and then she had briefly kissed him on the lips, and he did drop his shopping bag.

When he had crouched to pick it up and brushed the clinging drops of cold water off on his pants, and looked around, she was gone. He took a couple of steps toward the theater entrance, but the dozens of colorfully dressed strangers blocked his view, and he couldn't tell if she had hurried inside; and he didn't see her among the people by the photo booths or on the shiny black sidewalk.

Her lips had been hot—perhaps she had a fever.

He opened the plastic bag and peered inside, but the book didn't seem to have got wet or landed on a corner. A first edition of Colleen Moore's *Silent Star*, with a TLS, a typed letter, signed, tipped in on the front flyleaf. The Larry Edmunds Bookstore a few blocks east was going to give him fifty dollars for it.

And he thought he'd probably stop at Boardner's afterward and have a couple of beers before walking back to his apartment. Or maybe a shot of bourbon, though it wasn't yet noon. He knew he'd be coming back here again, soon, frequently—peering around, lingering, almost certainly uselessly.

Still, *I'll see you again,* she had said. *I like you.*

Well, he thought with a nervous smile as he started east down the black sidewalk, stepping around the inset brass-rimmed pink stars with names on them, I like you too. Maybe, after all, it's a rain-damp street girl that I can fall in love with.

She wasn't at the Chinese Theater when he looked for her there during the next several days, but a week later he saw her again. He was driving across Fairfax on Santa Monica Boulevard, and he saw her standing on the sidewalk in front of the big Starbucks, in the shadows below the aquamarine openwork dome.

He knew it was her, though she was wearing jeans and a sweatshirt now—her red hair and freckled face were unmistakable. He honked the horn as he drove through the intersection, and she looked up, but by the time he had turned left into a market parking lot and driven back west on Santa Monica, she was nowhere to be seen.

He drove around several blocks, squinting as the winter sunlight shifted back and forth across the streaked windshield of his ten-year-old Honda, but none of the people on the sidewalks was her.

A couple of blocks south of Santa Monica he passed a fenced-off motel with plywood over its windows and several shopping carts in its otherwise empty parking lot. The 1960s space-age sign over the building read RO IC MOTEL, and he could see faint outlines where a long-gone T and P had once made "tropic" of the first word.

"Eroic," he said softly to himself.

To his own wry embarrassment he parked a block past it and fed his only quarter into the parking meter, but at the end of his twenty minutes she hadn't appeared.

Of course she hadn't. "You're acting like a high-school kid," he whispered impatiently to himself as he put the Honda in gear and pulled away from the curb.

Six days later he was walking east toward Book City at Cherokee, and as was his habit lately he stepped into the Chinese Theater forecourt with three pennies in his hand, and he stood wearily beside the souvenir shop and scanned the crowd, shaking the pennies in his fist. The late afternoon crowd consisted of brightly dressed tourists, and a portly, bearded man making hats out of balloons, and several young men dressed as Batman and Spider-Man and Captain Jack Sparrow from the *Pirates of the Caribbean* movies.

Then he gripped the pennies tight. He saw her.

She was at the other end of the crowded square, on the far side of the theater entrance, and he noticed her red hair in the moment before she crouched out of sight.

He hurried through the crowd to where she was kneeling—the rains had passed and the pavement was dry—and he saw that she had laid three pennies into little round indentations in the Gregory Peck square.

She grinned up at him, squinting in the sunlight. "I love the idea," she said in the remembered husky voice, "but I didn't want to come between you and Jean Harlow." She reached up one narrow hand, and he took it gladly and pulled her to her feet. She could hardly weigh more than a hundred pounds. He realized that her hand was hot as he let go of it.

"And hello," she said.

She was wearing jeans and a gray sweatshirt again, or still. At least they were dry. Sydney caught again the scent of pears and cumin.

He was grinning too. Most of the books he sold he got from thrift stores and online used-book sellers, and these recent trips to Book City had been a self-respect excuse to keep looking for her here.

He groped for something to say. "I thought I found your 'Heroic' the other day," he told her.

She cocked her head, still smiling. The sweatshirt was baggy, but somehow she seemed to be flat-chested today. "You were looking for me?" she asked.

"I—guess I was. This was a closed-down motel, though, south of Santa Monica." He laughed self-consciously. "The sign says blank-R-O-blank-I-C. Eroic, see? It was originally Tropic, I gather."

Her green eyes had narrowed as he spoke, and it occurred to him that the condemned motel might actually be the place she'd referred to a couple of weeks earlier, and that she had not expected him to find it. "Probably it originally said 'erotic,'" she said lightly, taking his hand and stepping away from the Gregory Peck square. "Have you got a cigarette?"

"Yes." He pulled a pack of Camels and a lighter from his shirt pocket, and when she had tucked a cigarette between her lips—he noticed that she was not wearing lipstick today—he cupped his hand around the lighter and held the flame toward her. She held his hand to steady it as she puffed the cigarette alight.

"There couldn't be a motel called Erotic," he said.

"Sure there could, lover. To avoid complications."

"I'm George," he said. "What's your name?"

She shook her head, grinning up at him.

The bearded balloon man had shuffled across the pavement to

them, deftly weaving a sort of bowler hat shape out of several long green balloons, and now he reached out and set it on her head.

"No, thank you," she said, taking it off and holding it toward the man, but he backed away, smiling through his beard and nodding. She stuck it onto the head of a little boy who was scampering past.

The balloon man stepped forward again and this time he snatched the cigarette from her mouth. "This is California, sister," he said, dropping it and stepping on it. "We don't smoke here."

"You should," she said, "it'd help you lose weight." She took Sydney's arm and started toward the sidewalk.

The balloon man called after them, "It's customary to give a gratuity for the balloons!"

"Get it from that kid," said Sydney over his shoulder.

The bearded man was pointing after them and saying loudly, "Tacky people, tacky people!"

"Could I have another cigarette?" she said as they stepped around the forecourt wall out of the shadows and started down the sunlit sidewalk toward the soft-drink and jewelry stands on the wider pavement in front of the Kodak Theater.

"Sure," said Sydney, pulling the pack and lighter out again. "Would you like a Coke or something?" he added, waving toward the nearest vendor. Their shadows stretched for yards ahead of them, but the day was still hot.

"I'd like a drink drink." She paused to take a cigarette, and again she put her hand over his as he lit it for her. "Drink, that knits up the raveled sleave of care," she said through smoke as they started forward again. "I bet you know where we could find a bar."

"I bet I do," he agreed. "Why don't you want to tell me your name?"

"I'm shy," she said. "What did the Michelin Man say, when we were leaving?"

"He said, 'tacky people.'"

She stopped and turned to look back, and for a moment Sydney was afraid she intended to march back and cause a scene; but a moment later she had grabbed his arm and resumed their eastward course.

He could feel that she was shaking, and he peered back over his shoulder.

Everyone on the pavement behind them seemed to be couples moving away or across his view, except for one silhouetted figure standing a hundred feet back—it was an elderly white-haired woman in a shapeless dress, and he couldn't see if she was looking after them or not.

The girl had released his arm and taken two steps ahead, and he started toward her—

—and she disappeared.

Sydney rocked to a halt.

He had been looking directly at her in the bright afternoon sunlight. She had not stepped into a store doorway or run on ahead or ducked behind him. She had been occupying volume four feet ahead of him, casting a shadow, and suddenly she was not.

A bus that had been grinding past on the far side of the parking meters to his left was still grinding past.

Her cigarette was rolling on the sidewalk, still lit.

She had not been a hallucination, and he had not experienced some kind of blackout.

Are you always so nice to dead people?

He was shivering in the sunlight, and he stepped back to half-sit against the rim of a black iron trash can by the curb. No sudden moves, he thought.

Was she a ghost? Probably, probably! What else?

Well then, you've seen a ghost, he told himself, that's all. People see ghosts. The balloon man saw her too—he told her not to smoke.

You fell in love with a ghost, that's all. People have probably done that.

He waited several minutes, gripping the iron rim of the trash can and glancing in all directions, but she didn't reappear.

At last he was able to push away from the trash can and walk on, unsteadily, toward Book City; that had been his plan before he had met her again today, and nothing else seemed appropriate. Breathing wasn't difficult, but for at least a little while it would be a conscious action, like putting one foot in front of the other.

He wondered if he would meet her again, knowing that she was a ghost. He wondered if he would be afraid of her now. He thought he probably would be, but he hoped he would see her again anyway.

The quiet aisles of the book store, with the almost-vanilla scent of old paper, distanced him from the event on the sidewalk. This was his familiar world, as if all used book stores were actually one enormous magical building that you could enter through different doorways in Long Beach or Portland or Albuquerque. Always, reliably, there were the books with taped-over spines that you had to pull out and identify, and the dust jackets that had to be checked for the dismissive words *Book Club Edition,* and the poetry section to be scanned for possibly underpriced Nora May French or George Sterling.

The shaking of his hands, and the disorientation that was like a half-second delay in his comprehension, were no worse than a hangover, and he was familiar with hangovers—the cure was a couple of drinks, and he would take the cure as soon as he got back to his apartment. In the meantime he was gratefully able to concentrate on the books, and within half an hour he had found several P. G. Wodehouse novels that he'd be able to sell for more than the prices they were marked at, and a clean five-dollar hardcover copy of Sabatini's *Bellarion.*

My books, he thought, and my poetry.

In the poetry section he found several signed Don Blanding books, but in his experience *every* Don Blanding book was signed. Then he found a first edition copy of Cheyenne Fleming's 1968 *More Poems,* but it was priced at twenty dollars, which was about the most it would ever go for. He looked on the title page for an inscription, but there wasn't one, and then flipped through the pages—and glimpsed handwriting.

He found the page again, and saw the name *Cheyenne Fleming* scrawled below one of the sonnets; and beside it was a thumbprint in the same fountain-pen ink.

He paused.

If this was a genuine Fleming signature, the book was worth about two hundred dollars. He was familiar with her poetry, but he didn't think he'd ever seen her signature; certainly he didn't have any signed Flemings at home to compare this against. But Christine would probably be able to say whether it was real or not—Christine Dunn was a book dealer he'd sometimes gone in with on substantial buys.

He'd risk the twenty dollars and call her when he got back to his apartment. And just for today he would walk straight north to Franklin, not west on Hollywood Boulevard. Not quite yet, not this evening.

✢ ✢ ✢

His apartment building was on Franklin just west of Highland, a jacaranda-shaded old two-story horseshoe around an overgrown central courtyard, and supposedly Marlon Brando had stayed there before he'd become successful. Sydney's apartment was upstairs, and he locked the door after he had let himself into the curtained, tobacco-scented living room.

He poured himself a glass of bourbon from the bottle on the top kitchen shelf, and pulled a Coors from the refrigerator to chase the warm liquor with, and then he took his shopping bag to the shabby brown-leather chair in the corner and switched on the lamp.

It was of course the Fleming that interested him. He flipped open the book to the page with Fleming's name inked on it.

He recognized the sonnet from the first line—it was the rude sonnet to her sister . . . the sister who, he recalled, had become Fleming's literary executor after Fleming's suicide. Ironic.

He read the first eight lines of the sonnet, his gaze only bouncing over the lines since he had read it many times before:

To My Sister
Rebecca, if your mirror were to show
My face to you instead of yours, I wonder
If you would notice right away, or know
The vain pretense you've chosen to live under.
If ever phone or doorbell rang, and then
I heard your voice conversing, what you'd say
Would be what I have said, recalled again,
And I might sit in silence through the day.

Then he frowned and took a careful sip of the bourbon. The last six lines weren't quite as he remembered them:

But when the Resurrection Man shall bring
The moon to free me from these yellowed pages,
The gift is mine, there won't be anything
For you—and you can rest through all the ages
Under a stone that bears the cherished name
You thought should make the two of us the same.

He picked up the telephone and punched in Christine's number.

After three rings he heard her say, briskly, "Dunn Books."

"Christine," he said, "George—uh—here." It was the first time he had spoken since seeing the girl disappear, and his voice had cracked. He cleared his throat and took a deep breath and let it out.

"Drunk again," said Christine.

"Again?" he said. "Still. Listen, I've got a first here of Fleming's *More Poems,* no dust jacket but it's got her name written below one of the poems. Do you have a signed Fleming I could compare it with?"

"You're in luck, an eBay customer backed out of a deal. It's a *More Poems,* too."

"Have you got it right there?"

"Yeah, but what, you want me to describe her signature over the phone? We should meet at the Biltmore tomorrow, bring our copies."

"Good idea, and if this is real I'll buy lunch. But could you flip to the sonnet 'To My Sister'?"

"One second." A few moments later she was back on the phone. "Okay, what about it?"

"How does the sestet go?"

"It says, '*But when the daylight of the future shows / The forms freed by erosion from their cages, / It will be mine that quickens, gladly grows, / And lives; and you can rest through all the ages / Under a stone that bears the cherished name / You thought should make the two of us the same.*' Bitter poem!"

Those were the familiar lines—the way the poem was supposed to go. "Why," asked Christine, "is yours missing the bottom of the page?"

"No—I've—my copy has a partly different sestet." He read to her the last six lines on the page of the book he held. "Printed just like every other poem in the book, same typeface and all."

"Wow. Otherwise a standard copy of the first edition?"

"To the best of my knowledge, I don't know," he said, quoting a treasured remark from a bookseller they both knew. He added, "We'll know tomorrow."

"Eleven, okay? And take care of it—it might be worth wholesaling to one of the big-ticket dealers."

"I wasn't going to use it for a coaster. See you at eleven."

He hung up the phone, and before putting the book aside he touched the ink thumbprint beside the signature on the page. The paper wasn't warm or cold, but he shivered—this was a touch across decades. When had Fleming killed herself?

He got up and crossed the old carpets to the computer and turned it on, and as the monitor screen showed the Hewlett Packard logo and then the Windows background, he couldn't shake the mental image of trying to grab a woman to keep her from falling into some abyss and only managing to brush her outstretched hand with one finger.

He typed in the address for Google—*sounds like a Chinaman trying to say something*—and then typed "cheyenne fleming," and when a list of sites appeared he clicked on the top one. He had a dial-up AOL connection, so the text appeared first, flanking a square where a picture would soon appear.

Cheyenne Fleming, he read, had been born in Hollywood in 1934, and had lived there all her life with her younger sister Rebecca. Both had gone to UCLA, Cheyenne with more distinction than Rebecca, and both had published books of poetry, though Rebecca's had always been compared unfavorably with Cheyenne's. The sisters apparently both loved and resented each other, and the article quoted several lines from the "To My Sister" sonnet—the version Christine had read to him over the phone, not the version in his copy of *More Poems*. Cheyenne Fleming had shot herself in 1969, reportedly because Rebecca had stolen away her fiancée. Rebecca became her literary executor.

At last the picture appeared on the screen—it was black and white, but Sydney recognized the thin face with its narrow eyes and wide humorous mouth, and he knew that the disordered hair would be red in a color photograph.

The tip of his finger was numb where he had touched her thumbprint.

I'm Shy, she had said. He had thought she was evading giving him her name. Shy for Cheyenne, of course. Pronounced Shy-*Ann*.

He glanced fearfully at his front door—what if she was standing on the landing out there right now, in the dusk shadows? He realized, with a shudder that made him carry his glass back to the kitchen for a refill, that he would open the door if she was—yes, and invite her in, invite her across his threshold. I finally fall in love, he thought, and it's with a dead woman. A suicide.

A line of black ants had found the coffee cup he'd left unwashed this morning, but he couldn't kill them right now.

Once his glass was filled again, he went to the living room window instead of the door, and he pulled the curtains aside. A huge orange full moon hung in the darkening sky behind the old TV antennas on the opposite roof. He looked down, but didn't see her among the shadowed trees and vines.

And in a Windingsheet of Vineleaf wrapped,
So bury me by some sweet Gardenside.

He closed the curtain and fetched the bottle and the twelve-pack of Coors to set beside his chair, then settled down to lose himself in one of the P. G. Wodehouse novels until he should be drunk enough to stumble to bed and fall instantly asleep.

As he trudged across Pershing Square from the parking structure on Hill Street toward the three imposing brown brick towers of the Biltmore Hotel, Sydney's squinting gaze kept being drawn in the direction of the new bright-yellow building on the south side of the square. His eyes were watering in the morning sun-glare anyway, and he wondered irritably why somebody would paint a new building in that idiotic kindergarten color.

He had awakened early, and his hangover seemed to be just a continuation of his disorientation from the day before. He had decided that he couldn't sell the Fleming book. Even though he had met her two weeks before finding the book, he was certain that the book was somehow his link to her.

Christine would be disappointed—part of the fun of bookselling was writing catalogue copy for extraordinary items, and she would have wanted to collaborate in the description of this item—but he couldn't help that.

His gaze was drawn again toward the yellow building, but now that he was closer to it he could see that it wasn't the building that his eyes had been drawn toward, but a stairway and pool just this side of it. Two six-foot brown stone spheres were mounted on the pool coping.

And he saw her sitting down there, on the shady side of one of the giant stone balls.

He was smiling and stepping across the pavement in that direction even before he was sure it was her, and the memory, only momentarily delayed, of who she must be didn't slow his pace.

She was wearing the jeans and sweatshirt again, and she stood up and waved at him when he was still a hundred feet away, and even at this distance he was sure he caught her pears-and-cumin scent.

He sprinted the last few yards, and her arms were wide so he hugged her when they met.

"George," she said breathily in his ear. The fruit-and-spice smell was strong.

"Shy," he said, and hugged her more tightly. He could feel her breastbone against his, and he wondered if she had been wearing a padded bra when he had first seen her. Then he held her by her shoulders at arm's length and smiled into her squinting, elfin eyes. "I've got to make a call," he said.

He pulled his cell phone out of his jacket pocket, flipped it open and tapped in Christine's well-remembered number. He was already ten minutes late for their meeting.

"Christine," he said, "I've got to beg off . . . no, I'm not going to be home. I'm going to be in Orange County—"

Cheyenne mouthed *Overnight.*

"—overnight," Sydney went on, "till tomorrow. No, I . . . I'll explain it later, and I owe you a lunch. No, I haven't sold it yet! I gotta run, I'm in traffic and I can't drive and talk at the same time. Right, right— 'bye!"

He folded it and tucked it back into his pocket.

Cheyenne nodded. "To avoid complications," she said.

Sydney had stepped back from her, but he was holding her hand— possibly to keep her from disappearing again. "My New Year's resolution," he said with a rueful smile, "was not to tell any lies."

"My attitude toward New Year's resolutions is the same as Oscar Wilde's," she said, stepping around the pool coping and swinging his hand.

"What did he say about them?" asked Sydney, falling into step beside her.

"I don't know if he ever said anything about them," she said, "but if he did, I'm sure I agree with it."

She looked back at him, then glanced past him and lost her smile. "Don't turn around," she said quickly, so he just stared at her face, which seemed bony and starved between the wings of tangled red hair. "Now look around, but scan the whole square, like you're calculating if they could land the Goodyear blimp here."

Sydney let his gaze swivel from Hill Street, across the trees and broad pavement of the square, to the pillared arch of the Biltmore entrance. Up there toward the east end of the square he had seen a gray-haired woman in a loose blue dress; she seemed to be the same woman he had seen behind them on Hollywood Boulevard yesterday. He let his eyes come back around to focus on Cheyenne's face.

"You saw that woman?" she said to him. "The one that looks like . . . some kind of featherless monkey? Stay away from her, she'll tell you lies about me."

Looking at the Biltmore entrance had reminded him that Christine might have parked in the Hill Street lot too. "Let's sit behind one of these balls," he said. And when they had walked down the steps and sat on the cement coping, leaning back against the receding under-curve of the nearest stone sphere, he said, "I found your book. I hope you don't mind that I know who you are."

She was still holding his hand, and now she squeezed it. "Who am I, lover?"

"You're Cheyenne Fleming. You—you're—"

"Yes. How did I die?"

He took a deep breath. "You killed yourself."

"I did? Why?"

"Because your sister—I read—ran off with your fiancée."

She closed her eyes and twined her fingers through his. "Urbane legends. Can I come over to your place tonight? I want to copy one of my poems in the book, write it out again in the blank space around the printed version, and I need you to hold my hand, guide my hand while I write it."

"Okay," he said. His heart was thudding in his chest. Inviting her over my threshold, he thought. "I'd like that," he added with dizzy bravado.

"I've got the pen to use," she went on. "It's my special pen, they buried me with it."

"Okay." Buried her with it, he thought. Buried her with it.

"I love you," she said, her eyes still closed. "Do you love me? Tell me you love me."

He was sitting down, but his head was spinning with vertigo as if an infinite black gulf yawned at his feet. This was her inviting *him* over *her* threshold.

"Under," he said in a shaky voice, "normal circumstances, I'd certainly be in love with you."

"Nobody falls in love under *normal* circumstances," she said softly, rubbing his finger with her warm thumb. He restrained an impulse to look to see if there was still ink on it. "Love isn't in the category of normal things. Not any worthwhile kind of love, anyway." She opened her eyes and waved her free hand behind them toward the square. "Normal people. I hate them."

"Me too," said Sydney.

"Actually," she said, looking down at their linked hands, "I didn't kill myself." She paused for so long that he was about to ask her what had happened, when she went on quietly, "My sister Rebecca shot me, and made it look like a suicide. After that she apparently *did* go away with my fiancée. But she killed me because she had made herself into an imitation of me, and without me in the picture, *she'd* be the original." Through her hand he felt her shiver. "I've been alone in the dark for a long time," she said in a small voice.

Sydney freed his hand so that he could put his arm around her narrow shoulders, and he kissed her hair.

Cheyenne looked up with a grin that made slits of her eyes. "But I don't think she's prospered! Doesn't she look *terrible?*"

Sydney resisted the impulse to look around again. "Was that—"

Cheyenne frowned. "I've got to go—I can't stay here for very long at a time, not until we copy that poem."

She kissed him, and their mouths opened, and for a moment his tongue touched hers. When their lips parted their foreheads were pressed together, and he whispered, "Let's get that poem copied, then."

She smiled, deepening the lines in her cheeks, and looked down. "Sit back now and look away from me," she said. "And I'll come to your place tonight."

He pressed his palms against the surface of the cement coping and pushed himself away from her, and looked toward Hill Street.

After a moment, "Shy?" he said; and when he looked around she was gone. "I love you," he said to the empty air.

"Everybody did," came a raspy voice from behind and above him.

For a moment he went on staring at the place where Cheyenne had sat; then he sighed deeply and looked around.

The old woman in the blue dress was standing at the top of the stairs, and now began stepping carefully down them in boxy old-lady shoes.

Her eyes were pouchy above round cheeks and not much of a chin, and Sydney imagined she'd been cute decades ago.

"Are," he said in a voice he made himself keep level, "you Rebecca?"

She stopped in front of him and nodded, frowning in the sun-glare. "Rebecca Fleming," she said. "The cherished name." The diesel-scented breeze was blowing her white hair around her face, and she pushed it back with one frail, spotted hand. "Did she say I killed her?"

After a moment's hesitation, "Yes," Sydney said.

She sat down, far enough away from him that he didn't feel called on to move further away. Why hadn't he brought a flask?

"True," she said, exhaling as if she'd been holding her breath. "True, I did." She looked across at him, and he reluctantly met her eyes. They were green, just like Cheyenne's.

"I bet," she said, "you bought a book of hers, signed." She barked two syllables of a laugh. "And I bet she's still got her fountain pen. We buried it with her."

"I don't think you and I have much to say to each other," said Sydney stiffly. He started to get to his feet.

"It was self-defense, if you're curious," she said, not stirring.

He paused, bracing himself on his hands.

"She came into my room," said Rebecca, "with a revolver. I woke up when she touched the cold muzzle to my forehead. This is thirty-seven years ago, but I remember it as if it were last night—we were in a crummy motel south of Santa Monica Boulevard, on one of her low-life tours. I sat up and pushed the gun away, but she kept trying to get it aimed at me—she was laughing, irritated, cajoling, I wasn't playing along properly—and when I pushed it back toward her it went off. Under her chin. I wrote a suicide note for her."

The old woman's face was stony. Sydney sat back down.

"I loved her," she said. "If I'd known that resisting her would end up killing her, I swear, I wouldn't have resisted." She smiled at him belligerently. "Crush an ant sometime, and then smell your fingers. I wonder what became of the clothes we buried her in. Not a sweatshirt and jeans."

"A black linen suit," said Sydney, "with a white blouse. They were damp."

"Well, groundwater, you know, even with a cement grave-liner. And a padded bra, for the photographs. I fixed it up myself, crying so hard I could barely see the stitches—I filled the lining with bird-seed to flesh her out."

Sydney recalled the vines that had seemed to be embroidered on Cheyenne's bra, that first day. "It sprouted."

Rebecca laughed softly. " 'Quickens, gladly grows.' She wants something from you." Rebecca fumbled in a pocket of her skirt. "Bring the moon to free her from these yellowed pages."

Sydney squinted at her. "You've read that version of the sonnet?" Rebecca was now holding out a two-inch clear plastic cylinder with metal bands on it. "I was there when she wrote it. She read it to me when the ink was still wet. It was printed that way in only one copy of the book, the copy you obviously found, God help us all. This is one of her ink cartridges. You stick this end in the ink bottle and twist the other end— that retracts the plunger. When she was writing poetry she used to use about nine parts Schaeffer's black ink and one part her own blood."

She was still holding it toward him, so he took it from her.

"The signature in your book certainly contains some of her blood," Rebecca said.

"A signature and a thumbprint," said Sydney absently, rolling the narrow cylinder in his palm. He twisted the back end, and saw the tiny red ring of the plunger move smoothly up the inside of the clear barrel.

"And you touched the thumbprint."

"Yes. I'm glad I did."

"You brought her to this cycle of the moon. She arrived on the new moon, though you probably didn't find the book and touch her thumb till further on in the cycle; she'd instantly stain the whole twenty-eight days, I'm sure, backward and forward. Do you know yet what she wants you to do?"

If I'd known, Rebecca had said, *that resisting her would end up killing her, I swear, I wouldn't have resisted.* Sydney realized, to his dismay, that he believed her.

"Hold her hand, guide it, I guess, while she copies a poem," he said.

"*That* poem, I have no doubt. She's a ghost—I suppose she imagines that writing it again will project her spirit back to the night when she originally wrote it—so she can make a better attempt at killing me three years later, in 1969. She was thirty-five, in '69. I was thirty-three."

"She looks younger."

"She always did. See little Shy riding horseback, you'd think she was twelve years old." Rebecca sat back. "She's pretty physical, right? I mean, she can hold things, touch things?"

Sydney remembered Cheyenne's fingers intertwined with his.

"Yes."

"I'd think she could hold a pen. I wonder why she needs help copying the poem."

"I—" Sydney began.

But Rebecca interrupted him. "If you do it for her," she said, "and it works, she won't have died. I'll be the one that died in '69. She'll be seventy-two now, and you won't have met her. Well, she'll probably look you up, if she remembers to be grateful, but you won't remember any of . . . this interlude with her." She smiled wryly. "And you certainly won't meet me. That's a plus, I imagine. Do you have any high-proof liquor, at your house?"

"You can't come over!" said Sydney, appalled.

"No, I wasn't thinking of that. Never mind. But you might ask her—"

She had paused, and Sydney raised his eyebrows.

"You might ask her not to kill me, when she gets back there. I know I'd have left, moved out, if she had told me she really needed that. I'd have stopped . . . trying to *be* her. I only did it because I loved her." She smiled, and for a moment as she stood up Sydney could see that she must once have been very pretty.

"Goodbye, Resurrection Man," she said, and turned and shuffled away up the cement steps.

Sydney didn't call after her. After a moment he realized that he was still holding the plastic ink-cartridge, and he put it in his pocket.

High-proof liquor, he thought unhappily.

Back in his apartment after making a couple of purchases, he poured himself a shot of bourbon from the kitchen bottle and sat down by the window with the Fleming book.

But when the Resurrection Man shall bring
The moon to free me from these yellowed pages,
The gift is mine, there won't be anything
For you.

The moon had been full last night. Or maybe just a hair short of full, and it would be full tonight.

You might ask her not to kill me, when she gets back there.

He opened the bags he had carried home from a liquor store and a stationer's, and he pulled the ink cartridge out of his pocket.

One bag contained a squat glass bottle of Scheaffer's black ink, and he unscrewed the lid; there was a little pool of ink in the well on the inside of the open bottle's rim, and he stuck the end of the cartridge into the ink and twisted the back. The plunger retracted, and the barrel ahead of it was black.

When it was a third filled, he stopped, and he opened the other bag. It contained a tiny plastic 50-milliliter bottle—what he thought of as breakfast-sized—of Bacardi 151-proof rum. He twisted off the cap and stuck the cartridge into the vapory liquor. He twisted the end of the cartridge until it stopped, filled, and even though the cylinder now contained two-thirds rum, it was still jet-black.

He had considered buying lighter-fluid, but decided that the 151-proof rum—seventy-five percent alcohol—would probably be more flammable. And he could drink what he didn't use.

He was dozing in the chair when he heard someone moving in the kitchen. He sat up, disoriented, and hoarsely called, "Who's there?"

He lurched to his feet, catching the book but missing the tiny empty rum bottle.

"Who were you expecting, lover?" came Cheyenne's husky voice. "Should I have knocked? You already invited me."

He stumbled across the dim living room into the kitchen. The overhead light was on in there, and through the little kitchen window he saw that it was dark outside.

Cheyenne was sweeping the last of the ants off the counter with her hand, and as he watched she rubbed them vigorously between her palms and wiped her open hands along her jaw and neck, then picked up the half-full bourbon bottle.

She was wearing the black linen skirt and jacket again—and, he could see, the birdseed-sprouting bra under the white blouse. The clothes were somehow still damp.

"I talked to Rebecca," he blurted, thinking about the ink cartridge in his pocket.

"I told you not to," she said absently. "Where do you keep glasses? Or do you expect me to drink right out of the bottle? Did she say she killed me in self-defense?"

"Yes."

"Glasses?"

He stepped past her and opened a cupboard and handed her an Old Fashioned glass. "Yes," he said again.

She smiled up at him from beneath her dark eyelashes as she poured a couple of ounces of amber liquor into the glass, then put down the bottle and caressed his cheek. The fruit-and-spice smell of crushed ants was strong.

"It was my fault!" she said, laughing as she spoke. "I shouldn't have touched her with the barrel! And so it was little Shy that wound up getting killed, *miserabile dictu!* I was . . . *nonplussed* in eternity." She took a deep sip of the bourbon and then sang, "'Take my hand, I'm nonplussed in eternity . . .'"

He wasn't smiling, so she pushed out her thin red lips. "Oh, lover, don't pout. Am I my sister's keeper? Did you know she claimed I got my best poems by stealing her ideas? As if anybody couldn't tell from reading *her* poetry which of us was the original! At least I had already got that copy of my book out there, out in the world, like a message in a bottle, a soul in a bottle, for you to eventually—"

Sydney had held up his hand, and she stopped. "She said to tell you . . . not to kill her. She said she'd just move out if you asked her to. If she knew it was important to you."

She shrugged. "Maybe."

He frowned and took a breath, but she spoke again before he could.

"Are you still going to help me copy out my poem? I can't write it by myself, because the first word of it is the name of the person who killed me."

Her eyes were wide and her eyebrows were raised as she looked down at the book in his hand and then back up at him.

"I'd do it for you," she added softly, "because I love you. Do you love me?"

She couldn't be taller than five-foot one-inch, and with her long neck and thin arms, and her big eyes under the disordered hair, she looked young and frail.

"Yes," he said. I do, he thought. And I'm going to exorcise you. I'm going to spread that flammable ink-and-rum mix over the page and then touch it with a cigarette.

It was printed that way in only one copy of the book, Rebecca had said, *the copy you obviously found, God help us all. A soul in a bottle.*

There won't be another Resurrection Man.

He made himself smile. "You've got a pen, you said."

She reached thin fingers into the neck of her blouse and pulled out a long, tapering black pen. She shook it to dislodge a thin white tendril with a tiny green leaf on it.

"May I?" he asked, holding out his hand.

She hesitated, then laid the pen in his palm.

He handed her the book, then pulled off the pen's cap, exposing the gleaming, wedge-shaped nib. "Do you need to dip it in an ink bottle?" he asked.

"No, it's got a cartridge in it. Unscrew the end."

He twisted the barrel and the nib-end rotated away from the pen, and after a few more turns it came loose in his hand, exposing a duplicate of the ink-cartridge he had in his pocket.

"Pull the cartridge off," she said suddenly, "and lick the end of it. Didn't she tell you about my ink?"

"No," he said, his voice unsteady. "Tell me about your ink."

"Well, it's got a little bit of my blood in it, though it's mostly ink." She was flipping through the pages of the book. "But some blood. Lick it, the punctured end of the cartridge." She looked up at him and grinned. "As a chaser for the rum I smell on your breath."

For ten seconds he stared into her deep green eyes, then he raised the cartridge and ran his tongue across the end of it. He didn't taste anything.

"That's my dear man," she said, taking his hand and stepping onto the living room carpet. "Let's sit in that chair you were napping in."

As they crossed the living room, Sydney slid his free hand into his pocket and clasped the rum-and-ink cartridge next to the blood-and-ink one. The one he had prepared this afternoon was up by his knuckles, the other at the base of his palm.

She let go of his hand to reach out and switch on the lamp, and Sydney pulled a pack of Camels out of his shirt pocket and shook one free.

"Sit down," she said, "I'll sit in your lap. I hardly weigh anything. Are there limits to what you'd do for someone you love?"

Sydney hooked a cigarette onto his lip and tossed the pack aside. "Limits?" he said as he sat down and clicked a lighter at the end of the cigarette. "I don't know," he said around a puff of smoke.

"I think you're not one of those normal people," she said.

"I hate 'em." He laid his cigarette in the smoking stand beside the chair.

"Me too," she said, and she slid onto his lap and curled her left arm around his shoulders. Her skirt and sleeve were damp, but not cold.

With her right hand she opened the book to the sonnet "To My Sister."

"Lots of margin space for us to write in," she said.

Her hot cheek was touching his, and when he turned to look at her he found that he was kissing her, gently at first and then passionately, for this moment not caring that her scent was the smell of crushed ants.

"Put the cartridge," she whispered into his mouth, "back into the pen and screw it closed."

He carefully fitted one of the cartridges into the pen and whirled the base until it was tight.

George Sydney stood up from crouching beside the shelf of cookbooks, holding a copy of James Beard's *On Food*. It was his favorite of Beard's books, and if he couldn't sell it at a profit he'd happily keep it.

He hadn't found any other likely books here today, and now it was nearly noon and time to walk across the boulevard to Boardner's for a couple of quick drinks.

"There he is," said the man behind the counter and the cash register. "George, this lady has been coming in every day for the last week, looking for you."

Sydney blinked toward the brightly sunlit store windows, and in front of the counter he saw the silhouette of a short elderly woman with a halo of back-lit white hair.

He smiled and shuffled forward. "Well, hi," he said.

"Hello, George," she said in a husky voice, holding out her hand.

He stepped across the remaining distance and shook her hand. "What—" he began.

"I was just on my way to the Chinese Theater," she said. She was smiling up at him almost sadly, and though her face was deeply etched with wrinkles, her green eyes were lively and young. "I'm going to lay three pennies in the indentations in Gregory Peck's square."

He laughed in surprise. "I do that with Jean Harlow!"

"That's where I got the idea." She leaned forward and tipped her face up and kissed him briefly on the lips, and he dropped the James Beard book.

He crouched to retrieve the book, and when he straightened up she had already stepped out the door. He saw her walking away west down Hollywood Boulevard, her white hair fluttering around her head in the wind.

The man behind the counter was middle-aged, with a graying moustache. "Do you know who your admirer is, George?" he asked with a kinked smile.

Sydney had taken a step toward the door, but some misgiving made him stop. He exhaled to clear his head of a sharp sweet, musty scent.

"Uh," he said distractedly, "no. Who is she?"

"That was Cheyenne Fleming. I got her to sign some copies of her books the other day, so I can double the prices."

"I thought she was dead by now." Sydney tried to remember what he'd read about Fleming. "When was it she got paroled?"

"I don't know. In the '80s? Some time after the death penalty was repealed in the '70s, anyway." He waved at a stack of half a dozen slim dark books on the desk behind him. "You want one of the signed ones? I'll let you have it for the original price, since she only came in here looking for you."

Sydney looked at the stack.

"Nah," he said, pushing the James Beard across the counter. "Just this."

A few moments later he was outside on the brass-starred sidewalk, squinting after Cheyenne Fleming. He could see her, a hundred feet away to the west now, striding away.

He rubbed his face, trying to get rid of the odd scent. And as he walked away, east, he wondered why that kiss should have left him feeling dirty, as if it had been a mortal sin for which he couldn't now phrase the need for absolution.

✜ AUTHOR'S NOTE ✜

This story originated in my frustration that the poet Edna St. Vincent Millay died two years before I was born. The character Cheyenne Fleming ended up deviating widely from Millay—certainly poor Fleming's sonnet can't hold a candle (lit at both ends or not) to Millay's! But I think Millay was the best sonnetist since Shakespeare, so I guess Fleming shouldn't feel too bad.

My wife and I did encounter a balloon seller one day in the forecourt of the Chinese Theater, and he did snatch a cigarette out of my wife's mouth; the man was wearing a top hat, and she knocked it off. The used-book store, Book City, isn't there anymore, unfortunately. Not in the present, anyway—you can still find it in 2000, if you can get there.

⊰ PARALLEL LINES ⊱

IT SHOULD HAVE BEEN their birthday today Well, it was still hers, Caroleen supposed, but with BeeVee gone the whole idea of "birthday" seemed to have gone too. Could she be seventy-three on her own?

Caroleen's right hand had been twitching intermittently since she'd sat up in the living room day-bed five minutes ago, and she lifted the coffee cup with her left hand. The coffee was hot enough but had no taste, and the living room furniture—the coffee table, the now-useless analog TV set with its forlorn rabbit-ears antenna, the rocking chair beside the white-brick fireplace, all bright in the sunlight glaring through the east window at her back—looked like arranged items in some kind of museum diorama; no further motion possible.

But there was still the gravestone to be dealt with, these disorganized nine weeks later. Four hundred and fifty dollars for two square feet of etched granite, and the company in Nevada could not get it straight that Beverly Veronica Erlich and Caroleen Ann Erlich both had the same birth date, though the second date under Caroleen's name was to be left blank for some indeterminate period.

BeeVee's second date had not been left to chance. BeeVee had swallowed all the Darvocets and Vicodins in the house when the pain of her cancer, if it had been cancer, had become more than she could bear. For a year or so she had always been in some degree of pain— Caroleen remembered how BeeVee had exhaled a fast *whew!* from time to time, and the way her forehead seemed always to be misted with sweat, and her late-acquired habit of repeatedly licking the inner edge of her upper lip. And she had always been shifting her position

313

when she drove, and bracing herself against the floor or the steering wheel. More and more she had come to rely—both of them had come to rely—on poor dumpy Amber, the teenager who lived next door. The girl came over to clean the house and fetch groceries, and seemed grateful for the five dollars an hour, even with BeeVee's generous criticisms of every job Amber did.

But Amber would not be able to deal with the headstone company. Caroleen shifted forward on the day-bed, rocked her head back and forth to make sure she was wearing her reading glasses rather than her bifocals, and flipped open the brown plastic phone book. A short silver pencil was secured by a plastic loop in the book's gutter, and she fumbled it free—

—And her right hand twitched forward, knocking the coffee cup right off the table, and the pencil shook in her spotty old fingers as its point jiggled across the page.

She threw a fearful, guilty glance toward the kitchen in the moment before she remembered that BeeVee was dead; then she allowed herself to relax, and she looked at the squiggle she had drawn across the old addresses and phone numbers.

It was jagged, but recognizably cursive writing, letters:

Ineedyourhelpplease

It was, in fact, recognizably BeeVee's handwriting.

Her hand twitched again, and scrawled the same cramped sequence of letters across the page. She lifted the pencil, postponing all thought in this frozen moment, and after several seconds her hand spasmed once more, no doubt writing the same letters in the air. Her whole body shivered with a feverish chill, and she thought she was going to vomit; she leaned out over the rug, but the queasiness passed.

She was sure that her hand had been writing this message in air ever since she had awakened.

Caroleen didn't think BeeVee had ever before, except with ironic emphasis, said *please* when asking her for something.

She was remotely glad that she was sitting, for her heart thudded alarmingly in her chest and she was dizzy with the enormous thought that BeeVee was not gone, not entirely gone. She gripped the edge of the bed, suddenly afraid of falling and knocking the table over, rolling into the rocking chair. The reek of spilled coffee was strong in her nostrils.

"Okay," she whispered. "Okay!" she said again, louder. The shaking in her hand had subsided, so she flipped to a blank calendar page at the back of the book and scrawled OKAY at the top of the page.

Her fingers had begun wiggling again, but she raised her hand as if to wave away a question, hesitant to let the jigging pencil at the waiting page just yet.

Do I want her back, she thought, in any sense? No, not *want,* not *her,* but—in these nine weeks I haven't seemed really to exist anymore, without her paying attention, any sort of attention, to me. These days I'm hardly more than an imaginary friend of Amber next door, a frail conceit soon to be outgrown even by her.

She sighed and lowered her hand to the book. Over her OKAY the pencil scribbled,

Iambeevee

"My God," Caroleen whispered, closing her eyes, "you think I need to be told?"

Her hand was involuntarily spelling it out again, breaking the pencil lead halfway through but continuing rapidly to the end, and then it went through the motions three more times, just scratching the paper with splintered wood. Finally her hand uncramped.

She threw the pencil on the floor and scrabbled among the orange plastic prescription bottles on the table for a pen. Finding one, she wrote, *What can I do? To help*

She wasn't able to add the final question mark because her hand convulsed away from her again, and wrote,

touseyourbodyinvitemeintoyourbody

and then a moment later,

imsorryforeverythingplease

Caroleen watched as the pen in her hand wrote out the same two lines twice more, then she leaned back and let the pen jiggle in air until this bout too gradually wore off and her hand was limp.

Caroleen blinked tears out of her eyes, trying to believe that they were entirely caused by her already-sore wrist muscles. But—for BeeVee to apologize, to her . . . ! The only apologies BeeVee had ever made while alive were qualified and impatient: *Well I'm* sorry *if . . .*

Do the dead lose their egotism? wondered Caroleen; their one-time need to limit and dominate earthly households? BeeVee had maintained Caroleen as a sort of extended self, and it had resulted in isolation for the two of them; if in fact they had added up to quite as many as two, during the last years. The twins had a couple of brothers out there somewhere, and at least a couple of nieces, and their mother might even still be alive at ninety-one, but Caroleen knew nothing of any of them. BeeVee had handled all the mail.

Quickly she wrote on the calendar page, *I need to know—do you love me?*

For nearly a full minute she waited, her shoulder muscles stiffening as she held the pen over the page; then her hand flexed and wrote,

yes

Caroleen was gasping and she couldn't see the page through her tears, but she could feel her hand scribbling the word over and over again until this spasm too eventually relaxed.

Why did you have to wait, she thought, until after you had died, to tell me?

But *use your body, invite me into your body.* What would that mean? Would BeeVee take control of it, ever relinquish control?

Do I, thought Caroleen, care, really?

Whatever it might consist of, it would be at least a step closer to the wholeness Caroleen had lost nine weeks ago.

Her hand was twitching again, and she waited until the first couple of scribbles had expended themselves in the air and then touched the pen to the page. The pen wrote,

yesforever

She moved her hand aside, not wanting to spoil that statement with echoes.

When the pen had stilled, Caroleen leaned forward and began writing, *Yes, I'll invite you,* but her hand took over and finished the line with *exhaustedmorelater*

Exhausted? Was it strenuous for ghosts to lean out or in or down this far? Did BeeVee have to brace herself against something to drive the pencil?

But in fact Caroleen was exhausted too—her hand was aching—and she blew her nose on an old Kleenex, her eyes watering afresh in the menthol-and-eucalyptus smell of Bengay, and she lay back across the day-bed and closed her eyes.

A sharp knock at the front door jolted her awake, and though her glasses had fallen off and she didn't immediately know whether it was morning or evening, she realized that her fingers were wiggling, and had been for some time.

She lunged forward and with her free hand wedged the pen between her twitching right thumb and forefinger, and then the pen travelled lightly over the calendar page. The scribble was longer than the others, with a pause in the middle, and she had to rotate the book to keep the point on the page until it stopped.

The knock sounded again, but Caroleen called, "Just a minute!" and remained hunched over the little book, waiting for the message to repeat.

It didn't. Apparently she had just barely caught the last echo—perhaps only the end of the last echo.

She couldn't at all make out what she had written—even if she'd had her glasses on, she'd have needed the lamplight too.

"Caroleen?" came a call from out front. It was Amber's voice.

"Coming." Caroleen stood up stiffly and hobbled to the door. When she pulled it open she found herself squinting in noon sunlight filtered through the avocado tree branches.

The girl on the doorstep was wearing sweatpants and a huge T-shirt and blinking behind her gleaming round spectacles. Her brown hair was tied up in a knot on top of her head. "Did I wake you up? I'm sorry." She was panting, as if she had run over here from next door.

Caroleen felt the fresh air, smelling of sun-heated stone and car exhaust, cooling her sweaty scalp. "I'm fine," she said hoarsely. "What is it?" Had she asked the girl to come over today? She couldn't recall doing it, and she was tense with impatience to get back to her pen and book.

"I just," said Amber rapidly, "I liked your sister, well, you know I did really, even though—and I—could I have something of hers, not like valuable, to remember her by? How about her hairbrush?"

"You—want her hairbrush."

"If you don't mind. I just want something—"

"I'll get it, wait here." It would be quicker to give it to her than to propose some other keepsake, and Caroleen had no special attachment to the hairbrush—her own was a duplicate anyway. She and BeeVee had of course had matching everything—toothbrushes, coffee cups, shoes, wristwatches.

When Caroleen had fetched the brush and returned to the front door, Amber took it and went pounding down the walkway, calling "Thanks!" over her shoulder.

Still disoriented from her nap, Caroleen closed the door and made her way back to the bed, where she patted the scattered blankets until she found her glasses and fitted them on.

She sat down and switched on the lamp, and leaned over the phone book page. Turning the book around to follow the newest scrawl, she read,

bancaccounts

getmyhairbrushfromhernow

"Sorry, sorry!" exclaimed Caroleen; then in her own handwriting she wrote, *I'll get it back.*

She waited, wondering why she must get the hairbrush back from Amber. Was it somehow necessary that all of BeeVee's possessions be kept together? Probably at least the ones with voodoo-type identity signatures on them, DNA samples, like hair caught in a brush, dried saliva traces on dentures, Kleenexes in a forgotten waste-basket. But—

Abruptly her chest felt cold and hollow.

But this message had been written down *before* she had given Amber the hairbrush. And Caroleen had been awake only for the last few seconds of the message transmission, which, if it had been like the others, had been repeating for at least a full minute before she woke up.

The message had been addressed to Amber next door, not to her. Amber had read it somehow, and had obediently fetched the hairbrush.

Could all of these messages have been addressed to the girl?

Caroleen remembered wondering whether BeeVee might have needed to brace herself against something in order to communicate from the far side of the grave. Had BeeVee been bracing herself against Caroleen, her still-living twin, in order to talk to Amber? Insignificant *Amber?*

Caroleen was dizzy, but she got to her feet and kicked off her slippers, then padded into the bedroom for a pair of outdoor shoes. She had to carry them back to the living room—the bed in the bedroom had been BeeVee's too, and she didn't want to sit on it in order to pull the shoes on—and on the way, she leaned into the bathroom and grabbed her own hairbrush.

✢ ✢ ✢

Dressed in one of her old church-attendance skirts, with fresh lipstick, and carrying a big embroidered purse, Caroleen pulled the door closed behind her and began shuffling down the walk. The sky was a very deep blue above the tree branches, and the few clouds were extraordinarily far away overhead, and it occurred to her that she couldn't recall stepping out of the house since BeeVee's funeral. She never drove anymore—Amber was the only one who drove the old Pontiac these days—and it was Amber who went for groceries, reimbursed with checks that Caroleen wrote out to her, and the box of checks came in the mail, which Amber brought in from the mailbox by the sidewalk. If Caroleen alienated the girl, could she do these things herself? She would probably starve.

Caroleen's hand had begun wriggling as she reached the sidewalk and turned right, toward Amber's parents' house, but she resisted the impulse to pull a pen out of her purse. She's not talking to *me*, she thought, blinking back tears in the sunlight that glittered on the windshields and bumpers of passing cars; she's talking to stupid *Amber*. I won't *eavesdrop*.

Amber's parents had a Spanish-style house at the top of a neatly mowed sloping lawn, and a green canvas awning overhung the big arched window out front. Even shading her eyes with her manageable left hand Caroleen couldn't see anyone in the dimness inside, so she puffed up the widely spaced steps, and while she was catching her breath on the cement apron at the top, the front door swung inward, releasing a puff of cool floor-polish scent.

Amber's young dark-haired mother—Crystal? Christine?—was staring at her curiously. "It's . . . Caroleen," she said, "right?"

"Yes." Caroleen smiled, feeling old and foolish. "I need to talk to Amber." The mother was looking dubious. "I want to pay her more, and, and see if she'd be interested in balancing our, my, checkbook."

The woman nodded, as if conceding a point. "Well, I think that might be good for her." She hesitated, then stepped aside. "Come in and ask her. She's in her room."

Caroleen got a quick impression of a dim living room with clear plastic covers over the furniture, and a bright kitchen with copper pans hung everywhere, and then Amber's mother had knocked on a bedroom door and said, "Amber honey? You've got a visitor," and pushed the door open.

"I'll let you two talk," the woman said, and stepped away toward the living room.

Caroleen stepped into the room. Amber was sitting cross-legged on the pink bedspread, looking up from a cardboard sheet with a rock and a pencil and BeeVee's hairbrush on it. Lacy curtains glowed in the street-side window, and a stack of what appeared to be textbooks stood on an otherwise bare white desk in the opposite corner. The couple of pictures on the walls were pastel blobs. The room smelled like cake.

Caroleen considered what to say. "Can I help?" she asked finally.

Amber, who had been looking wary, brightened and sat up straight. "Shut the door."

When Caroleen had shut it, Amber went on, "You know she's coming back?" She waved at the cardboard in front of her. "She's been talking to me all day."

"I know, child."

Caroleen stepped forward and leaned down to peer at it, and saw that the girl had written the letters of the alphabet in an arc across the cardboard.

"It's one of those things people use to talk to ghosts," Amber explained with evident pride. "I'm using the crystal to point to the letters. Some people are scared of these things, but that's one of the good kind of crystals."

"A Ouija board."

"That's it! She made me dream of one over and over again just before the sun came up, because this is her birthday. Well, yours too I guess. At first I thought it was a hopscotch pattern, but she made me look closer till I got it." She pursed her lips. "I wrote it by reciting the rhyme, and I accidentally did *H* and *I* twice, and left out *J* and *K*." She pulled a sheet of lined paper out from under the board. "But it was only a problem once, I think."

"Can I see? I, uh, want this to work out."

"Yeah, she won't be gone. She'll be in me, did she tell you?" She held out the paper. "I drew in lines to break the words up."

"Yes. She told me." Caroleen slowly reached out to take the paper from her, and then held it up close enough to read the pencilled lines:

I/NEED/YOUR/HELP/PLEASE
Who R U?

I/AM/BEEVEE
How can I help U?
I/NEED/TO/USE/YOUR//BODY/INVITE/ME/IN/TO/YOUR/
    BODY IM/SORRY/FOR/EVERY/THING/PLEASE
R U an angel now? Can U grant wishes?
YES
Can U make me beautiful?
YES/FOR/EVER
OK. What do I do?
EXHAUSTED/MORE/LATER
BV? It's after lunch. Are U rested up yet?
YES
Make me beautiful.
GET/MY/HAIRBRUSH/FROM/MY/SISTER
Is that word "hairbrush?"
YES/THEN/YOU/CAN/INVITE/ME/IN/TO/YOU
How will that do it?
WE/WILL/BE/YOU/TOGETHER
+ what will we do?
GET/SLIM/TRAVEL/THE/WORLD
Will we be rich?
YES/I/HAVE/BANC/ACCOUNTS GET/MY/HAIRBRUSH/
    FROM/ HER/NOW
I got it.
NIGHT/TIME/STAND/OVER/GRAVE/BRUSH/YR/HAIR
    /INVITE/ME/IN

"That should be B-A-N-*K*, in that one line," explained Amber helpfully. "And I'll want to borrow your car tonight."

Not trusting herself to speak, Caroleen nodded and handed the paper back to her, wondering if her own face was red or pale. She felt invisible and repudiated. BeeVee could have approached her own twin for this, but her twin was too old; and if she did manage to occupy the body of this girl—a more intimate sort of twinhood!—she would certainly not go on living with Caroleen. And she had eaten all the Vicodins and Darvocets.

Caroleen picked up the rock. It was some sort of quartz crystal.

"When," she began in a croak; she cleared her throat and went on more steadily, "when did you get that second-to-last message? About the bank accounts and the hairbrush?"

"That one? Uh, just a minute before I knocked on your door."

Caroleen nodded, wondering bleakly if BeeVee had even known that she was leaving *her* with carbon copies—multiple, echoing carbon copies—of the messages.

She put the rock back down on the cardboard and picked up the hairbrush. Amber opened her mouth as if to object, then subsided.

There were indeed a number of white hairs tangled in the bristles.

Caroleen tucked the brush into her purse.

"I need that," said Amber quickly, leaning forward across the board. "She says I need it."

"Oh of course, I'm sorry." Caroleen forced what must have been a ghastly smile, and then pulled her own hairbrush instead out of the purse and handed it to the girl. It was identical to BeeVee's, right down to the white hairs.

Amber took it and glanced at it and then laid it on the pillow, out of Caroleen's reach.

"I don't want," said Caroleen, "to interrupt . . . you two." She sighed, emptying her lungs, and dug the car keys out of her purse. "Here," she said, tossing them onto the bed. "I'll be next door if you . . . need any help."

"Fine, okay." Amber seemed relieved at the prospect of her leaving.

Caroleen was awakened next morning by the pain of her sore right hand flexing, but she rolled over and slept for ten more minutes before the telephone by her head conclusively jarred her out of the monotonous dream that had occupied the last hour or so.

She sat up, wrinkling her nose at the scorched smell from the fireplace and wishing she had a cup of coffee, and still half-seeing the Ouija board she'd been dreaming about.

She picked up the phone, wincing. "Hello?"

"Caroleen," said Amber's voice, "nothing happened at the cemetery last night, and BeeVee isn't answering my questions. She spelled stuff out, but it's not for what I'm writing to her. All she's written so far this morning is—just a sec—she wrote, uh, 'You win you'll do—We've always been a team, right—' Is she talking to you?"

Caroleen glanced toward the fireplace, where last night she had burned—or charred, at least—BeeVee's toothbrush, razor, dentures, curlers, and several other things, including the hairbrush. And today she would call the headstone company and cancel the order. BeeVee ought not to have an easily locatable grave.

"Me?" Caroleen made a painful fist of her right hand. "Why would she talk to me?"

"You're her twin sister, she might be—"

"BeeVee is dead, Amber, she died nine weeks ago."

"But she's coming back, she's going to make me beautiful! She said—"

"She can't do anything, child. We're better off without her."

Amber was talking then, protesting, but Caroleen's thoughts were of the brothers she couldn't even picture anymore, the nieces she'd never met and who probably had children of their own somewhere, and her mother who was almost certainly dead by now. And there was everybody else, too, and not a lot of time.

Caroleen was resolved to learn to write with her left hand, and, even though it would hurt, she hoped her right hand would go on and on writing uselessly in air.

At last she stood up, still holding the phone, and she interrupted Amber: "Could you bring back my car keys? I've got some errands."

✢ AUTHOR'S NOTE ✢

Like a lot of people of my generation, my wife and I spent a year—2007, in our case—visiting elderly parents in "assisted living homes," the kind of places where the dining room has tables but no chairs because all the diners will arrive in wheelchairs, and there are banners advancing sentiments like, "Sunsets are as beautiful as sunrises," which can come to seem bitterly ironic.

In one of these places I was standing against the wall of a corridor so that two extremely elderly ladies could be wheeled past one another— and as they crossed, one of them croaked at the other, "Bitch!"

It occurred to me that a story about conflicts between two very old people would be intriguing—and of course I had to put a ghost in it.

I teach one class a week at the Orange County High School of the Arts—the other end of the age spectrum!—and the school building used to be a nineteenth-century church. My classroom is the basement catacombs, and one afternoon when I had given the students an assignment and they had all dispersed throughout the church to write, I found two of the girls huddled over a box that they had converted into a makeshift Ouija board, using a crystal for a planchette. When I said, "What the hell!" one of them quickly explained, "It's okay, Mr. Powers, it's one of the good kind of crystals!"

Oh. Well then.

So I had to give Amber their Ouija board.

⊰ FIFTY CENTS ⊱
written with James P. Blaylock

ENCHILADAS, Lyle thought. Sonora style, like you get out here away from the coast.

He listened to the engine of the old blue Fairlane as he sped east down Interstate 10, into the glare of the desert. The engine was shaking perceptibly, missing a stroke—probably a fouled spark plug. But he had spare spark plugs, and tools. He even had a spare starter-motor, alternator and water pump, just in case, in the trunk. The thing about old cars was that you could pretty much keep them going forever if you didn't outright kill them. That was ironic when you thought about it—newer cars were as fragile as hothouse flowers.

He had rebuilt the Fairlane's engine a few years back, and had some transmission work done, and there were a couple of weeks when a bad coil had given him fits, but the car had never been towed while he owned it, and it had never left him stranded. With any luck it would be the last vehicle he would ever need. A car wasn't infinitely fixable, of course, but who cared about the infinite? Time and chance happened to cars just as much as they happened to people, but if you were well-prepared you could get past most of the obstacles, until the last one.

He had filled up the tank in Cabazon, and he wouldn't be surprised if he got all the way out into Arizona today; there were lots of thrift stores and used bookstores in Arizona.

He'd know the book when he saw it. *The Golden Treasury of Songs and Lyrics,* selected by Francis T. Palgrave. Not today, probably, but

325

one day. When it came to finding old books you usually stumbled on them by chance, like so many things out here.

He could see Mount San Gorgonio now in the rearview mirror, becoming more distant with every mile, and within a few minutes he would leave it behind over the horizon and start the long haul into some real desert, out through Coachella and Desert Center and on into Blythe. There was a Mexican restaurant in Quartzsite, he recalled, just twenty minutes into Arizona, that served good enchiladas, and if he held it to sixty miles an hour, which was plenty fast enough for him, he would pull in around noon; and he hadn't checked the Quartzsite thrift-stores in months. Then he might very well angle on up Parker way for a look, and back home again along Highway 62. He would cross the river twice that way.

The air was clear out in the desert, almost like no air at all, and the sky was a deep cloudless blue. He rolled the window down and let the warm air blow through the car, sluicing out the old smells of map-paper and gun-oil with the timeless scents of hot stone and creosote. He wondered whether you could still buy the old burlap water bags that you strapped to the front bumper. There was something about that water, which always tasted a little like burlap and maybe a little like exhaust, that was better than just about anything.

A big tumbleweed came blowing along the right shoulder of the highway now, and a gust of wind sent it rollicking across in front of the Fairlane. It bounced once before clipping his front fender and rolling straight across the hood, showering the windshield with broken twigs. For a moment he couldn't see a damned thing, but the highway was empty ahead of him anyway, and he held the car in the lane, and within half a second the windshield was clear again. And then he could.

He saw a roadside phone booth up ahead on the left, still a couple of hundred feet away, and there was a man standing beside it, though there was no car. Put up a phone booth anywhere on earth, Lyle thought, and somebody will need to make a call there.

He checked his rearview mirror and then pressed the brake, eased across the oncoming lane and pulled off onto the shoulder, rolling to a stop just on the far side of the booth.

The man looked like a desert prospector of some kind—grizzled white hair and beard, stained khaki pants and a T-shirt, red suspenders. His pant legs were rolled up, and he had on a pair of work boots that had seen some hard times. He was a big man, tall and heavy, obviously well fed. The wind blew his white hair like streamers of old newspaper caught in a fence.

"Need a lift?" Lyle called through the open window. He switched off the engine, and the desert was dead quiet except for the whisper of wind.

The man peered around the phone booth at him indecisively, clearly puzzled, although it didn't seem to be Lyle's question that had him snowed. His whole face showed a deep confusion, like a man who had just waked up in unfamiliar surroundings and hadn't remembered yet where he was or why he was there.

Nut case, Lyle thought, but all the more reason to give him a lift.

"Nope," the man said abruptly. "You got a couple of quarters for the phone? Mine don't work." He had a voice like a shovel in a gravel pit, but it was airy and a little high, as if there was just a shade of helium in the mix.

"Probably bent," Lyle said, leaning away to open the glove box. He took out a little leather coin purse and unsnapped it, digging out a couple of quarters and then clicking it shut, tossing it back in and closing the glove box. For a moment he considered digging under the driver's seat too, but decided that quarters would do.

"Name's Lyle," he called to the man as he levered open the door and stepped out onto the packed shoulder sand. "George Lyle." He trudged up to the booth, holding out the two coins on the palm of his hand.

The man stared back at him, as if names in general meant nothing to him. He didn't take the quarters. On the other side of the highway a little wind devil spun up out of the desert, whirling toward them across the broad pavement, and as it swept over them Lyle could hear sand grains ping against the metal phone-booth hood.

"You got one of them cellulite phones?" the man asked, oblivious to it. The wind devil whirled away past them and out of existence.

"No, sorry," Lyle said, repressing a smile. "I don't know much about that kind of thing." He waved his open hand. "Try these two quarters on for size, Bub."

The man took the coins awkwardly, as if he had arthritis. His fingers were cold, Lyle noticed. Imminent heatstroke? It wasn't a hot day, especially, not for the desert, but it was a good eighty degrees or more and the man must have walked a ways; Lyle couldn't see a broken-down car anywhere ahead, and he hadn't passed any in the last hour or so. "You feeling all right?" he asked. The man was standing there looking at the coins, as if he still wasn't quite sure about something. "I'll be happy to give you a lift. East or west, doesn't matter a damn bit. I'm just out . . . on a scavenger hunt."

"I got a call to make," the man said, turning around and feeding the coins into the slot. "I've got to talk to my daughter."

Lyle heard him say this clearly enough, although the man by now seemed to be talking to the wind. Slowly he pushed the buttons, hesitating between each. He started to push a button and then abandoned it for another one as if digging the number out of the deep recesses of his mind. He held the receiver tight to his ear finally and stood looking east toward where the Chuckwalla Mountains stood out against the blue like an etching. Above the mountains were five white vapor trails, as if God were fixing to write music in the sky.

Lyle heard the *boo-dee-weet* of a missed connection.

"Can't get through yet," the man muttered, hanging up the phone. He picked the quarters out of the coin-return slot and idly rattled them in his right fist like dice, and then turned away from the telephone and blinked at Lyle, as if he had forgotten that he wasn't alone. "Thanks for the kindness," he said awkwardly. "Name's Swinger Campbell."

"Glad to meet you," Lyle said, and held out his hand again, hoping the man would realize he hadn't given back the two quarters—But Campbell didn't move to shake his hand, just licked his lips and looked east again.

"I was a good hard-rock silver miner in them days."

"Well I'm happy to give you a lift. You can tell me your story in the car. That way you won't get sandblasted by this wind."

"Broke a ton of rock and drank a quart of whiskey every day. It was our way of life."

"I'll bet it was," Lyle said.

"We had a claim up in the Panamints, me and Wino Larsen and Shave-and-Lotion MacDuff." He laughed a little now. "By God we were as hard as the rocks we busted, and that's the damned truth. I'll have to owe you that fifty cents."

"I'll put it on the tab," Lyle said. Oh well, he thought, less than a dollar at least. "Why'n't you get in the car, Swinger? Take a load off. I'll run you up to Desert Center or wherever else. Hell, I've got nothing better to do than give a man a lift. We can hash it over in the car."

But Swinger Campbell had started walking away, not down the highway, but straight out into the desert, and within seconds he was in among the Joshua trees and greasewood, his form rippling in the heat haze rising from the desert sand and rock. Lyle stood for a moment watching him, undecided, but then wearily set out after him. He couldn't just let the man walk to his death, for God's sake. The ground was fairly hard, but was rocky, and he had to pick his way. And a hundred feet from the highway there was a dry wash, where the sand was softer, and it slowed him down even more. The wind gusted around him, and he turned away, shielding his face from blowing sand, and when he straightened up again he saw that Campbell was already a surprising distance ahead, farther than seemed possible. Lyle turned to look back toward the car. He hadn't come more than a hundred feet, and already Campbell seemed to have covered three or four times that distance.

"Swinger!" Lyle shouted, cupping his hands to his mouth, but either Campbell didn't hear or he didn't care. The heat haze was obviously distorting things, because all Lyle could see now were Campbell's black boots rising and falling and the crossed red lines of his suspenders. Then he disappeared from sight altogether, hidden for a moment by a big Joshua tree. He reappeared momentarily, then disappeared again.

There was no way Lyle was going to catch him. Apparently Swinger hadn't been kidding about being as hard as the rocks he busted, because he was moving like a damned coyote. Lyle trudged back to the phone booth and the car; he could at least call the Highway Patrol and tell them to send someone out with some kind of off-road vehicle . . .

Of course, Swinger Campbell might not be crazy, or sick either. He might have a shack a few miles out there, and this could well be the closest phone. There were plenty of shacks out in the desert, scattered across the hundreds of miles, mostly cinderblock cubes with aluminum patios hung on the side for a little shade. Now and then you'd see one with an old broken-down windmill alongside.

There was no sign of Campbell at all now, nor of any shack, either, just unending desert. Lyle opened the Fairlane's passenger side door and fetched two more quarters out of the purse in the glove box, but when he walked back to the pay phone and lifted the receiver, he could hear nothing.

Campbell at least got sounds out of it, Lyle thought, and dutifully dropped his two quarters into the slot. He heard them clank somewhere inside the box, but still no sound came from the receiver. He might as well be holding a rock to his ear. And when he worked the coin-return lever, nothing appeared in the slot. He hung the receiver back on its hook and made himself walk away from it without getting angry.

Lyle climbed into the parked Fairlane, started up the engine, and waited as two cars sped past, going like there was no tomorrow. Then he crossed back over into the eastbound lane and pushed it up to sixty again.

Restore some random guidance to the day, he thought ten minutes later when he saw the hitchhiker. Like with the book he was after: a directed search finds nothing. He swung the wheel to the right and pulled to a stop so close that the young man in the denim jacket just had to lean forward and take hold of the door handle. Again there was no parked car in sight. A day for lost souls.

The boy appeared to be in his early twenties, and he fumbled a pack of Camel non-filters out of his shirt pocket as soon as he had sat down and pulled the door closed. "You, uh, got a light?" he said in a high, nasal voice. He seemed to be wary of Lyle—but that was only sensible, being picked up by a stranger.

"Cigarette lighter on the dash," Lyle said over his shoulder as he looked behind and accelerated back onto the pavement.

The cigarette pack wavered in the pale hands. "I, uh—guess I've quit. You want one?"

"Sure, thanks." Lyle took the pack with his right hand and tapped one out against the wheel, then put the pack down on the seat and pushed the lighter button in. A moment later it popped back out again, and he pulled the lighter out and held the tiny red coils to the end of the cigarette.

"You're welcome, Mr. Lyle."

Lyle made himself keep his eyes on the road. Probably this kid did electrical work, and had been to his store in Fontana. "All right," said

Lyle around his newly lit cigarette, "you know my name—so who are you?"

The young man didn't answer for several seconds, not until Lyle finally turned to squint at him. Then he said, "I'm you. From the future."

Lyle exhaled one syllable of surprised laughter. "Oh—oh, right? The future? You don't look anything like me. What do you do, get new bodies in the future?"

The young man shifted uneasily on the seat, and the shoulders of his worn denim jacket heaved in a shrug. "Sometimes." He kept brushing his lanky brown hair back to touch his forehead, gingerly, as if he'd been stung there.

Beyond the dusty windshield the Mojave Desert spread out to either side of the highway. Lyle reflected that this was pretty much the sort of thing he hoped for, in his long receptive drives—random input, rolling dice. "Okay, if you're me, what was my favorite restaurant back when I lived in Tucson?"

"I don't remember a lot of old stuff."

"I'd think you'd remember the camarones."

"Don Juan's. It was called Don Juan's."

"No. La Perlita. Was that gonna be your next guess?"

"Yes." There was an edge of defiance in the nasal voice. "You've got a gun under your seat. It's a .38 Special, Smith and Wesson, loaded with Hydra-Shok hollow-points." He turned to look squarely at Lyle for the first time. The wind through the open window was blowing his hair around his narrow face. "You've never been to Tucson."

Lyle's heart was thumping in his suddenly cold chest, but he forced a laugh. "I sold that gun. All I carry under the seat now is a Thomas Brothers map book—see?" He leaned forward over the steering wheel to reach under the seat with his left hand, and when he sat back again he was holding the .38 pointed across his lap at his companion. His right arm was straight, holding the wheel at the top. "I'm gonna pull over, sonny, and you're going to step out of the car."

Had this kid glimpsed the gun when he'd climbed in?—but he wouldn't have been able to tell what it was loaded with. He must somehow have seen the car before, searched it while Lyle had been in some store or diner or swap-meet; and he could have learned Lyle's name then, from the registration in the glove box.

The young man giggled nervously. "You can't kill me now."

"Nobody's killing anybody. I just don't want your company."

"Sometimes you can't choose, Mr. Lyle." He shrugged, holding his hands up as if to imply that there was nothing he could do about anything. "Look, I'm sorry. This is all my fault. I won't bother you again."

Roadside gravel was popping and grinding under the car's tires now, and the brakes were squealing. Dust obscured the view behind. No buildings or signs broke up the stony landscape that stretched away to remote mountains in the south, and the road ahead was as empty as the sky. This was as desolate a spot as the place where Lyle had picked him up. The young man opened the door and leaned forward, ready to step out.

"What is your name, by the way?" Lyle said, still pointing the revolver at him as the Fairlane rocked to a halt.

The young man paused, one foot on the dirt outside. "I told you," he said, staring out at the desert. "Albert Erlich. I won't see you again. I'm sorry for all the hassle. I hope you're all right. I was . . . desperate, as I recall." He looked back over his shoulder at Lyle and grinned, miserably. "Well, you take the high road and I'll take the low road, right?"

"How did you know about the gun?"

Albert Erlich stepped down and closed the door. Through the open window he said, "I've seen it before." He exhaled and stepped away from the car to look back the way they'd come, his hands shoved in the pockets of his denim jacket now. "A couple of times."

Lyle considered asking him when this had been, but he knew the answer would just be more nonsense.

"Goodbye, Albert," he said instead, and when Albert had closed the door Lyle drove along the shoulder for a dozen feet or so, raising dust, even though he couldn't get back into the lane until a bus had roared on past him, just because he suddenly wanted very badly to get away from Albert Erlich.

When he did gun the old car up into the clear lane in the bus's wake, he leaned forward to tuck the revolver back under the seat, and he gasped at a sudden pain in his stomach. Ulcers? The enchiladas should settle that question, for better or worse.

I'll have to make that call, he thought. *Crazy old guy, calls himself*

Swinger Campbell, wandering around in the desert north of the 10, near that phone booth that's a hundred miles from anywhere. And ideally he'd find a thrift store somewhere, a used bookstore, a yard sale; the *Golden Treasury,* squat little book issued with a yellow dust jacket, and if the dust jacket was gone the binding was gray cloth with silver stamping on the spine.

Ten minutes later he saw the figure of another hitchhiker rippling in the heat waves ahead, and without thinking he lifted his foot from the accelerator—again there was no car in sight on the shoulder—and when he had coasted to within a few hundred feet of the figure, he recognized the denim jacket and the stringy brown hair. It wasn't another hitchhiker, it was the same one. Albert Erlich again.

Lyle's foot had touched the brake pedal before he had even consciously decided to stop. The backs of his hands were chilled on the steering wheel in spite of the hard sunlight through the windshield, and his ribs tingled as if he had soda water for blood.

Nobody's even passed me, Lyle thought, since I made the kid get out of the car.

For a moment he earnestly dredged his memory for some recollection of having turned the car around; but the sun was still in the morning half of the empty sky ahead of him. You didn't turn around, he told himself. God help you, you didn't.

There were no vehicles behind him, so it didn't matter that he hit the brakes too hard because he was leaning forward again to get the revolver. For a moment after the car rocked to a halt in a cloud of dust, he couldn't see Erlich at all; then he could see the lean figure standing very close, with one hand spread and raised in a questioning gesture.

Lyle held the gun out of sight by his left thigh, and nodded; and the door was pulled open and Erlich leaned in, gripping the roof of the car as if to steady it.

"You drive like you're mad about something," he said in the remembered nasal voice. "Let me get my friend." He straightened up and turned around, and Lyle heard him yell, "Swinger! Hey, Swinger, our ride's here!" The flat voice didn't seem to carry at all in the desert air, and there were no echoes.

"Swinger Campbell," said Lyle in a careful, conversational tone.

Erlich crouched beside the open passenger-side door. "Right, that's the guy," he said, squinting out at the desert. "He's gone. He was just here a second ago. He's looking for a phone booth."

"Has to," Lyle began, but he was out of breath. He inhaled deeply, then said, "Has to call his daughter."

"Right. Oh well." Erlich climbed into the car and pulled the door closed, then fished a pack of Camels out of his jacket pocket and peeled off the wrapper and the foil.

Lyle sniffed—the young man's breath reeked of onions and salsa and enchilada sauce.

Lyle heard himself ask, "Who *are* you?" He was pleased that his voice was steady, so he ventured to go on. "Last time you said you were me, from the future."

"Did I? Last time? Actually—" Erich's voice was solemn, "—I'm your father, from the past."

"*Goddammit—*"

"Whoa, watch your driving! My name's Albert Erlich!"

"I know that, you told me that, I meant . . ."

"Jesus, you gonna shoot me?"

Lyle realized that he had raised the gun and pointed it across his lap. "I hope not."

"I didn't catch *your* name," said Erlich, apparently not cowed by the sight of the gun.

"You know it," said Lyle hoarsely. "Just like you know I've never been to Tucson. Just like you know this is a Smith and Wesson .38 Special, loaded with Hydra-Shok hollow-point rounds."

"Sounds like they're full of water, hydra shock," said Erlich absently, looking out at the desert sweeping past. "Well, Tucson's no big deal. So remind me?"

"Remind you of what?"

"Your name. I can't just call you Don Juan."

Lyle sighed wearily and took his foot off the gas pedal. The car had got up to eighty miles an hour. "Lyle. George Lyle."

"We were getting along so well at first, Mr. Lyle. My fault, I'm man enough to admit it."

"How did you—get here ahead of me? I dropped you off ten miles back."

"Oh." Erlich shook his head. "Just once more?"

"How did you get here so fast?"

"Here?" said Erlich, suddenly angry. "Here from . . . from *there*? I didn't, you—" He was scratching his forehead again. "*You* should know how I—and what did you do to that old Swinger guy? *You* get to drive *forward*, and we—"

Erlich thrashed suddenly in the seat, perhaps intending to attack Lyle; and then Lyle's wrist was twisted painfully as a brief, deafening explosion compressed the air in the car.

I shot him. Oh my God, Lyle thought, and the car slewed in the lane as he gaped at the figure of the young man beside him.

But there was a hole in the door panel; and Albert Erlich was sitting stiffly in the seat with no blood visible on him.

Lyle's hands were shaking; he dropped the pistol onto the floor, and used both hands to steer the car toward the shoulder. Gunpowder smoke burned in his nose. "I'm sorry," he was saying, though because of the ringing in his ears he could hear his own voice only in the bones of his head. "I'm sorry, I didn't mean to shoot—"

"I know, I know!" Erlich said loudly. "Just let me out, and then you can go kill *everybody*."

When the car stopped, Erlich got out without a word, and slammed the door; and as Lyle once again steered the old car onto the asphalt, panting with what he supposed was mainly relief, he could hear the young man behind him calling, out toward the desert, "Swinger? Hey, Swinger?"

Lyle was still shaking, and consciously watching the speedometer; he could imagine coasting to a stop without being aware of it, or distractedly gunning the old vehicle up to impossible speeds.

After five miles or so he saw another figure ahead to the right, out in the desert. It was an older man, standing beside an aluminum Edison relay shed some distance from the highway down a dirt track. Mercifully, it was clearly not Swinger Campbell. Lyle didn't even slow down, and anyway the figure stepped behind the shed as he drove past.

The Colorado River was as incongruous as he remembered it— water flowing in a line from north to south through the desert ahead of him, cold and blue-green under the sky—a true border, truer than any simple demarcation laid out by surveyors. The concrete bridge over it seemed to arch over the blue to a different world.

The old Ford Fairlane rumbled up the slope of the bridge, and in the moment when the car was barrelling over the crest he glanced around at the river and the land ahead. Though the landscape behind him was barren, on the far side of the river the desert was patched with irrigated fields, squares and disks of green.

But the irrigated tracts were clustered by the river, and soon he had driven through them and on into deeper desert. He was glad to see the highway sign ahead.

Quartzsite, the green sign said, *Food—Gas—Lodging,* and Lyle pulled off the interstate and turned right onto the dusty main street, where the first thing he saw was a Goodwill thrift store in a rundown strip mall.

He slowed down, assessing it. There were weedy flowerbeds with big lumps of white rock in them, meant for decoration probably, and the stores all had some kind of silver film over the windows to keep out the sun. A big, ragged sheet of it was peeling off one of the thrift store windows, giving it a desolate look, but desolate or not, it might be the place.

His wife had given him Palgrave's *Golden Treasury* on his birthday, in 1960. It had got lost somehow when he had sold the house in Adelanto in '88, after the lung cancer killed her. It was his own carelessness that cost him the book, and he hadn't even noticed the loss until a year or so ago, but he'd been devoting his time to searching for the *Golden Treasury* ever since, dropping into thrift stores and bookstores along the highway. *Time and chance,* he thought again, and sighed heavily. Phyllis had had a hell of a nice voice when he met her, back when they were young. She knew enough show tunes to fill a shoe box, and every now and then he had tried to help out on their old piano, but he wasn't worth much in that way, and he had left the piano to the new owners when he'd sold the house.

He would check the book section in this Goodwill—and he'd call the Highway Patrol—but right now he needed several beers to calm him down, along with lunch. The beers would be medicine, to slow his alarming heartbeat, which hadn't really throttled back since the damned gun had gone off. How the hell had the gun gone off? It had been a case of nerves. He shouldn't have been holding the thing, let alone had a finger on the trigger, for God's sake. And he shouldn't have picked up Erlich the second time and set himself up for something like that.

There was the Mexican restaurant on the corner past the Goodwill, and he had turned into the parking lot, switched off the engine, and got out of the car before he looked at the sign over the door and noticed the name of the place.

Don Juan's.

He opened the door but didn't get out, and after a while he pulled his shirt out from under his belt, picked up the revolver from the floor and tucked it into his waistband, right behind his belt buckle. Then he took the last two quarters out of the coin purse in the glove box—tip money, if he needed something other than bills. When he got out of the car he smoothed his now-untucked shirt over the angularity of the gun. It didn't show.

He locked the car door and walked across the sun-softened asphalt parking lot to the restaurant. Before he went in he looked back at the car, and from this angle he could see the hole where the bullet had punched through the door. Christ, he had shot his own car. He pulled open the restaurant door, clanging a set of bells hung on the inside of it.

The restaurant was dark inside, and cool, and it smelled just as it should, like beer and salsa and corn tortillas, and a little like mildewy air circulated through a swamp cooler. A middle-aged waitress motioned him in and waved him to a booth.

"Budweiser," he said to her when he had sat down on the side facing the front door and she had laid a menu in front of him. "Make it two, please."

"Hot out there?" she asked.

He exhaled, as if he'd been holding his breath, and smiled at her. "Not bad yet. Give it a couple of hours, though." She looked a bit like his wife Phyllis. More than a little bit. She had that sparkle in her eye and the same who-gives-a-damn hair.

"Anything to eat?" she asked, glancing at the menu on the table.

There it was again on the front of the menu: Don Juan's. Probably Erlich was familiar with this place, and had pulled the name out of his hat.

He pushed the menu away. "A couple of cheese enchiladas, please," he said, "with beans and rice."

"Coming up," she said, picking up the menu and walking away toward the kitchen.

There were dividers between the booths, wooden slats and potted plants, but he could see enough of the restaurant to know that the place was mostly empty. There was someone, a man, over across the way, just the white hair on the top of his head visible from here, and he heard another man's voice saying something to someone, probably to the waitress, but he couldn't see them either. He sat back and stretched his legs out under the table. Here came his beer, right on time, God bless it. The waitress set both bottles down and poured half of one into a small glass. The bottles were sweating heavily, and right now he couldn't think of anything that looked better.

He saw that her nametag read *Donna*. "Thanks, Donna," he said, toasting her before drinking off half the beer in the glass. He set it down and sat back again, feeling considerably better. The pistol's hammer pinched the flesh on his stomach, and he wished that he hadn't brought the damned thing in with him—although if he hadn't, sure enough that goddamn Erlich would show up and steal it out of the Fairlane.

He felt another twinge of pain in his gut, deep inside, but just then Donna brought the enchiladas. Ulcer or no ulcer he was going to eat the damned things. Out of habit he tried the beans and rice first, and they were good. You could tell a lot about a Mex restaurant from their side dishes—whether they put any effort into them or not. This was first rate. The enchiladas were hot all through and bursting with cheese and onions, and the sauce didn't taste like it was out of a can. Someone knew how to cook. When they finally came to hang him, and time was at a premium, this was what he would want to eat—cheese enchiladas, rice and beans, and a cold beer.

Before he slowed down he was halfway through the food and well into his second beer. He heard Donna's voice now from over near the register, and he half stood up to wave his emptied Budweiser bottle at her. He could see the man beyond the booth divider now.

"Swinger," he said, surprised, and the man looked up. It was him all right, right down to the red suspenders. Lyle wouldn't have to call the Highway Patrol after all. Campbell had a fork full of tamale halfway to his mouth. Lyle asked impulsively, "You get through to your daughter?"

Swinger squinted back at him, and not happily. "My daughter's been dead since before the war," he said flatly. "What the hell are you talking about?" He set the fork down on his plate. "Do I know you?"

The poor bastard's brains are fried, Lyle thought in embarrassment. "Back down the highway," Lyle said, gesturing vaguely toward the west, "across the river." But Swinger obviously didn't know him from a Chinaman, or if he did, he wasn't going to admit it. First Erlich and now Swinger Campbell, Lyle thought. Fast travellers, both of them.

"My mistake," Lyle said. "Sorry to bother you." He sat back down, remembering suddenly that Erlich had known Swinger, too. Maybe they were up to some kind of incognito thing. That's just what he needed, to get mixed up in a lot of tomfoolery, or worse. To hell with both of them. Give a man fifty cents and he acts like he doesn't know you. Maybe that was the deal, Lyle thought, draining the rest of his beer: Swinger was playing stupid to keep Lyle from mentioning the fifty cents. He looked for the waitress again. He hated like hell to have an empty beer glass. She was standing by the register, looking hard at the man facing her. A young man.

And Lyle's face was suddenly cold, and his stomach knotted up again. *Christ almighty,* he thought, *it's Erlich.* He peered at the young man, hoping he was wrong.

But it had to be. Same blue denim jacket and scraggly hair. Swinger Campbell's presence suddenly seemed sinister to him, and he hunched over his plate.

Wait 'em out, he told himself tensely. Give them a minute and they'd be gone, and he could drink another beer in peace. If it came down to it he would show them the gun in his waistband. It would mean plenty to Erlich, anyway. Lyle cut out a piece of enchilada, but he chewed it without tasting it now, and without thinking he picked up his empty beer glass and tilted it up to his mouth, only then remembering that it was empty.

He sighed, then lifted one of the bottles and waved it toward Donna, but when they made eye contact he saw right away that something was wrong. Her mouth was a tight line, and her face was white—she was obviously scared stiff. Lyle bent forward, watching closely, his heart starting to hammer in his chest.

He saw that Erlich had something in his fist, and it wasn't a twenty dollar bill. It was a small automatic pistol, no more than .22 or .25

caliber. Donna started to turn away, putting her hands out, and Lyle stood up, sliding out of the booth and reaching into his waistband for his own gun.

"Hey!" he shouted, drawing the revolver.

Peripherally he saw Swinger Campbell stand up, too, but the man staggered sideways out of his booth, sweeping his plate and beer glass off onto the floor and then collapsing face down on top of them.

At the clatter of china and glass Erlich had swiveled around, looking wildly back toward where Swinger was sprawled on the linoleum. The kid was clearly scared, shaking with fear. He saw Lyle and his revolver then, and he waved his own little pistol at Lyle.

"Keep away, old man!" he shouted. "It's not worth it! Nobody moves!"

But then Donna screamed, and Erlich twisted furiously back toward her, and his gun popped loudly.

Just like that she fell backward, disappearing entirely from Lyle's view, the whole thing happening in a single long moment. Lyle stood frozen in shocked surprise, as did Erlich, whose shoulders were twitching. Suddenly coming to life, Erlich reached over the counter into the open register and took out a handful of bills.

"Erlich," Lyle said, stepping toward him and raising his revolver. Erlich spun around in surprise, pointing his pistol at Lyle, and it popped again in the same instant that Lyle pulled the revolver's trigger.

The hard crack battered his eardrums, and he swung the barrel down toward the floor, for he had seen Erlich go down but didn't know if the shot had hit him or not; then past the spot of muzzle-glare in his vision Lyle saw that Erlich was sitting on the floor, slumped against the cash-register counter, with a black hole in the center of his forehead. His gun had tumbled away somewhere, but the bills were still clutched in his dead hand.

The restaurant was silent, and reeked of the burnt-metal smell of gunpowder. Lyle heard a back door slam—the cook and busboy getting the hell out, probably—as he started toward the counter to help Donna. He was strangely winded, as if he had run half a mile, and the pain in his stomach nearly doubled him over now.

Swinger Campbell lay face down on the floor—probably his heart—but one way or another he would have to wait.

Lyle stepped over Erlich's sprawled legs and grabbed the counter-edge with his left hand to steady himself, and he blinked cold sweat out of his eyes as he peered behind the counter.

Erlich's blood was spattered on the cash register and the street-side wall, but Donna was crouched behind a stool, blinking fearfully up at him; and he was relieved to see blood staining a hole torn in the shoulder of her blouse. Not a lot of blood, nothing arterial.

He let the revolver clank onto the counter and then knelt beside her and touched her arm. "It's okay," he said. "It's okay, honey."

She looked into his eyes, and nodded, taking his word for it. But then she looked down and her eyes widened.

He glanced down at himself. There was a broad red stain on his shirt, visibly expanding: Erlich had shot him in the stomach. I'll be damned, he thought, and he sat down hard on the floor, the pain moving through him now like a hot iron.

"Telephone," Donna said to him, pushing herself up with her good arm.

And then without any jolt he was back out in the sunny desert, standing, holding two quarters in the palm of his hand as if to give them to Donna, who was gone, so that she could make the call, and he whispered, "Try these on for size."

But Donna wasn't here, he was talking to no one but himself, and he closed his fist on the two coins.

Had he left his car in Quartzsite? How had he got here? He could see that he was on the California side of the river again.

Apparently he *had* crossed the river twice that day—just as he had planned. He looked back the way he had come, remembering his car in the parking lot, the torn metal where the bullet had gone through the door, and then remembering Donna, and then Phyllis and the life they'd had together. He could still taste the enchiladas and the beer, and it occurred to him that he hadn't ever got the third Budweiser. But then he hadn't paid for it either, not in that way, and he hadn't left Donna a tip, which was worse.

He was standing in the sand beside an aluminum shed with a big, faded Edison decal on the padlocked door. The black line of Interstate 10 lay a hundred feet to the north, and a blue car was approaching from the east, still far enough away to be lapped in watery mirage; Lyle took a step forward, then heard the uneven drone of the car's engine, clearly missing a stroke.

He stepped behind the shed before the Fairlane got too close—he didn't want to be seen, or, God help him, recognized—but he tried to project a thought to the agitated driver: *Go to the Goodwill store before you eat. This is your last chance to find the book.*

He'd have known the book first by its binding, then by the inscription on the flyleaf—*Happy birthday, George—Love, Phyllis.* Too late now. No more birthdays now.

He realized abruptly that he would head out into the desert, and he started plodding away from the shed and the highway even as the thought came into his mind. Swinger had got that right. Get off the highway. There was no point lingering, no point going on skipping backward like a stone across a lake.

He felt light, as if a burden had fallen away, and the rocks and soft sand of the desert floor were no longer any kind of problem at all. He heard the Fairlane speed past, heading toward Arizona, but he didn't look back. He wondered whether he would run into Swinger again out here, somewhere on up ahead, and it seemed to him then that he could see the red suspenders and the black boots through the heat haze in the remote distance. He hoped so; he could use the company. Sometimes you couldn't choose.

✥ AUTHOR'S NOTE ✥

At the enormous Acres of Books used bookstore in Long Beach—you have to take the 1975 freeway offramp to get there now—Jim Blaylock and I met an old man going through the labyrinthine poetry shelves, and he told us he was looking for a copy of Palgrave's Golden Treasury. *We told him we'd let him know if we saw it. "It has a yellow dust jacket," he said; and later he added, "There's an inscription on the flyleaf—'For my husband Ernie, with love, your wife Edna.'"*

He was looking for one particular copy *of the book.*

So Blaylock and I decided to expand the old guy's search to thrift stores and other used book stores, east across the desert into Arizona— and of course to get him into some supernatural trouble.

⚜ NOBODY'S HOME ⚜
An Anubis Gate Story

"Eternal process moving on,
From state to state the spirit walks;
And these are but the shattered stalks,
Or ruined chrysalis of one."
　　　　　—Tennyson, *In Memoriam*

OVER THE CLATTER of rain on the canvas awning above her head and the more remote background hiss of it on the pavement of Cannon Street in the darkness below, she could hear a faint, repeated crunching splash, as if someone were laboriously plodding down the narrow, gravel-paved street; but the sound didn't change its position.

Jacky Snapp shifted forward on the stone ledge and peered down. A streetlamp raised yellow gleams on an umbrella a dozen feet below her and to her left, out in front of St. Swithin's Church, and the umbrella was bouncing up and down as it moved forward eight steps, then stopped, whirled and jumped eight steps back.

Midnight was long past, and the London streets were quiet except for the occasional rattle of a carriage and horses, or a distant bell from out on the river. Jacky had spent the evening tracking down a beggar who was rumored to have fur growing all over him like an ape, but when she had cornered the man in the basement of an old pub off Fleet Street, her hand tense on the flintlock pistol under her coat, he had turned out to be only a very hairy old fellow with a prodigious beard— not the half-legendary man she had devoted her life to finding and killing.

Another false trail.

Her cold hand went to her chest, and under the fabric of her shirt she felt the glass cylinder she wore on a ribbon around her neck. I won't give up, Colin, she thought— I promise.

The umbrella below her was still hopping back and forth on its eight-step course, and it occurred to her that the person holding it might be playing hopscotch, jumping through the pattern of squares in the children's game. Alone, at midnight, in the rain. Jacky had only arrived in the city a couple of weeks ago, but she was sure this must be uncommon.

She pushed her wide-brimmed hat more firmly down onto her cut-short hair and prodded the false moustache glued to her upper lip, then leaned out from the first-floor window ledge to grip the wet drain-pipe by which she had climbed up to this perch; it still felt solidly moored, so she swung out and slid down the cold metal till her boots stopped at a bracket. From here she could stretch a loose-trousered leg sideways onto the granite sill of a ground-floor window, and a moment later she had dropped lightly to the street.

The figure under the umbrella was a girl, facing away now, her wet skirt flapping around her ankles under the hem of a dark coat as she hopped forward on one foot.

Jacky had decided simply to steal away in the other direction, toward the dim silhouette of St. Paul's cathedral dome, when the umbrella abruptly began to glow; in the same moment it was tossed aside and Jacky saw that bright flames had sprung up on the girl's shoulders and in her hair.

Jacky leaped forward and drove her shoulder into the girl's back, and when the girl tumbled forward onto her hands and knees on the wet gravel, Jacky pushed her over sideways and leaned in over the burning coat and tried to roll the girl's head into a puddle. The heat on Jacky's face made her squint and hold her breath, and her hands and wrists were scorching, and the glass vial had fallen out of her shirt and was swinging in the flames.

And another person was crouched beside her, trying to push her hands back; Jacky swung a fist in the person's direction, but it connected with nothing but cold rainy air. Finally she was able to roll the girl over onto her back, extinguishing the coat, and with stinging hands splash water onto the girl's head.

With the flames put out, the street seemed darker than ever; Jacky flinched to see glowing spots on the pavement, but at a second glance she saw that they only shone a dim green. Even as she blinked at them they faded, but not before she noticed that they had been arranged in a long row of foot-wide rectangles.

Hopscotch! she thought. She leaned back, gasping in the wonderfully cold air, and quickly looked around, but whoever it was who had tried to interfere in her rescue was gone. The girl lying on the street was panting and moving feebly.

On its now-charred ribbon, the vial that hung around Jacky's neck was too hot to touch, so she let it swing free for now. She started to get to her feet—

And with a start she noticed figures standing in the dimness of an alley on the south side of the street, scarcely a dozen feet away from where she crouched. She couldn't tell how many.

They wavered in the rainy breeze, as if they were silhouettes painted on an unmoored canvas, but their hands were moving and their heads turned back and forth, perhaps in whispered conversation.

Jacky's face suddenly felt colder than the rain, and her ribs tingled. As cautiously as if the alley figures were a pack of feral dogs, Jacky took hold of the girl's still-hot lapels and pulled her to her feet.

"He was supposed to go," the girl was saying, but Jacky put one hand over her mouth and gripped her elbow with the other.

"Walk quiet," she whispered, and took a tense step away, toward St. Paul's.

But with a flutter like birds the shadowy silhouettes came spinning out of the alley. They seemed to suffer in the rain, squeaking and ducking and cringing, but Jacky yanked her companion around and shoved her toward the drain pipe and yelled, "Climb!"

To her relief, the girl scrambled rapidly up the pipe, bracing her feet in the gaps between the blocks of the wall, and Jacky followed so closely that her head was between the girl's ankles until they had both scrambled onto the window ledge under the awning.

For several seconds neither of them spoke as they caught their breath.

Then, "You knew not to just run," panted the girl. "Away down the street."

Jacky was hugging herself and shivering. One of the things down there had been in profile for a moment, and the shape of the face, and the angle of the elbow and shoulder below it, had jarred her.

She touched the glass vial that dangled on her chest, and it was still too hot to tuck into her shirt.

The girl was sitting to her right, a foot away on the three-foot-wide ledge. "I should have let you burn," said Jacky bleakly as she flexed her stinging hands.

She looked down—the shadowy crowd was milling aimlessly on the narrow street between St. Swithin's on one side and a dark chemist's shop on the other. She looked away quickly.

The girl pulled her knees up and clasped her arms around them. "Can we get up to the roof from here?"

"Why? Those are . . . *ghosts*, aren't they? Whatever *you* are, catching fire in the street like that." Jacky was trying to fit into her experience the idea that she had apparently actually seen ghosts, and even perhaps one particular ghost, and she hoped she wasn't going to giggle or start crying. "Ghosts can only see footprints, I've heard," she went on, remembering the girl's earlier remark. "That's why I didn't run."

The girl nodded. "My name's Harriet. Living folk will be drawn to this, and living folk are likely to look up." She turned toward Jacky, and even in the deep shadow Jacky could see Harriet's wide eyes and pinched mouth. "And it's not a kindly sort of living folks who'd be drawn to it."

Jacky took a deep breath and exhaled, then nodded and touched her false moustache to make sure it was secure against more rain. "I'm Jacky," she said. Then she got up on her knees and leaned out to grip the drain-pipe again. "On up the pipe for two more floors. Don't slip."

She led the way this time, pushing herself upward with the edges of her boots between the blocks and letting the cold wet pipe slide soothingly through her linked hands and trying to peer upward through the rain, and after two welcomely distracting minutes of the strenuous exercise she had swung a leg over the cornice and rolled across the coping and landed on all fours on a tar-papered roof.

A moment later Harriet landed on top of her.

Jacky pushed her off and then leaned back against the low wall, scowling. The night was not as dark up here above the street, and she could see that Harriet was not much older than herself—perhaps nineteen or twenty.

Jacky dug a pewter flask out from an inside pocket of her coat—the back of her hand brushed the glass vial, which was still hot—and unscrewed the cap gingerly with her burned fingers.

After she had taken a long swallow of the warm brandy, she passed the flask to her companion, who was now sitting cross-legged a yard away. The rain was abating, and a less-dark patch in the clouds overhead might have been the emerging moon.

Harriet tilted the flask up and took a long sip. "You saved me from burning to death," she said hoarsely, exhaling. "Thank you."

Jacky shrugged. "I don't think you'd have burned to *death*," she said, "with the rain and all." She wagged her hand for the flask, and Harriet passed it back to her.

"Oh he'd have made sure of it," said Harriet with a visible shudder. "My husband's ghost—he even tried to push you off me when you were trying to put me out." She shook her head, her wet hair flapping around her narrow face. Perhaps talking to herself more than to Jacky, she went on softly, "I don't know what I'm going to *do*! That hopscotch in front of the London Stone was supposed to send him off to Purgatory. Or Hell."

Jacky recalled that a round piece of rock called the London Stone, about the size of a watermelon, was mounted in an alcove beside the front doors of St. Swithin's Church. "Why did—" she began.

But Harriet had been peering at Jacky's face, and now interrupted her. "Why've you got a sham moustache on?"

Jacky felt as if her life were unravelling tonight. The wrong hairy man at the pub, the disturbing ghost in the street, and now her necessary disguise seemed to be useless.

"Sham?" she said, belatedly remembering to speak in her usual assumed lower pitch.

"And the short hair." Harriet touched a bristly patch on her own scalp. "Though I'm one to talk, now."

"Er . . . I don't know what you—"

"Go on, I watched how you moved when you were climbing," Harriet said. "And your voice, till just now. You're a girl. Why the fakery?"

"Oh, hell." Jacky sighed and abandoned the pretense. "I, uh, have to mingle with some rough folk, in bad places. A girl would be . . . at a disadvantage."

"Have to?"

Jacky took another mouthful of brandy from the flask instead of answering. Then she bust out, "What—*happened*, down there?"

"Your waked-up ghost got tangled with mine," said Harriet, "my husband, when you knocked me down. And that pretty much got a whole lot of 'em waked up."

"My waked-up ghost?" Colin, she thought, does she mean *you*? Don't have been that ghost in the street, please! Stay—remote.

"Somebody whose ghost you're tied to," said Harriet. "Husband?"

"I'm not married!"

"Well, common-law, or any sort of, you know, informal but consummated. Your body is where you . . . overlapped, with him."

"I—we—never did. That. We were engaged to be married. He was a poet," she added.

"Oh. Somebody else then?"

Jacky shook her head.

"You're a virgin? Then you must be carrying around a piece of him . . . ?" She stared at Jacky curiously.

"No! Wait—" She touched the glass vial, which was impossibly still hot. "I—took his—dottle."

Harriet's eyes were wide. "You took his *head*?"

Jacky couldn't help barking out one syllable of a laugh. "Not noddle, *dottle*. The ash from a clay pipe of his." She pointed at the glass vial. "Ceneromancy, it's called. Magic you do with ashes. It's kept him near me, since . . . since he was killed."

Near enough for me to feel his presence, at least, she thought, and for him to put up lines of his poetry into my head when I'm nearly asleep—but not to appear in front of me, *looking* at me!

Harriet reached out hesitantly, and when Jacky warned her that it was somehow still hot from having swung over the fire, she only brushed the vial with the back of a finger.

"Well that's how come your man's ghost got awake," she said, leaning back. "That fire on me was lit by my mad dead husband. He was a lascar from Dumdum in India, a sailor. We were married two-and-some years ago—Spring of 1807—and he couldn't go back to India because marrying me broke his caste, and he'd be killed for it. He was a decent enough husband, though our two babies were born dead, but after he died he turned horrid—he wants me to do *sattee*, do you know what that is?"

Jacky thought it might be some sort of curried Indian stew, but she shook her head.

"That's where they burn the widow of a dead man. He'd never have wanted such a thing when he was alive, and I think it's really for higher castes than what he was—but his damned ghost thinks he's a brahmin or something now, and fancies a proper escort to his, his *heathen hereafter.*" She looked anxiously toward the edge of the roof as if she expected to see her husband's ghost come clambering over the cornice. The only sounds from the street, though, were faint echoes of someone running, clearly not a ghost.

Jacky handed her the flask, and when Harriet had finished it and handed it back empty, and Jacky had opened her coat to tuck it back into the inner pocket, Harriet sat back suddenly.

"You've got a gun?" she said.

"Oh. Well, yes." Jacky buttoned her coat self-consciously. "Like I said, I have to associate with some bad sorts sometimes." She stared at Harriet, then went on, speaking more rapidly, "I mean to find the man, the creature, that murdered Colin, my fiancee, and kill him. It's why I left home and came to London, it's why I can't be a girl while I'm here, looking for him in the low sort of places he's likely to be found. It's . . ." She rubbed her eyes, lowered her hands, and shrugged. "Well, to tell you the truth, it's all I've got left." She gave the other girl a frail smile. "Revenge."

"You know who he is, the man who murdered him?" Harriet seemed glad to be distracted from talk of her husband.

"Not in any . . . lasting sense."

"You know what he looks like?"

"Sometimes. But a description of him is only good for a couple of days. And sometimes he's covered with fur, like an ape."

Harriet's eyes were wide. "Are you joking?" When Jacky shook her head, Harriet went on, "You mean that werewolf, Doggy Joe? I thought he was made up."

"Dog-Face Joe. And no, he's real enough. He's not a werewolf—he grows fur all over himself, because of some curse, but then he can switch bodies with you, so you're suddenly in his old furry body and he's in yours—" She paused to catch her breath, "—and just before he leaves his old body, he eats poison, so you—" Her voice faltered to a stop, and she looked away over the rooftop chimneys, blinking and biting her lip.

"And that's how your fellow died, this Colin?"

Jacky nodded.

"Well . . . damn. It's no use talking to his ghost, though. A ghost's just not the person it's a ghost of."

Jacky shuddered. "I don't want to talk to him. It."

Harriet seemed surprised by her vehemence.

Jacky stood up, a bit unsteadily. "Let's get down from here. There's bound to be an easier way at the back."

They descended one floor on an iron ladder bolted to the north side of the building, and then a fire escape with ornamental iron balusters led them to another ladder, which extended down to the pavement of a narrow alley. By the yellow glow in a couple of smoke-fogged windows they were able to pick their way over the wet cobblestones, around a right-angle turn, and then a silvery rectangle ahead showed them a moonlit segment of Cannon Street.

"I hope they're gone," whispered Jacky as they moved forward.

"Has your *dottle* cooled off?"

Jacky touched the pendant. "Maybe a bit. I *should* have let you burn."

Harriet exhaled shakily. "You might get another chance shortly."

But when they stepped out of the shadowed alley mouth onto the crushed gravel pavement of Cannon Street, it wasn't ghosts they met. Jacky saw a man sprint heavily past from right to left with a puppet jouncing on strings clutched in his fist, and then two men came loping along right behind him, their coats flapping. The men passed Jacky and Harriet standing in the alley mouth, but a moment later Jacky saw the jiggling puppet's head swivel around to face backward. Its little face was as sunken and folded as a dried apple, and moonlight glittered on a pair of spectacles attached over the withered nose.

One of the men behind apparently noticed the action, and his boots scraped on the gravel as he stopped and turned to look in the same direction.

"It's looking at those two," the man barked.

The one with the puppet looked toward Jacky and Harriet and nodded, then immediately sat down in the wet street and began crooning to the puppet and stroking its patchy scalp. The other two ran directly toward Jacky and her companion.

Jacky caught her balance and spun to run back down the dark alley, but a loud boom shook the air, and she looked back over her shoulder as the echoes batted away between the close building-fronts.

Her pursuers had halted, peering to Jacky's right, and an operatically deep voice from that direction called, "Not in Billingsgate, Thames Street or Cheapside, creepers!"

A prolonged metallic squeaking followed this, and Jacky caught Harriet's arm and whispered, "Hold up, I know this one."

The man with the puppet struggled to his feet. "You fired your gun," he said in a nasal voice. "And we're three and you got your legs off."

A low little wheeled cart rocked into view from the right, and on it sat a burly man with no legs, his face entirely hidden by a bushy dark beard and a big pair of spectacles and a cap pulled low over them. His massive arms flexed as he braked by pressing his hands against the gravel.

"I've got another gun," he said; then he raised his hands and clenched them into big fists. "And I can break the legs off all three of you. Come and see if I can't."

The man stepped back and tucked his unsavory puppet under his coat. "Are you with Horrabin's beggars' guild or Captain Jack's?"

"Captain Jack's," said the legless man, "but one of Horrabin's lot probably sniffed this uproar too, and may shortly appear. Neither guild is happy with trespassing shade-dealers."

The three men darted venomous glances at Jacky and Harriet, but after a moment's hesitation they began walking away east on Cannon Street, and soon they were swaggering as if to show that they hadn't been intimidated.

The man on the cart wheeled around to face Jacky and Harriet. "And you two fools! Are you *trying* to get killed? You know how the shaders pluck awakened ghosts from haunted folk?"

"Hullo, Skate," said Jacky, in her deeper voice.

The man pulled the spectacles off his face and peered. "Mother of God, young Jacky is it? When did you turn stupid? Parading around Eastcheap wearing a wide-awake ghost! Boy, you—"

"It wasn't wide-awake till this girl's dead husband tried to set her on fire!" protested Jacky. "Mine is ashes in a little flacon around my neck, and when I tried to *extinguish* her, it got heated up in *her* ghost's flames."

Skate hooked the spectacles on his nose again, then hastily took them off. "Yours is plenty lively now—it'll be kicking and blowing for days, I expect. And you," he said, squinting at Harriet, "why have you got your dead husband onstage?—especially if he wants to burn you up?"

"I was trying to hopscotch him off by the London Stone," said Harriet defensively.

"Ach, idiot child, that hasn't been a good trap-door since the stone broke in two in the Great Fire—though it's still good enough to wake the lads up, worse luck." He shook his head. "Through the devil glasses you both shine like dishes of burning brandy. You can't walk the streets—the flash of you will draw more fellows like your man there with the mummied head on a puppet, and I don't actually have another gun." He snapped his fingers impatiently. "You don't dare leave footprints—even hopping on one foot's no good, as your friend found out." He sighed and shook his head.

Jacky touched the vial hanging outside her shirt, and it was still too hot to tuck in against her skin under the fabric. Kicking and blowing for *days*? she thought in alarm.

After a pause, Skate said, "There's no help for it. Have you got two shillings?"

"Yes," said Jacky. "They're rightfully the Captain's, though. I got 'em doing the thimble and pea trick in a pub."

"I'll acquaint Captain Jack with the circumstances," said Skate. "You've got to—"

"What do we need two shillings for?" interrupted Harriet.

Skate glared at her. "There's no way you two can swim a mile upriver at this hour, wouldn't you agree? Your only hope is to find a coach—wheels make no footprints, I can tell you that—so *run* now to St. Paul's, you'll be able to find a coach on the Strand. Take it to the horse ferry below Westminster Palace. There's probably a barge moored there, by what used to be Thorney Island in long ago times—you've heard of Nobody's Home?"

Jacky shook her head, but Harriet drew in her breath. "Is he real?" she asked. "And does he really take blood for pay?"

"So I've heard," said Skate. "But I've known people go to him and come back no worse. Those shaders or their kind, on the other hand, will leave you dead."

Jacky glanced up and down the moonlit street, trying to see if a waving shadow lurked in some recessed doorway. "Who is he?" she asked.

"Nobody, who else?" said Skate impatiently. "The barge is his home. Go!"

Skate wheeled his cart to the wall of St. Swithin's as Jacky and Harriet began running west through the patches of moonlight and darkness, and when Jacky glanced back over her shoulder she saw the legless man swing the spectacles against the London Stone.

"Thimble and pea?" asked Harriet breathlessly when the two of them had waved down a stray hackney coach by the broken statue of Queen Anne in front of the cathedral, paid the driver and told him their destination, and climbed in and pulled the door closed. The leather seats were still warm, and the interior of the coach smelled of very recent perfume and cigar smoke.

Jacky yawned, more from nervousness than because of the late hour, and she flexed her hands gingerly. "I put a pea under one of three pewter thimbles on a table, and slide them around, and then chaps bet on which thimble the pea is under. But I switch in a hollow pea made of India rubber, and I can hide it flat between my fingers and make it appear, or not, under any thimble. They lose their money. What do you mean, he takes blood for pay?"

She heard the driver flip the reins, and then she was rocked back in her seat as the horses stepped briskly forward and the coach lurched into motion.

"You say your Doggy Joe fellow is real," said Harriet, "not just a frighty tale—maybe Nobody is too. Folks say he lives on a boat, and can shuffle ghosts up or down. I've heard he's a ghost himself, which likely makes it easier."

"But why blood?"

"I don't know," said Harriet, more loudly to be heard over the grinding of the wheels on the pavement, "Ghosts like blood?" She touched her neck. "I'm glad you knocked me down. Even so I've got blisters and I can feel a good deal of my hair's gone."

Neither of them spoke then, and for several minutes they simply huddled in their coats and watched rows of dark buildings shift past like derelict galleons on an outgoing tide.

The Strand widened as the coach rattled past St. Clement Dane's on its island in the middle of the road, and Jacky told herself that she had not just seen a cluster of dark, waving figures between the pillars of the western portico. Clouds had again eclipsed the moon, and outlines and relative distances were obscure.

"Why hopscotch?" she asked quickly.

"Well, hopscotch there, by the stone," replied Harriet. "In times past, anyway. It's supposed to wake up your ghost, so he's right clinging to you, and then you hop him through the seven squares of Purgatory, saying his name at each square, and then jack him right out at the top. He's supposed to disappear—not set you on fire." She shook her head. "It's a sin, too, unnatural, like you're trying to force God's machinery. You got to do it on one foot, so you're touching the ground some, but not all the way. I wonder if it's still a sin if it doesn't work."

Jacky thought it probably was, but didn't say anything.

They alighted from the coach in front of a pub called the Portman Arms at the corner of Wood and Millbank Streets, a hundred yards down from the ornately Gothic south wall of the Palace of Westminster. The pub's windows were dark, and the warehouses on the east side of the street looked abandoned. Jacky forlornly watched the coach rattle away north, back toward streets with occasional lighted windows, and shivered.

A very dark alley between two of the warehouses led away in the direction of the nearby river, and Harriet waved toward it.

"The horse-ferry is that way," she said, her soft voice barely audible in the cold wind that funneled down the street.

Jacky eyed the dark gap unhappily. "Maybe our ghosts have gone back to sleep again, now that we're so far away. We could wake up the landlord at the Portman, just get a room."

Harriet reached out and touched the glass vial hanging on Jacky's shirt, and then jerked her hand back. She quickly looked up and down the patchily-moonlit street, and she stiffened when she looked north, toward the palace.

"To the river," she whispered, "fast."

Jacky glanced north as she hurried after her companion, and she broke into a sprint when she saw two dark figures up at that end of the street, moving toward them as smoothly as billows of smoke.

The alley echoed to the fast knocking of the girls' footsteps—ghosts can see footsteps! thought Jacky—and the air between the close brick walls was heady with the scents of tobacco and cinnamon. When they burst out into the moonlight again, between two docks that stretched out over the black water, Jacky was panting and glad of the fresh breeze in spite of its biting chill.

Harriet was looking up and down the dark pebbled shore, her hair whipping around her face. A couple of barges were canted over against scaffolding up on the slope, a set of steel tracks led down the slope and right into the river, a row of stout posts stood up in the shallows—but Jacky couldn't see any particular barge that might be Nobody's Home, and over the wind she could hear flapping and echoing whispers from the alley behind them.

"There!" cried Harriet, pointing north and breaking into a run.

Jacky followed without having seen what her companion might have pointed at, and the breath whistled through her teeth as her boots pounded over the clattering wet stones. Her hat flew away, unnoticed. For a moment the two girls were hunched over in fish-reeking darkness as they dodged pilings under one of the docks, and then they were out under the cloudy sky again and a low vessel was visible anchored in the shallows to their right, with dim green light showing at three portholes barely above the water line.

Harriet ran splashing straight out into the water, so Jacky followed, hooting in whispers at the icy chill of the water surging up quickly from her ankles to her thighs. She peered ahead at the vessel—it was a low wooden barge with a smokestack and no masts, perhaps twenty feet long from its blunt bow to its raised stern, and she could now see a ladder amidships that hung down into the water between a couple of the portholes. Canvas-bag fenders hung at the bow and stern.

Harriet had lunged forward and was swimming now, and Jacky gritted her teeth and did the same, rigidly keeping her head above the rippling water. She craned her neck to look back—two wavering manlike shapes hung where the waves lapped the stones.

At the ladder, the two girls clung to a rung above the water, panting and shivering. "Why are you," gasped Harriet, "so desperate to—lose your lover's ghost?"

Jacky just shook her head miserably, freezing in the water but dreading the wet climb up into the cold wind.

"I mean—" Harriet's voice came out in spasmodic rushes, "*he* doesn't want—to burn *you* up—does he?"

"I—don't want to have to—burn *him* up."

Harriet waited another moment, then resolutely climbed up the ladder. Jacky followed, gripping the rungs with numbed hands, and when she pulled herself up to the gunwale she heard Harriet say, "Permission to—come aboard—sir."

Jacky rolled over the gunwale and fell onto the deck and hugged herself in the momentary shelter from the wind; the flintlock pistol in her belt dug into her stomach, and it occurred to her that it wasn't going to be useable any time soon. She could see Harriet crouched beside her, and, focusing past her, a short man standing on the deck a few yards away in a slouch hat and a long oilskin coat. In the intermittent moonlight Jacky saw the gleam of spectacles on the man's round face.

The face looked up, toward the shore, and then down again at the two girls on the deck.

"Permission yes," the man said softly.

Below deck the main cabin was in the stern, and the ceiling was high enough for them to stand up straight, and wide enough so that the three occupants weren't crowded together. A big upright boiler in the stern radiated welcome heat from the closed iron door of its firebox, and the smells on the warm air were a peculiar mix of chocolate and the juniper reek of gin; and two lamps with green glass panes shed an underwater glow over everything.

Jacky looked around the cabin nervously. A narrow linen tent was set up against the forward bulkhead, between two low doors; closer to hand, a wooden table was bolted to the deck, and on it, beside three octavo-size leatherbound books, stood a clay jar with Greek letters pressed into its sides and a small hole near the bottom; and railed shelves at every height held an assortment of books and glass jars and mismatched shoes.

Jacky was avoiding looking at their host, and when she glanced down at the puddles she and Harriet were leaving on the deck she noticed a line of seven foot-wide squares and a wide circle painted in pale green, or possibly white, on the polished boards. Hopscotch again. The pattern might have extended farther, for the circle at the far end of the squares was right up against the skirts of the tent.

"Oftentimes, more than you suppose," the man said in a quiet uninflected voice as he shrugged out of his oilskin coat and hung it and his hat on a bulkhead hook, "swimming is the way to this. Clothing that's wet should be put in there," he said with a wave toward the low doors forward, "and dry ones put on."

At last Jacky lifted her head and looked at him. He was hardly more than five feet tall, and his nondescript flannel shirt and corduroy trousers didn't look new. The spectacles seemed to make his eyes appear smaller and more distant than they could really have been, and his face was round and smooth under wisps of fine fair hair that looked green in the peculiar lamplight. It occurred to her that it was an entirely unmemorable face—if she were to meet him again she wouldn't be sure it was the same man.

Whenever Jacky shifted her position on the gently rocking deck, she was freshly and uncomfortably aware of her cold, sodden clothing, and "dry ones" sounded wonderful, but she began, "What we want—"

The man held up a pale hand, then nodded toward the clay jar on the table. "A clepsidra there, a water clock. Into it can be put a ghost, so refreshment of the water keeps in your house his spirit. Into those books, as well, if one reads them every month. Or lamps he'll bide in, while the oil goes replenished." Jacky looked anxiously at the two green lamps mounted at shoulder height on the port and starboard bulkheads, and the man was faintly smiling at her when she looked at him again.

"But it's not for keeping the ghost that you've come, I think. It's expulsion through," he said, glancing at the hopscotch pattern on the floor, "Purgatory. Forever away from here."

Jacky touched the vial that still hung around her neck—and it was as hot as ever. "No, I want to keep mine. I just want him put back the way he was before tonight. Not . . . waked up and following me."

"Was?" said the man.

Jacky stepped closer to the boiler firebox and held her hands out to the radiated heat; the gin-and-chocolate smell was beginning to make her feel sick. "Like in your aspidistra," she said, nodding toward the water clock. "I just want his spirit near me, so I can feel him with me still, but doing no more than putting his rhymes into my head when I'm sleepy, like before. Not . . . *banishing* him. I just want you to cool the ashes of his dottle again."

"That means ashes from a pipe," spoke up Harriet, moving to stand beside Jacky by the firebox, "not his head." Jacky nodded and touched the hot glass vial hanging on her shirt.

"Who is your ghost?" the man asked Jacky. His voice was no louder, but it seemed to echo as if he spoke from some distance down a tunnel.

"His name? Colin Lepovre. He was my fiancee. A poet." He kept staring at her, so she added, "He was murdered by Dog-Face Joe, if you've heard of him?—can switch bodies with people?—and has to do it a lot because each body he takes for himself starts to grow fur all over it?" The man nodded again, still with no expression, so Jacky went on, forcing her voice to be level. "Dog-Face Joe took Colin's body, and switched Colin into a cast-off body—one with fur all over it and a, a stomach freshly full of poison."

"Were you once in a different body yourself?"

Jacky blinked at him. "What? No. Why—oh hell. The moustache is a fake." She touched it, and found that it was already askew on her upper lip; she pulled it off and shoved it into a pocket. "I'm a girl." Somehow she had thought this magician, or whatever he was, would have known that.

"Ah." He stared into her eyes for several uncomfortable seconds, then looked away. "Pardon—living bodies are not prominent in my vision."

After another pause, Harriet said quietly, "I'm a girl too, just for clearness sake. And I want my ghost all the *way* gone, like you said."

The man nodded. "Compelling them can be done." He waved in the direction of the shore. "Thorney Island this was once, straddled away from the mainland by branches of the Tyburn, a stream under pavement now. On the island King Canute eight hundred years ago ordered stopping to the tide—that is, the ghosts in the river. The river didn't stop, but the ghosts did. Still they do, here."

Jacky turned around to warm her back and stare at the man. "Are you Nobody?"

"Who else?"

"You take blood, in payment for your services?"

"A drop." He shrugged. "Two drops, maybe three."

Jacky bared her teeth and rolled her eyes—she recalled Harriet saying, *it's a sin, too, like you're trying to force God's machinery*—and finally she stamped on the deck. "If I don't do this," she said, her voice catching in her throat, "will he follow me, face me?" She hoped that if tears spilled down her cheek they'd be mistaken for river water. "Speak to me?"

Nobody pointed a pudgy finger at the vial on her chest. "Yes. You saw him, I think. Nearby now he waits for you."

Jacky exhaled shakily. "Then I can spare quite a few drops." She stepped away from the boiler toward the doors in the forward bulkhead, and Harriet was right behind her.

Jacky and Harriet each crouched through one of the doors on either side of the narrow linen tent, and in the darkness beyond hers, Jacky felt her way for a couple of feet and soon touched the back bulkhead of what must have been a storage closet. Her boots had tangled in a length of cloth, and when she unsnagged it and felt it, she concluded that it was some sort of heavy woolen nightshirt. After a moment's wary hesitation she decided that it would do, and that the possibility of her clothing being stolen here was remote, and so she tugged her wet clothes and boots off and pulled the woolen garment on over her head. She was unarmed, but the Nobody fellow didn't seem strong, and if he tried anything she'd brain him with his clytemnestra or whatever the thing was called.

She pushed open the door and was startled again by the green radiance from the two lamps—*lamps he'll hide in,* she thought, *while the oil goes replenished*—as the other door opened and Harriet came out on her hands and knees, blinking. Jacky saw that they were both now wearing white robes—her own a bit wet and grimy in spots from being stepped on. The deck was chilly under her bare feet.

"The pistol would be good to have," spoke up Nobody, who had pulled a stool out from under the table and was now sitting down. His hands were open and palm-up in front of him.

"It's, uh, soaked," Jacky pointed out.

"Good to have," repeated Nobody.

Jacky shrugged, stepped back into the storage locker and returned with her dripping flintlock; after glancing around the cabin, she laid it beside the clay jar on the table.

The man smiled, exposing two rows of little rounded teeth, and the boat shook as if it had run aground. White light flickered for a moment outside the portholes.

He took no visible notice of it. He opened a cabinet on the

starboard bulkhead and fetched out an inkpot, a pen, and two sheets of paper, and he laid them on the table beside Jacky's pistol.

"Dip the pen in the ink," he said to Harriet, "and hold it and one of the papers." When she had complied, he asked her, "Who is your ghost?"

She visibly took a deep breath and squared her shoulders. "My husband, Moraji. He was from India. We were married almost three years ago, had two babies who died. He died a month ago, falling from a roof. Now that he's dead he wants to burn me up."

The man nodded, as if this was not uncommon. He turned again to the cabinet, and this time it was a pint bottle of gin and a bowl of chocolate squares that he set down on the table. For a grotesque moment Jacky thought he was offering them refreshments.

But, "Ghosts will come to candy and liquor," he said, stepping away now toward the tent.

"Moraji didn't like candy," said Harriet unsteadily, "and he didn't drink."

"I said *ghosts*," said Nobody. "Where you stand is up here, by the circle. Both, both." Jacky and Harriet padded across the deck and stood beside the tent, and Nobody pulled the linen flap to one side; within stood a rough column of stone, four feet high and two feet wide, broken off on top. It looked like impure jade in this light, but when Nobody took off his spectacles and struck them against the stone, Jacky guessed what it was.

"The other piece of the London Stone," she said.

"We were just there," said Harriet faintly.

Dropping the eyeglasses, both lenses of which were shattered, Nobody turned to the girls; his face was blank, and his eyes still seemed unnaturally small in his round face, like two raisins in a pudding.

The gin bottle rattled on the table, and several of the chocolate squares burst apart.

"Yes," he said, and his voice was now definitely echoing. "The greater piece. A hundred years ago the Worshipful Company of Spectacle Makers used to break eyeglasses like these on it, on holy days, with priests in attendance and green stones in a hopscotch pattern on the street. And I've broken on it the lenses that held your ghosts."

A sudden cold wind was blowing across Jacky's bare ankles, and when she spun around she saw a streak of white moonlight on the ladder that led to the upper deck; the hatch-cover was open, or gone. She wondered if it might have blown off its hinges until she saw two undissipating smoky columns standing now over there by the ladder; even as she watched, branching wisps coalesced into arms that bent and straightened and bent again, and billows at the tops paled and condensed into angular heads.

She looked away quickly, her heart pounding in her chest. Was one of those awful figures Colin's ghost? Her hand darted to her chest, but the vial on the ribbon wasn't there; she realized that she had left it with her clothes in the storage locker.

Harriet was looking past her toward the ladder, and her face was pale green in the emerald lamplight, her lips sucked tightly over her teeth. Jacky knew her own face must look the same.

"Write his name on the paper," Nobody called to Harriet, "and then go stand on the first square. Both feet, no need of hopping while we're on flowing water." When she hesitated and threw a frightened glance toward Jacky, he added, "He won't molest you—he will be bound by all he is now, his name."

Harriet bowed her head and scribbled on the paper, using her left hand as a backing—Jacky was relieved to see that she knew how to write—and then, looking only down at the deck, she hurried to stand in the first square.

One of the spidery figures by the ladder waved its jointed arms over its head, and a windy hissing from it contorted into recognizable words: "*You come with me!*"

"Do not speak!" said Nobody quickly to Harriet. "Write the name again, and step into the second square."

The hissing kept up as Harriet slowly made her way through six more squares, spasmodically writing the name again before stepping into each one, but after its first statement the faintly articulated noise sounded only like the twittering of birds.

When Harriet was standing unsteadily in the seventh square, Nobody told her to halt. From a shelf near the cabinet he took a glass jar and another pen and crossed to where Harriet stood swaying. Peering more closely, Jacky saw that the new pen appeared to be made of bone, and that it was bristly with points at the nib end.

He handed Harriet the pen and with trembling pudgy fingers unscrewed the lid of the jar. "River water," he said. "Dip the pen and write the name once more."

Harriet winced as she gripped the pen, and when she dipped it into the jar Jacky saw blood on the girl's fingers. Harriet gingerly scribbled the name one more time, though the water left no visible track on the paper.

"Crumple the paper," said Nobody hoarsely, "and drop it into the circle below the stone."

Jacky was glancing at Nobody when the ball of paper tapped the deck, and she saw him inhale deeply—and her ears popped and the tent flap twitched; and just for that moment the man's blank face was darker, and sharpened into distinct features, and a deep sigh escaped the now-clearly-drawn mouth; and looking the other way, Jacky saw that only one dark swaying figure stood by the ladder now.

Her gaze swung back to Nobody, and his face had subsided into its previous pallidly unlined anonymity.

The ghost didn't go away to any afterlife, she thought dizzily, it never made it as far as the stone. This Nobody fellow ate it. Nobody's prickly bone-pen took Harriet's blood and then through that link he inhaled her husband's ghost.

Jacky yawned, and her ears popped back to normal hearing.

"It's gone," said Nobody, and Harriet sat down abruptly and buried her face in her hands, breathing deeply. Both pens rolled away across the deck.

"Now yours," said Nobody, turning his moon face to Jacky. "To be put back quiescent into that small bottle—" He leaned closer to her, blinking. "Which you have put where?"

The wind over the river must have picked up; a draft had begun whistling somewhere in the cabin.

Jacky's face was cold with sweat. "I left it in that closet. But is he going to *speak* to me?" She pointed at Harriet. "Hers *spoke* to her."

Harriet, still sitting on the floor, looked up at her bleakly. "You're more afraid of yours than I was of mine."

Jacky looked toward the ladder; the wobbling form still stood there, slowly bending its arms and twisting its head. Then she crouched beside Harriet.

"He came to my house," she said to her in a fast whisper, "my parents' house. He was in a stranger's body, covered with fur and dying of poison, and Dog-Face Joe had chewed the tongue to ribbons before he switched Colin into it, but—Colin managed to *come to me*, because—because he loved me." Jacky took a deep, hitching breath. "Damn it, it was midnight and—and I heard the front door bang open, and then what seemed to be a big gorilla with blood all over its mouth came rushing up the hall at me! There was a pistol—" She nodded toward the table, "—that one—and I—how in *Hell* could I have known it was Colin?"

Harriet whispered, "You shot him?"

The windy whistling was louder.

Jacky closed her eyes and nodded. "And when he was dying there on the floor in front of me, I looked into his eyes and—his eyes were the wrong color of course, but—we recognized each other. We both knew I had killed him. And then he died." She balled her fists. "I can't face him, have him speak to me!"

"But it was that, that Dog-Face Joe person who really *killed* him."

Jacky shook her head. "I fired the ball that pierced his heart."

The blowing draft had a hollow sound now, not whistling anymore, and then it rose in pitch and formed the word *Jacky*.

Jacky spun, still crouching, and stared at the thing by the ladder. ". . . Colin . . . !"

The wind said, "*Is it you? I can't see.*"

"Do not be approaching it," said Nobody. "Fetch your pendant and I will put the ghost back in, and cool it to sleep."

"Yes," said Jacky, looking away from the ghost and getting to her feet, "quickly." He inhaled Harriet's husband's ghost, she thought, but he can't do that with Colin's. I'll be able to sense it if Colin's ghost—sleeping again, merciful God!—is put back in the vial.

She had taken two steps toward the storage locker when the ghost voice said, "*Let me go.*"

Jacky turned to the infuriatingly empty face of Nobody. "Is he—it—aware? Of us, what we're saying?"

"As an imbecile would be."

Harriet had stood up too, and now put her hand on Jacky's shoulder. "It's not him," she said. "There's not enough there to really want anything."

Jacky heard a high, whispered note that might have been a wail. "*Jacky,*" said the voice, "*are you here? I'm alone.*"

Even as Nobody opened his small mouth to forbid it, Jacky turned to face the thing across the deck and called, "I'm here, Colin!" Her voice scraped her throat. "And you won't be alone, you'll be with me all the time, just like you were before tonight!"

"*Let me go where I am.*"

The airy voice had no inflection. Jacky blinked tears out of her eyes and peered at the dim figure in the green radiance, trying to see any expression, any face in it.

Go where I am? she thought. Does it want to rejoin Colin's departed soul? She thought of figures in dreams, and wondered if they felt lost when the dreamers awakened and turned their attention to the affairs of the day.

Harriet was peering at the fingers of her own right hand, which had held the wounding pen, and then she looked narrowly at Nobody.

"Don't do the hopscotch," she said to Jacky.

Jacky glanced to the side at her, and momentarily wondered if Harriet guessed that Nobody had cheated her and simply consumed the ghost of her husband.

"If it says—" began Jacky.

"It doesn't *know* what it's saying," Harriet said.

"Its words are like numbers on rolled dice," said Nobody. He did his boneless-looking shrug again. "Fetch the pendant or pick up the pens."

It doesn't matter, Jacky thought, what the ghost may want, even if it is distinct enough to want something; if I do the hopscotch trick, Nobody will inhale Colin's ghost, and I will *not* permit that, I will *not* see Colin's remembered features briefly animate Nobody's stagnant face.

"I'll get the pendant," said Jacky, and she trudged barefoot across the deck to the door in the forward bulkhead and pulled it open. When she was in the narrow locker and had pulled the door closed behind her, she crouched and felt through her tumbled wet clothing, and she found a fold of cloth that was hot; she flipped the fabric this way and that, and soon disentangled the ribbon with the vial attached to it.

But she had felt something hard in another bundle of wet cloth, and she dug around until her fingers found their way into a pocket and closed on three little cylinders—her thimbles. Probably the India rubber pea was in that pocket too, but she didn't bother to feel for it.

She stood up in the darkness and draped the ribbon around her neck; immediately she could feel the heat of the vial through the cloth of the robe. And after a long moment's thought she closed her fist on the three pewter thimbles.

She opened the door and stepped back into the cabin. Harriet and Nobody were still standing on this side of the hopscotch pattern, and Colin's ghost bobbed its shadowed head on the far side by the ladder.

"What do I do?" she asked.

The man reached out to the green-glass lamp on the starboard bulkhead and lifted the conical iron cap from the top of it; Jacky winced, for it must have been very hot, but Nobody's face continued to show no expression as he reversed the cap and set it back in place. It was now a concave vessel, and he began picking up the chocolate squares from the bowl and dropping them into the inverted cap. Smoke sprang up immediately, and the coffee-like smell of burned chocolate filled the cabin.

He lifted the bottle of gin, but just held it and extended his other hand toward Jacky.

"Give me the pendant," he said.

"What will you do?"

His little eyes darted to the smoking chocolate and back to her. "Quickly," he said.

"But—what?"

"I will put it into the burning candy, which will draw and hold the ghost, and then pour the liquor in. It will burn, and his false alertness will burn away with it. Sleep again . . . is what he will have again, in the little glass jar of yours."

The ghost's windy whisper intruded then, repeating her name.

"Oh please!" she cried to the thing without looking at it, "just be silent for a minute!"

It said her name again.

"Speaking to it is not good," said Nobody.

But Jacky discovered that she had to. "We'll be like we were," she called in a pleading tone, still not looking in that direction, "you—quiet, invisible, but—there." In a blessedly minimal way, she added to herself. "Us together. I—*need* you—like that. *Damn* it," she added, and with her free hand she pulled the ribbon off over her head and thrust it toward Nobody. "Do it fast."

The whistling voice formed words again: "*It spreads its wings, unmindful of the height . . ."* and Jacky helplessly recalled the second line of the couplet: *And takes the wind in half-forgotten flight.* It was the end of one of Colin's sonnets, about a long-confined bird finally set free. Jacky turned a stricken look on the agitated ghost across the cabin.

She caught Nobody's loose-skinned wrist. "I didn't know it was you," she said in a quiet but intense voice, speaking now to the pendant in Nobody's hand. She forced the words out. "God help me, I didn't know I was killing *you.*"

"*Forgive,*" said the thing by the ladder.

Jacky raised her head and made herself look at it. "Do you," she whispered hesitantly, "mean you . . . forgive me?"

"*All,*" it said.

Jacky found that she took that statement, vague as it was and from a doubtful source, as definitive assent. Tears were running down her cheeks, but her shoulders relaxed and she wondered if they had been tensed ever since Colin's death a month ago.

She released Nobody's wrist.

The ghost went on, "*He yearns to be away who cherished thee,*" it said, "*let nothing of his spirit here remain.*" Those lines were paraphrased from another of Colin's poems. And then the voice added, "*I forgive, you forgive. Forgive all, release all.*"

After two jolting heartbeats Jacky seized Nobody's hand, which had now moved so close to the hot iron cup that she burned her knuckles against its edge.

And she pulled the pendant and ribbon out of Nobody's fist.

"No," she said dully, "I must lose him twice." In her other hand she squeezed the three thimbles, and she said to Nobody, "Let's do the hopscotch."

Jacky wrote *Colin Lepovre* in ink on the other piece of paper.

"Drop the vial onto the first square," said Nobody, "and then stand in it."

Seven squares of Purgatory, she thought as she stepped into the square. It was rings, in Dante. *It's a sin, too,* Harriet had said. Was this token Purgatory for Colin's ghost, or for herself?

Six more times she wrote his name and picked up the vial to drop into the next square, and each time she picked it up the vial seemed cooler. At last she stood in the seventh square, with the circle and the London Stone in front of her.

"Halt," said Nobody.

She looked to the side and saw him dipping the bristly bone pen into the jar of river water; and while he was doing that she slipped the pewter thimbles onto her thumb and the first two fingers of her right hand. And when he handed her the dripping pen she kept the tips of her fingers folded in.

Harriet opened her mouth to say something, but Jacky frowned and shook her head at her.

She made sure to wince realistically as she gripped the bristly pen with her shielded fingertips and clumsily wrote Colin's name one last time, in water, unreadably. The bone-spines scratched harmlessly against the thimbles; no blood was drawn.

"Crumple the paper," said Nobody hoarsely, "and drop it and the pendant into the circle below the stone."

This time Jacky didn't look at Nobody; she watched the paper and the glass vial strike the deck, and she saw a thin streak of light that shifted from green to bright white as it sprang from the vial and made a momentary spot of light on the surface of the stone.

She heard the wind of Nobody's inhalation—and it didn't stop. Again her ears popped, and the flap of the linen tent was fluttering in a new breeze.

She spun to look toward the ladder, and the cloudy figure was smaller—a patch of fog, a curl of diaphanous silk, a ripple in moonlight.

Over the whistling of Nobody's continuing inhalation, she heard a tiny voice whisper, clearly, "*Finish it, my love—act it out the same—I need it to look the same—you again, and me again, and the same pistol . . .*"

She didn't even need to hear the flintlock pistol rattling on the table to know what it meant. Finish it, she told herself, finish it for God's sake.

She stumbled past the inflating figure of Nobody to the table, shook the thimbles from her hand and snatched up the pistol. Blinded with tears, she pointed the barrel toward the ladder, tugged the hammer back with her thumb and then pulled the trigger. The hammer struck the empty flash-pan with a tiny click.

She heard a sound that might have been a distant glad cry, and then the barge began to shake itself to pieces.

The boards of the deck overhead were splintering and bending downward in the gale that suddenly seemed to be coming from all directions, and jars were leaping off the shelves to burst in wild spray, but all sounds were muffled as Jacky caught Harriet's arm and pushed her toward the forward bulkhead, in which the storage locker doors were already open and swinging back and forth. The two girls grabbed up their flapping wet clothing and turned toward the ladder.

The figure of Nobody was a huge balloon now, the face just a scatter of bobbing eyes and nostrils around the wide, sucking hole of a mouth on the top of the expanding sphere, the shirt and trousers just torn rags flapping in the wind around the bulbous limbs. Somehow he was still inhaling, uselessly but powerfully, and everything, even the air, was being pulled into him.

The green lamps went dark as they sprang from their hooks. Jacky tugged Harriet forward, and the two of them scrambled in sudden darkness across the deck, covering their faces with their hands to block flying pieces of wood and ignoring fragments of glass cutting their bare feet, and then they were hurriedly climbing up the flexing ladder.

Out in the moonlight and cold fresh air, they took two running steps across the concave deck and sprang over the gunwale.

The water, when she crashed into it, was colder than Jacky remembered. After she had kicked her way to the churning surface she wasn't able to take a deep breath, and she found it hard to swim while holding the pistol in one hand and what she hoped was most of her clothing in the other, but within a few yards the water was shallow enough for her to wade toward the pebbled shore.

Behind her she heard a loud boom that echoed back from the buildings on the east side of the river, followed by a prolonged tumult of falling water; even as she shifted around against the current to look back, boards were spinning down out of the sky to splash into the river. The wind carried a gust of chilly spray across her face.

At last she and Harriet were panting on their hands and knees on the wet stones of the shore. Harriet lifted one hand to push her dripping hair away from her face.

"What'd you *do*?" she gasped.

Jacky had laid down her pistol in order to spread her sopping jacket out on the pebbles, though she was shivering so violently that her hands were clumsy. "I—cheated him, I suppose," she managed to say through clenched teeth. Pushing her numbed fingers into the side pocket of the jacket, she fumbled out the soggy false moustache. It looked like a tangle of hair someone might pull from a clogged drain, but she jerkily combed it out with her fingernails and pressed it hard against her upper lip.

"It won't—stick," said Harriet.

"It will if I keep my hand on it." Jacky picked up the pistol again. "Men coming."

A square of lamplight shone in the darkness of sheds and docks that made a jagged silhouette against the distant moonlit wall of Westminster Palace, and from moment to moment the yellow light was interrupted by figures running toward the shore. The thudding of their boots grew louder.

"Here's two survivors!" came a nearby call, and then a man in a heavy coat was crouching by them as boots in the darkness crunched closer.

"Are there others?" the man gasped. "We can get boats out."

"Nobody but us," said Jacky, speaking in her deeper voice.

"Nobody? Where is he?"

"He'd be dead," said Harriet. She was sitting on the pebbles, trembling and hugging herself. "We're all that's left."

"I think he—exploded," added Jacky.

"Ah! I follow you. That's good then. Are you injured?"

Jacky thought of their cut feet, but said, "No. Just freezing to death."

"Right, we'll get you into blankets in the watermen's shed. Here, you fellows, give these two a hand. I believe they've rid the river of Nobody."

Huddled in a rough blanket that smelled of old dock pilings but was blessedly dry, and sipping brandy from a tin cup, Jacky kept the knuckle of her free hand pressed against the false moustache. She had explained to their rescuers that her nose would bleed if she let off the pressure.

Two men in worn woollen pea coats and canvas trousers leaned forward from a bench against the wall, their hard faces lit in amber chiaroscuro by the glow from the open door of a coal stove. Smoke curled from a blackened clay pipe clenched between the teeth of one of them.

"But what blew him up?" he asked, speaking around the clay stem, after Jacky and Harriet had described their time on Nobody's Home.

"He cheated me," said Harriet, who was crouched in another blanket beside Jacky. "He used my blood to eat my husband's ghost, instead of sending it on to the hereafter. Inhaled the ghost, is what it was. But when it was Jacky-boy's turn, he somehow avoided getting cut by the needles on the pen, and so Nobody didn't get the ghost of . . . Jacky's brother." Jacky was pleased that her companion was going along with her pretense and her version of the story. "He inhaled, though," Harriet went on, "and when he didn't catch the ghost, it seemed like he couldn't stop inhaling. He blew up like a balloon, and then I suppose he just—popped."

The other man sat back and nodded with evident satisfaction. "It might be years, decades, before he collects again." To Jacky and Harriet he explained, "Ghosts from upriver get snagged here, God knows why, like leaves caught by a drain, and when a whole lot of 'em clump up, they make a sort of man, something very like a man, good enough to talk and naturally good at handling ghosts. It's never what you'd call a particular person—it's Nobody, in that way. And it lives on the smell of fresh blood, like they say jungle plants live on just smells in the air."

"Jungle air, it's got to be," put in his companion. "Damp."

The other man frowned at the interruption. "It wasn't smart for you two to go and try to do business with him. Maybe you know what the priests would say about it. But," he added, shrugging, "it worked out tolerably well. The River Police never really believed the story, and that barge was sometimes there and sometimes not, like some kind of black rainbow that only shows up in moonlight."

The two rivermen got to their feet, and the one with the pipe laid it down on the windowsill. "Dawn soon," he said. "We've got to get the boats out for custom at the stairs. You two can stay here till your things dry out."

"God bless you for rescuing us," said Harriet.

The other man laughed shortly. "You probably saved some *further* idiots that would else have gone aboard that graveyard barge." His companion nodded solemnly.

When they had opened the door to the chilly pre-dawn wind and then closed it behind them, Harriet looked at Jacky.

"Nobody was a ghost himself," she said. "A compost of a bunch of them, that is. I don't think it was a sin to blow him up."

Jacky gave a brief, mirthless laugh. "Right. What did I do? I killed Nobody."

Harriet nodded uncertainly. "You can toss the moustache now. You've got a mum and da back home? I expect you'll be going back there."

Jacky lifted her hand hesitantly away from her upper lip, and then let her hand fall into her lap when the moustache stayed in place.

"It's sticking again," she said, "now that it's dried out a bit."

"But you can be a girl again now. No need for," Harriet waved toward the pistol that lay on the wooden floor beside Jacky, "*that*, nor the moustache—no need anymore for you to be going into the hell-holes and rookeries."

Jacky frowned at her in puzzlement. "It was Nobody that got killed, not Dog-Face Joe. Nothing about that changed tonight."

The brandy bottle stood on a shelf by the door, and Harriet got up to refill her cup, and then refilled Jacky's too. "We'll have to buy these watermen a new bottle," she said. And when she had sat down beside Jacky and tucked up her blanket, she went on, "You freed yourself from your ghost. He's not there to haunt you anymore."

Jacky swallowed half of the brandy in her cup and closed her eyes as it spread a replacing sort of warmth through her chest. "Was he ever there? Now I think he was never in that flacon of ashes. I believe I only ever imagined his . . . presence."

Harriet was clearly upset; and as if she were trying to talk Jacky out of another sort of sin, she went on, "He used to recite his poems to you, when you were half asleep!"

"When I was dreaming."

"But you remember—"

"What I remember about this grotesque night I'm sure I'll soon forget. I think the River Police had the story right. What barge? What ghost man?"

"Your—your feet are cut, from broken glass. Mine too."

Jacky nodded. "We were fools to go walking barefoot on the shore at night."

The wind shivered around the watermen's shed.

"Ah." Harriet frowned at Jacky for several seconds, then said, "It was the forgiveness."

Jacky turned to her and said, furiously, "You and I were the only people aboard that barge, if there was a barge at all. What, did I forgive you for something?"

"Your Colin said, 'Forgive . . . forgive all.' You were glad when it meant he forgave you. For shooting him."

"Colin's been dead for a month. I doubt he has a lot to say now. A ghost's not the person it's a ghost of, you said it yourself."

"If he had stopped with only the one word, when it sounded like he was forgiving you, you wouldn't be doubting all this."

"I don't—"

"He meant for you to forgive the thing that truly killed him, this Dog-Face Joe. He was asking you to give up your revenge."

Jacky clenched her fists. "What if he was? He's gone, taken away from me—if he wasn't gone before tonight, he certainly is now—and I can't . . . live, I can't resume my life—until that creature that killed him is dead. It's all I have, for now." She exhaled and shook her head. "He's still out there, somewhere."

"But—but you could go home!"

"Until I do this I don't have a home." She held her right hand out in front of her and flexed her fingers. "I feel like I killed myself, too, when I killed Colin a month ago. I'm the ghost of the girl he was engaged to. Until I do this . . . I'm nobody myself." She gave Harriet a strained smile and touched her hand. "I'm sorry. In other circumstances I think you and I could have been friends."

Harriet nodded. "I can't argue with you—talk you away from this course."

"No," Jacky agreed. Her shoulders were tense, and she stretched, blinking at the window. "The sun's up, I think. Our clothes and boots should be dry enough to walk away in soon."

Harriet sighed and got up again to refill their tin cups. She paused at the window and looked out at the river, and Jacky could imagine what she was seeing—the early traffic on the river, clouds still edged with coral, the highest wheeling seagulls flashing white in the dawn sunlight.

Jacky's gaze fell to the flintlock pistol on the floor. And she reminded herself that she would have to clean it and oil it soon, so that it wouldn't rust.

"He is not here; but far away
The noise of life begins again,
And ghastly through the drizzling rain
On the bald street breaks the blank day."
—Tennyson, *In Memoriam*

✥ AUTHOR'S NOTE ✥

Bill Schafer at Subterranean Press asked me if there was any story left to be told in connection with the characters and events of my novel The Anubis Gates—*and it occurred to me that the character Jacky Snapp had not got all the attention she deserved, in that novel. So I wrote this personal prequel for her. And since it's a prequel, you don't need to know anything about the novel when you read it.*

My wife and I saw the London Stone, on a visit to England, and it's such a disappointment these days that there's almost a kind of rewarding irony to it—it's now just a melon-sized hunk of rock in the window of a convenience store. And it's at ankle level, so to see it you have to crouch down on the sidewalk or go into the store and step behind the magazine rack, and crouch there. If we hadn't been looking for it, we'd no more have noticed it than do the hundreds of Londoners who must walk past this little piece of British history every day.

⚔ A TIME TO CAST AWAY STONES ⚔

⚔ I ⚔

May 1825

> "Though here no more Apollo haunts his Grot,
> And thou, the Muses' seat, art now their grave,
> Some gentle Spirit still pervades the spot,
> Sighs in the gale, keeps silence in the Cave . . ."
> —Lord Byron

> "Oh, thou Parnassus!"
> —from *Childe Harold's Pilgrimage,*
> Canto I, LXII

SOMEWHERE AHEAD in the windy darkness lay the village of Tithorea, and south of that the pass through the foothills to the crossroads where, according to legend, Oedipus killed his father. Trelawny and his young wife would reach it at dawn, and then ride east, toward Athens, directly away from Delphi and Mount Parnassus.

But it was only midnight now, and they were still in the Velitza Gorge below Parnassus, guiding their horses down the pebbly dry bed of the Kakoreme by the intermittent moonlight. It was half an hour since they had left behind the smells of tobacco smoke and roasted pigeon as they had skirted wide through the oaks around the silent tents of Ghouras's palikars at the Chapel of St. George, and now the night wind in Trelawny's face smelled only of sage and clay, but he still listened for the sound of pursuing hoofbeats . . . or for stones clattering or grinding, or women's voices singing atonally out in the night.

The only sound now, though, was the homely thump and knock of the horses' hooves. He glanced to his right at Tersitza—huddled in her shaggy sheepskin cape, she seemed like a child rocking in the saddle, and Trelawny recalled Byron's words:

And then—that little girl, your warlord's sister?—she'll be their prey, and change to one of them—supposing that you care about the child.

Byron had said it only three months after dying in Missolonghi last year, and at the time it had not been a particularly important point— but now Tersitza was Trelawny's wife, and Trelawny was determined to get her free of her brother's ambitions . . . the ambitions which until a few months ago had been Trelawny's too. A man had to protect his wife.

A great man?

The intruding thought was so strong that Trelawny almost glanced around at the shadows among the twisted olive trees here to see who had whispered it; but he kept his eyes on Tersitza. He wished she would glance over at him, show him that she was still there, that she still had a face.

Percy Shelley hadn't protected his wife—his first wife, at least, Harriet. He had abandoned her in England and run off to Switzerland to wed Mary Godwin, and Harriet had in fact died a year or two later, in the Serpentine River in Hyde Park. Shelley had been a great man, though, one of the immortal poets—a true king of Parnassus!—and such men couldn't be bound by pedestrian moralities out of old holy books. Trelawny had been proud to call Shelley his friend, and had eventually overseen the poet's cremation and burial. Shelley had been a braver man than Byron, who for all his manly posturing and licentious ways had proven to be a willing prisoner of . . . convention, propriety, human connections.

A warm wind had sprung up now at their backs, tossing the loose ends of Trelawny's turban across his bearded face, and he smelled jasmine. *All the kingdoms of the world, and the glory of them,* he thought. I am even now literally turning my back on them.

With the thought, he was instantly tempted to rein in the horses and retrace their course. The British adventurer, Major Francis Bacon, would be returning here, ideally within a few weeks, and if Bacon kept his promise he would be bringing with him the talisman that would . . . would let Trelawny do what Byron had advised.

But he bitterly recognized the dishonesty of his own rationalization. Major Bacon would probably not be able to make his way back here before Midsummer's Eve, and after that it would almost certainly be too late. And—and Trelawny had told Tersitza that their expedition tonight was to rescue her brother, the *klepht* warlord Odysseus Androutses, from his captivity in the Frankish Tower at the Acropolis in Athens. Odysseus had been imprisoned there two weeks ago by his one-time lieutenant, Ghouras, whose palikars were already camped in several places right here in the Velitza Gorge. Trelawny knew that Ghouras meant soon to blockade the mountain entirely, and that tonight might be the last chance he and Tersitza would have to escape.

He had no choice but to turn his back on the mountain, and on the glamorous damnation it offered.

Not for the first time, he forced down the forlorn wish that Byron had never spoken to him after dying in Missolonghi.

A year ago, in April of 1824, Edward Trelawny had ridden west from Athens toward Missolonghi with a troop of armed palikars, eager to show Lord Byron that an alliance with certain maligned old forces really *was* possible, and would be the best way to free Greece from the Turks. Previously, especially on the boat over from Italy, Byron had laughed at Trelawny's aspirations—but shortly after their arrival in Greece, Trelawny had left the dissolute lord's luxurious quarters in Cephalonia and struck out on his own across the war-ravaged Greek countryside, and had eventually found the *klepht*, the Greek warlord, who knew something of the ancient secret ways to summon such help and to virtually make gods of the humans who established the contact.

As Trelawny had furtively guided his band of palikars westward through the chilly mountain passes above the Gulf of Corinth, hidden by the crags and pines from the Turkish cavalry on the slopes below, he had rehearsed what he would say to Byron when they reached Missolonghi: *The klepht Odysseus Androutses and I have already paid the toll, in rivers of Turkish blood on the island of Euboaea, and in blood of our own drawn by the metal that's lighter than wood—we have our own army, and our headquarters are on Mount Parnassus itself, the very home of the Muses! It's all true—join us, take your rightful place on Parnassus in the soon-to-be-immortal flesh!*

Byron wasn't nearly the poet that Shelley had been, in Trelawny's estimation, but surely any poet would have been flattered by the Parnassus allusion, Parnassus being the home of the goddesses called the Muses in classical Greek myths, and sacred to poetry and music. Trelawny would not remind Byron that Mount Parnassus was also reputed to be the site where Deucalion and Pyrrha landed their ark, after the great flood, and repopulated the world by throwing over their shoulders stones that then grew up into human form.

And Trelawny would not mention, not right away, his hope that Byron, who had once had dealings with these powers himself before foolishly renouncing them, would act in the role the Arabs called *rafiq*: a recognized escort, a maker of introductions that otherwise might be dangerous.

Trelawny had imagined that Byron would finally lose his skeptical smirk, and admit that Trelawny had preceded him in glory—and that the lord would gladly agree to serve as *rafiq* to the powers which Trelawny and Odysseus Androutses hoped to summon and join—but on the bank of the Evvenus River, still a day's ride west of the mudbank seacoast town of Missolonghi, Trelawny's band had passed a disordered group of palikars fleeing east, and when Trelawny had asked one of the haggard soldiers for news, he learned that Lord Byron had died five days earlier.

Damn the man!

Byron had died still intolerably imagining that Trelawny was a fraud—*If we could make Edward tell the truth and wash his hands, we will make a gentleman of him yet,* Byron had more than once remarked to their mutual friends in Italy—and that all Trelawny's reminiscences about having captured countless ships on the Indian Ocean as second-in-command to the noble privateer de Ruyters, and marrying the beautiful Arab princess Zela, were fantasies born of nothing but his imagination. Trelawny had always been sourly aware of Byron's amiable skepticism.

✢ ✢ ✢

His horse snickered and tossed its head in the moonlight, and Trelawny glanced at Tersitza—who still swayed in the saddle of the horse plodding along beside his, still silently wrapped in her shaggy cape—and then he peered fearfully back at the sky-blotting bulk of Mount Parnassus. It hardly seemed to have receded into the distance at all since they had left. If anything, it seemed closer.

Only to himself, and only sometimes, could Edward Trelawny admit that in fact he *had* concocted all the tales of his previous history—he had *not* actually deserted the British Navy at the age of sixteen to become a corsair and marry a princess who died tragically, but had instead continued as an anonymous midshipman and been routinely discharged from the Navy in Portsmouth at twenty, with not even the half-pay a lieutenant would get. A sordid marriage had followed a year later, and after the birth of two daughters his wife had eloped with a captain of the Prince of Wales's Regiment. Trelawny, then twenty-four, had vowed to challenge the man to a duel, though nothing had come of it.

But his stories had become so real to him, as he had repeated them in ever-more-colorful detail to Shelley and Mary and the rest of the expatriate British circle in Pisa in the early months of 1822, that Trelawny's memory served them up to his recall far more vividly than it did the tawdry, humiliating details of the actual events.

And now he *was* living the sort of life he had only imagined—only foreseen!—back in Italy. He habitually dressed now in Suliote costume, the red and gold vest and the sheepskin *capote,* with pistols and a sword in his sash, and he was second-in-command to Odysseus Androutses, a real brigand chief, and together they had killed dozens of Ali Pasha's Turkish soldiers on the occupied island of Euboaea.

But the memories of ambushing Turks and burning their villages on Euboaea brought up bile to the back of his throat now, and made him want to goad the horses into a foolhardy gallop through the patchy moonlight. It wasn't the fact of having killed the men, and women and children too, that twisted his stomach, but the knowledge that the killings had been an offering, a deliberate mass human sacrifice.

And he suspected that when Odysseus had afterward performed the blood-brother ritual with him in the vast cave high up on Mount Parnassus, in which Trelawny had cut a gash in his own forearm with the knife made of lightweight gray metal, that had been a human sacrifice too. A *humanity* sacrifice, at any rate.

With an abrupt chilling shock he realized that the wind at his back shouldn't be warm, nor smell of jasmine. Quickly he reached across to take the slack reins of Tersitza's horse, but he had no sooner grabbed the swinging leather strap than a cracking sound to his left made him look back over his shoulder—

—the sound had been like a rock splitting, and for an instant he had been afraid that he would see again, here, the black bird-headed thing, apparently made of stone, that had been haunting his dreams and had seemed in them to be the spirit of the mountain—

—but it was a girl that he saw, pacing him on a third horse; and her horse's hooves made no sound on the flinty riverbed. Her luminous eyes were as empty of human emotion as a snake's, though by no means empty of emotion.

But he recognized her—she could be no one else than Zela, the Arabian princess who had died while pregnant with his child thirteen years ago. Her narrow little body was draped in pale veils that were white in the moonlight, but he was certain that they were actually yellow, the Arab color of mourning.

The smell of jasmine had intensified and become something else, something like the inorganically sweet smell of sheared metal.

She smiled at him, baring white teeth, and her soft voice cut through the clatter of the wind in the olive branches:

"Out of this wood do not desire to go,
Thou shalt remain here whether thou wilt or no."

His face went cold when he abruptly remembered that Zela had never existed outside his stories.

Even as he called, "Tersitza!" and goaded his own horse forward and pulled on the reins of hers, he recognized the lines the phantom girl had quoted—they were from *A Midsummer Night's Dream*, and it was on this upcoming midsummer's eve that he was to be consecrated to the mountain.

Tersitza was still slumped in her saddle, and Trelawny pulled his mount closer to hers and then leaned across and with a grunt of effort lifted her right out of the saddle and sat her limp form on his thighs as her cape came loose and blew away. Glancing down at her in the moment before he kicked his horse into a gallop, he saw that her eyes were closed, and he was profoundly reassured to feel for a moment her warm breath on his hand.

With one arm around her shoulders he leaned forward as far as he could over the horse's flexing neck and squinted ahead to see any low branches he might be bearing down on. Tersitza's riderless horse was falling behind, and the hoofbeats of Trelawny's were a rapid drumming in the windy gorge.

Peripherally he could see that Zela was rushing forward right beside him, a yard away to his left, though her horse's legs were moving no faster than before, and the moonlight was luminously steady on her even as it rushed past in patches all around her, and her voice was still clear in his ears:

"I am a spirit of no common rate.
The summer soon will tend upon my state,
And I do love thee. Therefore stay with me."

Trelawny didn't spare her a glance, but from the corner of his eye he could see that her veils were not being tossed in the headwind. His breath was choppy and shallow, and the wind was cold now on his sweating face.

The village of Tithorea couldn't be more than five miles ahead of them now, and this phantom didn't appear to be a physical body. As long as his horse didn't stumble in the moonlight—

Abruptly the Zela phantom was gone, but after a moment of unreasoning relief Trelawny cursed and pulled back on the reins, for somehow they weren't in the Velitza Gorge anymore.

His horse clopped and shook to a panting halt. Trelawny could feel cold air on his bared teeth as he squinted around at the dozens or hundreds of tumbled skeletons that webbed the sides of the path now, below the rocky slopes; many of the further ones straddled the bigger skeletons of fallen horses, and the bony hands of those closer clutched ropes tied around the skulls of camels on the rocky ground. The jagged moonlit ridges far above seemed as remote as the stars they eclipsed, and faintly on the wind he could hear high feminine voices combining in alien harmonies.

He made himself breathe deeply and unclench his fists from the reins and stretch his fingers. He recognized the place, at least—the devils of Parnassus hadn't transported them to some hellish valley on the moon.

They were in the Dervenakia Pass, where the army of the Turkish general Dramali Pasha had been trapped and massacred by the wild mountain Greek tribes nearly two years ago. The smell of decay was only a frail taint now on the night wind.

But the Dervenakia Pass was in the Morea—across the Gulf of Corinth, easily fifty miles south of where Trelawny and Tersitza had been a moment ago.

Very well, he thought stoutly, nodding as he forced down his panic—very well, I know the way to Argos from here, we can—

A clanking of stones on the road ahead jerked his head in that direction, and his tenuous hope flickered out.

A tall spidery thing like a black animated gargoyle stood in the moonlit path now, a hundred feet ahead. More rocks were breaking away from the walls of the pass and tumbling across the ground to attach themselves to it, adding to its height as he watched. Its stone beak swung heavily back and forth in the moonlight.

Its lengthening black shadow shifted across the scattered white ribcages and skulls behind it, and the high faraway voices were singing louder now, spiralling up toward a crescendo beyond the range of human hearing.

Trelawny's eyes were wide, and he wasn't breathing, or even thinking. His horse was rigidly still.

The figure ahead of them was even taller when it straightened somewhat, its long, mismatched stalactite arms lifting toward the horse and riders—and though it only roughly resembled a human body, Trelawny was certain that it was female. And when it spoke, in an echoing voice like rushing water choked and sluiced and spilled by a slow millwheel—

"And I will purge thy mortal grossness so
That thou shalt like an airy spirit go,"

—he knew it was the same creature that had seemed to be riding at his left hand in the Velitza Gorge.

His face and palms tingled in the cold wind, as if damp with some moisture more volatile than sweat. *Thy mortal grossness.*

The thing ahead of them was hideous, but that wasn't why Trelawny ached uselessly to tear his eyes from it—the stones it was animating were crude, but they weren't *it*. The entity confronting him was an immortal ethereal thing, "an airy spirit" that only touched matter as a well-shod man might carelessly leave bootprints in mud, while Trelawny and Tersitza *consisted* of matter—fluids and veined organic sacs and tangled hairs, pulsing and *temporary.*

Trelawny yearned to hide from the thing's intolerable attention, but he couldn't presume to move. Abruptly he began breathing again, a harsh hot panting, and it humiliated him.

He was still holding Tersitza's limp, gently breathing little body in front of himself, as if it were an offering, and for a moment of infinite relief he felt the thing ahead shift its attention to her before fixing its psychic weight on him again.

The voice came only in his head now, again using lines from his memory but no longer bothering to cater to his fleshy ears by agitating the cold air:

I claim the ancient privilege of Athens:
As she is mine, I may dispose of her.

Since the thing had referred to Tersitza, Trelawny was able to look down at the girl. And though she was obviously as miniscule and ephemeral a thing as he now knew himself to be, her helpless vulnerability couldn't be ignored, and he scraped together the fragments of his crumpled identity enough to answer.

"No," he whispered.

The thing in the path ahead of them was growing still taller and wider, its misshapen head beginning to blot out part of the night sky, but with adamantine patience it spoke again in his head:

All the kingdoms of the world, and the glory of them.

That was what Satan had offered Christ, in the gospel of Matthew. Edward Trelawny realized that this vast thing was offering him a chance to become something like its peer, to purge him of his body-bound mortality.

How I would have soared above Byron here, he thought.

But he wrapped his awkwardly jointed arms around Tersitza and pulled her bony form to himself.

"No," he said again, and his voice was clearer now.

He looked up from under his eyebrows, blinking away the stinging sweat—and then clenched his eyes shut, for the thing was rushing at him, expanding in his view—

—but there was no obliterating impact. After some tense length of time he began breathing again, and the taint of old decay was gone, and what he smelled on the chilly mountain breeze now was tobacco and roasted pigeon.

He opened his eyes. Tersitza was still slumped unconscious across his lap on the saddle, but the giant stone form whose slopes began a mile in front of them was Mount Parnassus, its high shoulders hidden behind clouds in the moonlight. His horse stamped restlessly in damp leaves.

They were back in the Velitza Gorge again, as abruptly as they had been taken out of it—if indeed they *had* actually been out of it, and the spirit of the mountain had not simply manifested itself to him in a scene conjured, as its statements and first appearance had been, from Trelawny's memory and imagination.

To his right through the dark tangles of the oak branches he could see the cooking fires and the palikars' tents around the ruined Chapel of St. George.

He hugged Tersitza to him, already beginning to wish he could have accepted the stone thing's magnanimous offer.

The girl stirred at last, then sat up and glanced around.

"We're no further than this?" she whispered, shivering in his arms.

She had spoken in her native Greek, and he answered haltingly in the same language. "We were turned back." He was suddenly exhausted, and it was an effort to recall the Greek words. "We lost your horse."

"And my cape is gone." She ran her hands through her long black hair, feeling her scalp. "Was I hurt? I can't remember meeting Ghouras's soldiers!" She turned her pale little face up to him and her dark eyes looked intently into his. "Were you wounded?"

"No." For a moment he considered letting her believe that it had indeed been the palikars of Odysseus's rival who had forced them back to the mountain—but then he sighed and said, "It wasn't Ghouras who stopped us. It was—magic, enchantment." He wished he dared to tell her that he had been trying to save her from a fate literally worse than death—the opposite of death, in fact—and that it was her brother who had put her in that peril. "It was the mountain, your brother's mountain, that drove us back. Pulled us back."

"*Enchantment?*" She kept her voice down, but her whisper was hoarse with scorn. "Are you a coward after all? Odysseus is your blood-brother, and you are scared away from rescuing him by some . . . nymphs, dryads? *Fauns?*"

"You—" he whispered furiously, "—would be dead now, if I had not. And *I* would be . . ."

"Dead as well," she said. "Turn back—I would rather be dead than have a coward for a husband."

Trelawny was mightily tempted to do as she said. I could be with Zela, he thought. Again. At last.

But he whispered, "Keep your voice down," and he waved toward the campfires at the old monastery, dimly visible through the trees. "Do you want to rouse Ghouras's men too?"

Yes, he could be with Zela—but Zela was a phantom who had never existed, and this girl, for all her maddening irrationality, was real, vulnerable flesh and blood.

You protect the ones you love. He clung to the thought. Even if they ignorantly resent you for it.

"We're not turning back," he said. Somewhere an owl whistled its low note through the trees.

"Give me a couple of pistols," Tersitza hissed, "and I'll go by myself!"

She was serious, and he found that his anger was gone. He admired courage, even—or especially—pointless courage. "On foot?" he asked with a smile. "It wasn't fauns and dryads."

For a few moments she was silent, and the wind rattled the dark branches around them. "I suppose it was a *vrykolakas*," she said with apparent carelessness, though he felt her shudder as she spoke the word. *Vrykolakas* was the Greek term for vampire.

"It was," he said, "but one made of stone instead of flesh." He remembered the vision of Zela riding beside them. "Though it could mimic flesh."

She exhaled a wavering breath, and seemed to shrink in his arms.

He opened his mouth to say something more, but she gripped his wrist with cold fingers.

"I—have seen it," she said humbly, almost too softly for him to hear. "It *was* the mountain, the ghost of the mountain. I—" She looked ahead toward the imposing silhouette of Mount Parnassus, which now blocked half the sky in front of them. "I had hoped we were escaping it tonight."

"So," said Trelawny, "had I."

He flicked the reins, and the horse started forward along the familiar track to its stable in the guardhouse at the foot of the mountain, near the path that would lead Trelawny and his wife back up to the ladders that mounted to their house in Odysseus's cave, eight hundred feet above the gorge.

⊰ II ⊱

June 1824

> ". . . and fortunate is he
> For whom the Muses have regard! His song
> Falls from his lips contented. Though he be
> Harried by grief and guilt his whole life long,
> Let him but hear the Muses' servant sing
> Of older beings and the gods, and then
> His memory is cleared of everything
> That troubled him within the world of men."
> —Hesiod's *Theogony,*
> the Ceniza-Bendiga translation,
> lines 96-102

AFTER ENCOUNTERING the fleeing palikars just east of Missolonghi a year ago, and learning from them that Byron had died only a few days earlier, Edward Trelawny had pressed on with his own party of palikars and reached the marshy seacoast town the next day.

Down at the end of a row of shabby wooden houses under a gray sky, the house Byron had worked and died in stood on the shore of a wide, shallow lagoon. Trelawny had been escorted upstairs by Byron's old servant Fletcher, and had found the lord's coffin laid out across two trestles in the leaden glow of narrow uncurtained windows.

Fletcher had pulled back the black pall and the white shroud, and Trelawny had scowled and pursed his lips at the evidences of an autopsy—the aristocratic face bore an expression of stoic calm, though thinned by the fever that had killed him, but the disordered gray-streaked brown hair half-concealed a crude ring cut in his scalp where physicians had removed part of his brain, and the body's torso was divided by a long incision.

When Fletcher left the room, Trelawny drew his Suliote dagger and forced himself to cut off the small toe of Byron's twisted left foot. Byron was gone, but even a relic of the man might have some value as a *rafiq*.

Byron had been a corepresentative in Greece of the London Greek Committee, which had put together a Stock Exchange loan to fund the war for Greek independence, and though a big sum of cash was daily expected, all that had been provided so far in Missolonghi were several cannons. By claiming to be Byron's secretary, Trelawny prevailed on the remaining representative—an idealistic but naive British colonel called Stanhope—to let him take away a howitzer and three three-pounders and ammunition, for the defense of eastern Attica by Odysseus Androutses. Trelawny even managed to commandeer fifty-five horses and twenty artillerymen to haul the guns across the seventy-five miles back to the Velitza Gorge and the foot of Mount Parnassus, where Odysseus's soldiers built a crane to hoist the guns and crates up to the fortified cave.

Mavre Troupa, the Black Hole, was what the Greeks called the cave, but Trelawny had been relieved to get back to its lofty security.

The climb up to its broad lip was exhilarating—the last sixty feet of the eight hundred were a sheer vertical face, negotiated by clambering up ladders made of larch branches bolted to the crumbling sandstone, and the last twenty-foot ladder had a tendency to swing like a pendulum in the wind, for it was attached only at the top so that it could be pulled up in case of a siege.

The cave itself was a fairly flat terrace two hundred feet wide, with a high arching stone ceiling; the cave floor shelved up in rocky platforms as it receded into the shadows of the mountain's heart, and the various levels were wide enough for several small stone-and-lumber houses to have been built on them—Odysseus's mother and siblings lived in several of them—and the remote tunnels were walled off as storerooms, filled with sufficient wine and oil and olives and cheese to last out the longest conceivable siege. There was even a seasonal spring in the southern corner of the enormous cave, and an English engineer had begun work on a cistern so that the citizens of the cave could have water on hand even in the summer.

Philhellenes, the Englishmen who had come to fight for Greece's freedom—mostly young, mostly inspired by Byron's old poetry and recent example—seemed to Trelawny to be underfoot throughout the country these days, and, though he was one of them himself, he felt that unlike them he had shed his old links and actually become a Greek . . . as dark as any, attired identically, and second-in-command to a genuine mountain king right out of Sophocles.

One of these Philhellenes was the artillery officer who had come along with him on the arduous trip to Parnassus from Missolonghi, a Scotsman in his thirties who claimed to have fought in the Spanish wars; his last name was Fenton, and he had faced the rain and the muddy labor of carting the cannons to the mountain with a kind of tireless ferocious cheer—and he frequently quoted the poetry of Robert Burns. Trelawny admired him.

Trelawny's newly acquired artillerymen stayed at the guardhouse and tents below, with the bulk of Odysseus's soldiers, but Odysseus welcomed Trelawny and Fenton when they had climbed up the final ladder to the fortified cave and stood panting on the wooden platform that projected out over the misty abyss.

Trelawny had been a little nervous about the introduction, and ready to speak up for Fenton, but Odysseus seemed almost to recognize the wiry Scotsman—not as if they had met before, but as if Odysseus was familiar with some category of men that included Fenton, and had a wry and cautious respect for its members.

The bandit-chief's eyes narrowed under his striped head-cloth as he smiled, and in the mix of Italian and Greek by which he communicated with Westerners he said, "I can see that you will be of assistance and encouragement to my dear friend Trelawny," and led him away to show him where the new guns might best be mounted on the battlements that lined the cave's rim.

Satisfied that his peculiar friends would find each other's company tolerable, and eager to get out of the glaring daylight at the front of the cave, Trelawny hurried past the groups of palikars who were clustered around the several fire-pit rings on the cave floor, and leaped up the natural stone steps to the more shadowed level where his own small wooden house had been built.

He pulled his sword and pistols free of his sash and clanked them on the table, struck a flame with his tinderbox and lit a candle, then carefully lifted out of a pocket the handkerchief that was wrapped around Byron's toe. Byron was now, in a sense, physically on Mount Parnassus, *in* the mountain, but Trelawny had no idea how he might use the toe to facilitate contact with the species with whom he and Odysseus hoped to make an alliance: the creatures referred to in the Old Testament as the Nephelim, the giants that were "in the earth in those days."

There was no contact between that species and humanity now, but there had been, as recently as two and a half years ago; and Byron had been one of their partners before the bridge between them had been broken. Trelawny believed they left some physical trace on the bodies of their human symbiotes, and so Byron's toe might at least be a reminder to them of the lost alliance—and the Nephelim, the Greek Muses, could not now even in spirit venture far from Mount Parnassus, so Trelawny had brought it to them.

He laid the little cloth bundle on the table and flipped aside the hemmed edges. Byron's toe had turned black during the month since Trelawny had taken it in Missolonghi, and he touched it gingerly.

Over the vaguely buttery smell of the candle, Trelawny was startled to catch the scent of the Macassar oil Byron had always used on his hair.

And then Byron spoke to him.

The voice was faint, and seemed to shake out of the candle flame: "Trelawny, man! This is—a huge mistake."

Trelawny became aware that he had recoiled away from the table and banged the back of his head against one of the upright beams of the house; but he took a deep breath and walked back and leaned his hands on the table to stare into the flame.

"Will you—" he began, but the voice interrupted him.

"How did you do this? How am I returned?"

"After Shelley drowned," stammered Trelawny, glancing nervously at the narrow window that looked out on the dim upper levels of the cave, "we recovered his boat—it was rammed in the storm by an Italian vessel, a *felucca*—"

"It wasn't rammed," whispered Byron's voice, "he drowned deliberately, foundered his boat and sank, to save his wife and last child." The flame quivered, as if with a sigh. "But you did retrieve his boat."

Trelawny frowned, for he was certain that their mutual friend Shelley had not committed suicide; but he let the point pass and went on.

"And," he said, "and one of his notebooks was aboard, and legible once I dried it out. I let Mary take it, but not before I cut several pages out of it. In those pages Shelley explained how a man might become immortal."

"And save Greece too," said Byron's voice, fainter but even now still capable of conveying dry mockery, "just incidentally."

"Yes," said Trelawny loudly, and then he went on in a whisper, "and save Greece. That's no . . . mere excuse. I'm a Greek now, more than I was ever an Englishman."

"And now you mean to be a slave." The voice was almost too faint for Trelawny to hear. "To live forever, yes, perhaps—but not your own man any longer—not a man at all, but just a . . . shackled traitor to your race." The flame wavered. "Is there a second candle you could light?"

Trelawny snatched another candle from a wicker basket hung on the wall and lit its wick from the flame of the first candle. Not seeing a candle-holder, he drew his dagger and cut the bottom of the candle into a wedge which he jammed between two boards of the table-top.

"Our bodies," came Byron's voice again, stronger now emanating from the two flames, "those of us who wed those things, are sacramentals of that marriage bond. And Shelley meant his carcass to be lost, or burned. He was half one of them from birth, he said, and had begun to turn to stone like them. If you could bring his poor bones here, and break away what's human from what's stone, you might undo this . . . *overture* of yours."

"I'm not you," said Trelawny hoarsely. "I'm not afraid of becoming a god."

"Did Shelley—in this notebook that you found—*describe* these things that might be summoned back? Do you know what the Muses *look* like now?"

Trelawny didn't answer right away, for Shelley had in fact drawn a sketch of one of his supernatural mentors, on a page Trelawny hadn't cut out and taken away; the thing was grotesque, an awkward hunchbacked, bird-beaked monster.

"The physical forms they might take," Trelawny said finally, "on one occasion or another—"

"You've got two children, daughters, haven't you?" Byron went on. "Still back in England? Shelley didn't say what sort of . . . *fond attentions* these things pay to families of humans they adopt? If you and your mad *klepht* call up these things, your daughters won't survive, rely on it. And then—that little girl, your warlord's sister?—she'll be their prey, and change to one of them—supposing that you care about the child. All *human* family is sacrificed—"

Boots were echoingly scuffing up the stone levels toward Trelawny's house, and he hastily pocketed Byron's toe and swatted the two candles. Both went out, though the one wedged in the table stayed upright.

Trelawny strode to the flimsy door and pulled it open. The broad silhouette of Odysseus seemed to dwarf the figure of Fenton against the distant daylight as the pair stepped up the last stone rise.

"Come down to the edge," said Odysseus in Italian; he went on in Greek, "where the guns will go."

Trelawny followed the two men down the steps to the wide flat area at the front of the cave. Four six-foot sections of the stone wall had been disassembled so that the cannons might be mounted in the gaps, and Trelawny, squinting uncomfortably in the sunlight that slanted into the front of the cave, noted that only the two notches in the center of the wall threatened the road that wound its way up the gorge.

"But why aim the other two out at the slopes?" he asked Odysseus. "The Turks are hardly likely to come blundering in among the trees."

"To everything there is a season," said Fenton with a smile, "a time to gather stones together, and a time to cast away stones." His Scottish accent was especially incongruous in this cave sacred to ancient Hellenic gods. It was apparently too great a strain on Odysseus's frail grasp of English, for he turned to Trelawny and raised his bushy black eyebrows.

Trelawny slowly translated what Fenton had said.

The *klepht* nodded. "When you are consecrated," he said to Trelawny, "we will sow the same seeds as Deucalion and Pyrrha did."

"Deucalion and Pyrrha," said Fenton, rubbing his hands together and bobbing his head as he blinked out at the gorge, "I caught that bit. The giants in the earth."

Trelawny glanced at Odysseus, but the squinting eyes in the sun-browned face told him nothing.

To Fenton, Trelawny said, carefully, "You seem to know more about our purpose than you told me at first." He shivered, for the gusts up from the gorge were chilly.

"Ah, well I had to see, didn't I," said Fenton, "that you were the lot

I've been looking for, before I did any *confiding*. But your *klepht* has it right—sow our army from up here."

Trelawny let himself relax—the man's caution had been natural enough, and he was clearly an ally—and he tried to imagine thousands of kiln fired clay pellets spraying out over the Velitza Gorge on some moonlit night, the boom and flare of the guns and then the clouds of pale stones fading as they fell away into the echoing shadows.

And then in the darkness of the forest floor the things would lose their rigidity and begin to move, and burrow through the mulch of fallen leaves into the soil, like cicadas—to emerge in manlike forms at the next full moon. And Trelawny would be the immortal gate between the two species.

He laughed, and nearly tossed the coward Byron's toe out into the windy abyss; but it might still be useful in establishing the link.

"My army," he whispered.

Fenton might have heard him. "When," he asked, "will you—?" He stuck a thumb into his own waistcoat below his ribs and twisted it, as if mimicking turning a key.

Odysseus clearly caught his meaning. "*Uno ano,*" he said.

Trelawny nodded. One year from now, he thought, at Midsummer's Eve. But even now the sun seemed to burn his skin if he was exposed to it for more than a minute or so. During the long trek from Missolonghi he had worn his turban tucked around his face during the day—and even then he had been half-blinded by the sun-glare much of the time—but he wasn't wearing his turban now.

"We can talk later," he said, "around the fires."

The other two nodded, perhaps sympathetically, and Trelawny turned away and hurried back up the stone steps into the shadows of the cave's depths.

Back in his room with the door closed, he pulled back the baggy sleeve of his white shirt and stared at the cut in his forearm. As Odysseus had predicted, it hadn't stopped bleeding. According to Odysseus it wouldn't heal until next year's midsummer, when a more substantial cut would be made in his flesh, and a transcendent healing would follow. The bigger incision would have to be made with a new, virgin knife, but apparently Mount Parnassus had several veins of the lightweight gray metal.

Trelawny leaped when something twitched in his pocket—he was

"'Deucalion and Pyrrha,'" came Byron's faint whisper from the flame. "'Consecrated.'"

Trelawny sat down on his narrow bed, then sagged backward across the straw-filled mattress and stared at the low ceiling beams. "Why do you care," he said. "You're dead."

"I hoped to see you," said the flame, "back in Missolonghi—before I died. I don't have many friends that I relied on, but you're one of them."

"You liked me the way you'd like a dog," said Trelawny, still blinking at the ceiling. The candle-smoke smelled of Macassar oil and cigars. "You always said I was a liar."

"I never flattered friends—not trusted friends. I never let dissimulations stand unchallenged, when I wanted honesty." The frail flame shook with what might have been a wry laugh. "I only wanted it from very few."

"I never gave you honesty," said Trelawny belligerently, and a moment later he was startled at his own admission—but, he thought, it's only a dead man I'm talking to. "My mentor, the privateer captain de Ruyters—my Arab wife, Zela—none of it was true."

"I always knew, old friend. 'Deucalion and Pyrrha,' though—and 'consecration.' What ordeal is it they're planning for you, here?"

"'Old friend.'" Trelawny closed his eyes, frowning. "Odysseus has a surgeon—he's going to put a tiny statue into my abdomen, below my ribs. A statue of a woman, in fired clay."

" 'He took one of his ribs, and closed the flesh where it had been.' And you want to reverse what Yahweh did, and put the woman back." Byron's tone was light, but his faint voice wobbled.

Trelawny laughed softly. "It frightens you even *now?* Reversing history, yes. When clay is fired in a kiln, the vivifying element is removed from the air—wood can't burn, it turns into charcoal instead—and this is how all the air was, back in the days when the Nephelim flourished. For the right man, the clay can still . . . wake up."

Byron's voice was definitely quivering now. "The Carbonari, charcoal-burners, try to dominate their trade, because of this. They work to keep it out of hands like . . . yours."

"The Carbonari," said Trelawny scornfully, "the Popes, the Archbishops of Canterbury! And you too—all of you afraid of a power that might diminish your—your dim, brief flames!"

Byron's ghost had begun to say something more, but Trelawny interrupted, harshly, "And *your* flame, 'old friend,' is out."

And with that he leaped off of the bed and smacked his palm onto the candle, and the room was dark again.

For a moment he thought of Byron's question—*Shelley didn't say what sort of . . .* fond attentions *these things pay to families of humans they adopt?*—but then he thought, *My army,* and stepped to the door to join the others, regardless of the sunlight.

⊰ III ⊱

June 11, 1825

> ". . . it is our will
> That thus enchains us to permitted ill—
> We might be otherwise—"
> —Percy Shelley,
> "Julian and Maddalo"

IN THE MONTH since he and Tersitza had been turned back in their attempted midnight flight from the mountain, she had several times asked Edward Trelawny about the *vrykolakas* that had barred their escape. It seemed to him that she was morbidly fascinated by it, though she wouldn't elaborate on her claim, that night, to have seen it herself.

On this Saturday noon, though, Trelawny made his hopping and shuffling way down from his house in the high inner reaches of the cave to find her sitting at a table in the sunlight on the broad stone floor at the front of the cave and talking to Fenton about it.

And another young English Philhellene, a newly arrived friend of Fenton's named Whitcombe, was leaning on the parapet close enough to hear. He had only been staying at the cave for four days now, and Trelawny hadn't yet talked to him at any length.

A cannon barrel gleamed fiercely in the sunlight just beyond their table, and even up here, hundreds of feet above the treetops in the

Velitza Gorge, the air was stiflingly hot. Fenton was bareheaded, but Tersitza was wearing a white turban with the loose ends tucked across her face.

Reluctant to venture out into the direct rays of the sun, Trelawny had hung back in the shadows, and though he could hardly focus his eyes on the figures out in the glaring light, he had heard Fenton laugh.

"In ten days your teeth will be fine," said the Scotsman now in his cacophonous Greek. "You'll be able to bite through stone."

Trelawny recalled that Tersitza had been complaining of a toothache for the last several days.

"And throats," Tersitza said lightly. "I wish I had had the courage to approach her, on those nights I glimpsed her on the mountain. She *wasn't* threatening, I now believe—just—bigger than me, in all ways. Bigger than flesh."

Whitcombe turned to look toward Tersitza and Fenton, but Fenton shifted his head to glance at him; Trelawny couldn't see Fenton's expression, but Whitcombe looked away and resumed staring out over the gorge.

Fenton turned back to face Tersitza. "It's good you didn't," he said. "You're not family quite yet."

Tersitza shifted on her chair and held up her arm so that her shawl fell back. Trelawny noticed a narrow band of white cloth above her elbow, and he thought he saw a spot of blood on it.

"Almost I am, now." She let the shawl fall forward, covering the band. "But I wish I had been awake, last month, when she stopped Edward and me from leaving her. For a while, he says, she took the form of a beautiful woman."

"No more beautiful than yourself, I'm sure," purred Fenton, "and no more immortal than you'll be, in ten days."

Whitcombe moved away to the right along the parapet, toward one of the cannons that was aimed out at the hillside of the gorge. Two rifles leaned against the low wall near him.

She'll be their prey, and change to one of them, Byron had said a year ago; *supposing that you care about the child.*

At the time, Trelawny had not cared about Tersitza. *The troubles of humans was not a concern of mine.* Now his belly was cold with the certainty that her arm had been ritually cut in the same way that his had, by the lightweight gray-metal knife. Odysseus was imprisoned in Athens—could Fenton have presided over the ceremony?

Trelawny stepped soundlessly back into the deeper shadows. Ten days from now would be Midsummer's Eve, when Trelawny was expected to undergo the consecration to the mountain. He was supposed to have had the fired-clay statue inserted into his abdomen weeks ago, and the surgeon here was increasingly suspicious of Trelawny's excuses and postponements.

Where the hell was Bacon? It was almost four months now since he had gone off to retrieve the talisman from Captain Hamilton of the frigate *Cambrian*. Hamilton was the senior British Navy officer in the Aegean Sea, and his father-in-law had reportedly acquired the talisman when Percy Shelley's ashes were buried at the Protestant Cemetery in Rome two years ago.

Trelawny recalled his meeting in February with Major Francis D'Arcy Bacon, on indefinite leave from the 19th Light Dragoons.

It had been the last time Trelawny had seen Odysseus; they had ridden with a dozen of Odysseus's palikars to the abandoned ruins of Talanta, ten miles east of Parnassus, to meet with the Turk captain Omer Pasha and arrange a private three-month truce. "It is the only way in which I can save my people from being massacred," Odysseus had told Trelawny; "if Ghouras will send me no supplies for my army, I can't defend the Athenian passes, and I must find what allies I can."

Trelawny had been uneasy about making a secret peace with the Turkish enemy, and he had remembered Byron's posthumous warnings about Odysseus's purpose. But he had just nodded, as if Odysseus's explanation of the meeting with Omer Pasha was entirely satisfactory.

Rain had been thrashing down outside the ruined Greek church on the night of the meeting, and an attack from Ghouras's troops in the area seemed likely, so the horses had been brought into the church still saddled, and the mutually mistrustful Turks and Greeks kept their rifles and swords close by them as they crouched against the walls or sat around the fire on the cracked marble floor.

After Odysseus and Omer Pasha had concluded their pact, and a dinner of roasted goat had been followed by coffee and the lighting of pipes, several of Odysseus's palikars had stepped in from the rainy night escorting a couple of disheveled strangers and announced that they had captured two Franks.

One of the captives, a tall sandy-haired man of perhaps forty, looked around at the scowling crowd of Greek and Turkish soldiers in the firelight and said in English to his companion, "What a set of cut-throats! Are they Greeks or Turks?"

Trelawny sat against the cracked plaster wall not far from the fire, puffing at a clay pipe, but he knew he was indistinguishable from the rest of Odysseus's men.

"Mind what you say," the other man said quietly.

"Oh, they only want our money," the first man went on. He took off his wet hat and shook rainwater onto the floor. "I hope they'll give us something to eat before they cut our throats—I'm famished."

In halting but comprehensible Greek, the man explained to Odysseus that he and his companion were neutral travelers simply out to see the country, and though neither Odysseus nor Omer Pasha appeared to believe him, Odysseus invited him to sit down and have some of the no-longer-hot goat meat.

The tall man, who introduced himself as Major Bacon, sat down beside Trelawny; and as he gnawed at a rib he stared at Trelawny.

After a while he muttered quietly, "You've got the Neffy brand, then, haven't you?"

"'Neffy,'" repeated Trelawny, also speaking quietly. "As in Nephelim? The 'giants that were in the earth in those days,' in the sixth chapter of Genesis?"

Bacon had dropped the goat bone he'd been holding, and now asked Odysseus for *raki,* the local brandy. Odysseus spoke to one of his palikars, and the man stood up and handed Bacon a cup of wine.

"If they're robbers," Bacon called to his unhappy companion on the other side of the fire, "they're good fellows, and I drink success to their next foray."

Lowering his voice, he said to Trelawny, "You're English? You certainly don't look it. No, I said you're a . . . hefty man." He forced a laugh. "But hardly a giant."

"It's all right," Trelawny told him, staring into the pile of burning logs on the ruined marble floor. "I do have the, the 'Neffy' brand, I know." He touched his forearm, but he knew that the mark showed in his face too, in his eyes.

"Ah." The major retrieved his goat bone and stared at it thoughtfully. "Not . . . altogether happy about it, are we?"

Trelawny glanced at Bacon, wondering what this stranger might know about the ancient race that slept unquietly in Mount Parnassus, and their imminent awakening.

"Not altogether," he ventured.

"Would you . . . get away, if you could?"

Trelawny thought of young Tersitza, asleep in his bed back in the cave on the mountain, and sighed. "Yes."

Bacon pursed his lips and seemed to come to a decision. "Think of an excuse for you and I to talk away from these men."

After a pause, Trelawny nodded, then got up and crossed to where Odysseus sat, and whispered to him that Bacon was willing to carry a letter to the British Navy asking for Odysseus's safe passage to Corfu or Cephalonia in the Ionian Sea. With Ghouras in charge of Athens now and already trying to arrest Odysseus, it would in fact be a valuable option to have.

But ever since the day he had talked to Byron's ghost, Trelawny had been trying to figure out a way to get a message to Captain Hamilton of the HMS *Cambrian*.

"Good," said the *klepht*. "Have him write it."

Trelawny straightened, nodded to Bacon, and then led the way to a doorless confessional in the shadows away from the fire.

When Major Bacon had joined him, carrying his cup of wine, Trelawny told him about the proposed letter.

"Very good," said Bacon, settling onto the priest's bench in the confessional's center booth. "I can write such a letter, in fact."

"I do want you to write to this Captain Hamilton," said Trelawny. There was only a leather-covered kneeler in his booth, in which parishioners had once knelt to confess their sins, so he leaned against the plaster wall. "I have another purpose."

"You can tell me what to write. But—you're marked with the metal from fossile alum! And I gather you have some idea of what sort of . . . antediluvian creature you're a vassal to."

"Not just any vassal." Trelawny smiled unhappily and quoted Louis XV. '*Après moi le déluge.*' Who are you? How do you know about these things?"

The older man grinned, though not happily.

"I was a vassal to them myself, boy, until two and a half years ago, when the link between the two species was broken in Venice. Before it was broken, I watched my wife and my infant son die, and—and met them again later, when they had crawled back up out of their graves." His voice was flat, not inviting comment on events that he had clearly come to some sort of costly terms with. "None of it troubled me at the time. I was . . . married, to one of the Nephelim, and the troubles of humans was not a concern of mine."

"But it—is, now," Trelawny hazarded cautiously.

"There are other wives and sons," Bacon said, "besides mine. I make what amends I can, for the sake of my soul. When I learned that some fugitive members of the Hapsburg royalty were in Moscow, hoping to interest Czar Alexander in reviving the Nephelim connection, I went there, and—prevented it. Then I learned that a Greek warlord had taken possession of the Muses' very mountain and had lately performed human sacrifices in the villages of Euboaea, so I came here." He looked at Trelawny curiously. "The warlord had a partner in those sacrifices, a foreigner."

Trelawny looked back toward the fire. "Already," he said hoarsely, "the troubles of humans was not a concern of mine."

"But it is now?"

"I didn't know—quite how jealous these things are—until an old friend told me. I have two daughters back in England, and, lately, a wife."

"Stay in touch with your old friend," advised Bacon. "We tend to need reminding."

"He's dead. He was dead when he told me."

Bacon laughed. "I'm dead myself, in every important respect." He nodded toward the men around the fire. "My traveling companion is one of the Philhellene rabble, whom I hired as a guide in Smyrna. He still fears death."

Trelawny wasn't sure if he himself did or not. "Listen," he said, "you've got to convince Captain Hamilton of the facts you and I know, and then have him get from his father-in-law a . . . piece of bone that he once stole as a souvenir."

"Ah?"

"When I got to Rome in April of '23, I supervised the reburying of Percy Shelley's ashes. You've heard of Shelley?"

"Atheist poet?"

Trelawny frowned. "Among other things. He . . . apparently! . . . killed himself to save his own wife and son from these things. He was *born* into the family of these creatures, and even before his death he had begun to petrify. I was at his cremation in Viareggio in August of '22, and when we scraped his ashes into a wooden box, I noticed that his jawbone had not burned. But when I arrived in Rome I found that his ashes had been buried in an anonymous corner of the cemetery, and I insisted that the box be dug up again and re-buried in a more prominent spot—and I looked in the box before I buried it."

"The jawbone was gone?"

Trelawny nodded. "I questioned everyone, and eventually learned that Captain Hamilton's father-in-law had been present, and had been seen to take something out of the box, as a, a *souvenir*. My dead friend said that if I could break one of Shelley's bones right in Mount Parnassus itself, and sever the Nephelim element from the human element, that might, I don't know, constitute a *rupture* or *defilement* of the arrangement I've made with them."

Bacon shook his head. "I know the *Cambrian* is in the Aegean Sea somewhere," he said, "but it'd be God's own chore to find him and then try to get this bone, just—I'm sorry!—to save one man's family."

"I'm not 'just one man,'" said Trelawny, and to his alarm he felt the old pride welling up in him; "I'm to be the bridge," he went on quickly, "they're going to implant a fired-clay statue into my ribs, and then at this Midsummer's Eve I'll be consecrated as the overlap, the gate between the species! *I'll* be—don't you see?—the restoration of the link."

For several seconds Bacon was silent in his booth. "No," he said finally with a smile that made his gleaming face look haggard in the firelight, "I won't gain anything by killing you, will I? You *klepht* will only find another racial traitor to do it with. No lack of candidates, I imagine." He stared toward the fire. "I wonder if killing your bandit-chief would effectively prevent it."

"His one-time ally and now chief rival, Ghouras of Athens, would step in. Already he's trying to."

"And others behind him, I suppose. The Greeks can't forget Deucalion and Pyrrha or the Muses in Parnassus." He sighed and stood up. "Write your letter, I'll take it—and I'll return with this atheist's jawbone as quickly as I'm able."

Trelawny stepped away from the wall. "Before Midsummer's Eve," he said, suppressing a shiver that might have been fear or shameful hope, "or you may as well give it back to Hamilton's father-in-law to use as a paperweight."

Standing in the shadows near the cave's glaringly sunlit edge now, the words Fenton had spoken a moment ago rang in Trelawny's head:

No more beautiful than yourself, I'm sure, and no more immortal than you'll be, in ten days.

"Tersitza," Trelawny said loudly, stepping forward, "you and I must leave here, at once. I believe Ghouras will listen to an offer of ransom for your brother."

Tersitza's covered face turned to him, and her eyes told him nothing. "My brother knows that Ghouras will kill him," she said. "He knew it when he surrendered to him. He'll come back to us afterward—stronger."

"And you've got a spot of *surgery* to undergo, haven't you?" added Fenton cheerfully, pushing his chair back across the uneven stone floor and standing up. "Time's short."

Behind him, the newcomer Whitcombe was staring in evident alarm at the three people by the table. The wind from below tossed his blond hair.

"Do it today," said Tersitza. "You need time to heal from it. You don't want to be carried down the mountain to Delphi on a stretcher, on Midsummer's Eve!"

"I'll have the surgery tomorrow, or the day after," said Trelawny, wishing he didn't have to blink tears out of his eyes in the glare. "Today you and I ride to Tithorea."

"But Ghouras's men have blockaded the gorge," said Tersitza patiently. "Wait, and we'll be able to ride right over them." She laughed. "*Fly* right over them."

"You're not getting cold feet, are you, old man?" said Fenton. "Not the pirate prince of the Indian Ocean?"

"I keep my word," said Trelawny stiffly. I did vow at our wedding to protect her, he told himself. That takes precedence, even if she doesn't want protection.

"But—are you serious?"

"Completely."

"Ghouras will just arrest you both and lock you up with her brother."

"Ghouras wants this cave, he wants the mountain, not us—and he knows he can't take it by force. He'll negotiate." This is good, he thought—it almost makes sense.

"And you think it will help to take Tersitza with you."

Trelawny could think of no plausible reason for that condition, so he only said, "Yes."

Fenton frowned and shrugged. "Odysseus told us that you're in command here while he's away. If you're confident you can come back, and if you *want* to be carried to Delphi with a bleeding incision . . ."

"I heal fast," said Trelawny. He turned to Tersitza and said, "We can meet with Ghouras at Tithorea, I'm certain. We'll be back here in two days at most."

And I hope I'm wrong, he thought. I hope Ghouras's men *do* simply arrest us, and forcibly take us to Athens, away from this monstrous mountain.

Tersitza's eyes were shadowed by her turban, and Trelawny couldn't tell whether she was looking at him or at Fenton.

But after a pause her shoulders slumped and she sighed, fluttering the cloth over her face. "Very well, my husband."

"I *would* advise keeping your pistols handy," Fenton said.

"Yes of course," said Trelawny.

"Why not at least get in a bit of target practice, then?" Fenton said. "Just while the palikars climb down to get your horses saddled? Whitcombe here can join us." He peered with apparent sympathy at Trelawny. "Though I must say you look a little shaky to compete this afternoon."

"Even with a pistol I'm a better shot than you two with your carbines," Trelawny muttered, "any day."

Relieved that they had given in to his proposal so easily, Trelawny quickly called for the Italian servant he always addressed as Everett, and told him to set up a plank for a target at the far left side of the terrace.

Both Fenton and Whitcombe had rifles ready and leaning against the parapet, and now they picked them up and checked the flints and the powder in the pans.

Trelawny drew a pistol from his sash and stepped between them and the target to shoot first. When Everett had set up the board and hurried back into the shadows, Trelawny swung his arm up and fired, and though the smoke stung his already watering eyes and the boom of the shot set his ears ringing, he heard the plank clatter forward onto the stone.

He stepped forward to prop the board up again, but paused when he heard Tersitza shout urgently to one of the Greeks, "Fire the cannons!"

Trelawny knew the cannons were aimed out over the gorge, loaded with the fired-clay pellets that were to come alive at the next full moon —but it wouldn't work *now*, the statue hadn't been implanted in him yet.

He opened his mouth to ask her why—

And a sudden hard blow to his back and jaw sent him staggering forward as a rifle-shot cracked behind him; he caught his balance and straightened, dizzy and stunned and choking on hot blood, and then he coughed and spat blood down the front of his shirt and cried hoarsely, "I've been shot!"

Dimly he was aware that Fenton had rushed up and was supporting him now, shouting something, but Trelawny turned to Tersitza, who was waving at someone behind him; and a moment later the stone floor shook under Trelawny's feet as the unmistakable boom of a cannon shot jarred the terrace.

Fenton was shouting, "He's good on his own for another minute, at least! It'll take! He's—" The man's voice choked off then in a gasp, and Trelawny blinked tears out of his eyes to see Tersitza.

She was pointing a pistol of her own at him, or at Fenton.

"Not *me*, not *yet*!" Fenton screamed, and then he wrenched Trelawny around by the shoulder and spoke directly into his face: "She's pregnant, she's carrying your still-human—"

Tersitza's shot struck Fenton squarely in the chest, and he pitched over backward and rolled onto his face, his head against the base of the parapet.

Trelawny abruptly sat down on the stone floor and bent forward to let the blood run out of his mouth, and two teeth and an object like half of a big pearl tumbled out past his lips to clink in the widening red puddle on the stone. But his sight was dimming and he remotely realized that he wasn't breathing, and his ribs and skull seemed to be shattered and held together only by the confinement of his skin.

As if from far away in a ringing distance, he heard the other three cannons being fired in rapid succession.

The clay pellets flew tumbling through the hot air, still moving out away from the cave terrace but already beginning to fall toward the treetops and the Kakoreme riverbed. Trelawny was leaping with them out over the world, though at the same time he was still sitting hunched forward on the stone floor of the cave terrace on the mountain.

His right arm was numb and useless, but with his left hand he picked up the half-pearl and rubbed away its coating of bright red blood. Now he could see that it was half of a ceramic ball, with half of a tiny grimacing face imprinted on it.

He laid it back down in the puddle and moved his hand away.

Someone was kneeling beside him, and when he squinted he saw that it was Zela, the Arab princess whose marriage to him had been cut short by her youthful death—in his stories.

"Swallow it," Zela said. "I—can't force you!" Trelawny thought blurrily that she seemed surprised to realize that she couldn't.

Trelawny's consciousness had expanded as far as the mouth of the gorge to the east, and north to the three standing pillars on the round stone dais at the Oracle of Delphi, but he bent his attention downward over Mount Parnassus to look at the figures on the terrace of Odysseus's cave.

He saw the sitting figure that was himself; two holes in the back of his white shirt, to the right of his spine, showed where the rifle balls had struck him.

A figure that must have been young Whitcombe had snatched off its turban and tied one end of it to the crane boom at the edge, and was rapidly climbing down it toward the highest of the moored ladders on the cliff-face below.

The woman who was either Tersitza or Zela was speaking, and the hovering spirit of Trelawny discovered that he could hear what she said:

"Swallow it." There was urgency in her voice. "You've only got half of the statue inside you now. Swallow it and it will reform itself, and reform you. I *can't* force you! You're dying, Edward, my love—you'll *die* here, now, if you don't do what I say. Or you can be healed, and live forever with us."

He was able, too, to look in another, entirely unsuspected direction, and there he saw the Trelawny figure step toward the fallen target-plank, as behind him Fenton aimed a rifle at his back and pulled the trigger—but the gun didn't fire; Fenton gestured at Whitcombe, who raised his own rifle and fired it at Trelawny's back, and two balls flew from the muzzle in slow motion across the terrace and struck Trelawny just to the right of his spine. From this vantage point, the hovering Trelawny spirit could even see the balls—one silver, one ceramic—punch through his flesh; the ceramic one split as it glanced off his shoulder-blade and broke his collar bone, one half of the ball tearing up through his neck muscles to break his jaw and lodge in his mouth.

This was the recent past. Trelawny looked in the other new direction, but could see nothing in the future. Did that mean he would very shortly die?

You'll die here, now, if you don't do what I say. Or you can be healed, and live forever with us.

The direction which was the future must be blank because he had not yet chosen.

The Trelawny figure's shocked lungs were at last able to take a spluttering breath.

The air smelled of tobacco, sweat, and the Indian rum known as arrack.

Trelawny was sitting at a table in a lamp-lit Bombay tavern he remembered well, and it was an effort of his unbodied will to remember too that the place had never actually existed. In a few seconds he was able to hear noises, and then he either noticed or it became the case that the low-ceilinged room was crowded. Slaves carrying trays threaded their way between tables full of young British midshipmen in blue jackets, but Trelawny stared at the man sitting across the table from him—he was perhaps thirty years old, with black hair pulled back from his high tanned forehead, and he puffed tobacco smoke from the hose of a hookah. Unlike anyone else in the place, he had a cup of steaming coffee in front of him.

The man pressed his lips together in a way Trelawny remembered well—it used to indicate impatience at an unexpected obstacle.

"You died," Trelawny said to him carefully, "off the Barbary Coast, in a fight with an English frigate." He realized that he *could* speak, and that his wounds were gone, and that he could flex both arms. He took a deep effortless breath, wondering if it might be his last, but forced himself to go on: "And in fact you never existed at all outside my imagination." For this man at the table with him was the privateer de Ruyters, who in Trelawny's stories had taken him in as a raw, wild sixteen-year-old deserter and taught him discipline and self-control.

"If you like," said de Ruyters with a tight smile. "At that rate, of course, you're about to bleed to death on Mount Parnassus, and your Tersitza will be a widow. And you and I will never have—oh, where do I start? We'll never have stormed St. Sebastian, and saved your bride Zela from the Madagascar pirates. Zela, in fact, will never have existed." His smile was gone. "Perhaps you've forgotten her already."

Trelawny had not. He remembered, as if it had actually occurred, his first meeting with Zela: when de Ruyters's French and Arab crew had routed the slave traders of St. Sebastian before dawn and burst into the slave-huts, where Trelawny had been only moments too late to save Zela's bound father from being stabbed by one of the pirate women. Trelawny had killed the woman and freed the dying old Arab, who as he took his last breaths had drawn a ring from his own finger and put it on Trelawny's, and had joined Trelawny's hand with his young daughter's, and had then spoken a blessing and died.

The Arab's daughter had been Zela.

Later Trelawny had learned that this had constituted a betrothal, and he had devoted the next several weeks to the strictly chaperoned courtship that Arab tradition required; when at last he had been permitted to hold Zela's hand and meet her unveiled eyes, he had known that this was, as he had put it to himself, the first link of a diamond chain that would bind him to her forever.

"She," said Trelawny, "died too. After not having ever existed either."

After? he thought, impatient with himself.

"We *can* exist," said de Ruyters irritably. "We *do,* in some branches of reality. Would you not rather have the adventurous life you had with us, than what—if you insist!—you actually had?—an undistinguished Naval career and a shabby marriage and divorce?"

De Ruyters reached across the table and gripped Trelawny's shoulder, and a confident comradely smile deepened the lines in his cheeks.

"Look, man," he said softly, waving around at the crowded tavern—which abruptly faded away, revealing a landscape that was deeper and clearer than anything Earth could provide: a remote horizon of green-sloped mountains lit by slanting amber light, crowned with castles whose towers cleaved the coral clouds; wide bays glittering in the sunset glow, stippled with the painted sails of splendid ships; parrots like flaming pinwheels shouting among the leafy boughs closer at hand. Faintly on the cool sea breeze Trelawny caught the lilt of festive music.

He couldn't see de Ruyters, but a girl stood beside him now on this grassy meadow, her slim brown body visible under her blowing yellow veils, and he knew that she would be young forever. "All these things will I give you," she told him, "if you will worship me."

Trelawny knew that it was the spirit of the mountain that was speaking to him and had been speaking to him.

"You need not surely die," the girl said earnestly. "When you swallow the stone, then your eyes shall be opened, and you shall be a god among gods, knowing neither good nor evil."

And Trelawny remembered what this same creature had said to him a month ago, when he had tried to escape with Tersitza from Parnassus:

And I will purge thy mortal grossness so
That thou shalt like an airy spirit go . . .

For a moment he glimpsed again the pale, sweating, tortured figure sitting on the terrace-edge of the Parnassus cave, a string of blood dangling from its mouth to the spreading puddle of blood in which lay several teeth . . . and the half-sphere stone.

One image or the other would have to be erased—the bright sensual immortality or the suffering organic thing in the cave. The one was imaginary and the other was real, but what hold had real things ever had on him?

A god among gods, Trelawny thought dizzily, "king of kings," as Shelley had written—"look on my works, ye mighty, and despair."

But the thought of Shelley's poetry brought back Byron's words about him: *he drowned deliberately, foundered his boat and sank, to save his wife and last child.*

Trelawny had been proud to call Shelley his friend.

The young girl still stood beside him on the green slope, near enough to touch, but Trelawny made himself look away from her. "Tersitza," he said, bracing himself and almost apologetic, "is pregnant with my child."

Then, abruptly, he was in the reeking Bombay tavern again, and in the dim lamplight de Ruyters was staring at him across the table. "Zela was pregnant too. Is."

Somewhere beyond this hallucination, Trelawny felt the cannon-propelled clay pellets clatter down onto the dirt and pebbles of the Velitza Gorge, bounding and skittering until they came to rest. They would germinate if the link between humanity and the Nephelim was established—if he swallowed the broken-off half of the little stone statue so that it could be whole inside him.

If I do it, he thought, Tersitza, with the wound of the gray metal knife in her arm, will change to one of them . . . and so will my child . . . supposing that I care about them.

Hating himself for his cowardice, Trelawny closed his eyes and reached out again with his left hand, brushed at the puddled stone surface that it encountered until his fingers closed around the split stone sphere, and again picked it up.

Torn nerves made a bright razory pain in his ribs, his neck, his jaw. He opened his eyes and saw Tersitza staring anxiously at him.

"Be healed," she said.

And he flung the stone out sideways, into the abyss.

"No," he grated to Tersitza and the mountain.

⊰ IV ⊱

August 1825

"For the first twenty days after being wounded, I remained in the same place and posture, sitting and leaning against the rock, determined to leave everything to nature. I did not change or remove any portion of my dress, nor use any extra covering. I would not be bandaged, plastered, poulticed, or even washed; nor would I move or allow anyone to look at my wound. I was kept alive by yolks of eggs and water for twenty days. It was forty days before there was any sensible diminution of pain; I then submitted to have my body sponged with spirit and water, and my dress partly changed. I was reduced in weight from thirteen stone to less than ten, and looked like a galvanized mummy."

—Edward John Trelawny,
Records of Shelley, Byron and the Author

IT WAS NEARLY two months later that Major Bacon came at last to the cave, climbing barefoot up the ladders in the noonday sun because the height was too unnerving for him to attempt the ascent in boots. At the top of the second ladder, hanging over a drop of more than seven hundred feet, he had to shout several times to the suspicious faces that peered down at him from the parapet twenty feet above.

"Trelawny!" he yelled up at them. "I'm looking for *Edward Trelawny*, you ignorant brigands!"

You clods, you stones, you worse than senseless things, he thought worriedly. Midsummer's Eve was more than a month past, and though Shelley's charred jawbone was wrapped in an altar cloth in Bacon's haversack, it would be of no use if Trelawny had already been transformed into the new link between humanity and the Nephelim. He hoped poor idiot Whitcombe had been able to accomplish something.

Bacon allowed himself a moment to stare at the pitted limestone directly in front of his rung-clutching hands—looking up was even more terrifying than looking down past his feet at the distant rocky gorge, and he felt as if his bowels had turned to ice water. But at a scuffling sound from above he looked up again.

A girl's face had appeared now at the cave's rim, scowling down at him. "Bacon?" she called.

His stomach was too fluttery on this windy, vertiginous perch for him to do more than scream back the Greek word for assent, "*Neh!*"

The girl disappeared, and after sixty fast, shallow breaths Bacon had begun considering the ordeal of feeling for the next rung down with his bare right foot, and then putting his full weight on that rung and doing it again, back down forty feet of rickety ladders to the narrow ledge that was still seven hundred vertical feet above the roofs of the barracks and stables at the foot of the mountain . . . but then he heard a clattering from above and saw that several men were angling another ladder out from the cave and lashing its top end to a boom that projected out over the low wall at the edge.

Bacon had to duck when the ladder swung free, and the bottom end of it swished through the air a foot over his head.

He stayed crouched at the top of the second ladder until the third one had largely stopped swinging. It stood out at right angles from the cliff-face, and the high-altitude breeze chilled Bacon's sweating face as he reached up with one hand and gripped the bottom rung. A moment later his other hand had clutched it too, and he climbed up it rapidly, before it could swing away from the fixed ladder and leave his feet flailing free.

No more than a minute later he was sitting on the cave floor several yards back from the edge, panting and pressing his palms against the solid stone.

Five or six disreputable Greeks with rifles stood around him in the shade of the cave's roof, but their scowls might have been habitual, for the rifles were pointed at the floor.

"Trelawny?" said the girl who had peered at him over the edge. She was standing beside Bacon, dressed in a loose white chiton that left her arms bare to the shoulders, and she seemed very young. The big dark eyes in her thin face stared intently at him.

Bacon stared back, and did not see the feverish hunger he remembered seeing in the eyes of his unnaturally resurrected wife and son.

After a pause, "*Neh*," Bacon said again. "Here?"

She nodded, perhaps just at the affirmative, and rocked her head toward the back of the cave, and then began walking up the shelved layers of stone into the deeper shadows.

Bacon sighed mightily and got to his feet.

Several little houses had been built of wood and stone on the higher levels, and the girl led him to one of them and pulled open the flimsy door.

The room within, lit by a lantern on the table, smelled like an ill-kept dog kennel, and at first the frail figure on the bed did seem to show the sick, predatory alertness of those favored by the Nephelim—but a second glance convinced Bacon that it was only extreme physical illness that gave the sunken eyes their glittering semblance of eagerness.

A dirty cloth was visible under the bearded jaw, bound over the top of the head, and the figure apparently couldn't speak; but when its eyes lit in recognition and a skeletal hand wobbled toward him, Bacon recognized the man.

"My God," he said. "Trelawny?"

The man on the bed looked toward Tersitza and touched his jaw. The girl crossed to him and worked with both hands at the knotted cloth, and when it fell away, Trelawny opened his mouth and said, clearly, "Yes."

Bacon leaned against the wall and ventured to smile. Clearly Trelawny had somehow not been granted the near-godhood that had been planned for him.

"Here I am," Bacon said, "come to redeem my pledge of rendering you a service—" He paused to look around the room, "—and to enable you to quit Greece."

"You," said Trelawny hoarsely, "are a friend indeed."

Bacon unslung the haversack from his shoulder and crouched to unstrap it. He lifted out the altar-cloth and unfolded it, exposing the arch of dark bone with its row of knobby teeth.

Tersitza was looking on anxiously, and a couple of bearded faces were peering in through the door, but there was no comprehension in their expressions.

Half of the jawbone-section was gray stone, and the hinge-end was blackened yellow bone.

"Shall I break it?" Bacon asked.

"No," said Trelawny. "It's for me to do."

He held out his skeletal arm again, and Bacon straightened up and crossed to the bed and laid the bone in Trelawny's withered palm.

Trelawny's right arm seemed to be useless, but he gripped the bone between the fingertips and the heel of his left hand, and then the tendons stood out like cords on his trembling forearm as he squeezed the thing.

Tersitza opened her mouth and took a half-step forward, then hesitated.

The bone snapped.

The floor shook, as if the whole mountain had been massively struck.

Bacon flinched, then with hollow flippancy quoted the Book of Judges: "With the jawbone of an ass you have slain your thousands."

He noticed tears glittering on the girl's cheeks, though she made no sound.

Trelawny opened his shaking hand and two pieces fell onto the floor, the stone half separate from the organic half.

"Give me the bit that was Shelley," said Trelawny, "the human half of him."

Bacon bent down and retrieved it, and handed it to Trelawny.

By the dim lantern-light Bacon looked around at their audience, and decided he could talk safely if he spoke in rapid English.

"You aren't the link between the species," he said. "It didn't happen, obviously. Why not?"

"A young man shot me," said Trelawny, "in the back, before the appointed day. He fled directly after. My people here," he added with a nod toward the girl and the men in the doorway, "caught him and wanted to kill him, but I let him go two weeks ago."

"Ah," said Bacon. After a moment he asked, "Why'd you let him go?"

"He was—trying to *save* me, actually. When he shot me. Well, save Tersitza and my unborn child, at any rate." Trelawny clutched the fragment of Shelley's jaw. "Odysseus and his agents—" He looked toward the wall, and Bacon guessed that he was deliberately not looking at the girl, "—had arranged to insert the fired-clay statue into me by a more conventional sort of surgery, since I was reluctant to have it done with a scalpel; they loaded a rifle with it."

Bacon raised his eyebrows and looked at the wasted figure on the bed—clearly Trelawny's jaw and right arm had been injured. It seemed unlikely that a shot in the back could have done all this damage.

"But Whitcombe shot you first?" he hazarded.

The girl and the men in the doorway shifted at the mention of the name.

And Trelawny was staring at him. "You—know him?"

"I *sent* him, man."

"Sent him to shoot me in the back?"

"If that was what the situation called for." Seeing Trelawny's sunken eyes fixed on him, he grinned and added, "The troubles of humans is still not a *big* concern of mine. But his shot obviously didn't kill you, quite—didn't they then shoot the statue into you?"

Trelawny was shaking, and he seemed to spit. "Did I call you a *friend*, a moment ago?"

"Yes, and I am your friend. I don't indulge my friends when hard measures are needed to save them—save their souls, if not their lives." He smiled. "I have very few friends."

"God help them."

"Rather than another, yes."

Trelawny scowled at him. "Whitcombe didn't shoot me *first*—it was him that shot the bloody statue into me."

"He *did?*" Bacon shook his head. "I don't understand. Why are you—as you are, then?"

"Your man Whitcombe loaded their rifle with a *second* ball, too—one made of silver. And he made sure that he was the one who fired it, so the addition wouldn't be noticed."

Bacon laughed softly. "Ah, clever boy! Silver repels vampires, certainly. And that . . . *cancelled* the stone one?"

"No, damn you. The stone ball, the statue, broke, as it broke my bones; half of it broke my jaw and came out through my mouth. 'Jawbone of an ass' there, if you like. All the *silver* ball accomplished was to restrain *them*—" Now he did glance at the girl, "—from forcibly feeding it to me, shoving it back in." He exhaled harshly. "I had to *choose* to throw away the mountain's offer of salvation—and accept," he added, waving his frail hand at his diminished body, "this, instead."

Bacon nodded and crossed his arms. "I learned some things about your chum Shelley," he said, "while I was off fetching that there bit of bone. It seems he made a costly choice too, finally, at the end—and he didn't get the privilege of complaining about it, after."

Trelawny managed to draw himself up in the bed, and Bacon was more able to recognize the man he had met on that rainy night in the ruined chapel at Talanta six months ago. "I'm not complaining," said Trelawny. "Just giving you honesty." He closed his eyes and sighed deeply. "I only give it to a very few."

Four days later at noon they left the cave—Trelawny and his Italian servant, Bacon, Tersitza and her younger brother. Odysseus's mother and his palikars chose to stay behind in the Muses' mountain. A rope had to be tied under Trelawny's arms and run through the pulley on the boom, for he couldn't negotiate the ladders.

At the foot of the mountain at last, Trelawny was lifted into a saddle, and it was all he could do to keep from falling off the horse as their party wound slowly down the dry Kakoreme riverbed. Trelawny was squinting in the sun-glare, but now only because of his long stay in the dimness of the cave.

Tersitza sat cross-legged on a mule, and she replied only in curt monosyllables to the remarks Trelawny was able to articulate. They passed the stones marking Fenton's grave without comment.

The bone fragment of Shelley's jaw was tucked into Trelawny's sash beside his pistols and his sword, and he touched the angular lump of it and wished he believed in God so he could pray.

From behind them a deep boom rolled down the gorge, followed a moment later by another, and Trelawny knew that the palikars in the cave were firing the guns as a parting salute, with no projectiles loaded. The ready tears of long convalescence blurred his vision.

In the dirt and pebbles and fallen leaves all around them, he knew, were the kilned clay pellets that had been fired from those same cannons two months ago—and he wondered now if they had quivered with newborn alertness, in the moment between their landing and his rejection of Parnassus's offered gift.

Another cannon shot boomed away between the ridges of the gorge.

For a moment as the echoes faded he was sure he caught, faintly, the high female voices he had heard singing on the night four months ago when he had tried to take Tersitza and himself away from the mountain—but they were very faint now, and he was bleakly sure that they no longer sang to him.

He thought of Odysseus, the real Odysseus of Homer, tied to the mast and intolerably hearing the song of the sirens fading away astern.

And in a vision that he knew was only for himself, he saw the great stone spirit of the mountain rise beyond the trees to his right; its vast sunlit shoulders eclipsed the southern ridges, and its dazzling face, though it was an expanse of featureless gleaming rock, somehow expressed immortal grief.

And I do love thee, it had said to him on that night. *Therefore stay with me.*

As he shifted his head the thing stayed in the center of his vision as if it were a lingering spot of sun-glare, or else his gaze helplessly followed it as it moved with voluntary power, and he found that he had painfully hitched around in the saddle to keep it in sight, until it overlapped and merged with the giant that was Mount Parnassus, receding away forever behind him.

✥ AUTHOR'S NOTE ✥

Trelawny was a real historical person. He was certainly a liar who eventually came to believe his own melodramatic fabulations—though his last words were, "Lies, lies, lies"—but his adventures on Mount Parnassus did happen. He really was the right-hand man of the mountain warlord Odysseus Androutsos, really did marry the thirteen-year-old Tersitza, and he really was shot by William Whitcombe in the high Parnassus cave, and with no medical aid simply waited out his recovery. His injuries were exactly as I describe them, and he really did spit out, along with several teeth, half of one of the two balls Whitcombe's rifle had been loaded with.

He survived, and in later years asked Mary Shelley to marry him (she declined the offer), swam the Niagara River just above the falls, and in his old age was lionized in Victorian London society as the piratical friend of the legendary Byron and Shelley—and even of Keats, though in spite of the many colorful stories he would tell about his acquaintance with that poet, Trelawny had never actually met him. His life story was a patchwork of grand facts and shabby lies, and it wasn't until eighty years after his death that researchers were able to sift one from the other. I admire him.

⚔ DOWN AND OUT IN PURGATORY ⚔

For Michael and Laura Yanovich

"I've always thought that death puts an end to the possibilities of revenge."

—PETER O'DONNELL

Before you embark on a journey of revenge, dig two graves.

—CONFUCIUS

⚔ I ⚔

"THIS WAY. Keep the clipboard visible and don't meet anybody's eye. Look like you work here, right?"

The young man in the white lab coat led the way down the fluorescent-lit hallway, past several tall stacks of cardboard boxes labeled *Can Liners,* and Holbrook momentarily wondered if they were very big can liners. The cool air smelled only of Lysol and the young man's after shave. Holbrook had to step ahead and look at the man's blue badge to remember his name.

"I need to see his face, Matt," he said, fairly steadily. "And if he has a tattoo on his shoulder."

"Push on the plastic to look, I'm not cutting it open for a measly hundred bucks."

Holbrook was resolved to cut the plastic with the rental car key if he had to, but he nodded. His mouth was dry, and tasted of airline peanuts.

Four hours ago in San Francisco his life had still had a purpose, but the phone call from the private detective had effectively shattered it.

"Your friend finally showed up," the detective had said.

"Who is this?" Holbrook had replied impatiently. "What friend? I don't have any friends."

"That's good. I'm talking about your man John Atwater. I'm afraid he's dead. The L.A. County Coroner's Office sent his prints in to the FBI, and they identified him."

Holbrook had found himself sitting on his kitchen floor, watching his coffee cup spin away across the linoleum. "It's—dammit, it's not over yet—there can be errors. With fingerprinting. Did he have the tattoo?"

The man hadn't known that.

Matt paused now beside a steel door, a printed sign on it read STAND CLEAR WHEN DOOR IS IN MOTION. Holbrook was breathing deeply. Several printed announcements or bulletins were thumbtacked to the wall beside the door, but he couldn't read those.

Matt took hold of the metal handle and slid the door open. Inside, under recessed white lights and roaring ceiling-mounted blowers, long shapes in plastic bags filled metal shelves and lay on narrow wheeled tables. The air in here was very cold.

Matt stepped in and slid the door shut when Holbrook had joined him. "These ones tied with ropes have been autopsied," Matt said, each syllable a puff of steam. "Your man's on the far end, not cut up yet."

Holbrook walked slowly past the angular bagged shapes on the tables, his shoes scuffing on textured strips on the concrete floor. Some of the bodies were wrapped in a silvery plastic, but most of the bags were fairly clear, and through them he could see flesh colors, and here and there patches of red which he assumed were blood. Absently he laid the meaningless clipboard on one of the bags.

The walls were lined with steel shelves divided by partitions, and most of the spaces were occupied by still more plastic wrapped shapes.

Holbrook nodded toward them. "You've got room for more."

"Those shelves on the far wall are for ones that weigh more than two-hundred-and-twenty-five pounds," commented Matt. "Your pal was up there till they moved him in line here." He paused beside one of the wheeled tables and waved at the shape on it. "He-e-re's Johnny."

Holbrook took a deep breath of the cold air, then stared at the face blurrily visible below the rippled plastic. He hadn't seen John Atwater for more than ten years, and the man had been athletically trim in those days, while this face was wide. With both hands Holbrook pressed the plastic down against the cheeks, and now the face was narrower and clearly visible. And Holbrook couldn't pretend that he didn't recognize it.

He lifted his hands away, then pressed one hand against the plastic over the body's bare shoulder—and saw the word *THINGS* tattooed in stark sans-serif letters on the pale skin.

Involuntarily he touched his own shoulder; under his jacket and shirt the word *APART* was tattooed in the same lettering. And for a moment he let himself remember the woman whose shoulder had borne the word *FALL*.

He blinked back tears. "You think you're safe now?" he whispered.

The private detective had said that Atwater had been found on a Malibu balcony overlooking the sea, dead of a sudden massive stroke, with a drink beside him and a girlfriend in bed in the room behind him.

Holbrook looked up at Matt. "He died happy."

"We done here? Get your clipboard and let's go." Matt hurried back toward the steel door. "Happy? Well, that's good, isn't it? Come on."

Holbrook turned away from the body. "It's . . . intolerable."

Far out of Los Angeles to the east on the old Route 66, late afternoon sunlight threw the shadows of tumbleweeds and an occasional mesquite tree across the two highway lanes that were the only evidence of humanity in an endless flat plain under an empty sky. In the distance, the horizon was the uneven line of the remote Providence Mountains.

Holbrook watched the odometer as he drove, and when he was fourteen miles southeast of the one-gas-station town of Ludlow he slowed the rental Kia and began peering through the windshield for a dirt road slanting off the highway. "Middle of nowhere" seemed to have been an accurate description.

He saw it, or at least saw some cleared track on which tire treads had worn a pair of flattened lines in the sandy dirt. The Kia was only rolling along at about twenty miles per hour now, and he easily steered it off the pavement onto the dirt road.

The car coasted slowly as he kept his foot lifted from the gas pedal. It had been a long, tense drive from Los Angeles—and a longer trip from San Francisco—and he tried to remember when he had last eaten. Last night, in his apartment on Telegraph Hill?

All at once he was shaking, and he gripped the wheel tightly—what if there were no trailer out here at the end of it all, what if the alleged psychic had lied? The phrase *middle of nowhere* seemed suddenly literal, and Holbrook had to resist the impulse to reverse back onto the highway while there still was a highway behind him, while he could still hope to get back to the world, even just the tiny outpost that was now-distant Ludlow. The ragged band that was the remote mountains seemed thinner and even farther away, and for one breathless instant he was sure that if he were to drive across the desert toward them they would recede.

His hand snapped forward defensively, and it hit the button for the radio, and then piano music shook the air-conditioned breeze in the car, at least partly restoring the external world; but after a moment he turned the radio off. He bad only heard a couple of bars, and it couldn't have been Ravel's Piano Concerto in G. He could hardly hope to recognize it these days, in any case—it had been Shasta's favorite performance piece, but more than ten years had passed since he had heard her play it.

The engine whined and the car rocked on its shock absorbers as he gave it more gas, and the rear-view mirror showed only dust.

He touched his shoulder, remembering the drunken night in the summer of 2001 when the six members of their close-knit college group had decided to get a set of farewell tattoos.

Shasta and John had just graduated, and two of the others were moving out of state, and after many pitchers of beer at Chasteen's on Sunset, they had all driven over to a tattoo parlor in El Segundo. It had been Tom Holbrook, hopelessly in love with Shasta ever since they had both been freshmen—wondering dejectedly how he might maintain any sort of contact with her after this—who had suggested that each of them be be tattooed with one word from the Yeats line, *Things fall apart, the center cannot hold.* And the alcohol and the melancholy mood of the evening had led them all to agree. The line had one too many words for their group, but none of them had wanted *the* anyway. Pete Calvert, nowadays a school janitor in San Bernardino, had got *CANNOT;* Ed Rocha had got *HOLD,* and at last report he was a real estate millionaire; Dylan Emsley had got *CENTER,* and died in a car crash in '03 at the age of twenty-five.

Shasta DiMaio had got *FALL.* John Atwater had got *THINGS.* Tom Holbrook had wound up with *APART,* which had seemed bleakly appropriate.

The Kia's temperature needle was a bit on the right side of straight up, and Holbrook was ready to switch off the air conditioning and turn on the heater to get a second radiator cooling the engine, when the car crested a low rise and he saw the tan-colored trailer tucked behind a low cluster of cottonwood trees.

It appeared to be corrugated aluminum or fiberglass, and its roof slanted up higher at the far end, with a little window in the long triangle, perhaps to make room for a bunk. There were two wide windows in the flank and a door with a window in it at the near end. It was dusty and its two visible wheels appeared to be flat, but its deliberate lines and angles looked as incongruous in this natural wasteland as a spacecraft on the moon. When Holbrook swerved into the cleared patch in front of it and turned off the car's motor, he could hear the clatter of the trailer's rooftop air conditioner. Feeling unmoored from everything in his life, Holbrook got out of the car and walked through the jarringly hot dry air to the trailer.

The man who opened the trailer's door when Holbrook knocked on it appeared to be in his fifties, thin and clean-shaven, with long gray hair pulled back in a ponytail. He wore jeans and a gray sweatshirt with a nearly faded out peace-sign across the front, and on the cool breeze from inside the trailer Holbrook could smell incense and patchouli oil.

"Holbrook," the man said, in a nasal voice that carried a trace of a British accent. When Holbrook nodded, the man went on, "I'm Martinez, obviously. Whatever it is you want, it will be expensive— nobody ever brings small problems out here." He stood back and waved to the trailer's dim interior. "Sit down."

Holbrook stepped up onto pale blue carpet, and after a few

moments he was able to make out upholstered benches along both walls, and wide, curtained windows. Electric light behind pebbled ceiling panels threw a weak yellow glow on the glass-topped table between the benches. The only things on the table were a legal pad, several pencils, and a black laptop computer.

Holbrook edged around the table and sat down. "I want to kill somebody."

Martinez shut the door and slid onto the opposite bench. "By supernatural means, I presume, or you wouldn't have come to me. Well, I can listen, at least. Where is this person?"

Holbrook sighed. "In a plastic bag in the morgue at the Los Angeles County Coroner building."

Martinez sat back and gave him a quizzical look.

"Yes, yes," said Holbrook impatiently, "he's dead, but—that won't do. *I* didn't kill him. And he died happy! Now—I now see that I need to make him cease to exist at all, in any form. He must be—" He lifted a hand and let it drop.

"Really most sincerely dead?" suggested Martinez.

Holbrook didn't smile. "You contact dead people all the time, right? You come highly recommended. So how do you destroy, negate, eradicate, a ghost? And—to the extent that ghosts can be aware of things—I want him to know who did it to him."

Martinez leaned forward to peer at Holbrook. "Who . . . is he?"

"You might have heard of him. John Atwater. He murdered his wife six years ago, and a year later he was acquitted after a lot of inadmissible evidence and two hung juries. He was a lawyer, and he had high-powered lawyer friends. There were stories in the L. A. *Times.* He went invisible after that; dark, off the grid, in hiding, with a lot of stashed money. When he finally reappeared two days ago, it was because he had died."

In the cool interior of the trailer, Holbrook could smell his own sweat over the scent of patchouli.

"I think I remember it." Martinez leaned back. "The murdered wife had a peculiar name . . ."

"Shasta."

Holbrook had tried to speak the name levelly, but Martinez nodded slowly. "That's the way of it, eh? You don't want to talk to her?"

"Would she be . . . available?"

"Well probably not, actually, after six years. They tend to move out from the center, out of Ouija range." He shook his head. "But we can certainly banish the Atwater fellow—block him from manifesting himself, even block him from any awareness of events in . . . this *mortal coil*. I'll need to find out where they bury him, or at least where they incinerate him, and my expenses will be—"

"But if you banish him, won't he still exist, on the, I don't know, on the other side?"

Martinez shrugged. "For a while, at least, probably. I don't know what becomes of them after they've moved outward, beyond my sphere of perception."

"I want to kill him there. I want him to stop existing there." The trailer shook in a gust of desert wind.

Martinez laughed softly. "My dear fellow, to have any hope of accomplishing that, you'd have to be there yourself. That is to say, dead."

"I'm sure he only went into hiding because he knew I meant to find him and kill him. Now he thinks he's eluded me absolutely, but—I mean to follow him." Holbrook nodded. "Yes, of course, dead."

Martinez was tapping one of the pencils on the tabletop. "Is it . . . are you certain it's worth that? He *is dead*, after all."

Holbrook wiped his damp palms down his thighs. "Nothing else is worth anything."

Martinez stared at him expressionlessly for several seconds. "I imagine you're aware that people die every day, hm? Quite a lot of them, actually. Before we go any further, let's see if we can get a trace on your man."

He stood up and opened a polished wooden cabinet in the forward wall, and lifted out a square wooden board and a glass jar with a screw-top lid. When he set them on the table, Holbrook saw that letters were printed on the board in a circle, and the jar contained a dozen or so little shiny black insects—peering uneasily, he saw that the scurrying things were earwigs.

"This works better, for a cold call, than the traditional board and sliding planchette," said Martinez, resuming his seat. "There has to be motion, and the bugs have virtually no wills of their own to interfere with the spirit's promptings." He unscrewed the lid of the jar and quickly turned it upside-down on the center of the board, as if he were playing bar dice.

"When I lift it," he told Holbrook, "you say your man's name. It has to be your voice."

Holbrook bared his teeth. "I don't want to talk to him, *converse* with him! Can't you—"

Martinez held up his free hand. "If he answers, we'll hang up. We just want to see if he answers."

Holbrook blew air out through his lips. "Okay. Go."

Martinez snatched the jar away, and Holbrook said, "John Atwater" as the wiggling creatures spread out across the board. Holbrook slid down the bench away from them.

Several of the earwigs had simply stopped, and a few others had crawled off the board and begun exploring the tabletop. None of them moved in any evidently organized or purposeful way. Holbrook wanted to brush back the ones closest to him, but was afraid it might interfere with the procedure.

After a full minute of watching the bugs in tense silence, Martinez said, "No, there's no response from your man. He may be just gone. Ah—wait a moment." He stared at the insects still on the board, and then lifted a hand to point down at several that had clustered near the letter H in the last few seconds. "Aha! I know where he was, as it were, recently, so to speak. It makes sense, since he died in Los Angeles."

Martinez sat back with a sigh, and smiled at Holbrook. "I think we may come to an arrangement. And if we can, I won't require payment in money."

"So you'll . . . assist?"

"Advise. Guide. Expedite, possibly."

Expedite? thought Holbrook. But how can I object? He's being generous. "Oh. Yes." He exhaled. "Well, I need to know . . . the geography of the place, the customs, if they have customs. How ghosts interact, what I can do." Holbrook spread his hands. "Everything."

"Yes. Well it's not a particular place; it's more like a lot of different realities simultaneously occupying the same space, just as all sorts of radio frequencies occupy the same air. You find that you've tuned in to one, and you're unaware of the others. But they're all generally described as a vast dome, with new arrivals appearing on the top, and then gradually making their way outward—down the sides. Spirits of Western cultures have traditionally referred to these consensual realities as Purgatory, though these Purgatories don't seem really to correspond to the Roman Catholic idea of that state."

"Consensual realities," said Holbrook, "and I'll tune in to one of them." He frowned doubtfully. "Can decisive things happen in a consensual reality?"

Martinez said drily, "You'd be surprised how much of the substance of *this* world is consensual. Yes, I believe decisive things can happen. Relevant to your purpose, it's generally thought that a mirror can destroy a ghost—not here, but there. It makes a sort of sense; a reflection in a mirror would *be* substantially the ghost who looked into it. They hardly consist of any more than their self-projected appearance, and that frail quantity can apparently jump across to the observed image in the mirror, and the original ghost-figure fades— and if you shatter the mirror then, while his image is in it, you shatter him. There'll be nothing left of him to go on to definition."

"Definition . . . ?"

"That's what they call it when they move out of my perception."

"So a mirror can destroy one."

"They believe so."

"And I can find a mirror there?"

"Not a real mirror, no. There's nothing actually *real*, there. But I suspect that if you hold up your empty hand, or two hands with your fingers outlining a rectangle, and *say* it's a mirror, with some confidence, you may be able to make an adequate substitute appear."

Holbrook frowned. "That's weak."

"Yes," said Martinez. He nodded toward the board on the table. "Your quarry is out of my Ouija range, we got no answer—but the H those bugs gathered around is the distinctive dial-tone, you might say, of a specific Purgatory. There's a fairly articulate, coherent ghost there who calls himself Hubcap Pete. I can generally raise him. Unlike most of his kind, he has been a resident, if you will, of his particular Purgatory for at least ten years of our time, and his gets a lot of local expirations—I think he lived in Los Angeles, or died there anyway. When you, er, arrive, he'll probably be willing to explain the place and its ways to you."

Arrive there, thought Holbrook with a shiver. *When I arrive there.* He forced a casual tone into his voice and said, "He doesn't stray from the top of the *dome,* this Hubcap guy?"

"I believe he travels all over it, actually. There are apparent highways. He's forever driving a virtual car of some sort. In fact, I suspect it's his attention that sustains this particular Purgatory gyre or wavelength. Now listen carefully, and remember—for this expedition, you and I will be able to communicate via Ouija software, just as we'll shortly be communicating with him, and the payment I ask is that you find out who Pete was when he was alive. Where he lived, what his name was, when he died, as much as you can learn."

"He won't tell you himself?"

"No."

"Why do you want to know who he was?"

"Why, I want to lay flowers on his grave, don't I? Adopt his dogs, finish his crossword puzzles? What do you care? Only do this for me."

Holbrook sat back and closed his eyes for a moment, resting his head against the curtained window behind him. "Okay." He opened his eyes when he heard Martinez tapping the computer keyboard. "You can get online out here?"

"No," said Martinez absently, "there's no DSL out here, and with satellite internet the ping time is annoying." He glanced up. "Not the sort of online you mean, anyway. And this has to be done well away from populated areas, in any case—Pete is what they call an over-easy spirit, meaning that he died while he was actually engaged in contact with the afterworld. He already had one foot in the door, you might say, half his weight there, so the crossover wasn't as traumatic and damaging for him as it is for most ghosts. He still has a good deal of mental power. We'll see to it that you're an 'over-easy' too. But such ghosts are dangerous to summon. Sometimes lethal."

Holbrook managed a smile. "He might kill me?"

"Unlikely. You seem firmly in touch with your surroundings, if a bit stressed at the moment. But you'll feel the mental impact when I get Pete on the line, and 'over-easy' ghosts like him have been known to bump a living soul right out of its body, if it was shaky or inexperienced, and take its place. The ancient Jewish mystics called such entities *dybbuks*. I'm fairly sure that my man Pete would never do that deliberately, but such ghosts *are* drawn to weak souls. Hence my remote location. Nobody should ever use Ouija in a populated area."

"So I should do my dying here?" *Tonight?* Holbrook thought. He was all at once aware of his heartbeat, the pulse in his temples, the seesaw flex of his lungs.

Martinez was still tapping away at the keyboard. "Hm? Oh—yes, definitely, if I can get hold of Pete." He nodded toward the door. "It's a big desert, no morgue for you. Part of the service."

Holbrook swallowed to quell a surge of nausea. It *is* worth it, he told himself. And after I've broken the mirror with Atwater in it, I'll look in a mirror myself, and it'll break when I disappear and it hits the pavement. If I can conjure up a couple of mirrors.

"Is there pavement in Purgatory?" he asked.

Martinez looked up impatiently. "There seem to be streets, so I suppose there's pavement. The spirits say they walk around. It's just consensual gravity, too, at least at the top of the dome. Ghosts don't have near enough mass to have any measurable weight."

"Ghosts have *any* mass?"

"Of course they do, or they'd move at the speed of light." Martinez pushed his chair back. "Now then—I'm about to call Hubcap Pete. He communicates via some sort of keypad on his end, but in order to leapfrog over the barrier from the other side, his words need to have some physical manifestation here, motion, like my scurrying bugs or the moving planchette on traditional Ouija boards; pixels on a monitor aren't macro enough. So I route him through TTS, text-to-speech software, and sound waves in air and vibrating eardrums are agitation enough to do the trick. He'll be a synthesized voice, lacking intonation and stress. And in order to maintain himself, his precariously autonomous self, he always talks in rhyme when he's talking across the mortal gulf. A counterentropy move, you see. You remember how you'll pay me?"

"Information about who Hubcap Pete was," said Holbrook, "when he was alive."

"Right. Let's have at it then—put off, and sitting well in order, smite."

Martinez stood up and opened the wooden cabinet again, and a moment later he stepped toward the door, hefting a big black gun. Holbrook's heart was thumping hard in his chest as he made himself look squarely at the weapon, and he saw that it was a pump-action 12-gauge shotgun, with a pistol grip instead of a shoulder stock. Only after a shocked moment did Holbrook notice that the man had also fetched from the cabinet a roll of Saran Wrap.

"Would you bring the laptop?" Martinez said. "Obviously we do this outside."

Holbrook couldn't immediately stand up. "Whoa, with a *shotgun?* Wouldn't something like . . . I don't know, cyanide . . . ?"

"Induce confusion and unpredictable behavior? Yes. Almost certainly break your connection with Pete? Yes. Instantaneous is better." Martinez opened the door, and a hot breeze swept into the trailer, spicy with the scent of sage. The light outside was the amber glow of sunset. "You can still reconsider, naturally, and simply pay me for this past twenty-minute consultation."

Holbrook thought of Shasta as he had last seen her—she and John had been in L.A. for a week in 2006, and she had invited him to join them for an early dinner at Mastro's. Shasta had been thinner than he remembered, with new lines under her eyes and down her cheeks. John had looked fit and tanned, and had paid the whole tab with a Platinum American Express card. Shasta had kissed Holbrook, perhaps wistfully, when they left.

And he remembered the murder trial—one of the exhibits had been a mannequin wearing a brown-spotted sweater of Shasta's, with wooden dowels projecting like arrows from the chest to indicate the paths of the bullets.

"No," he said, getting to his feet and reaching for the laptop, "I'm on board." He followed Martinez out through the door. The rattle of the rooftop air-conditioner was louder outside.

Martinez led him around to the shaded far side of the trailer, where a wrought iron table and four chairs stood on a cleared patch of sandy dirt. The table and chairs had once been painted white, but were flecked with rust now. Beyond them stood a Jeep half covered by a blue tarpaulin, and beyond that the desert stretched away in copper light and long shadows toward the distant mountains.

"You take the chair facing away from the trailer," Martinez said. He laid the shotgun and the roll of Saran Wrap on the iron table, then took the laptop from Holbrook and sat down on the other side.

Martinez opened the computer and tapped some more keys, and now he spoke into it.

"Pete? Come over here." The desert breeze drew low veils of sand around the sides of the trailer, and a hawk hung in the purple sky. "Pete? I want you to meet a fellow."

Holbrook sat down slowly. He found that be was hoping Hubcap Pete wouldn't make the connection, and then he despised himself for that hope. *She* died, he thought; can't you?

Abruptly his view of the table and Martinez faded; a moment later he could see clearly again, and he hastily wiped his mouth and blinked around, reminding himself of where he was.

"He's on," whispered Martinez. "You felt his arrival, didn't you?"

Then a flat, not-quite-continuous voice buzzed out of the laptop's speaker. Holbrook had to lean closer to hear it clearly.

"I know why your boy came . . . he's been looking for some dame." After a pause, the voice went on, "Has he found her . . . is this just fan mail from some flounder."

"No," said Holbrook, glancing from the black cover of the computer to Martinez, and back. He was sweating, still disoriented. "No, I'm looking for the man who killed her. His name is Atwater, John Atwater."

Martinez whispered, "They prefer not to use—"

"We mostly don't tell each other who we were," said Hubcap Pete. "It's too much of a lure."

"—their real names there," Martinez finished.

For a moment the air conditioner rattled more loudly in a gust of hot wind.

Holbrook pressed on, "How do I find a ghost, a spirit, there? Will you be able to direct me?"

"You do not—" began the voice; and then it stopped.

Holbrook held his breath, staring at the laptop on the iron table. After a few seconds he let his breath out and looked up at Martinez, raising his eyebrows.

"Wait a bit," said Martinez. "He's probably just going through a tunnel." He met Holbrook's puzzled gaze. "I told you he drives all the time. Do you have any identifying marks? For when I call you. Spirits there won't know your name."

Holbrook hesitated, then lifted his shoulder. "A tattoo. It says 'Apart.'"

"That'll do fine. It'll probably make itself visible. You're vulnerable if the ghosts know your real name, so don't—"

But the voice from the computer was speaking again: "Well . . . was that all you wanted me to tell."

"We didn't hear your answer," said Martinez to the computer. "Please repeat."

"I said, You do not need me to direct . . . call him like you called me collect."

"No," said Holbrook, "I mean if I'm there, where you and he are, can you tell me how to find him there?"

"Ha ha ha," came three measured syllables from the computer's speakers. "You would have to die . . . to get here guy."

Martinez pushed back his chair and stood up. "That's his plan, Pete. He wants to be an over-easy ghost, like what you are." He picked up the roll of Saran Wrap, unreeled a couple of feet of the clear film and tore it off.

The synthesized voice said, "Is that true . . . what he says about you."

Martinez draped the film over the computer and tucked the edges under it. He gestured for Holbrook to keep talking.

"That's right," Holbrook said hoarsely.

He doesn't want to get blood and brains on his computer, he thought. He's going to shoot me from behind; from up close—there's hardly four feet between the trailer wall and the back of my head. More loudly, he went on, "Yes, it's true."

The voice from the computer was not muffled by the plastic film. "Not likely you find him among all the expansions . . . in our father's halfway house are many mansions."

Martinez spoke. "We believe he's in the same mansion you're in, Pete."

After a pause, "Please think again son," said the voice from the laptop's speaker, "this thing can't be undone."

Martinez leaned down and whispered to Holbrook, "Keep him talking. This won't take but a moment." He reached over and picked up the shotgun, then stepped behind Holbrook's chair.

Holbrook's hands were shaking, and he stuffed them into his jacket pockets. His vision seemed to have narrowed, and a high keening wailed in his mind, and he couldn't take a deep breath.

He made himself think again of the mannequin with the dowels protruding from its chest.

"I want to do it," he said. "Now. While I'm talking to you."

He heard Hubcap Pete's flat voice say, "You're a chump . . . but hang onto my shirt tail sonny and jump."

From behind him, Holbrook heard the fast clatter and click of a shell being chambered in the shotgun.

Holbrook's teeth were clenched so hard that his jaw hinges ached. This call is collect, he thought. This is on your credit card, John. You're paying for all of this.

"I'm holding on," he grated. "Don't drop me."

Two endless seconds passed.

Then with a silent but incomprehensibly profound cleaving he was kicked forward, out across the desert, and the low hills and scrub brush hurtled past beneath him. He tried to blink against an expected headwind, but in fact there didn't seem to be any air around him at all, and he didn't have eyelids in any case. He realized that his vision swept a full 360 degrees—he perceived the mountains rushing up at him and the trailer receding in an infinite distance; and the dark sky and the racing sand were simultaneously visible too.

There was no sound at all, until he heard a voice say, "I'll drop you near the town square,"—and it was a human voice, gruff and deep, not the synthesized voice any longer.

Holbrook stumbled, and a street tilted itself so that he didn't fall.

"Want it or not?" said a dim figure sitting behind a counter in front of him. On the counter was a beige plastic knob the size of a quarter, with string wrapped around a short metal post on one side of it.

Holbrook looked around quickly, and he knew there was air because he was panting; and he had eyes again, because he was blinking. The breeze smelled of diesel fumes and was very cold; and though he saw that he was now wearing only a damp T-shirt and ragged cut-off jeans and sneakers, it was not the chill, but relief—to see that he actually had a body—that made him shiver. He stood in a narrow street between tall buildings; at one moment their walls were featureless, but as he shifted his head he saw that they were peppered with tiny hinged windows all opening and shutting rapidly, and then the walls were smooth again. Looking up, he saw gray clouds churning in the gap between the angular rooftops.

He could feel a rapid heartbeat in his chest. I'm okay? he thought tentatively. I still exist, at least.

He turned back to the figure that had spoken—it was apparently a woman, almost completely hidden under a profusion of multicolored shawls—and he pointed at the little knob on the counter.

He found that he was able to speak. "What is it?" he asked dizzily.

"I think it's a yo-yo," the figure answered.

Holbrook picked it up, and for a moment it was as light as a shred of styrofoam; then his hand sagged as it assumed several pounds of weight. If it was a yo-yo it was awfully small, and one side of it was missing.

A white-haired man in khaki shorts and a Polo shirt jostled Holbrook and leaned in over the counter, and said something to him that sounded like "Take it apart."

Holbrook laid the plastic knob back down on the counter and stepped back, across a two-inch sidewalk into the street. "Not," he said carefully, "today. Thank you."

The pavement felt spongy for a moment, but when he turned and began walking, his sneakers scuffed solidly against it.

A cold hand caught at his elbow. He turned and saw that the old man in the Polo shirt had followed him and was insistently waving what appeared to be a white patent leather boot with an antenna sticking out of the top. "I think it's for you, Apart," he said.

Holbrook peered more closely at the object and saw that it was an old Motorola mobile phone from the 1980s. He took it from the old man and held it up to his ear.

"Uh," he said. He had not stopped panting. "Who is—"

"Rhyme, remember," interrupted a voice from up near the antenna. "Apart, this is Martinez. Type an answer in whatever sort of keypad you see. It has to rhyme, remember. Apart, this is—"

Holbrook held the bulky old instrument away, and he saw that the keys on the inner side of it bore letters but no numbers.

He tapped the keys and the space bar for GUY JUST GAVE ME THIS PHONE and then IM NOT ALONE

He gasped when he tapped the E key, for in that instant the gray daylight was extinguished and he could see only a dark plain with one spark in the center of it; but a moment later the narrow street surged back into visibility around him, and the old man in the Polo shirt was still frowning at him.

"Ah!" came Martinez' voice from the phone's speaker, "good, good! Give that person some money for the phone, keep it with you if you can. But spell out words how you want them pronounced—and you don't have to rhyme when you're talking to others of your—now—sort. Find Pete."

The phone was silent. Holbrook dug in his pants pocket and pulled out a roll of bills. For a few seconds the denominations were hard to read, then he saw that they were all hundred-dollar bills. He peeled one off, with difficulty, and handed it to the old man.

"Did you call me . . . Apart?" Holbrook asked. He flexed his hand, which was tingling as if he had slept on it.

The old man scowled and pointed at Holbrook's shoulder; and when Holbrook glanced sideways and down, he saw that the black letters of his tattoo were clearly visible through the T-shirt's damp, threadbare fabric—the letters even seemed to be bigger.

Holbrook took a deep breath and let it out, and the cityscape seemed to settle down, the silhouettes of buildings and streetlamp poles straightening out and subsiding to vertical.

Now other figures were visible in the shadowed street—two children were hopping past, each with one leg in a canvas sack, though as they receded they looked more like one three-legged child, a couple of shadowy young men shook hands in a doorway opposite, and kept on doing it; a cluster of teenage girls hurried by with faint cries like parakeets, and after a few steps he lost sight of them and could see only an old woman hobbling away—and Holbrook became aware that the old man in khaki shorts was still frowning up at him.

"I got a Bluetooth!" said the old man. "But it's fake, I made it out of candy wrappers." He stepped back. "You think you're so big. You say you got this, and you got that, and you got this shiny telephone that works."

Holbrook's teeth were cold in the chilly breeze that funneled down the street, and he closed his mouth.

"Uh," he said finally, "what? The telephone? You gave it to me." The two young men were still shaking hands, with no sign of stopping soon, or ever. He added, "And I gave you a hundred bucks for it."

"Monopoly money. And the call was for you." For a moment the man's hair was dark brown, and slicked back in a 1950s-style ducktail; then it was sparse and white again. "I never get calls. I'm as good as you."

The mobile phone had softened in Holbrook's grip—his fingers were sinking into it, wetly, and he opened his hand and let it fall to the cobblestones. It broke into quivering pieces like an upended panful of vanilla pudding.

"Holy Toledo," exclaimed the old man. "Now you got no phone at all." He took Holbrook's hand and led him several yards down the street, past the shoulder of a building on the left and into brighter light.

Holbrook freed his hand and stopped. They were in one corner of a broad square now, between stark concrete Bauhaus-style buildings with black windows and empty gray balconies. A few evidently human figures were visible near a fountain out toward the center of the square, and a bridge like a Roman aqueduct was visible between two of the buildings on the far side, under a turbulent ash-colored sky.

Holbrook quailed at the volume of the open space, after the close walls of the street behind them.

"Do you," he said quietly, "know a guy called Hubcap Pete?"

"Sure. Watch the bridge there and you'll see him. Can I have another hundred bucks?"

"In a second." Holbrook peered at the bridge in the distance, but though he saw several rectangles like semi-trailers moving across the top of it, he didn't see any sort of car.

"I need to find somebody," he went on. "How do I find somebody, here? No, not Pete, somebody else—his real name is John Atwater." He pulled the roll of bills out of his pocket and tugged one free.

The old man snatched it from him. "The stud," he said, nodding. "You want to find the stud."

"Is that what he says?" Holbrook's face was real enough to feel suddenly hot. "He's a liar, he abused his wife—"

His companion giggled and looked around, though none of the other figures were nearby. "No, it's how you find a stud—you knock along the wall, right? Boom boom boom boom rap! There's no use putting a nail in the plaster if there's no stud behind it. You knock in all directions till it sounds different, and you know that's where it is."

"Oh!" Holbrook exhaled and made himself relax as he stuffed the rest of the money back into his pocket. "How do I . . . *knock on the wall*, then?" The old man's face wrinkled in a baffled frown, and Holbrook went on quickly, "I get it, it's like knocking on a wall to find the wood, the stud, behind the plaster—so how do I do that to find somebody here?"

"Well you call his real name, don't you?" the man said irritably. "What did you think? The fountain there is the top of the bell, you can face in all directions from there."

"Okay. Thanks. Uh, keep the change." Holbrook began hesitantly shuffling forward, away from the high walls.

Behind him, the old man shouted, "You got a shadow! *I* got no shadow!"

The pavement of the square was bricks fitted together in a herringbone pattern, and when Holbrook glanced down, he saw that there was indeed a blurry patch of shade on the red bricks around his sneakers. Well, he thought, I'm an over-easy ghost. I bet I'm not likely to turn into a three-legged child or a group of teenagers.

The sea of bricks was perceptibly rippled in concentric rings around the fountain; the ripples bent around the corner of the building behind him. Holbrook made his way out across the square, stepping carefully over the humped rows of brick. The ridges were lower toward the center of the square.

Water cascaded from the bowl at the top of the white stone fountain and fell down through rings of stone petals into a wide pool with a knee-high coping. Children were splashing in the pool, but Holbrook had already developed a reluctance to look too closely at the inhabitants of Purgatory.

The spray from the fountain was stingingly cold when Holbrook had got to within a yard of the pool, and he held out his hands and tried forcefully to imagine a quilted jacket to pull on over his clinging T-shirt—a well-remembered jacket that he had once owned, red nylon, with an overlapping zipper—and for a moment a wisp of red fog curled around his fingers before blowing away.

Abandoning the effort, he hugged himself against the wind and turned away from the fountain. "John Atwater!" he called across the square.

He felt no change, and there was no response, not even an echo from the Soviet-looking apartment building fifty yards away. He was still shivering, and now his leg itched and he couldn't scratch it properly through the denim.

He edged several steps to the right, and tried calling Atwater's name again. Again there was no response, though the children in the fountain splashed water on him, having perhaps heard only the last two syllables of his call.

He didn't waste breath in cursing them, but stepped a yard farther to the right, and this time called the hated name toward a tall cement cube that might have been a prison. No faces appeared at the narrow windows, and there was still no echo. Holbrook paused to scratch his leg again, though the itching persisted.

Holbrook was sweating in spite of the cold. What if he's not here? he thought. What if I died for nothing?

After six more shuffling, shivering, hoarsening tries, he was facing the gap in the buildings through which he could see the distant bridge—and now he saw a brightly lime-green car moving across the span. Even from this distance he could make out its tall tailfins, and while he watched it move, all the frail traces of other colors vanished from the drab cityscape.

And when he again cried, "John Atwater!" the warehouse to the left of the gap quivered on its unguessable foundations, and for a few moments it was a one-story brick building with curtained windows— and, as if borrowing color from the passing distant car, green-leafed magnolia trees stood on either side of the open front door. And it seemed closer.

Then it was just the warehouse across the square, its streaked concrete walls and spinning rooftop air vents as solid-seeming as before.

Ping, Holbrook thought.

He had recognized the briefly visible smaller building; it was Chasteen's, the restaurant in which the six of them used to spend long evenings over bock beer and Turkish coffee. On the last night they had all gathered there, shortly before deciding to get the group tattoo, Holbrook had drunkenly recited to Shasta two lines from an A. E. Housman poem—*May will be fine next year, as like as not: /Oh aye, but then we shall be twenty-four.* And in fact they had both been twenty-three then, and by the following May Shasta was married to John and living far away.

Find the stud, Holbrook thought; he's in that direction. He stepped away from the fountain and hurried across the square toward the street that opened beside the warehouse.

As he stepped over one of the higher curved pavement ridges he glanced down, and then paused. The uptilted bricks had fallen aside at one point, and he noticed a square gray box wedged in the gap. He took a moment to crouch and peer at it—it was a model of a building, with tiny windows on its sides and a cluster of miniature air-conditioning ducts on its roof. It didn't move at all when he reached down and tugged at it, and he only succeeded in crushing in one side with his thumb, so he straightened and hurried away.

The street alongside the warehouse was paved with asphalt, and broadened out as it extended away from the square. Within a block it took on a residential look—the buildings on either side were only two or three stories tall, set well back from the curbs, with bay windows and forests of TV antennas on the roofs, and many of the front yards were cluttered with various sorts of litter, among which Holbrook noted mismatched couch cushions and piles of broken crockery. People were picking through the stuff, and Holbrook concluded that these were yard sales. He could hear someone down the street trying to get a car started, and he caught different smells on the air now— tobacco, and corn tortillas, and chlorine. A profusion of shoes with the laces tied together swung like little pendulums on street-spanning cables, and beyond them the monochrome silhouette of an airplane moved across the sky in quick jumps, like a spider.

Abruptly the asphalt shivered under Holbrook's feet, and he hopped sideways to keep his balance. A woman in a pink skirt and jacket who had been standing on the curb ahead of him was now sitting in the street; when the shaking subsided he hurried over to her, glancing nervously at the cables and shoes swinging overhead.

"We shouldn't be under the power lines," he said, extending a hand to help her up. "There might be aftershocks."

Blonde hair had fallen across the woman's face, and she brushed it aside with one hand and took Holbrook's hand with the other. Her face, blinking up at him in surprise, was smooth—Holbrook guessed that she was in her early twenties. When he pulled her to her feet, her weight was hardly more than he would have expected from just lifting her velvet skirt and jacket.

"Aftershocks?" she said, and Holbrook almost flinched, for her voice was like the squeak of iron nails being pried out of wood. "Where you been, honey? There aren't any earthquakes." She didn't release his hand, and squeezed it several times.

"So what was that?" asked Holbrook. He glanced upward again. "A bomb?"

"The bell has to stretch when it grows out, doesn't it? And it has to grow out to make up for the bits that fall off the bottom edge, where the gravity's real and hard. I stay up here." She was still squeezing his hand. "And there's no electricity in those wires, and they can't fall anyway." She looked down at his feet. "You're a diplomatic, aren't you, Mister Apart? A real big spender, didn't go through Customs." She laughed, a sound like glass breaking. "Listen, take me with you—I can have a body temperature with the right fella, and I know a million songs."

Holbrook realized that she had seen his faint shadow on the asphalt. "I don't know where I'm going, I'm just looking for a guy—"

"Don't take *him,* what do you want to take him for? You're not *queer,* are you? Take me!"

"I'm not taking anyone anywhere!" He tugged, but she still gripped his hand.

"Aww, why go alone? I could wash your hair, teach you to juggle, remind you of things—"

Holbrook looked around him at the street; the visible people had resumed picking among the junk laid out in the yards, and the starter motor was still whining farther down the street, and he remembered her saying *I stay up here.* "For God's sake, where is it you think I'm going?"

"Don't tease me, honey—everybody knows you over-easy fellas can jump right off the bell and start over again in real life, as a baby."

"What, like reincarnation?"

"That's it. We can be a couple while you do it. I like you."

"A couple—" Her jacket was unbuttoned, and he could see that she wasn't wearing anything under it. "A couple," he repeated.

Then, for a moment so brief that she didn't notice it herself, three wooden dowels stood out from her breasts, and when Holbrook jerked back he pulled his hand free of hers.

"I," he stammered, stepping away from her, "I've got something to do. I'm sorry." He turned and began walking quickly away down the street, the breeze chilling his sweaty face.

From behind him he heard her despairing wail, "I could have been your twin!"

He waved without looking back.

A moving shape in the street caught his eye, and when he had walked closer be saw that it was a gleaming black motorized wheelchair with a skeletal man elaborately strapped into it. The man's finger flicked back and forth on the control lever, and the wheelchair buzzed forward a yard, then back, then a yard to the side, and at one point Holbrook had to hop to avoid being bumped by the wide tires. Peering more closely, he saw that the man's eyes were tightly shut and that a pair of headphones were clamped onto the bald head. A faint darkness of shade moved back and forth on the pavement beside the wheelchair, but Holbrook couldn't think of anything to be gained by distracting the man, and he hurried past.

Before he had taken twenty long steps away from the bobbing wheelchair, he heard "*Apart!*" called from somewhere in front of him; and the source seemed oddly close to his face, though the nearest person was a man sitting behind the wheel of an old white Dodge Dart a dozen yards ahead. The starter motor chattered on, and the car shook, and smoke and fragments of birds' nests blew out of the exhaust pipe, but the engine still didn't start.

Over the noise of it he again heard a voice call the word tattooed on his shoulder. He blinked around at the preoccupied figures on the street, none of whom were close to him or looking at him, and then he walked over to the Dodge. The driver's side window was cranked down, and the man in the car was opening and closing his mouth, perhaps cursing.

"Excuse me," said Holbrook loudly, leaning down to peer in. The man behind the wheel was wearing a suit and tie, and his white shirt was blotted with sweat.

"It's an emergency, officer," the man gasped without looking up from the dashboard. His hand kept the ignition key twisted to the right, and the harsh noise continued. "My daughter's wedding—"

"Did you hear—" Holbrook began, then realized that this man couldn't have heard anything above the unceasing snarling of the starter motor.

"My daughter," the man said through clenched teeth. "It'll all be okay between us if I can get there."

Holbrook stepped back, shrugged helplessly, then turned and resumed walking down the street. He was leaning back slightly as he walked, though the street ahead didn't visibly deviate from level; the sensation was as if the whole world were tilting. The buildings on either side didn't quite stand up at right angles to the pavement now, but were tilted a few degrees in the direction of the square behind him.

Soon a low buzz was louder than the receding starter motor, and when Holbrook glanced to the side he saw a little girl on a skateboard slanting toward him across the mottled gray asphalt.

"You're the guy, I bet," she piped as she swerved to a stop beside him, her dark pigtails flying. "The guy the jukebox is calling for." She glanced at his shoulder and nodded, then waved toward a hot-dog-and-bun-shaped stuccoed structure ahead on the right; on a sign over its long windows was painted LOSSAGE SAUSAGE.

Again Holbrook heard the word *Apart* shiver the air in front of him, and the sound did seem to come from the direction of the odd little diner.

"Like that," the girl said. She was wearing a yellow gingham dress with white ribbons, and Holbrook thought she looked dressed up for a birthday party.

"Probably," he said. "Uh, do you know why it's doing that?"

"Somebody from the original world wants to talk to you, I guess. Everybody who's staying up here is retarded—you're smart to be heading downhill."

Holbrook looked back the way he'd come. "That guy in the car—*that's* not Hubcap Pete, is it?"

The girl shook her head solemnly. "No, Hubcap Pete never turns his big green car off. *That guy? Him?* He's been there for years—his car won't ever start, and you can't even talk to him. I've tried to, a lot. He's never gonna go down to graduation." She shrugged. "I probably wouldn't either, if I was him."

"Graduation?"

"You know, when you fly off the bottom edge of the bell and find out what grade you're in. I bet *he'd* just be in detention—he was real mean to his daughter."

Holbrook was glancing toward the diner, and so it was only in his peripheral vision that he saw the girl's silhouette flicker and become taller; when he looked back at her she was the little girl in pigtails.

She pushed off, crouching on the skateboard to gain speed downhill. "See you later," she called back, "if we're in the same class!"

Holbrook watched her ride away down the street, then sighed and began trudging toward the red-and-brown-painted diner.

He heard scratchy music from inside the place as he approached the screen door, and when he was still a couple of steps away from the threshold the door was pushed open as a heavyset man in a football jersey stumbled out, fell, and began rolling quietly down the pavement; Holbrook caught the door and stepped inside.

The interior was narrow, with red vinyl booths along the wall opposite the close streetside windows, and he could hear a tired disco rhythm from the glowing jukebox at the uphill end of the place. The warmer air smelled of sauerkraut. He stepped past half a dozen translucent figures slouched in the booths, and just as he stopped in front of the jukebox the vague music paused and a voice from the speaker said, "Apart."

He was not surprised to see that the buttons on the front panel were the twenty-six letters of the alphabet and a space bar. His hand was tingling again, but he stretched his fingers and then typed out, ITS ME WHAT OF THEE.

And when he pushed the E button for the last time, his narrow surroundings dimmed, and for a moment he again saw a broad dark plain with one spark visible on it, as he had when he'd tapped a message into the big mobile phone by the square; then the gaudy housing of the jukebox drove the glimpse away.

"You'll compromise yourself with such lousy rhymes," said Martinez's voice from the jukebox. "I'm glad I finally caught you— you're nearly out of range, I've been trying for days."

It's been days, there? thought Holbrook. He breathed deeply to shake off a wave of dizziness, wondering where his real body might be—his no doubt headless body. He quickly scratched his scalp here.

Martinez went on from the tinny speaker, "You haven't stayed in touch with Hubcap Pete, damn it. I was just talking to him, and now he says he's been the verifier there long enough, he's ready to jump."

Holbrook lowered his hand and forced himself not to think about a mound of newly-turned dirt in some remote Mojave desert arroyo. Don't look back, he told himself. *You* don't *need* Pete—finding Atwater is all that matters now, it's all that's left, and you've got a line on him even without Pete's help.

As if he'd read his mind, Martinez said, "Apart, Pete is the verifier— he's an alert spirit that's always circulating around that Purgatory, observing every district of it, validating it all. If he jumps, if he goes away, that Purgatory gyre is likely to wobble and then simply implode.

The moon may exist even if nobody's looking at it, but I'm afraid this Purgatory won't, if Pete stops looking at it."

Holbrook bared his teeth, and his face had suddenly gone cold in spite of the warm air. It can't implode before I find Atwater! he thought. And somehow show him a mirror, and then break it.

He thought rapidly for a few moments, then typed, I SHOULD TALK HIM OUT OF IT THEN YOUR SAYING AND WITHOUT ANY FURTHER DELAYING.

"That's much better. Yes. I probably won't be able to contact you again for a while, till you get back to the center, but I told him he should hold off because you had something important to tell him. Don't ask, I have no suggestions. And remember what you're doing for me in exchange for all this!"

In exchange for you blowing my head off, thought Holbrook. But, "I remember," he muttered, and he typed, WORRY NOT I HAVENT FORGOT.

The jukebox shook, and then there was just the listless disco music quivering in the speaker.

A lanky-haired young man smoking a cigarette had sidled up while Holbrook had been listening to Martinez's voice, and now he spoke up. "You and me," he said, "we can always get reincarnated if this place collapses. We're over-easies, right? Not like the rest of these losers." He drew on the cigarette, and the tip glowed.

Holbrook noticed that smoke was now leaking from the young man's chest and from under his jaw; and he was sure that if they were outside, the young man would cast no patch of shadow. You're an over-easy only in your dreams, kid, he thought.

Still, Holbrook wanted to know about this alleged reincarnation option. It would be an unlooked-for salvation to be able to live a human life again, after eradicating Atwater here.

Looking past his companion toward the door, Holbrook said, "You sure you know how, sonny?"

"Duh! I was in and out of courtrooms all the time. Ask anybody. You just jump off, or fall off, and when you're arraigned you plead *nolo contendere*—*nolo contendere* spelled backward is reincarnation."

"Uh—no it's not."

"Yes it is. I heard it on the radio."

Holbrook shrugged. This was useless, and his leg was itching again; walking would be a relief. "Well, I'll see you in a nursery sometime, maybe, back in the original world."

The young man followed him down the aisle to the screen door, but stayed inside when Holbrook stepped out onto the street.

"I'm, uh, not supposed to be out in direct sunlight," he muttered, edging back toward the booths. "Skin cancer."

Direct sunlight? thought Holbrook, glancing at the churning overcast sky; but he waved and started away down the increasingly tilted street in the direction the girl on the skateboard had gone.

He passed a row of 1920s-style bungalows, most of them draped in canvas tents as if for termite extermination, and then he appeared to be in a little business district—he saw car repair garages with huge balloons in the shapes of apes and Santa Clauses bobbing on the roofs, and neon-lit smokeshops, and a movie theater with a dozen inflated tube men out front flailing their long arms around the letterless marquee. Holbrook could hear screaming from inside, and he wondered uneasily what movie might be playing.

At one point he crouched as another earthquake—or dome stretching—shook the street. He held his breath, hoping it wasn't the first shock of this Purgatory collapsing; and when the pavement and buildings remained standing, he straightened and hastily called, "John Atwater!"

Ahead of him and to the left, the multicolored boomerang-shaped buttresses of a car wash vanished, and Holbrook saw the brick walls and curtained windows and sidewalk magnolia trees of Chasteen's. And he was able to take several steps in that direction before the mirage vanished and the car wash reappeared.

I'm getting closer, he thought tensely; Atwater may be only a couple of streets away.

He stepped into the recessed doorway of a pawnshop and held up his left hand with the thumb extended; his right hand was still tingling uncomfortably.

"I'm holding a mirror," he whispered. He tried to make himself feel the edges of a rectangle of glass, and squinted at the space between his fingers, hoping to see the shop door reflected in it. And for a moment he was holding a flat white object; it felt rubbery, but it was a vastly better result than the jacket he had tried to imagine beside the fountain in the square.

The object faded to nothing after a few seconds, so he shook his fingers, took a deep breath and tried again—this time the rectangle that appeared felt like hard plastic, and in it he saw Martinez's trailer in the Mojave desert.

"Getting there," he told himself after it faded, and he pushed out of the recessed doorway and resumed walking down the street. The pavement was now so steep that he had to set his feet carefully to avoid sliding—though when he glanced back the way he'd come, the street ascended straight as a ruler, with no evident change in inclination along its visible length.

Ahead of him now were terraces tilted toward him, and he guessed that if he were standing there they would seem to be level. The Purgatory bell was evidently subject to optical illusions.

Another street crossed this descending one, and he made his way to the corner and turned to the left, walking on pavement that now slanted down at his right. At least the tattoo parlors and bars that he was passing, though set higher on one side, were all vertical. The chilly breeze here smelled of gasoline and bananas. He walked along the downhill side of the street, swinging around streetlamp poles and watching the crumbling curb under his feet.

He was panting and shivering in the breeze, and when he looked up at the high side of the street and again saw the brick wall and curtained windows of Chasteen's, he paused, watching the little restaurant and waiting for it to disappear. And he had stared at it for nearly thirty seconds before remembering that he had not called *John Atwater* this time.

This time it was not a mirage—this was the place his call had shown him and led him to, as real as any other place in Purgatory.

$$\rightleftharpoons \text{II} \rightleftharpoons$$

IS HE *IN* THERE? thought Holbrook.

He forced himself to take one slow step after another up the asphalt slope.

Holbrook knew that his real heart was stopped and cold in an unmarked grave in the original world, but he could nevertheless feel a pulse pounding in his temples, and he was dizzy enough to keep his hands spread to the sides as he walked up to the higher curb.

He remembered the broad face he had dimly seen through clear plastic at the Los Angeles Coroner's morgue. It seemed a very long time ago.

Will I shortly be looking into that face?

Atwater had still been handsome and fit-looking when Holbrook had had dinner with him and Shasta at Mastro's in 2006. Holbrook had at that time been a proofreader at a throwaway advertising paper in nearby Culver City, and Atwater had pretended to be very interested in hearing all the details of the job, while Shasta had just looked out the window and taken rapid sips of her Manhattan. Three years later she had been in a roped bag in the Coroner's building.

Up on the level sidewalk now, Holbrook turned around and looked down at the sloping skyline of Purgatory. He could see towers and steeples at a distance of at least a mile; all of them were tilted toward him. Clearly he must be on the descending skirt of the bell—but he had noticed no curvature of the pavement since leaving the fountain in the square, no convexity.

He dismissed the puzzle and turned to face the front door of Chasteen's. The round stained glass window and the iron latch were exactly as he remembered, and the door swung inward when he squeezed the latch and pushed. Familiar smells of tomato sauce and fennel and garlic rode the puff of warm air from the lamplit interior, and he saw a pitcher of dark beer on the table the six of them had customarily occupied.

He had closed the door against the cold breeze outside and taken two steps across the wooden floor when a chair scraped at the other end of the dining room and a voice called loudly, "Excuse me, you got a problem?"

Holbrook braced himself and then faced the figure that was now standing back there by the fireplace; but even in the relative dimness he could see that it was not John Atwater.

"Dylan?" said Holbrook softly. "Dylan Emsley!" Immediately he wondered if he should have said Center, the tattoo Emsley had got, instead of the man's real name.

Emsley shuffled forward, slightly facing away from Holbrook but peering at him sideways. "What're you looking at?" he demanded. "You know who I am?"

He wore black jeans and a black denim jacket, and he still looked twenty-five—the age he had been in 2003, when he had died in a car crash on the Hollywood Freeway.

"Have you," said Holbrook hesitantly, "been here—all this time?"

"I'll eat where I please! And take as long as I want! You wanna start some shit?"

"Center! *Dylan,* damn it! I'm Tom Holbrook, remember?"

Emsley was now holding a short knife. "How about I cut your face for you? You like that?"

Holbrook's chest went cold, and he was about to try conjuring a mirror when a mellow voice spoke from behind him. "You've got to wash dishes again, Dylan—you still don't have money for the check."

Emsley paused and frowned, and Holbrook glanced back toward their old table—and the figure now sitting on the far side of the pitcher of beer was John Atwater, lean and confident in a well-tailored suit and tie. "Here I am," Atwater said, "back of the bar in a solo game, right? Do you remember how to sit down?"

It occurred to Holbrook that he had not sat down since his death, and he was suddenly afraid that he would fall through the chair or something if he tried. He simply stood and stared at the man across the table, remotely aware of Emsley's footsteps receding into some other room.

Holbrook had been hunting Atwater for six years, in the real world and now in this flimsy makeshift post-mortem one, and he had at last come to the moment of confrontation—but the denunciations he had composed in a hundred sleepless nights had fled beyond his recall.

Instead he just burst out, "You killed her!"

Atwater smiled vaguely. "I don't remember things so well. Wait—the APART tattoo—I know who it is, you're a janitor—don't tell me—Calvert, Pete Calvert. Are you going to sit? Killed who?" He rocked his head to peer vaguely around at the room. "Dylan Emsley was just here."

"I'm *Tom Holbrook,* and you killed *Shasta.* I loved her, she was the most precious person on earth, but *you,* with no value at all, you took her away and killed her!"

"I'm sure you loved something, we all did. Yes, you're right, I *did* kill her, I do remember. With a gun. She disrespected me." He nodded. "One does what one has to do—I don't blame myself. I was always true to my own conscience." The last sentences had a rote sound, as if he'd said them many times.

"Your *conscience*? You were always true to your, your *narcissism*." Holbrook inhaled deeply. "I killed *myself* to get here, to find you. You're worth less than nothing, but I can at least make you into nothing." More loudly, he went on, "I'm going to make you cease to exist, do you understand that?"

He waited a few seconds for an answer, but Atwater just blinked at him; so Holbrook concentrated on his rage and frustration and thrust out his hand. And now he was holding a solid flat rectangle, and the back side of it was matte gray.

Atwater cocked his head, looking at the thing. "What have you got?"

"It's a mirror, damn you. Look into it."

"It's not a mirror. I remember what mirrors looked like."

Holbrook tilted the thing and looked down, but didn't see a reflection of the other side of the room; on the face of the rectangle was a picture of a man holding a baseball bat.

"That's a baseball card," explained Atwater. "They used to come with gum."

From another room came a shout from Emsley: "Soon as I'm done here I'm gonna kick your ass."

Atwater laughed softly. "You killed yourself? And then walked all the way down here—to find me? Downhill was easy, wasn't it? But you can't get back up again, it's too steep, go ahead and try it. Dylan figured that out before he got all the way down to the fringes. Stay with us— he likes you, I can tell. You can help him wash dishes for eternity."

Holbrook threw the rectangle at the floor—it disappeared before it hit the boards—and then took two running steps and lunged across the table, his clawed hands reaching for Atwater's throat.

But his hands struck gravel and he rolled across a pile of old headless Barbie dolls in suddenly cold air, under the gray sky. When he sat up, he was facing a rising cement slope; he looked over his shoulder and saw Atwater standing in the back doorway of Chasteen's.

"This is our place," Atwater said, "Center's and mine." For a moment he was gray-haired and fat, wearing a bathrobe, and then he was again the dark-haired man in the business suit. "I think you better go think up a place of your own."

"Fucker!" came Emsley's voice from inside.

Holbrook struggled to his feet, slipping on the dolls, and humiliation and despair helped him imagine a handgun in his right fist. A moment later he was gripping a soft, blurry object; he concentrated, and it hardened and focused into the shape of a big-caliber stainless-steel revolver.

He pointed it at Atwater and pulled the trigger, but there wasn't even a click as the hammer rose and fell. He pulled the trigger several more times, as Atwater looked on with raised eyebrows, and finally he thumbed the cylinder release and swung the cylinder out. All six chambers had jelly beans wedged in them, four of them with tiny firing pin dents.

Holbrook tossed the gun away, and didn't hear it strike anything. "The bell grows out!" he said loudly. His face was wet, and cold in the chilly breeze. "This will be the fringe soon! You'll fall off—" He kicked some dolls aside and straightened up, flexing his hands, and went on, "*I* won't be here—I know how to be reincarnated! You think I killed myself with no way back? Hah!" He pointed down at his sneakers. "See that shadow? I'm an over-easy, I died in contact with Hubcap Pete and he told me himself how to be born again back in the original world!"

He had flung that empty boast in sheer angry bravado, but Atwater reverted to the old man in the bathrobe again, and said, "Tom, tell me how!" His eyes were wide and his lower lip hung away from his teeth. "Tell me how and I'll tell you where Fall—*Sh-shasta*—is!"

Holbrook sighed deeply. "You're lying," he said unsteadily, "she's been dead six years, she wouldn't still—"

"How long do you think Emsley has been dead? Yes, the bell g-g-grows out, but you only have to shift uphill a bit from time to time, to stay even. She's in a . . ." He paused and smiled craftily, and he was dark-haired and wearing the suit again. "No, you tell me how, first."

Holbrook considered thinking up some arduous procedure to tell Atwater, but decided against giving the ghost any moments of hope at all.

"*Well* . . ." he said, "no. I can find her the same way I found you, and I'll tell *her* how. She and I will do it together. We'll meet up again in the original world, while you stay here forever with Emsley."

And it may even be possible, he thought, hardly daring to let himself entertain the idea. Two of the ghosts here mentioned the possibility of reincarnation—maybe it's more than just a fantasy. *We can be a couple while you do it,* the woman in pink had said.

"We'll—we'll get a Ouija board," he went on, a bit shrilly, "and send you a wedding announcement!"

Atwater had stepped back, out of the gray light, his appearance flickering now between the trim executive and the fat old man. "I remember," he said quietly, "you always did hide behind that delusion." He closed the door, and Holbrook was alone with the scattered dolls in the sharply-tilted alley.

A sudden pain in the base of his spine let him know that he had sat down.

For some indeterminate time his mind was as empty as a fired shotgun shell. When thoughts began to occur, they were fragments: *That's it? . . . six years I've . . . impossible? even after . . . I gave up my life for . . .*

Then one thought was a complete sentence: *Shasta is here somewhere.*

He got to his feet. I can learn to make a real mirror, he told himself, and come back here then, but in the meantime, Shasta is here somewhere. I *must* be able to find her.

He walked along the alley in the direction he'd come from, and eventually came to what might have been the same street he had been following down from the square. He stepped in under the awning of a watch-repair shop and waited for a couple of mumbling pedestrians to pass, then took a deep breath and said, "Shasta DiMaio." And when the view of the street didn't shiver, he turned a few degrees to his right and said it again.

During the course of the next minute Holbrook shifted by short increments all the way around, saying her name over and over again, to the dark shop window and out to the street again, but there was no slightest ripple in his vision.

His chest had gone cold, and he was considering making his way back to the imaginary Chasteen's and asking Atwater to tell him where Shasta was, when a bitter thought occurred to him.

Facing out into the street, he made himself say, "Shasta Atwater," and at once his view of an abandoned gas station across the street was momentarily replaced by a glimpse of a building he knew he recognized. The yellow sign over the door and wide windows was obscured by spreading acacia branches, but the place was . . . Book City, a bookstore on Hollywood Boulevard that had closed in the 1990s. Holbrook couldn't recall ever having gone there with Shasta.

When his vision cleared, a thirty-foot long Chinese dragon was being paraded down the street, animated by a dozen running men inside its framework, and its bright orange catfish-whiskered face bobbed and swung as firecrackers popped on both sides of the street and threw shreds of red paper like rose petals—but before it had passed Holbrook, the painted fabric skin had evaporated, leaving only a line of men trudging downhill with long poles under their arms. Holbrook sprinted across the street after they had passed, and when he glanced back he saw that even the dozen men had disappeared.

"Shasta Atwater," he said dizzily, and again for a moment he saw the bookstore ahead of him.

He held onto a streetlight pole as he rounded the corner into a new street, but he didn't immediately let go of it and hurry onward.

Only two or three close buildings stood in this direction, because the street ended a dozen yards ahead in a tangle of cracked pavement and twisted rebar. Some hundreds of feet beyond the edge, Holbrook could see a diagonal cliff matching the slant of the street he was on, with a sawtooth pattern of low, ranch-style houses mounting up its sloped brink from left to right. One of the houses was missing the wall on this side, and he could just make out the intermittent blue glow of a TV set in one of the exposed rooms.

He walked carefully toward the broken-off end of this street, moving along the downhill-side curb, and when he got to within a couple of yards of the crumbled edge he clung to a stop-sign pole and peered across the gap. A couple of telephone lines spanned the abyss from this street to a street on the other side, and several telephone poles dangled from the swinging lines. Holbrook concluded that the gap was the result of a piece of the bell having fallen away, for if the bell had simply split here, the power lines would have been stretched and snapped.

He inched closer and looked down; and though he expected it, he was disoriented to see that the far surface, exposed now in cross-section, was only a few hundred feet thick, with some crystalline regularities along the slanted bottom edge implying more structures on that side. Below it was just more gray sky.

Did she fall? he thought; and he shouted, "Shasta Atwater!" across the divide.

But the vision of the bookstore flashed for a moment in his sight, over there on the far side, and he sagged in relief; then he thought, *How am I to get there?*

The wind that blew up from the gulf was colder than the breeze in the streets behind him, and he turned, shivering, to retrace his steps—I can walk back up the slope of the bell to a point above the gap, he thought, no matter what Atwater said about the difficulty of it—when he heard a two-tone car horn, and, peering ahead, saw a bright green convertible stopped in the intersection, facing uphill. It looked like some late-1950s Cadillac, long and wide, with exaggeratedly tall tailfins.

He paused, expecting it to dissolve as the Chinese dragon had done, then realized that the driver must be Hubcap Pete himself.

Holbrook made his way as quickly as he could along the tilted street back to the intersection. The car horn honked again, and Holbrook could see the driver clearly now—it was a white-haired man with a bushy moustache, in a Hawaiian shirt, and he was waving one tanned arm.

"Apart!" the man yelled. "Quit clowning around and get over here."

Holbrook heard another car approaching, and looked up the street. The white Dodge Dart he had seen earlier, its engine running at last, was barreling down toward the green convertible; it swerved around it, its tires squealing, and went bobbing away downhill.

Holbrook saw no other traffic, and he hurried across the incline to the driver's side of the convertible; and when the driver waved impatiently at the passenger side, he scrambled around to that side and got in and closed the door.

"You're—Hubcap Pete," Holbrook said as the engine roared and he was pressed back into the seat by sudden acceleration uphill.

"Right," the man said. "You didn't hang around at the square. Didn't that Martinez fellow in the desert tell you to?" The car slanted to the right onto a freeway onramp that Holbrook had not noticed on his walk down the street.

"No." Holbrook spoke loudly over the fluttering headwind. "Anyway, I was looking for a guy."

"Martinez said you have something important to tell me. What is it?"

Holbrook had forgotten that Martinez had said that. "Uh," he said helplessly, "don't jump. This place will collapse if you do."

"Huh. That was it? Well, don't worry, this place won't collapse if I have anything to say about it."

The freeway rose above the surrounding buildings, and when Holbrook shifted around in the seat to glance back, he saw a figure swinging from one of the abyss-spanning telephone lines; from this distance he couldn't be sure, but it seemed to be a heavy-set man with a bathrobe flapping around his bare legs. Holbrook's chest suddenly felt empty.

"Damn, I think—" he began.

"Yeah, that's your guy," said Hubcap Pete, nodding without glancing away from the lanes ahead, "crossing to the other side. You got the plumb bob?"

"Can you get over there?" Holbrook asked anxiously, still bracing himself on his left arm to stare back at the distant dangling figure. "He's going to kill her again!" He squinted at the sections of the edge that he could see. "Is there a bridge you could take?"

"That gap just happened a day or so ago. Bridges don't grow that fast." Hubcap Pete took one hand from the wheel and pointed at the dashboard. "The air-conditioner control knob."

Holbrook noticed that the knob was missing. "So? No, I don't have it. Can you—"

"We'll loop around the inside edge of the gap. Probably be there before he is, even if he doesn't fall. And he can't kill anybody, they're all dead already. Didn't that woman in the booth give it to you, up by the square, right after you landed?"

"Well, hurry. What, the goddamn control knob of your air-conditioner? No, nobody—" Holbrook paused. "Oh. Yeah, it had a string wrapped around the post. She said it was a yo-yo."

The freeway curved to the right, and Pete steered into the right lane and stayed on it when it split away and became an offramp; a red traffic light hung over the cross street ahead, and Pete slowed to a stop. Lush oleander bushes screened the view to the sides. Holbrook was breathing fast, and he thought this area of Purgatory smelled like a newly-opened jar of vitamin pills.

"She didn't know what it was," Pete said. "You're supposed to use it as a plumb bob." He glanced around the interior of the car and sighed.

"I'll make you another." Before Holbrook could ask why, Pete went on, "What did that Martinez guy tell you about me? I've dealt with him before."

"He said that you died while you were in Ouija contact with somebody . . . here," Holbrook said, waving around at the street and the bushes. He rubbed his left arm, which had gone to sleep from being braced on the back of the seat.

"Somebody here." Pete nodded, staring at the red traffic light. "Yes, it was a man I had killed. I was trying to . . . apologize?" He laughed shortly. "Explain, excuse myself? But his wife, his widow I should say, had not gone to bed after all, and heard me speaking to him at the Ouija board, and she realized it was me who had killed him. She fetched a gun and shot me in the back." He squinted sideways at Holbrook. "Martinez wants you to find out about me, doesn't he, and then report back?"

After a pause in which the light turned green, Holbrook nodded.

Pete made a left turn onto a broad street between old wooden tenements that rapidly and noisily extruded balconies and then retracted them. Shingles and scraps of lumber whirled away in the wind. "Did he tell you why he wants to know about me? My real name, the names of my family, friends, the woman who killed me? Most of them are probably still alive in the original world—I haven't seen any of them come through here, anyway. No? He wants *leverage* on me."

Holbrook tried to lift his hand in an *and?* gesture, but his arm was still numb.

Pete went on, "He wants to get me to interrogate new arrivals, to learn their poor little secrets—Social Security numbers and bank passwords so he can empty accounts before survivors even know a person's dead, learn where stuff's hidden, maybe get insider trading tips, get medical and legal details for possible blackmail . . . spirits here are so dumb that they'd tell me all those things, but I won't do it." He looked away from the street to give Holbrook a piercing glance. "Would you?"

"No." Holbrook thought about it. "I don't know. It'd depend on whether he could get me something I badly want, I guess, from his side." Holbrook mentally reviewed the agreement he'd made with Martinez, which looked impossible to keep since Hubcap Pete knew what it was. "Wouldn't you like revenge on the woman who killed you?"

Pete grimaced. "Hell no. It was redundant when she shot me—I killed myself, everything that was worthwhile in myself, when I killed her husband. I think I've finally figured that out, in my time here. That's the value of this halfway house, it gives spirits a little while to get straightened out, to reconsider stuff." He glanced at Holbrook, who was craning his neck to try to see over the rooftops, and added, "We're getting there, we're getting there."

Holbrook slouched back down in his seat, massaging his arm, and he thought about the spirits he had met here. "Do they ever reconsider? They don't seem very bright, mostly."

"Some do. That fellow in the Dodge Dart that drove past me back there, I think he's finally ready to make what frail amends he can to his daughter. I hope he catches up to her before she flies off the rim—she's pretty quick on that skateboard."

Holbrook recalled the little girl talking about the man who'd been trying to get the Dodge started, and he remembered catching a momentary peripheral glimpse of her as a taller person. "She said that when you fly off the bottom edge of the bell you find out what grade you're in. And one guy seemed to think you wind up in a courtroom. Martinez called it definition."

"It's not a bell," said Pete irritably as he passed a slow-moving horse trailer with half a dozen identical children's faces at the barred windows. "Purgatory's a flat disk, spinning. It's centrifugal force, not gravity, that makes it seem as if the outer sections are tilted down. And as the edges break away, new buildings grow up out of the central square's pavement, and move outward."

Holbrook thought of the miniature building he had seen sticking up out of a fissure between the bricks in the square. And I caved in one wall of it, he thought, trying to pull it out. Don't mention that now.

"So what does happen," he asked, "when you fly off the edge?"

"Well, I haven't done it *yet*," said Pete, "but I get the idea there's a *real* primary out there, with something you could say was like actual gravity. Like a solar system, and every spirit finds its proper orbit, depending on what it consists of, around something that radiates and reciprocates . . . good stuff. Joy, you know? Contentment. Intelligence. Communication. The ones in the closer orbits get brighter, but the ones in the remote, colder orbits shrink down to hardly anything." He shrugged. "Yeah, I guess it's like definition, or getting assigned to a class level, or a verdict in a courtroom. But really it's more like plain physics."

And pleading *nolo contendere* probably wouldn't get you any second chance, thought Holbrook. Even if it *did* spell reincarnation backward.

Hubcap Pete had steered onto another freeway onramp, and within a hundred yards it had risen high above the surrounding streets and buildings. Looking over Pete's shoulder, beyond the rushing rail Holbrook could see the wedge of gray-sky emptiness that cleaved the cityscape below, though from this distance he couldn't hope to see a figure clinging to a telephone line that stretched from one edge of the gap to the other.

"A couple of these, these spirits," he said hesitantly, "mentioned the possibility of reincarnation. Is that . . . something that can happen?"

"Yeah," said Pete, apparently angry, "it can, for distinct over-easy spirits like you and me. You want to know how?" Without waiting for an answer, he went on, "I'll tell you. You find a spirit here who's in Ouija contact with someone in the original world—they'll be holding telephones or wearing headphones or something, and have their eyes closed, is how you can tell, and they'll be moving something back and forth, like with shuffleboard or croquet, or they'll be working a Rubik's cube with letters on the squares. What they're really moving is the sliding gadget on a Ouija board over in the original world. And you snatch their headphones and put them on yourself, and grab the Rubik's Cube or whatever, so now it's *you* that the poor sap back in the original world is in contact with."

Playing shuffleboard or croquet, thought Holbrook—or jigging a motorized wheelchair back and forth.

He spread the fingers of his right hand. "So?"

"Your other hand is numb, isn't it?" said Pete. "I know how that is. You've heard of amputees who feel itchy and cold in the missing limb? They call that a phantom limb. Same thing here—except that you're a whole phantom body. And you'd like to be reincarnated into a *real* one again. Shit."

"What, you take over the body of the, the *poor sap* in the original world, bump his soul out? Martinez said that could happen. But that's not really—"

"That's *dybbuks*," interrupted Pete, "and it doesn't work very well.

I've seen 'em come right back here after a little while. No, when you're in Ouija contact with somebody in the original world, you can see all the souls near him—it looks like a big dark plain, and the souls show up as sparks. For real reincarnation, you look for two that are overlapping, and you take the smaller, weaker one—bump it aside and step in."

"The smaller one . . ." began Holbrook.

"Forget about it. It's not something you'd do, or I'm wrong about you."

"Wrong about me? You don't know anything about me at all."

"I know you're here to figure out whether to blame a girl or not. Same as me."

"You've got it wrong. I'm here to—"

"I know, I know, delete a guy. Tell me another, phantom boy."

Holbrook opened his mouth to reply angrily, but remembered that Pete was apparently taking him to where Shasta was; and he had noticed the oval passenger-side mirror, which was attached only by a clamp to the door he had his elbow on. He sat back, resolved to bide his time.

From up here on the freeway bridge, he could just see the central square and the fountain off to his right, and beyond them more streets radiating outward. In the middle distance another freeway bridge arched above the domes and chimneys. It was clear that Purgatory was indeed flat—he could dimly make out the irregular far edge, miles away.

"If we didn't have to get *your* business settled," growled Pete, "I'd right now be driving over all the freeways and main streets, always counterclockwise, to keep it all spinning; this car has mass, inertia, traction. If I don't go around and look at it all, it gets blurry, and if the spinning slows down, more pieces fall off. Like they been doing! That's why you need a plumb bob." He shook his head. "God knows what's become of the one I left for you in the square—I'll have to make you another."

As the freeway bridge began to descend, Holbrook caught a last glimpse of the gap to the left, and he saw that they were now on the other side of it; and the car's turn signal indicator began clacking as Pete slowed the car and drifted it into the right lane.

He took the next offramp, a narrow gravel-paved path, and the car slewed almost broadside-on before Pete wrestled it back in line. At the end of the track was a cement-paved road with deep diagonal tining grooves.

As Pete steered the car left, across the grooves, he said, "Your girl's down this way. You should try that exit in the rain."

Holbrook peered through the windshield at the crowded barns and windmills alongside the lanes in front of them. "It rains here?"

"You think those clouds are just for show? Shit. You want to see some real rain?"

"Just get us to the bookstore," said Holbrook shortly, staring out to the side now at a fenced field dotted with rusted iron statues of dogs He hoped any rain here was no more substantial than the roofs.

"Sure," said Pete, "never mind if half of Purgatory turns to mush or falls off." He lifted one finger from the steering wheel to point ahead. "Her bookstore place is coming up on the right. Hop out—I'll catch you again, after."

With luck there won't be any after, thought Holbrook; Shasta and I can live forever in the bookstore, as Atwater and Emsley appear to be doing at Chasteen's. As long as Purgatory doesn't collapse!

But, "Okay," he said as the car rocked to a halt and he saw the yellow Book City sign over the long windows. "Now get back on your usual route," he added anxiously as he got out and closed the door.

Just as the car started to move forward and speed up, Holbrook grabbed the passenger-side door mirror with both hands; he was yanked off his feet, but as he rolled to a stop on the gravel road, his bleeding hands still clutched the mirror, and the green car was accelerating away. A church steeple and a water tower bowed perceptibly as the car passed between them.

Holbrook sat up, wincing, and then painfully got to his feet. He was reassured by each ache and twinge, though, for they were sensations that real bodies had—Hubcap Pete's remark about a *phantom body* had scared him.

When he turned toward the bookstore, the front door was open and Shasta herself was actually there, standing on the threshold no more than ten feet away. She was wearing a blue denim jacket and skirt, and she was the youthful college student he had recited the Housman lines to at their last night in Chasteen's, not the tired woman who had kissed him after the dinner at Mastro's in 2006.

For several seconds Holbrook simply stared at her.

At last, "I don't want that," she said, and it shook him to hear her well-remembered voice again.

"No, you don't," Holbrook said quickly. "It's poison, don't even look at it. Shasta, it's me, it's Tom Holbrook!" He looked back, in the direction of the long gap in Purgatory's fabric, but he didn't see a tall man in a business suit or a fat old man in a bathrobe.

"This thing," he went on, bending down to slap the cone-shaped back of the mirror, "is to protect you from—" He shook his head. "Can I come in?"

"Tom Holbrook," she said. "Yes, that was your original name, wasn't it? I remember you. You were one of the ones who got a tattoo." With her free hand she pulled the right side of the jacket away, and he could see the *FALL* tattoo partly covered by a white tank-top. "That's my handle."

Holbrook glanced down at his own shoulder; his T-shirt had dried out and didn't cling now, and he tugged it down to expose his own tattoo.

"Apart," said Shasta. "That's right. I married . . . Things, didn't I."

"Don't think about that now." Holbrook bent to pick up the mirror, then crouched to grip it with both abraded hands. "Heavier than it looks," he said, lifting it. "Let me just get this inside."

Shasta stepped aside, glancing at the streamlined mirror housing Holbrook carried. "That'll probably make the shop move downhill faster," she said.

"Oh!" Holbrook paused. "I'll leave it outside."

"No, bring it in. Who do you want to poison? Whatever's in that thing might make somebody sick, but nobody dies here."

"Well . . . John. Things. And this is a mirror."

"A mirror. And you want to break it, after he looks into it, *steps* into it." She pushed back her dark hair and looked directly at Holbrook. "Why?"

"Do you, uh, remember how you died?"

"Yes, he shot me. Is that why you want to erase him? That's between him and me."

Holbrook had shuffled in through the door, and he set the mirror cone-up, facedown on the counter by the cash register. Tall close-set bookshelves made narrow corridors of the building's interior, and in one corner by the window stood a dusty piano with boxes stacked on it.

He turned around to face Shasta. "Do *you* want to show him the mirror?—and then break it?"

She smiled in evident bafflement. "No."

Holbrook stared at her for a moment. "I trust you won't object when I do it," he said, in a tone that came out more defiant than he had intended.

She shrugged and leaned back against a wall of bookshelves, and Holbrook noticed that none of the spines had titles. "Apart," she said, "there's something you should know about me."

"What's that?"

"I don't know, but you should know it."

The wall behind her flickered as gold-stamped titles now appeared on all the book spines; it seemed to be the same title on all of them, but Holbrook was standing too far away to read it.

"We can stay here," he said. "You and I, forever. If Things comes, I'll break him in the mirror."

Shasta blinked around at the shelves, humming to herself, and jumped slightly when her eyes fell on him. "I'm sorry, what was it?"

"I said I'll break him in the mirror. Things, John Atwater, your one-time husband." She was still staring at him blankly, so he added, "I'm Tom Holbrook, remember?"

She reached toward him, and he saw that her hand touched his arm, though he didn't feel it. "Wait," she said, "I remember, if I concentrate." She nodded several times and then looked at him with evident recognition. "Apart," she said; "Tom—you're dead now. You don't need me, you don't need the excuse of me anymore, there's no one to hide away from anymore."

To his surprise, he was suddenly angry. "I'm not hiding from him! I got this mirror to kill him! I'm ready—"

"Not from him. You never got married, did you? You were never that close to anybody."

"I wanted to marry *you*—you know that!—but you married *him*, and he *killed* you."

She smiled. "And after that? You never found somebody, even then? It's been a long time."

"Nobody could replace *you*—and then I couldn't think of anything but finding him and killing him, for what he did."

"Yes. Even after I was dead, I was still your excuse." She stepped away from the wall, and before turning to face her again he peered at the shelves. The title on all the books was *The House At Pooh Corner,* though as he watched, it changed to *Los Angeles Extended Area Telephone Directory.*

"Don't snoop," she said from behind him.

When he turned around, she was buttoning up her jacket. She gave him an empty look, and he wasn't sure she still recognized him. "I don't know if this has done you or me any good," she said, "but I believe I'm finally tired of recasting this place uphill."

Holbrook raised one spread hand in mute inquiry.

"I suggest we stroll down by the terraces," she said, stepping toward the door.

"Down's not a good idea," Holbrook began, lifting the mirror from the counter, but a cry from across the street made him spin in that direction.

For a moment it was a shabby old man in a bathrobe and bedroom slippers who was stepping out from between two cartoon outhouses; and then it was John Atwater in his suit, and the outhouses flickered behind him with a glimpse of Chasteen's.

"Apart!" Atwater called again.

Holbrook stepped out onto the street, hefting his mirror. "Right here." The cold wind was from downhill, carrying the scent of wet stone.

Atwater was staring at the gravel below his polished shoes, and he took two more steps and then halted. "You found her," he said, and his voice was pitched higher than before, "Just as I said. Now come through with your part of the bargain."

"Things!" exclaimed Shasta; Atwater didn't reply to that, though her voice shook him into a few seconds of bathrobe-clad decrepitude.

Then, restored to his suit and tie and dark hair but still staring at his shoes, Atwater said, "Does he really know Hubcap Pete?"

"Does who?" asked Shasta. "Oh, this guy? Yes, Pete drove him here, in his big green car. He said, *I'll catch you later.* Oh! And it's Apart, you remember, with the tattoo?"

"Look at me!" called Holbrook, raising the mirror.

Atwater glanced up, then quickly lowered his eyes again. "So you've got a real mirror now! But you owe me—*tell me how to do it!* You two can do it together, like you said, but you promised to tell *me* how."

Shasta glanced at Holbrook. "He never did know how to do it," she said. "But *I'm* going to the terraces."

"I mean *reincarnation*," shouted Atwater, wavering like a body viewed under agitated water. "He knows how to be born again in the original world." When his appearance came back into focus, he tipped a quick glance at Holbrook. "You *do* know how, don't you?"

"It—doesn't matter to you," said Holbrook, turning away from him to face Shasta.

She rocked her head downhill and raised her eyebrows.

He looked uphill, at the road ascending between silos and lines of barbed wire fence, then sighed and stepped downhill beside her. The mirror seemed to be getting heavier.

Logs had been half-buried crosswise in the road, and the two of them stepped carefully from one to another for a hundred sloping feet, and then there was level flagstone pavement, with an ornate iron railing on the downhill side and stairs to right and left. A few figures were visible on the stairs, all shuffling downward. The gray light was dimmer now—the overcast sky was lower, and closer in front of them, and marbled with black. The wind from below was damp.

"Tut-tut," said Shasta as she guided them down the stairs on the right, past an old man struggling to get a walker down the steps, "it looks like rain."

The tall buildings on either side looked abandoned—row upon row of glassless windows in streaked cement cliffs, tangles of fallen lumber and cables between close walls, unmoored satellite dishes swinging like wind-chimes. After Holbrook and Shasta had descended several levels, the railings on the downhill side of the landings were weathered railway ties bolted together.

At one point Holbrook glanced back up the way they'd come, and saw Atwater's round head peering down over the wooden beam one flight above them, his scanty gray hair fluttering.

Shasta had seen him too. "Like old times," she said, "except in those days I'd be walking with him, and it'd be you who was following."

Holbrook shifted the ever-heavier mirror to a more comfortable position, and didn't answer. He promised himself that he would soon ask her, plead with her, to turn back; but he was afraid that she would insist on going on alone, if he did.

Their way grew steeper, and instead of a slope of terraces connected by stairways, they were now descending something like a broad concrete fire escape. They paused to rest on one of the decks, stepping to the rail to get out of the way as half a dozen men in business suits trotted past them, following one of their number who carried a small flag.

Holbrook took hold of the rail with his free hand and looked down, and he saw that the wall widened out in a roofed gallery a flight or two below, but beyond that there was nothing but churning clouds—and he remembered his view of the broken-away gap with the telephone lines stretching across it.

And he recalled what Hubcap Pete had told him: *Purgatory's a flat disk, spinning. It's centrifugal force, not gravity, that makes it seem as if the outer sections are tilted down.*

We must be perpendicular to the souls in the central square, he thought. Still gripping the rail, he leaned out, now squinting straight up—the wall extended vertically as far as he could see, and in the misty distance up there it did seem to bristle with what must be rooftops and towers.

If the Empire State Building were ever to grow in the square, he thought, from here I'd see it sticking out horizontally.

"For God's sake," he said finally, crouching to set the mirror at his feet, and then massaging his arm, "let's go back up while we still can." Even without the burden of the mirror, his phantom thigh muscles ached as he forced himself to stand up straight against the increased gravity.

Shasta turned to him with a concerned look. "But Tom, we *can't.* You can't—even if you leave that mirror behind here. Nobody ever makes it back up, from this far down. Didn't you know that?" Holbrook heard labored shuffling on the next floor above them, and Shasta waved up toward it. "Yes, that's Things. *He* knows it—he only followed us because he believes you *will* tell him the reincarnation secret. I don't think he could *do* it—I don't think he'd stretch that far, as he is—but you're right not to tell him about it."

Spots of chill touched Holbrook's hands and face, and he stepped back under the deck overhead as raindrops splashed on the rail and began to darken the floor on that side.

"And rain makes the fringe heavier," Shasta added.

Holbrook was breathing fast, from panic as much as from cumulative fatigue. "Stretch?" he said. "Do *you* know how to do it? How to—be reborn in the original world?"

She nodded. "I've been here long enough, and sometimes I've listened and remembered—though I couldn't reach, either."

"Listen," Holbrook said, "I have a shadow. You can't see it now, but maybe you noticed it when everywhere wasn't so tilted and dark. I think you *could* reach, if you did it *with* me." He waved in the direction the trooping businessmen had taken, and lowered his voice. "People come down here—surely one of them will have headphones on, be in Ouija contact with the someone in the original world, eventually. If we just wait here."

"Here won't be here for long, I think." Shasta laughed softly. "And you'd kill a child—two children, real ones!—to get us lives again? You always did strike *poses,* Tom."

It looks like a big dark plain, Hubcap Pete had said, *and the souls show up as sparks. For real reincarnation, you look for two that are overlapping, and you take the smaller one.*

"Oh," Holbrook said. "Oh." He sat down beside the mirror. "Weaker and inexperienced, sure—it's the soul of a child that hasn't been born yet, that you bump aside. Take the place of."

"Yes. You hadn't guessed that part of it?"

"I hadn't thought about it." He shrugged hopelessly. "Pete said I wouldn't do it."

"What if I told you that one of those tourists who marched past us just now was wearing headphones?"

Holbrook peered down the long cement floor in the direction those men had taken. They had either gone up or down the stairs that lay at that end, but he would certainly be able to follow the rhythmic drumming of their footsteps either way.

And then what? Snatch the headphones and put them on, scan the sparks on that dark plain and reach out for one of them? To steal a second life for myself by eliminating an innocent one?

He sighed and shook his head.

"I made it up," said Shasta, starting toward the stairs. "None of them had headphones."

Holbrook got wearily to his feet, hefting the mirror, which now weighed as much as a bowling ball. "They weren't moving right anyway, now that I think of it. Pete said that people in contact kind of jiggle back and forth."

He followed her to the stairs, and as he struggled down the steps after her, he saw that the stairs ended at the foot of this flight. They had reached the bottom, or outermost, level.

This was the wider area, the long roofed gallery that he had seen from the deck above, and as he stepped out of the stairwell he saw that it was a two-lane street, with a railing over on the abyss-facing side. Shasta hurried across the lanes and peered down over this last railing. Within moments her hair was pasted flat by the strengthening rain.

"Infinity," she called back to Holbrook, who had put down the mirror and was leaning against the inside wall. She waved at the cloudy emptiness beyond the rail. "Out there you find your level of buoyancy—inward, in the sunlight, or out in the cold dark." She peered down to the right, then pointed. "Look!"

The rain was gusting all the way to the inside wall now, and Holbrook pushed away from it and walked carefully across the glistening pavement to stand beside her at the rail. She was squinting through strands of dark wet hair, and he looked in the direction she was pointing.

The edge was uneven, and a hundred yards below them to the right a long section of masonry extended downward for several more levels—but it was swaying in the rain. Holbrook could see white faces and waving arms.

Then it separated from the Purgatory disk, and, along with a lot of chunks of tumbling cement, it spun away into the clouds. The whole edge shook, and Holbrook clung uselessly to the railing.

He was about to insist that they climb back up at least a couple of levels, when a hoarse shout from behind made him turn around.

John Atwater had fallen down the last few steps from the level above, and he was rolling on the wet cement in front of the stairwell, tangled in his bathrobe.

"Shasta!" he yelled, "make him take me with you! You both still owe me that much!"

"I've got what I owe you right here," said Holbrook, hurrying back across the street to where he had left the mirror.

Shasta turned to face both of them. "We're not doing the reincarnation," she called to Atwater. "And it's far too late to try to get back up." As if to emphasize her words, the pavement and walls shivered, and Shasta flailed her arms and then took two fast steps toward the wall as the railing fell away behind her. "We're all about to find our levels of buoyancy."

Get our verdicts, thought Holbrook, learn what grade we're assigned to, find the orbits our quotients of joy naturally fall into.

The roaring of a car engine was echoing now along the roofed roadway.

"Fine," said Atwater, perhaps sobbing, "but tell *me* how."

Holbrook was standing only a few yards to Atwater's right. "You couldn't do it," Holbrook told him, bending to once again lift the ponderous mirror in both hands, "and I won't tell you how anyway. But you can look into this."

"Shasta," said Atwater, crouching forward away from the wall, into the slanting rain, "*you'll* tell me. You love me."

"I'm sure I did love you," replied Shasta, with no animosity.

As you never managed to love me, thought Holbrook. Who wouldn't have *killed* you.

"But Tom's right," Shasta went on, "you couldn't do it. And I won't tell you either. You'd only hurt yourself if you tried."

Atwater's broad head, streaked now with wet gray hair, swiveled from her to Holbrook. "After everything," he said, more quietly, "you both betray me. You're both responsible—you *know* you're both responsible!—for the place in which I'd find *myself* on that . . . that judgmental periodic table!" He waved out toward the void. "The quickest to decay, in the remotest orbit, on the ocean floor with no buoyancy at all! Beyond the reach of any light, intelligence, wit! *Forever!*"

Atwater turned to face Holbrook, and he stood up straight, and for just a moment he was again the dark-haired man in the business suit. "Very well," he said. "Hold up your mirror."

Holbrook stared at him for several seconds, then spun around and hurled the mirror out at the space where the railing had been. He had thrown it as hard as he could, but it just cleared the edge.

"Work out your own damnation," he said breathlessly, "in fear and trembling."

The sound of a car engine had grown louder, and now headlight beams gleamed on their three wet faces and illuminated the slanting raindrops, and the big green convertible came nosing down the wall-side lane from the direction where the section of Purgatory had broken away.

The squeal of brakes echoed up and down the enclosed street, and

Hubcap Pete levered open the driver's side door and climbed out onto the puddled pavement. His moustache drooped and his Hawaiian shirt was clinging to him. He held out one hand with something dangling from it.

Holbrook pushed wet hair back from his forehead and squinted, and saw that it was a car's window crank swinging on a foot-long piece of string.

"A replacement plumb bob," said Pete, speaking loudly over the drumming of the rain. "Now you can't use the air conditioning *or* roll the window up. Don't lose this one."

Atwater shambled up to stand beside the front bumper, wrapping his sodden bathrobe around himself. "I'll give you a thousand dollars," he said distinctly, "to drive me up out of here."

"Talk to the new owner," Pete said, nodding toward Holbrook. "I've driven enough miles by now to know where I am. This boy's got a sense of direction, but he has some miles to go before he parks."

Atwater scrambled forward, but wound up sitting down heavily after Pete shoved him back with the palm of one hand.

Holbrook took hold of the string the window crank dangled from. "What do I do with it?"

"You hold it up," said Pete impatiently, "and see if the buildings are still vertical, still parallel with the string! If they seem to be tilted more than the string is, toward the central square, then you gotta drive around more, faster, to speed up the disk so it doesn't collapse. And *look* at everything, to keep it all distinct! These people deserve whatever time they care to take, here, to reconsider, if they can. Or maybe they don't deserve it—but I like to give it to 'em anyway."

He walked around the hood of the car and crossed the other lane to stand beside Shasta, near the gap where the railing had been. Atwater still sat where he had fallen beside the inner wall, staring emptily at Holbrook.

Holbrook looked away from him, and met Shasta's gaze.

He raised his eyebrows and waved toward the passenger side, but she smiled and shook her head.

"Honestly," she said, perhaps in emphasis, perhaps as a parting piece of advice.

He nodded, acknowledging this final refusal. "That's okay," he said; then, "Really, it's okay."

"Go," said Pete, "this section of the disk is going to fall off any minute. Straight ahead, and take the next ramp on your left, that'll get you back up onto the freeway. And drive careful—the right side mirror is gone."

Holbrook slowly climbed into the driver's seat and pulled the door closed. The dashboard glowed green in the dimness, and he saw that a big keypad was mounted above the radio, facing the driver.

The gear-shift lever was up in the Park position, and he tentatively gunned the engine; echoes rang away along the wet lanes.

"Will you *go*?" said Pete.

Holbrook pulled the lever down into Drive, and the car moved forward. He pressed the accelerator and the car sped up, and when he saw the ramp approaching on the left, he looked into the rear-view mirror. Atwater was still sitting on the pavement back there, and Hubcap Pete and Shasta were standing by the gap.

Shasta waved, and after a moment he sighed and lifted his right hand from the wheel and held it up, fingers spread in the rain; then he gripped the wheel with both hands and steered into the ramp.

It was steep and narrow, and he drove slowly, peering ahead at the curving walls; and he jumped when the glow of the headlights in the tight passage was dimmed by gray light from behind—when he glanced into the rear-view mirror, he saw that this curl of the ramp was now the lowest part of the Purgatory fringe, and the abyss yawned only a few yards in back of his rear wheels. He sped up, making the tires squeal around the turns.

The headlights again provided the only light after he had followed the spiral ramp a dozen yards farther, and then the cement walls were lit from ahead. The ramp straightened out and soon curved to the right, and he saw that he was on a freeway onramp under the eternal gray sky, with office buildings or warehouses on either side. A few indistinct cars moved along the lanes, and he signaled for a turn and merged into the left lane.

I'm moving clockwise, he thought. I'll have to find an interchange and get going the other way.

The radio popped and buzzed, and then a voice from the speaker said, "Pete? Come over here. Have you met up with Apart yet? Tom Holbrook? Pete, are you there?"

Holbrook unclenched his right hand from the steering wheel and reached for the keypad. One letter at a time, pausing frequently to look at the ghostly traffic ahead and ignoring the momentary glimpse of the dark plain, he typed in, NO AND I DONT THINK I EVER WILL JACK AND JILL HAVE GONE DOWN THE HILL.

He switched off the radio.

❖ AUTHOR'S NOTE ❖

A friend introduced me to the wonderful Modesty Blaise novels of Peter O'Donnell, and in The Impossible Virgin *I came across the statement, "I've always thought that death puts an end to the possibilities of revenge." Of course my immediate thought was, What if it didn't?*

Inevitably my "Purgatory" called to mind the Grey Town in C. S. Lewis' The Great Divorce, *with its adaptable infrastructure and mentally diminished inhabitants. And I found it just as inevitable that each of my characters would have to eventually face some sort of judgment, or weighing, or personal parabola. After all, Purgatory.*

And given the question, "Play with the gravity, or not?" the answer was obvious.

⚜ SUFFICIENT UNTO THE DAY ⚜

EVERYBODY AGREED that Nana Coldharp, well up in her eighties now, was at last clearly too old to manage the family Thanksgiving get-together anymore, so this year her late-in-life daughter Hibiscus, known as Biscuit, was to be in charge. Biscuit was the youngest of the Coldharps by more than twenty years, and there weren't likely to be any more of them, since her brother David still hadn't married—and, considering that he was now fifty and seldom left the house, he didn't seem likely to. Everybody called him Shortstack. The family, living and dead, was mostly Hoffmans now, since Biscuit's older sister Judith had married Hanky Hoffman in 1982. He had died fifteen years ago, but Biscuit still hadn't warmed to him.

At 4 PM on Thanksgiving afternoon she had put on an apron and tied her chestnut hair back in a ponytail and was preparing the accomodation water for certain of the expected guests. Under the sink was a board that swung up, and from the recess underneath she carefully lifted out the original bottle and unlooped the ribbon that held the glass stopper in place.

She poured half of it into a saucepan, restoppered the bottle and set it back where she'd got it, then filled the saucepan with water from the tap. It would warm gradually on an unlit burner as the turkey was finishing up in the oven.

While it worked at changing the ordinary water, she crossed the stone tile floor and looked out the window and down the long dirt driveway, streaked now with the shadows of a descending line of bearded palm trees. No guests yet, though six crystal prisms were hung on strings at the dining room's western window.

The house was a big old three-story neo-Victorian at the top of a hill in Moscone, an unincorporated little town only an hour east of Los Angeles by mapbooks but much farther away in demeanor. Grandpa Coldharp had built the house in the 1920s, and two generations of Coldharps had labored to keep the place from collapsing in the years since.

The kitchen was warm, and smelled of the roasting turkey and the bacon strips she'd laid over it for basting, and Biscuit walked out into the cooler living room and stood by the fireplace, where a couple of logs had been laid ready on the grate. The one-drop rhythm of reggae music was faintly audible from Shortstack's room down the hall, and she could hear Nana thumping around upstairs.

Through the screen door at the far end of the room now came the whirring rattle of a Volkswagen laboring up the driveway in too high a gear. That would be Amelia and her two kids, Jasper and Jackalyn. Biscuit sighed and lifted from the mantel the glass box with Grandpa Coldharp's oracular penny in it. It was an Indian head penny, minted in 1909, and when the box was shaken the penny bounced around inside but always came up heads; the family tradition was that you could ask it any question, as long as the answer was yes.

"Will this dinner turn out the way it should?" she asked in a whisper.

She shook the box, and when the penny stopped rattling around, it had come up heads for yes.

Biscuit put the box back on the mantel and returned to the kitchen. A couple of big pasta pots, already nearly filled with tap water, had been set on the formica counter, and now she lifted the saucepan from the stove and carefully poured the contents into the pasta pots. The saucepan was completely dry afterward, and she clanked it away into a cuboard beside the sink.

From the living room came the bang of the screen door and fast thumping on the carpet, and then ten-year-old Jasper was in the kitchen, pulling open the stove door and reaching in to break off a piece of the crisp bacon on the turkey.

Biscuit grabbed the back of the boy's T-shirt and yanked him away. "You go wait in the living room," she told him.

He shook his head. "I'm liable to upset Jackalyn." Jackalyn was thirteen, and things tended to break and fly around when she became agitated. "She's already in a bad temper because of her parakeet—

Mom's hair got all tied up in knots on the drive here." He looked around the kitchen. "Does Uncle Shortstack still have his gun?"

"None of your business." Biscuit closed the oven door. "And don't upset me, either." She was sixteen years older than Jasper, but was often intimidated by him.

The boy dragged a stool to the counter and stood on it, and a moment later he had fetched a coffee cup down from a cupboard and dipped it into one of the pots of accomodation water.

"Pea brain!" exclaimed Biscuit, slapping his hand so that he let go of the cup. "You don't *drink* that! You want to look like your grandfather's radiator that time?" Jasper just stared at her blankly, for in fact he hadn't even been born yet when Hanky Hoffman had blown a radiator hose in the driveway one Christmas morning and all the water had come gushing out of the bottom of the car.

"Never mind," Biscuit went on, "look, it's not ordinary water." She reached into the pot and fished out the coffee cup, and when she raised her arm out of the water her hand was dry and the cuff of her shirt was loose and undarkened. "And the cup's dry too."

Jasper's eyes were wide, and he immediately tore a paper towel off a roll on the counter and dipped the sheet into the liquid; and when he lifted it out, it was still bright and dry.

"*That's* what goes in the fishbowls?" he said.

"They're not fishbowls tonight, and get out of here. If you've got to upset your sister, see that you don't do it in the dining room." We don't need the Haviland china plates broken, she thought.

As he slouched out of the kitchen, she stirred the accomodation water with one finger; it was like stirring very fine fluffy sand, and her finger was dry and uncooling when she pulled her hand back. At least we know the seed water worked, she thought. And now we'll once again have a fresh batch to top up the original bottle with.

The bottle, replenished with newly extended substance every year at Thanksgiving, had reputedly been in the Coldharp family since the sixteenth or seventeenth century, and the story was that the original quantity of otherworldly water had been wrung from Dante Alighieri's cloak after he returned from his comedy.

In the living room Biscuit could hear Jasper complaining to his mother about her, and then Amelia telling him, "Be quiet or I'll give you something to be quiet about!"

A moment later Amelia stepped into the kitchen, carrying a Saran Wrap-covered pot of mashed potatoes and shaking her head. "You slapped him?"

"No. Pulled him away from the stove by his shirt, and then—oh yes, I did, I slapped his hand. He wanted to drink some of that." She nodded toward the pasta pots.

Amelia nodded and set her pot on the stove. To Biscuit she always looked as if she had just got out of bed in spite of having a bad cold—her nose and eyes looked as if she'd been rubbing them, and her lips seemed stretched to cover her prominent teeth. And today her thin blonde hair did look as if someone had been tying it in knots. As always, she was wearing a sweater that hung down to her knees.

"I wish you'd let him," she said. "He wouldn't be able to watch that damned TV if he spent the evening in the bathroom."

The TV set in the living room was analog, and when broadcasting switched to digital in 2009, Shortstack had taken the aerial antenna down from the roof and sunk it into the ground in the yard. Now the TV worked, but only got grotesque black-and-white cartoons with characters nobody ever heard of.

Biscuit shrugged. "It's just for one night a year."

"But he dreams about it for months after." Amelia looked at the two big pots on the counter. "We should get the accomodations out, the sun's going down. Oh—does Shortstack still have his gun?"

"Your son asked me that. Why?"

"Jackalyn's parakeet starved to death, and she won't admit it—she insists it's just real sick, and she wants your brother to put it out of its misery."

Biscuit opened her mouth, closed it, and then said, "Its nonexistent misery. With a .44 magnum."

"Whatever it is. Better than beating the thing with a shovel. Let's get the accomodations."

The door to the garage was on the other side of the stove, and Biscuit crossed to it and pulled it open. Six boxes were stacked on the cement floor by her Chevy Blazer, and Amelia opened one and lifted out a two-gallon fishbowl on her spread-fingered hand.

"Heavy," she said.

"Ten bucks each on Amazon," said Biscuit, hoisting another box.

"But you remember a couple of the cheap ones broke last year when . . . everybody got too excited."

"You mean Jackalyn. She's better now." Amelia touched her tangled hair with her free hand. "Mostly."

Biscuit nodded dubiously and stepped back into the kitchen.

Amelia hefted the fishbowl in both hands and followed her. "Oof," she said, adjusting her grip. "Where are all the cats? I'd think the smell would have 'em all in here."

"Out in the yard, on the roof. They'll be back in tomorrow, but they're scared of the accomodation water." Biscuit set her box on the floor, lifted out the fishbowl and slid it onto the counter beside the big pots. "Sometimes I think the cats are smarter than we are."

She dipped the fishbowl into the strange water and lifted it out full. "Jasper!" she called. "Jackalyn!"

Jasper came running in and Biscuit handed the bowl to him. "Put this on the dining room table, and do *not* play with it," she said firmly, and when he had shuffled out of the kitchen she went to the garage to fetch another box as Amelia was handing her filled bowl to young Jackalyn.

Biscuit heard Amelia say, "Oh, *that's* nice, *that's* mature. I just hope somebody spits in *your* accomodation one day, young lady."

They had finally got all six of the fishbowls filled and arranged at various places on the long dining room table, and Biscuit had shed her apron and was uncorking the last of four bottles of Zinfandel wine, when she heard a car pull up outside; it roared in neutral for a moment, and then went silent.

"That'll be Judith," Biscuit said. She set down the bottle and hurried through the living room to the front door. Peering through the screen, she saw her older sister, Amelia's mother, unfolding her lean frame from a middle-aged Honda and looking closely at Amelia's Volkswagen. She must have known that it was her daughter's car, but Judith had had a Volkswagen of her own stolen years ago, and, on the assumption that the thieves had changed the look of the car, had ever since viewed every Volkswagen with suspicion.

Biscuit was dismayed to see that Judith was now opening the trunk of her car and lifting out a foil-covered casserole dish, even though Biscuit had called her earlier and told her not to bother. Looking over her shoulder, back into the living room, she called, "Everybody remember the napkin routine!"

Various voices from the dining room acknowledged her.

Shortstack was just now shambling into the living room from the hall, his gray hair slicked down and, even from across the room, smelling sharply of Vitalis. He was wearing shorts and buttoning a long-sleeve shirt. "One day," he said, pausing to yawn, "I'm going to actually *eat* one of Judith's casseroles."

"Better you should drink the accomodation water," said Biscuit. "Jackalyn wants you to shoot her parakeet with your magnum, by the way."

"Good, good. You noticed a cushion missing from the back porch sofa? I cut it up and made a silencer with the foam rubber. Nobody'll hear a thing."

Biscuit shook her head tiredly. "That's swell. Judith!" she added then, for her burdened older sister had kicked open the screen door. "We've already got the accomodations set out, and the turkey should be ready any minute."

"*Excuse* me for not being here to help," snapped Judith. "I had a *colitis* attack."

Shortstack nodded. "I daresay. When is Nana likely to —"

"People arriving!" came a nervous call from young Jasper.

Biscuit left Judith to take her casserole to the kitchen and hurried into the dining room.

The prisms hanging at the western window were revolving on their strings, casting spots of colored light across the walls and over the tense faces of Amelia and her two children, and the water in the fishbowls was glowing pink. As Biscuit watched, grimacing faces formed in the bowls, and she tried to identify them.

There was Uncle Scuttle, who Amelia refused to sit next to because he had wrecked her Barbie town when she was eight; and across the table two emerging faces were recognizable as Judith's husband Hanky and his sister Anemone.

Down the table a face was rapidly opening and closing its mouth in another of the fishbowls, and Biscuit guessed it was her father, John, called Papa by everyone. He had died only three years ago, at the age of eighty-seven, and even though he had been increasingly vague during his last years, it was still disturbing for her to see him like this. She walked slowly down the room, hesitated, and then set her cell phone on the tablecloth next to him, marking her seat.

By the window a gray face with enormous eyes coagulated into view in another fishbowl, and even from the far end of the room Biscuit recognized Grandpa Coldharp. He had died more than a decade before she was born, and though everybody said he had been a fine man, his ghost was able and inclined to remotely goose and pinch women, and Biscuit was glad she'd be seated far away from him. She saw that Amelia apparently felt the same way, for she had set her purse on a chair at this end of the table.

"Jackalyn too," said Biscuit. "We don't need that."

Amelia nodded, her closed lips looking tighter than usual. "Old beast."

"I cast a horoscope today," announced Judith from the living room doorway, her narrow hands twisting the front of her long black dress. "The stars are all in an uproar."

"They'll have to wait," said Biscuit, hurrying back to the kitchen to turn on the microwave oven. She punched in two minutes, which ought to be enough time to reheat the rolls and gravy, and then she pulled open the oven door.

Shortstack wandered into the kitchen then, and he obligingly lifted the wide aluminum pan with the turkey in it onto a table against the wall. He opened his mouth, but whatever he intended to say was forgotten when a loud metallic clattering echoed from down the hall.

Nana's stair-traverse wheelchair platform was evidently misbehaving. Biscuit ran down the hall to the base of the stairs just in time to see the platform clank to an abrupt halt at the bottom of its track, throwing her mother forward against the restraining bar. The whole apparatus shook for a few seconds, then fell still.

"Don't tell me," gasped the old woman, "they're here, aren't they?" When Biscuit nodded, her mother went on, "All of them together *radiate*—over-amp the damn motor."

Shortstack had followed Biscuit down the hall, and he wrestled the restraining bar up as Biscuit pulled the wheelchair forward.

"Your father too?," growled Nana. "Tell him to leave the silverware alone."

Biscuit nodded, and rolled her eyes at Shortstack as she got behind the wheelchair and began pushing it down the hall. Their father had liked to demonstrate his psychokinetic ability to bend spoons without touching them, though to be fair he had not done it since his death.

Shortstack veered off to the kitchen to bring in the turkey as Biscuit wheeled her mother straight down the hall into the dining room. Young Jackalyn was agitated, muttering to herself about the absence of ice-cream this year, and Biscuit warily eyed the plates on the table, ready to hustle the girl out of the room if they started rattling.

Judith was still standing in the doorway. "The stars indicate that we won't all be here next year," she said, speaking more loudly, for Jasper had turned on the TV in the living room behind her.

The surfaces of several of the accomodation bowls vibrated into conflicting rings, producing faint voices that said, "What, what?"

"I said we won't all be here next year!" said Judith, more loudly still.

Amelia had fetched the rolls and set them on the table, and Judith told her, "Not by my chair, please! I'm gluten intolerant."

"What, what?" piped a couple of the ghosts, and another answered, "She says she's hootin' and hollerin'."

"My illnesses," Judith went on determinedly, "make me wonder if it's me whose chair will be empty. But we're all together tonight. I —"

"She sure is," agreed another of the ghosts. "Who are these people?"

Shortstack had found a platter to slide the turkey onto, and now he shuffled in and clanked it down on the table.

"I pray for you every night," Nana told Judith. "*You* should pray."

"I say *affirmations*," Judith told her.

"Half of 'em are Asians!" exclaimed another of the ghosts.

Biscuit had heard some of Judith's affirmations, on occasions when her older sister had spent the night at the house—*I am overflowing with joy,* and *I live in balance and harmony*—and Biscuit was tempted to suggest one or two new ones for her.

She pushed her mother's wheelchair to a place on the other side of Papa Coldharp's fishbowl.

"Oh," said Nana, glancing up and down the table, "not my good napkins!"

Judith was looking elsewhere, so Biscuit gave her mother a sympathetic look, then said "I'll go get Jasper," and stepped away.

The lights hadn't been turned on in the living room, and Jasper was sitting only a yard from the television screen, his face white in the glow.

Biscuit paused to look at the screen. Awkwardly drawn figures with exaggerated heads and triangular bodies that diminished down to tiny feet waved and moved their heads repetitively; the only sounds, at the moment, anyway, were grunts and an occasional giggle.

Behind her, Judith strode into the kitchen, her footsteps sounding angry.

"Jasper," Biscuit said, "come on, we're going to start eating."

The boy looked up at her; his mouth sagged open and a giggle exactly like the one from the television shook out of it.

"Stop it!" she said, louder than she had meant to, and she barely stopped her raised hand from slapping him.

He laughed in his normal voice then, and said, "Aunt Biscuit's scared of the cartoons!"

"Get in there," she said, bending down to shake his arm. He got to his feet, still laughing at her, and she pushed him ahead of her into the dining room. Judith was right behind them, and when Biscuit crossed to her place beside Papa Coldharp's fishbowl she saw that Judith was carrying the casserole she'd brought.

Beside Biscuit, Papa Coldharp's bowl vibrated softly, and she heard his voice say, "Hi, Biscus." It had been his jocular greeting to her for years, before he had forgotten everything.

Surprised at this evidence of alertness, she turned to blink at his fishbowl. "Hi, Dad," she said.

Shortstack had hacked the turkey into uneven pieces with a butter knife. Amelia had brought in her bowl of mashed potatoes, and she helped herself to a big spoonful and passed the bowl to Jackalyn, who pushed it across the table toward Biscuit without taking any.

"What was the yelling in there?" Amelia asked Biscuit.

"Aunt Biscuit's scared of the cartoons!" said Jasper again, then popped a whole roll into his mouth and made grunting noises.

"I wish you wouldn't watch that junk," Amelia said to him, and Nana shook her head in stern agreement.

"Moron dreams of buried people," she said. "David should shoot that TV set."

Shortstack raised a glass of wine. "Right after I shoot a parakeet, Ma!"

Biscuit glanced anxiously at Jackalyn—the girl was frowning at Shortstack, but the dishes were still motionless.

Amelia and Shortstack and Nana had served themselves spoonfuls of Judith's casserole, and Biscuit gave each of them a meaningful glance as she took a serving of it herself and then ostentatiously unfolded her napkin and laid it in her lap. She sighed, remembering her mother's exclamation: *not my good napkins!*

"Ulna's not here!" said her mother then, staring at a fishbowl on the other side of the table from her; its accomodation water was clear, with no face in it. Ulna was her younger sister, who had died six years ago at the age of sixty-eight.

"And the sun's down," noted Judith. "She's not coming."

Biscuit bit her lip and reached across her father's fishbowl to touch her mother's hand in condolence. Sometimes the relatives just stopped being able to come back, and there wasn't really any consolation in the customary statement that the person had moved on.

"She's moved on," spoke the water in her father's fishbowl.

Uncle Scuttle's fishbowl jittered wordlessly, and Shortstack got up and crossed to the telephone. When he had returned to his seat and sat down, he leaned back and closed his eyes, his right hand holding a pen over the message pad. After a few seconds his hand began moving, dragging the pen over the pad, though he still had his head against the back of his chair and his eyes were still closed. Uncle Scuttle's bowl went on churning.

"Are you going to put my parakeet out of its misery," said Jackalyn in a low voice, "or shoot the TV?"

Without moving or opening his eyes, Shortstack said, "We'll dispatch your bird right after dinner, sweetie. I made a silencer for the gun, it'll be very quiet."

Jackalyn's fist was white on her fork. Biscuit guessed that she didn't like being called sweetie.

Judith was frowning down the table at the girl, and Biscuit saw Nana sigh and then surreptitiously slide half of her serving of the casserole off her plate and into her lap. Aromatherapy was one of Judith's enthusiasms, and she was so devoted to it that she used the aromatic oils in her cooking, which, Shortstack had once observed, was like cooking with transmission fluid. Biscuit had taught her relatives how to make noise with cutlery and then, when Judith wasn't looking, slide half of whatever she had cooked into the napkins on their laps, and presently do it again with the other half. Later on they could ball up the napkins and one by one make some excuse to leave the table briefly, and step outside and toss the napkins onto the roof. Every year Shortstack had to climb up on a ladder and take them down.

"So what does my brother *say?*" Nana asked Shortstack. Uncle Scuttle had been mute since his death, never having got the trick of vibrating the water surface like a speaker diaphragm, and could only communicate by way of Shortstack's automatic writing.

Shortstack lowered his head and opened his eyes. "Uh . . . *make a shrine for Ulna,*" he read off the pad. "*Forgive and forget, bygones be bygones.*"

Amelia scowled down the table at Scuttle's fishbowl, and Biscuit knew she was remembering how Scuttle, Nana's younger brother, had wrecked her Barbie town more than a quarter of a century ago and to this day had never apologized.

Judith too was now looking toward Uncle Scuttle's fishbowl, possibly holding a grudge about the Barbie town debacle on her daughter's behalf, so Biscuit slid half of her own serving of the casserole off her plate onto her lap. Immediately the fishbowl of Judith's husband, Hanky, began vibrating.

"Hibiscus!" came his frail voice, "what do you—what do you think you're—Judy, she —"

Judith's head whipped around. "What did you do?"

"I—spilled some food," Biscuit said, "is all."

"Judith," began Nana, "Don't —" but Jasper interrupted her.

"They all do it!" the boy said. "They all dump your casserole into their napkins!"

Judith shoved Amelia's shoulder back and peered at the napkin on her lap.

"I'm sorry, Mom, I —" Amelia began, but Judith silenced her with a wave.

"Don't try to apologize unless you've got a lot of time," she said. She looked past her daughter at Jackalyn. "Has your brat done it too?" Turning her glare back on Amelia, she added, "Where *did* you get that Volkswagen?"

"Don't call me a brat," said Jackalyn in a dangerously low growl.

Judith swung her attention to Jackalyn again, and she pointed at the scraps of casserole that had not yet gone into the girl's napkin. "You will *eat that,* young lady."

"I won't," said Jackalyn.

"Judith," said Biscuit hastily, "it was my fault, I told —"

Judith didn't look away from Amelia's daughter. "Do I have to pry your mouth open and shove it in, like I used to with your mother? Eat it!"

"*I won't!*" repeated Jackalyn, and with a loud crack her plate sprang into several pieces that spun across the table, knocking over a couple of wine glasses.

Biscuit jumped, but it was because she had felt a sudden cold pressure slide up her ribs, under her shirt. Across from her, Amelia had squeaked at the same moment and now looked away from her embattled mother and daughter to glare down the table.

"Touch me again," she yelled at Grandpa Coldharp's fishbowl, "and I'll pour you down the toilet!" The water in Uncle Scuttle's bowl was jittering again, and Amelia picked up a roll and tossed it at him. "And when are *you* going to apologize for wrecking my Barbie town?"

Hanky, not having followed developments, was still repeating in his birdlike voice, "Hibiscus, what do you think you're doing? Hibiscus, what do you think you're doing?"

"Shut up," Biscuit yelled at him, "you . . . you dead busybody!"

Jackalyn covered her face with both hands. "*Everybody shut up!*" she yelled.

And with a staccato series of cracks and thuds, all the plates on the table broke, the bowl of mashed potatoes split and spilled its contents, and the ragged turkey rose spinning from the platter and fell heavily onto the tablecloth, knocking over two more wineglasses and one of the bottles. Red wine began glugging out of the neck. With the pop of an exploding lightbulb the illumination in the room diminished by half.

Beside Biscuit, the surface of the water in her father's fishbowl was high concentric rings. "Stop, stop!" piped her father's voice, overriding Hanky's broken-record droning. "Dad, Judy—ah —"

He seemed to sneeze, and Biscuit jumped again as all the silverware on the table leaped into the air in twisted shapes. Nana just sighed and flicked her husband's fishbowl with her fingers. From down the hall came the noise of her stair-traversing wheelchair platform banging to the top of its track and down and back up again.

Hanky was still monotonously asking Biscuit what she was doing, and Jackalyn had pushed her chair back and fled from the room in tears, closely followed by her brother; but now she had returned and was standing in the living room doorway, holding a shoe box and glaring at Shortstack.

"You put my parakeet out of its misery *now*," she said loudly.

Shortstack looked up and down the devastated half-lit table, then smiled at the girl. "Dinner does seem to be over." He pushed his chair back, lifted his balled-up napkin from his lap and got to his feet. "I'll meet you out back."

"Oh God," said Biscuit. She balled up her own napkin, but since Judith was glaring at her, she just dropped it on the floor under the table. "May I be excused?" she asked the room at large, and, getting no answer except a somewhat anxious wave from her mother and the repeating question from Hanky's fishbowl, hurried down the hall to pull the plug on the stair-traversing wheelchair platform motor.

The platform had come entirely free of its track and was canted against the wall across the hall from the stairs, and several framed pictures lay on the floor with their glass broken. Biscuit stepped over the platform and unplugged the smoking motor.

Shortstack came up the hall behind her and pulled open his bedroom door. "*My* napkin's on the *roof*," he said, looking at her empty hands.

"Mine's under the table." Biscuit stepped into the doorway and said, "Jackalyn's bird is dead already."

Shortstack's tiny room had one window facing out onto the backyard slope, but he had long ago boarded it up to make room for more bookshelves. The Murphy bed he had built for himself was folded into the wall, and he was just straightening up from a chest he kept beside his old white-painted desk.

"Oh," he said. "Then I won't need this."

He was holding what looked like an oversized metal megaphone, but when she looked at it more closely she saw that it was a broad foot-and-a-half-long cone wrapped in aluminum foil, with the walnut grip of a pistol sticking out at the narrow end.

"What the hell," she said.

"It's my .44," he told her, "but the big extension is a silencer. My own design. Usually you can't silence revolvers, since there's a gap where noise comes out between the cylinder and the barrel, but the foam rubber from the sofa covers everything."

He bent to put it back, but Biscuit said, "No, you still need to shoot the bird. She let it starve, is what happened, so she's pretending it's still alive, but sick."

Shortstack blinked, then nodded. "Right. Okay. I can participate in her delusion."

"Wonderful." Biscuit sank into a chair by the door. "Some Thanksgiving dinner, huh?"

"Shorter than usual, but memorable," he agreed. "What did Scuttle do to Amelia's Barbie town? In fact, what *was* her Barbie town?"

"Oh—do you remember that desert tortoise we used to have? Smudge?"

"Sure. Big as a truck tire."

"Well, Amelia—this was in '93—Amelia was eight and I was two, and she had set up a little village with all her Barbie and Ken and Skipper dolls, with toy cars, and houses with little kitchens and closets full of doll clothes, you know, and one afternoon Uncle Scuttle was drunk, wandering around in the yard, and he saw Smudge and took it in his head that it would be nice for Smudge to visit Barbie town." She leaned back against the wall and stared at the ceiling. "So he held Smudge upright and walked him over across the grass to the Barbie colony—but just as Smudge got there, maybe because Scuttle tilted him ninety degrees, Smudge started pissing. Like a firehose. It wiped out Barbie town, bodies flying everywhere, cars turning over . . . I had bad dreams about it. Amelia has never got over it. We had to wear latex gloves to bury all the Barbies and Kens and Skippers."

"Really!" Shortstack stepped past her into the hall, carrying his gun. "I'd have been twenty-six—same age you are now, I believe. How did I miss all this?"

"I don't know. Weren't you and Judith all astronomical then?"

Shortstack preceded her down the hall toward the dining room, and he nodded and looked back. "Sleep all day, watch the stars all night. And then Judy decided they were alive or something."

"Hard to tell what is and isn't sometimes."

She followed him out onto the back porch and down the steps to the yard, shivering in the early evening breeze and wishing she'd grabbed a sweater.

Jackalyn was crouched on the grass a few yards in front of her, and in the yellow glow from the back porch light her taut, tear-streaked face hung over the opened shoe box and, nearby, a pale lump with two twig-like feet.

"That your bird?" Shortstack asked her.

The girl looked up at him and nodded.

"You can fill a shot glass for him at dinner next year," Shortstack said,not unsympathetically.

He set his feet widely and lowered the barrel, holding the grip firmly in both hands. With one thumb he pulled back the hammer, and there seemed to be a lot of solid clicks as it went back to full cock.

He pointed the wide cone down at the lifeless parakeet, though Biscuit didn't see how he could aim, and for several seonds the wind in the mesquite trees was the only sound. Then he sighed, and Biscuit saw his trigger finger tighten.

But, no doubt due to some error in his acoustical calculations, instead of muting the explosion of the gunshot, his foam-and-foil apparatus monstrously magnified the sound. A wall of compressed air punched Biscuit off her feet and she sat down on the grass; she could hear nothing over the ringing in her ears, but she saw Jackalyn spring away, and Shortstack had dropped the encumbered gun, which was now on fire. Bits of foil and foam rubber spun in the air, and where the dead parakeet had lain was a wide, raised hole in the lawn. Biscuit turned toward the house and saw that all the windows on this side were now missing their glass.

It's a mercy, she thought, that the nearest neighbor is half a mile away.

She was still staring at the house when Amelia and Judith came running out onto the porch, their mouths working, and Biscuit waved to show them that no one was hurt; but the two women came hurrying down the steps, still visibly speaking and now gesturing back toward the house.

Biscuit got shakily to her feet, pointing a finger at her left ear and shaking her head; and she waved toward the house and raised her eyebrows.

Amelia grabbed her elbow and pulled her in that direction. Biscuit couldn't hear her own footsteps on the boards as she was marched up the steps and across the porch. She looked back over her shoulder and, before she was hurried through the dining room, saw Jackalyn laughing at Shortstack, who was stamping on his flaming gun.

Amelia tugged her into the dim living room, where Biscuit saw that Jasper was again sitting cross-legged in front of the television. She glanced at the scren, where several of the same, or similar, sketchy figures moved their limbs mechanically. The cartoon mouths changed shape, but she couldn't hear if they were producing words now or just giggling and grunting as before.

Amelia bent down and shook her son's shoulder. The boy spared her a glance devoid of recognition and quickly looked back to the screen. Amelia turned to Biscuit, her mouth opening and closing with obvious urgency; then, seeing that Biscuit couldn't hear her, she crouched and touched the screen, her trembling finger following one of the cartoon figures.

Biscuit peered bewilderedly at the figure, which was gesticulating more than the couple of others. Unlike the others, it seemed to be "looking at the camera"—addressing the viewers.

Amelia pointed at her distracted son and then again at the cartoon figure, nodding wide-eyed at Biscuit as if to ask if she understood; as if pleading that she understand.

The arms of the sketchy character on the screen were now bent so that its squiggle hands were at the sides of its oval head, and it was rocking back and forth—in distress, Biscuit thought.

Again Amelia pointed at her son and then at the cartoon character.

Suddenly the ringing in Biscuit's ears seemed louder, and her chest felt hollow and terribly cold. She reared back away from the television, pressing her fist against her open mouth.

She nodded at Amelia to show that she understood at last, and then she pushed past Judith and rushed back through the dining room—catching a glimpse of her alarmed mother still at the table—and leaped clear over the back steps. The ringing in her ears had abated enough so that she heard her shoes hit the grass.

Jackalyn was crouched over the ripped-up hole in the dirt, flicking at it, apparently hoping to find some fragment of her parakeet that she might bury, and Shortstack had gingerly picked up his gun and was tossing it from hand to hand. It appeared to be just a smoking bundle of exploded foil and blackened foam rubber.

"Shortstack!" Biscuit yelled, but he didn't look up. She stepped forward and waved her hand in front of his face, and when he turned to her she pointed across the yard and beckoned.

She had to wave in that direction again, with a frown and exaggerated nod, before he shrugged and followed her.

A cable hung from the roof-peak of the house to the dirt by the back fence, where Shortstack had buried the detached aerial television antenna, and Biscuit mimed shooting a gun at the spot where it entered the soil. This end of the yard was only dimly lit by the porch light, and Shortstack shook his head uncomprehendingly, so with both hands Biscuit pointed an imaginary gun at the cable and then jerked them up as if in recoil.

"Shoot the cable!" she shouted.

He raised his eyebrows and nodded, then tilted his head as if to ask if she were sure. She nodded, emphatically.

Shortstack held up a hand, then crouched and laid the gun on the grass so that he could firmly set one shoe on it. He dragged the gun out, scraping it against the sole of his shoe, and most of the mess of foam rubber and foil came off.

He straightened up, cocking the revolver and then pulling the trigger while his thumb let the hammer down gently; satisfied that the mechanism still worked, he gave Biscuit a puzzled half-smile and then cocked the gun again and aimed it at the point where the cable entered the dirt.

"Fingers in your ears!" he said loudly, and when Biscuit had hurriedly complied, he pulled the trigger. Biscuit heard the report as no more than a solid but muffled thump, but this time there was a blinding flare as flame leaped a yard out of the muzzle and burst from the gap between the cylinder and the barrel.

Unable to see past the smear of retinal glare in her vision, Biscuit took her fingers out of her ears and waved her arms out in front of herself until her hand brushed against the cable. It swung freely, no longer moored to the dirt.

She gave her brother a thumbs-up, then turned and hurried back into the house, her eyes raised so that she could see where she was going by peripheral vision. This time she heard her feet hit the boards of the steps and the porch, and she heard her mother call from her wheelchair, "Will someone tell me what's going on?" as she ran past the table and into the living room.

"In a minute, Mom!" she called back.

Her vision had cleared enough to see that the television screen showed only snow now, and she didn't hear any voices from the speaker. She blinked around the darkened room—Judith, she saw, was standing by the front door, her wide eyes glittering in the television screen's glow; and Amelia was sitting on the floor cradling Jasper, who was sobbing.

Biscuit crouched beside them, and was able to hear Amelia saying, "You're okay now. Never mind. You're okay."

Jasper hitchingly caught his breath and said, "They pulled me in! Mom! I—didn't know how to get out!" He noticed Biscuit then, and said gruffly, "What're you looking at?"

Amelia looked up at Biscuit and said, "You did something?"

"Shortstack shot the TV cable," said Biscuit, still panting.

"And Jackalyn?"

"Trying to find pieces of her parakeet."

Amelia nodded.

"I think it's time we called it a night," she said.

"Glad you could come," said Biscuit emptily.

"Thanks for having us," replied Amelia in the same tone.

Judith pushed away from the door and walked unsteadily toward the dining room. "I need to get my casserole dish."

"I'm sorry about . . . that," Biscuit called after her, but her sister just waved without looking back.

"Maybe we should all have just eaten the damn stuff," said Amelia quietly as she got to her feet and helped her son stand up.

"I don't think it would have helped much," said Biscuit, straightening up, "to have us all vomiting, in addition to everything else."

"I suppose not, on the whole. Come on, Jasper, let's fetch your demented sister." She took hold of his shoulder and led him out of the living room into the somewhat brighter dining room.

Biscuit sighed and twisted the television's on-off knob till it clicked, and the screen's glow shrank to a bright dot that slowly faded. She turned and peered at the shadowed objects on the mantel till she identified the glass box with Grandpa Coldharp's oracular penny in it, and after a moment's hesitation she took it down and carried it with her into the dining room, where Judith had picked up her dish and stepped wordlessly past her. A few seconds later the front door slammed.

Biscuit sat down at her place and set the glass box in front of her on the tablecloth. Some sounds like throat-clearing came from the fishbowls, but none of them ventured to comment.

Biscuit's mother was looking at her with raised eyebrows, and her father's accomodation water stirred uneasily.

Biscuit saw that her wine glass was one of the few that had not been spilled, and she picked it up. "Shortstack shot Jackalyn's dead bird," she said, "and Jasper got possessed by the cartoons in the TV, but Shortstack shot out the cable and Jasper came back." She tipped up the glass and drained it. From outside came the sound of Judith's Honda starting and shifting into gear.

"I'm glad of that," said her mother. "Don't let him hook the TV up again." She looked around at the broken windows and dishes and the spilled food and wine. "Another rout."

Biscuit shrugged and nodded.

Amelia came in from the backyard, herding Jasper and Jackalyn in front of her. "I'll call you tomorrow, Nana," she said, and after a nod to Biscuit she pushed her children on through the living room.

After a few seconds of silence, Biscuit gave her mother a cautious glance and said, "I'm sure Shortstack can carry you up and down the stairs till we get the machine working again."

"It's wrecked?" her mother asked, and Biscuit nodded glumly. Between them, Papa Coldharp's fishbowl stirred, and rings formed on the surface of the accomodation water. Biscuit saw that a crumb of stuffing from the abused turkey was floating in it.

The front door closed again, and shortly Biscuit heard the whir of the Volkswagen engine.

"Odd kids she's got," she observed.

Her mother shook her head. "God help us, every one."

Shortstack shambled in from the back porch, picking bits of blackened rubber from the barrel of his .44. He sat down and nodded to his mother and sister and his father's fishbowl.

"Good," came her father's frail voice from the water, "to have spent some—time with you all again."

"Yes," said Biscuit, and "Likewise," said Shortstack, and their mother closed her eyes and nodded.

"I believe," the water in the fishbowl went on, "it's time now, to—go gentle!—into that good night. Not rage, rage."

Her father had always liked Dylan Thomas' poetry. "You really think?" asked Biscuit. Shortstack had paused in prying at a black blob on the muzzle of his revolver.

"Dump us all," her father's voice said. "The—original bottle too."

Biscuit looked across his fishbowl at her mother. The old woman's eyes were still closed, but she nodded and reached out to touch her husband's fishbowl. "Go gentle, dear," she whispered.

Biscuit picked up the glass box and shook it, and as always the penny came up heads, for yes.

Her mother leaned over to look at it, then sat back and nodded again. "It'll be strange to have only a few people at Thanksgiving."

"They're enough," said Biscuit.

❖ AUTHOR'S NOTE ❖

There's always some elderly relative at family gatherings who misbehaves or says the wrong thing—before long it'll be me, if it isn't already—and it could only be worse if they still attended after their deaths.

In the first sentence of Anna Karenina, *Tolstoy famously said, "Happy families are all alike; every unhappy family is unhappy in its own way." He didn't comment on haunted families, and I figured that such families would be uniquely weird—with domestic difficulties only exacerbated by the necessities of dealing with eccentric family members both living and dead.*

This is as close as I'll probably ever get to writing a James Thurber story like "The Night the Bed Fell on Father"—"The Night Shortstack Killed Amelia's Parakeet."